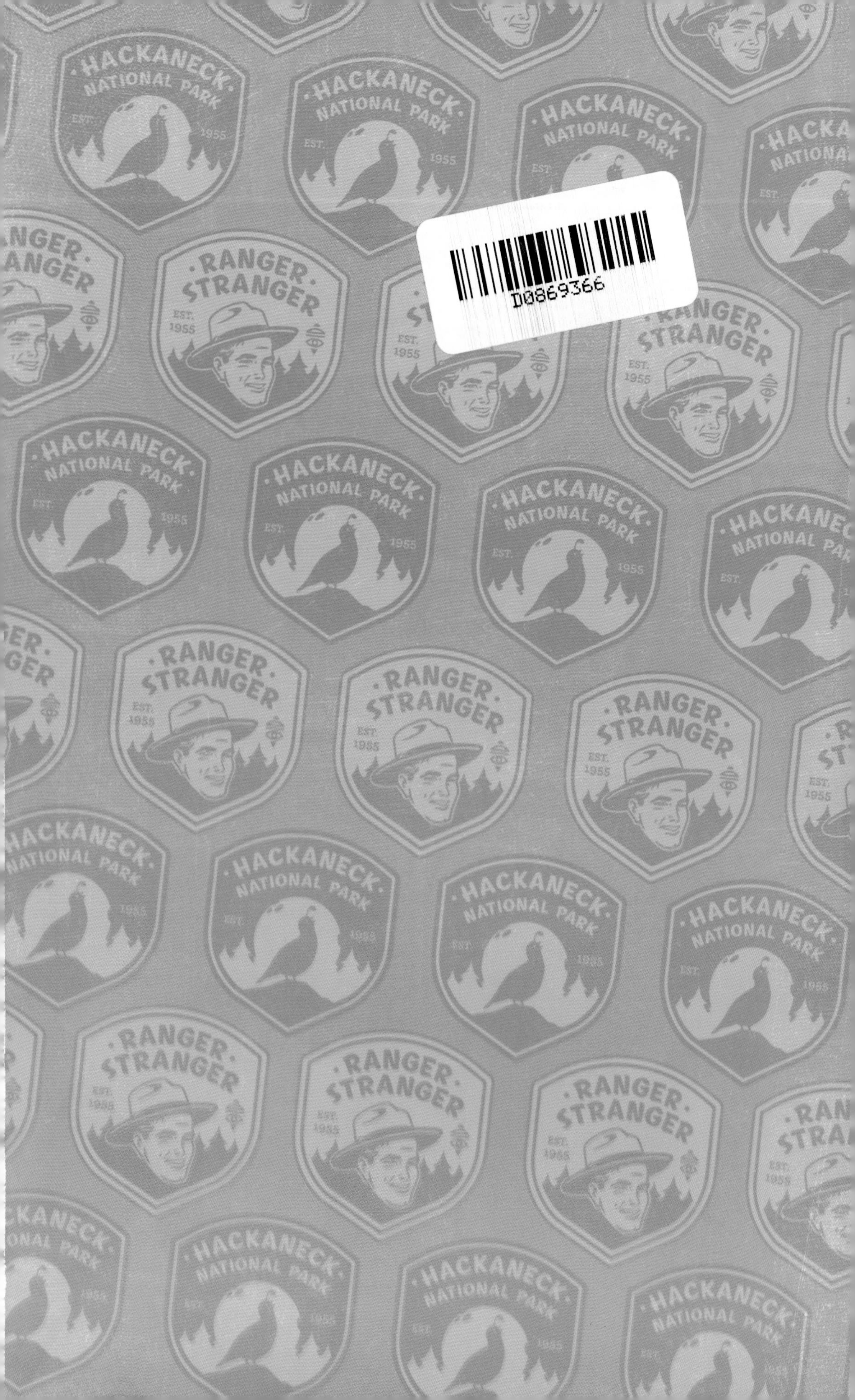
HACKANECK
NATIONAL PARK
EST.
1955
RANGER
STRANGER
EST.
1955

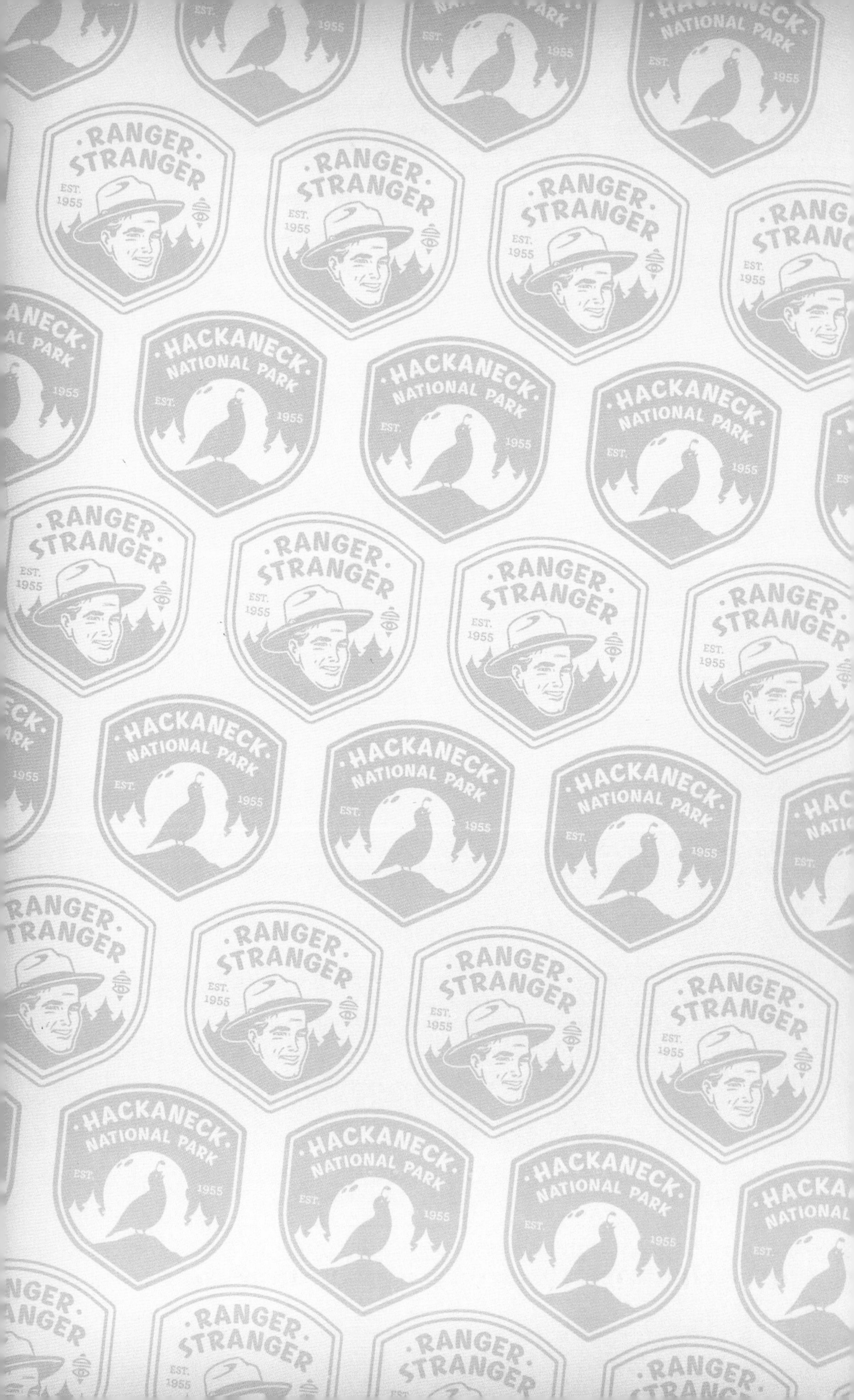
RANGER STRANGER
EST. 1955
HACKANECK NATIONAL PARK
EST. 1955

RANGER STRANGER

WRITTEN BY

ADAM BATTAGLIA & TYLER JENSEN

ART BY

TYLER JENSEN

EDITED BY

ANDREA LORENZO MOLINARI

PRODUCTION BY

MARCUS GUILLORY

GUEST WRITER:

CHRIS STEPHENS

SPECIAL THANKS TO:

TRINITY ANIMATION, RITO CUESTAS, ELI BARRACH, and ALLISON HUPP

Brendan Deneen, *Chief Executive Officer*
James Haick III, *President*
Don Handfield, *Chief Creative Officer*
Lesa Miller, *Chief Operations Officer*
Trent Miller, *General Counsel*

Richard Rivera, *Publisher*
Andrea Lorenzo Molinari, *Editorial Director*
Marcus Guillory, *Head of Design*
Nicole D'Andria, *Director of Digital Content*

 FB/TW/IG:
@Scoutcomics

LEARN MORE AT:
www.scoutcomics.com

HERE'S THE THING, WE WERE TRYING TO GET A BIG TIME A-LISTER TO WRITE THIS FORWARD. THAT DIDN'T HAPPEN, BUT WE THINK YOU'RE GOING TO BE THRILLED WITH WHO WE DID SCORE. SO WITHOUT FURTHER ADO, LARRY, FROM LARRY'S SPORTING GOODS. UN-EDITED DUE TO TIME CONSTRAINTS.

FOREWORD by Larry

DID YOU GET YOUR WORMS? NOW? OK... HI, THIS IS FOR THE THING? THE DIRTY COMICS THING? YEAH, I JUST KIND OF FLIPPED THROUGH SINCE YOU ONLY GAVE IT TO ME YESTERDAY AND I HAVE LOTS OF STUFF TO DO. LISTEN, YOU SEEM NICE ENOUGH BUT TO TELL YOU THE TRUTH I DON'T MUCH CARE FOR THIS SORT OF FILTH. I DIDN'T READ IT SO MUCH AS LOOKED AT THE PICTURES AND THAT'S ALL I NEEDED TO SEE. GOOD LUCK, BOYS."

Another WORD by Garland Woodburn

OH, HELLO. I'M RANGER GARLAND WOODBURN. HEAD RANGER IN CHARGE OF RANGERING HERE IN HACKANECK NATIONAL PARK. AND WELCOME TO THE END-ALL AND BE-ALL OF THE *RANGER STRANGER* COMIC EXPERIENCE. YEP, AFTER THIS I'LL BE DEAD. JUST KIDDING. I WON'T. BUT YOU MIGHT. BUT LET'S HOPE NOT. UNLESS YOU'VE DONE SOMETHING REALLY AWFUL, LIKE, PUNTED A POTBELLY PIG INTO A HOT TUB. OR SOLD LEECHES TO SOMEONE AS AN APHRODISIAC, BUT WHAT WAS LATER ADJUDICATED TO BE A PRACTICAL JOKE. THAT'S JUST NOT A FAIR TRADE OF GOODS OR SERVICES, Y'KNOW? ON THE FLIP SIDE, THIS BRAND SPANKIN' NEW GRAPHIC NOVEL IS. SURE, IT'S GOT ALL THE SEASONAL ISSUES FROM BEFORE, BUT THERE'S ALSO NEW STUFF. NEW COMICS, NATURE ARTICLES, AND BAD IDEAS THAT WERE JUST TOO AWFUL TO PUBLISH. THINK OF IT AS AN OMNIBUS OF OUTDOOR ODDITY. ALL THIS JUST TO SAY "THANK YOU" FOR BEING A FAN. AND FOR PLUNKING DOWN SOME CLAMS IN THE HOPES *RANGER STRANGER* MIGHT MAKE YOUR DAY A LITTLE LESS SHITTY. WE PROMISE THAT HARD-EARNED LEECH MONEY IS WORTH IT.

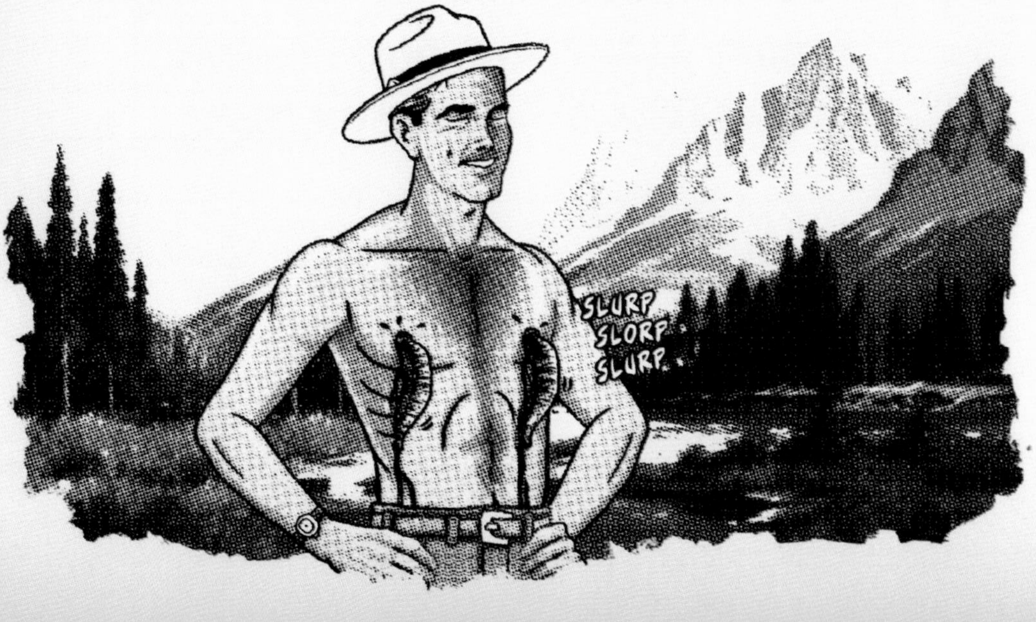
SLURP
SLORP
SLURP

Cheers & Jeers

Up To The Gills

Your article "Biggest Cutthroats" by Charles Nerny in the October issue was very misleading. It was nothing but practices and measures for catching creek trout. It hit a spot with me, and I had to take a walk. Next time just say "Fishing and other boring crap" or something so the rest of us can get back to more interesting productivity.

A. H. Goorin I   *(Lansing, Michigan)*

* * *

Your recent article "Biggest Cutthroats" is disgusting and mentions nothing about pirates. I've called your publisher and will also be following up with a letter.

Wilford Peebles   *(San Francisco, California)*

To Blow A Duck

I just finished your story by Bill Zorkins, "Learn to blow a Duck Call," in the September issue.

To begin, I was too slow getting out of the way of a baseball when I was 55, and when I came to nine months later, I had completely lost my hearing, most of my memory, and suffer from impotency. I am 67 now so I have no memory of what a duck sounds like and have no desire for sex.

I got tired of having friends ask me to have sex with them and then go duck hunting, so I decided to do something about it. I have a friend, Hank Toulson, who owns a hardware store, and I thought I'd check in with him. He was fine and looking handsome in his new sport coat, so I decided to purchase a duck call from him for $4.99. I tried it out at the store to see if I could work it. After some trial and instruction and a few tears, I asked him how it sounded. He said, "It's a good thing you can't hear for shit, Ray, because that duck call made my ears bleed. Why don't you just stick to having sex." Slappy Elkhart, who duck hunts hard five days a week and goose hunts harder the other days, was there and claimed that it sounded like a sick mule he once had that he ran over with his combine. (The mule died.) Anyway, I punched them both in the throat and said I wasn't going to have sex with them anymore.

Then I left without paying and went over to old Phil Langdon's house and got 18, second-hand decoys for $4.99. Then we had sex. Then I went down to the creek and made my best calls. And wouldn't you know--not a damn duck. Although, a coyote came in to investigate, probably thinking he had an easy meal. I tried to have sex him, but he wanted none of it. Truthfully, neither do I anymore.

Lastly, if you know where Buzz Aldrin gets his hair cut, please write me back and let me know.

Raymond T. Danforth   *(Woodstown, New Jersey)*

Watch n' Learn

Sarah Penfield's harrowing and detailed article "Play Deadly for Me" about lying still for seven hours while a grizzly bear ate all the members of her church group was very inspiring. It most surely has a place in hunter safety education.

D. L. Jenkins   *(Manitowoc, Wisconsin)*

* * *

We have incorporated this training into our Boy Scout camping course. Would it be possible to obtain Ms. Penfield's slides and photos for our boys?

Carl Borht, Scoutmaster 454 *(Andover, New Hampshire)*

"Man or Deer?"

Jubal Campocino's article "Man or Deer?" in the November hunting issue certainly stimulated some thought in our division. I was a fighter pilot in World War II and was closely associated with the Renshaw system for aircraft recognition, in which a tachistoscope was used. Carrying one of these in the field would be a useful tool and the difference between bringing home fresh venison for the family and burying a dead hunter out in the woods, driving his Pontiac into the river, taking his money, burning his wallet and clothes, keeping the secret from everyone, even your wife, and becoming an enraged alcholic because of the massive weight of guilt and remorse slowly eating your brain, running into his son at a swap meet several years later because you recognize an old photo of him in a picture frame that was for sale for $4.99, and you burst into tears, screaming "Why? Why?" as you try to cut your wrists with the frame glass as the son realizes and screams "It was you!" and pulls a hot, snubnose .38 from under a rag on his "talk to me behind the van" table, and shoots you, but the pistol is old and blows up in his hand, and your wife is screaming "What's happening?" and you're bleeding and crying and the son is bleeding out on the ground.

Dougal Shineberg, Game Biologist

Dept. of Conservation   *(Butte, Montana)*

* * *

We use a tachistoscope in our school for training adult businessmen to develop a competitive edge against weakness in the workplace. We are very much interested in knowing how we might conduct the training mentioned in this article, and how we might obtain the necessary materials.

John Palekis, Director

Palekis School of Vocational Business Education

(Lincoln, Nebraska)

* * *

The members of our weekly social group heartily approve of this article. We would like to know much more as it appeals tremendously to us as a club activity. I have been designated to ask you for details on how to conduct this and the materials necessary.

Isaac Faartz, Vice-President

Benevolent Order of Bison Social Club (B.O.O.B.S.)

(Portland, Oregon)

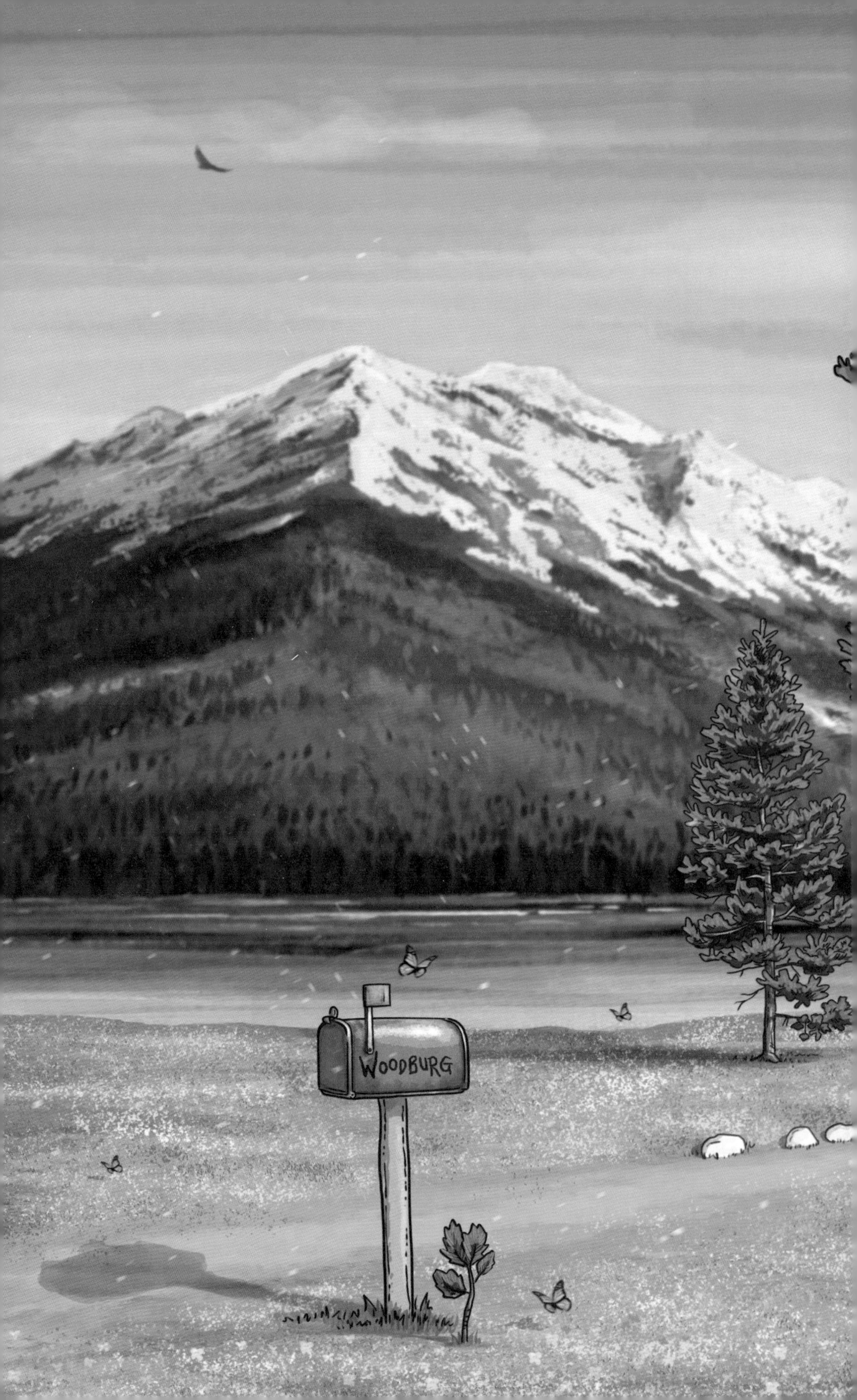
WOODBURG

SPRING

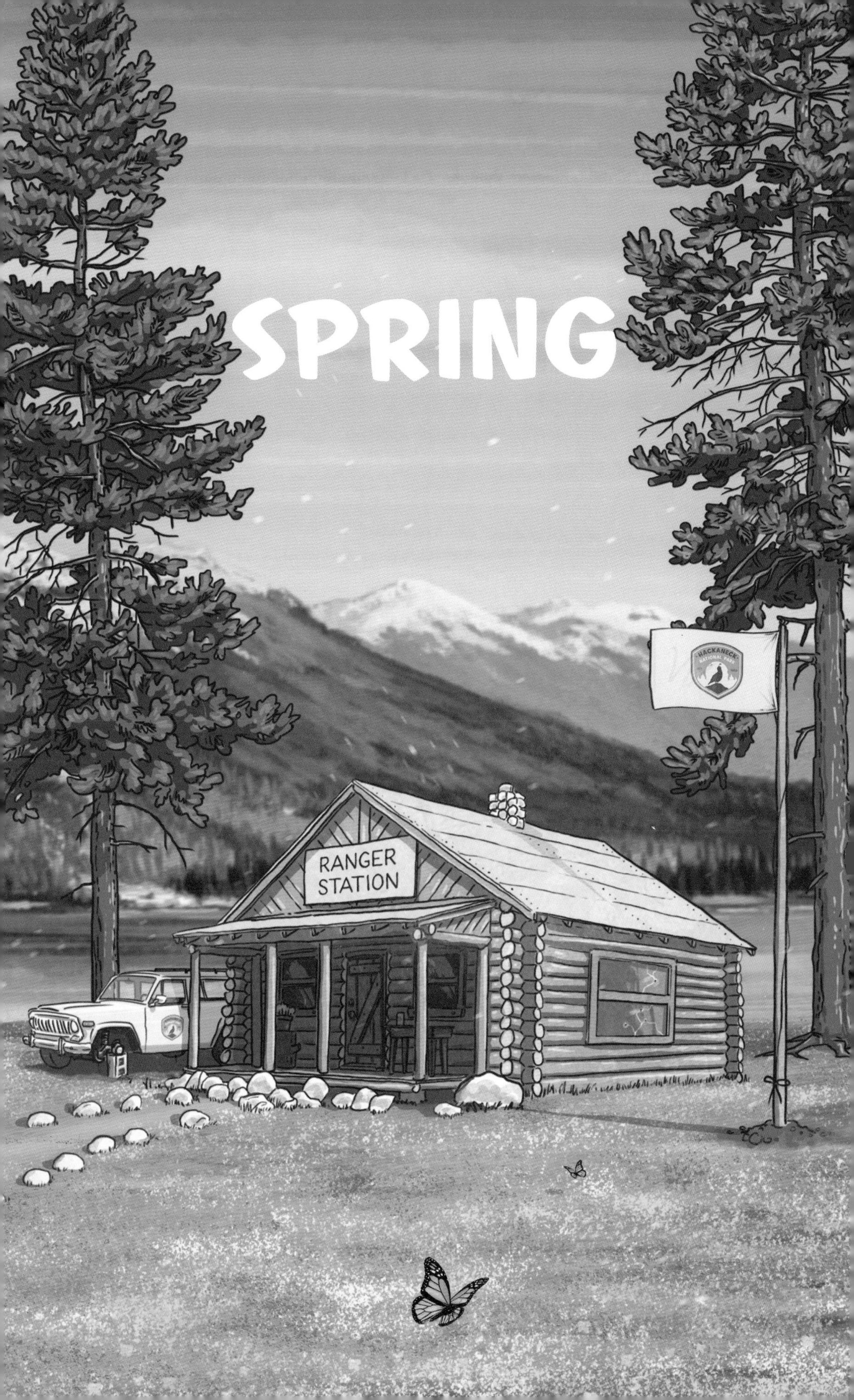
RANGER
STATION

SPRING HAS SPRUNG A LEAK

IT'S SPRING! AND LOVE IS IN THE AIR. ALONG WITH OTHER THINGS. LIKE POLLEN. AND KILLER BEES. WHEN YOU THINK ABOUT LOVE, WHAT COMES TO MIND? IS IT LOVE FOR YOUR FELLOW MAN? MOTHER EARTH IN ALL HER SPLENDOR? YOUR PET? IS IT CARNAL? FOR YOUR FELLOW MAN OR YOUR PET? IS IT GETTING WARM IN HERE?

AS THE DAYS RETURN, OUR THOUGHTS HERE IN HACKANECK RETURN TO NATURE, OF COURSE. AND SO, WE'VE COLLECTED AN OMNIBUS OF OUTDOOR COMICS IN PHYSICAL FORM FOR YOUR PLEASURE. HOW YOU DERIVE PLEASURE FROM THIS IS UP TO YOU, SICKO. PERSONALLY, I SUGGEST FINDING A NICE COZY SPOT IN THE WOODS, DO YOUR BUSINESS, AND THEN, LEAVE IT UNDER A PILE OF LEAVES FOR THE NEXT PERSON. LIKE THE OLDEN DAYS WHEN MEN WERE MEN, AND BOYS WERE MEN. AND ALSO, WOMEN WERE MEN. PAY IT FORWARD.

RANGER GARLAND WOODBURN
HACKANECK NATIONAL PARK

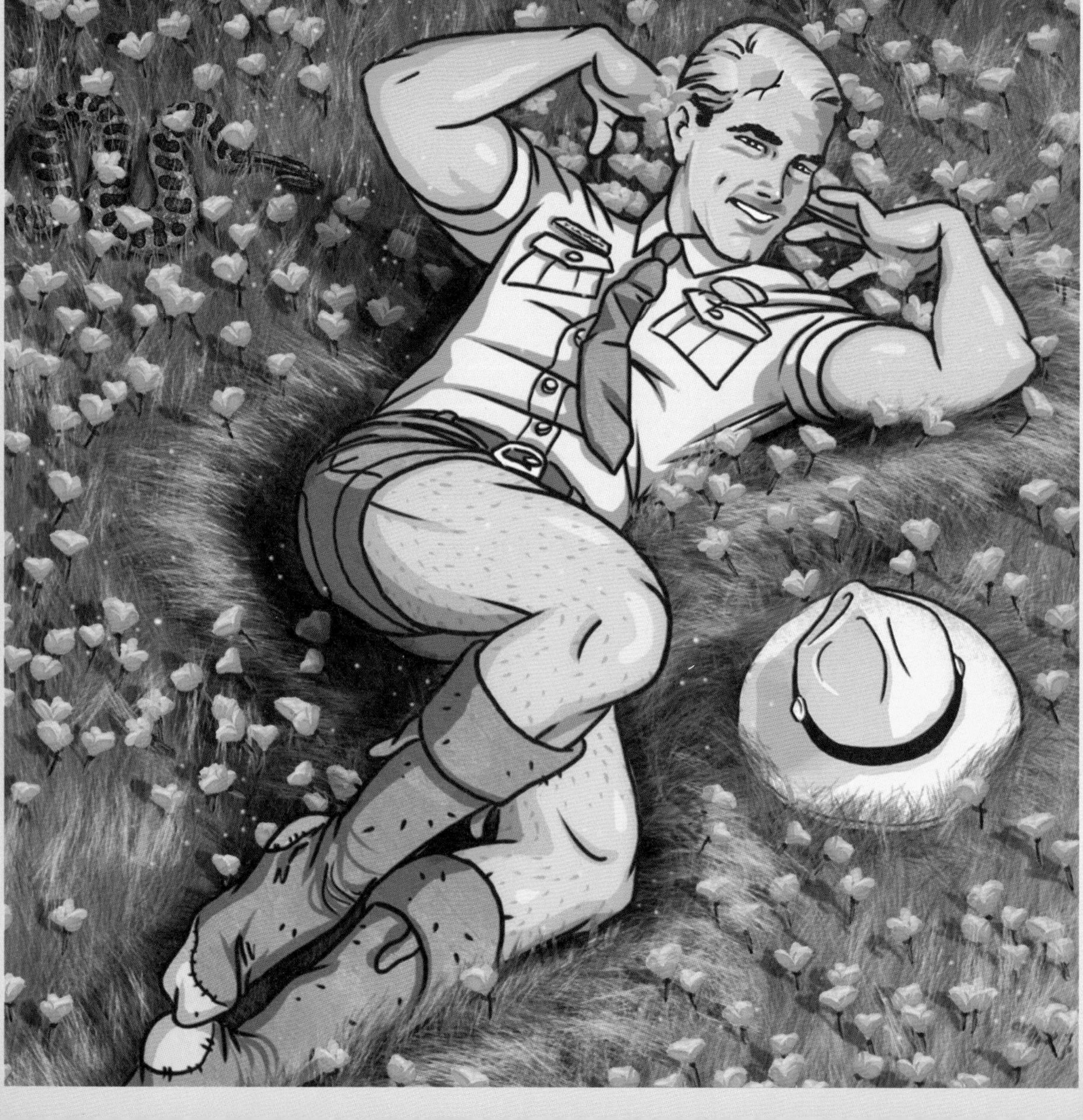

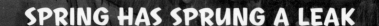

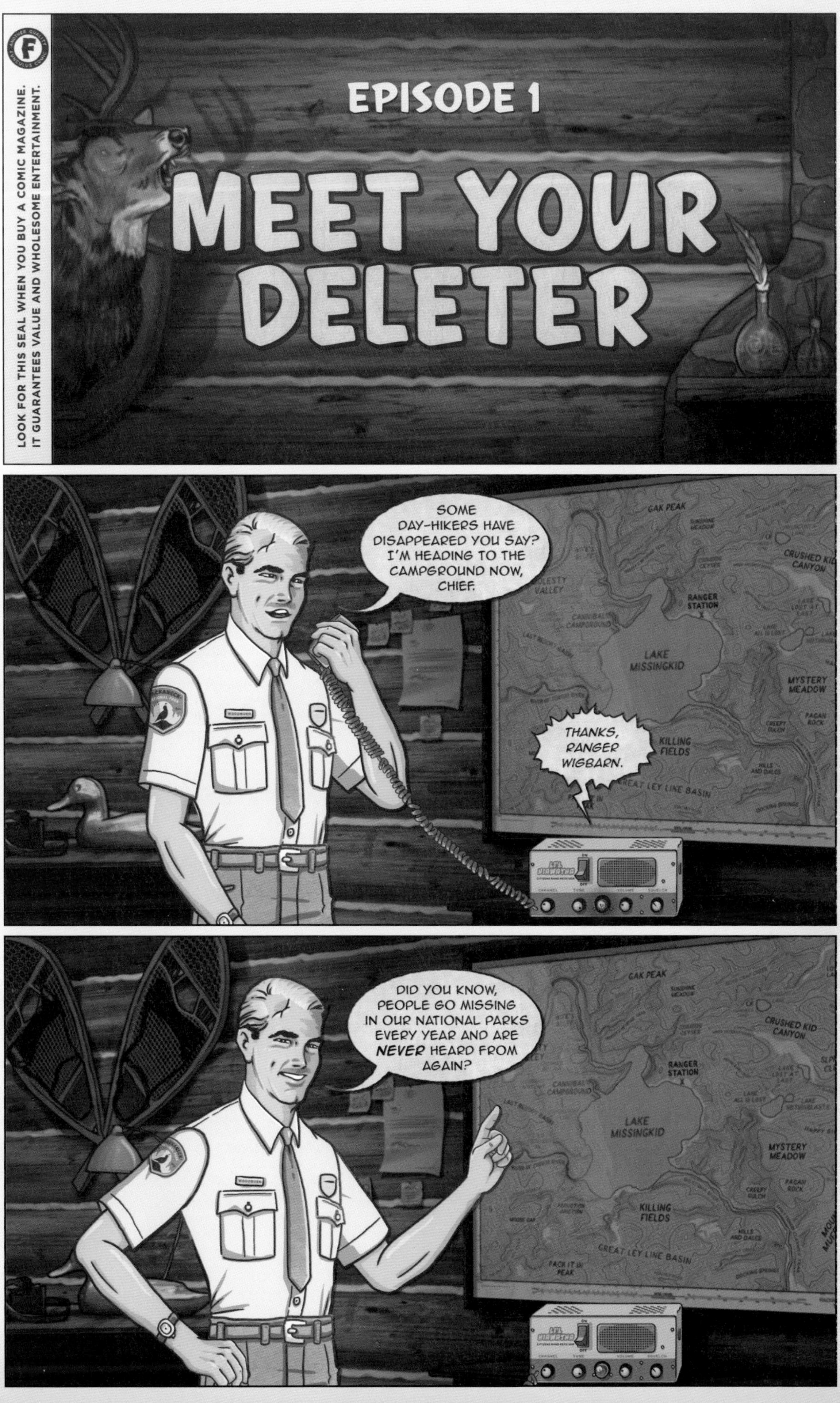
LOOK FOR THIS SEAL WHEN YOU BUY A COMIC MAGAZINE.
IT GUARANTEES VALUE AND WHOLESOME ENTERTAINMENT.
EPISODE 1
MEET YOUR DELETER
SOME DAY-HIKERS HAVE DISAPPEARED YOU SAY? I'M HEADING TO THE CAMPGROUND NOW, CHIEF.
THANKS, RANGER WIGBARN.
GAK PEAK
CRUSHED KID CANYON
RANGER STATION
LAKE MISSINGKID
MYSTERY MEADOW
KILLING FIELDS
GREAT LEY LINE BASIN
DID YOU KNOW, PEOPLE GO MISSING IN OUR NATIONAL PARKS EVERY YEAR AND ARE *NEVER* HEARD FROM AGAIN?
PACK IT IN PEAK

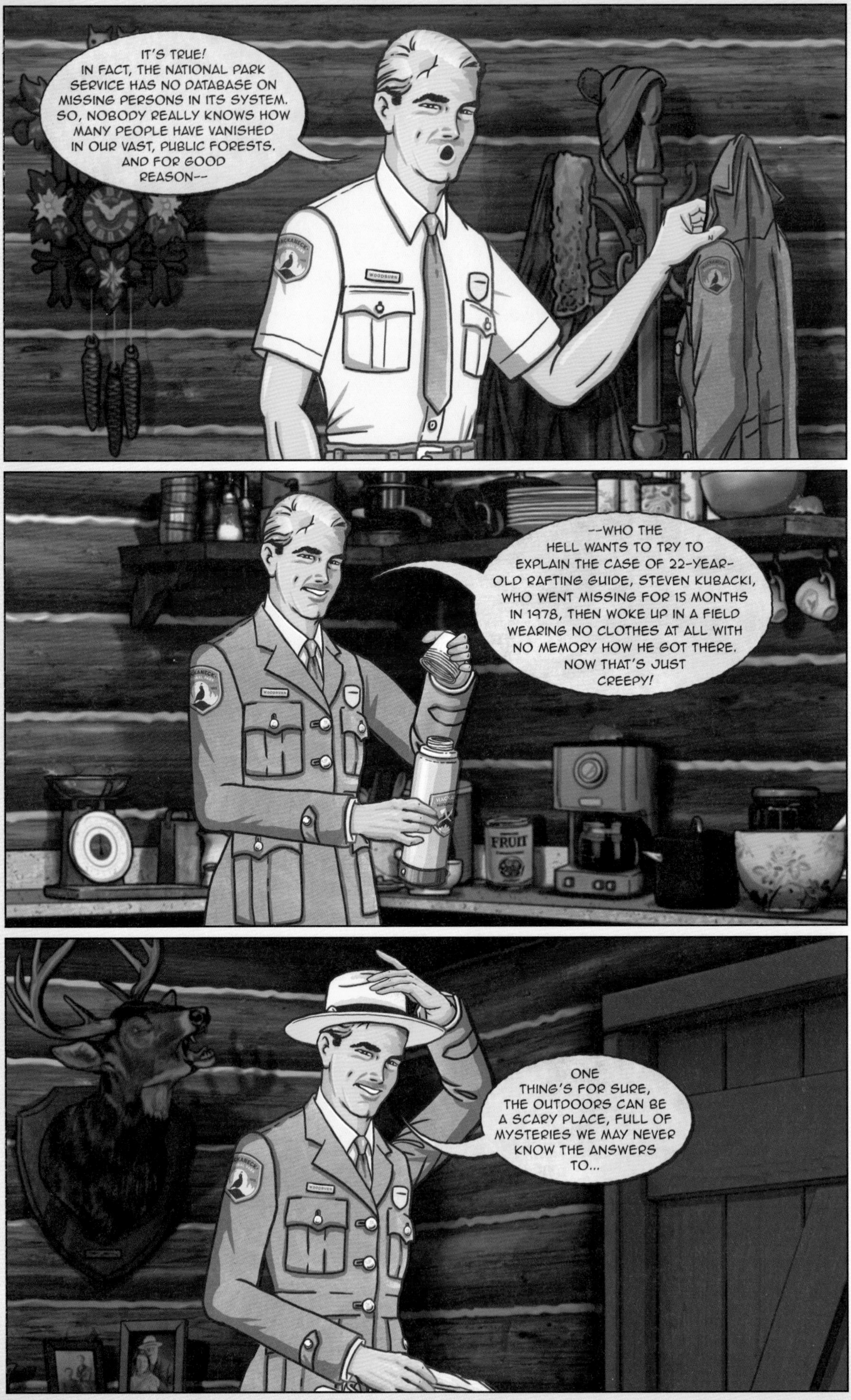
IT'S TRUE! IN FACT, THE NATIONAL PARK SERVICE HAS NO DATABASE ON MISSING PERSONS IN ITS SYSTEM. SO, NOBODY REALLY KNOWS HOW MANY PEOPLE HAVE VANISHED IN OUR VAST, PUBLIC FORESTS. AND FOR GOOD REASON--
--WHO THE HELL WANTS TO TRY TO EXPLAIN THE CASE OF 22-YEAR-OLD RAFTING GUIDE, STEVEN KUBACKI, WHO WENT MISSING FOR 15 MONTHS IN 1978, THEN WOKE UP IN A FIELD WEARING NO CLOTHES AT ALL WITH NO MEMORY HOW HE GOT THERE. NOW THAT'S JUST CREEPY!
ONE THING'S FOR SURE, THE OUTDOORS CAN BE A SCARY PLACE, FULL OF MYSTERIES WE MAY NEVER KNOW THE ANSWERS TO...

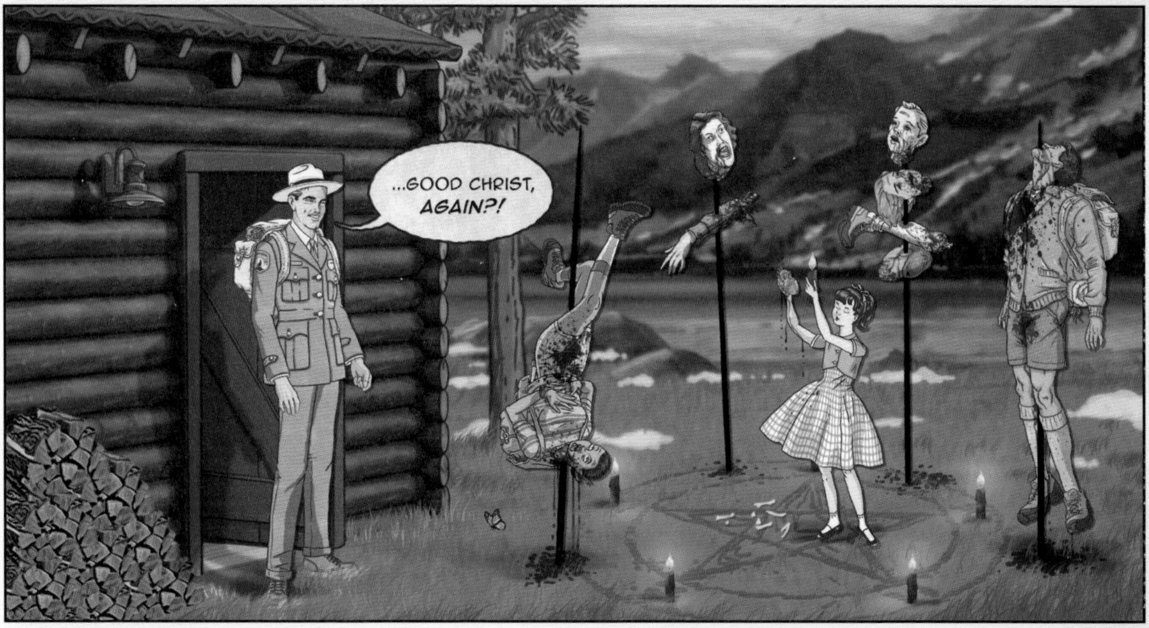
...GOOD CHRIST, AGAIN?!

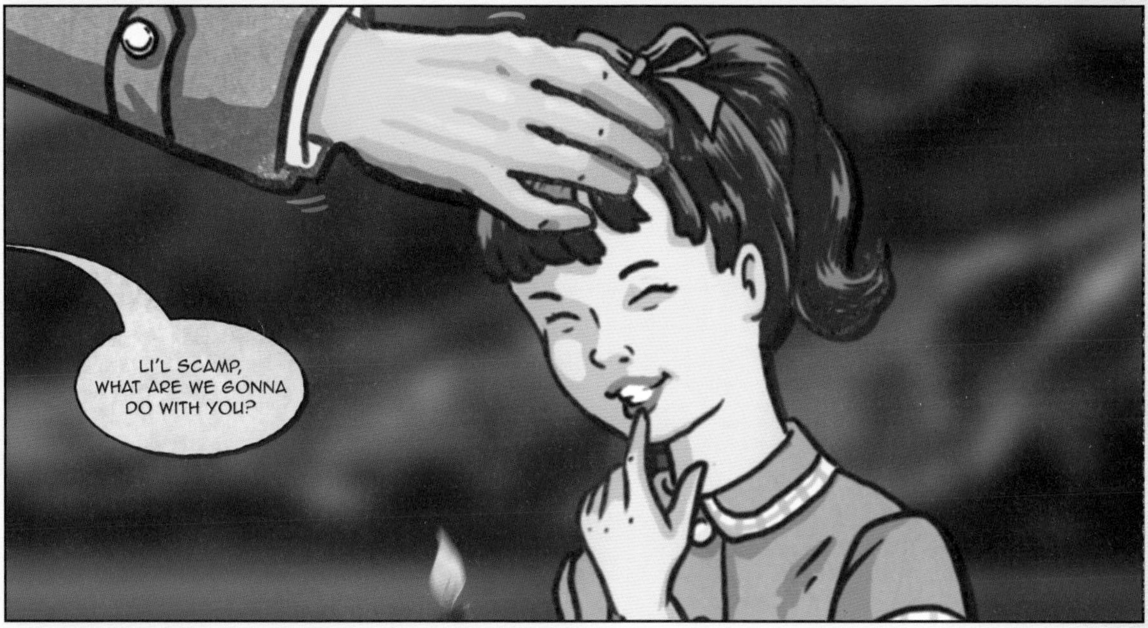
LI'L SCAMP, WHAT ARE WE GONNA DO WITH YOU?

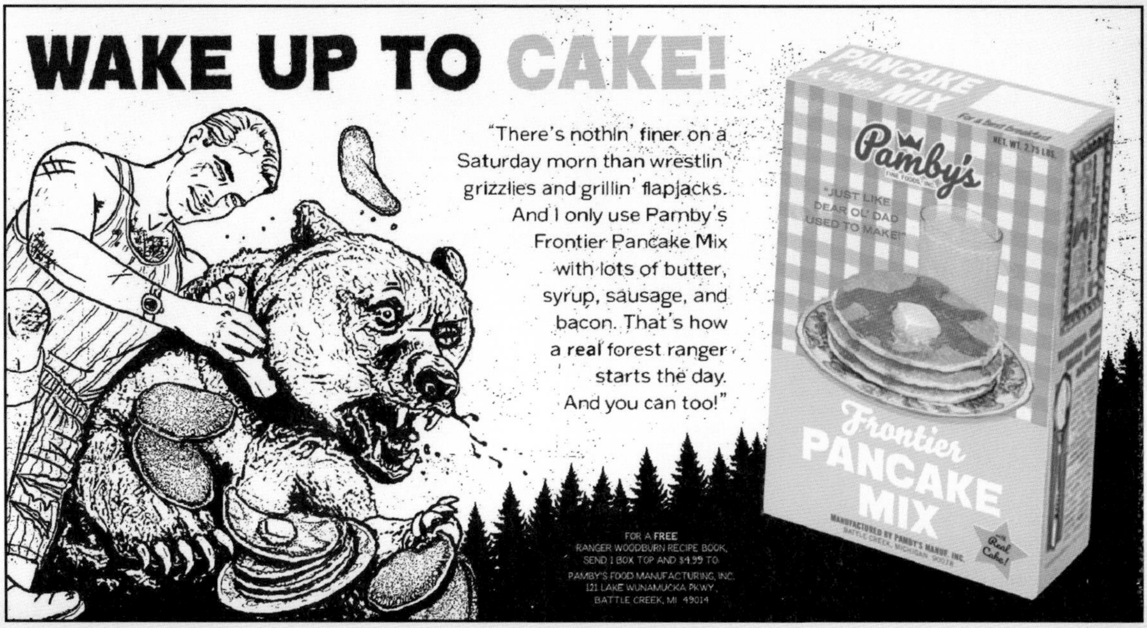
WAKE UP TO CAKE!
"There's nothin' finer on a Saturday morn than wrestlin' grizzlies and grillin' flapjacks. And I only use Pamby's Frontier Pancake Mix with lots of butter, syrup, sausage, and bacon. That's how a real forest ranger starts the day. And you can too!"
FOR A FREE RANGER WOODBURN RECIPE BOOK, SEND 1 BOX TOP AND $4.99 TO:
PAMBY'S FOOD MANUFACTURING, INC.
121 LAKE WUNAMUCKA PKWY.
BATTLE CREEK, MI 49014
PANCAKE MIX
NET. WT. 2.75 LBS.
Pamby's
FINE FOODS, INC.
"JUST LIKE DEAR OL' DAD USED TO MAKE!"
Frontier PANCAKE MIX
MANUFACTURED BY PAMBY'S MANUF. INC.
Real Cake!

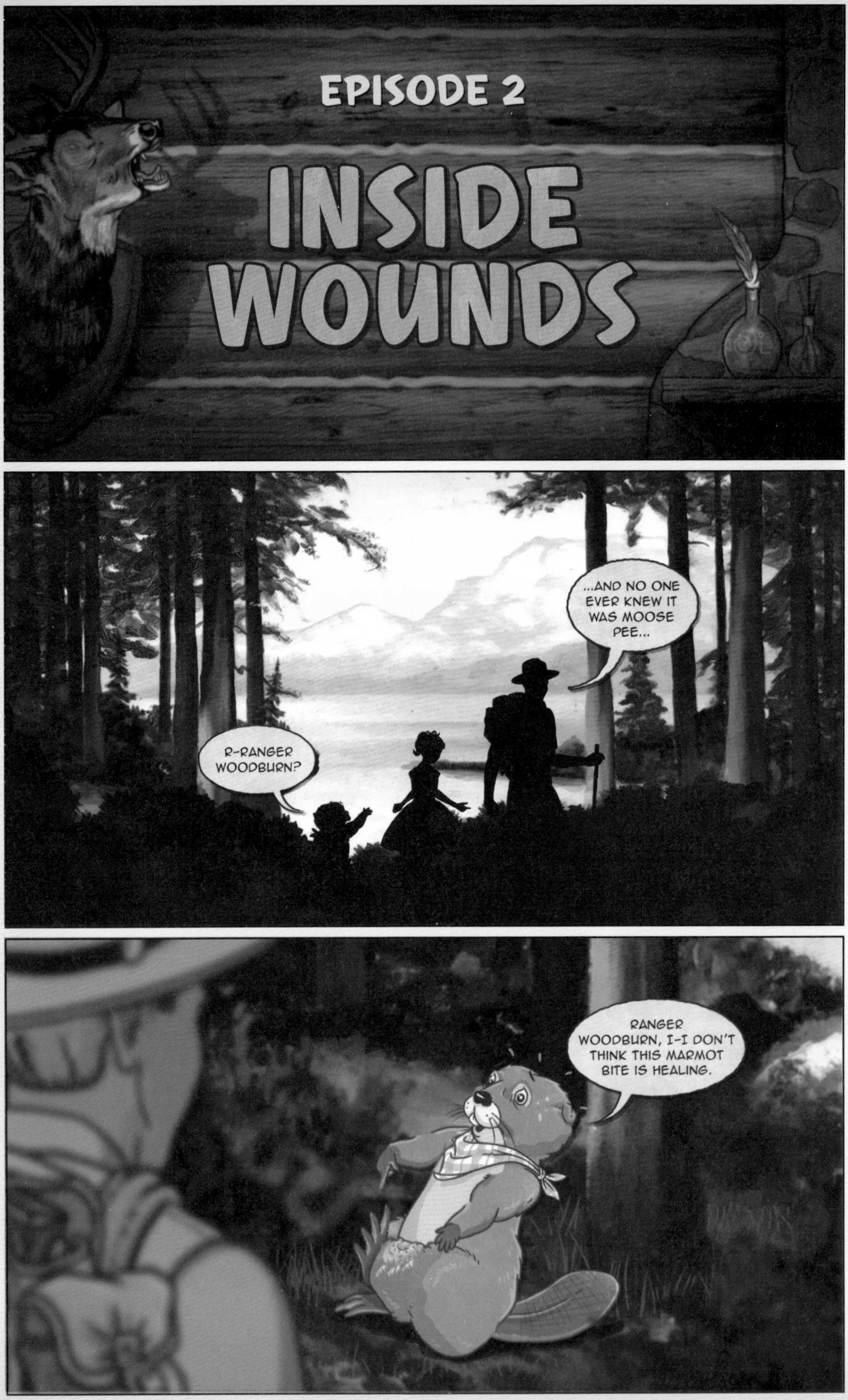
EPISODE 2
INSIDE WOUNDS
...AND NO ONE EVER KNEW IT WAS MOOSE PEE...
R-RANGER WOODBURN?
RANGER WOODBURN, I-I DON'T THINK THIS MARMOT BITE IS HEALING.

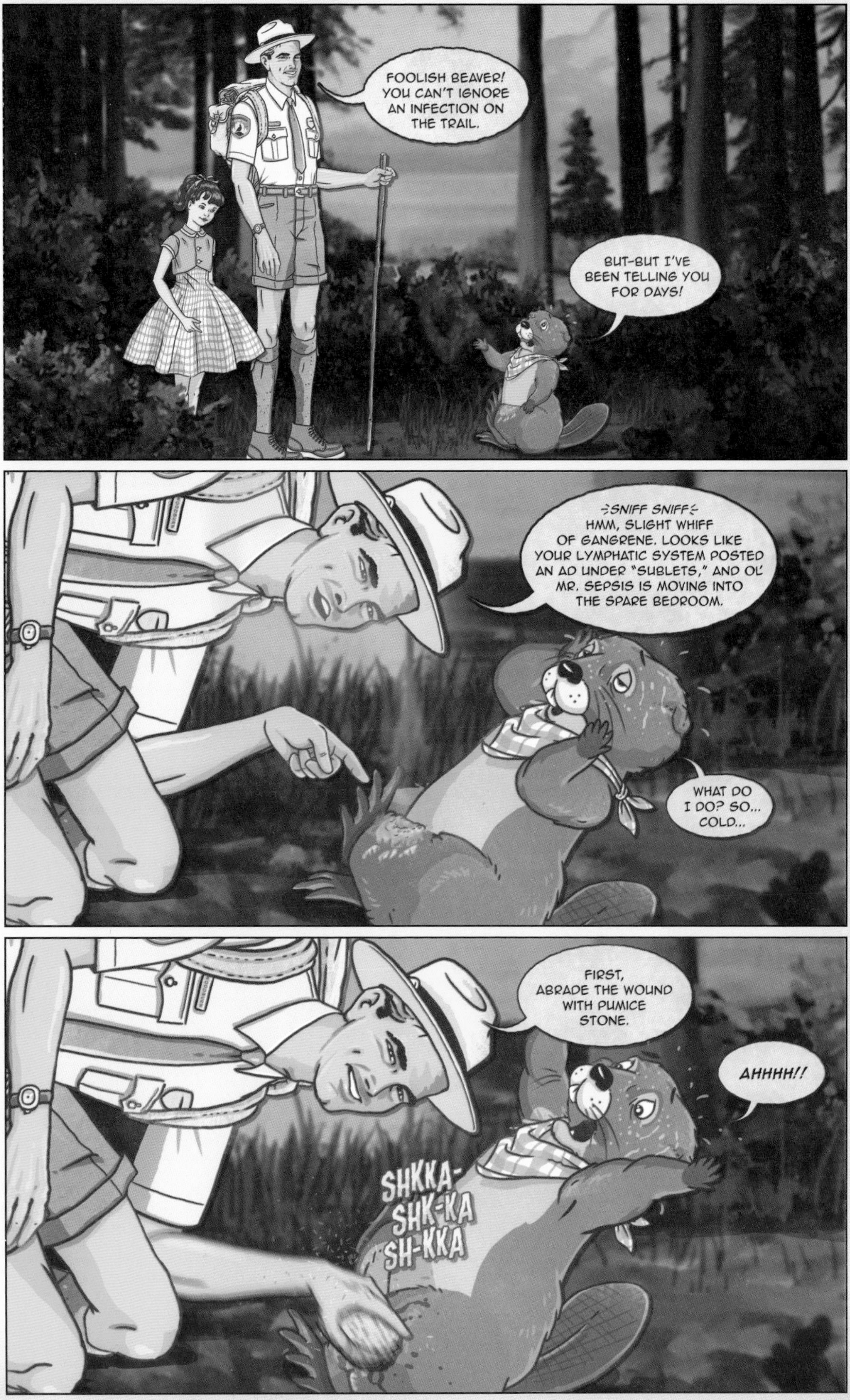
FOOLISH BEAVER! YOU CAN'T IGNORE AN INFECTION ON THE TRAIL.
BUT-BUT I'VE BEEN TELLING YOU FOR DAYS!
-SNIFF SNIFF- HMM, SLIGHT WHIFF OF GANGRENE. LOOKS LIKE YOUR LYMPHATIC SYSTEM POSTED AN AD UNDER "SUBLETS," AND OL' MR. SEPSIS IS MOVING INTO THE SPARE BEDROOM.
WHAT DO I DO? SO... COLD...
FIRST, ABRADE THE WOUND WITH PUMICE STONE.
AHHHH!!
SHKKA-SHK-KA SH-KKA

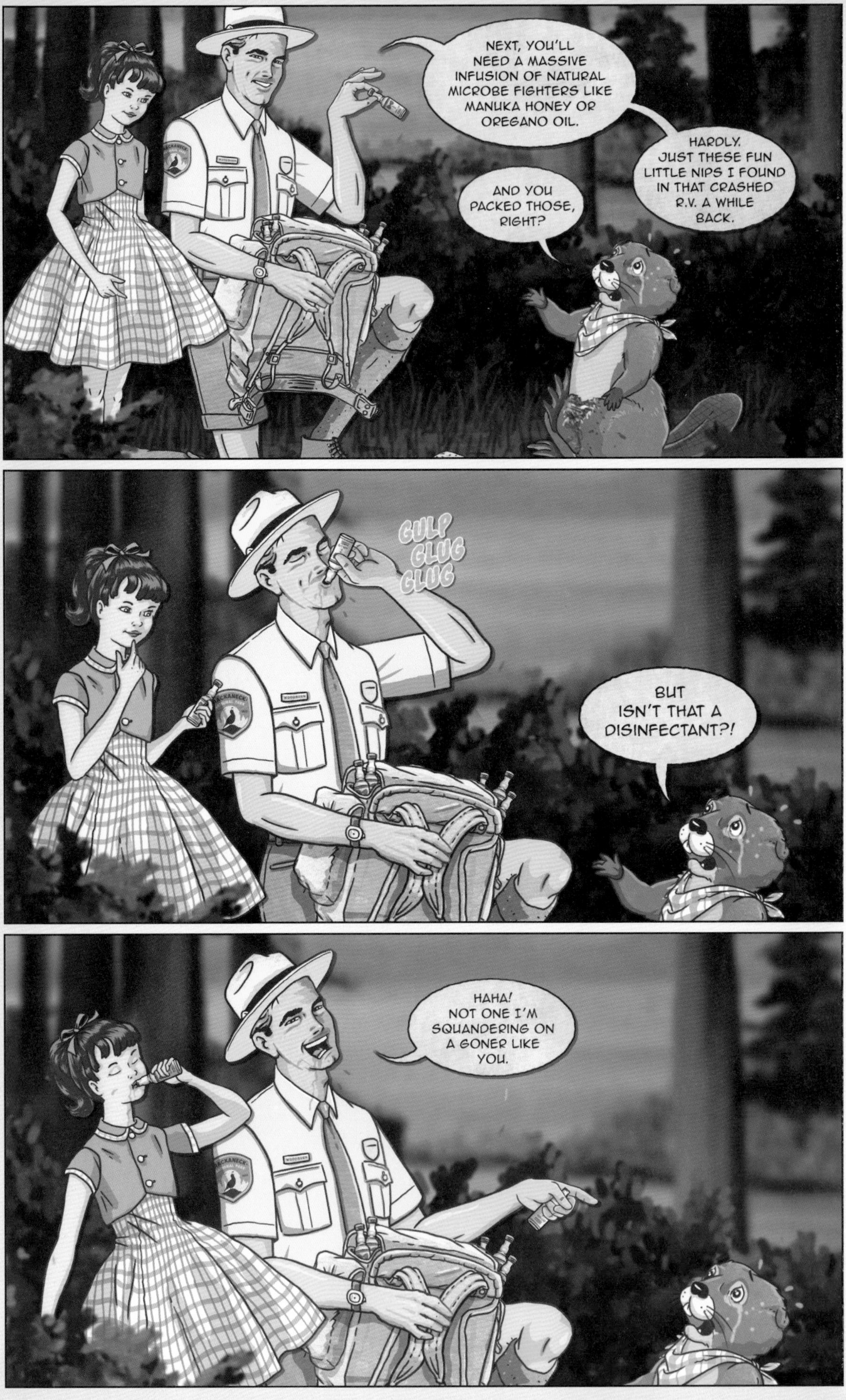
NEXT, YOU'LL NEED A MASSIVE INFUSION OF NATURAL MICROBE FIGHTERS LIKE MANUKA HONEY OR OREGANO OIL.
AND YOU PACKED THOSE, RIGHT?
HARDLY. JUST THESE FUN LITTLE NIPS I FOUND IN THAT CRASHED R.V. A WHILE BACK.
GULP GLUG GLUG
BUT ISN'T THAT A DISINFECTANT?!
HAHA! NOT ONE I'M SQUANDERING ON A GONER LIKE YOU.

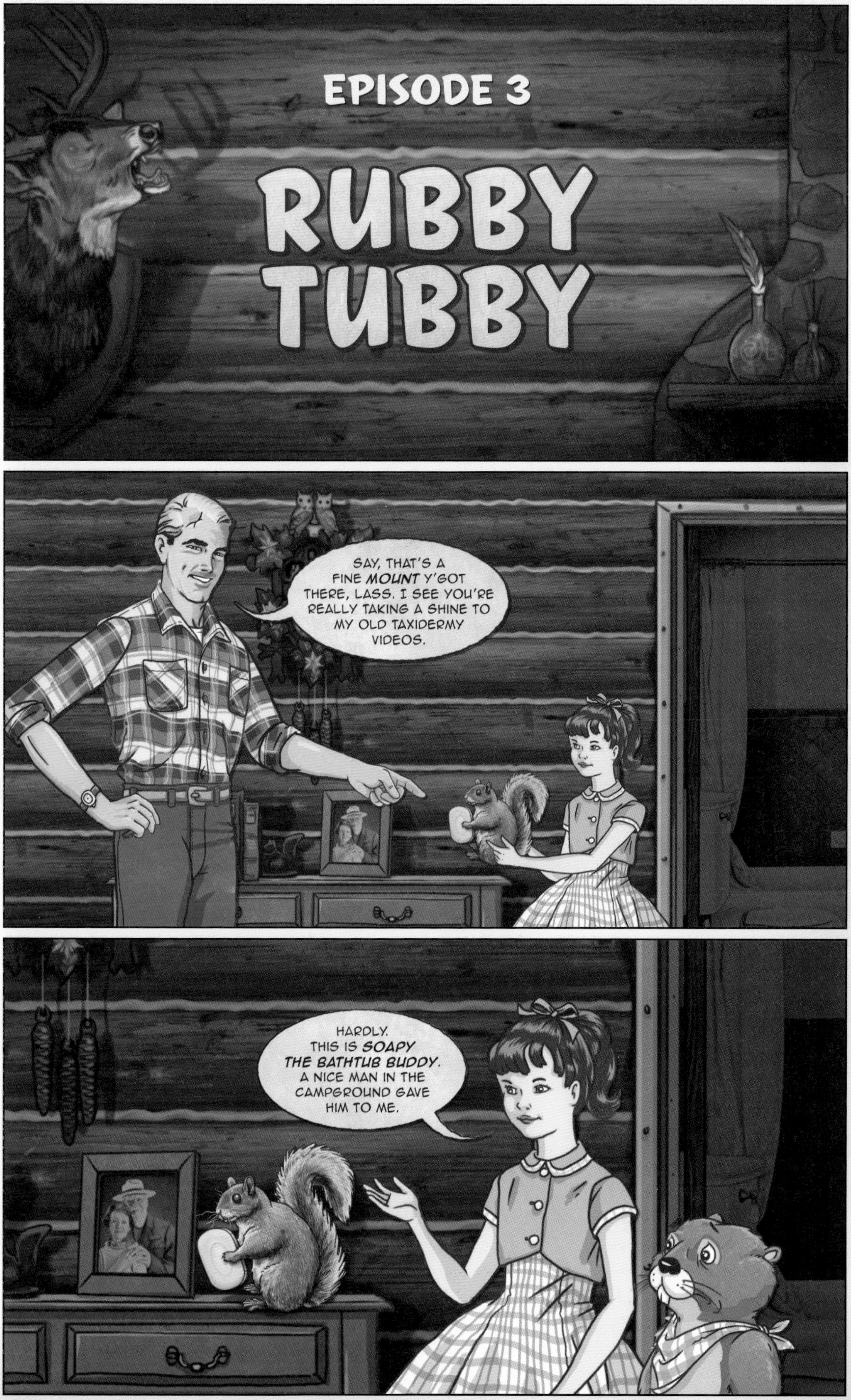
EPISODE 3
RUBBY TUBBY
SAY, THAT'S A FINE MOUNT Y'GOT THERE, LASS. I SEE YOU'RE REALLY TAKING A SHINE TO MY OLD TAXIDERMY VIDEOS.
HARDLY. THIS IS SOAPY THE BATHTUB BUDDY. A NICE MAN IN THE CAMPGROUND GAVE HIM TO ME.

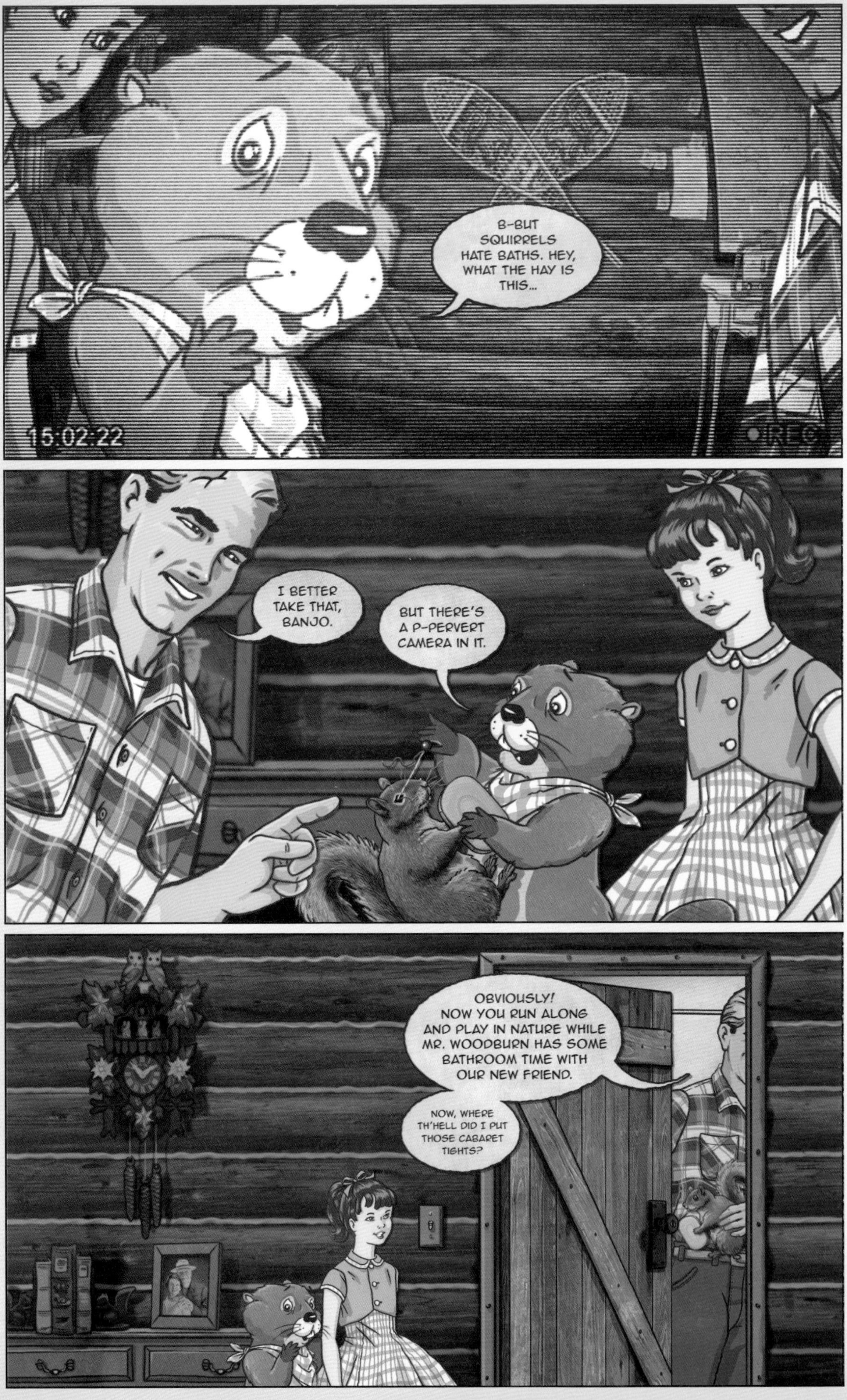
15:02:22
REC
B-BUT SQUIRRELS HATE BATHS. HEY, WHAT THE HAY IS THIS...
I BETTER TAKE THAT, BANJO.
BUT THERE'S A P-PERVERT CAMERA IN IT.
OBVIOUSLY! NOW YOU RUN ALONG AND PLAY IN NATURE WHILE MR. WOODBURN HAS SOME BATHROOM TIME WITH OUR NEW FRIEND.
NOW, WHERE TH'HELL DID I PUT THOSE CABARET TIGHTS?

EPISODE 4
TOO HOT IN THE HOT TUB

WHAT *MILLENNIALS* NEED IS SOME TIME AWAY FROM THE BIG CITY—TO ENJOY ALL THE BOUNTY MOTHER NATURE HAS TO OFFER.

WE'RE OPENING A DAY SPA!

PRETTY!

Welcome to
RANGER WOODBURN's
❀ DAY SPA ❀
ALL NATURUL HOT SPRING
(CLOTHING OPSHONEL)
NO SKINNYDIPPING!

DANG $15 OSED
SCALDING WATER - HIGH ACID

BLOOP!
BLURP

BLOOP!

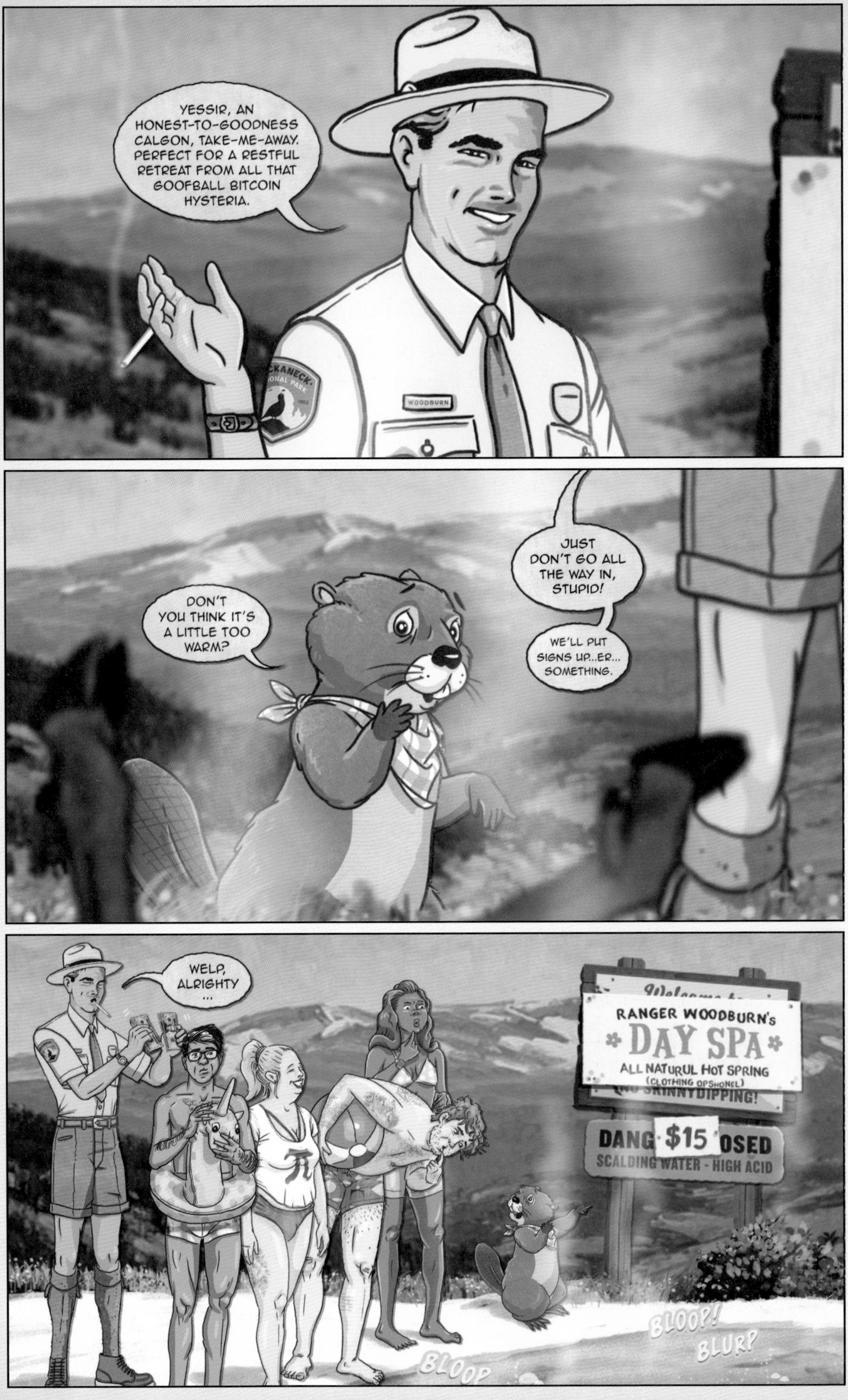
YESSIR, AN HONEST-TO-GOODNESS CALGON, TAKE-ME-AWAY. PERFECT FOR A RESTFUL RETREAT FROM ALL THAT GOOFBALL BITCOIN HYSTERIA.
WOODBURN
DON'T YOU THINK IT'S A LITTLE TOO WARM?
JUST DON'T GO ALL THE WAY IN, STUPID!
WE'LL PUT SIGNS UP...ER... SOMETHING.
WELP, ALRIGHTY ...
RANGER WOODBURN's
DAY SPA
ALL NATURUL HOT SPRING
(CLOTHING OPSHONEL)
SKINNYDIPPING!
DANG $15 OSED
SCALDING WATER - HIGH ACID
BLOOP!
BLURP
BLOOP

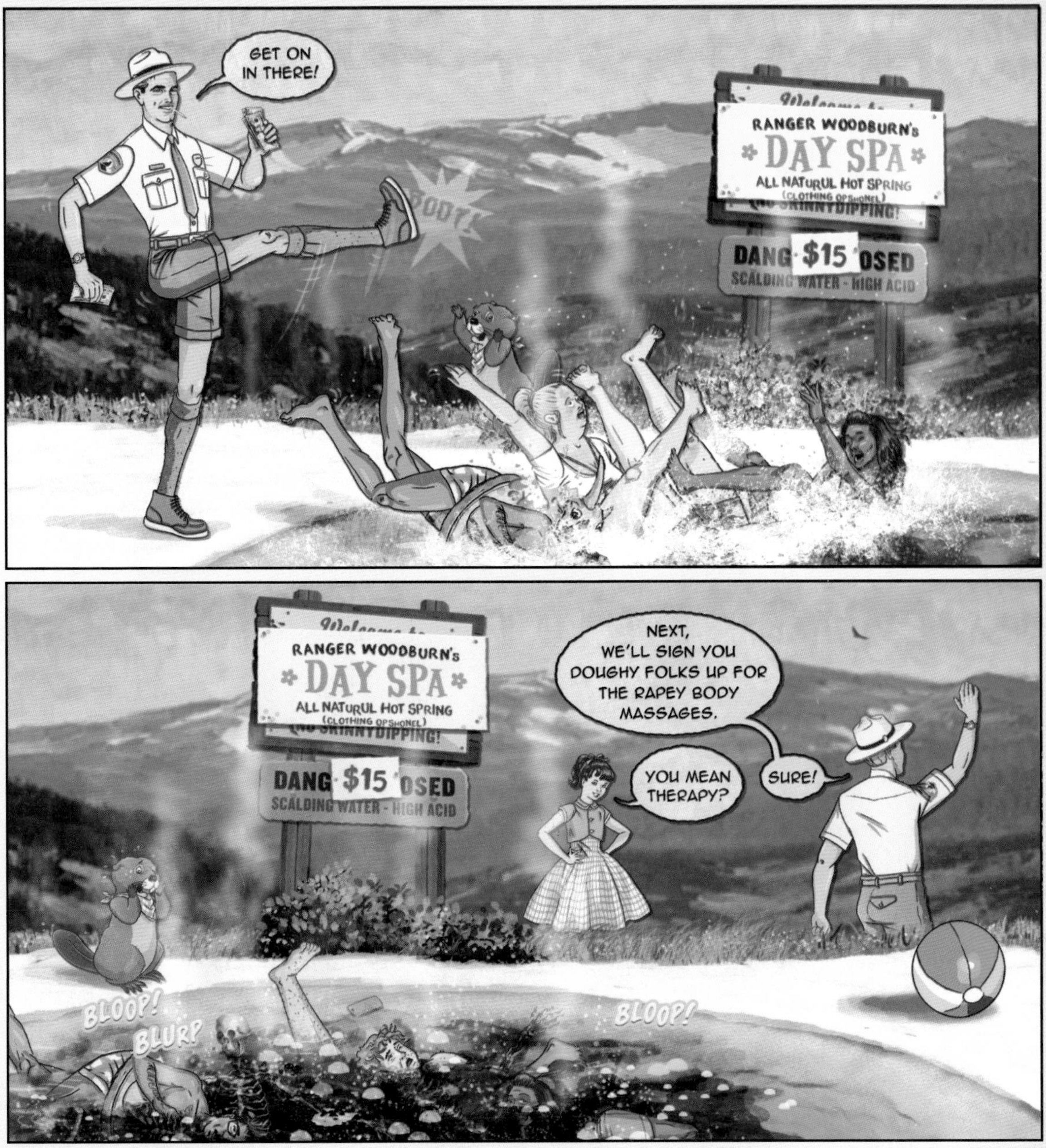

GET ON IN THERE!
RANGER WOODBURN's
DAY SPA
ALL NATURUL HOT SPRING
(CLOTHING OPSHONEL)
DANG $15 OSED
SCALDING WATER - HIGH ACID
NEXT, WE'LL SIGN YOU DOUGHY FOLKS UP FOR THE RAPEY BODY MASSAGES.
YOU MEAN THERAPY?
SURE!
BLOOP!
BLURP
BLOOP!
DID SOMETHING DIE IN HERE? YOU BET IT DID.
BOURBON
OLD BUCK
DOUBLE-FISTED
Old Buck bourbon is for a refined pallet, like that of your boss. It goes down hard, like that time in 5th grade when you got punched in the stomach, and everyone laughed. The smooth spice and rich finish come from the unique charring process of this oak-aged bourbon whiskey. Yep, with Old Buck by your side, now YOU'LL have the last laugh.
·OLD· BUCK
DOUBLE-FISTED BOURBON
PAMBY'S DISTILLERS CORPORATION • ARIZONA BOURBON WHISKEY • 90 PROOF

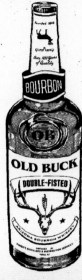

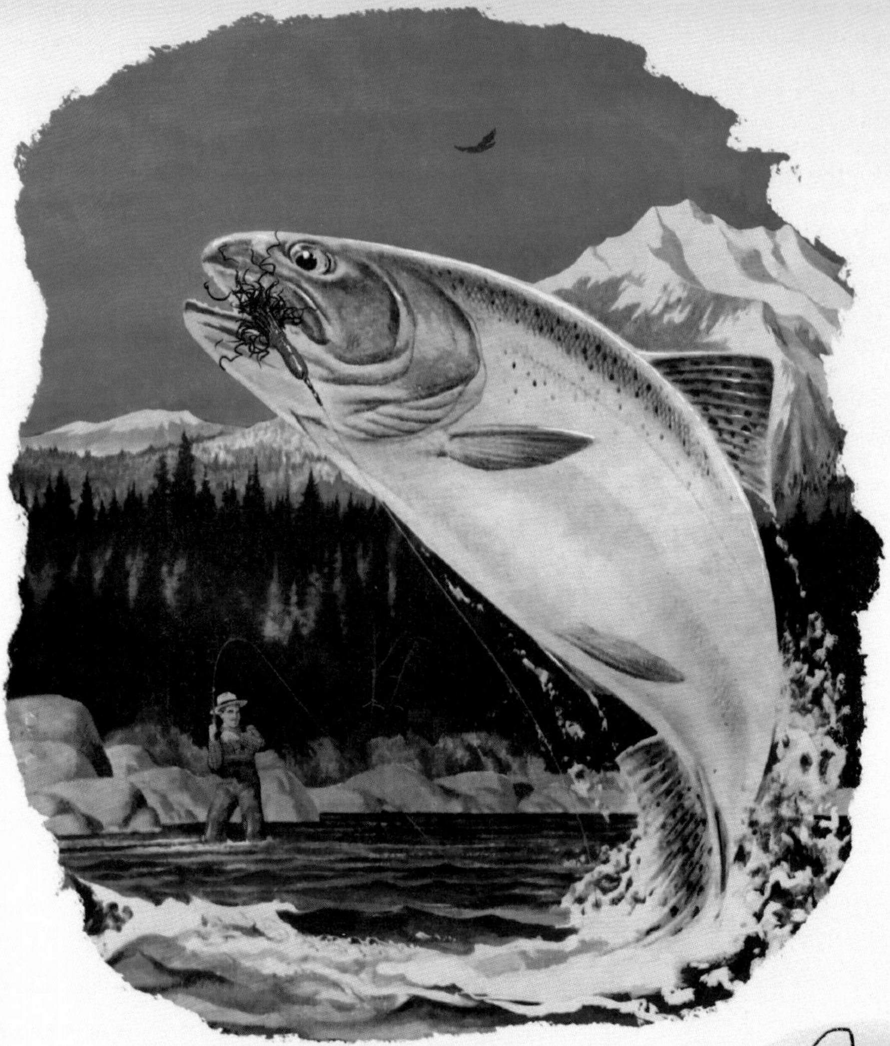

THE BEST HAIR IS YOUR CHEST HAIR

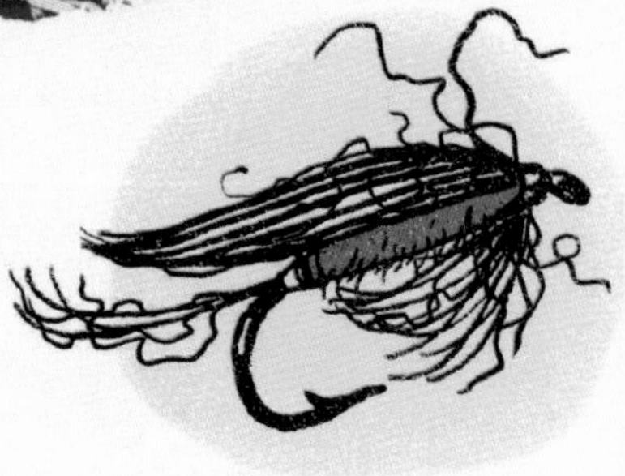

The Carpet Coachman

By Garland Woodburn

Is there anything more manly than making your own fishing lure? Yes, of course there is! Fighting a grizzly bear, jumping a gorge on a motorcycle, or drinking scotch with a wild cougar. So to make sure your fishing lure is as manly as possible let me suggest making it out of the manliest part of your body: chest hair. Because there's nothing that catches a fish's eye like gross hair from your torso.

To start your lure, grab a healthy chunk of chest hair and pull as hard as possible. This may lead to wincing, grimacing, or yelling "Ouchie, Mama!" Next, figure out what type of lure you want to make. There are jigs, spinnerbait, spoons, flies, or a tangled mess of chest hair. Let me suggest the last one since that's what you're working with. Take your clump of hair and any shiny piece of garbage you can find and slap them together using something sticky. You can use glue, tar, chewing tobacco, or honey which may lead you to fighting that grizzly bear I mentione earlier. Now you can check that off your bucket lis Because you're probably going to die doing it. Tak your sticky substance and slather it on real goo Next find yourself a hook. Not the kind of fresh son melody musicians use in their songs to make ther catchy. That's crazy! Why would you even mentio that? Boy, are you dumb. I'm talking about th curved, metallic kind that's sharp on one end. Tak the hook and make sure not to stab yourself to many times jamming it into the chest hair, meta glue combo. If you do manage to hook yourself b accident, congratulations! You've caught yoursel a human! Once the hook has been placed, hold i there for anywhere from 60-90 minutes. Hope yo didn't have anything to do for the next hour or hav anything baking in the oven. Which reminds me, m brownies should be done. Hooray!

Back to your lure. After it's dried it's finally me to attach it to your fishing line. Take your fishing ne and tie it around the lure like you would tie our shoes. Don't know how to tie your shoes? Not problem. Make a knot, then make two bunny ears nd knot those. Not sure what bunny ears are? That's problem. Use the internet to look it up. Now that ou have your lure attached to your line, you need a shing pole. Fishing poles are expensive. But the good ews is you can steal one from just about anywhere: our neighbor's garage, a fish and tackle store, or ome guy you see fishing. Now you have everything ou need to fish. At least that's what those fishermen isisted when I asked them at gunpoint. Finally, it's me to head down to the ol' fishing hole which is what call the river. When you get down there, remember shing takes patience, luck, and fish. That last one hould be pretty obvious. And that's it, just like that ou're a fisherman. That human hair lure should atch a gazillion fish or your money back! Which to e clear, you put very little money into this endeavor, o we're talking pennies. Valuable pennies which you ould have saved up to buy yourself an actual fish to at from the grocery store and not wasted all your time itting around catching nothin' at the ol' fishing hole. ut it's too late for that. You're already committed. A elpful side note: if you don't have chest hair to start, ou can always use other kinds of hair like beard hair, g hair, or human hair from that hair doll you made hat you don't tell anyone about. Because why would ou, there's nothing weird about it at all, is there?! If ou don't have any of those aforementioned types of air, well, you're out of luck. You're also out of hair, hich is equally as bad.

Good luck fishin'. Remember if you don't atch anything the first time you're out there, then ou're a damn failure and wasting your time. You hould probably quit fishin' and bury your head in the and! The world has enough unsuccessful fishermen n it. Trust me, I'm one of them.

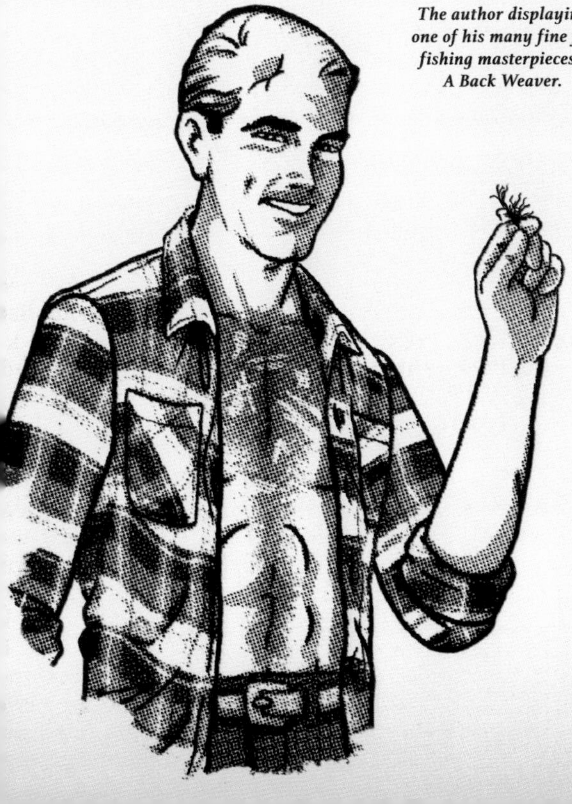

The author displaying one of his many fine fly fishing masterpieces - A Back Weaver.

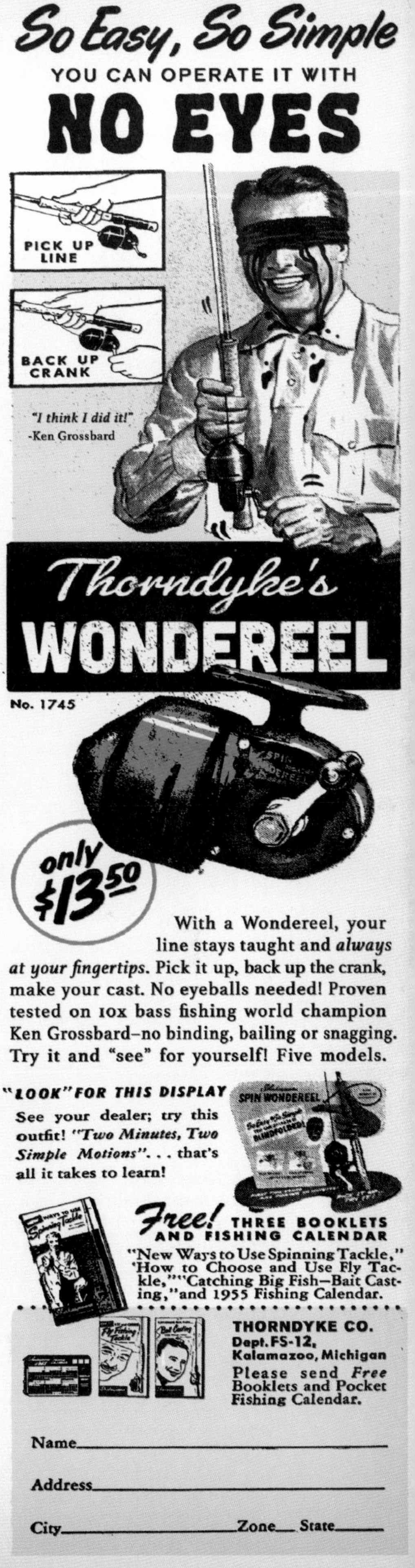
So Easy, So Simple
YOU CAN OPERATE IT WITH
NO EYES
PICK UP LINE
BACK UP CRANK
"I think I did it!"
-Ken Grossbard
Thorndyke's
WONDEREEL
No. 1745
only $13.50
With a Wondereel, your line stays taught and always at your fingertips. Pick it up, back up the crank, make your cast. No eyeballs needed! Proven tested on 10x bass fishing world champion Ken Grossbard–no binding, bailing or snagging. Try it and "see" for yourself! Five models.
"LOOK" FOR THIS DISPLAY
See your dealer; try this outfit! "Two Minutes, Two Simple Motions". . . that's all it takes to learn!
SPIN WONDEREEL
Free! THREE BOOKLETS AND FISHING CALENDAR
"New Ways to Use Spinning Tackle," "How to Choose and Use Fly Tackle," "Catching Big Fish–Bait Casting," and 1955 Fishing Calendar.
THORNDYKE CO.
Dept. FS-12,
Kalamazoo, Michigan
Please send Free Booklets and Pocket Fishing Calendar.
Name
Address
City
Zone
State

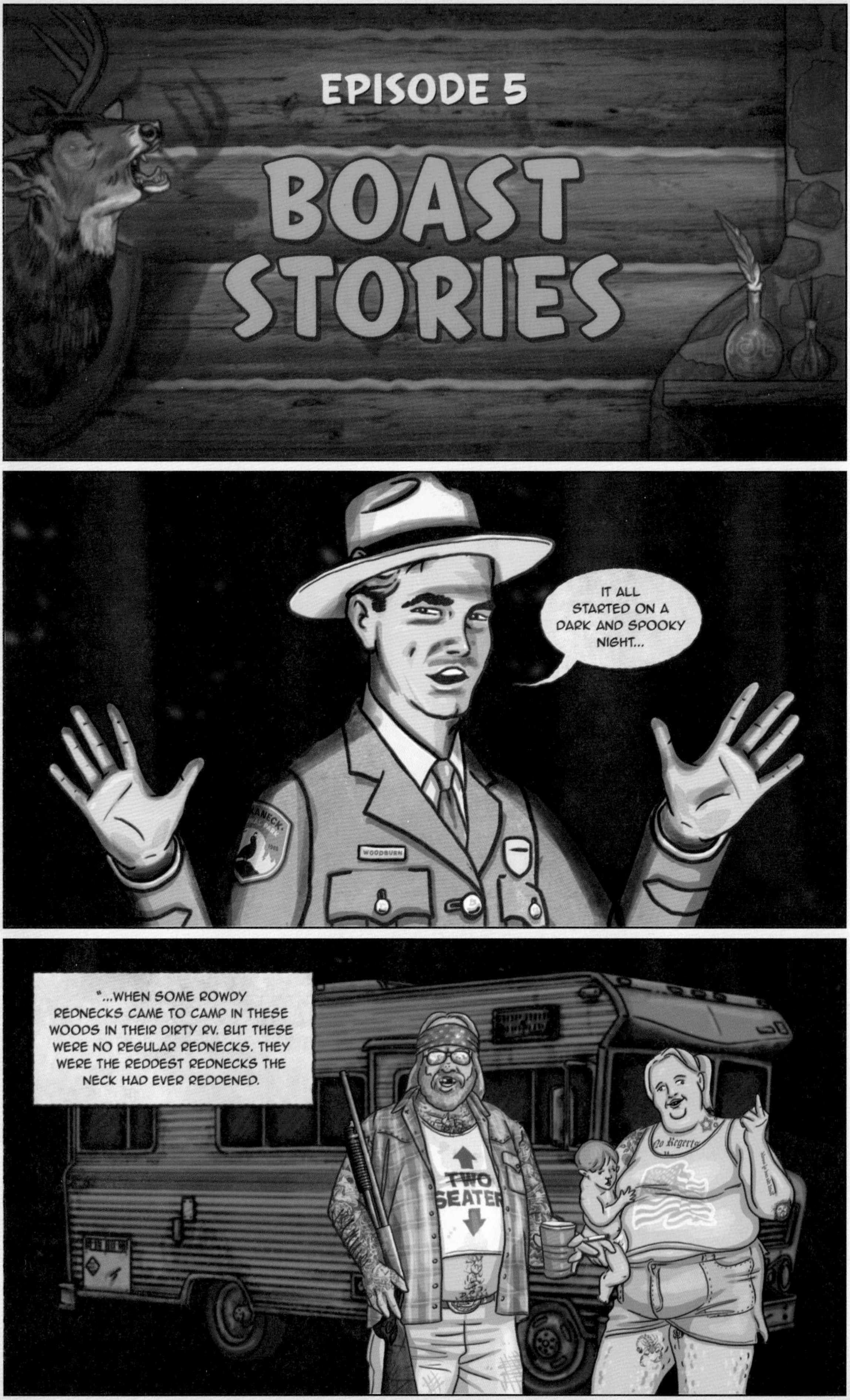
EPISODE 5
BOAST STORIES
IT ALL STARTED ON A DARK AND SPOOKY NIGHT...
WOODBURN
"...WHEN SOME ROWDY REDNECKS CAME TO CAMP IN THESE WOODS IN THEIR DIRTY RV. BUT THESE WERE NO REGULAR REDNECKS. THEY WERE THE REDDEST REDNECKS THE NECK HAD EVER REDDENED.
TWO SEATER
No Regerts

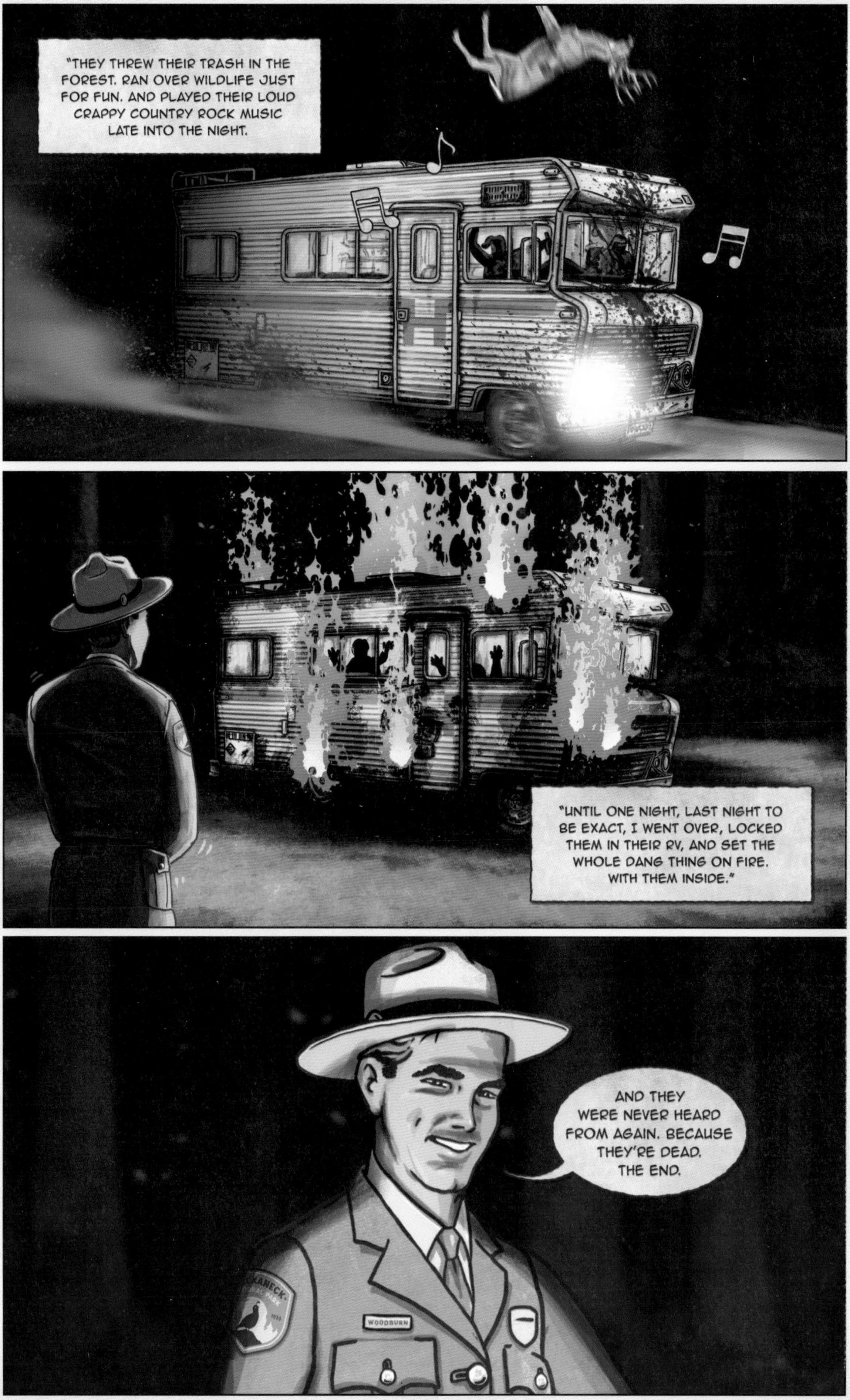
"THEY THREW THEIR TRASH IN THE FOREST. RAN OVER WILDLIFE JUST FOR FUN. AND PLAYED THEIR LOUD CRAPPY COUNTRY ROCK MUSIC LATE INTO THE NIGHT.
"UNTIL ONE NIGHT, LAST NIGHT TO BE EXACT, I WENT OVER, LOCKED THEM IN THEIR RV, AND SET THE WHOLE DANG THING ON FIRE. WITH THEM INSIDE."
AND THEY WERE NEVER HEARD FROM AGAIN. BECAUSE THEY'RE DEAD. THE END.
WOODBURN

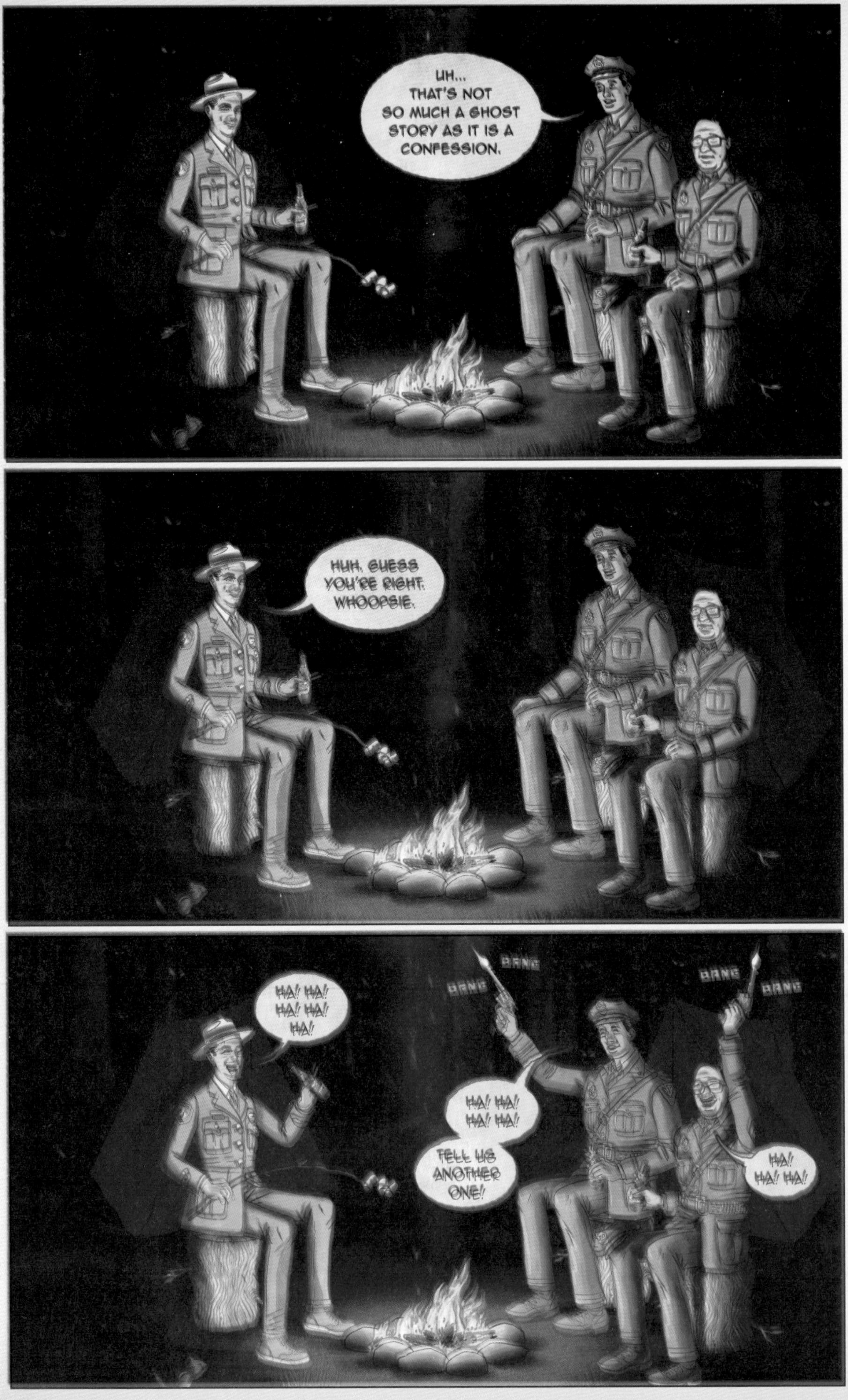
UH... THAT'S NOT SO MUCH A GHOST STORY AS IT IS A CONFESSION.
HUH. GUESS YOU'RE RIGHT. WHOOPSIE.
HA! HA! HA! HA! HA!
BANG
BANG
BANG
BANG
HA! HA! HA! HA!
TELL US ANOTHER ONE!
HA! HA! HA!

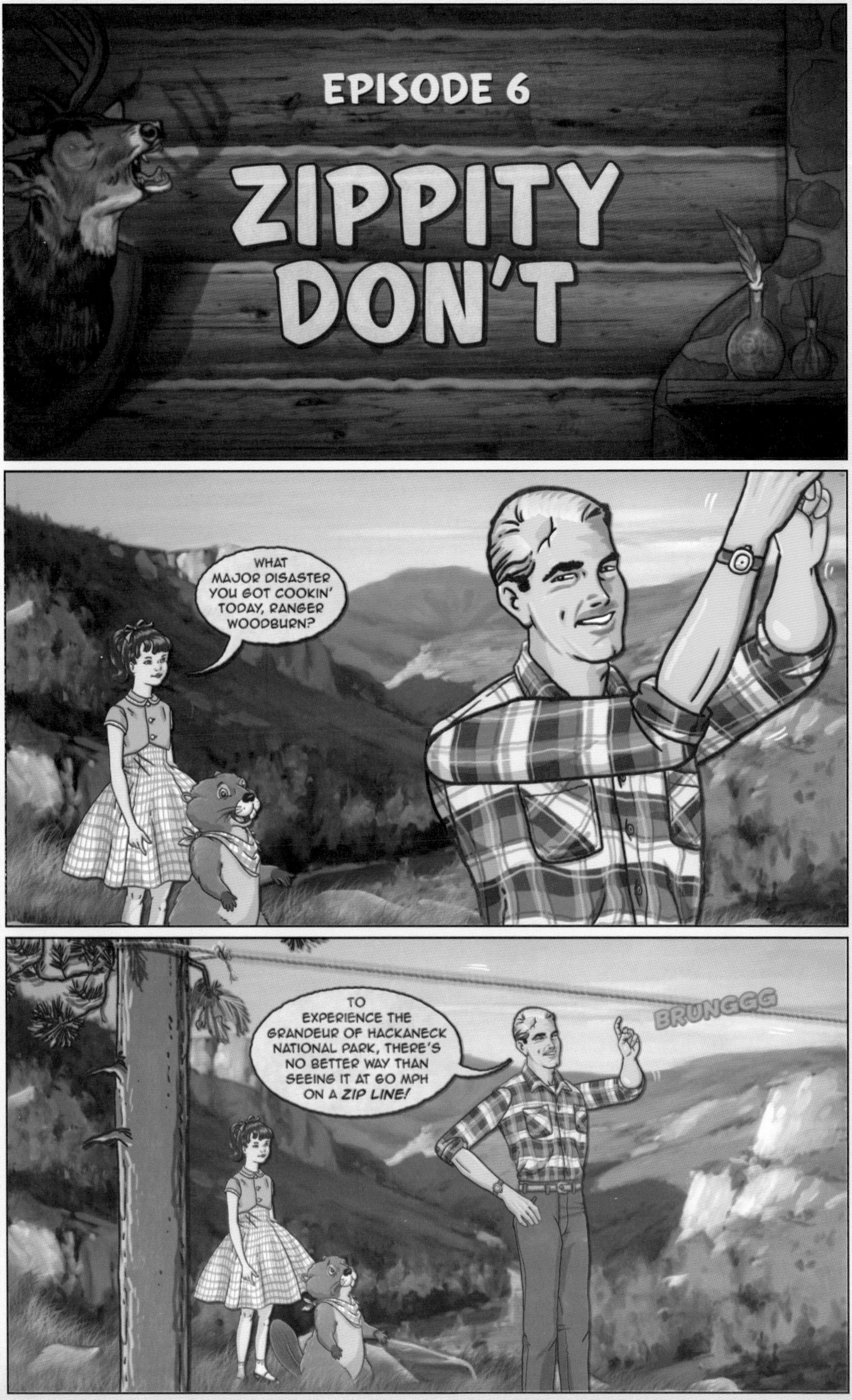
EPISODE 6
ZIPPITY DON'T
WHAT MAJOR DISASTER YOU GOT COOKIN' TODAY, RANGER WOODBURN?
TO EXPERIENCE THE GRANDEUR OF HACKANECK NATIONAL PARK, THERE'S NO BETTER WAY THAN SEEING IT AT 60 MPH ON A ZIP LINE!
BRUNGGG

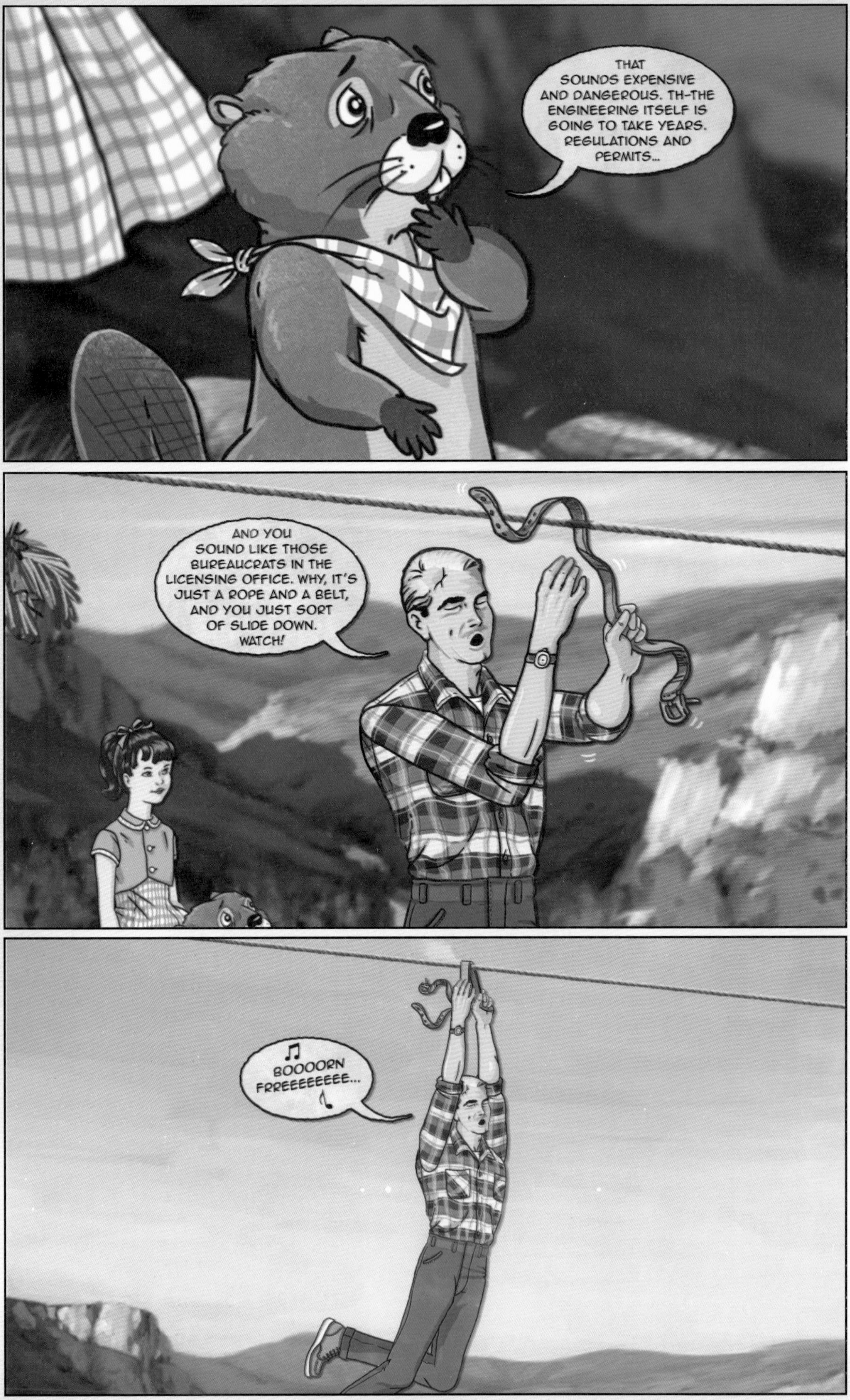
THAT SOUNDS EXPENSIVE AND DANGEROUS. TH-THE ENGINEERING ITSELF IS GOING TO TAKE YEARS. REGULATIONS AND PERMITS...
AND YOU SOUND LIKE THOSE BUREAUCRATS IN THE LICENSING OFFICE. WHY, IT'S JUST A ROPE AND A BELT, AND YOU JUST SORT OF SLIDE DOWN. WATCH!
♫ BOOOORN FRREEEEEEEE... ♪

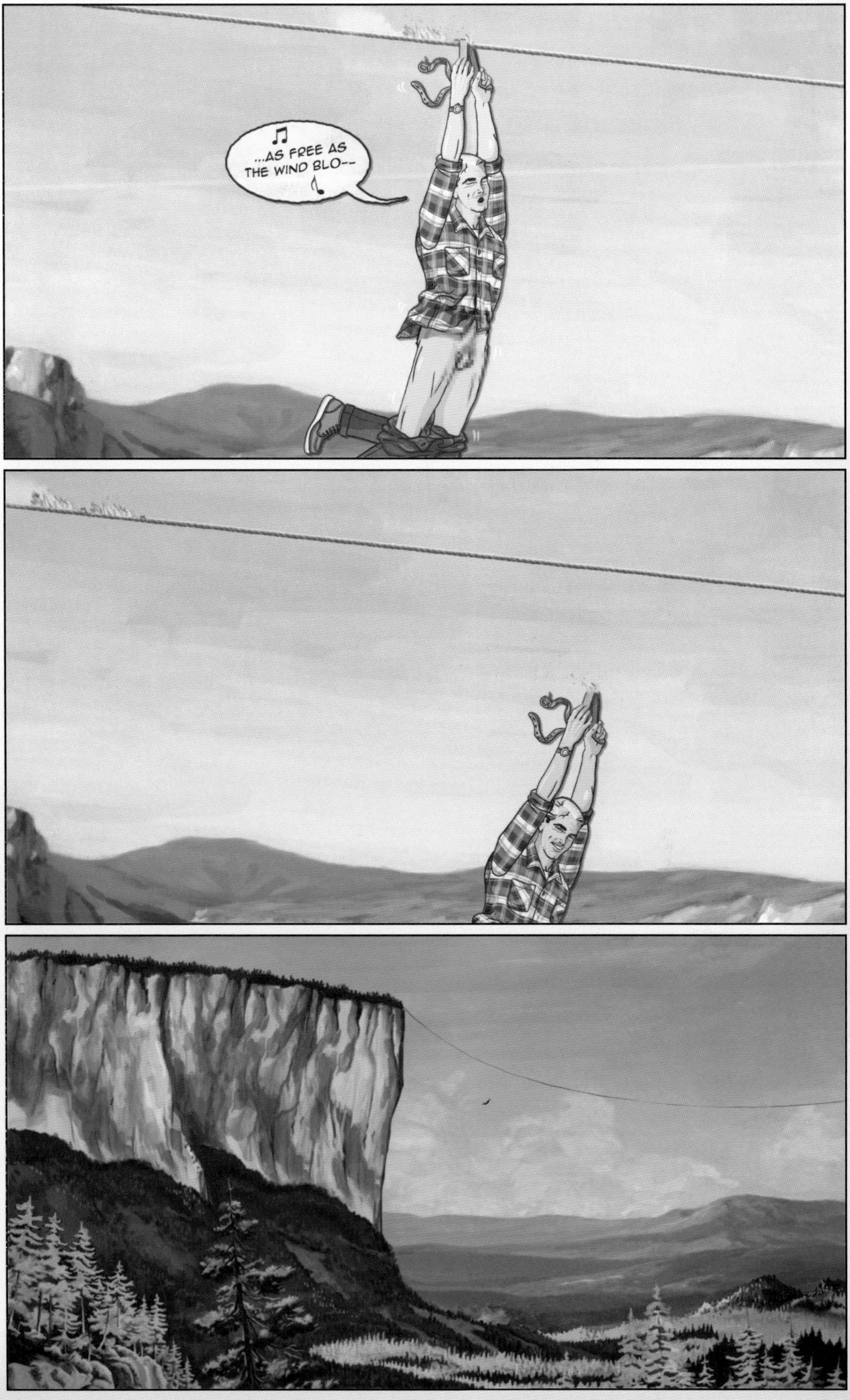
...AS FREE AS THE WIND BLO--

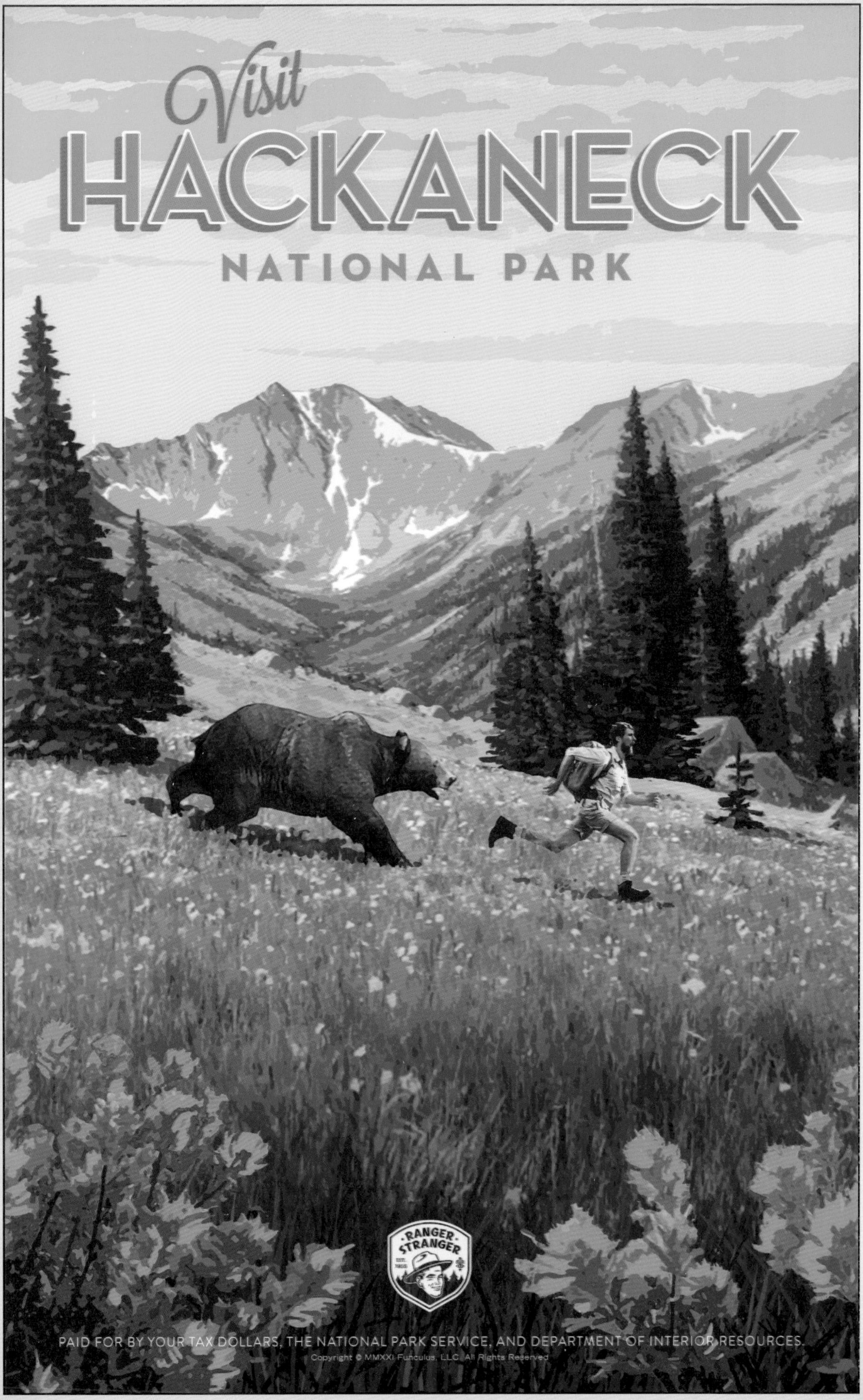
Visit
HACKANECK
NATIONAL PARK
RANGER
STRANGER
PAID FOR BY YOUR TAX DOLLARS, THE NATIONAL PARK SERVICE, AND DEPARTMENT OF INTERIOR RESOURCES.
Copyright © MMXXI Funculus, LLC. All Rights Reserved

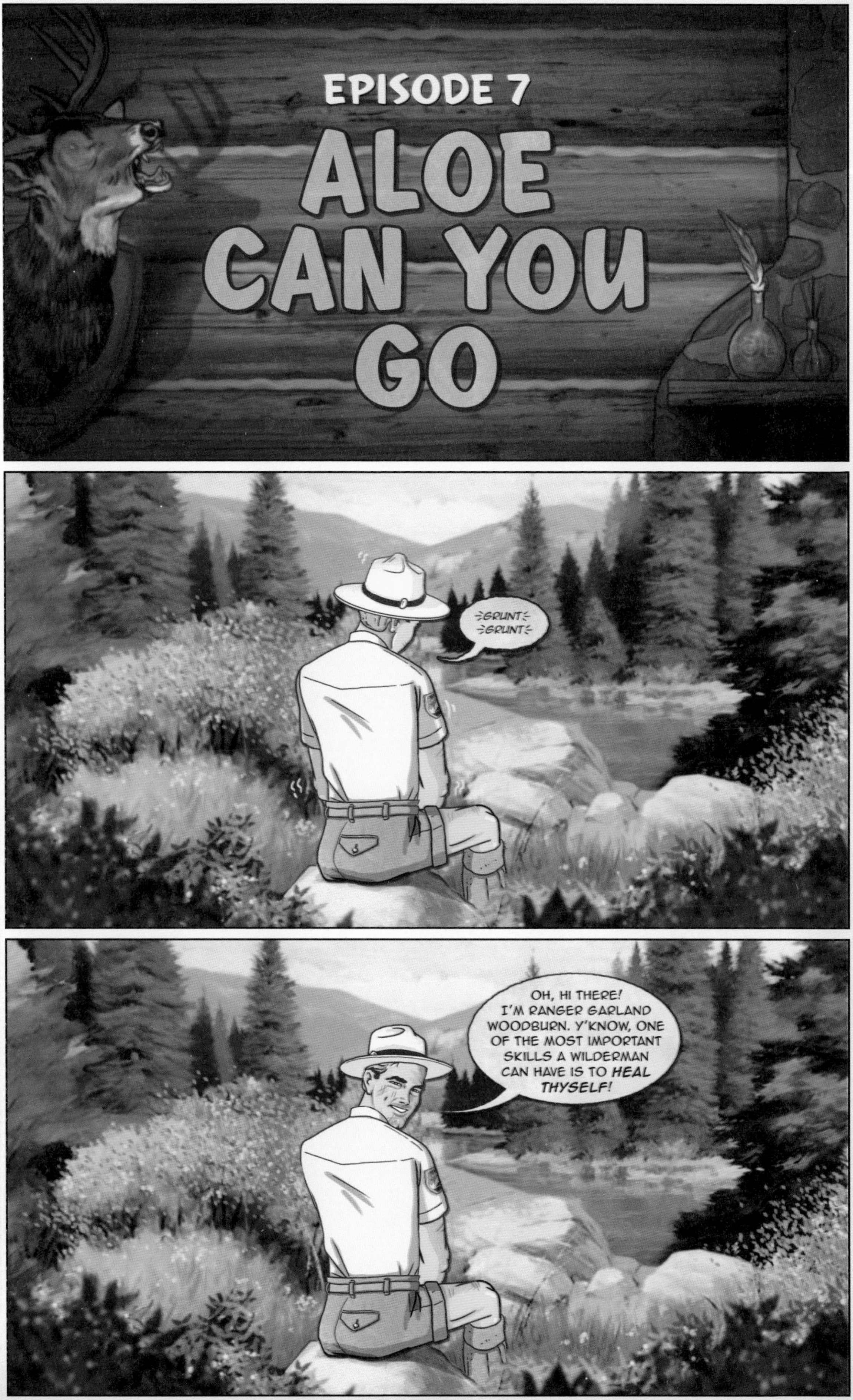
EPISODE 7
ALOE CAN YOU GO
GRUNT GRUNT
OH, HI THERE! I'M RANGER GARLAND WOODBURN. Y'KNOW, ONE OF THE MOST IMPORTANT SKILLS A WILDERMAN CAN HAVE IS TO *HEAL THYSELF!*

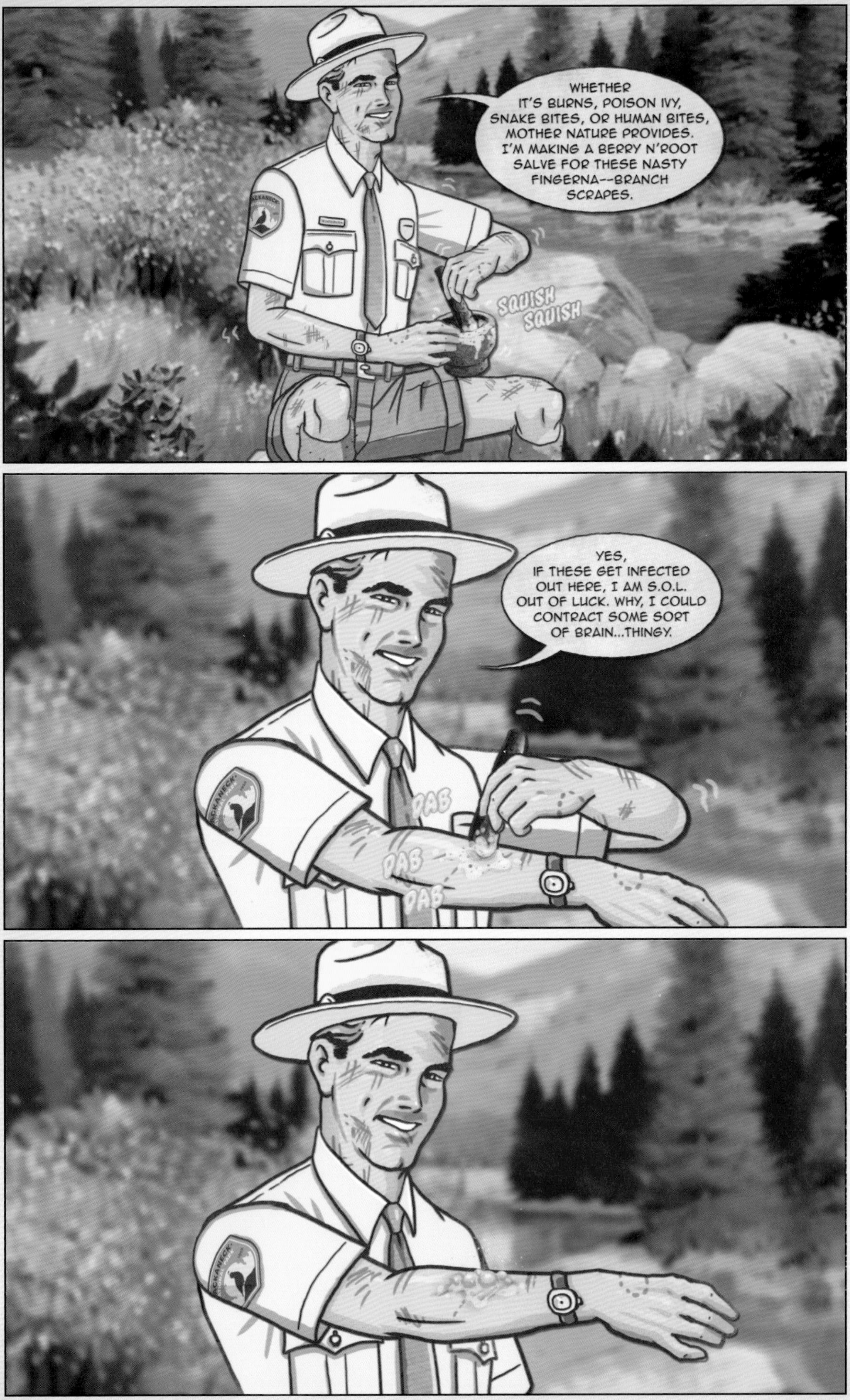
WHETHER IT'S BURNS, POISON IVY, SNAKE BITES, OR HUMAN BITES, MOTHER NATURE PROVIDES. I'M MAKING A BERRY N'ROOT SALVE FOR THESE NASTY FINGERNA--BRANCH SCRAPES.
SQUISH SQUISH
YES, IF THESE GET INFECTED OUT HERE, I AM S.O.L. OUT OF LUCK. WHY, I COULD CONTRACT SOME SORT OF BRAIN...THINGY.
DAB
DAB
DAB

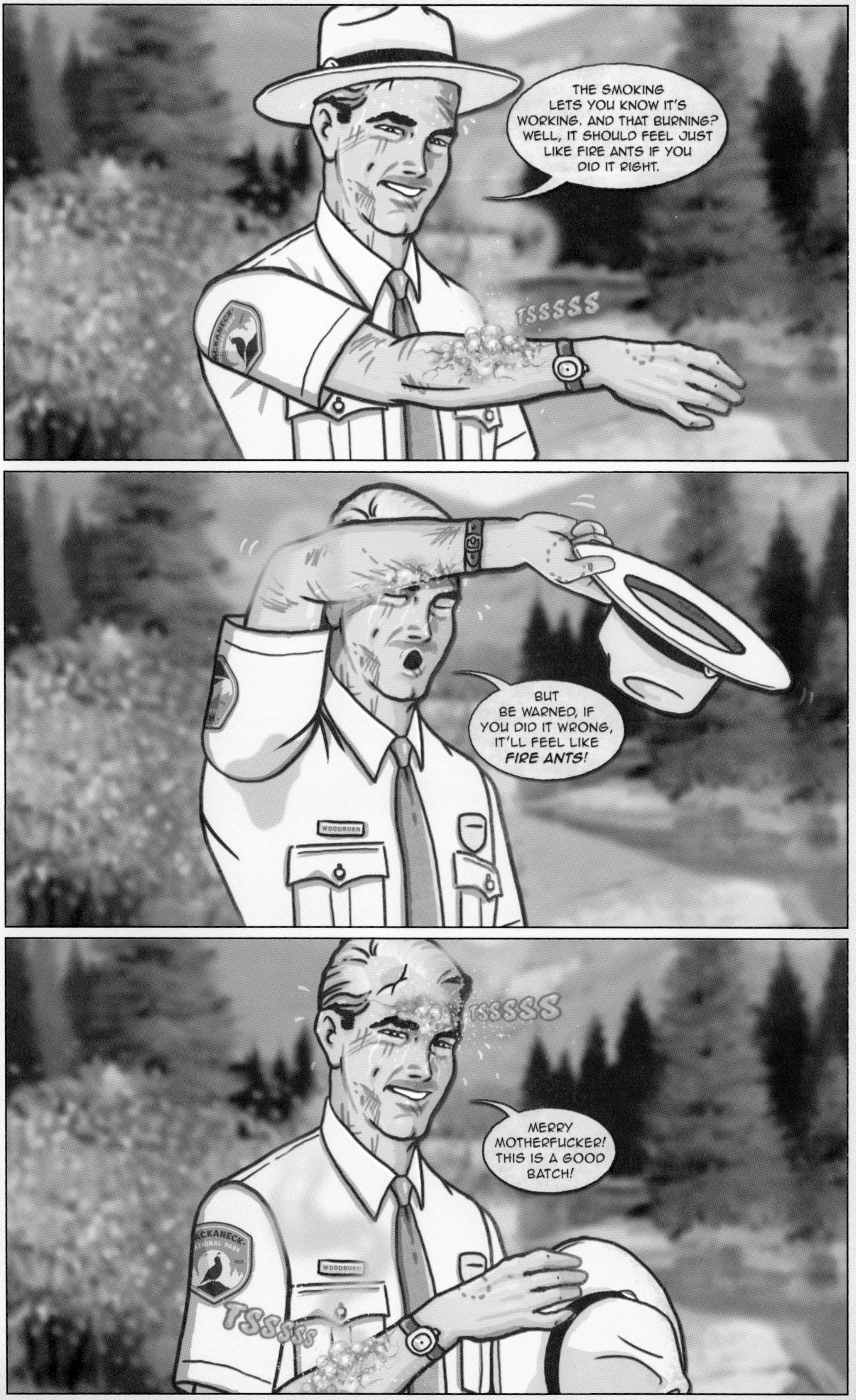
THE SMOKING LETS YOU KNOW IT'S WORKING. AND THAT BURNING? WELL, IT SHOULD FEEL JUST LIKE FIRE ANTS IF YOU DID IT RIGHT.
TSSSSS
BUT BE WARNED, IF YOU DID IT WRONG, IT'LL FEEL LIKE *FIRE ANTS!*
TSSSSS
MERRY MOTHERFUCKER! THIS IS A GOOD BATCH!
WOODBURN
TSSSSS

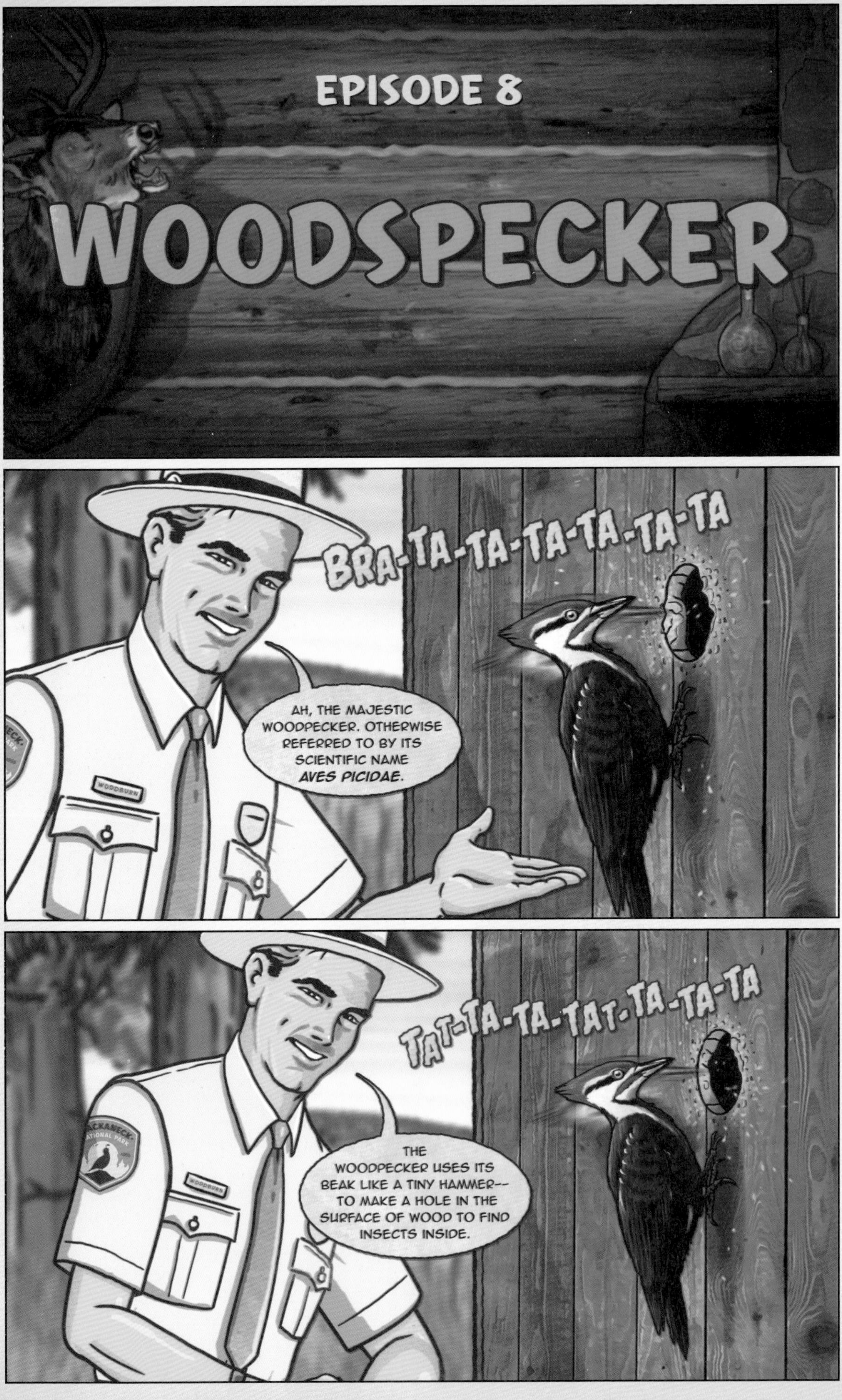
EPISODE 8
WOODSPECKER
BRA-TA-TA-TA-TA-TA-TA
AH, THE MAJESTIC WOODPECKER. OTHERWISE REFERRED TO BY ITS SCIENTIFIC NAME *AVES PICIDAE*.
TAT-TA-TA-TAT-TA-TA-TA
THE WOODPECKER USES ITS BEAK LIKE A TINY HAMMER-- TO MAKE A HOLE IN THE SURFACE OF WOOD TO FIND INSECTS INSIDE.

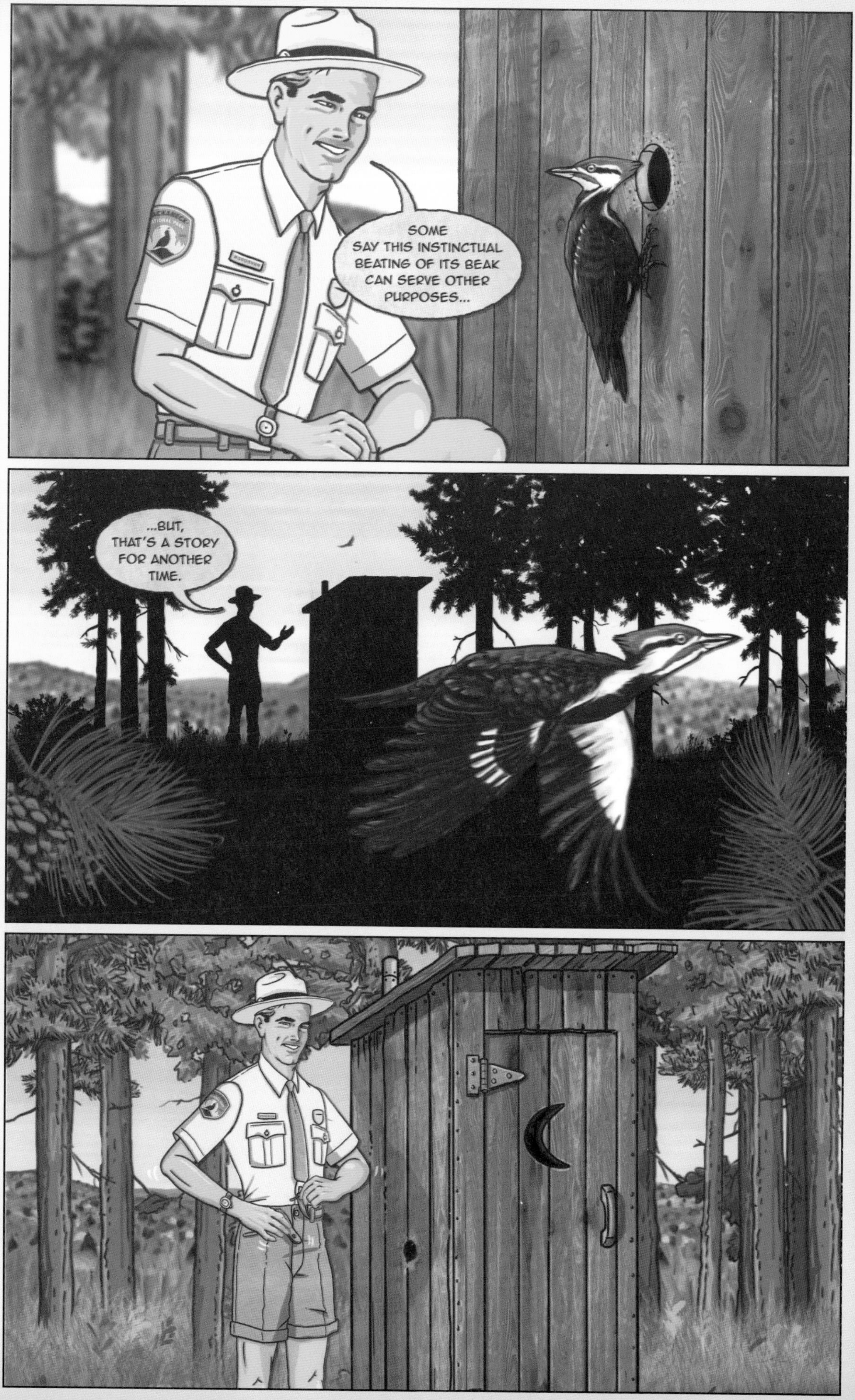
SOME SAY THIS INSTINCTUAL BEATING OF ITS BEAK CAN SERVE OTHER PURPOSES...
...BUT, THAT'S A STORY FOR ANOTHER TIME.

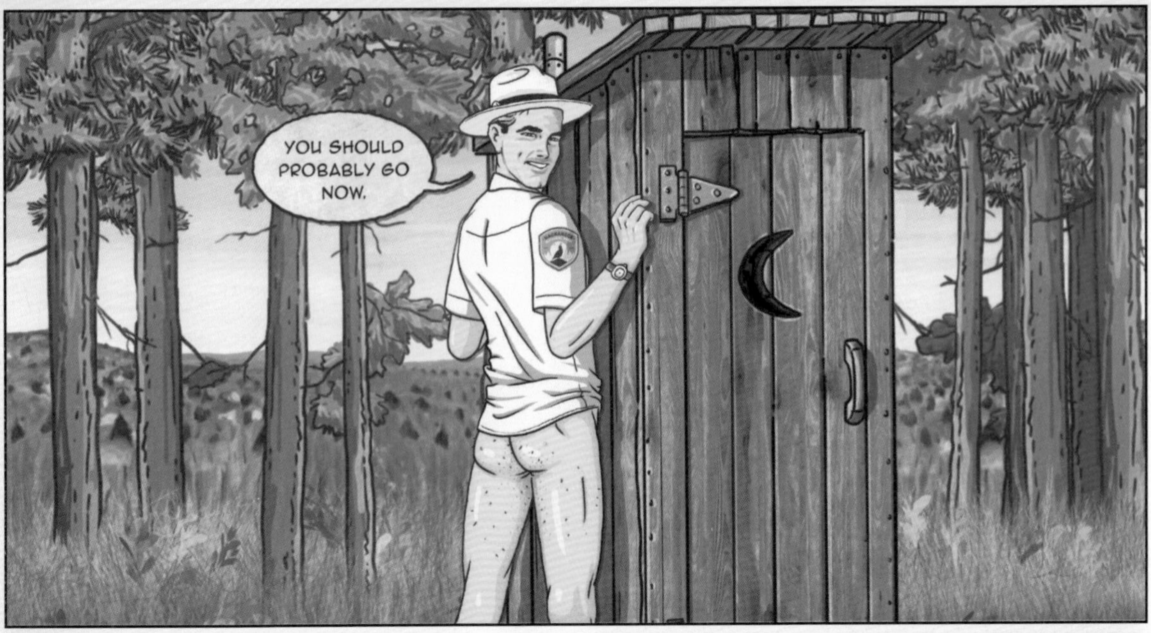
YOU SHOULD PROBABLY GO NOW.

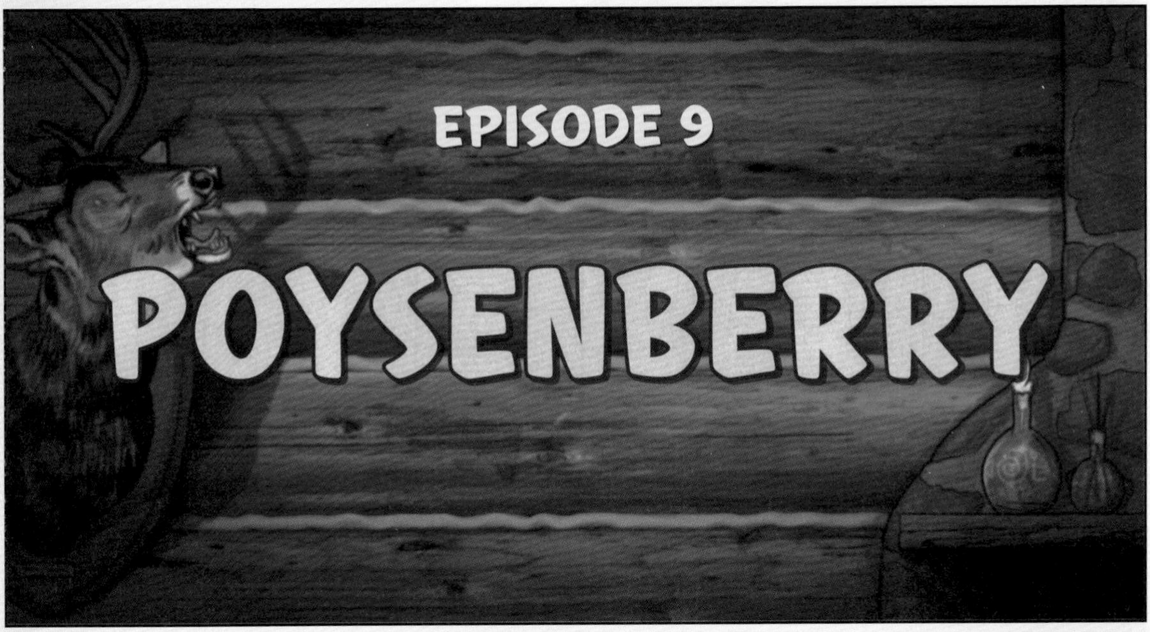
EPISODE 9
POYSENBERRY

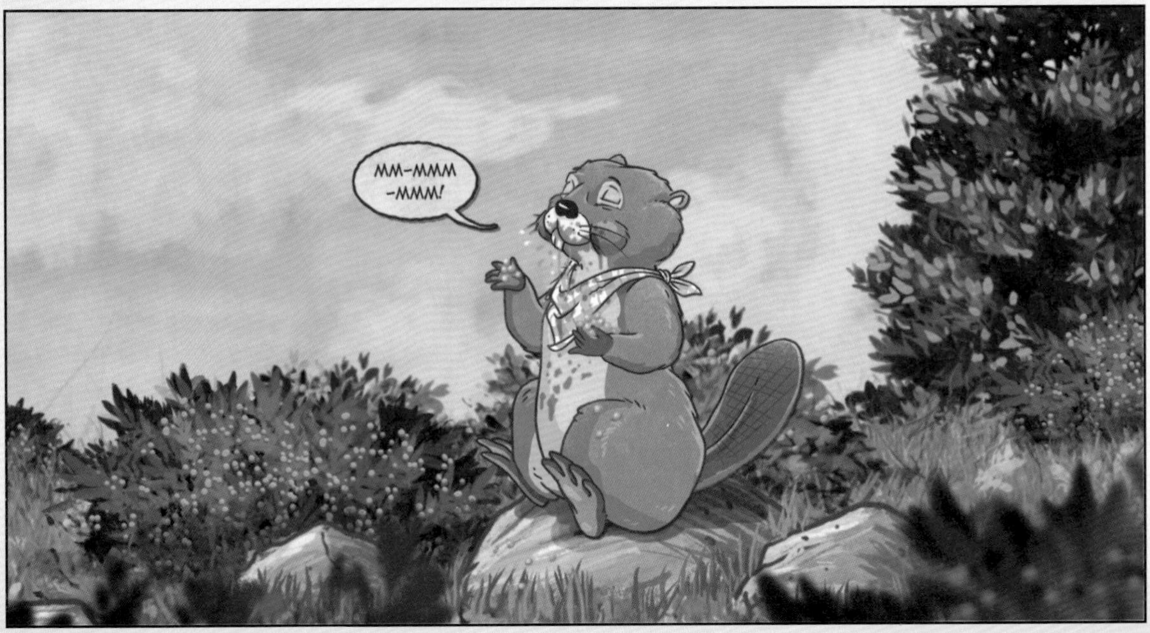
MM-MMM -MMM!

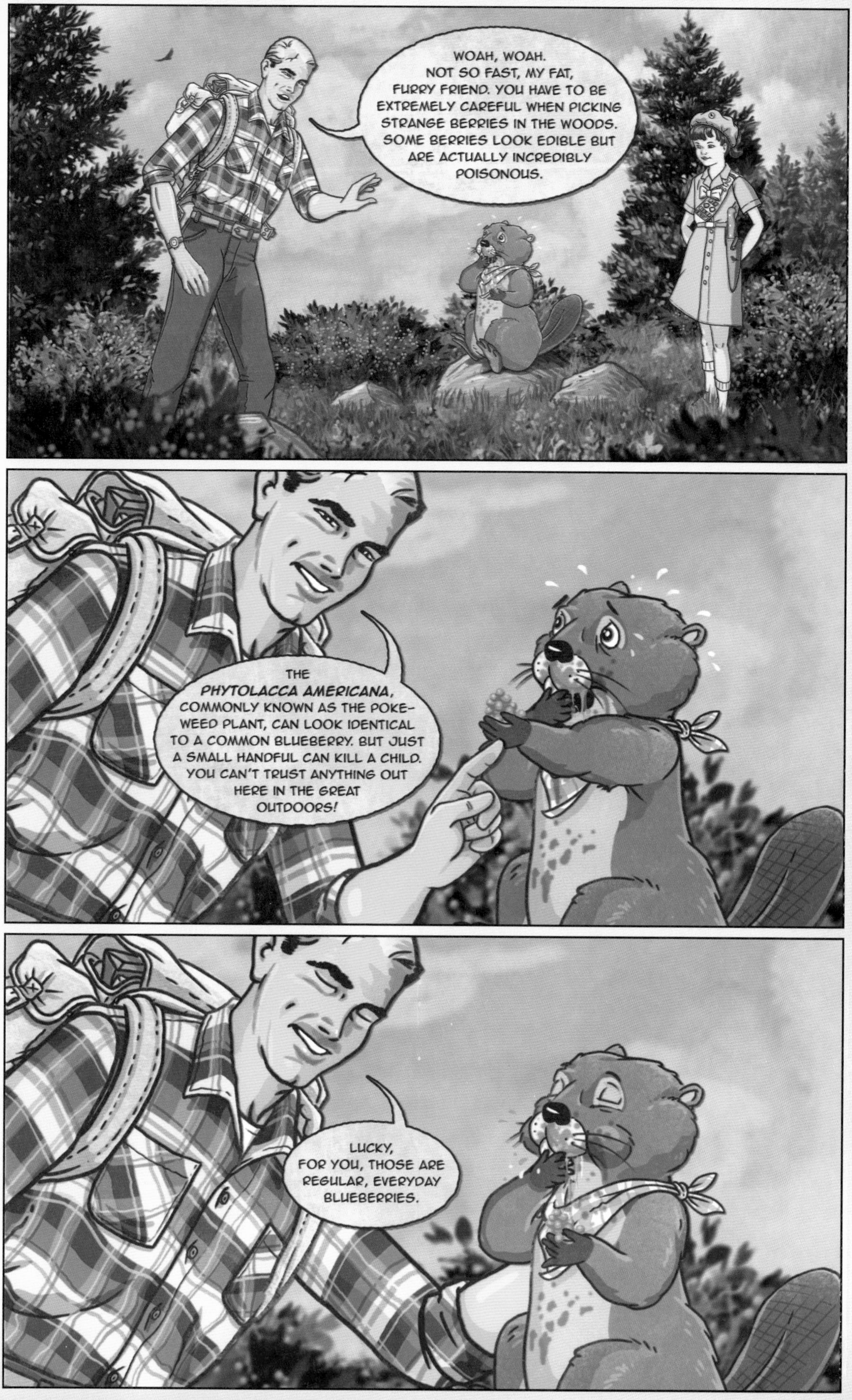
WOAH, WOAH. NOT SO FAST, MY FAT, FURRY FRIEND. YOU HAVE TO BE EXTREMELY CAREFUL WHEN PICKING STRANGE BERRIES IN THE WOODS. SOME BERRIES LOOK EDIBLE BUT ARE ACTUALLY INCREDIBLY POISONOUS.
THE *PHYTOLACCA AMERICANA*, COMMONLY KNOWN AS THE POKE-WEED PLANT, CAN LOOK IDENTICAL TO A COMMON BLUEBERRY. BUT JUST A SMALL HANDFUL CAN KILL A CHILD. YOU CAN'T TRUST ANYTHING OUT HERE IN THE GREAT OUTDOORS!
LUCKY, FOR YOU, THOSE ARE REGULAR, EVERYDAY BLUEBERRIES.

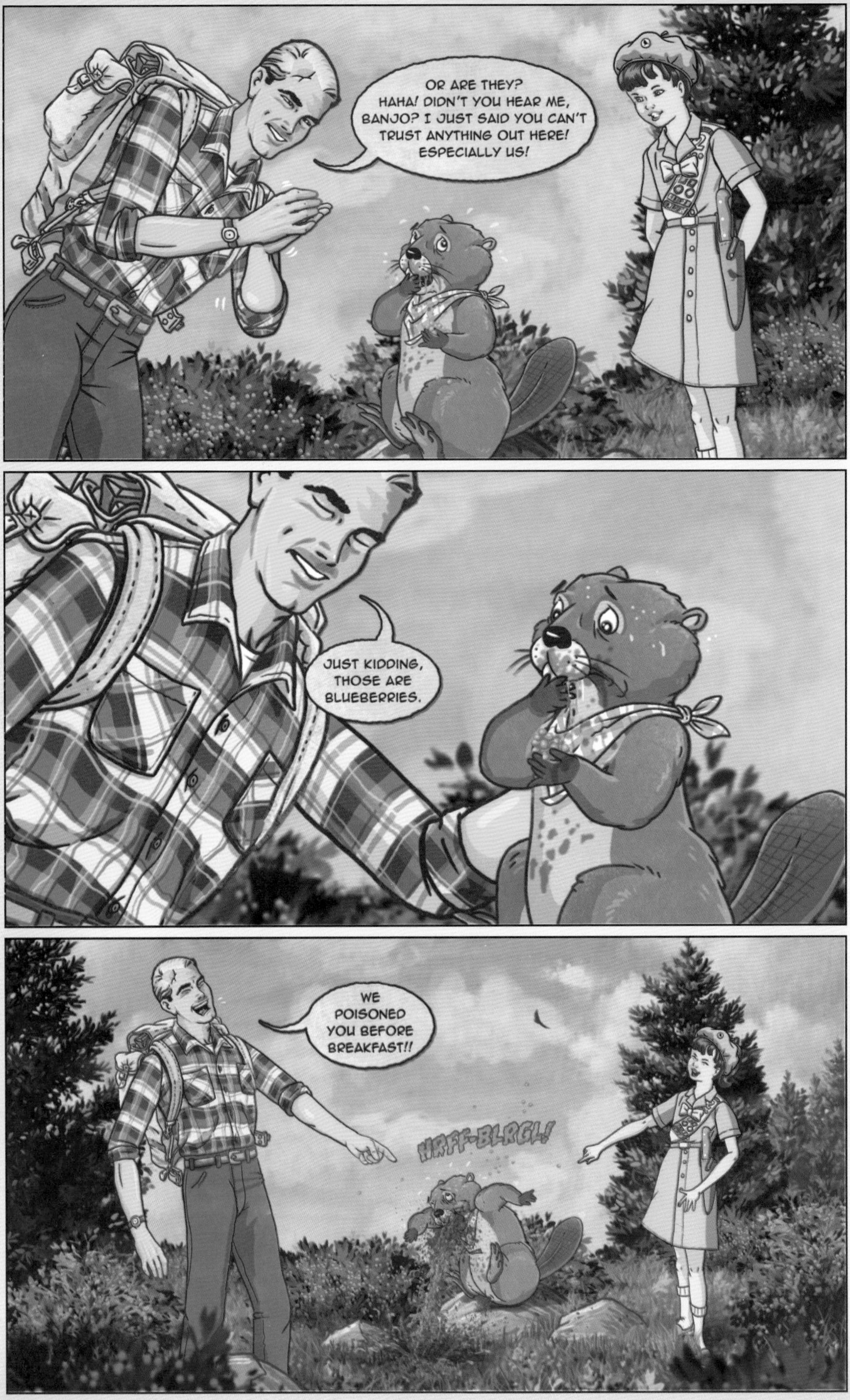
OR ARE THEY?
HAHA! DIDN'T YOU HEAR ME, BANJO? I JUST SAID YOU CAN'T TRUST ANYTHING OUT HERE! ESPECIALLY US!
JUST KIDDING, THOSE ARE BLUEBERRIES.
WE POISONED YOU BEFORE BREAKFAST!!
HRFF-BLRGL!

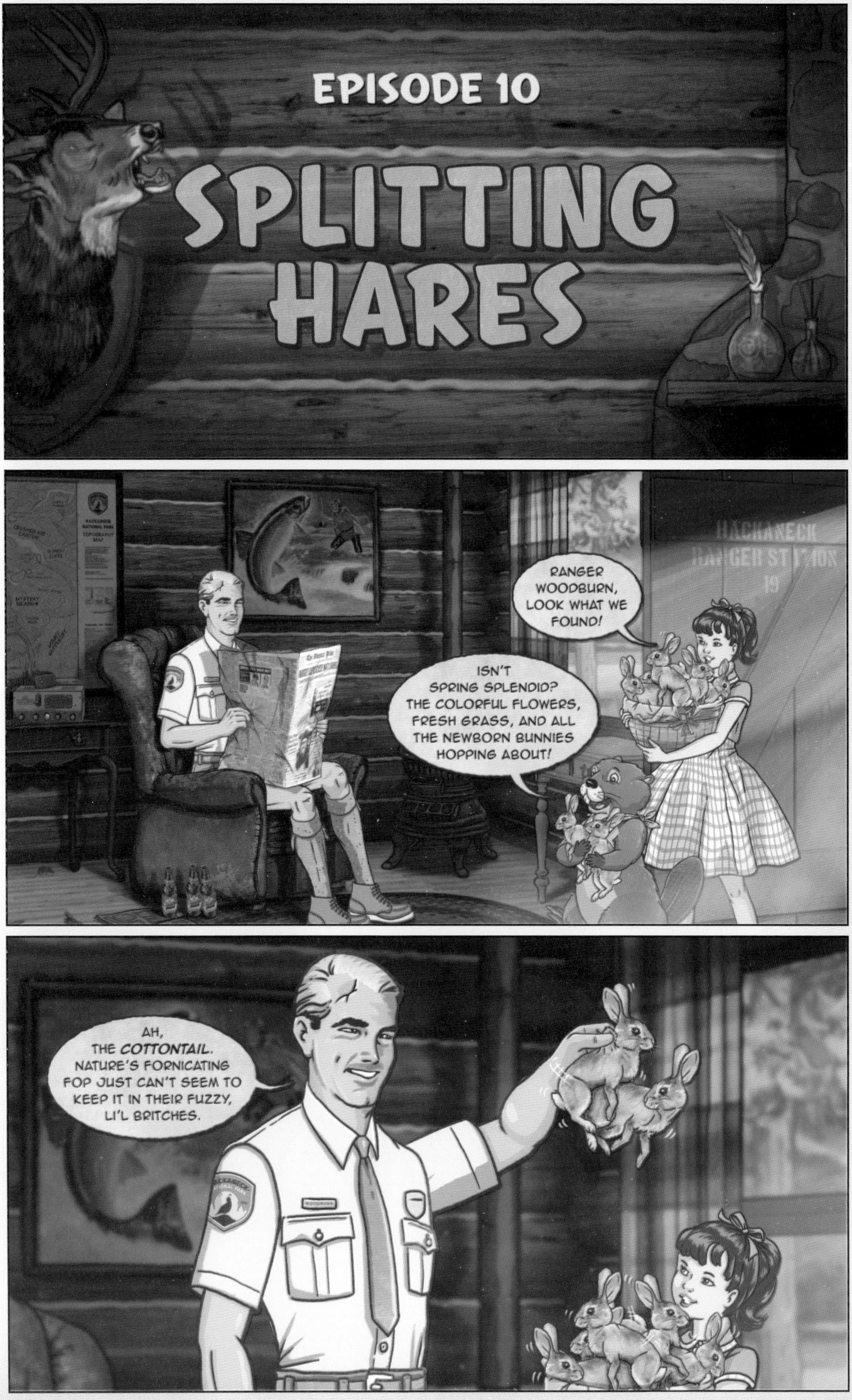
EPISODE 10
SPLITTING HARES
RANGER WOODBURN, LOOK WHAT WE FOUND!
ISN'T SPRING SPLENDID? THE COLORFUL FLOWERS, FRESH GRASS, AND ALL THE NEWBORN BUNNIES HOPPING ABOUT!
AH, THE *COTTONTAIL*. NATURE'S FORNICATING FOP JUST CAN'T SEEM TO KEEP IT IN THEIR FUZZY, LI'L BRITCHES.

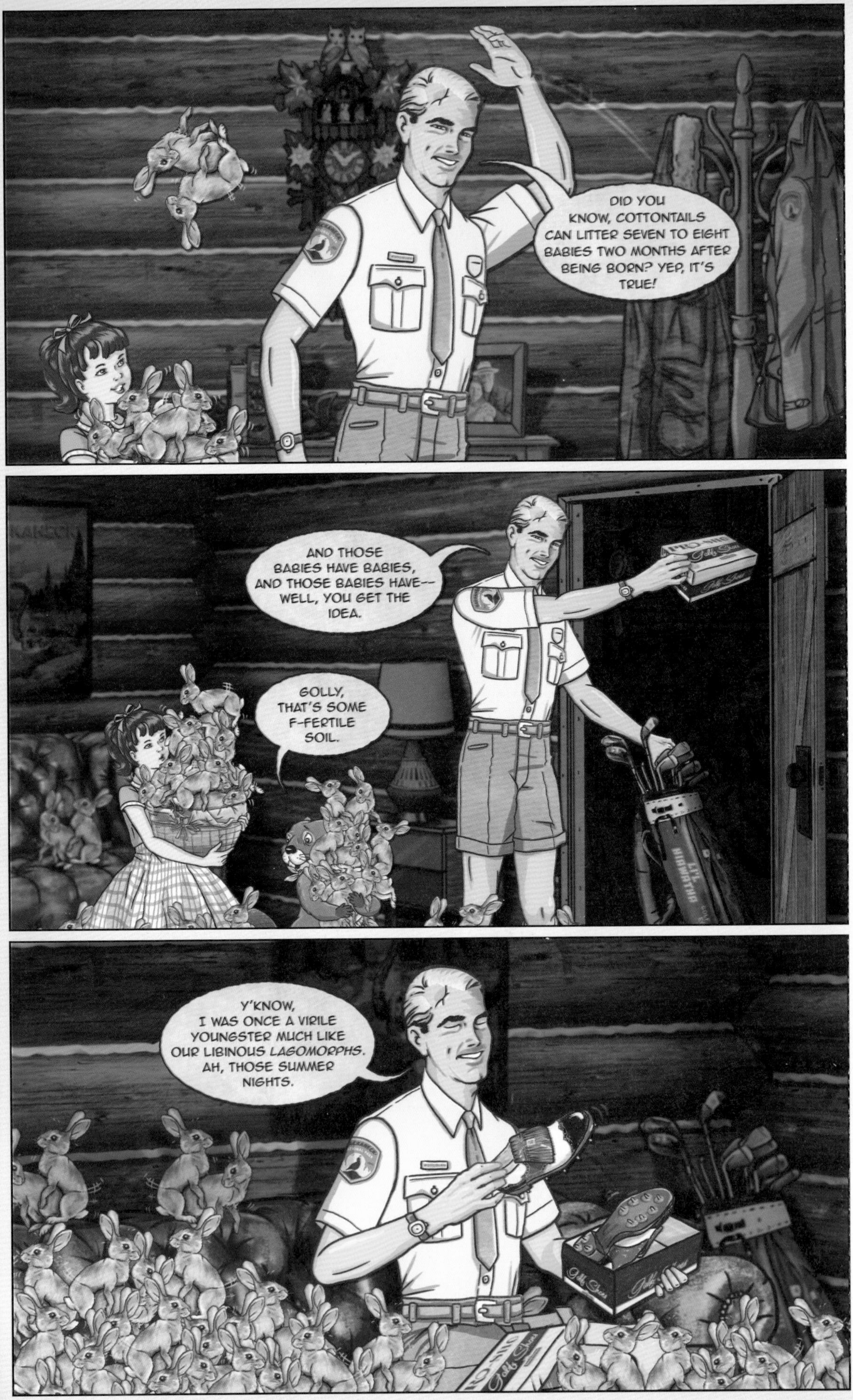
DID YOU KNOW, COTTONTAILS CAN LITTER SEVEN TO EIGHT BABIES TWO MONTHS AFTER BEING BORN? YEP, IT'S TRUE!
AND THOSE BABIES HAVE BABIES, AND THOSE BABIES HAVE-- WELL, YOU GET THE IDEA.
GOLLY, THAT'S SOME F-FERTILE SOIL.
Y'KNOW, I WAS ONCE A VIRILE YOUNGSTER MUCH LIKE OUR LIBINOUS *LAGOMORPHS*. AH, THOSE SUMMER NIGHTS.

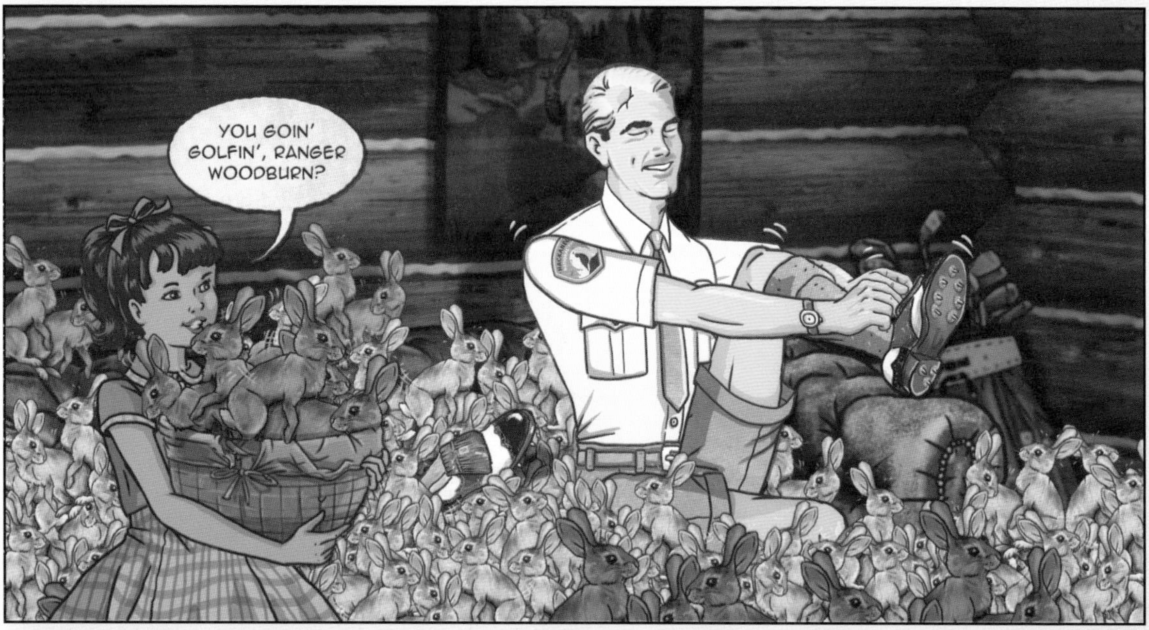
YOU GOIN' GOLFIN', RANGER WOODBURN?

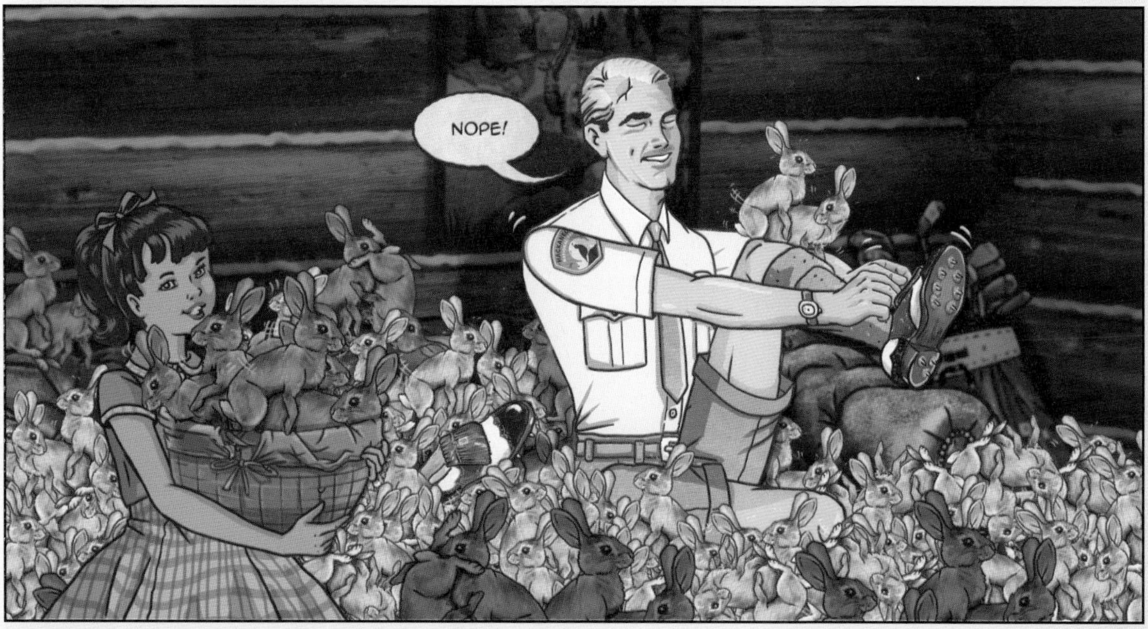
NOPE!

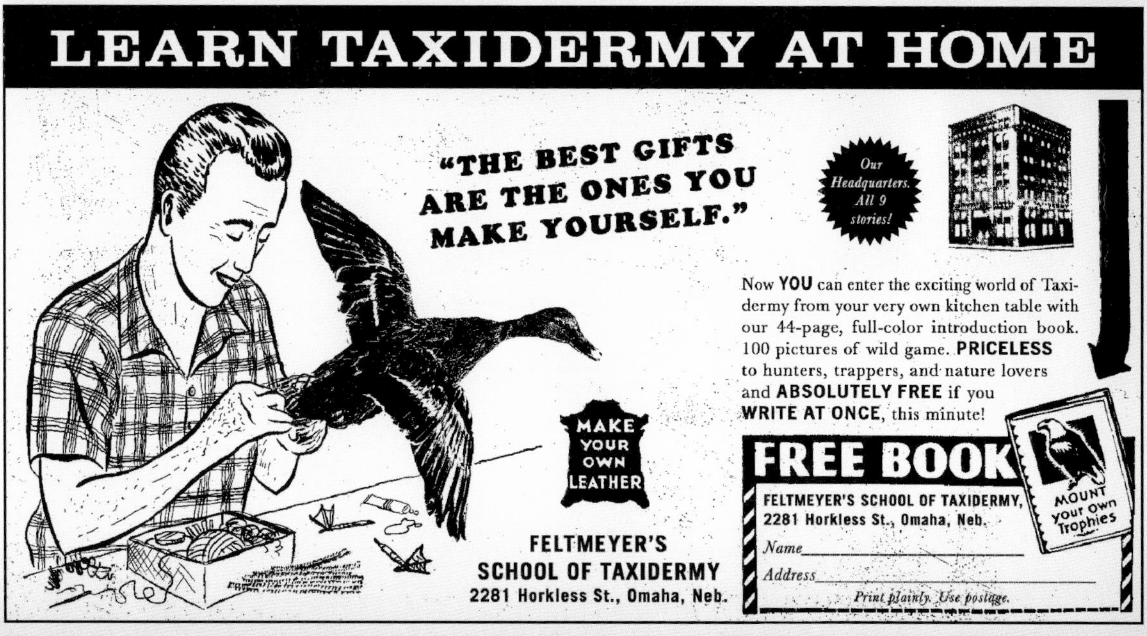
LEARN TAXIDERMY AT HOME
"THE BEST GIFTS ARE THE ONES YOU MAKE YOURSELF."
Our Headquarters. All 9 stories!
Now YOU can enter the exciting world of Taxidermy from your very own kitchen table with our 44-page, full-color introduction book. 100 pictures of wild game. PRICELESS to hunters, trappers, and nature lovers and ABSOLUTELY FREE if you WRITE AT ONCE, this minute!
MAKE YOUR OWN LEATHER
FELTMEYER'S SCHOOL OF TAXIDERMY
2281 Horkless St., Omaha, Neb.
FREE BOOK
FELTMEYER'S SCHOOL OF TAXIDERMY,
2281 Horkless St., Omaha, Neb.
Name
Address
Print plainly. Use postage.
MOUNT Your Own Trophies

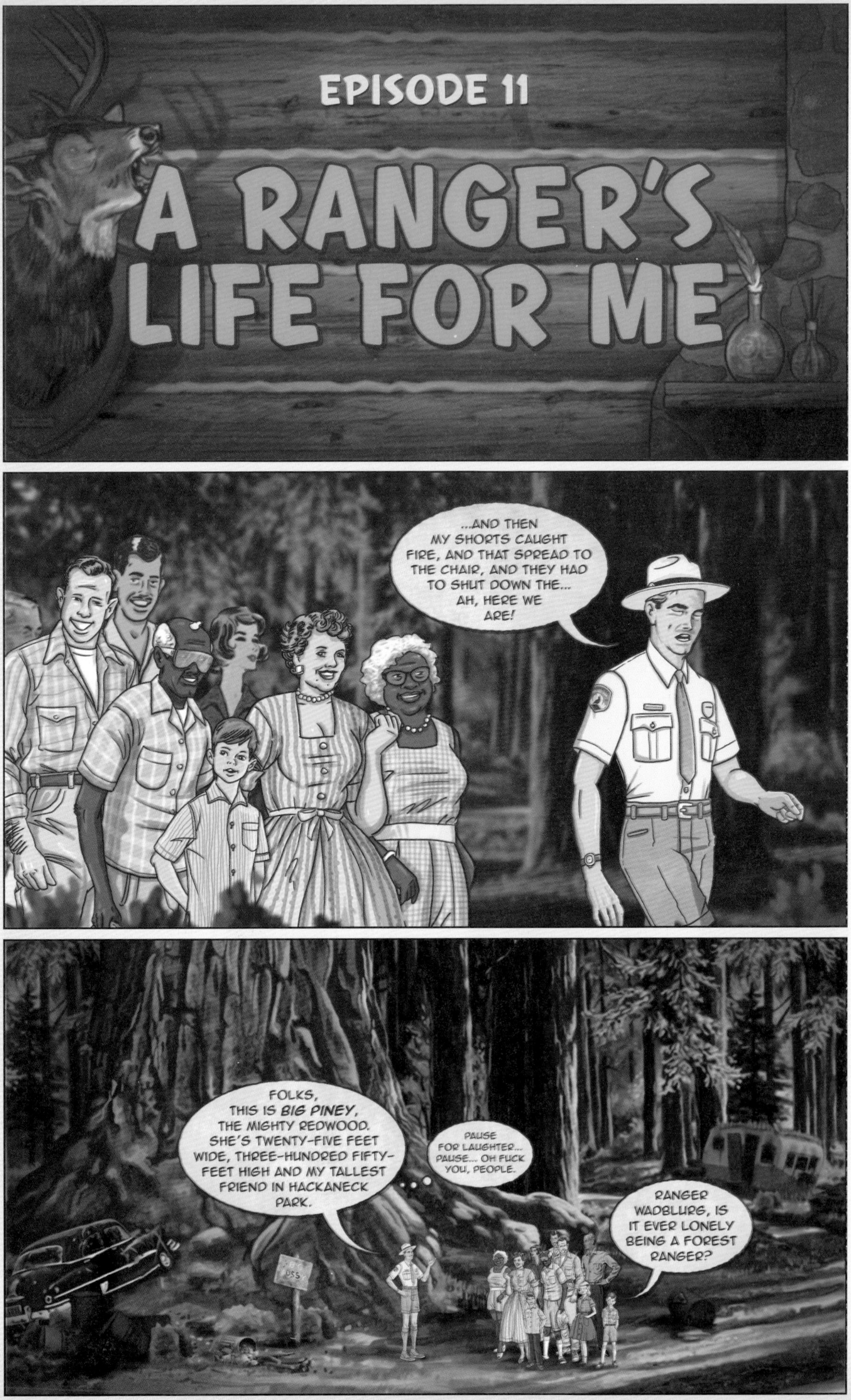
EPISODE 11
A RANGER'S LIFE FOR ME
...AND THEN MY SHORTS CAUGHT FIRE, AND THAT SPREAD TO THE CHAIR, AND THEY HAD TO SHUT DOWN THE... AH, HERE WE ARE!
FOLKS, THIS IS *BIG PINEY*, THE MIGHTY REDWOOD. SHE'S TWENTY-FIVE FEET WIDE, THREE-HUNDRED FIFTY-FEET HIGH AND MY TALLEST FRIEND IN HACKANECK PARK.
PAUSE FOR LAUGHTER... PAUSE... OH FUCK YOU, PEOPLE.
RANGER WADBLURG, IS IT EVER LONELY BEING A FOREST RANGER?

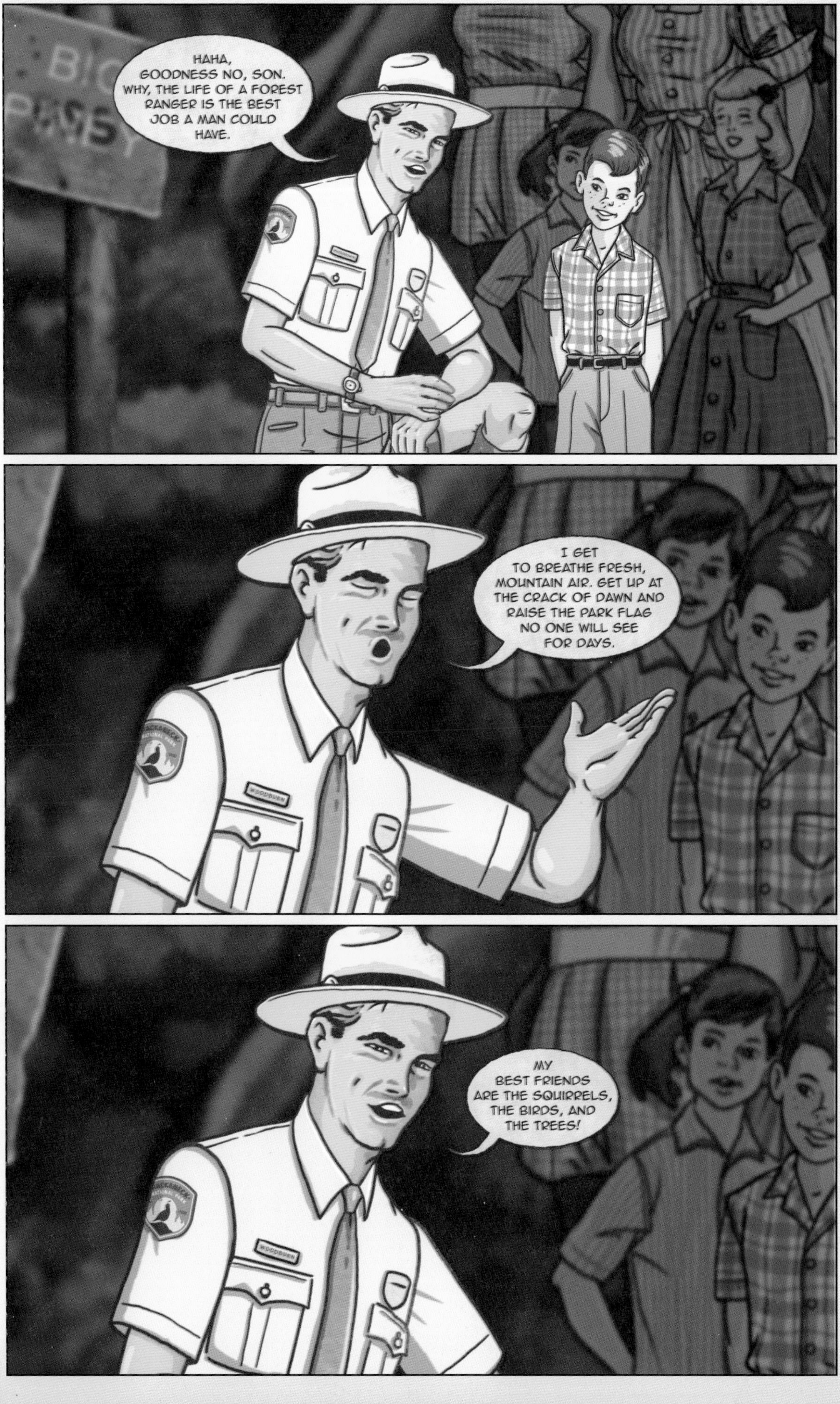
HAHA, GOODNESS NO, SON. WHY, THE LIFE OF A FOREST RANGER IS THE BEST JOB A MAN COULD HAVE.
I GET TO BREATHE FRESH, MOUNTAIN AIR. GET UP AT THE CRACK OF DAWN AND RAISE THE PARK FLAG NO ONE WILL SEE FOR DAYS.
MY BEST FRIENDS ARE THE SQUIRRELS, THE BIRDS, AND THE TREES!

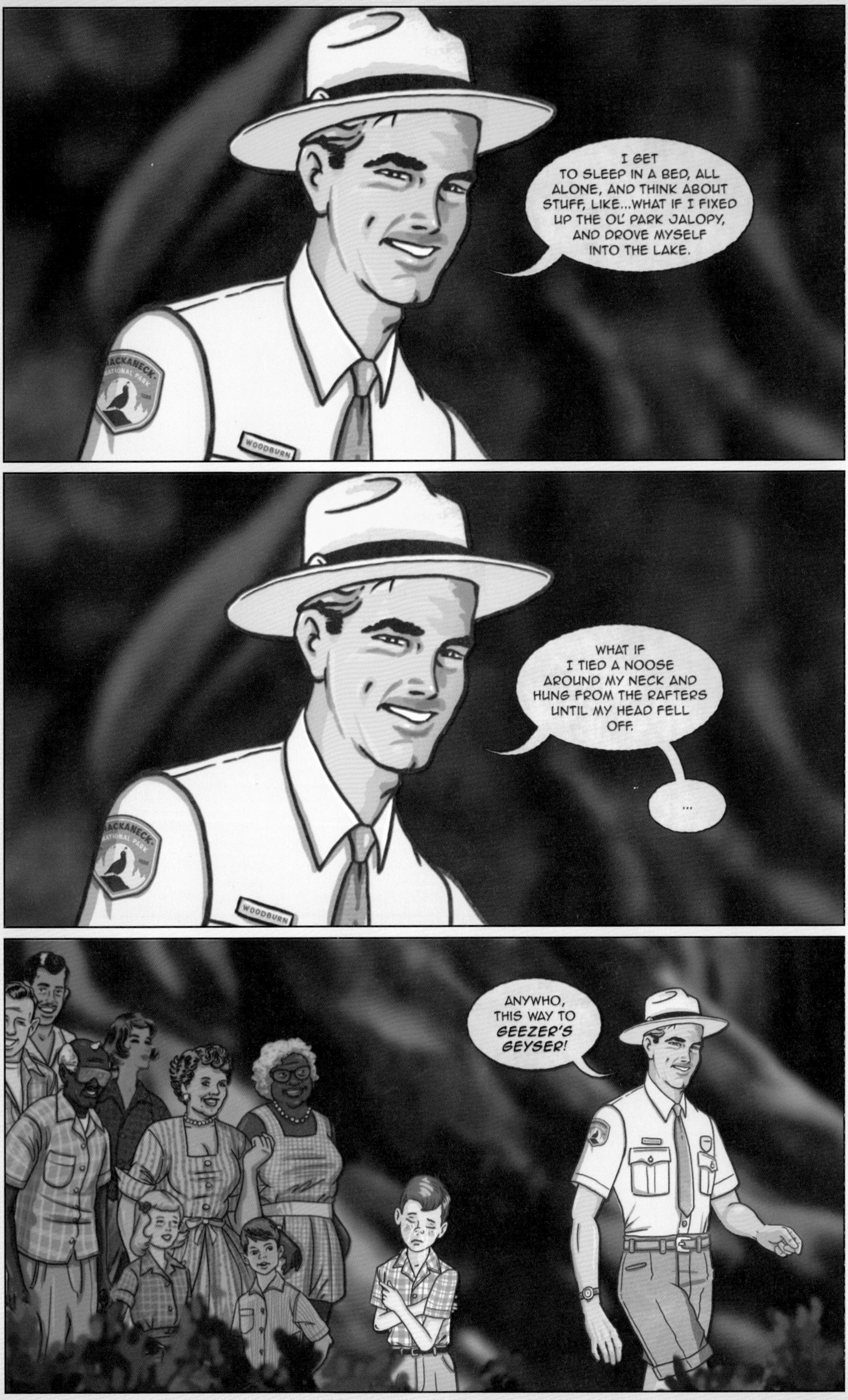
I GET TO SLEEP IN A BED, ALL ALONE, AND THINK ABOUT STUFF, LIKE...WHAT IF I FIXED UP THE OL' PARK JALOPY, AND DROVE MYSELF INTO THE LAKE.
WOODBURN
WHAT IF I TIED A NOOSE AROUND MY NECK AND HUNG FROM THE RAFTERS UNTIL MY HEAD FELL OFF.
...
WOODBURN
ANYWHO, THIS WAY TO *GEEZER'S GEYSER!*

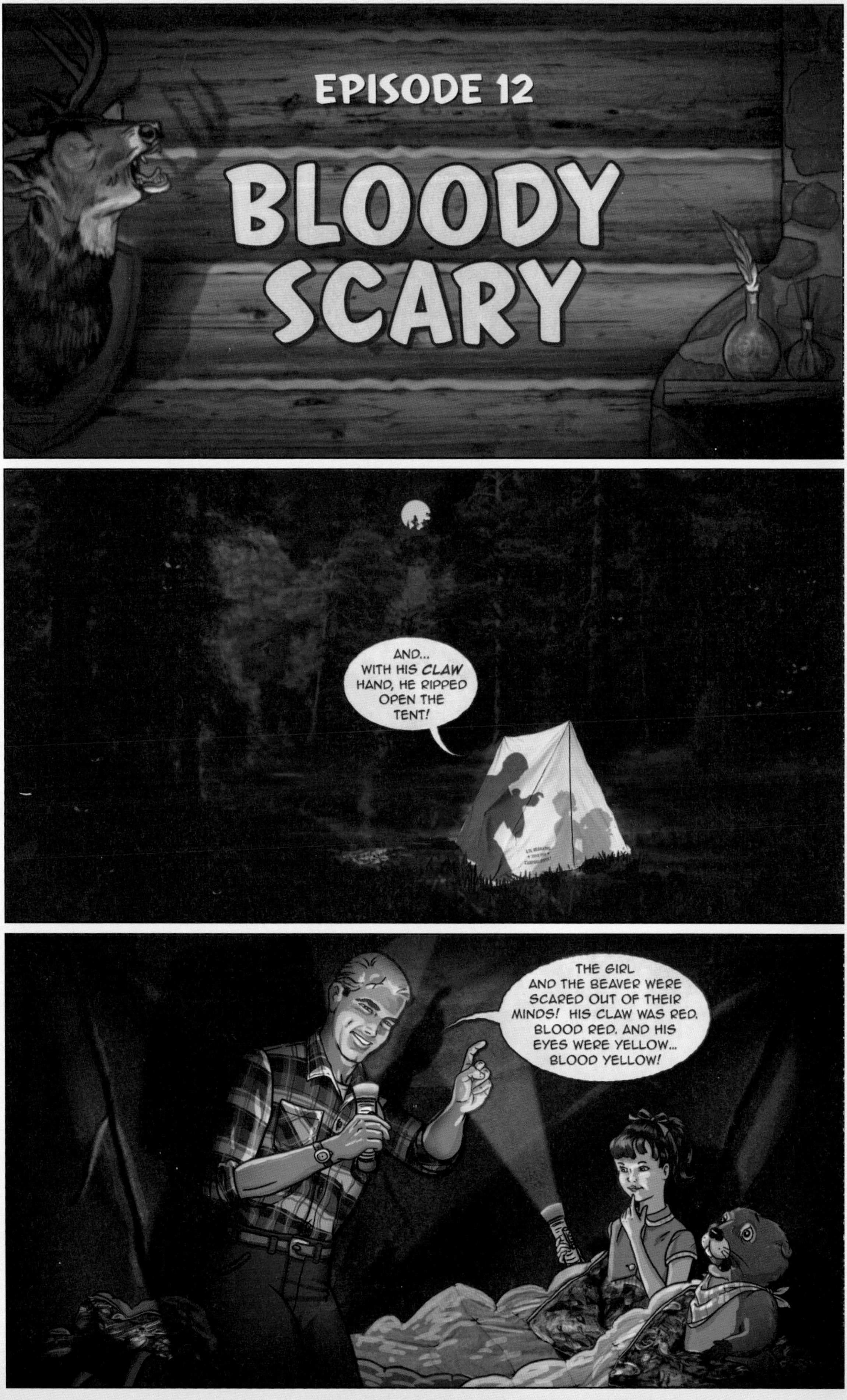
EPISODE 12
BLOODY SCARY
AND... WITH HIS CLAW HAND, HE RIPPED OPEN THE TENT!
THE GIRL AND THE BEAVER WERE SCARED OUT OF THEIR MINDS! HIS CLAW WAS RED. BLOOD RED. AND HIS EYES WERE YELLOW... BLOOD YELLOW!

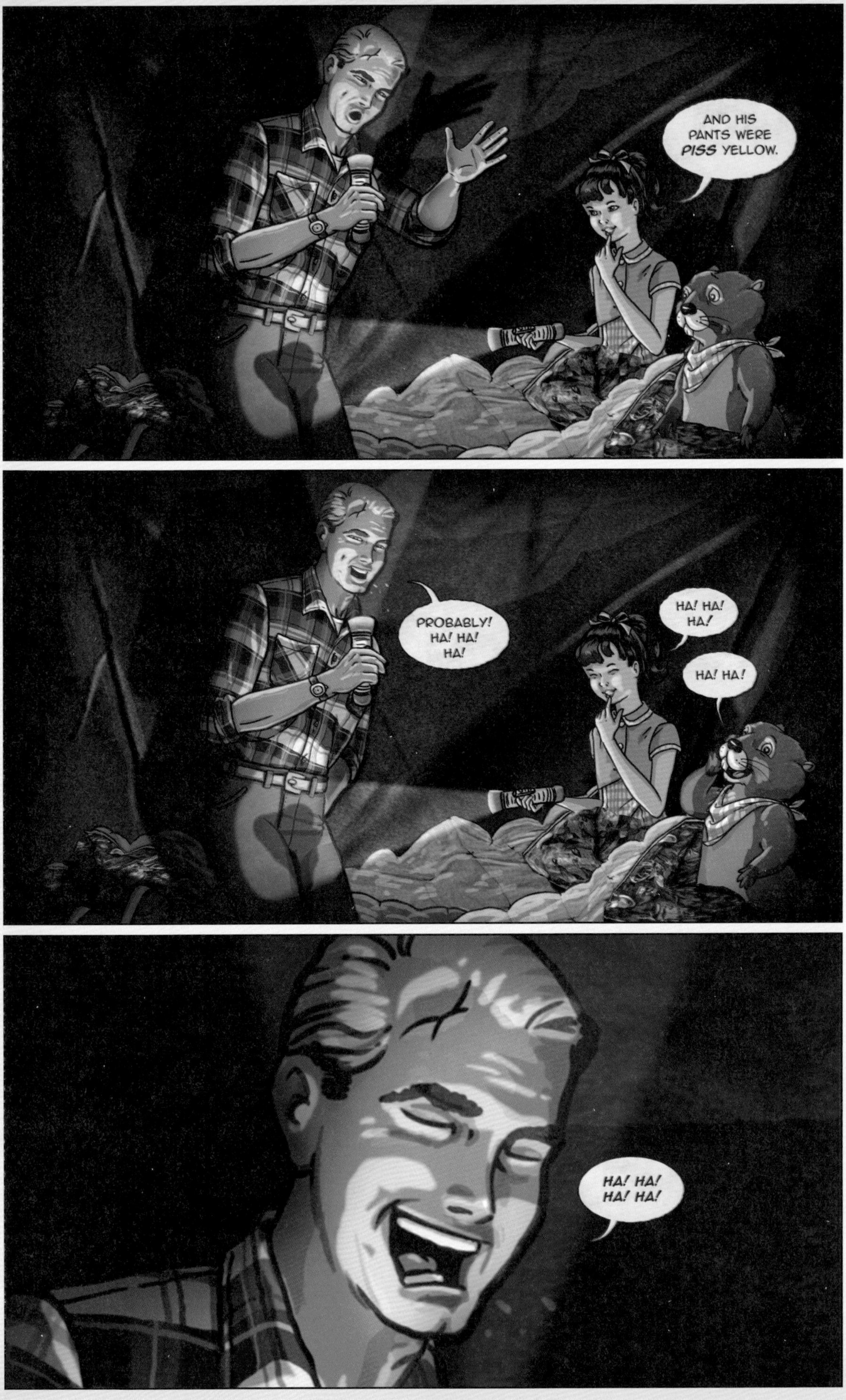
AND HIS PANTS WERE PISS YELLOW.
PROBABLY! HA! HA! HA!
HA! HA! HA!
HA! HA!
HA! HA! HA! HA!

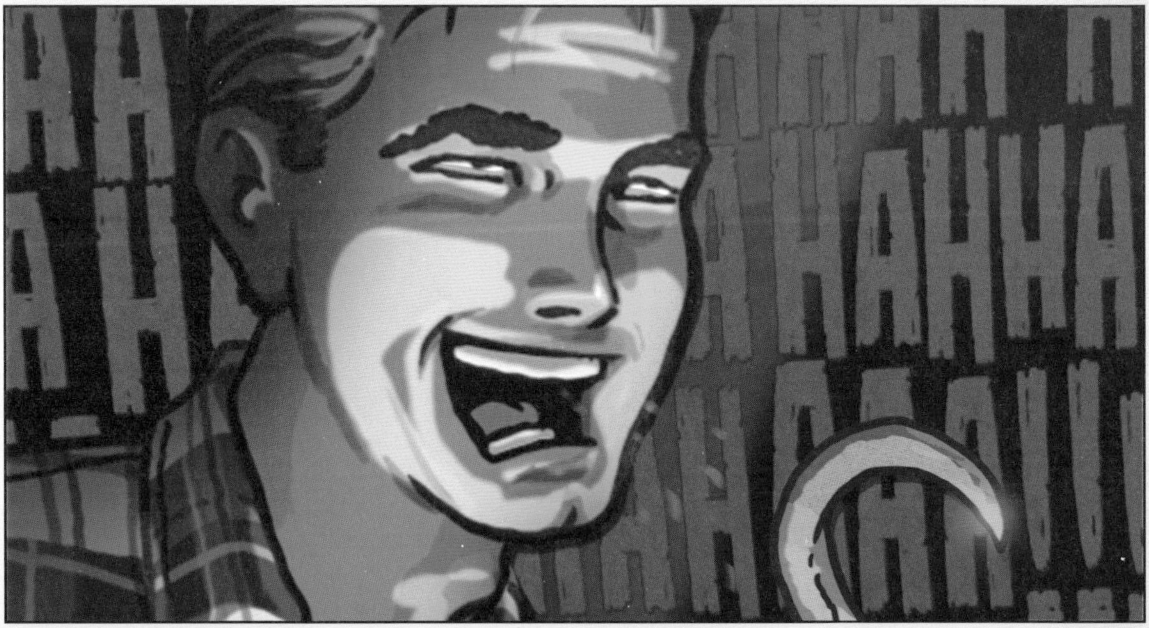
HAHAHA

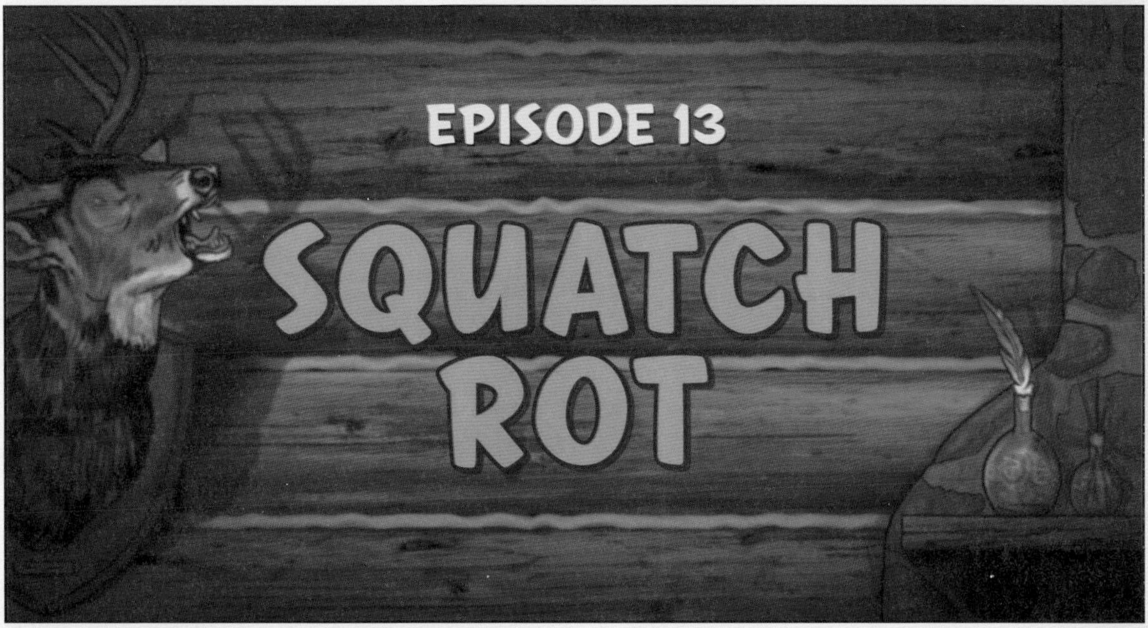
EPISODE 13
SQUATCH ROT

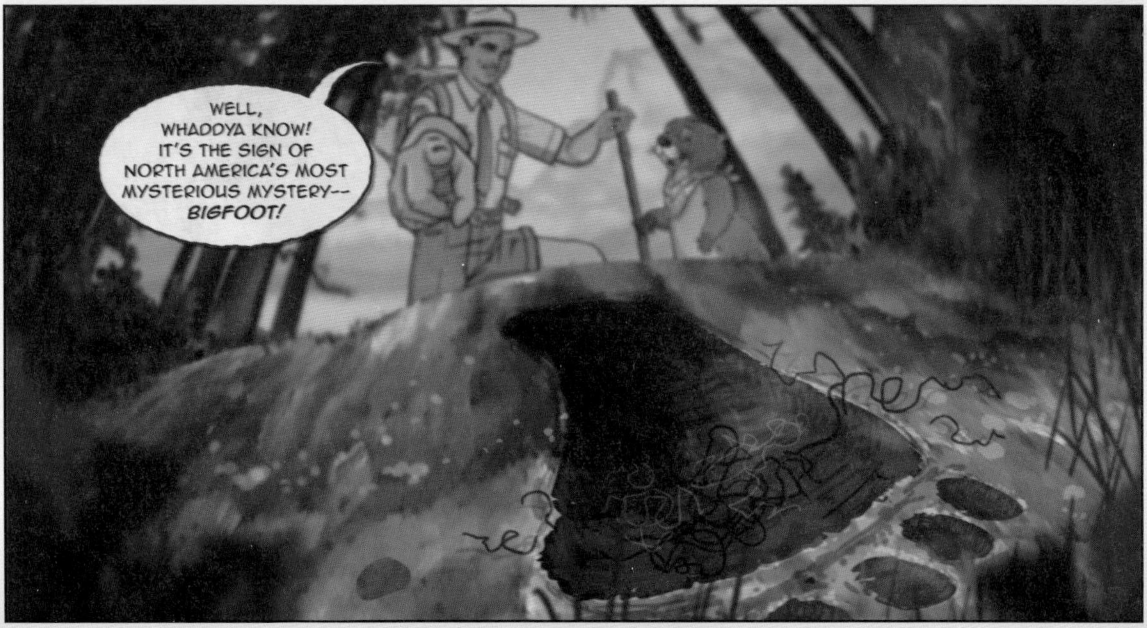
WELL, WHADDYA KNOW! IT'S THE SIGN OF NORTH AMERICA'S MOST MYSTERIOUS MYSTERY-- BIGFOOT!

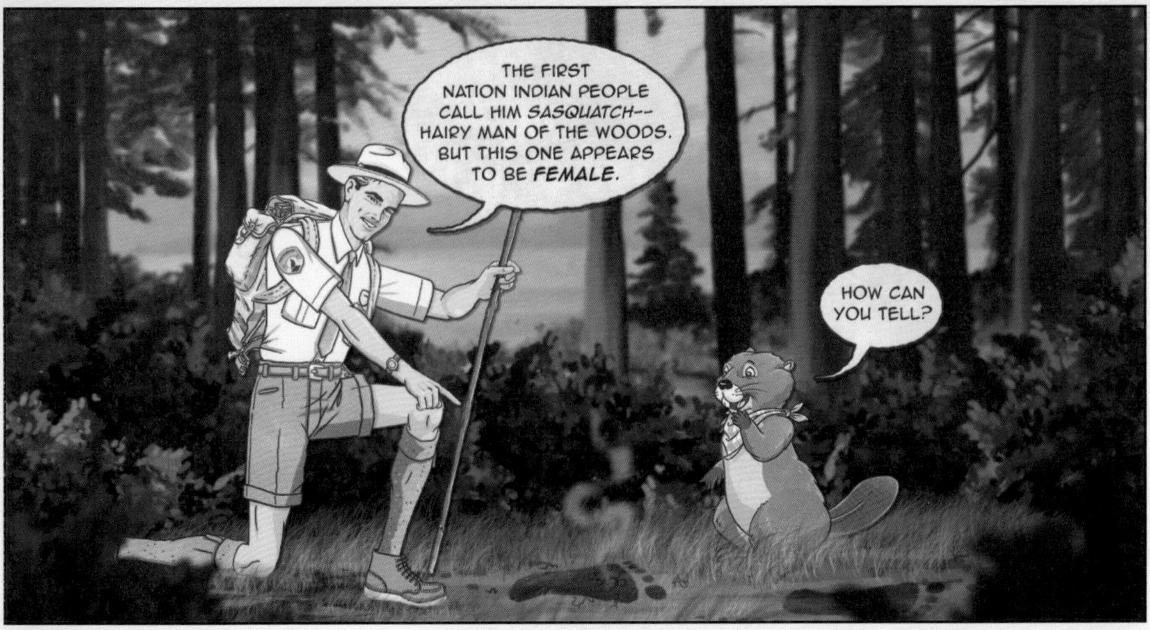
THE FIRST NATION INDIAN PEOPLE CALL HIM *SASQUATCH*-- HAIRY MAN OF THE WOODS. BUT THIS ONE APPEARS TO BE ***FEMALE***.
HOW CAN YOU TELL?

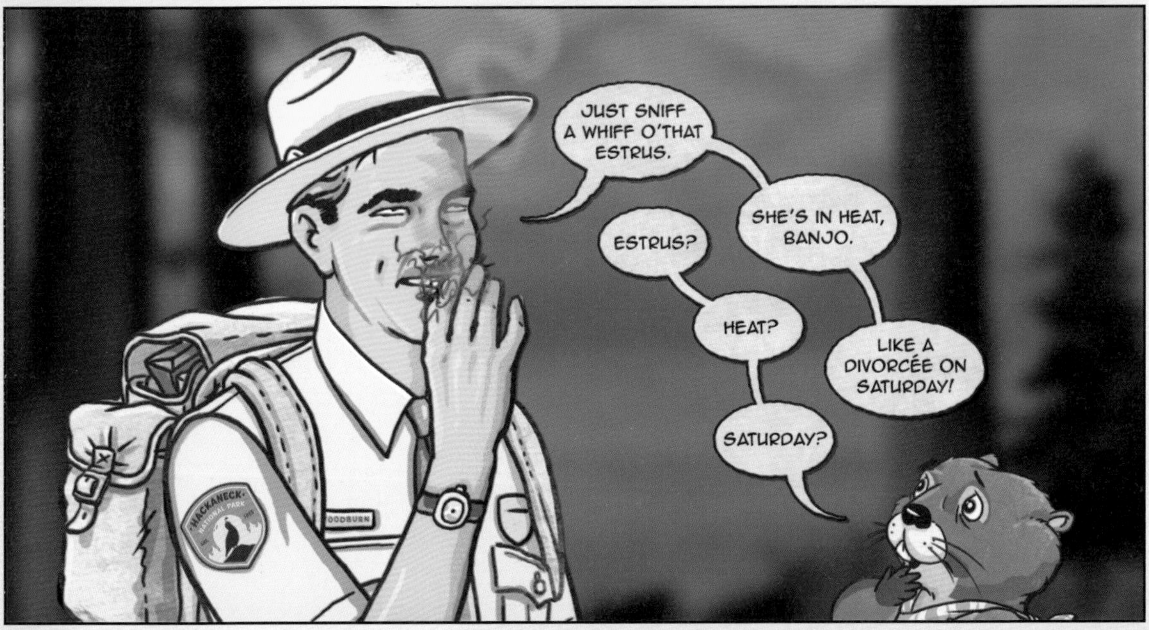
JUST SNIFF A WHIFF O'THAT ESTRUS.
ESTRUS?
SHE'S IN HEAT, BANJO.
HEAT?
LIKE A DIVORCÉE ON SATURDAY!
SATURDAY?
HACKANECK NATIONAL PARK
WOODBURN

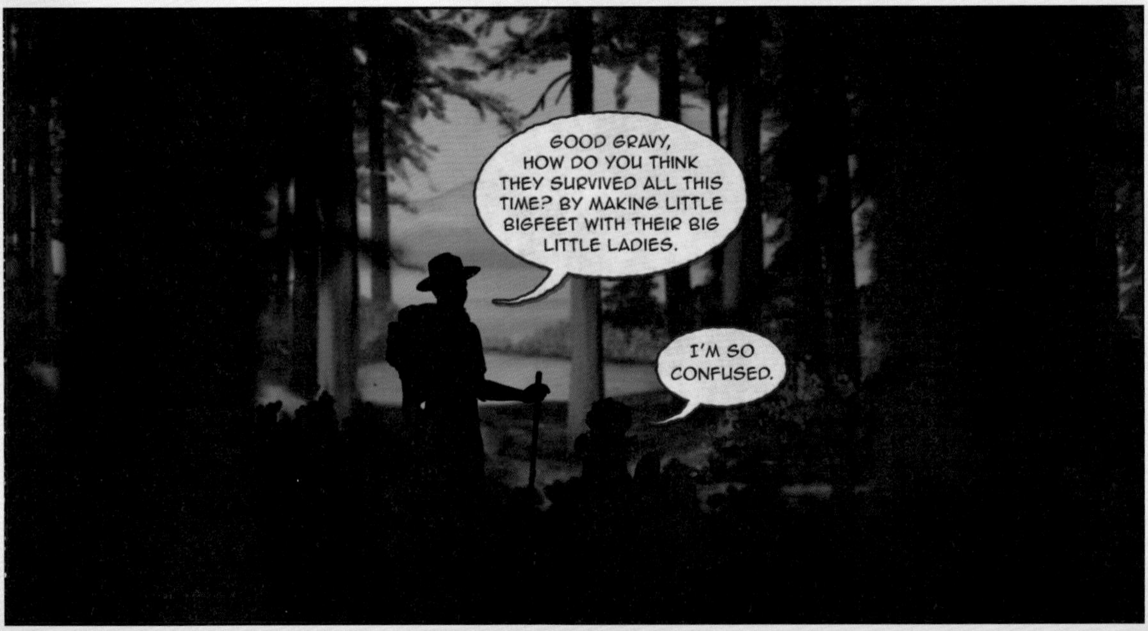
GOOD GRAVY, HOW DO YOU THINK THEY SURVIVED ALL THIS TIME? BY MAKING LITTLE BIGFEET WITH THEIR BIG LITTLE LADIES.
I'M SO CONFUSED.

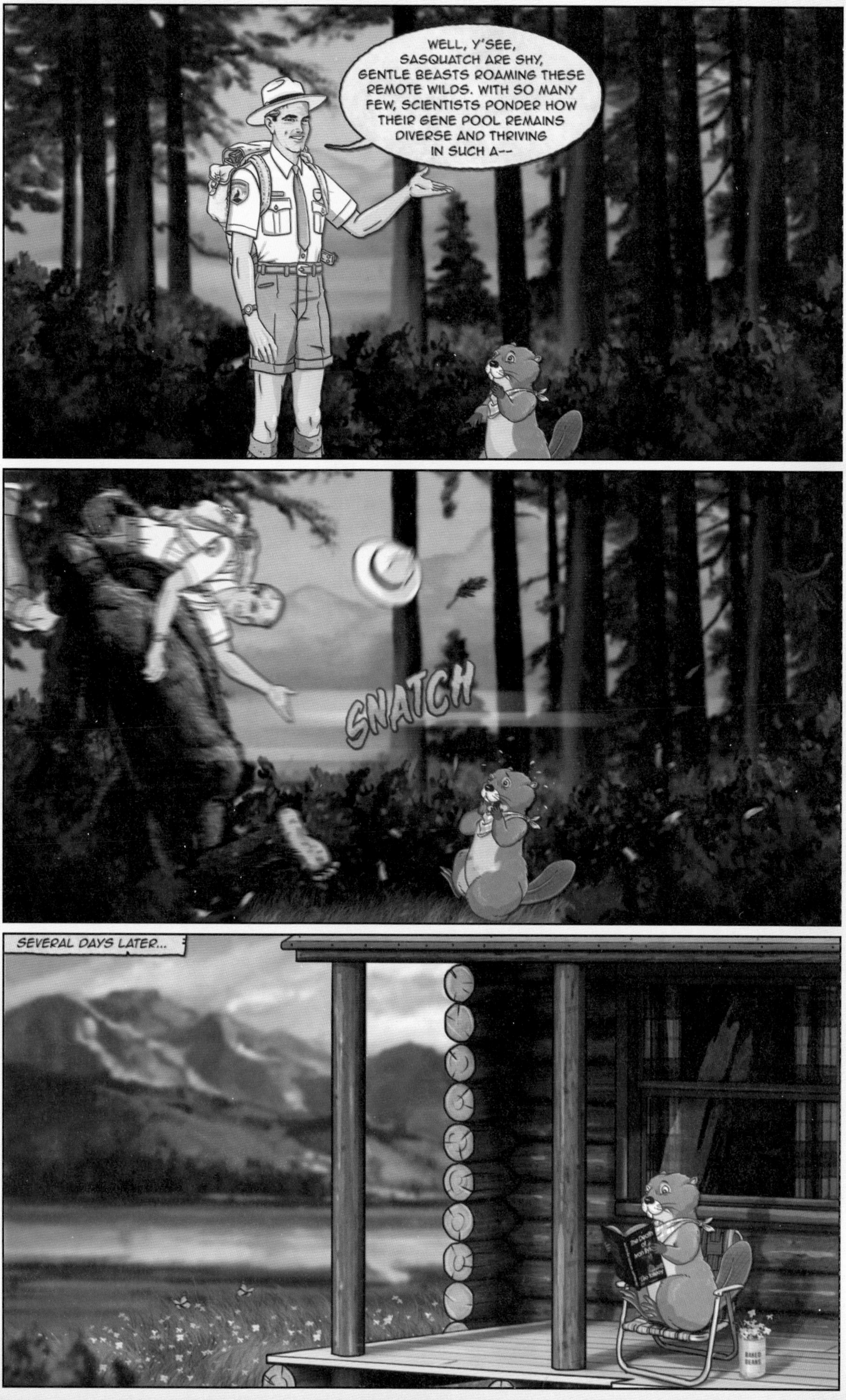
WELL, Y'SEE, SASQUATCH ARE SHY, GENTLE BEASTS ROAMING THESE REMOTE WILDS. WITH SO MANY FEW, SCIENTISTS PONDER HOW THEIR GENE POOL REMAINS DIVERSE AND THRIVING IN SUCH A--
SNATCH
SEVERAL DAYS LATER...
BAKED BEANS

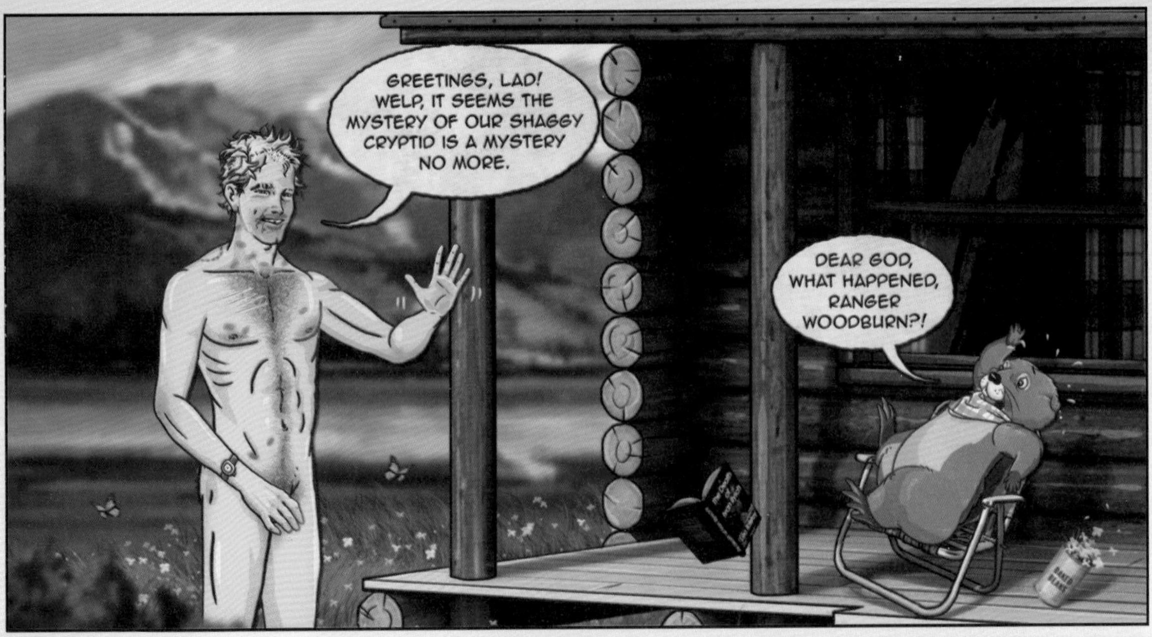
GREETINGS, LAD! WELP, IT SEEMS THE MYSTERY OF OUR SHAGGY CRYPTID IS A MYSTERY NO MORE.
DEAR GOD, WHAT HAPPENED, RANGER WOODBURN?!

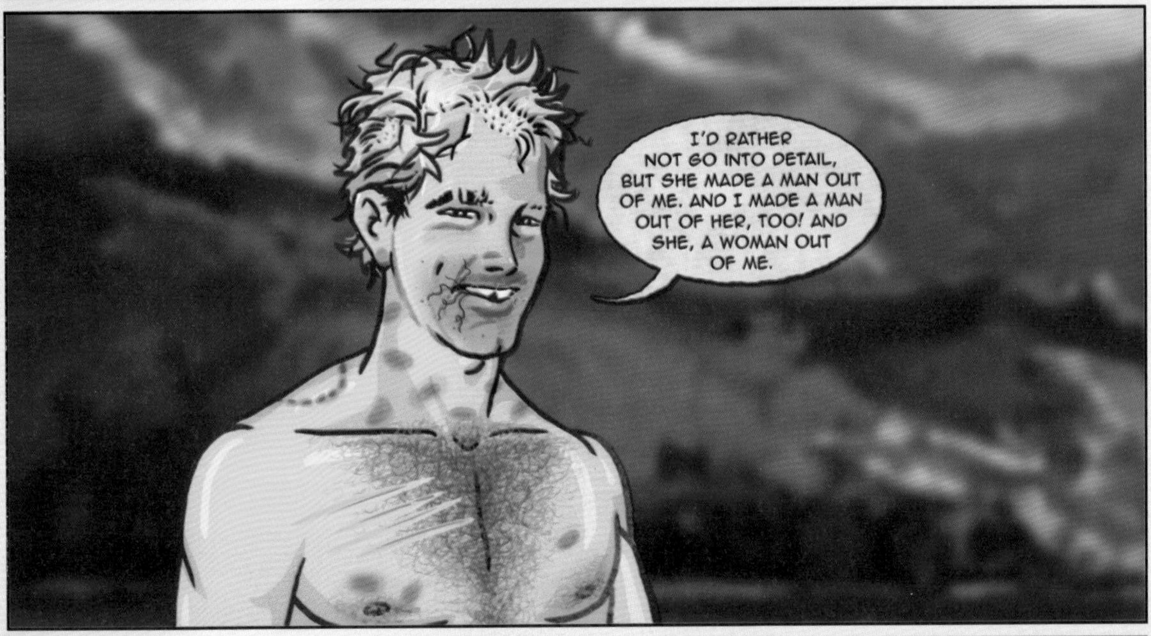
I'D RATHER NOT GO INTO DETAIL, BUT SHE MADE A MAN OUT OF ME. AND I MADE A MAN OUT OF HER, TOO! AND SHE, A WOMAN OUT OF ME.

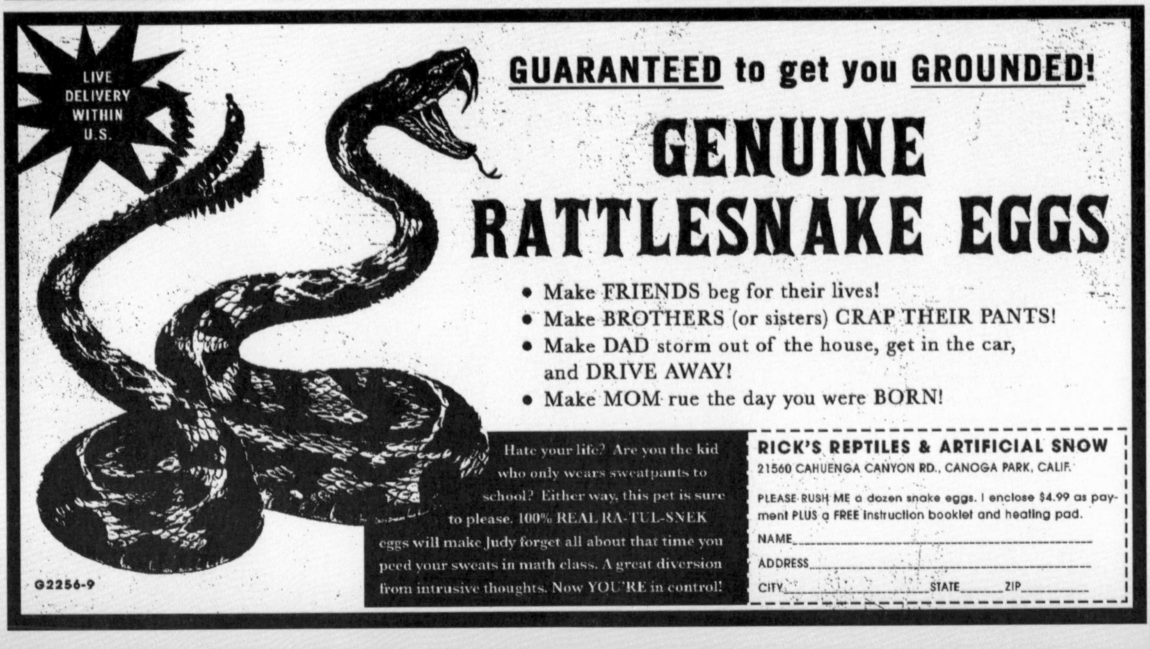
LIVE DELIVERY WITHIN U.S.
GUARANTEED to get you GROUNDED!
GENUINE RATTLESNAKE EGGS
• Make FRIENDS beg for their lives!
• Make BROTHERS (or sisters) CRAP THEIR PANTS!
• Make DAD storm out of the house, get in the car, and DRIVE AWAY!
• Make MOM rue the day you were BORN!
Hate your life? Are you the kid who only wears sweatpants to school? Either way, this pet is sure to please. 100% REAL RA-TUL-SNEK eggs will make Judy forget all about that time you peed your sweats in math class. A great diversion from intrusive thoughts. Now YOU'RE in control!
RICK'S REPTILES & ARTIFICIAL SNOW
21560 CAHUENGA CANYON RD., CANOGA PARK, CALIF.
PLEASE RUSH ME a dozen snake eggs. I enclose $4.99 as payment PLUS a FREE instruction booklet and heating pad.
NAME
ADDRESS
CITY STATE ZIP
G2256-9

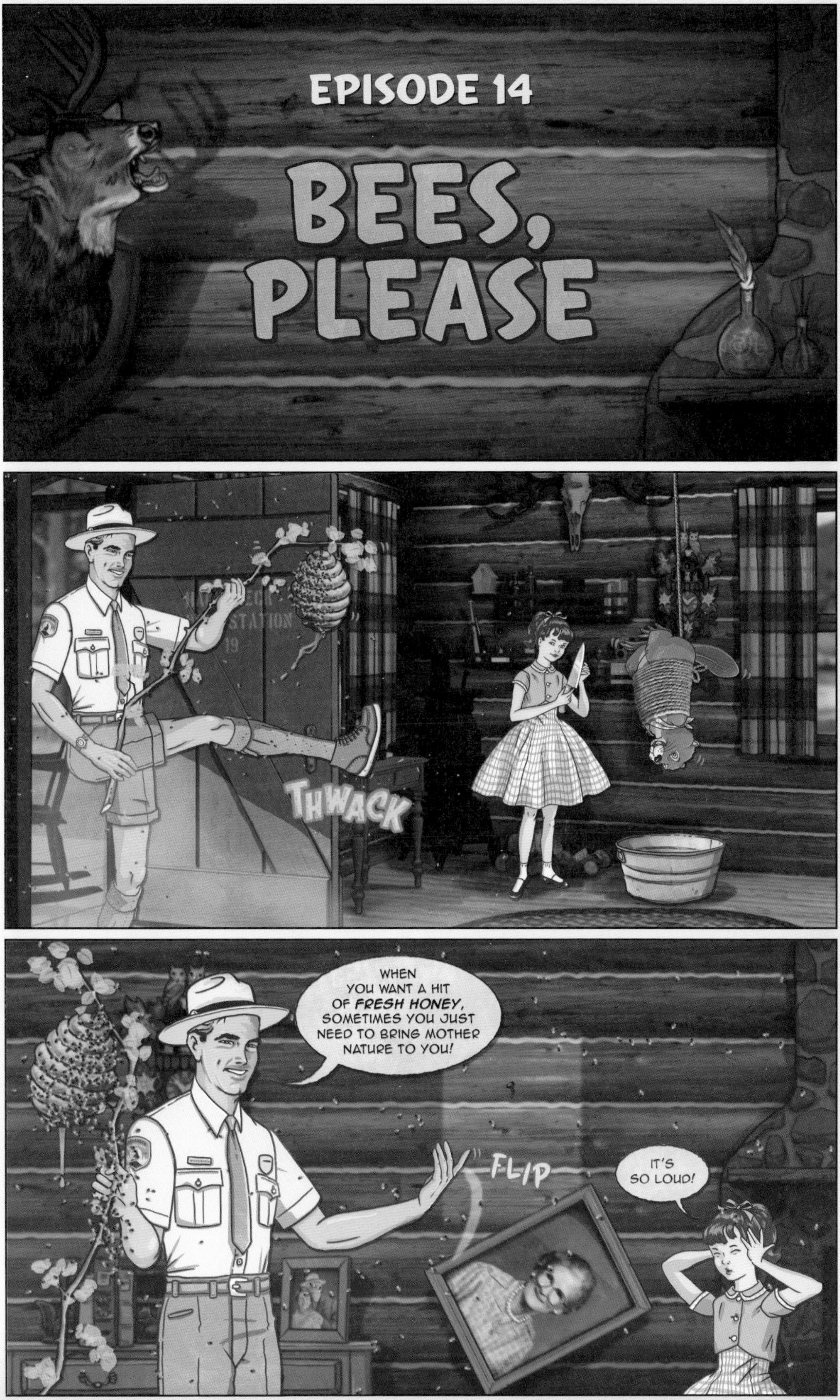
EPISODE 14
BEES, PLEASE
THWACK
WHEN YOU WANT A HIT OF *FRESH HONEY*, SOMETIMES YOU JUST NEED TO BRING MOTHER NATURE TO YOU!
FLIP
IT'S SO LOUD!

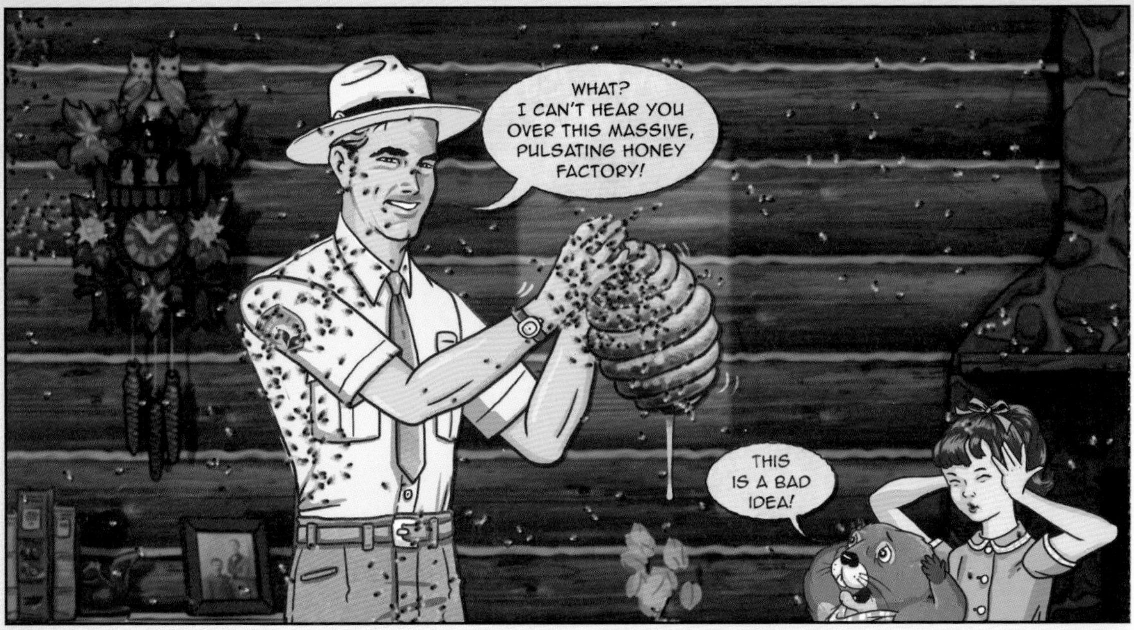
WHAT? I CAN'T HEAR YOU OVER THIS MASSIVE, PULSATING HONEY FACTORY!
THIS IS A BAD IDEA!

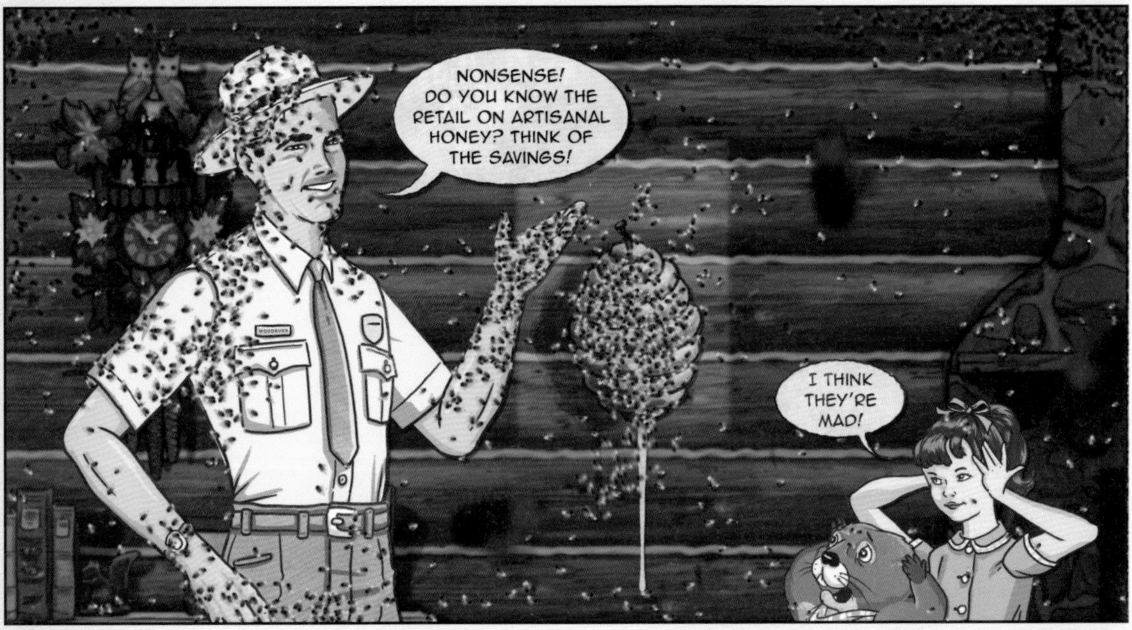
NONSENSE! DO YOU KNOW THE RETAIL ON ARTISANAL HONEY? THINK OF THE SAVINGS!
I THINK THEY'RE MAD!

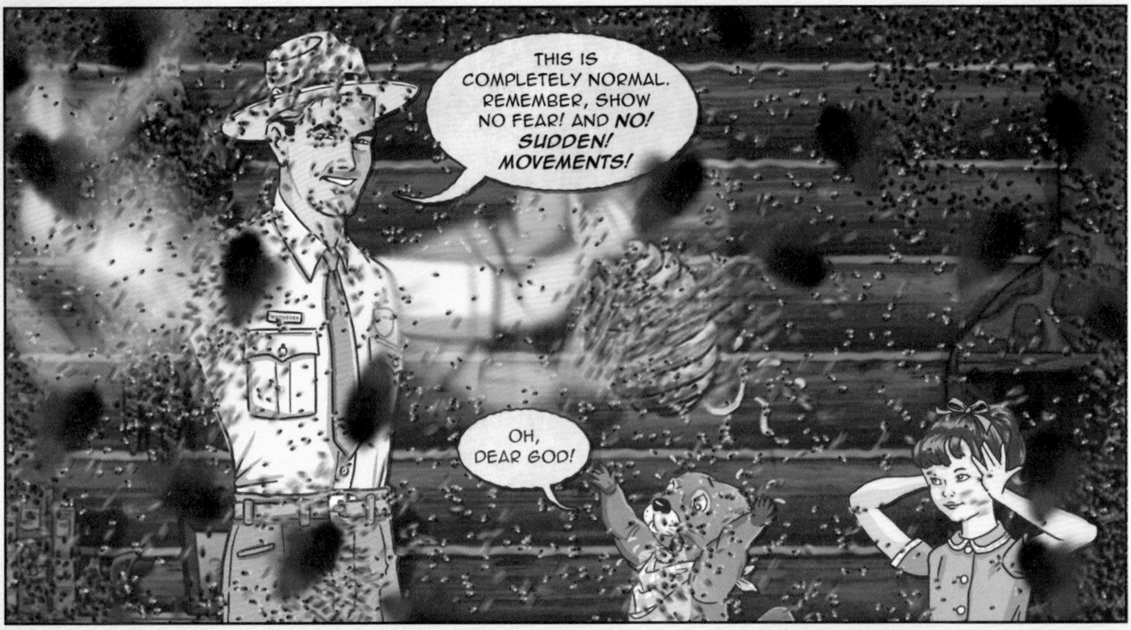
THIS IS COMPLETELY NORMAL. REMEMBER, SHOW NO FEAR! AND *NO! SUDDEN! MOVEMENTS!*
OH, DEAR GOD!

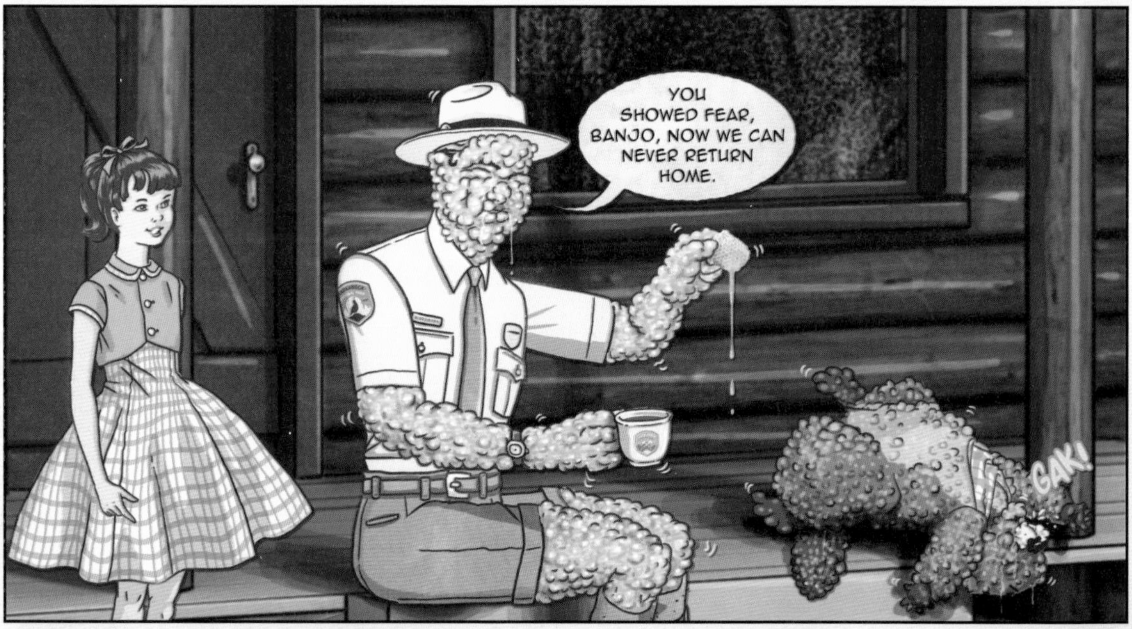
YOU SHOWED FEAR, BANJO, NOW WE CAN NEVER RETURN HOME.
GAK!

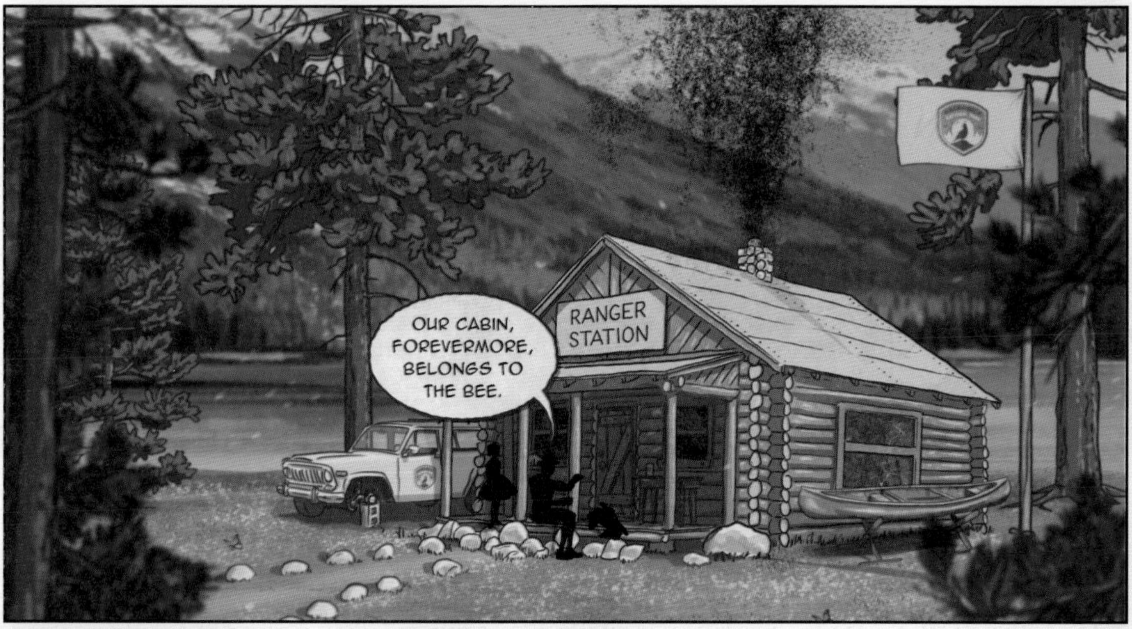
RANGER STATION
OUR CABIN, FOREVERMORE, BELONGS TO THE BEE.

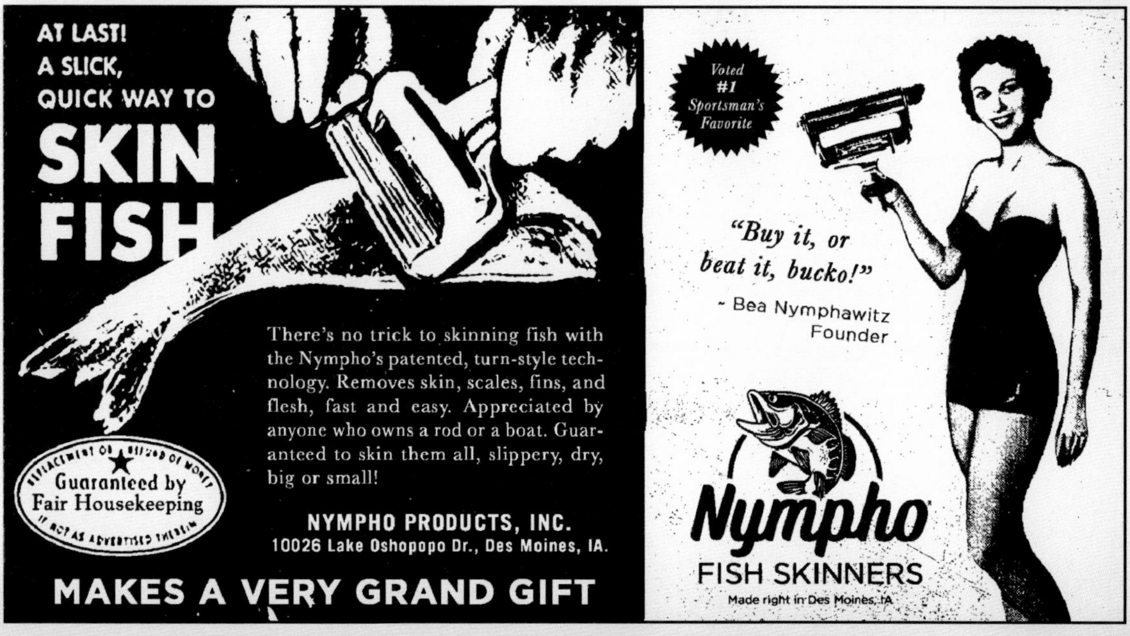
AT LAST! A SLICK, QUICK WAY TO
SKIN FISH
There's no trick to skinning fish with the Nympho's patented, turn-style technology. Removes skin, scales, fins, and flesh, fast and easy. Appreciated by anyone who owns a rod or a boat. Guaranteed to skin them all, slippery, dry, big or small!
Guaranteed by Fair Housekeeping
NYMPHO PRODUCTS, INC.
10026 Lake Oshopopo Dr., Des Moines, IA.
MAKES A VERY GRAND GIFT
Voted #1 Sportsman's Favorite
"Buy it, or beat it, bucko!"
- Bea Nymphawitz
Founder
Nympho
FISH SKINNERS
Made right in Des Moines, IA

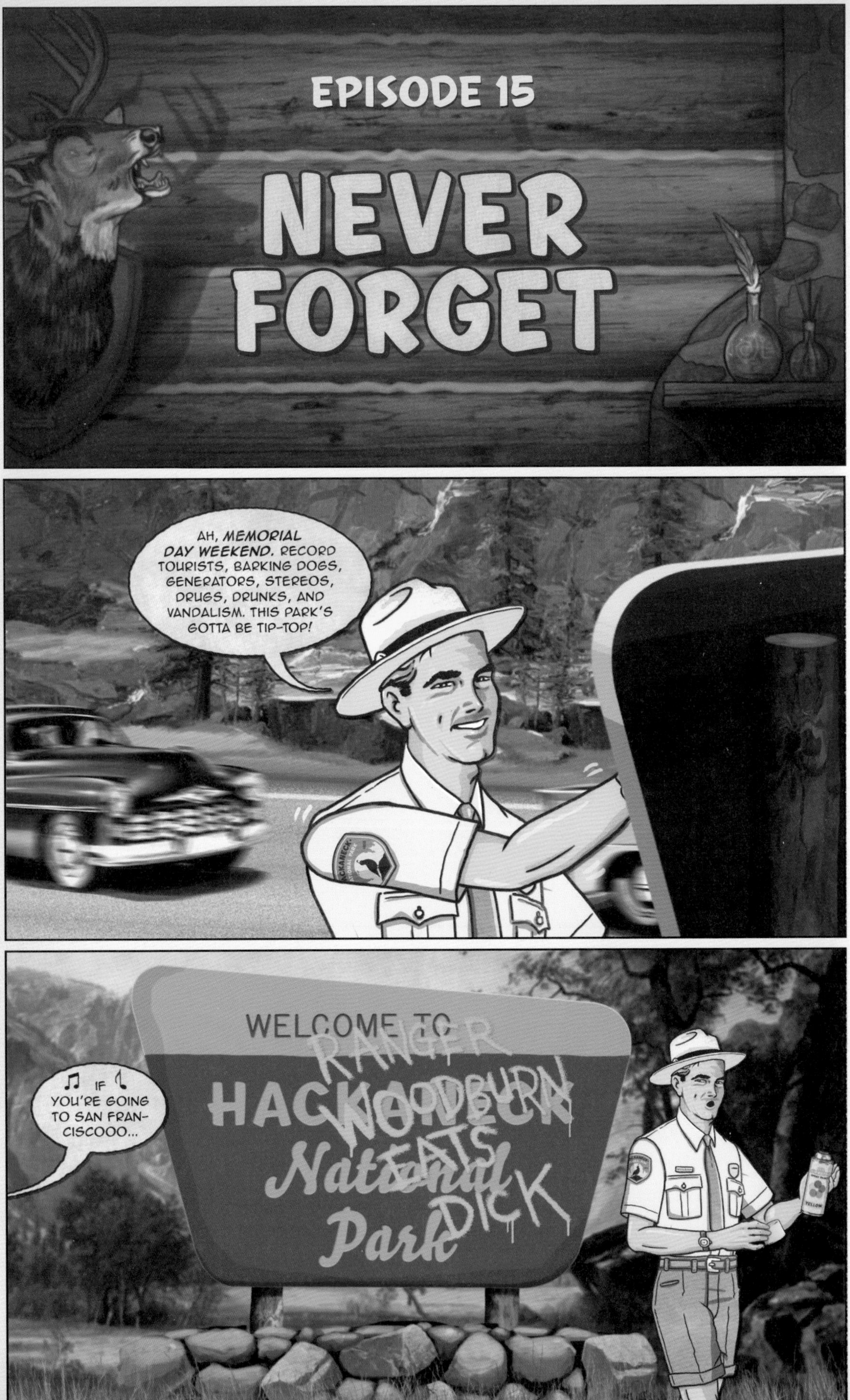
EPISODE 15
NEVER FORGET
AH, MEMORIAL DAY WEEKEND. RECORD TOURISTS, BARKING DOGS, GENERATORS, STEREOS, DRUGS, DRUNKS, AND VANDALISM. THIS PARK'S GOTTA BE TIP-TOP!
WELCOME TO
RANGER WOODBURN EATS DICK
National Park
♫ IF ♪ YOU'RE GOING TO SAN FRANCISCOOO...

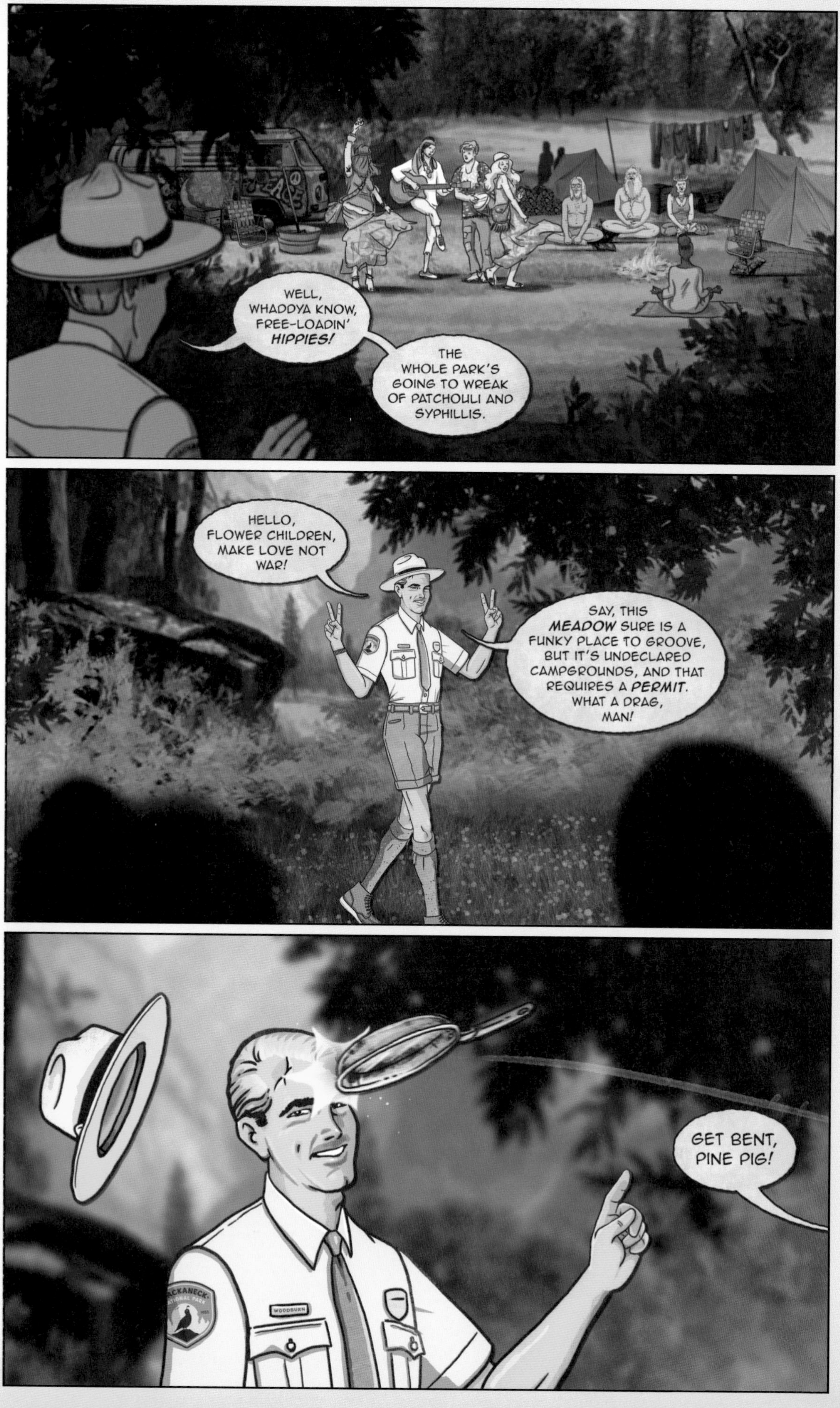
WELL, WHADDYA KNOW, FREE-LOADIN' *HIPPIES!*
THE WHOLE PARK'S GOING TO WREAK OF PATCHOULI AND SYPHILLIS.
HELLO, FLOWER CHILDREN, MAKE LOVE NOT WAR!
SAY, THIS *MEADOW* SURE IS A FUNKY PLACE TO GROOVE, BUT IT'S UNDECLARED CAMPGROUNDS, AND THAT REQUIRES A *PERMIT*. WHAT A DRAG, MAN!
GET BENT, PINE PIG!

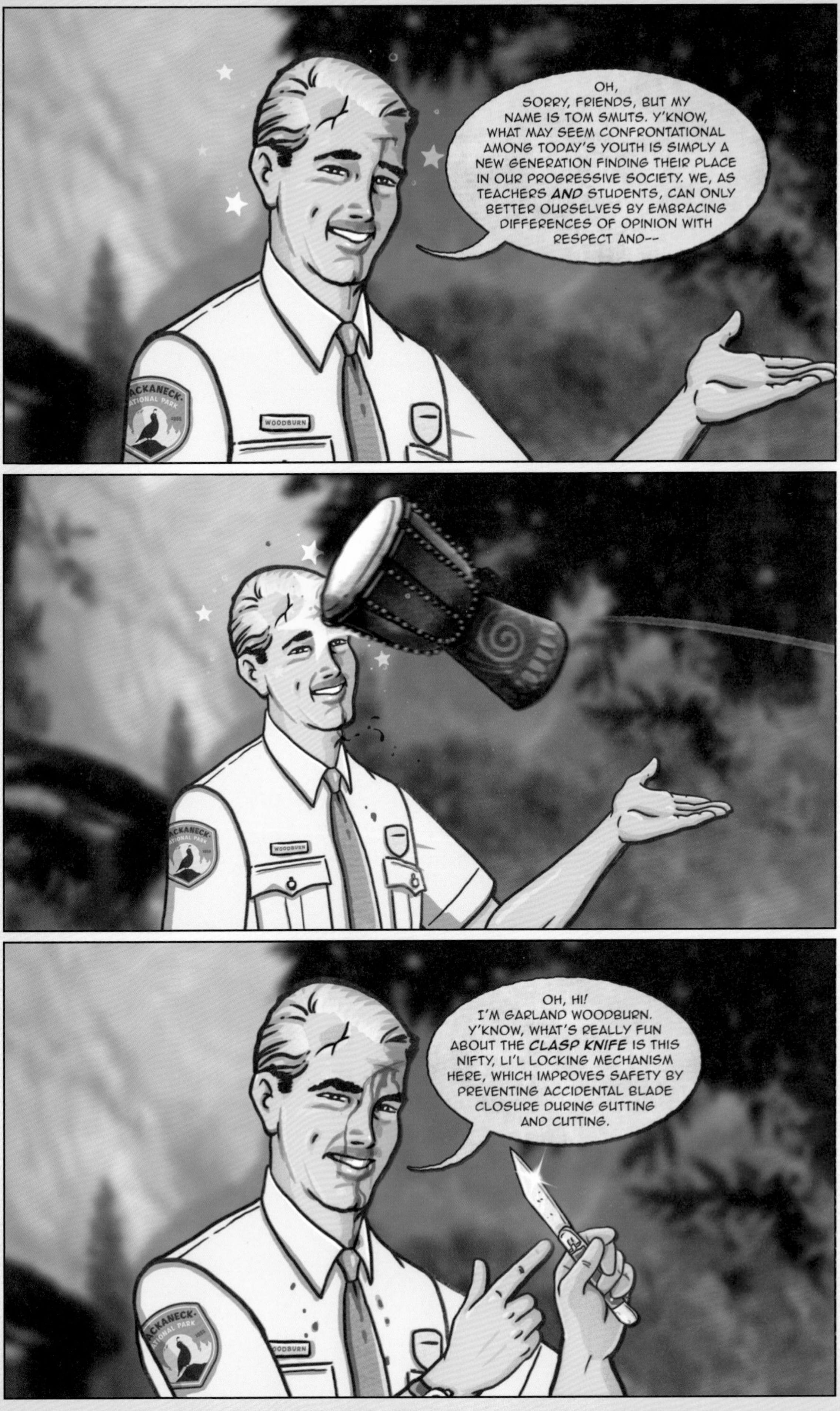
OH, SORRY, FRIENDS, BUT MY NAME IS TOM SMUTS. Y'KNOW, WHAT MAY SEEM CONFRONTATIONAL AMONG TODAY'S YOUTH IS SIMPLY A NEW GENERATION FINDING THEIR PLACE IN OUR PROGRESSIVE SOCIETY. WE, AS TEACHERS ***AND*** STUDENTS, CAN ONLY BETTER OURSELVES BY EMBRACING DIFFERENCES OF OPINION WITH RESPECT AND--
OH, HI! I'M GARLAND WOODBURN. Y'KNOW, WHAT'S REALLY FUN ABOUT THE ***CLASP KNIFE*** IS THIS NIFTY, LI'L LOCKING MECHANISM HERE, WHICH IMPROVES SAFETY BY PREVENTING ACCIDENTAL BLADE CLOSURE DURING GUTTING AND CUTTING.

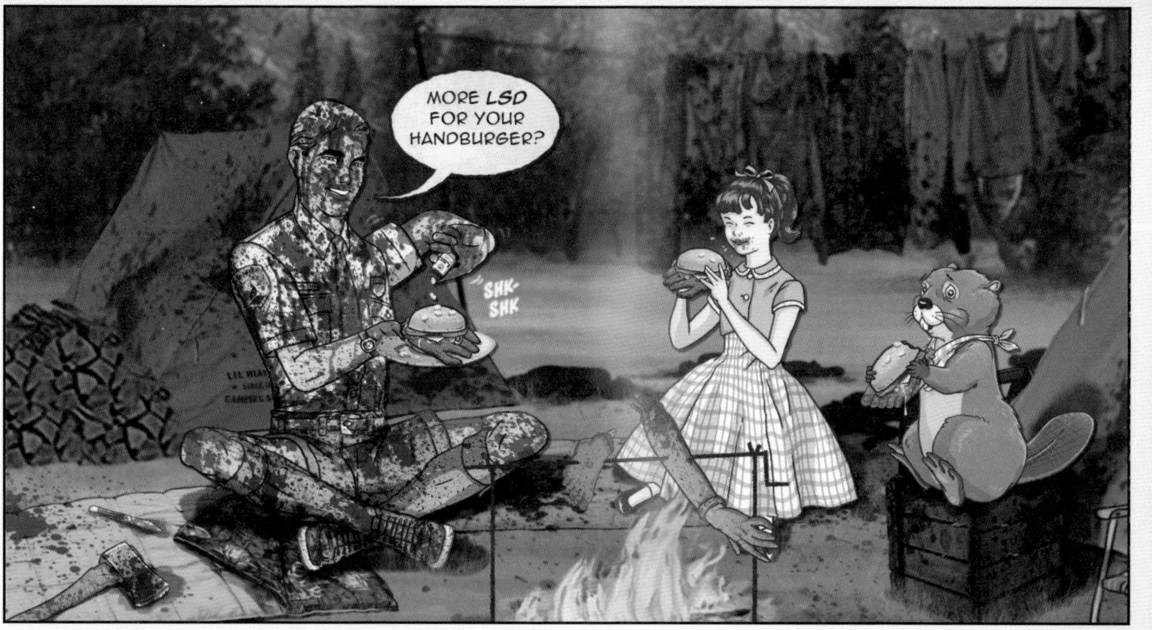
MORE LSD FOR YOUR HANDBURGER?
SHK-SHK

FIRESIDE STORIES: OLD FRIENDS

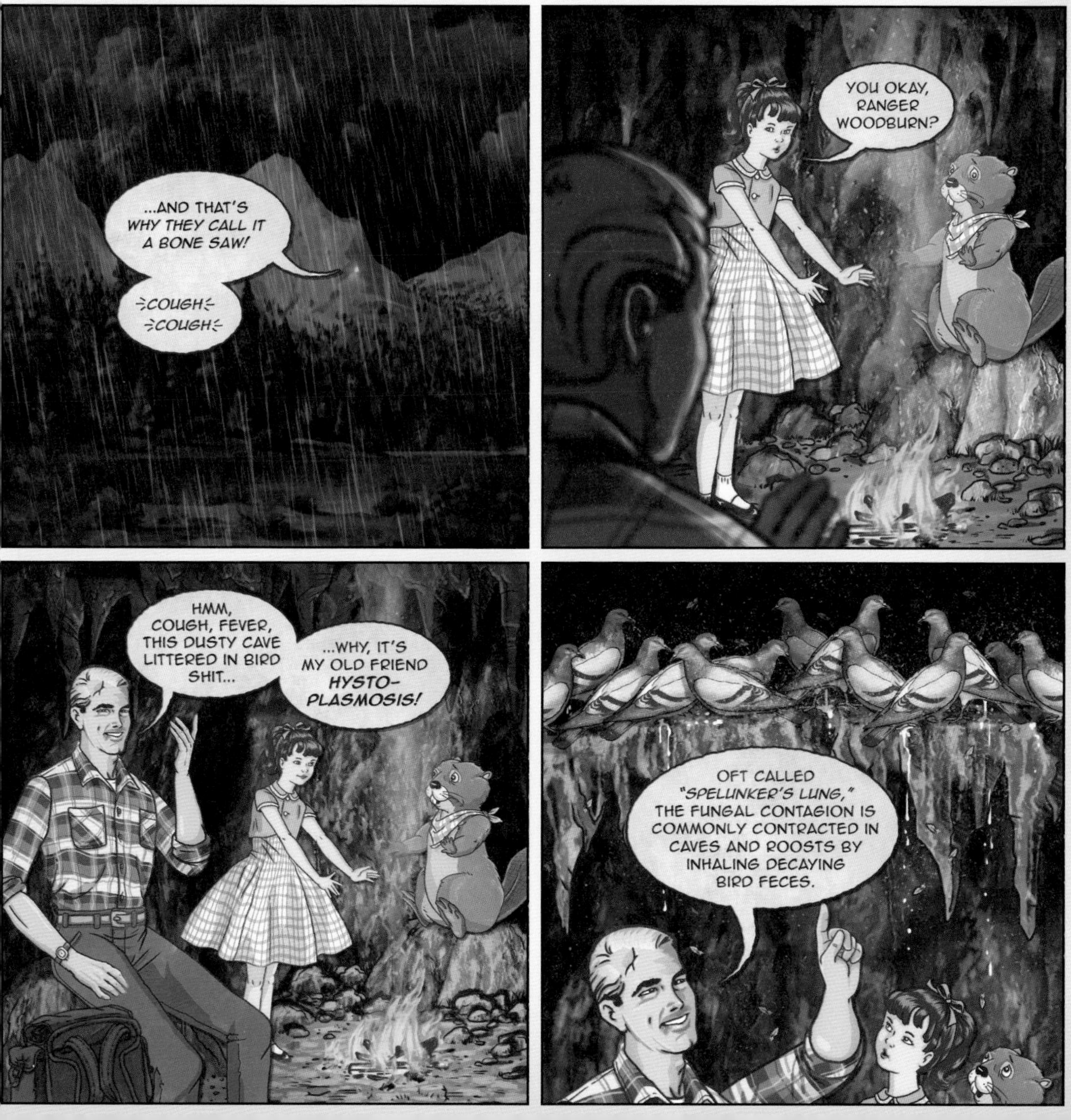
...AND THAT'S WHY THEY CALL IT A BONE SAW!
COUGH COUGH
YOU OKAY, RANGER WOODBURN?
HMM, COUGH, FEVER, THIS DUSTY CAVE LITTERED IN BIRD SHIT...
...WHY, IT'S MY OLD FRIEND HYSTO-PLASMOSIS!
OFT CALLED "SPELUNKER'S LUNG," THE FUNGAL CONTAGION IS COMMONLY CONTRACTED IN CAVES AND ROOSTS BY INHALING DECAYING BIRD FECES.

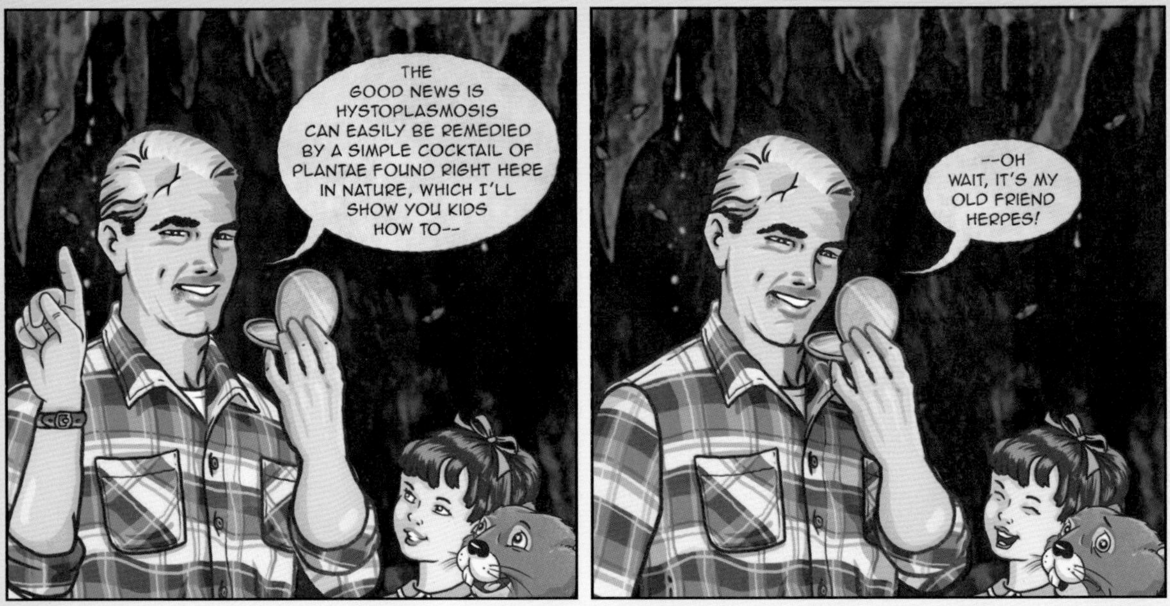
THE GOOD NEWS IS HYSTOPLASMOSIS CAN EASILY BE REMEDIED BY A SIMPLE COCKTAIL OF PLANTAE FOUND RIGHT HERE IN NATURE, WHICH I'LL SHOW YOU KIDS HOW TO--
--OH WAIT, IT'S MY OLD FRIEND HERPES!

FIRESIDE STORIES: ALL ABOUT SPLINTS

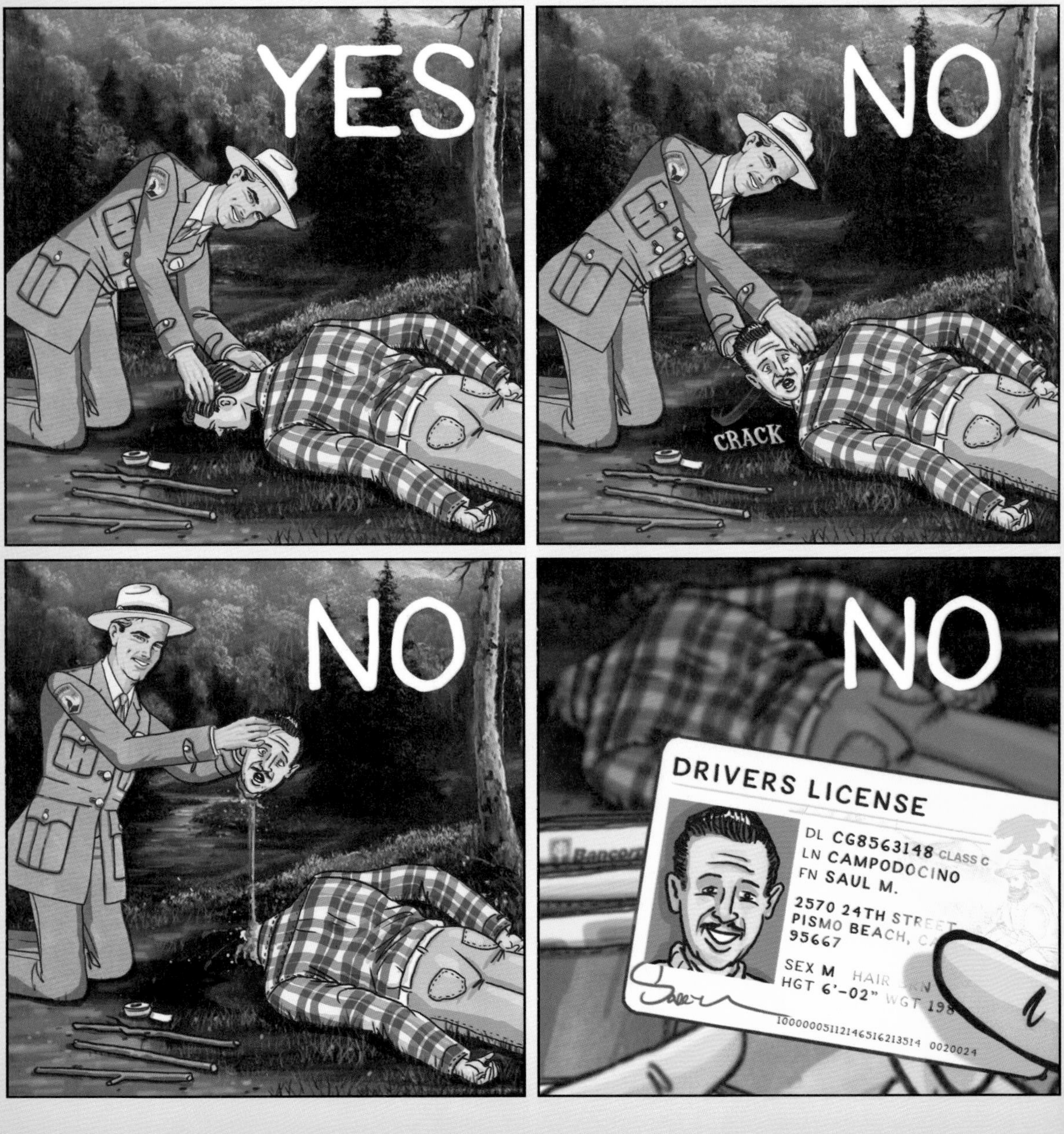
YES
NO
CRACK
NO
NO
DRIVERS LICENSE
DL CG8563148 CLASS C
LN CAMPODOCINO
FN SAUL M.
2570 24TH STREET
PISMO BEACH, C
95667
SEX M
HGT 6'-02"

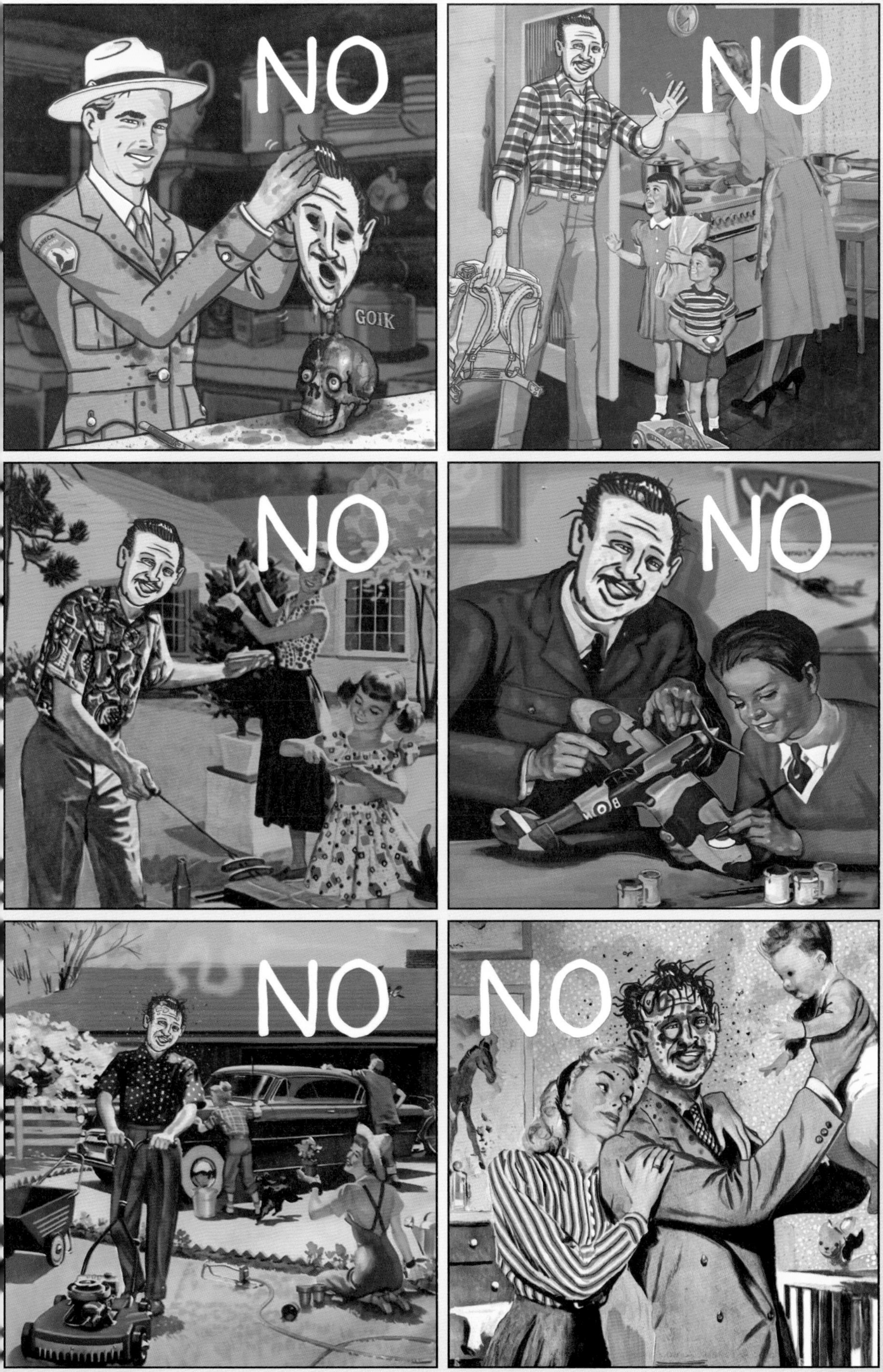
NO
GOIK
NO
NO
NO
NO
NO

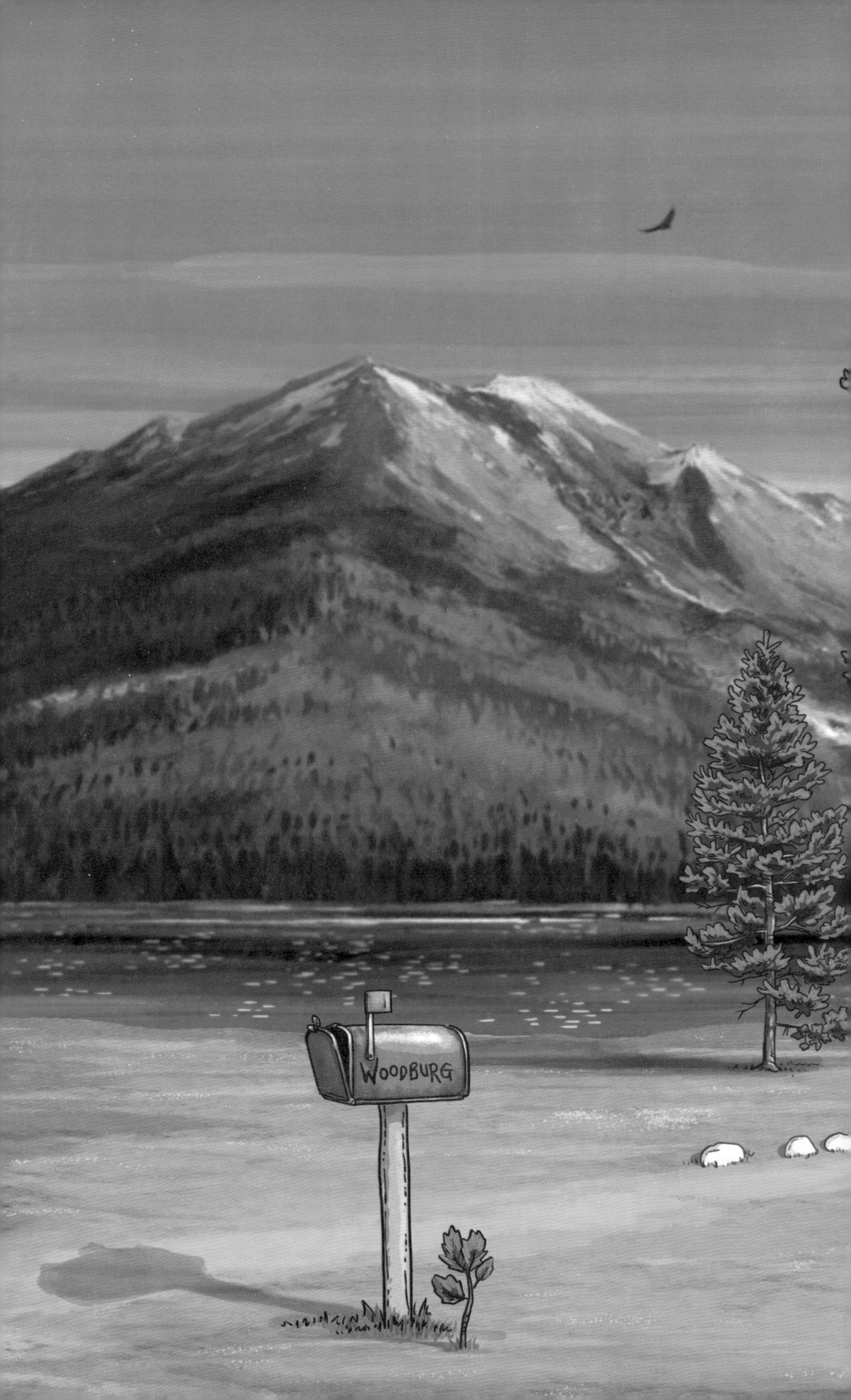
WOODBURG

SUMMER

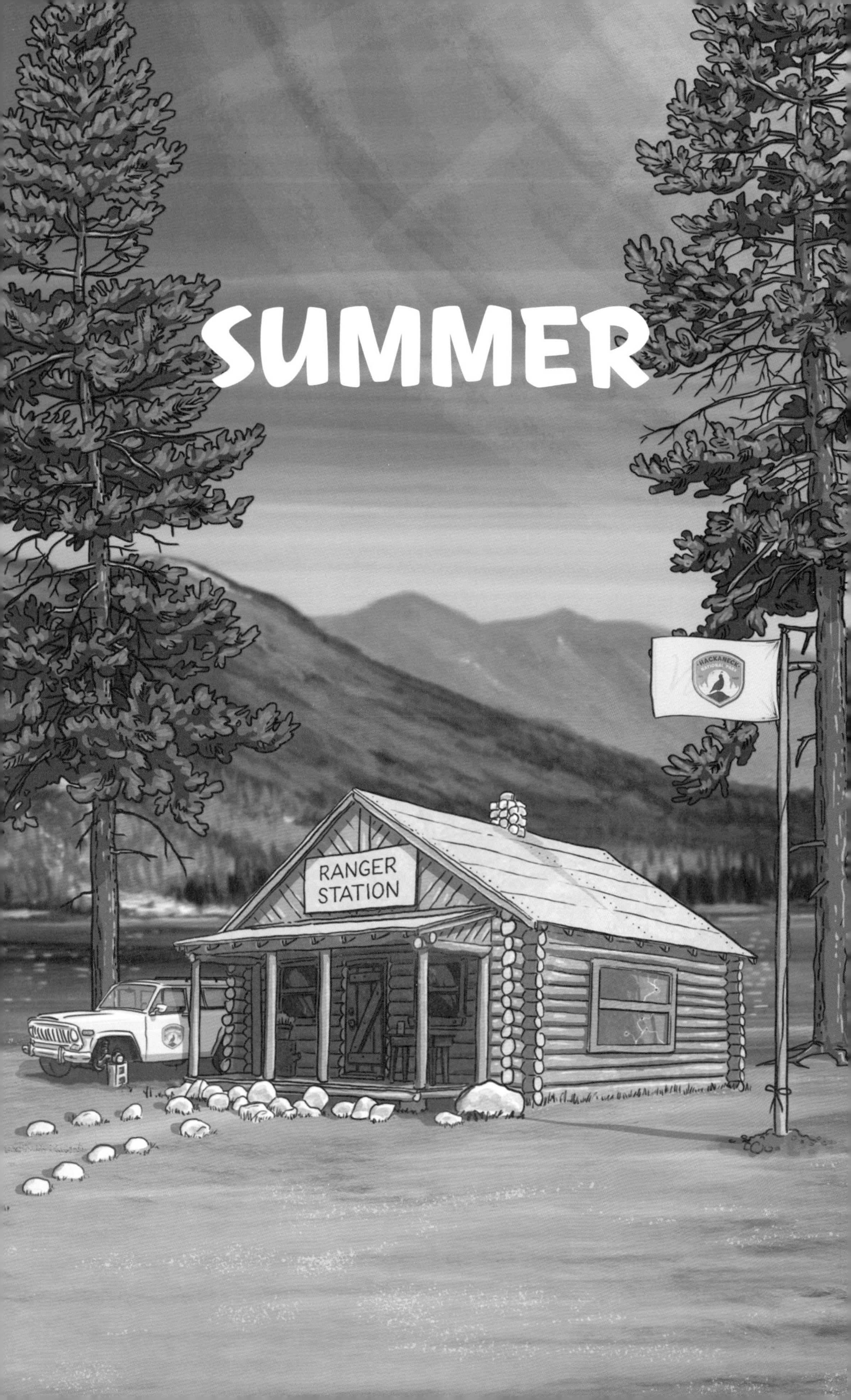
RANGER
STATION

HOT ENOUGH FOR YA?

HOWDY, CAMPERS! YOU SURVIVED ANOTHER SEASON. SPRING SPRANG, AND HERE WE ARE, ANOTHER HOT, FLAMING SUMMER. WE SPENT THE LAST FEW MONTHS RAKING THE FOREST FLOOR FOR YOUR BENEFIT, AND GUESS WHAT? MAN, THAT STUFF BURNED TOO. AT LEAST THE BLUEGILL ARE BITING. ANYWAY, BE THANKFUL YOU'RE ALIVE. FOR NOW. IT'S A NUMBERS GAME FOR THE OL' SEPARATOR OF SOULS, AND EVENTUALLY, WELL, YOU KNOW. PERSONALLY, I'M THANKFUL MY TAR-CAKED LUNGS ARE IMPERVIOUS TO VIRUSES AND WILDFIRE SMOKE IN ORDER TO BRING YOU ANOTHER COLLECTION OF CAREFULLY-CURATED CURIOS TO OGLE. SO, THROW BACK A COUPLE FIZZY LIZZIES, AND TAKE A BREAK FROM THE REAL WORLD. HAVE A LAUGH AT THE DARKER SIDE OF LIFE WHILE YOU WAIT.

RANGER GARLAND WOODBURN
HACKANECK NATIONAL PARK

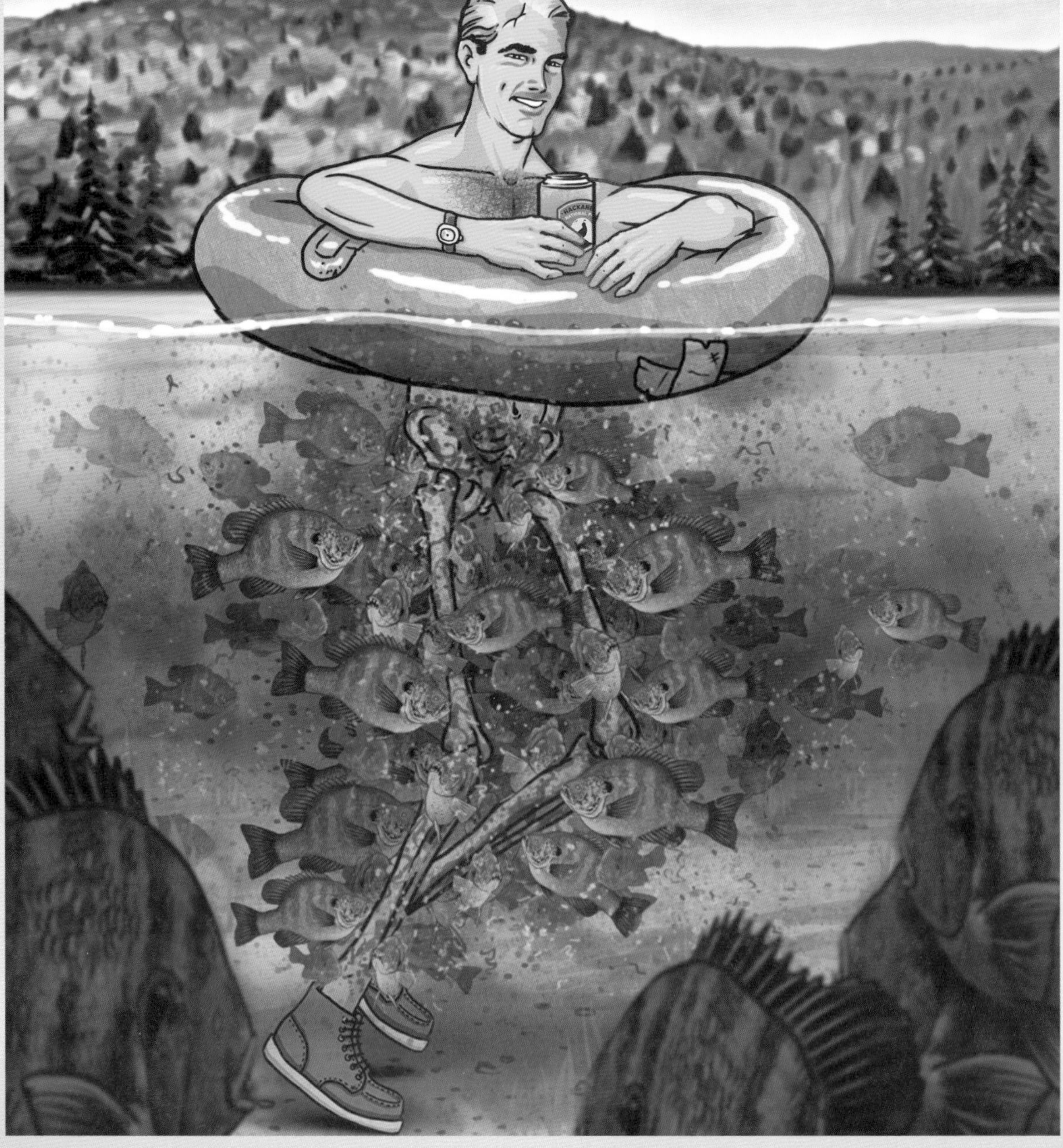

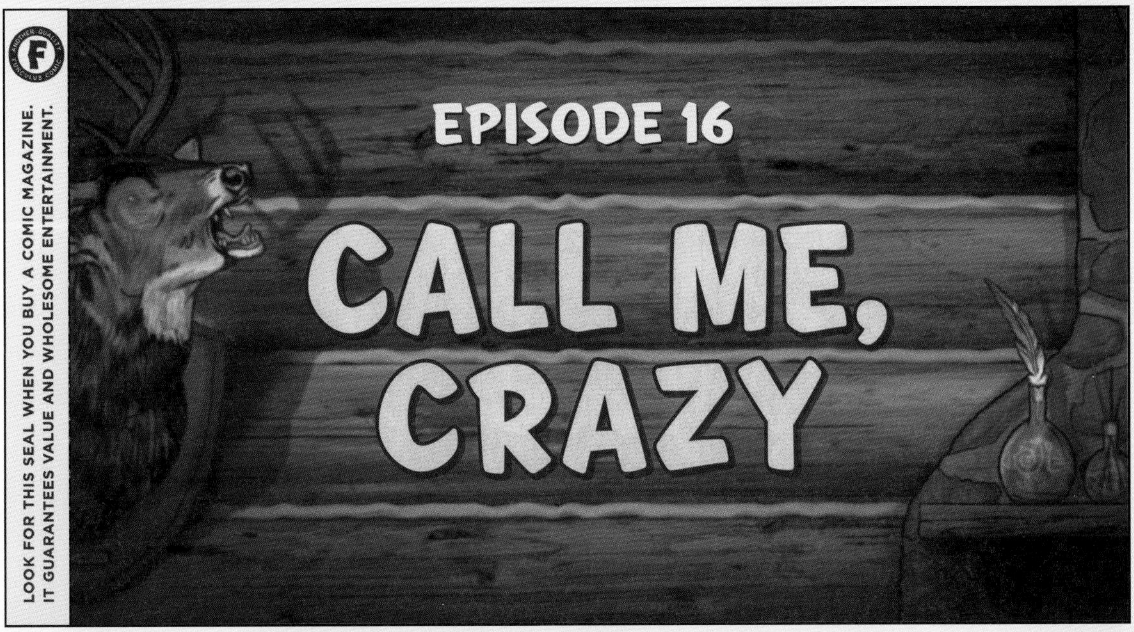
LOOK FOR THIS SEAL WHEN YOU BUY A COMIC MAGAZINE.
IT GUARANTEES VALUE AND WHOLESOME ENTERTAINMENT.
EPISODE 16
CALL ME, CRAZY

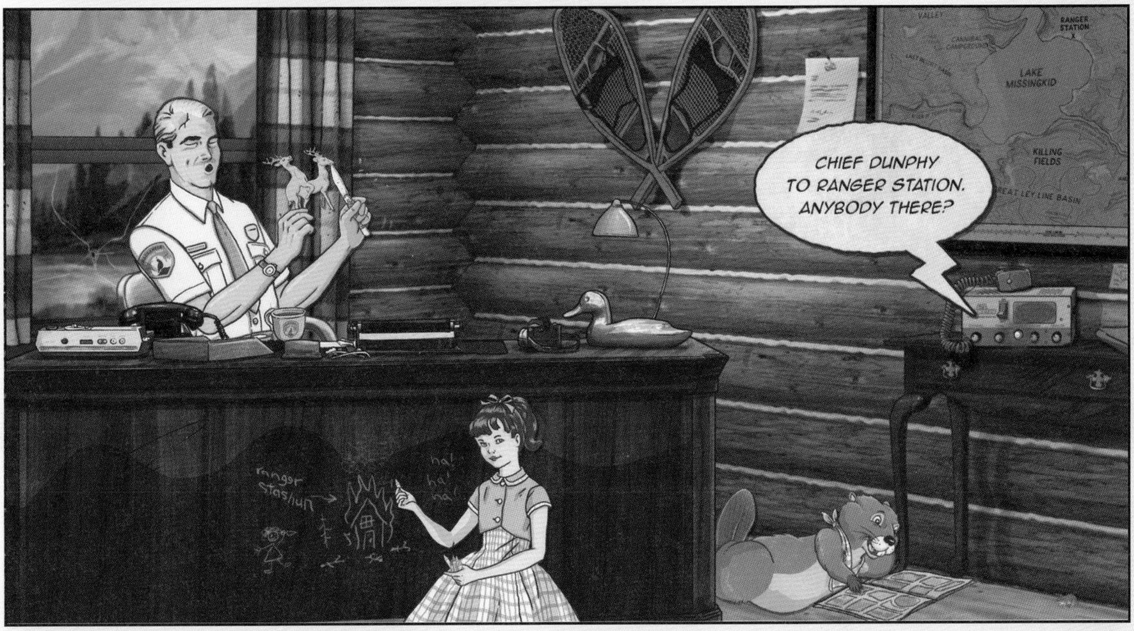
RANGER STATION
LAKE MISSINGKID
KILLING FIELDS
CHIEF DUNPHY TO RANGER STATION. ANYBODY THERE?
ranger stashun
ha! ha! ha!

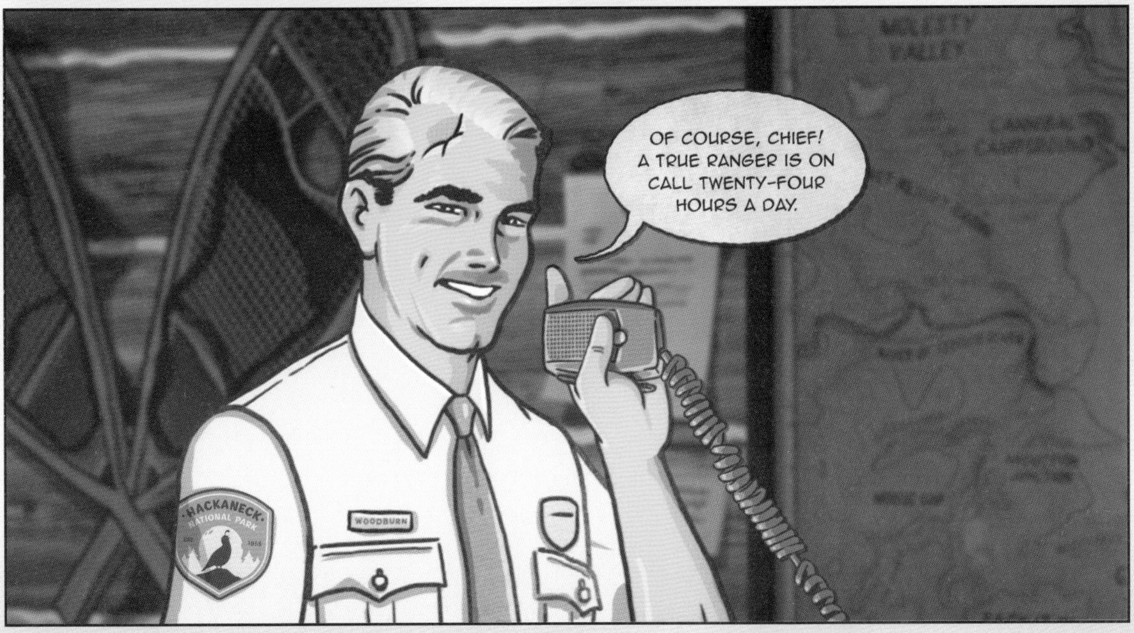
OF COURSE, CHIEF! A TRUE RANGER IS ON CALL TWENTY-FOUR HOURS A DAY.
HACKANECK NATIONAL PARK
WOODBURN

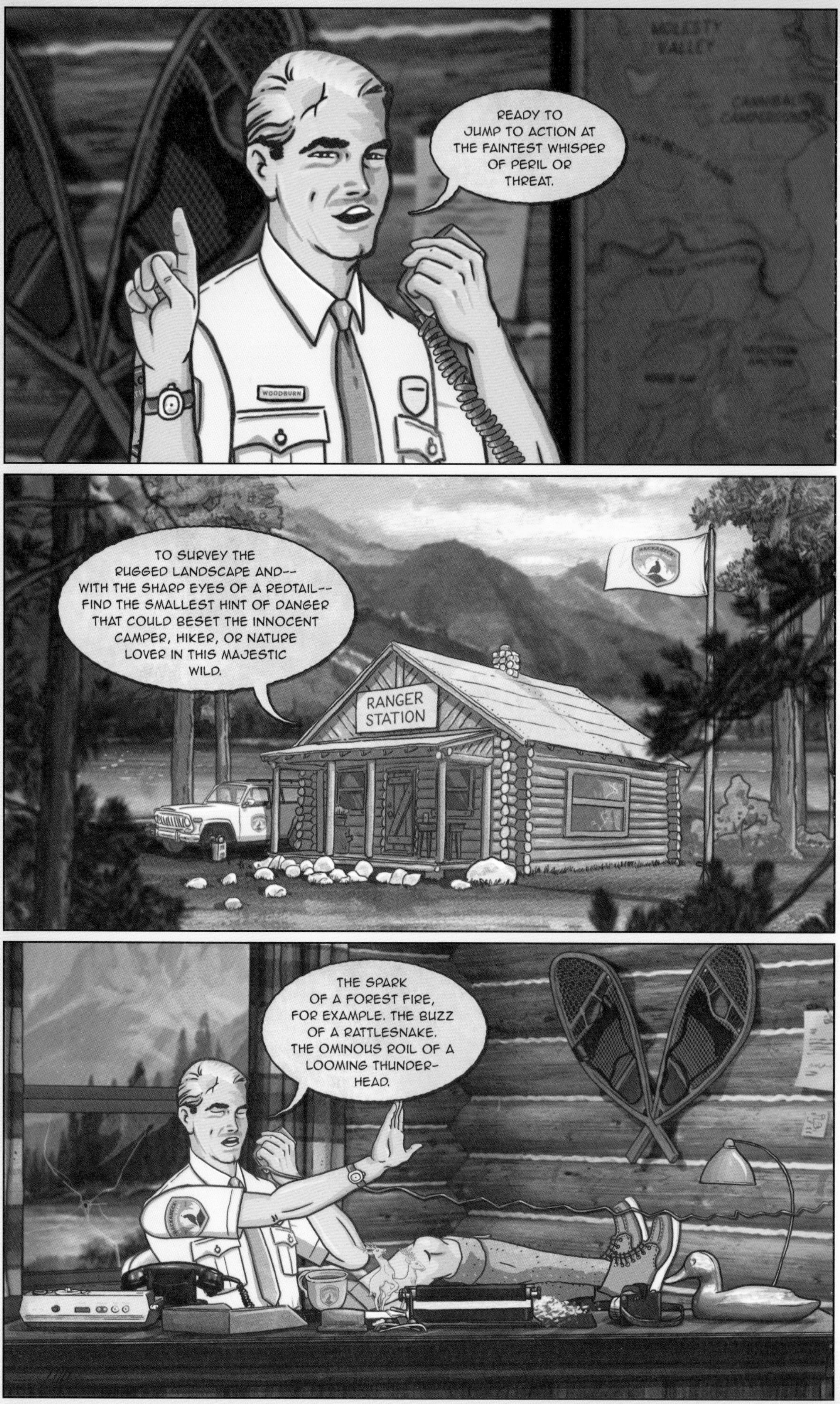
READY TO JUMP TO ACTION AT THE FAINTEST WHISPER OF PERIL OR THREAT.
WOODBURN
TO SURVEY THE RUGGED LANDSCAPE AND-- WITH THE SHARP EYES OF A REDTAIL-- FIND THE SMALLEST HINT OF DANGER THAT COULD BESET THE INNOCENT CAMPER, HIKER, OR NATURE LOVER IN THIS MAJESTIC WILD.
RANGER STATION
THE SPARK OF A FOREST FIRE, FOR EXAMPLE. THE BUZZ OF A RATTLESNAKE. THE OMINOUS ROIL OF A LOOMING THUNDER-HEAD.

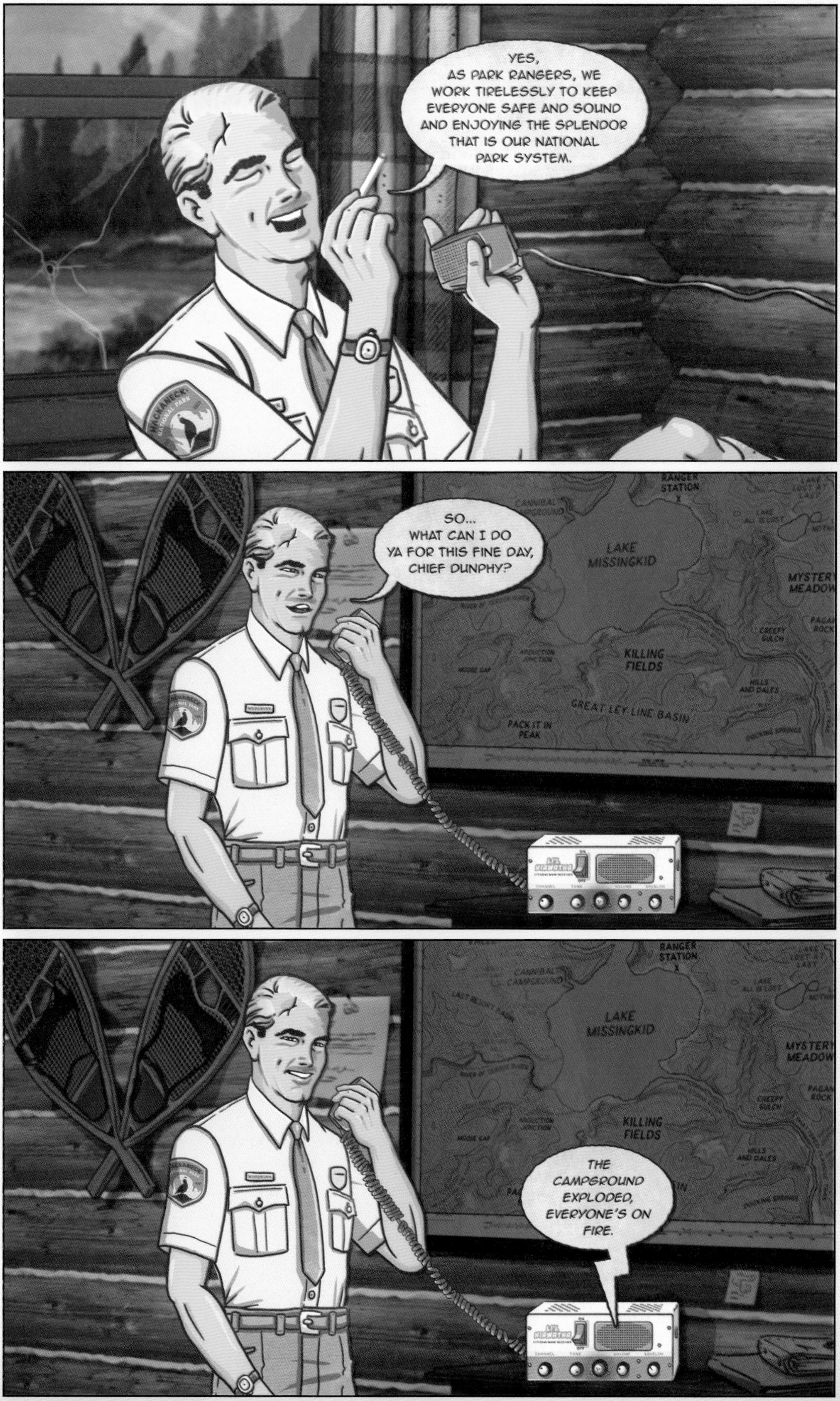

YES, AS PARK RANGERS, WE WORK TIRELESSLY TO KEEP EVERYONE SAFE AND SOUND AND ENJOYING THE SPLENDOR THAT IS OUR NATIONAL PARK SYSTEM.
SO... WHAT CAN I DO YA FOR THIS FINE DAY, CHIEF DUNPHY?
RANGER STATION
LAKE MISSINGKID
KILLING FIELDS
GREAT LEY LINE BASIN
PACK IT IN PEAK
CREEPY GULCH
HILLS AND DALES
THE CAMPGROUND EXPLODED, EVERYONE'S ON FIRE.

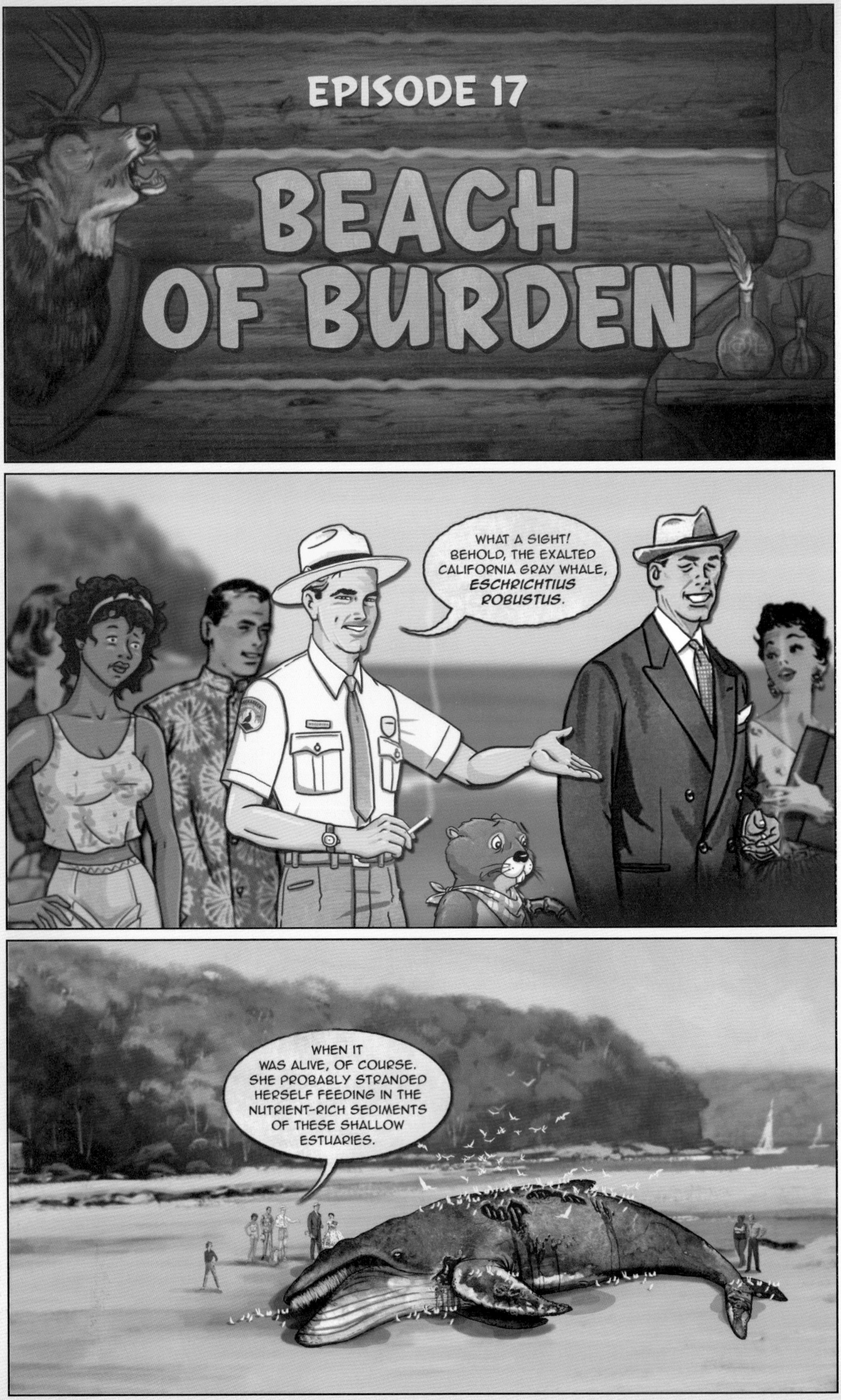
EPISODE 17
BEACH OF BURDEN
WHAT A SIGHT! BEHOLD, THE EXALTED CALIFORNIA GRAY WHALE, ESCHRICHTIUS ROBUSTUS.
WHEN IT WAS ALIVE, OF COURSE. SHE PROBABLY STRANDED HERSELF FEEDING IN THE NUTRIENT-RICH SEDIMENTS OF THESE SHALLOW ESTUARIES.

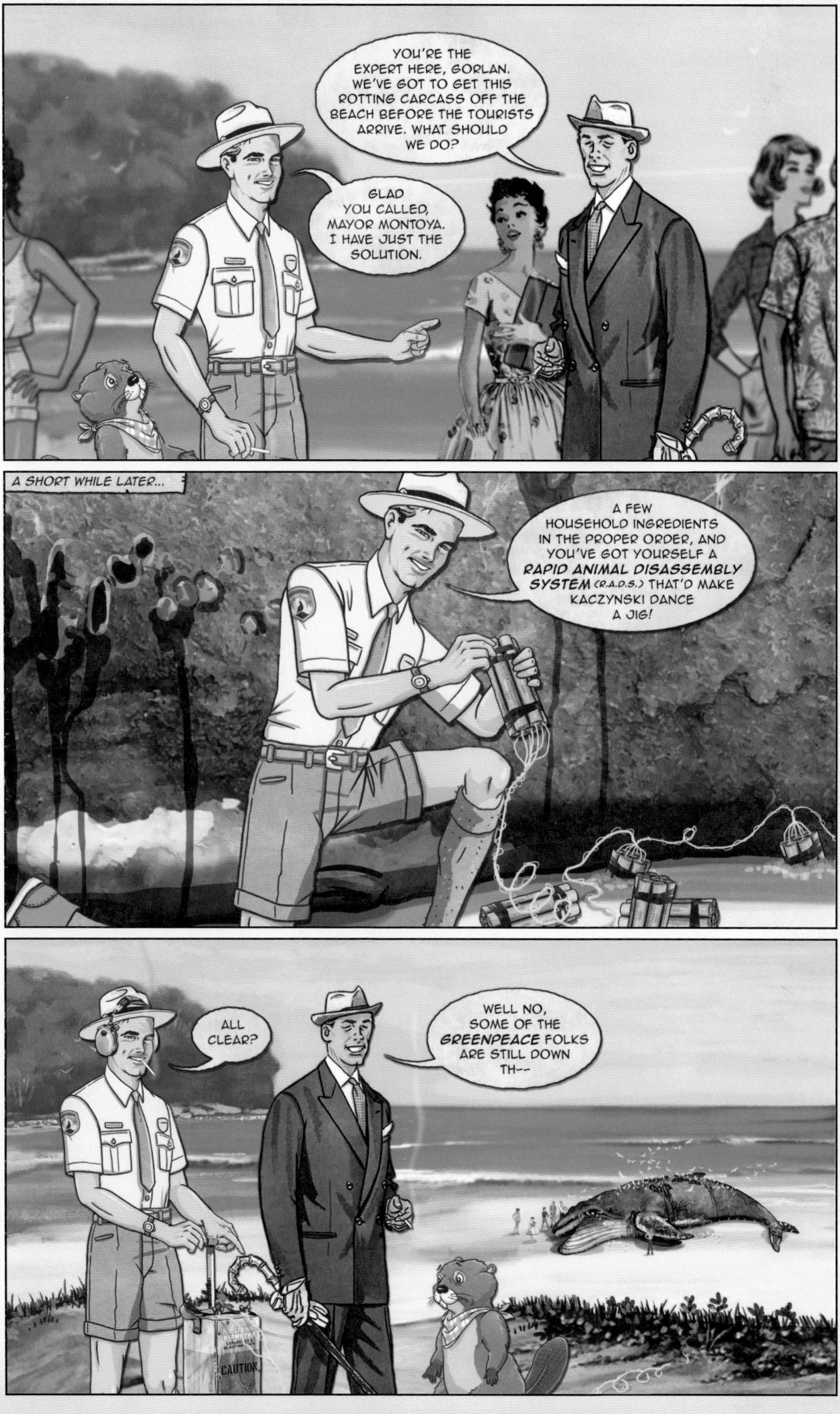
YOU'RE THE EXPERT HERE, GORLAN. WE'VE GOT TO GET THIS ROTTING CARCASS OFF THE BEACH BEFORE THE TOURISTS ARRIVE. WHAT SHOULD WE DO?
GLAD YOU CALLED, MAYOR MONTOYA. I HAVE JUST THE SOLUTION.
A SHORT WHILE LATER...
A FEW HOUSEHOLD INGREDIENTS IN THE PROPER ORDER, AND YOU'VE GOT YOURSELF A RAPID ANIMAL DISASSEMBLY SYSTEM (R.A.D.S.) THAT'D MAKE KACZYNSKI DANCE A JIG!
ALL CLEAR?
WELL NO, SOME OF THE GREENPEACE FOLKS ARE STILL DOWN TH--
CAUTION

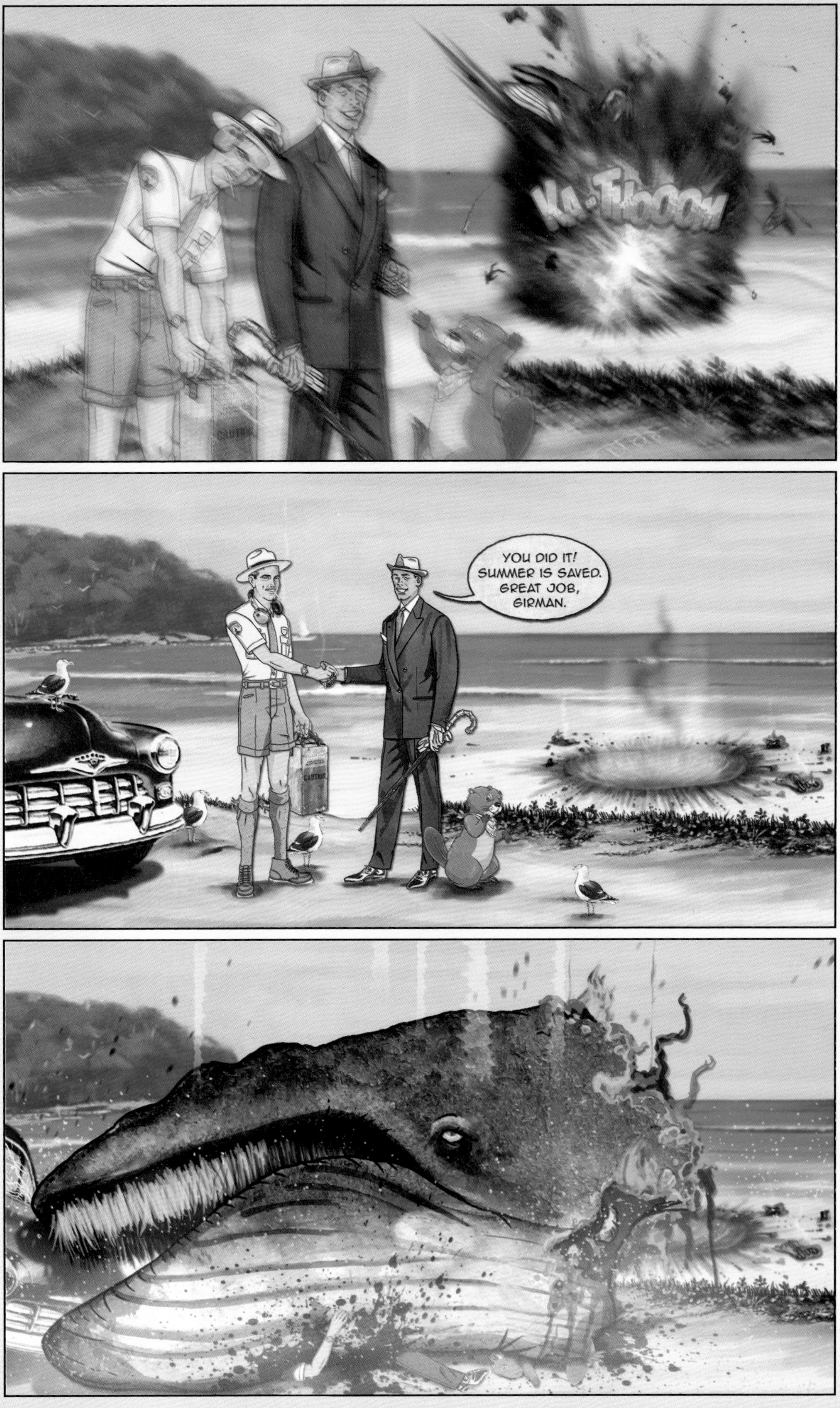
KA-THOOOM
CAUTION
YOU DID IT! SUMMER IS SAVED. GREAT JOB, GIRMAN.

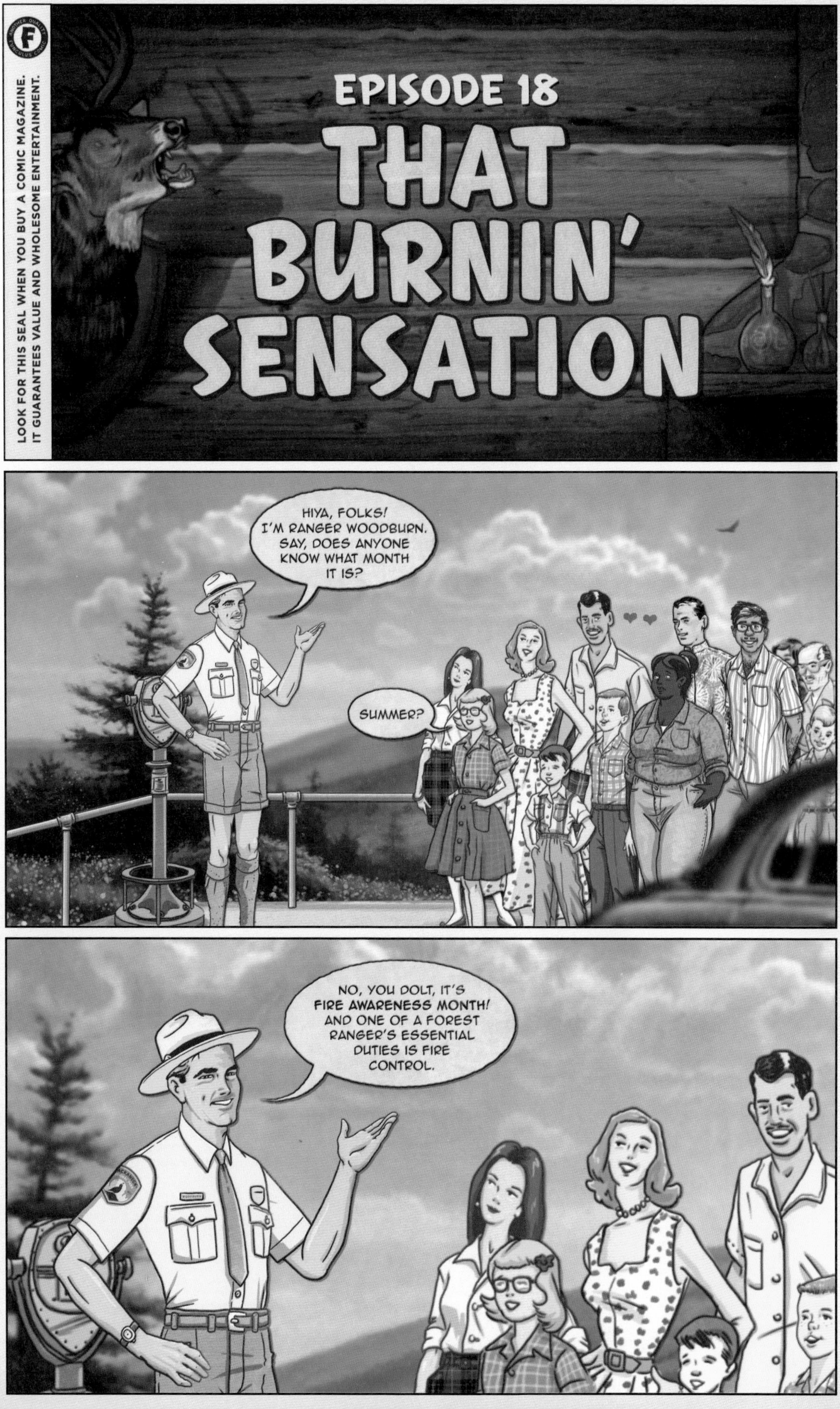
LOOK FOR THIS SEAL WHEN YOU BUY A COMIC MAGAZINE. IT GUARANTEES VALUE AND WHOLESOME ENTERTAINMENT.
EPISODE 18
THAT BURNIN' SENSATION
HIYA, FOLKS! I'M RANGER WOODBURN. SAY, DOES ANYONE KNOW WHAT MONTH IT IS?
SUMMER?
NO, YOU DOLT, IT'S FIRE AWARENESS MONTH! AND ONE OF A FOREST RANGER'S ESSENTIAL DUTIES IS FIRE CONTROL.

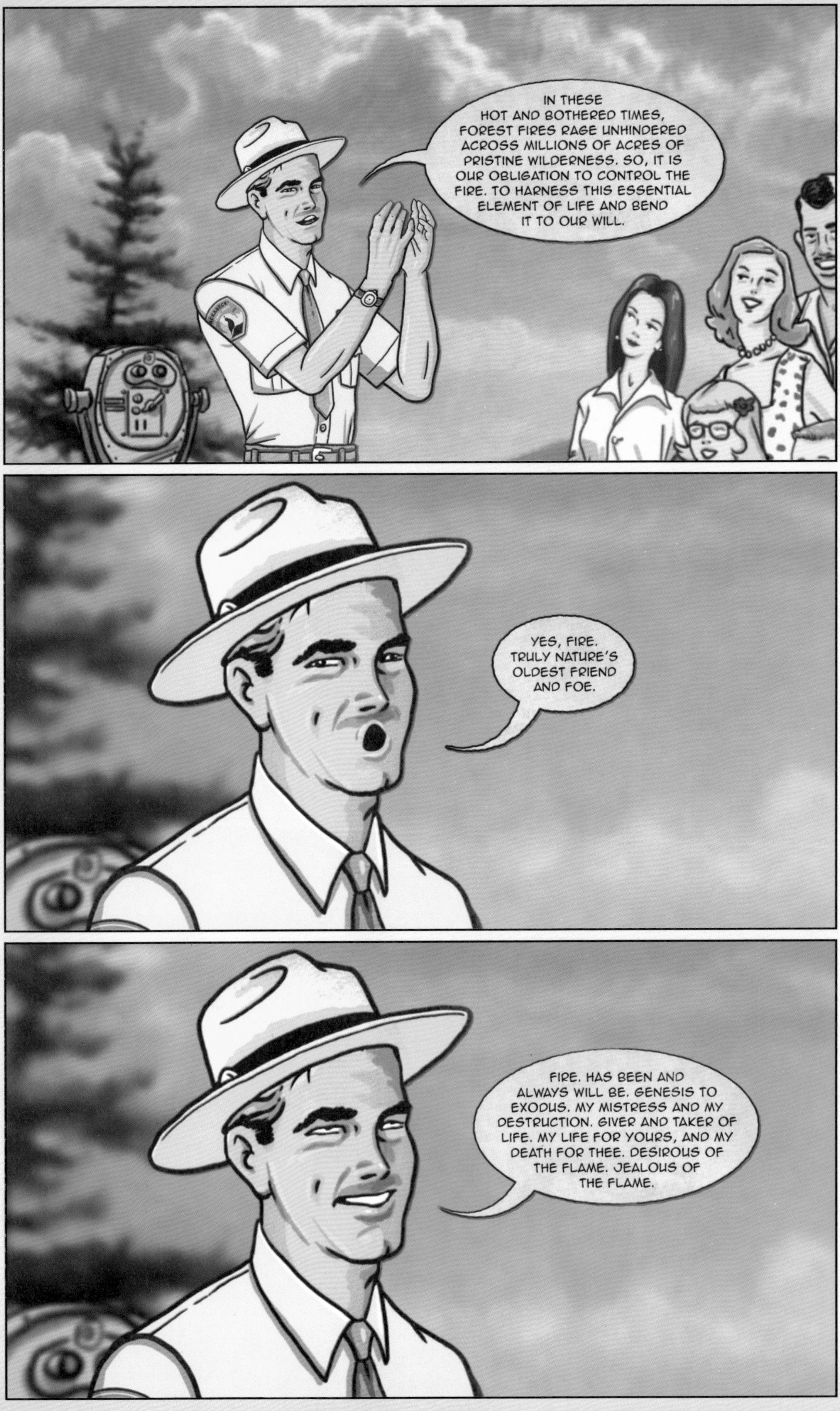
IN THESE HOT AND BOTHERED TIMES, FOREST FIRES RAGE UNHINDERED ACROSS MILLIONS OF ACRES OF PRISTINE WILDERNESS. SO, IT IS OUR OBLIGATION TO CONTROL THE FIRE. TO HARNESS THIS ESSENTIAL ELEMENT OF LIFE AND BEND IT TO OUR WILL.
YES, FIRE. TRULY NATURE'S OLDEST FRIEND AND FOE.
FIRE. HAS BEEN AND ALWAYS WILL BE. GENESIS TO EXODUS. MY MISTRESS AND MY DESTRUCTION. GIVER AND TAKER OF LIFE. MY LIFE FOR YOURS, AND MY DEATH FOR THEE. DESIROUS OF THE FLAME. JEALOUS OF THE FLAME.

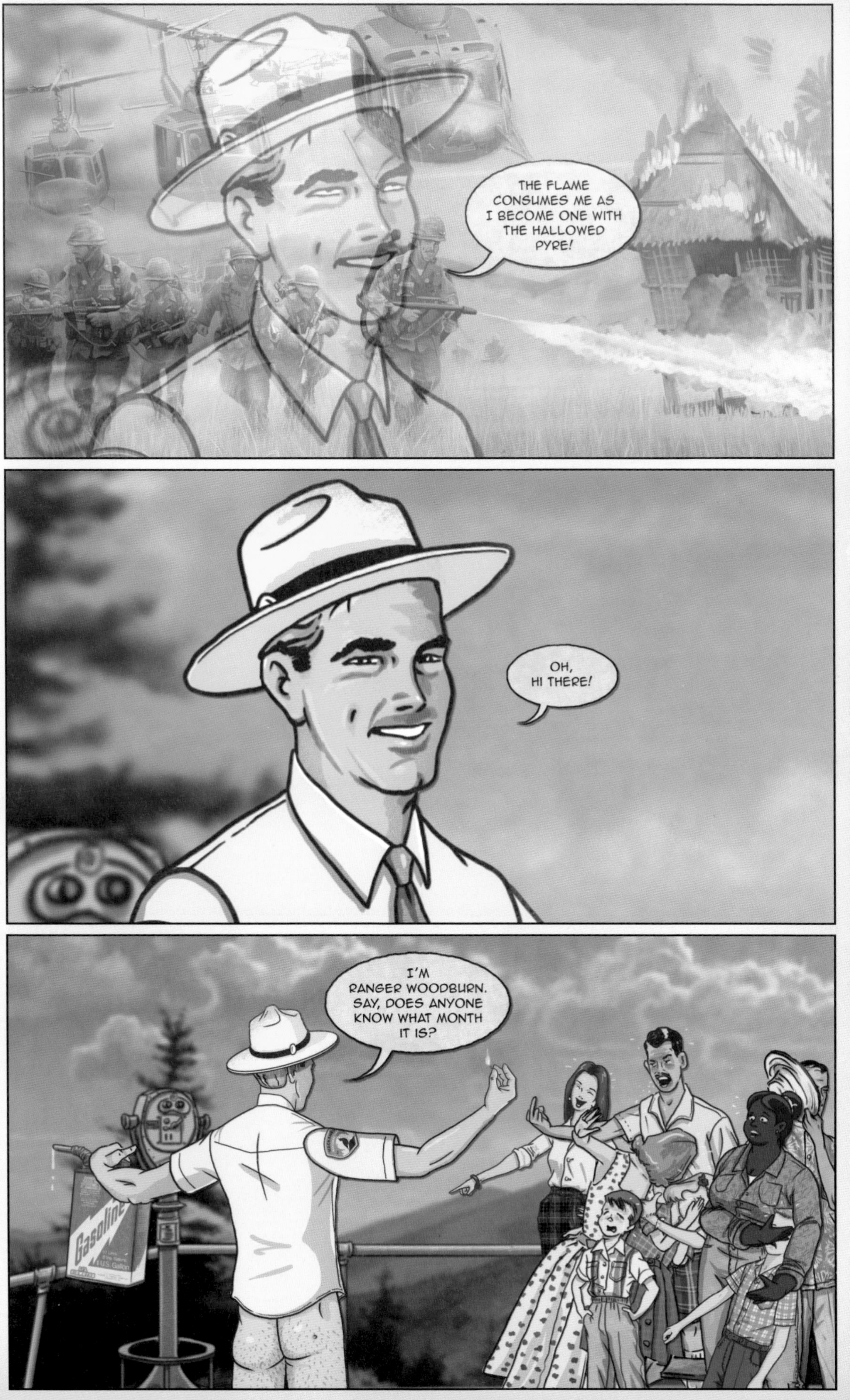
THE FLAME CONSUMES ME AS I BECOME ONE WITH THE HALLOWED PYRE!
OH, HI THERE!
I'M RANGER WOODBURN. SAY, DOES ANYONE KNOW WHAT MONTH IT IS?
Gasoline

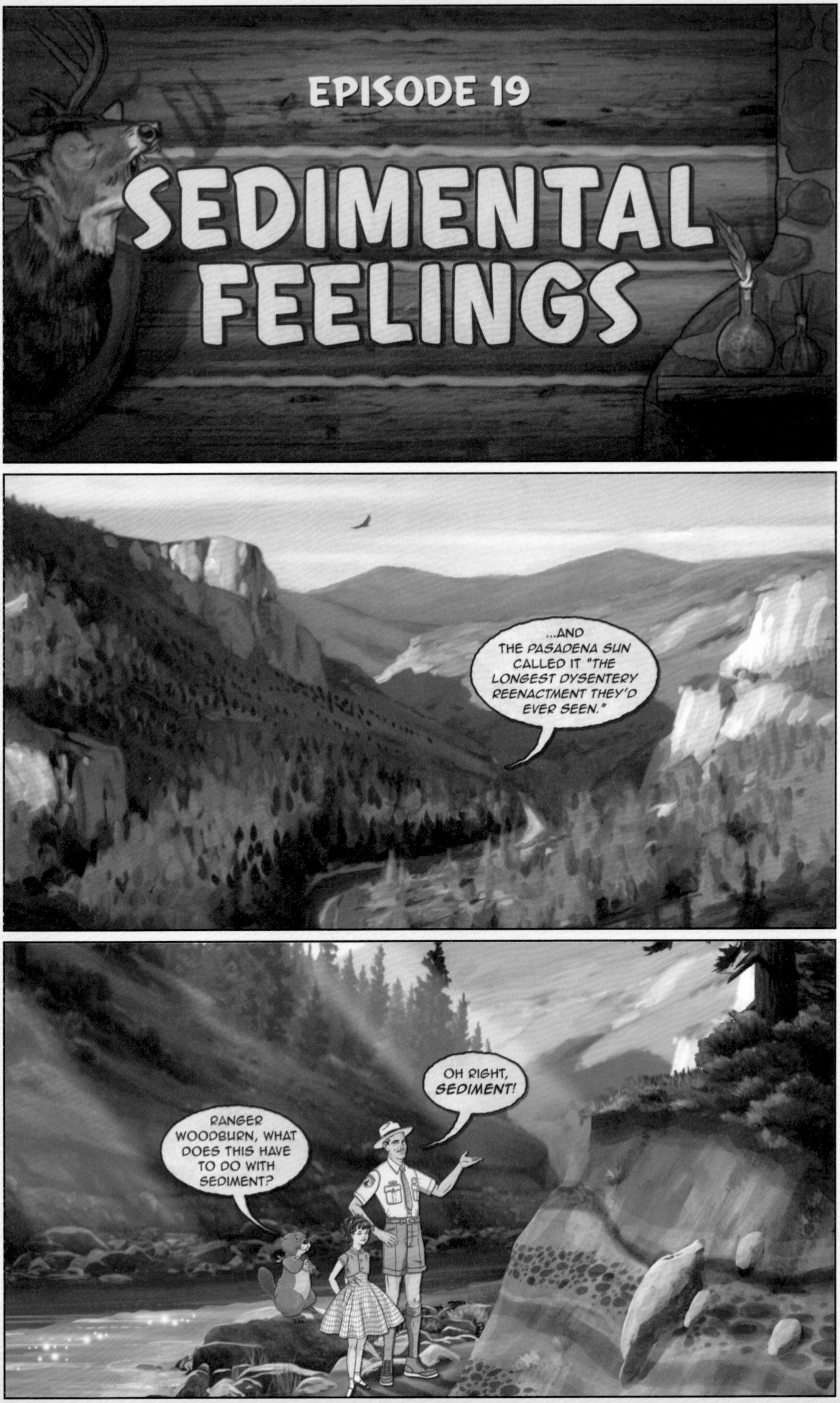
EPISODE 19
SEDIMENTAL FEELINGS
...AND THE PASADENA SUN CALLED IT "THE LONGEST DYSENTERY REENACTMENT THEY'D EVER SEEN."
OH RIGHT, SEDIMENT!
RANGER WOODBURN, WHAT DOES THIS HAVE TO DO WITH SEDIMENT?

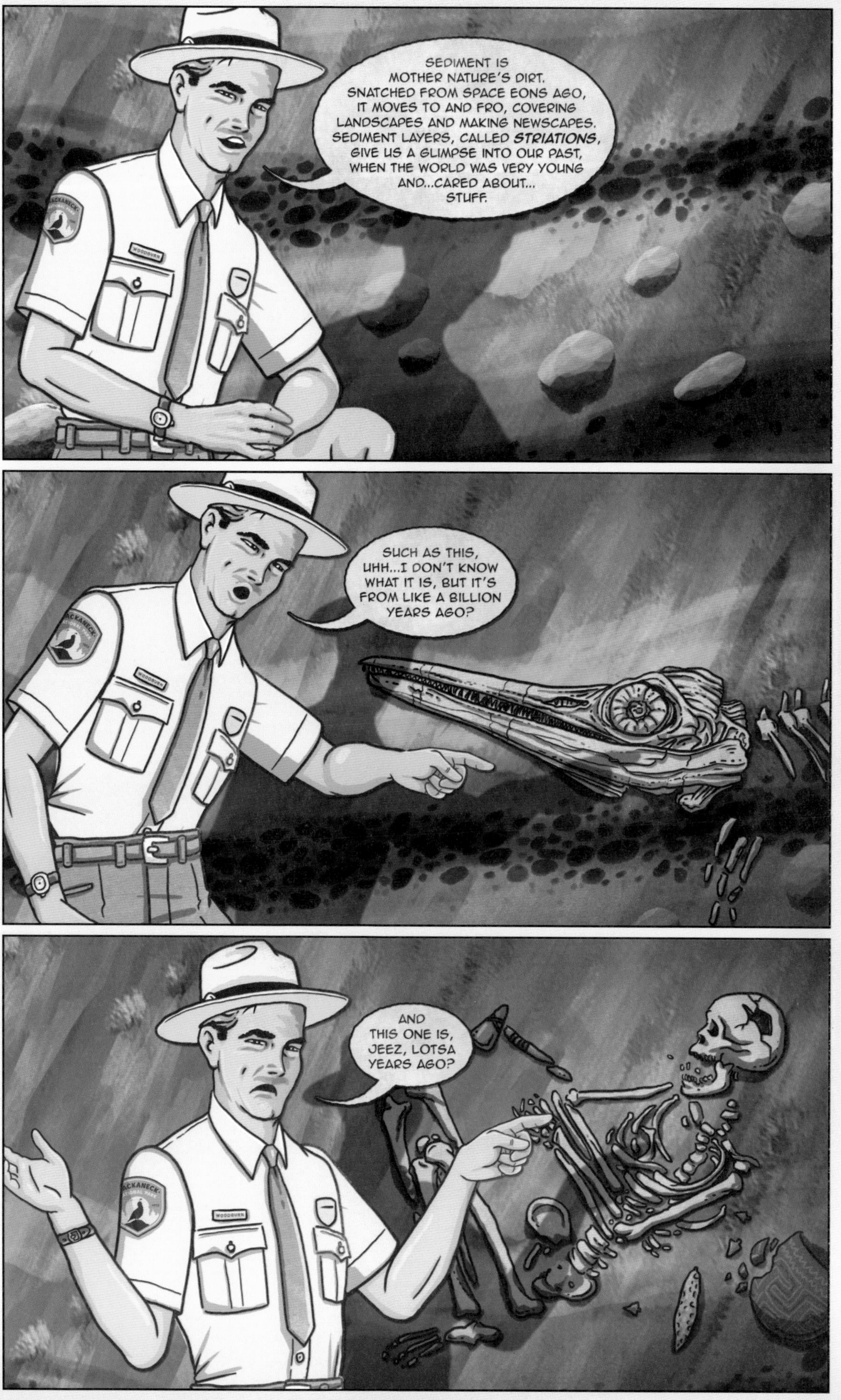
SEDIMENT IS MOTHER NATURE'S DIRT. SNATCHED FROM SPACE EONS AGO, IT MOVES TO AND FRO, COVERING LANDSCAPES AND MAKING NEWSCAPES. SEDIMENT LAYERS, CALLED *STRIATIONS*, GIVE US A GLIMPSE INTO OUR PAST, WHEN THE WORLD WAS VERY YOUNG AND...CARED ABOUT... STUFF.
SUCH AS THIS, UHH...I DON'T KNOW WHAT IT IS, BUT IT'S FROM LIKE A BILLION YEARS AGO?
AND THIS ONE IS, JEEZ, LOTSA YEARS AGO?

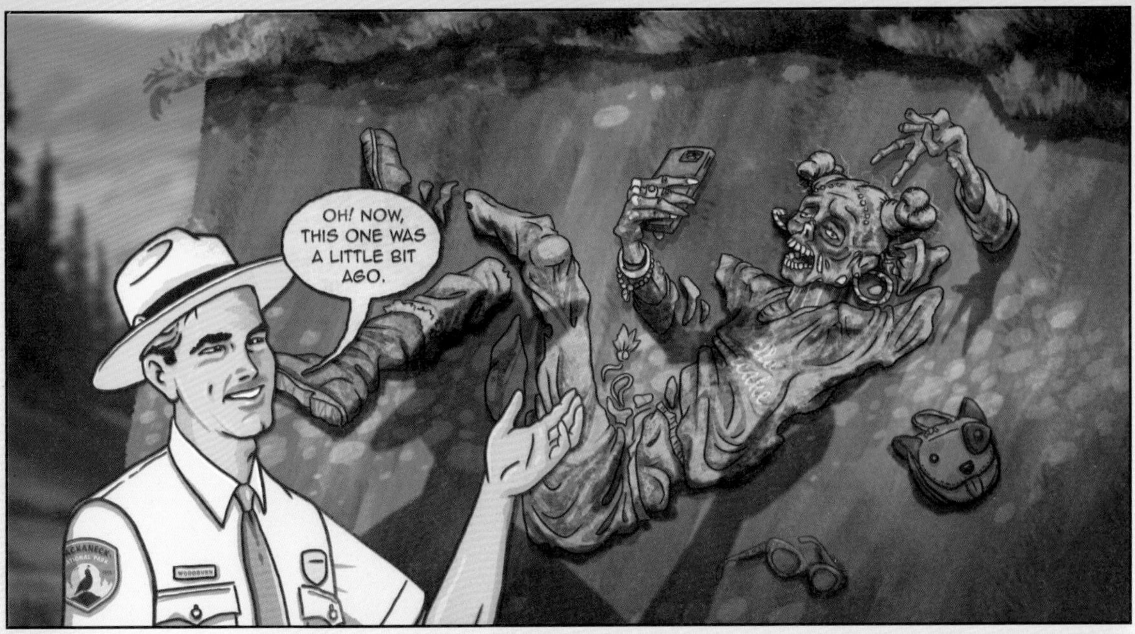
OH! NOW, THIS ONE WAS A LITTLE BIT AGO.
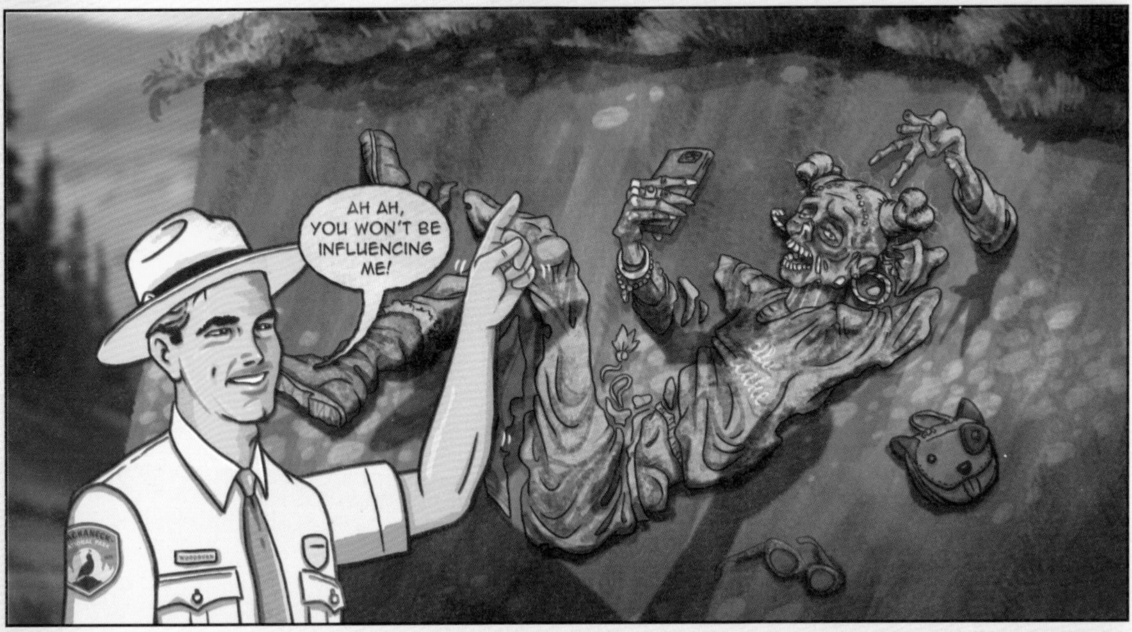
AH AH, YOU WON'T BE INFLUENCING ME!
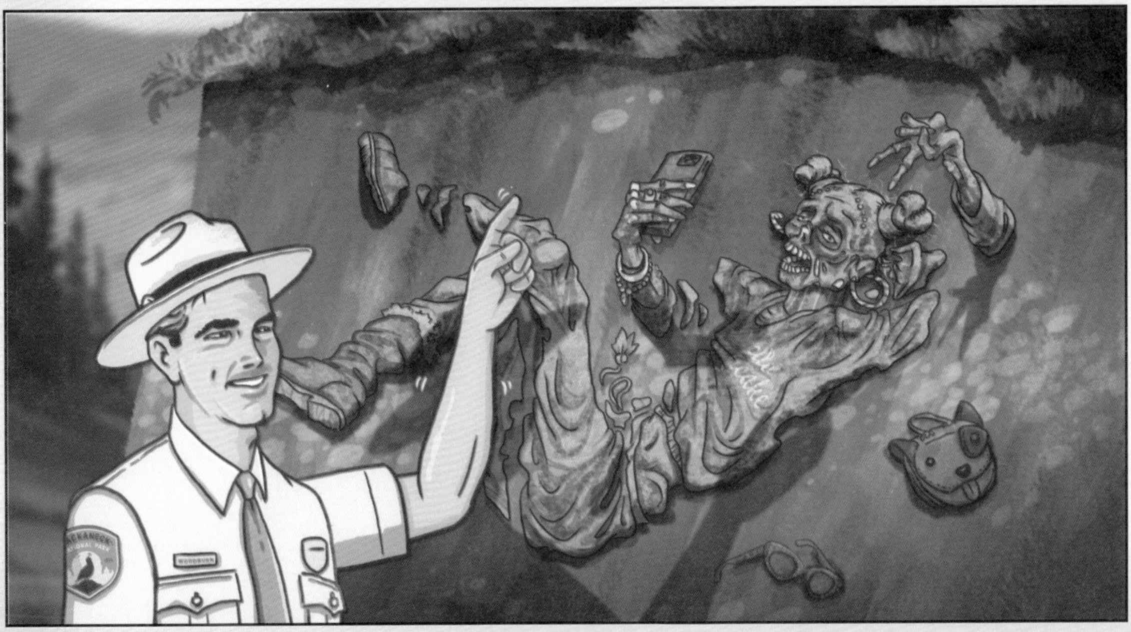

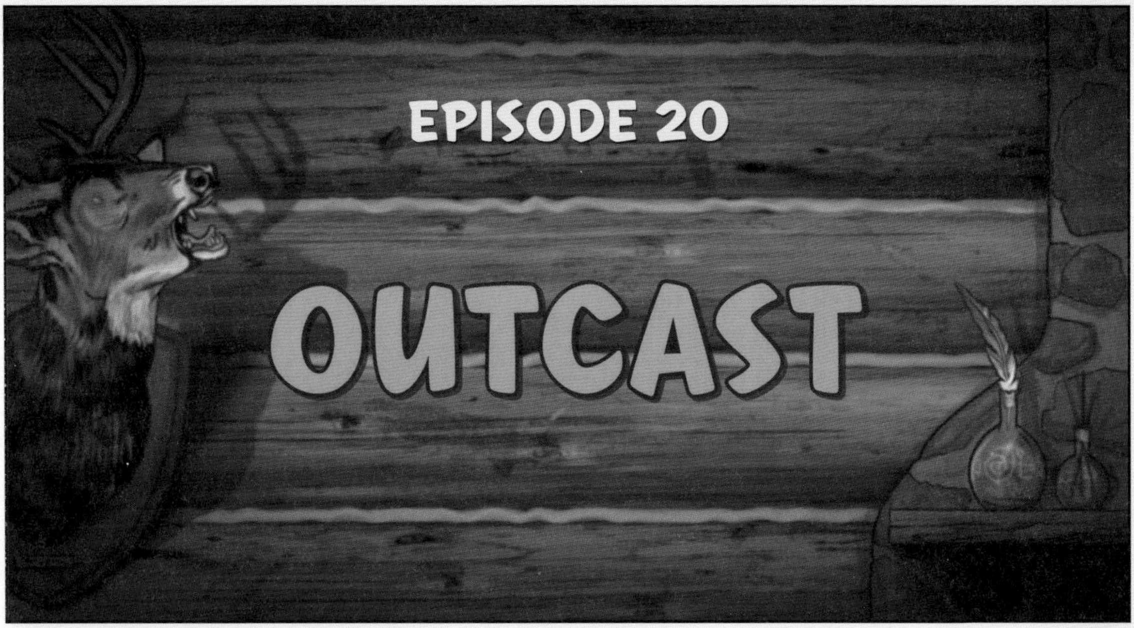
EPISODE 20
OUTCAST

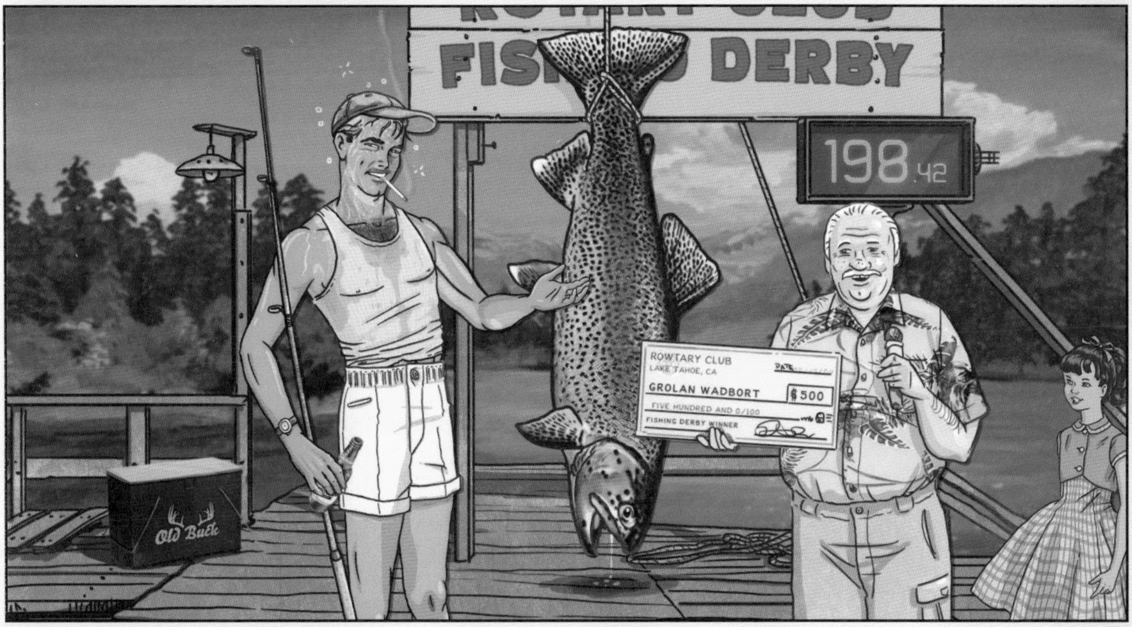
DERBY
198.42
ROWTARY CLUB
LAKE TAHOE, CA
GROLAN WADBORT
$500
FIVE HUNDRED AND 0/100
FISHING DERBY WINNER
Old Buck

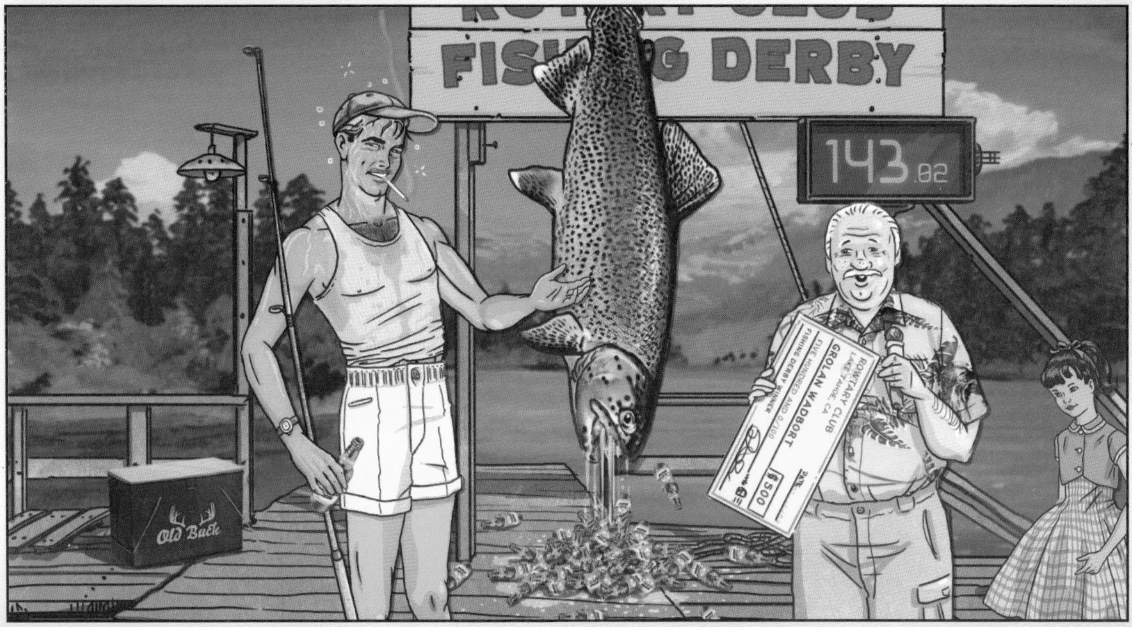
DERBY
143.82
ROWTARY CLUB
LAKE TAHOE, CA
GROLAN WADBORT
$500
FIVE HUNDRED AND 0/100
FISHING DERBY WINNER
Old Buck

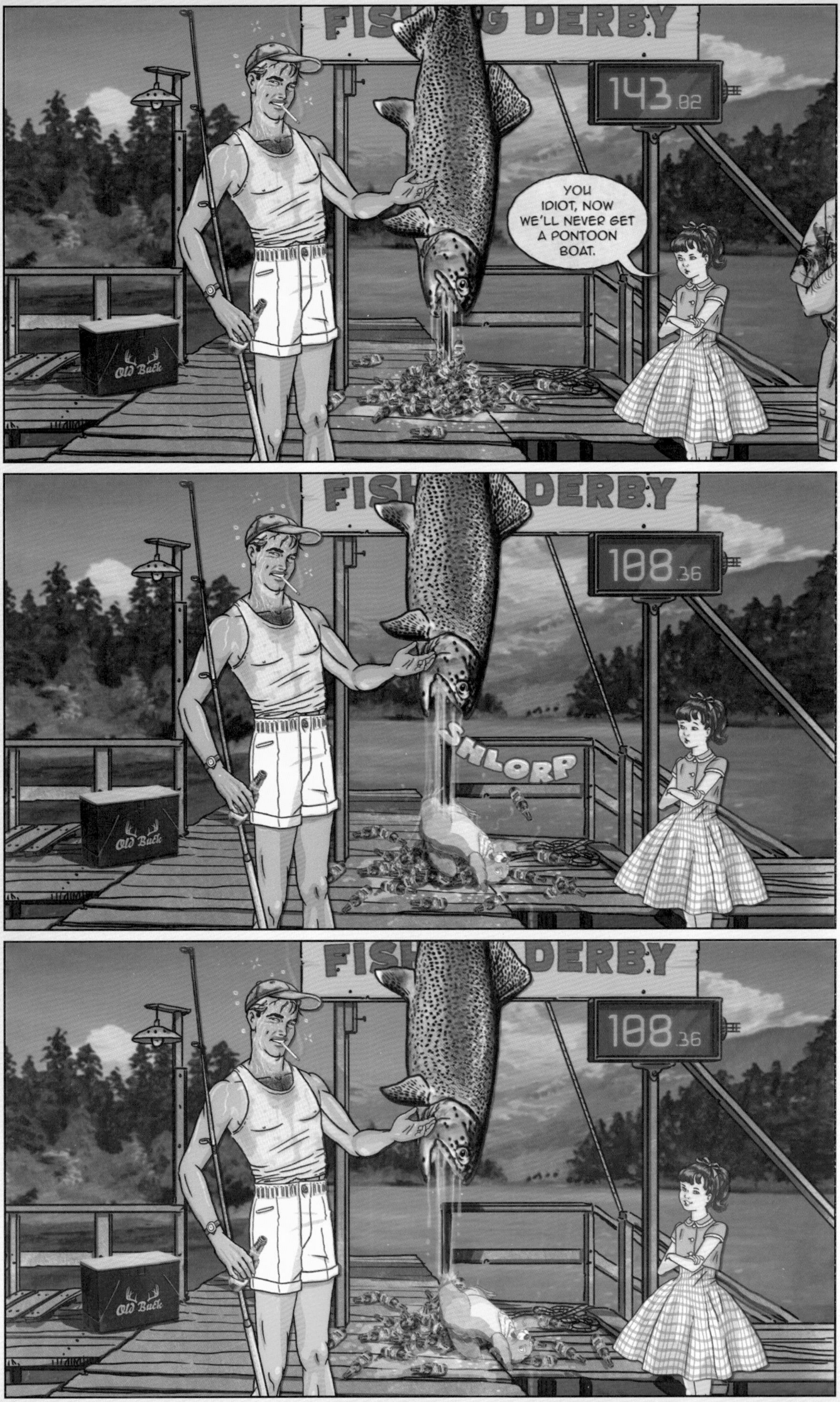
DERBY
143.82
YOU IDIOT, NOW WE'LL NEVER GET A PONTOON BOAT.
Old Buck
DERBY
108.36
SHLORP
Old Buck
DERBY
108.36
Old Buck

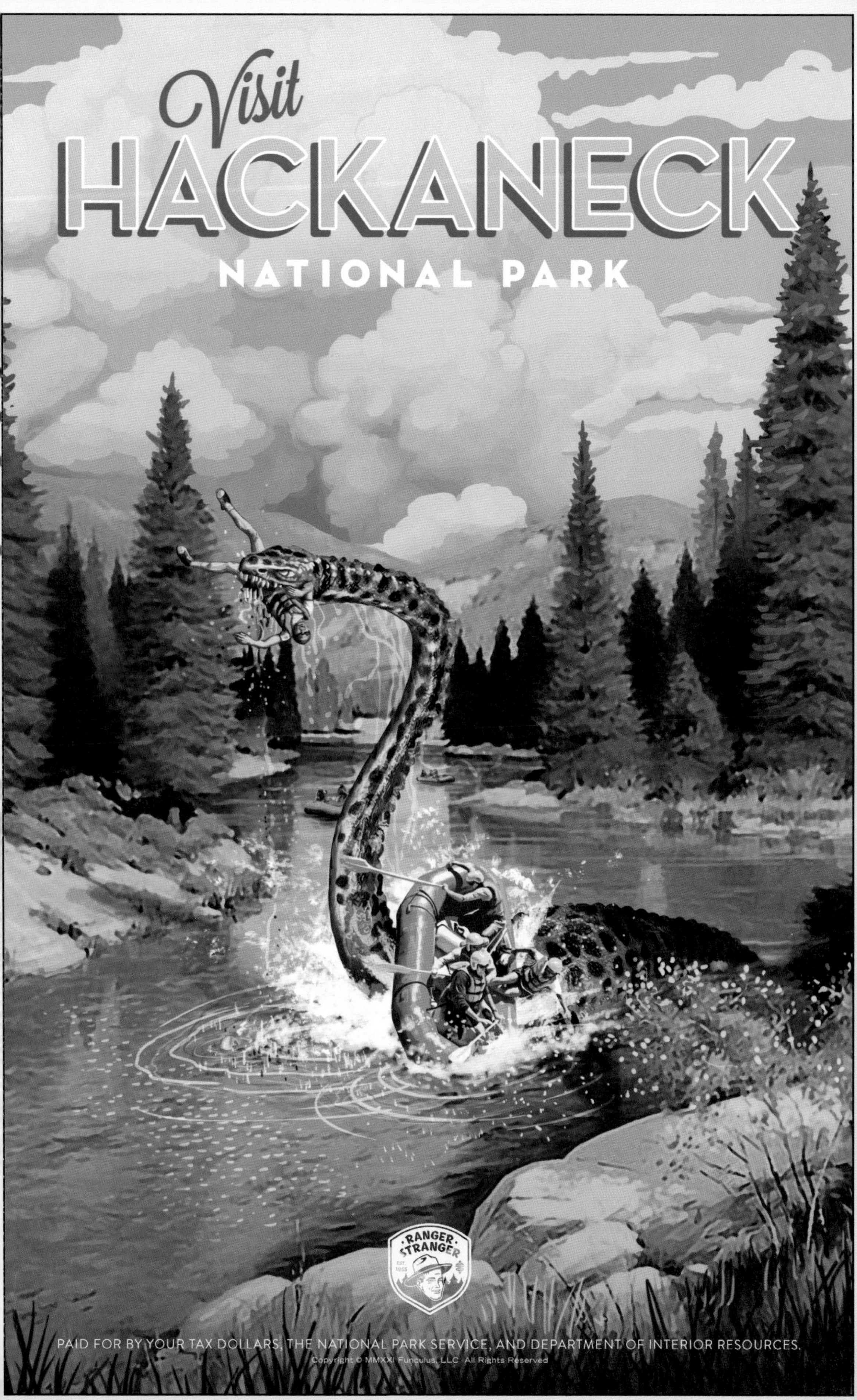
Visit
HACKANECK
NATIONAL PARK
RANGER STRANGER
EST. 1955
PAID FOR BY YOUR TAX DOLLARS, THE NATIONAL PARK SERVICE, AND DEPARTMENT OF INTERIOR RESOURCES.
Copyright © MMXXI Funculus, LLC All Rights Reserved

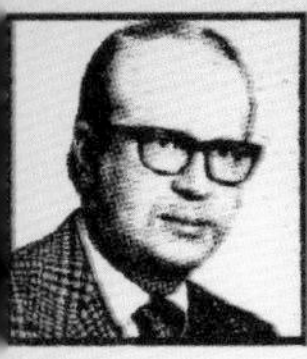

BOATIN' with DICKY BORDEN, Editor

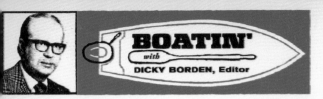

Tired of getting ripped off at the used boat dealership? Send 'em overboard and build one brand new.

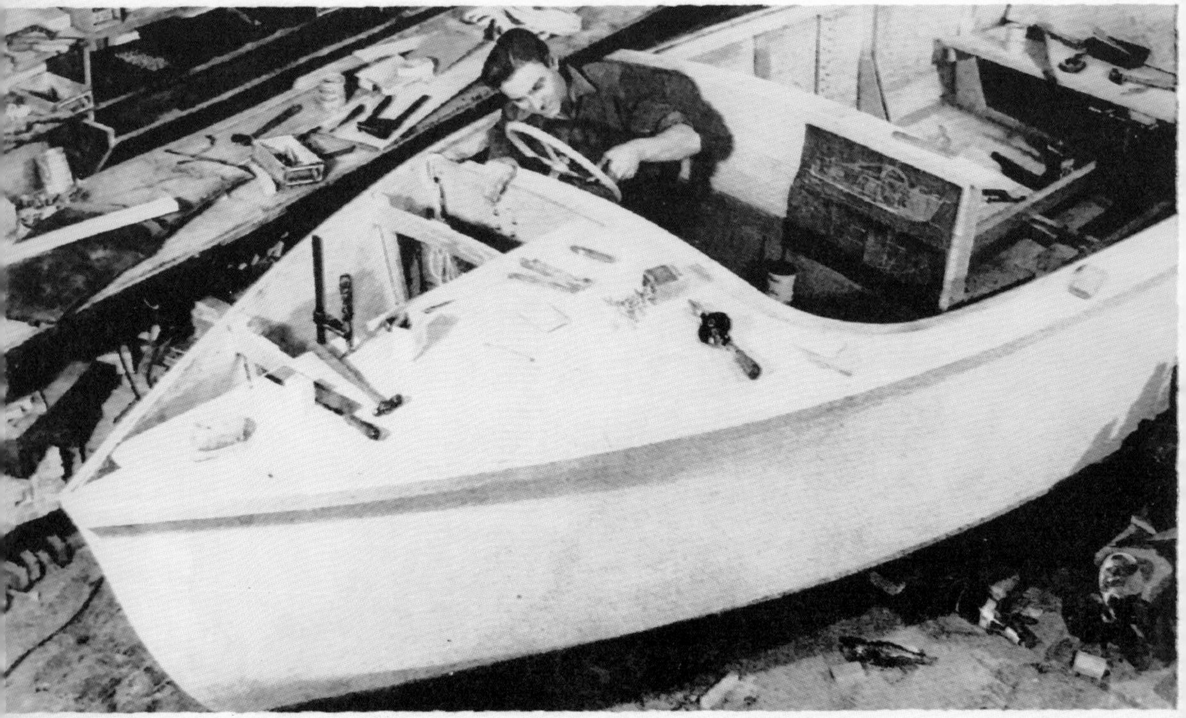

Easy as 1-2-3! Assembling a U-Mak-It, 18-foot inboard in your basement is every man's dream.

DO-IT-YOURSELF BOATS

Calling all Master Builders! It's a long lost art, that of picking up some pieces of wood with your hands and creating something you can float on and fish from. From as far back as ancient Egypt, and other early civilizations probably, everyone knew how to build a boat. If you didn't, you'd have something of a character deficit most likely and a deficit of *moral timbre* as well! Let's rectify that shall we? Your father was always looking for the easy way out, let's just get that out of the way.

First, we're gonna need to figure out what kind of boat you're looking for? A skiff, a catamaran, a ferry? Ha ha. We'll need to look at your budget of course, are you on a behind-the-deli, stale biscuit budget or a fast-food burger budget? Let's face it, if your budget is any more than that, just go buy yourself a boat. And you're most likely not working with your hands and probably don't have the moral timbre to build yourself a boat anyway! Your father works for an accounting firm.

Once you've decided on your type of boat and decided on your budget, it's time for the fun part! Wading through the morass of shit on the internet, looking to see if they still make do-it-yourself boat kits. It's not like times of yore, when you could flip through a Sears and Roebuck catalog, circle the boat you want, save up for postage, mail your order, wait a month, then build your boat. No, you can order it online and then call your grandfather who actually owns tools and can measure and cut things. Your father never got his hands dirty, and you can tell. He has a limp shake.

So you've waited patiently, and now it's new boat day! They've delivered the boat, right at the bottom of the driveway, completely encased in 500 yards of plastic wrap. What the fuck. How am I supposed to get this fucking thing in my garage? First, cut away the plastic wrap and move the boat parts piece by piece up to your garage. This is going to give your haunches a good workout. The delivery guys knew what they were doing. Pricks. It's like something your father would do. Oh sure, they saved themselves a minute unloading it at the end of the driveway, but that just shows you their *moral timbre*.

Step 1.	**Assemble the boat.**
Step 2.	**Apply fiberglass and epoxy.**
Step 3.	**Install seats and bulkheads.**
Step 4.	**Install hardware.**
Step 5.	**Paint or varnish.**

That was easy! Now it's launch day! All your ard work is going to pay off. Today is the day you're oing to launch that beautiful boat that you made vith your own two hands, your blood and sweat, ut no tears. Well, your father's tears. Christ, what a ucking baby.

First things first, attach your boat trailer to our trailer hitch, and make sure your vehicle is tow ated for the amount of weight. Your father owns a ontiac, so we'll take my truck. It's little details like hat, he doesn't think.

Even if you're a seasoned boat owner or ew to the boat game, getting your boat to the lake an be a tricky endeavor. Always remember, when acking your trailer down the boat ramp, everything s backwards. Also remember that everyone is udging you. When you turn your wheel to the left, our trailer wants to go right, then flip it around and everse it for the other way. And back and so forth, ow you're getting the picture! Your father's hand-ye coordination was abysmal.

But now, you've got it all cattywampus, and ou're gonna have to straighten her back out. You've ad to do this a couple times. You're sweating like pig at this point, your face is red. You told your ids to wait outside the truck because you needed o concentrate. And now they ran to the swingset ecause they're all embarrassed. A bunch of other ids are laughing at the guy on the boat ramp, and our kids are laughing along, embarrassed to say hat's their old man who's making a real mess of hings. There's a line forming, and now they're all ucking honking, and you can't get it down the ramp or Pete's sake. *"Just shut up and give me a second to hink!"* you screech. The line is snaking all the way hrough the lot, and it's backed up out onto the treet now. This is the fourth try, and a bunch of ther dads are trying to help, trying to scream above he incessant honking. *"Turn it to the left! Turn it right! ;o home!"* you hear them yelling.

Now, you're soaked with sweat and mbarrassed you even tried, your own kids won't get ack into the truck, and you just want to hide your ace. You might be crying a bit. And you say "To hell vith this!" and just fucking gas it straight ahead. But h no! The boat slipped off your trailer, and you're craping it along the parking lot at full speed. All hat work! And for what? This was a huge mistake, vhich is what they'll probably write on your father's ombstone. If he only had the *moral timbre,* things vould have turned out differently.

tay tuned for next month's article, "So you want to ent a boat!"

ON THE WATER IN 4 EASY HOURS...

"Way to go, Dad!"

★★★★★★★★★★★★★★★★★★★★★★★★★★★★

In just four hours,* you too can build your own boat and gain the respect of your family with a Chetek, flared-transom, plywood boat kit. Completely impervious to rot and marine growth with Chetek's patented space-age "Fiberglass" boat fabric from DuPants. Wait 'til your kids see your new found confidence! Easy to assemble, ideal for staying afloat on the lake or bay. Send $4.99 for a free brochure on all models today! Financing available. Freight not included.

★★★★★★★★★★★★★★★★★★★★★★★★★★★★

For Details See Your Dealer or Write 42 Dovre Road

Chetek BOATS

FLARED TRANSOM

CHETEK BOAT CORPORATION . Chetek, Wisconsin

Order today, and receive a Wisconsin-built trailer for your dinghie or cruiser. Transom support, some complete with tilting beds. Shipping not included.

DELIVERED RIGHT TO YOUR DRIVE-WAY!

**Avg. time 12-14 hours*

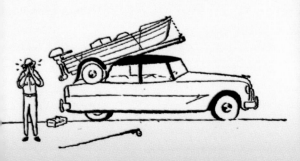

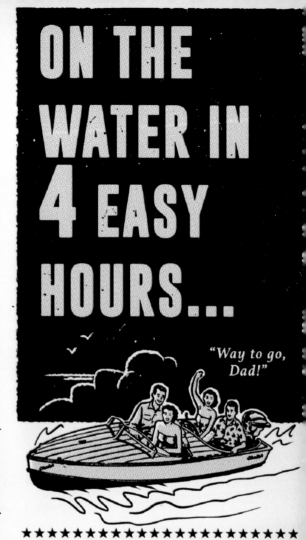

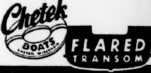

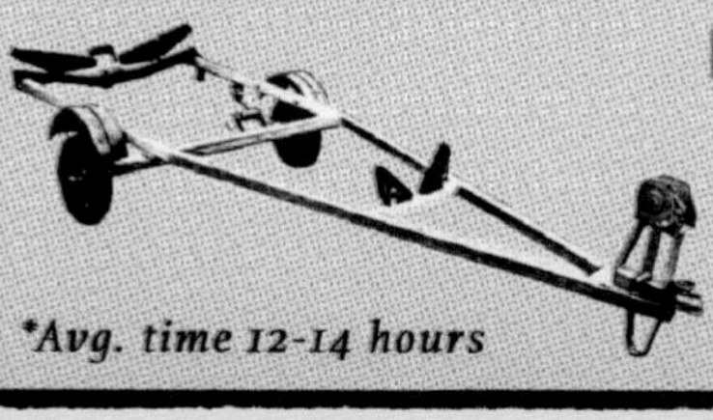

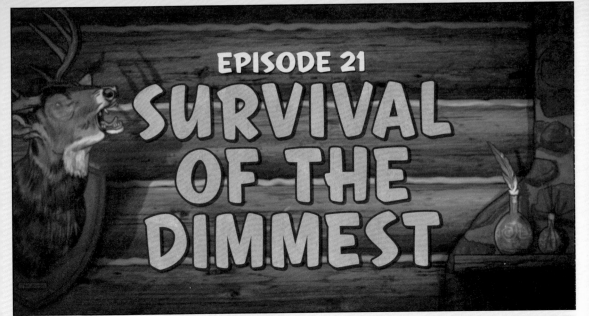

EPISODE 21
SURVIVAL OF THE DIMMEST

WHEN YOU'RE LOOKING TO SET UP CAMP IN THE WILDERNESS, IT'S IMPORTANT TO FIND THE RIGHT SPOT. REMEMBERING THE *FIVE W'S* CAN BE THE DIFFERENCE BETWEEN LIFE AND DEATH.

WATER. IT'S A LIFESAVING RESOURCE SO LOOK FOR A CAMPSITE NEARBY.

WEATHER. A DROP IN TEMPERATURE CAN BE LIFE THREATENING! SO BE CONSCIOUS OF IT.

WOOD. USED FOR WARMTH OR COOKING. MAKE SURE YOU HAVE PLENTY IN THE AREA.

WILDLIFE. BE AWARE OF THE DANGEROUS NATURE ALL AROUND YOU...

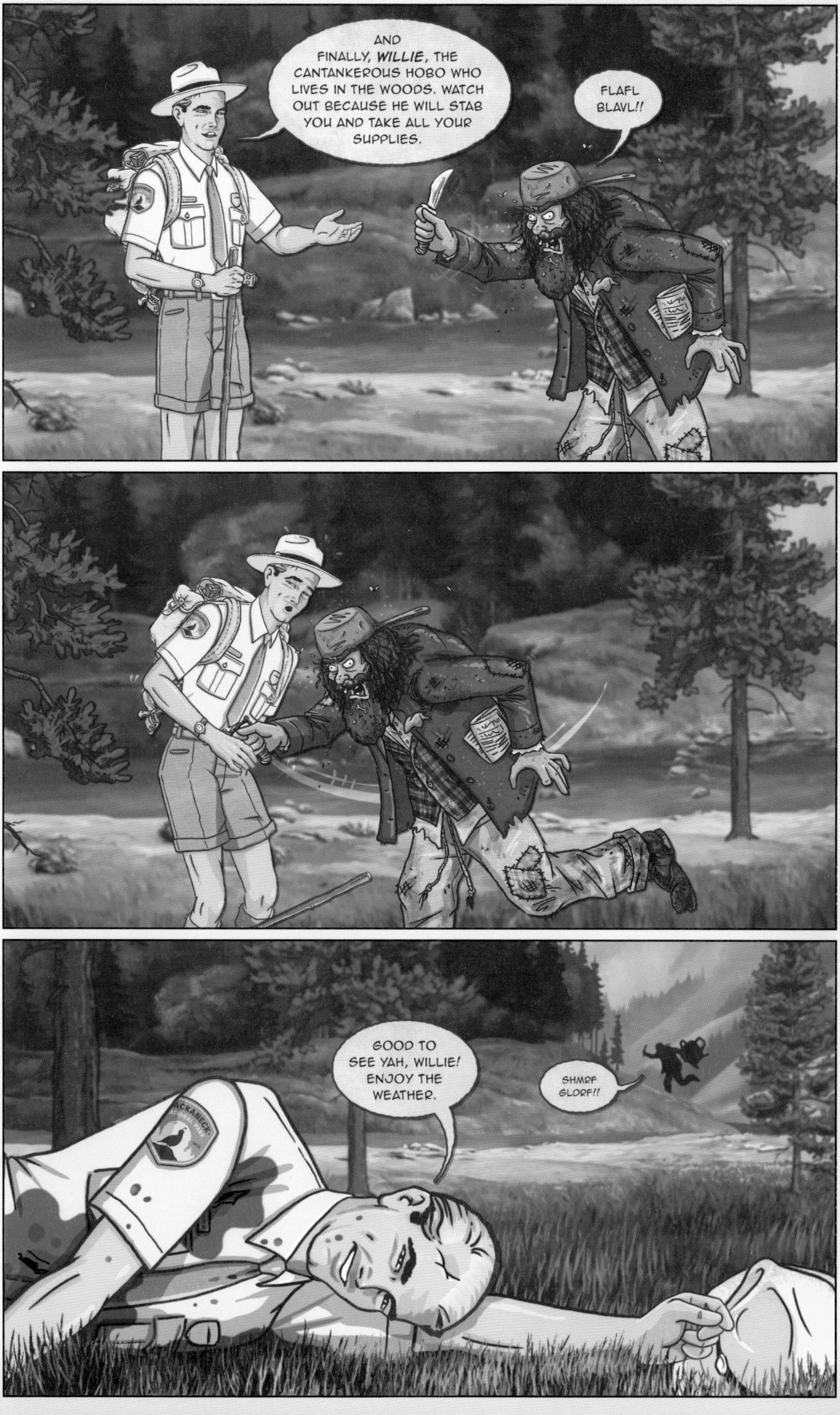
AND FINALLY, *WILLIE*, THE CANTANKEROUS HOBO WHO LIVES IN THE WOODS. WATCH OUT BECAUSE HE WILL STAB YOU AND TAKE ALL YOUR SUPPLIES.
FLAFL BLAVL!!
GOOD TO SEE YAH, WILLIE! ENJOY THE WEATHER.
SHMRF GLORF!!

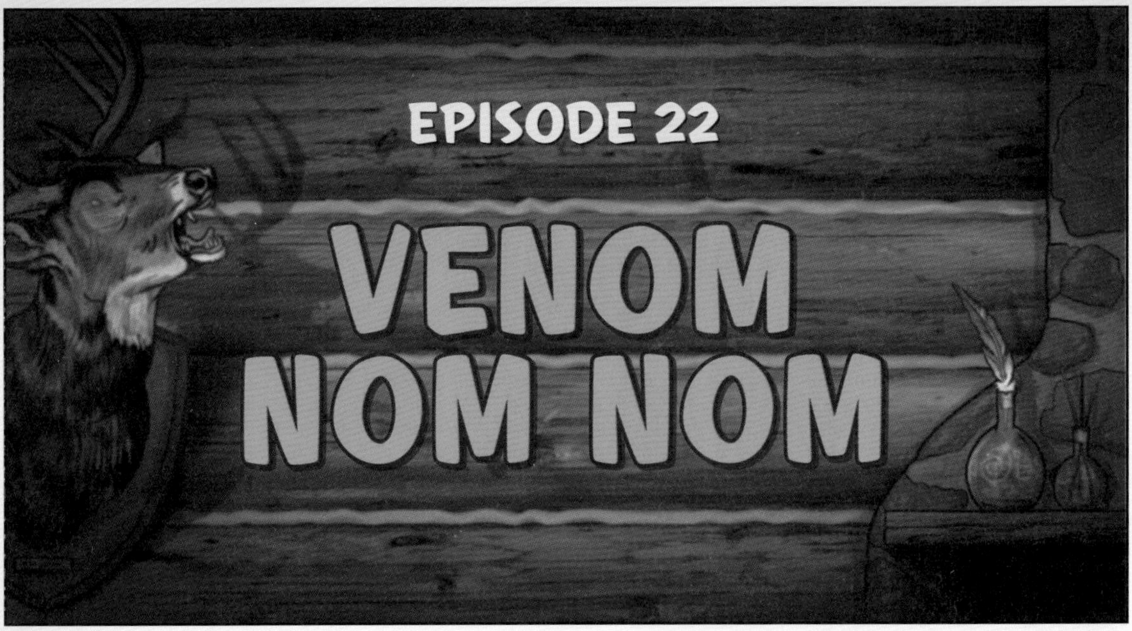
EPISODE 22
VENOM NOM NOM

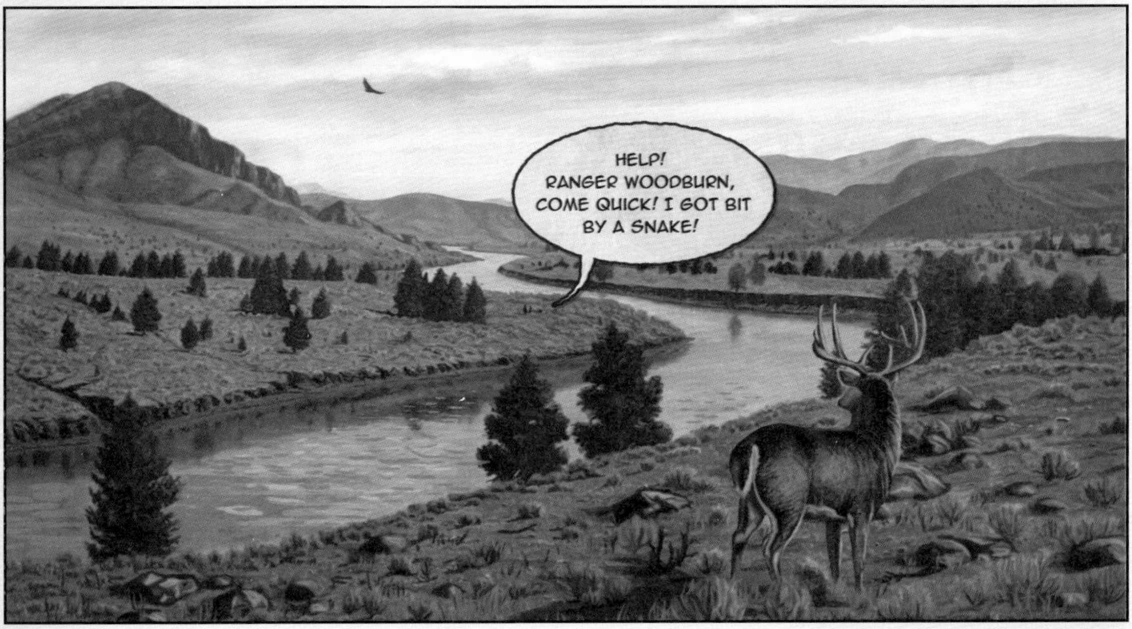
HELP! RANGER WOODBURN, COME QUICK! I GOT BIT BY A SNAKE!

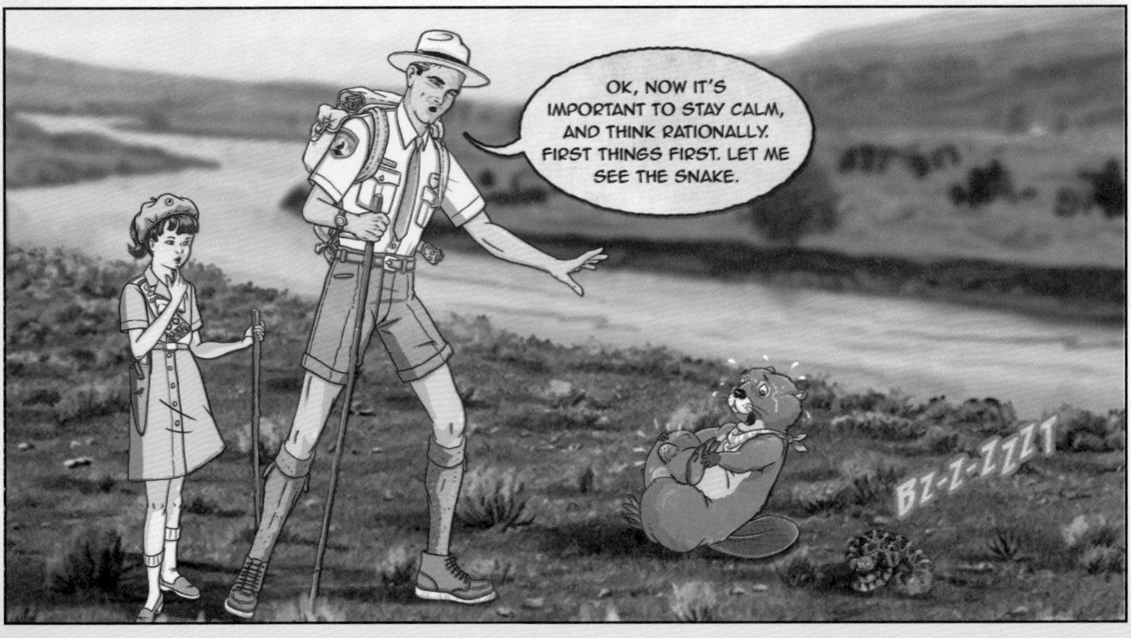
OK, NOW IT'S IMPORTANT TO STAY CALM, AND THINK RATIONALLY. FIRST THINGS FIRST. LET ME SEE THE SNAKE.
BZ-Z-ZZZT

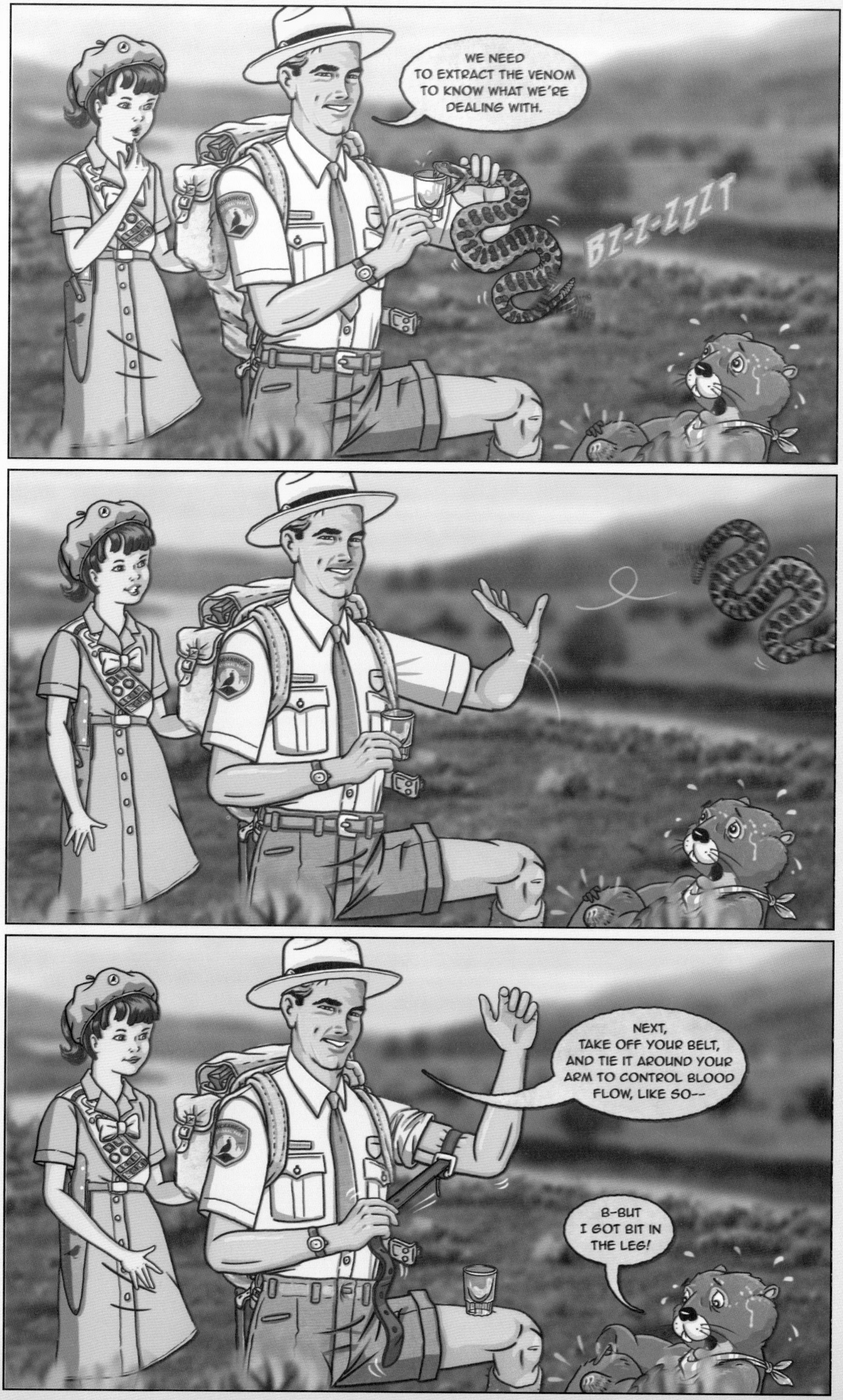
WE NEED TO EXTRACT THE VENOM TO KNOW WHAT WE'RE DEALING WITH.
BZ-Z-ZZZT
NEXT, TAKE OFF YOUR BELT, AND TIE IT AROUND YOUR ARM TO CONTROL BLOOD FLOW, LIKE SO--
B-BUT I GOT BIT IN THE LEG!

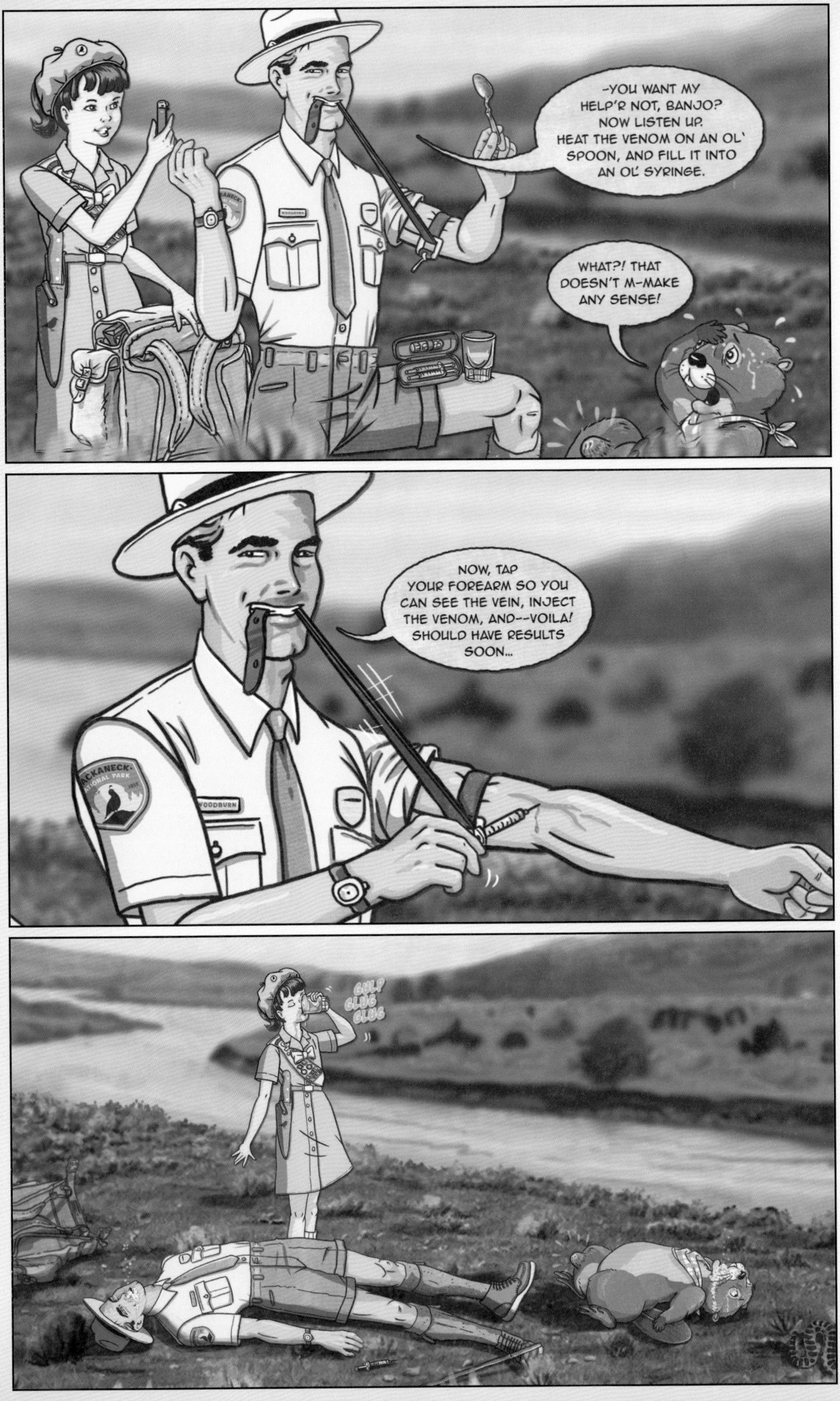
-YOU WANT MY HELP'R NOT, BANJO? NOW LISTEN UP. HEAT THE VENOM ON AN OL' SPOON, AND FILL IT INTO AN OL' SYRINGE.
WHAT?! THAT DOESN'T M-MAKE ANY SENSE!
NOW, TAP YOUR FOREARM SO YOU CAN SEE THE VEIN, INJECT THE VENOM, AND--VOILA! SHOULD HAVE RESULTS SOON...
WOODBURN
GULP
GLUG
GLUG

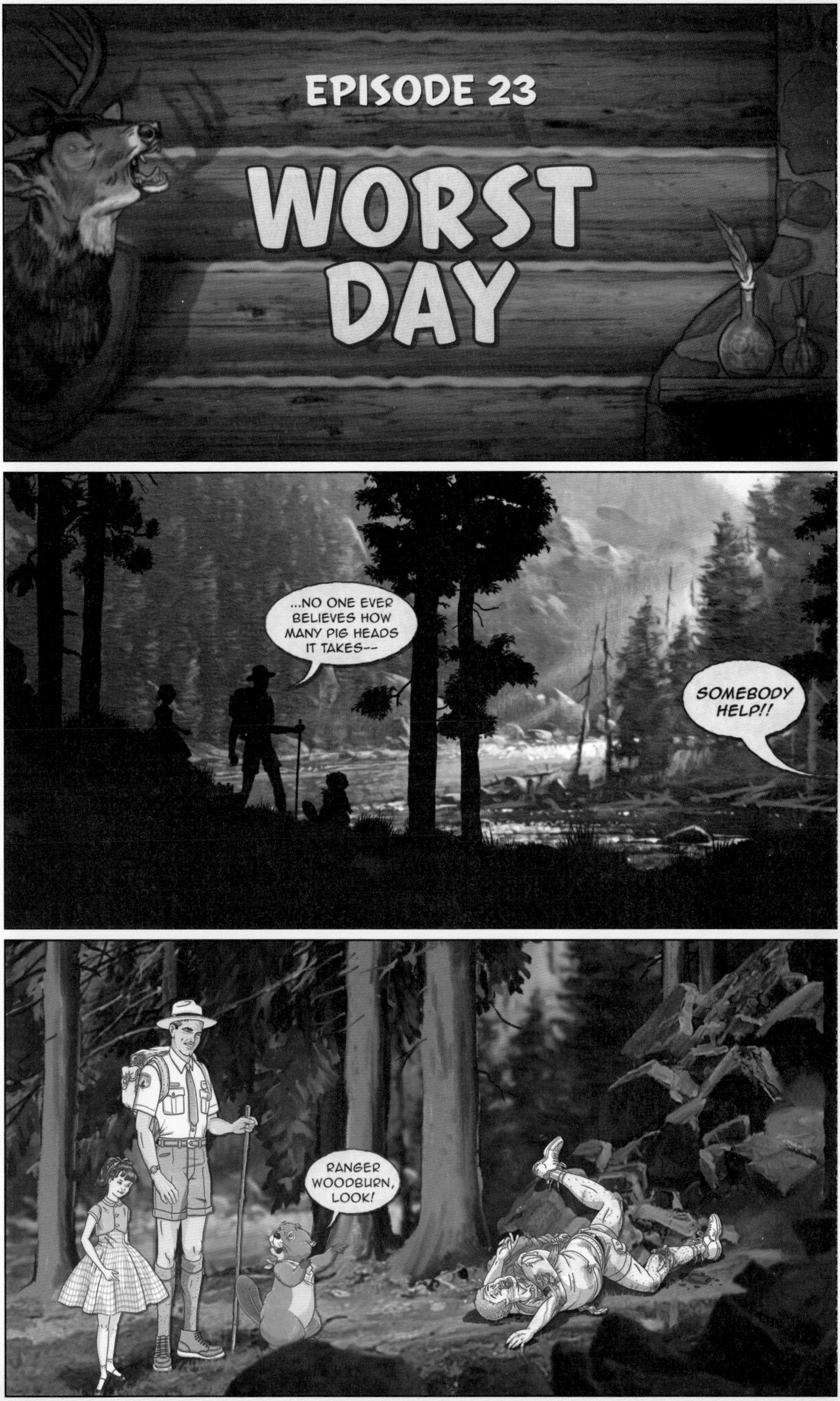
EPISODE 23
WORST DAY
...NO ONE EVER BELIEVES HOW MANY PIG HEADS IT TAKES--
SOMEBODY HELP!!
RANGER WOODBURN, LOOK!

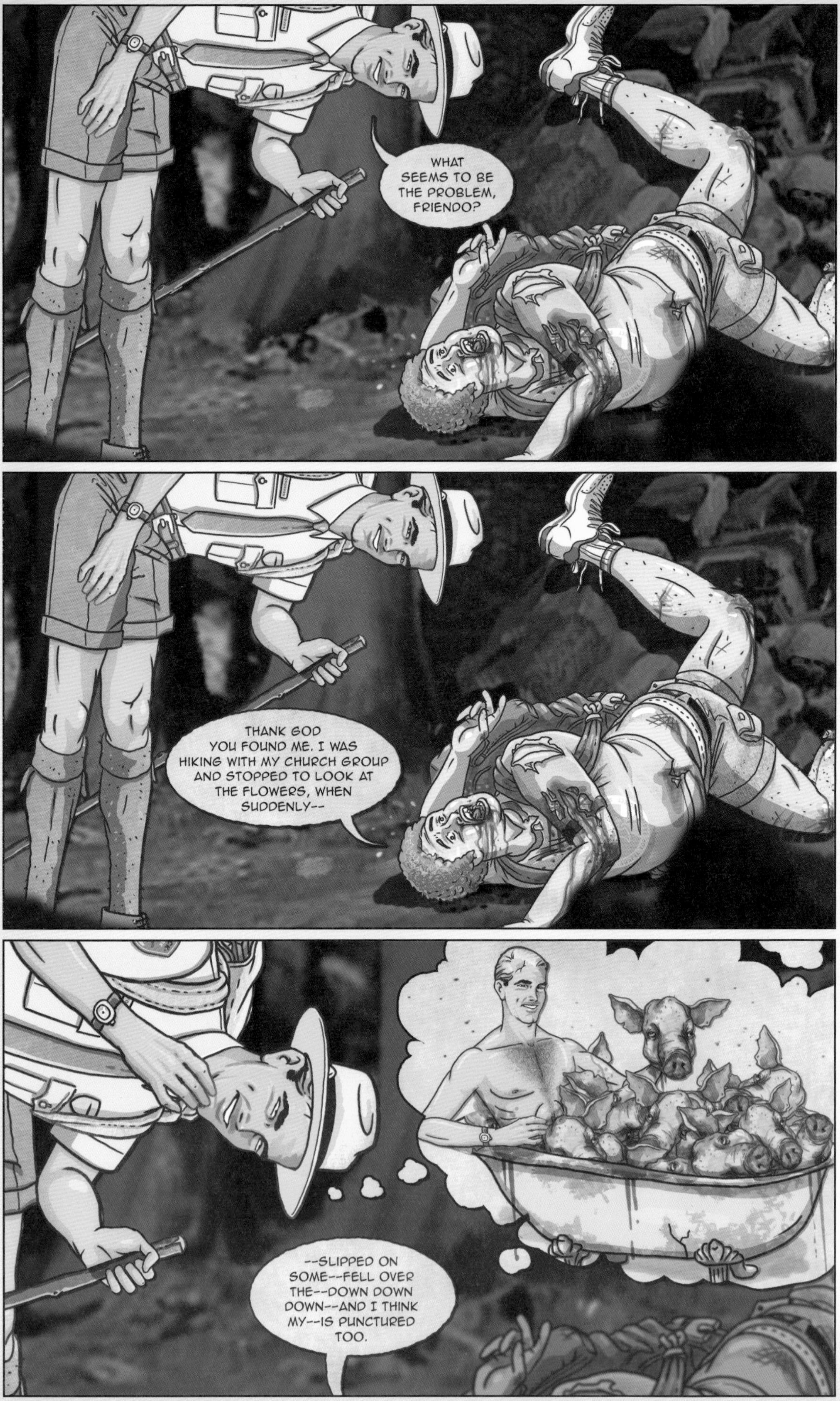
WHAT SEEMS TO BE THE PROBLEM, FRIENDO?
THANK GOD YOU FOUND ME. I WAS HIKING WITH MY CHURCH GROUP AND STOPPED TO LOOK AT THE FLOWERS, WHEN SUDDENLY--
--SLIPPED ON SOME--FELL OVER THE--DOWN DOWN DOWN--AND I THINK MY--IS PUNCTURED TOO.

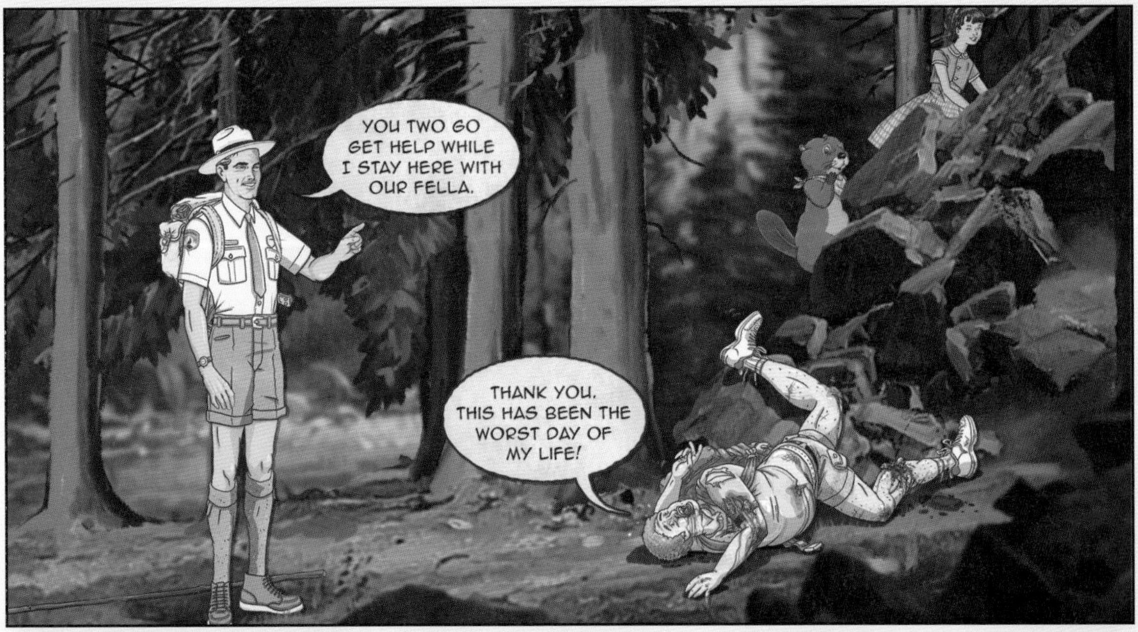
YOU TWO GO GET HELP WHILE I STAY HERE WITH OUR FELLA.
THANK YOU. THIS HAS BEEN THE WORST DAY OF MY LIFE!

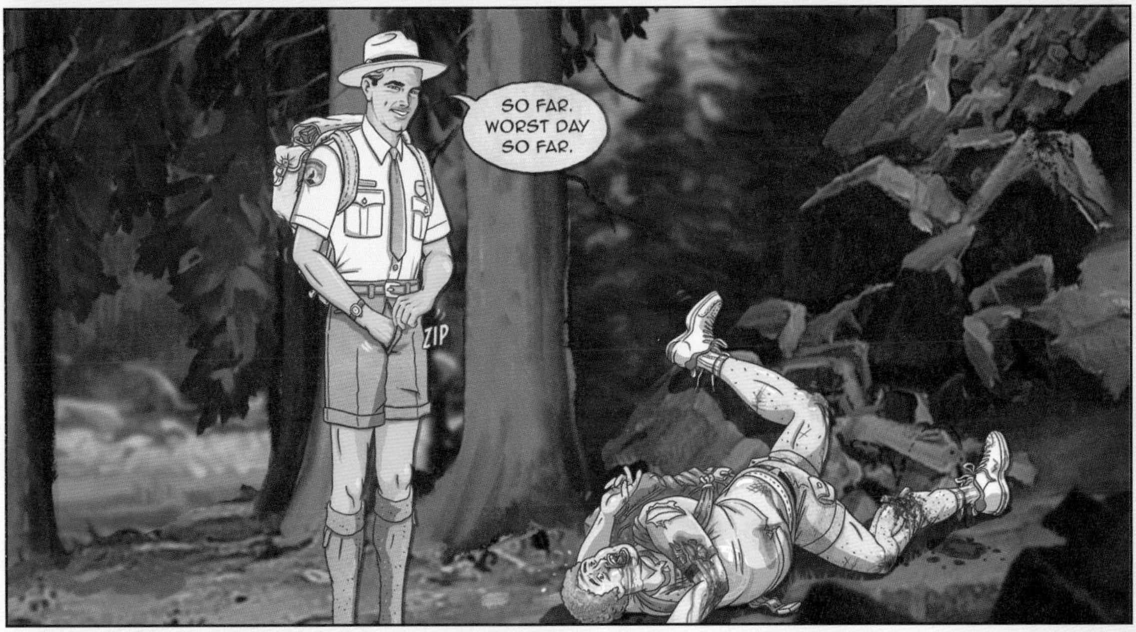
SO FAR. WORST DAY SO FAR.
ZIP

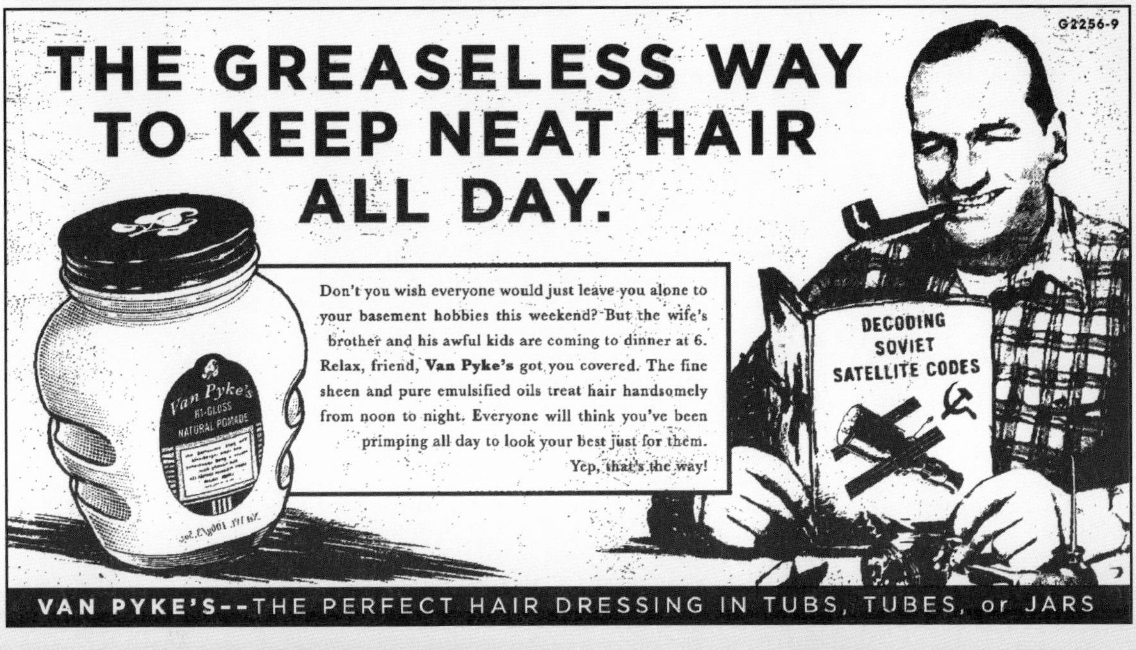
G2256-9
THE GREASELESS WAY TO KEEP NEAT HAIR ALL DAY.
Don't you wish everyone would just leave you alone to your basement hobbies this weekend? But the wife's brother and his awful kids are coming to dinner at 6. Relax, friend, Van Pyke's got you covered. The fine sheen and pure emulsified oils treat hair handsomely from noon to night. Everyone will think you've been primping all day to look your best just for them.
Yep, that's the way!
Van Pyke's
HI-GLOSS
NATURAL POMADE
DECODING SOVIET SATELLITE CODES
VAN PYKE'S--THE PERFECT HAIR DRESSING IN TUBS, TUBES, or JARS

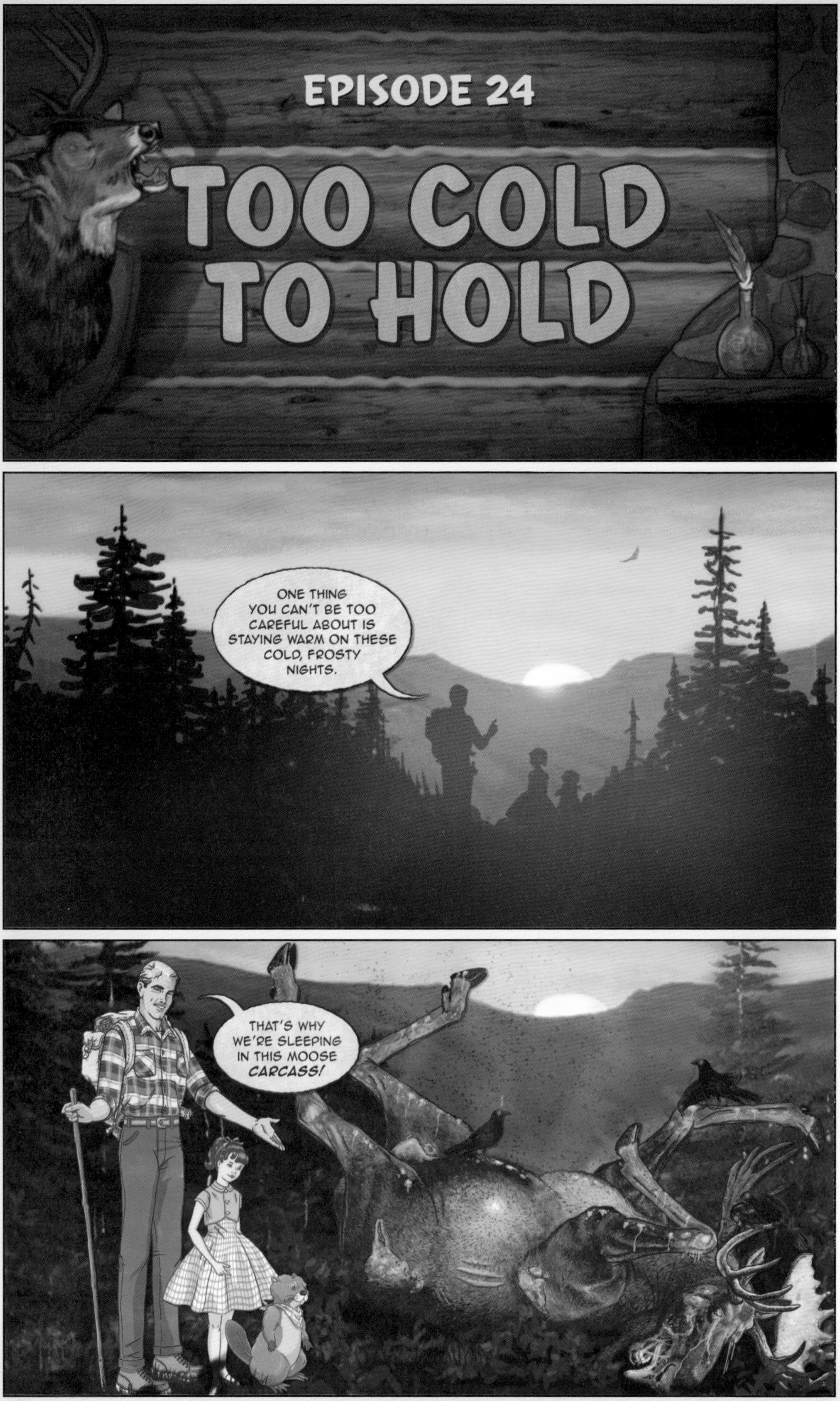
EPISODE 24
TOO COLD TO HOLD
ONE THING YOU CAN'T BE TOO CAREFUL ABOUT IS STAYING WARM ON THESE COLD, FROSTY NIGHTS.
THAT'S WHY WE'RE SLEEPING IN THIS MOOSE *CARCASS!*

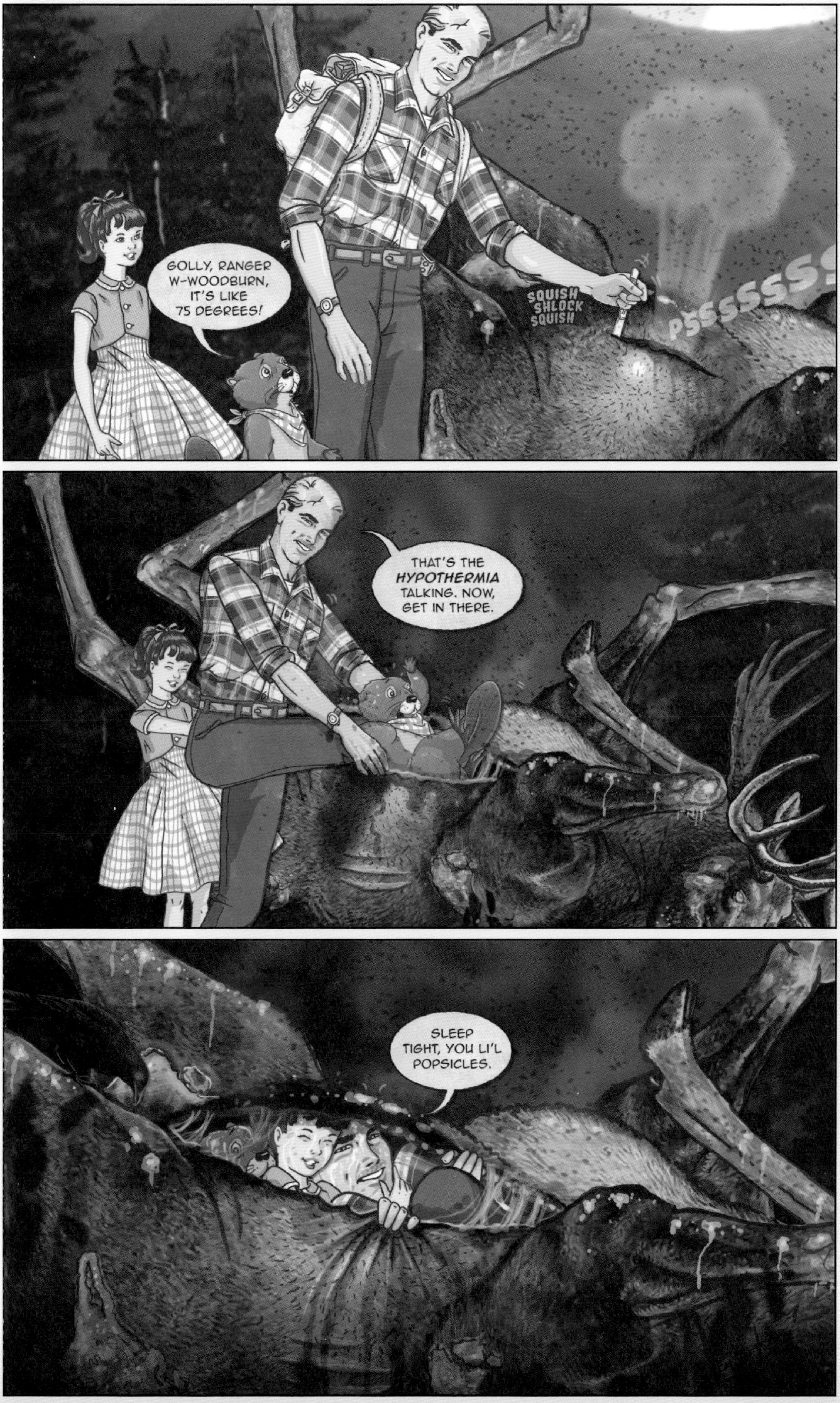
GOLLY, RANGER W-WOODBURN, IT'S LIKE 75 DEGREES!
SQUISH SHLOCK SQUISH
PSSSSSSSS
THAT'S THE *HYPOTHERMIA* TALKING. NOW, GET IN THERE.
SLEEP TIGHT, YOU LI'L POPSICLES.

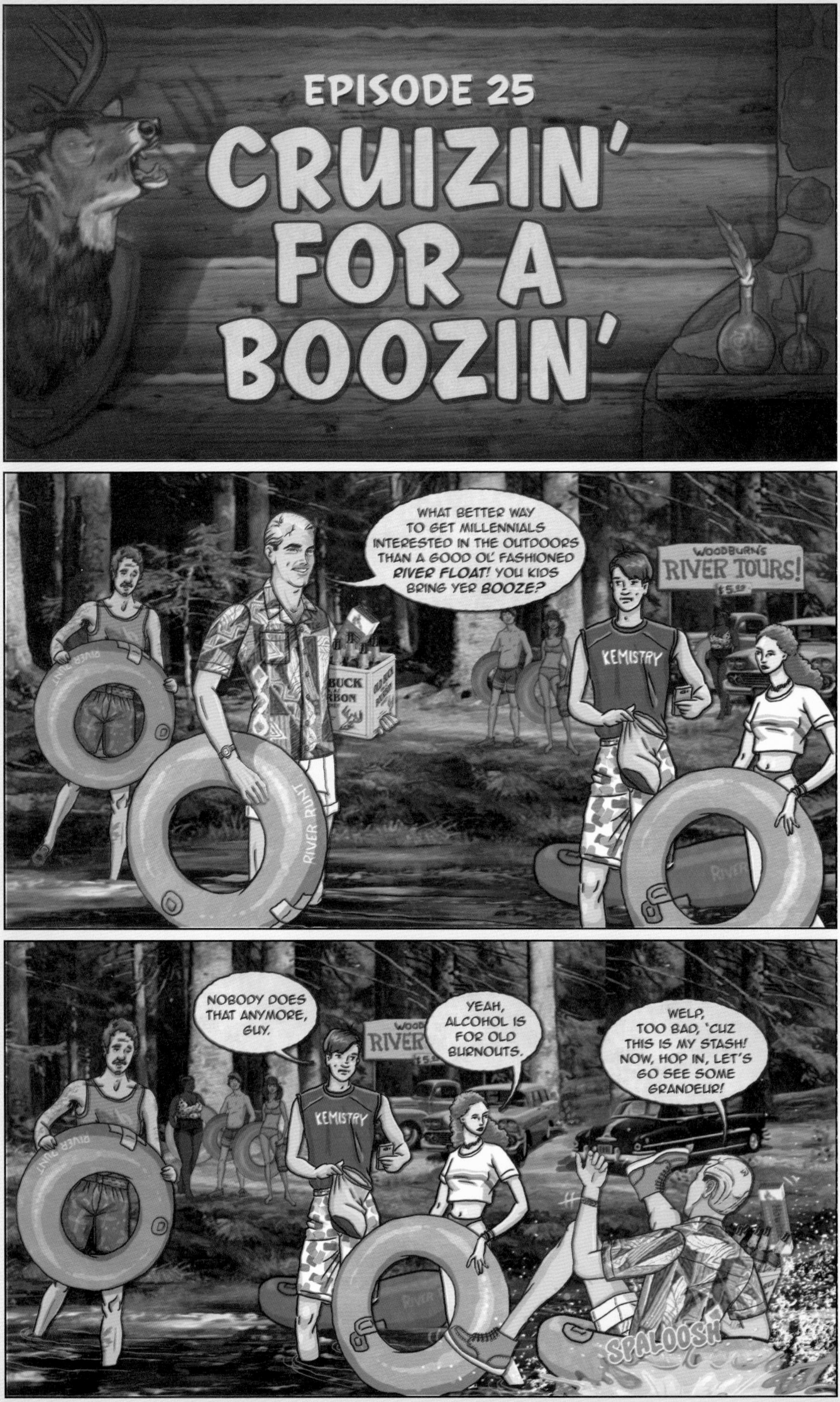
EPISODE 25
CRUIZIN' FOR A BOOZIN'
WHAT BETTER WAY TO GET MILLENNIALS INTERESTED IN THE OUTDOORS THAN A GOOD OL' FASHIONED *RIVER FLOAT!* YOU KIDS BRING YER *BOOZE?*
WOODBURN'S RIVER TOURS!
KEMISTRY
RIVER RUNT
NOBODY DOES THAT ANYMORE, GUY.
YEAH, ALCOHOL IS FOR OLD BURNOUTS.
WELP, TOO BAD, 'CUZ THIS IS MY STASH! NOW, HOP IN, LET'S GO SEE SOME GRANDEUR!
SPALOOSH

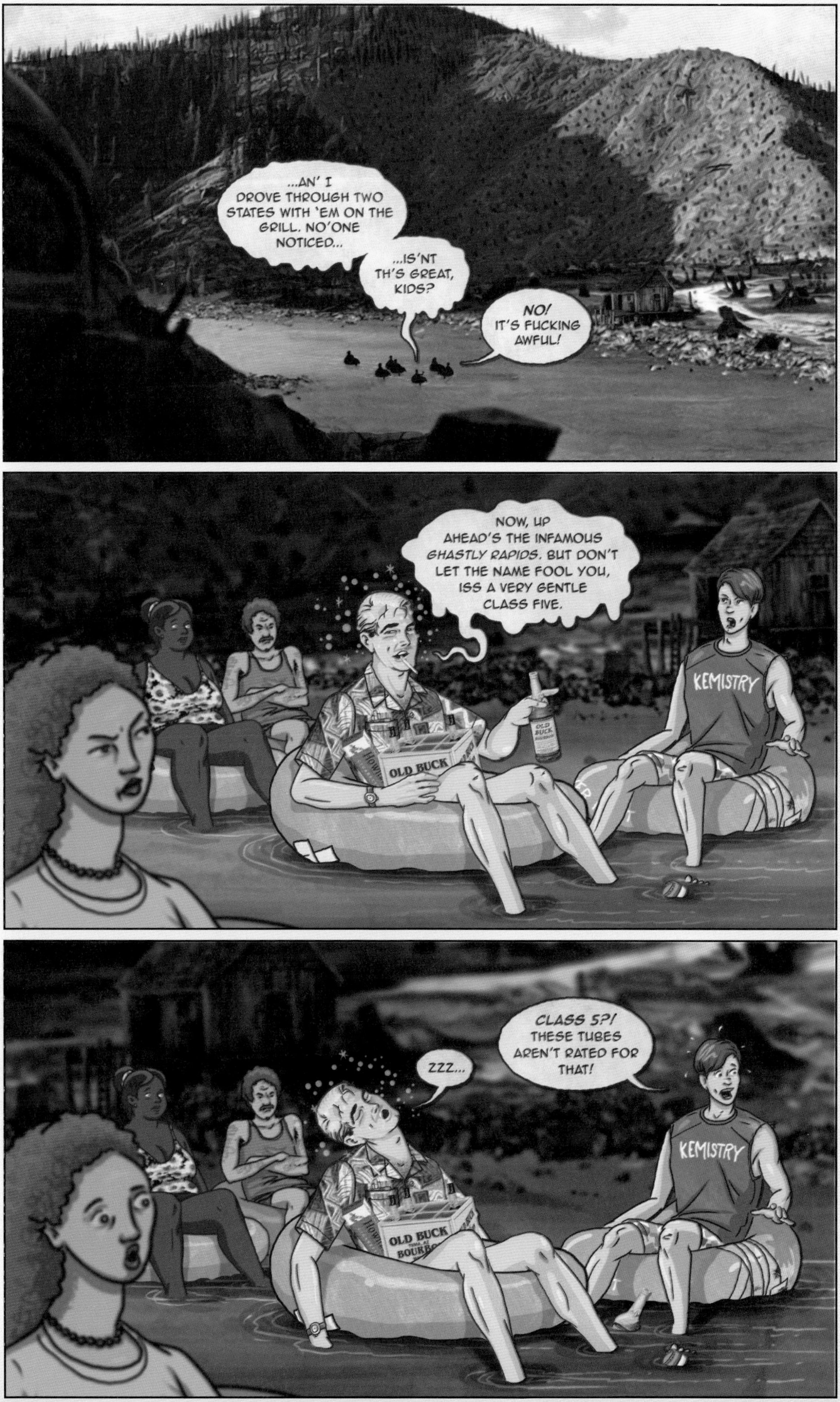
...AN' I DROVE THROUGH TWO STATES WITH 'EM ON THE GRILL. NO'ONE NOTICED...
...IS'NT TH'S GREAT, KIDS?
NO! IT'S FUCKING AWFUL!
NOW, UP AHEAD'S THE INFAMOUS *GHASTLY RAPIDS*. BUT DON'T LET THE NAME FOOL YOU, ISS A VERY GENTLE CLASS FIVE.
OLD BUCK
KEMISTRY
ZZZ...
CLASS 5?! THESE TUBES AREN'T RATED FOR THAT!
OLD BUCK
KEMISTRY

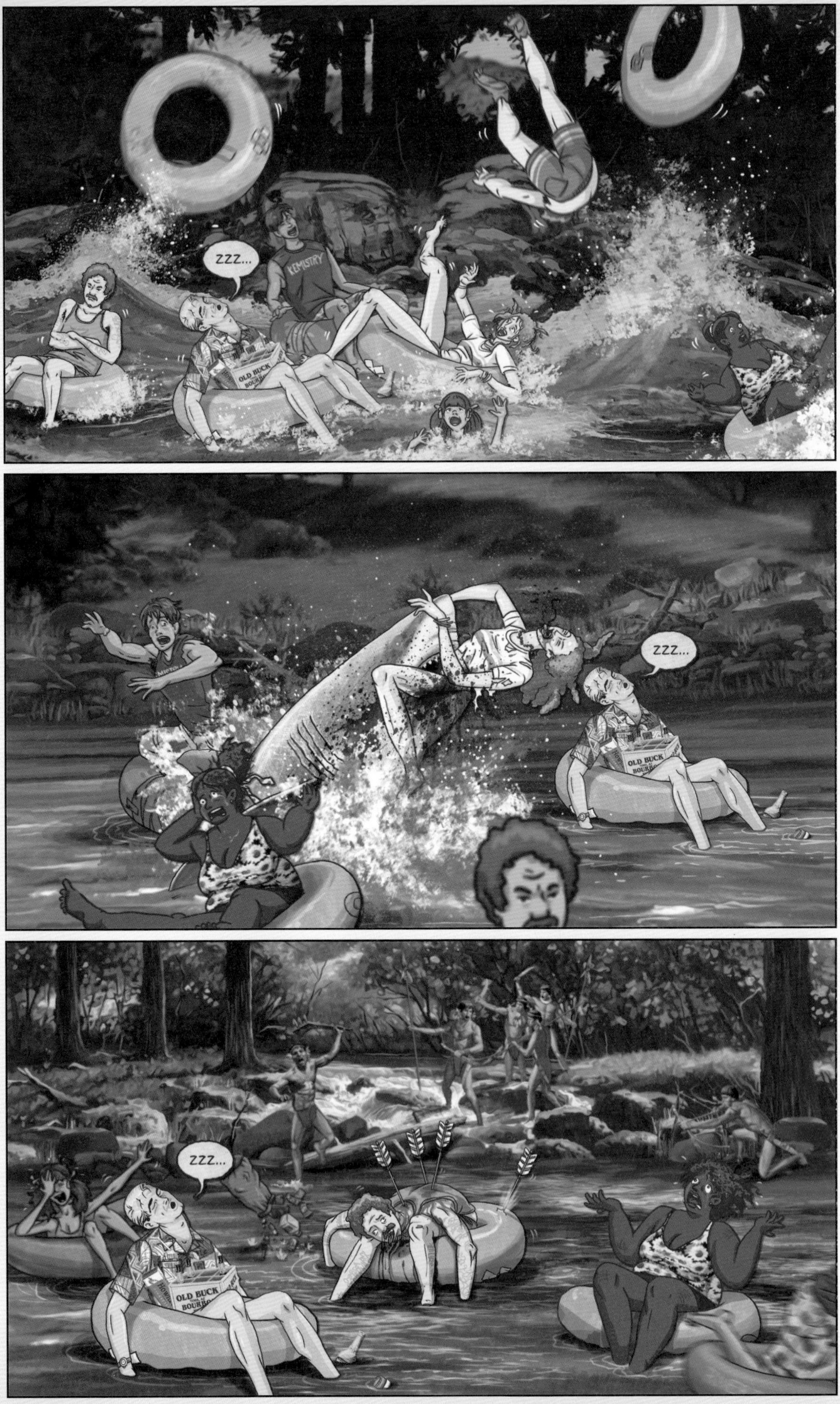
ZZZ...
KEMISTRY
OLD BUCK
ZZZ...
OLD BUCK
ZZZ...
OLD BUCK

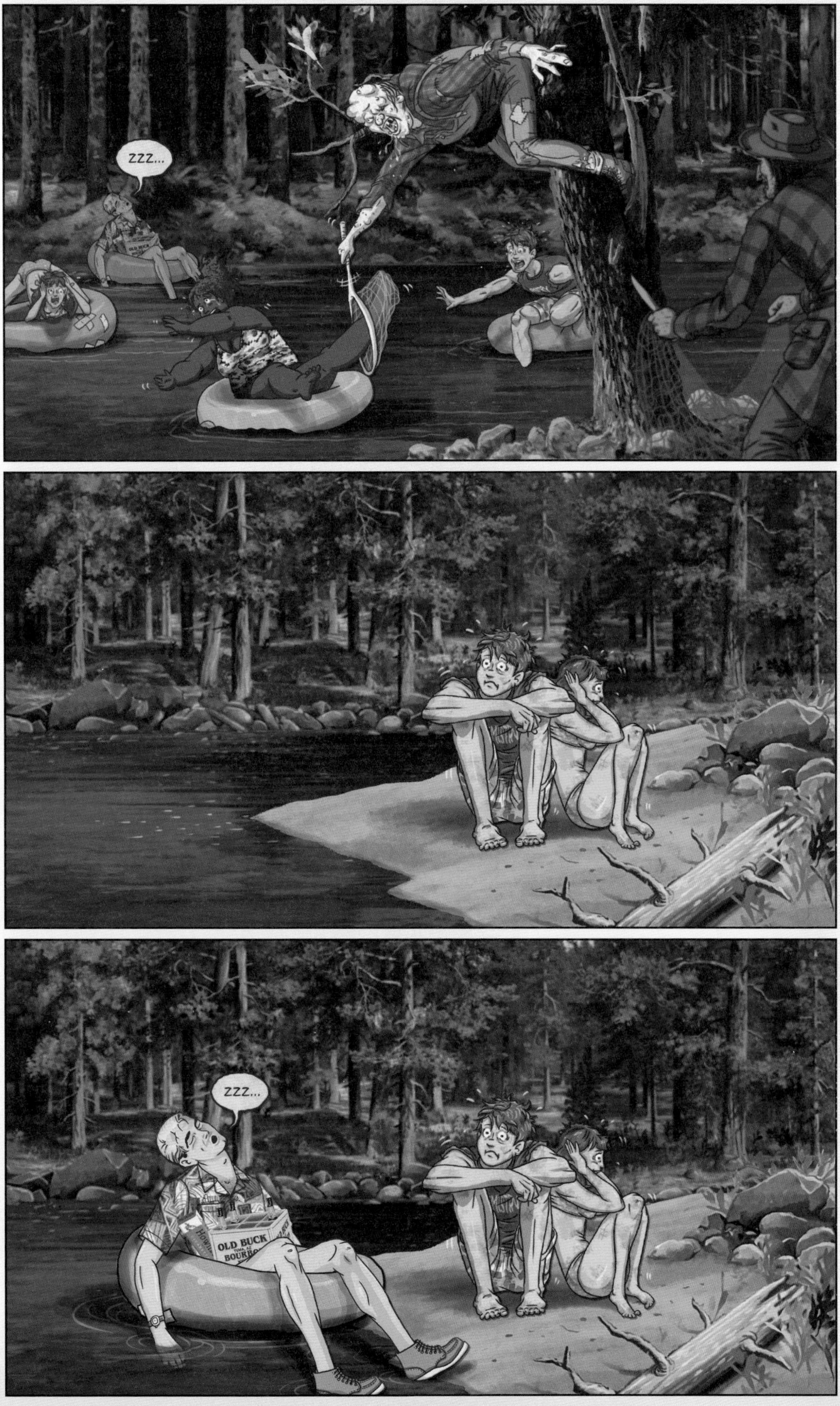
ZZZ...
ZZZ...
OLD BUCK

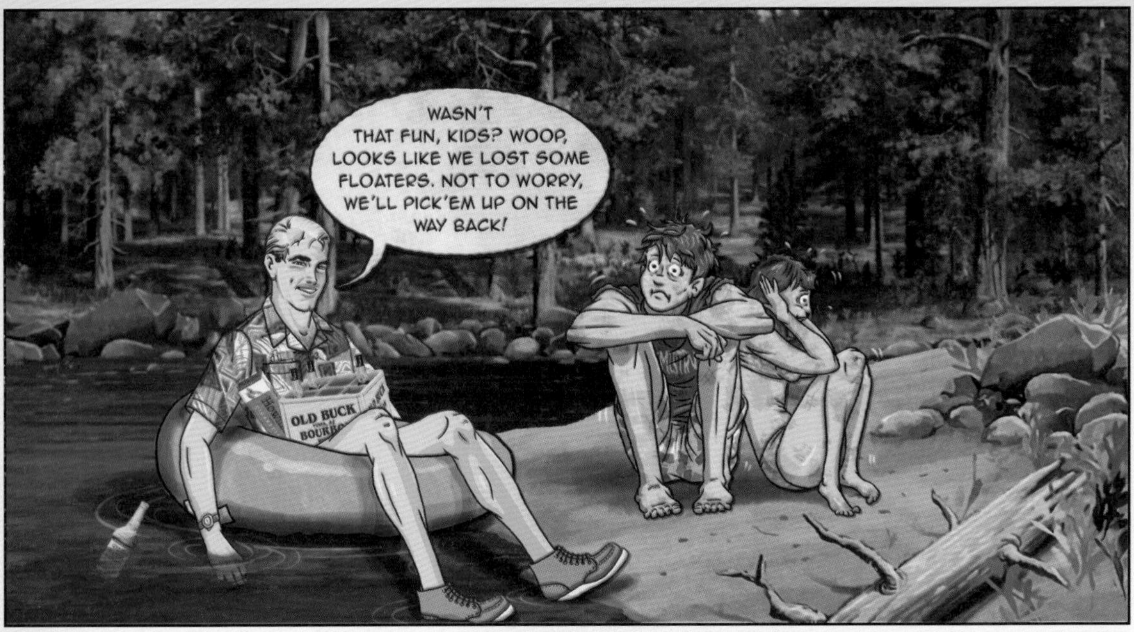
WASN'T THAT FUN, KIDS? WOOP, LOOKS LIKE WE LOST SOME FLOATERS. NOT TO WORRY, WE'LL PICK'EM UP ON THE WAY BACK!
OLD BUCK
BOURBO

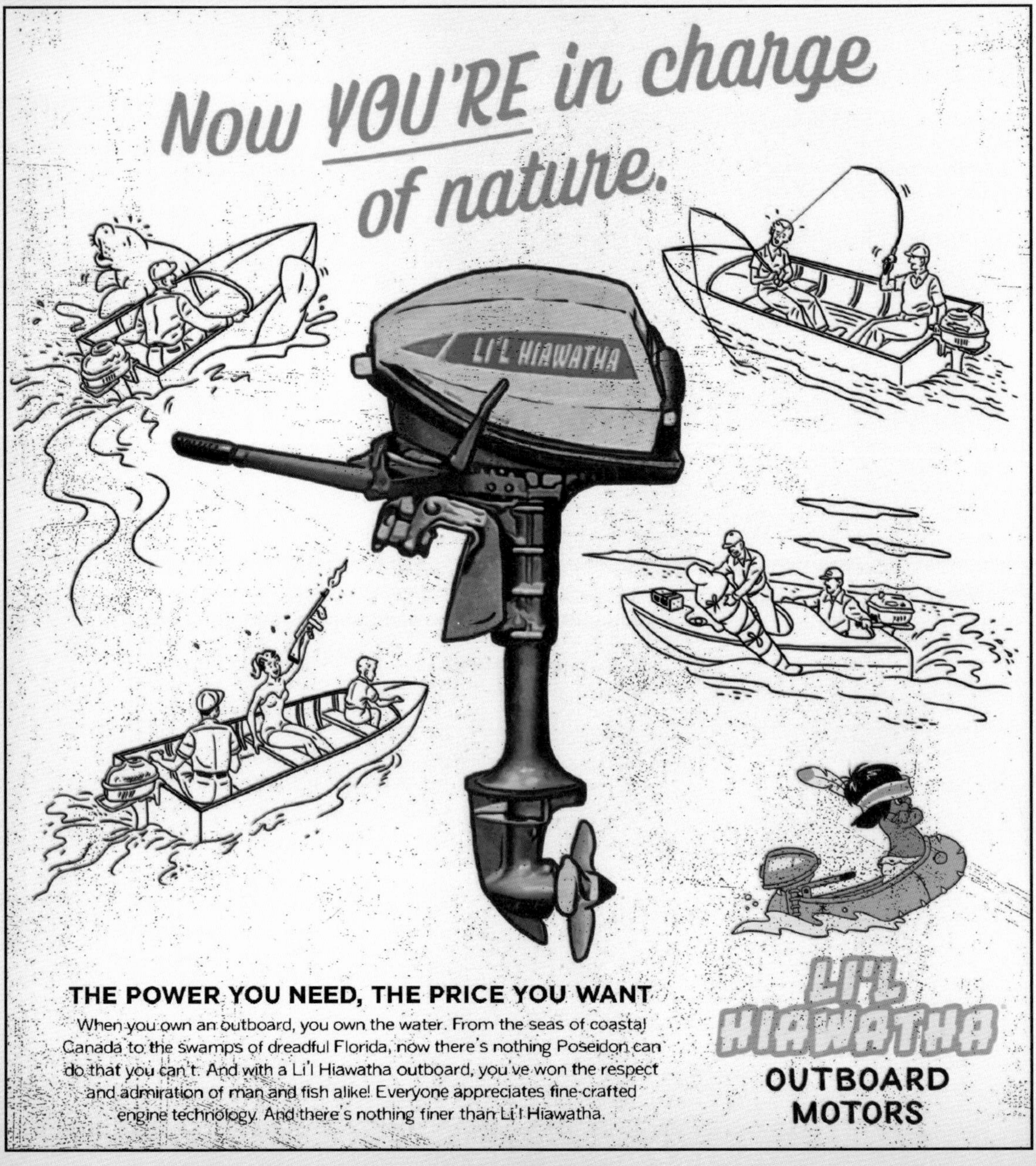
Now YOU'RE in charge of nature.
LI'L HIAWATHA
THE POWER YOU NEED, THE PRICE YOU WANT
When you own an outboard, you own the water. From the seas of coastal Canada to the swamps of dreadful Florida, now there's nothing Poseidon can do that you can't. And with a Li'l Hiawatha outboard, you've won the respect and admiration of man and fish alike! Everyone appreciates fine-crafted engine technology. And there's nothing finer than Li'l Hiawatha.
LI'L HIAWATHA
OUTBOARD MOTORS

FIRESIDE STORIES: ON DEADLY TIDES

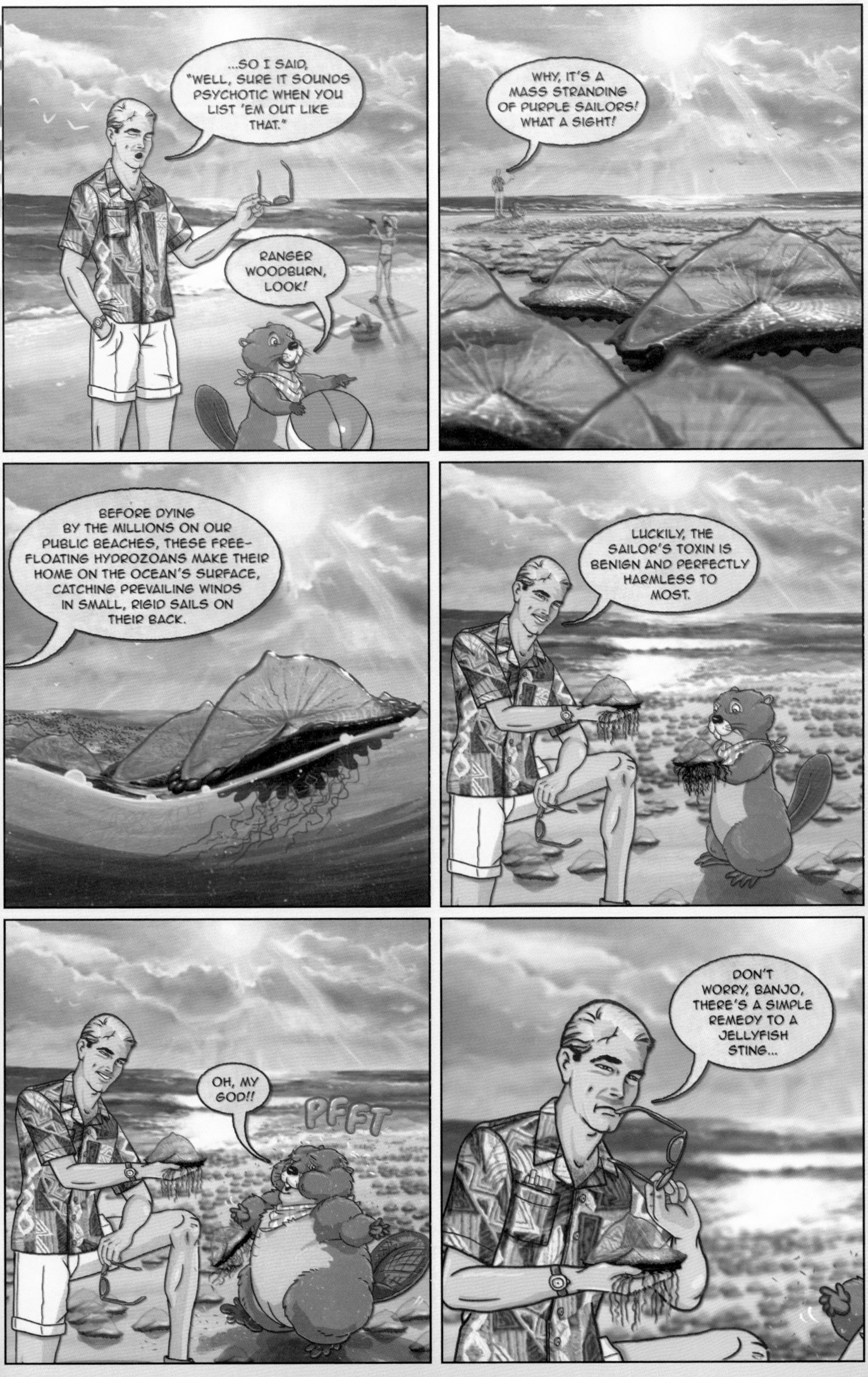

...SO I SAID, "WELL, SURE IT SOUNDS PSYCHOTIC WHEN YOU LIST 'EM OUT LIKE THAT."
RANGER WOODBURN, LOOK!
WHY, IT'S A MASS STRANDING OF PURPLE SAILORS! WHAT A SIGHT!
BEFORE DYING BY THE MILLIONS ON OUR PUBLIC BEACHES, THESE FREE-FLOATING HYDROZOANS MAKE THEIR HOME ON THE OCEAN'S SURFACE, CATCHING PREVAILING WINDS IN SMALL, RIGID SAILS ON THEIR BACK.
LUCKILY, THE SAILOR'S TOXIN IS BENIGN AND PERFECTLY HARMLESS TO MOST.
OH, MY GOD!!
PFFT
DON'T WORRY, BANJO, THERE'S A SIMPLE REMEDY TO A JELLYFISH STING...

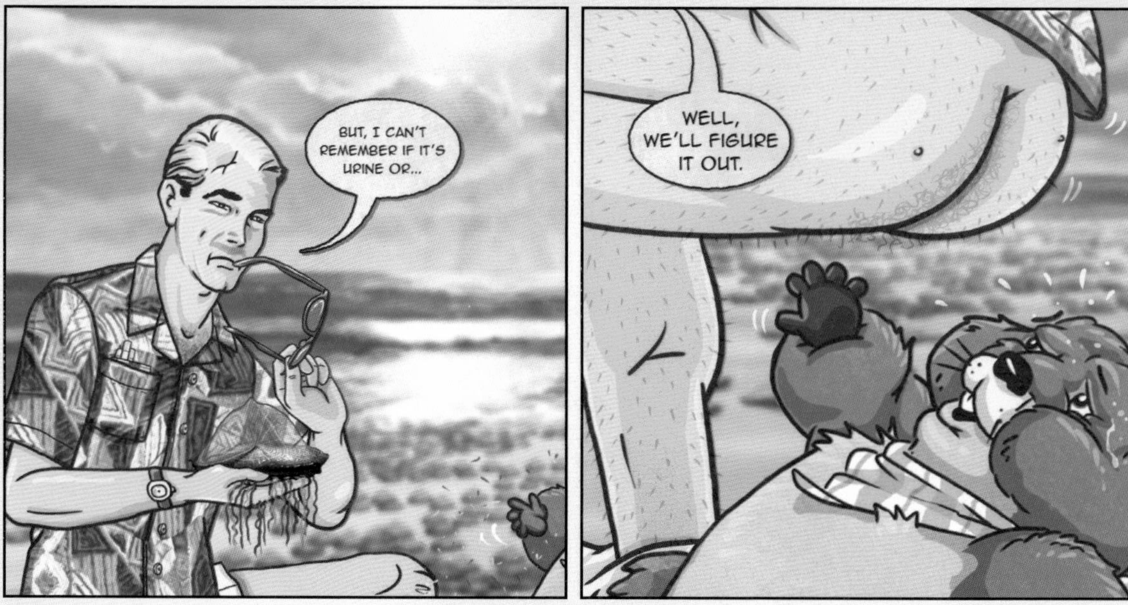

BUT, I CAN'T REMEMBER IF IT'S URINE OR...
WELL, WE'LL FIGURE IT OUT.

FIRESIDE STORIES: TICK TOCK

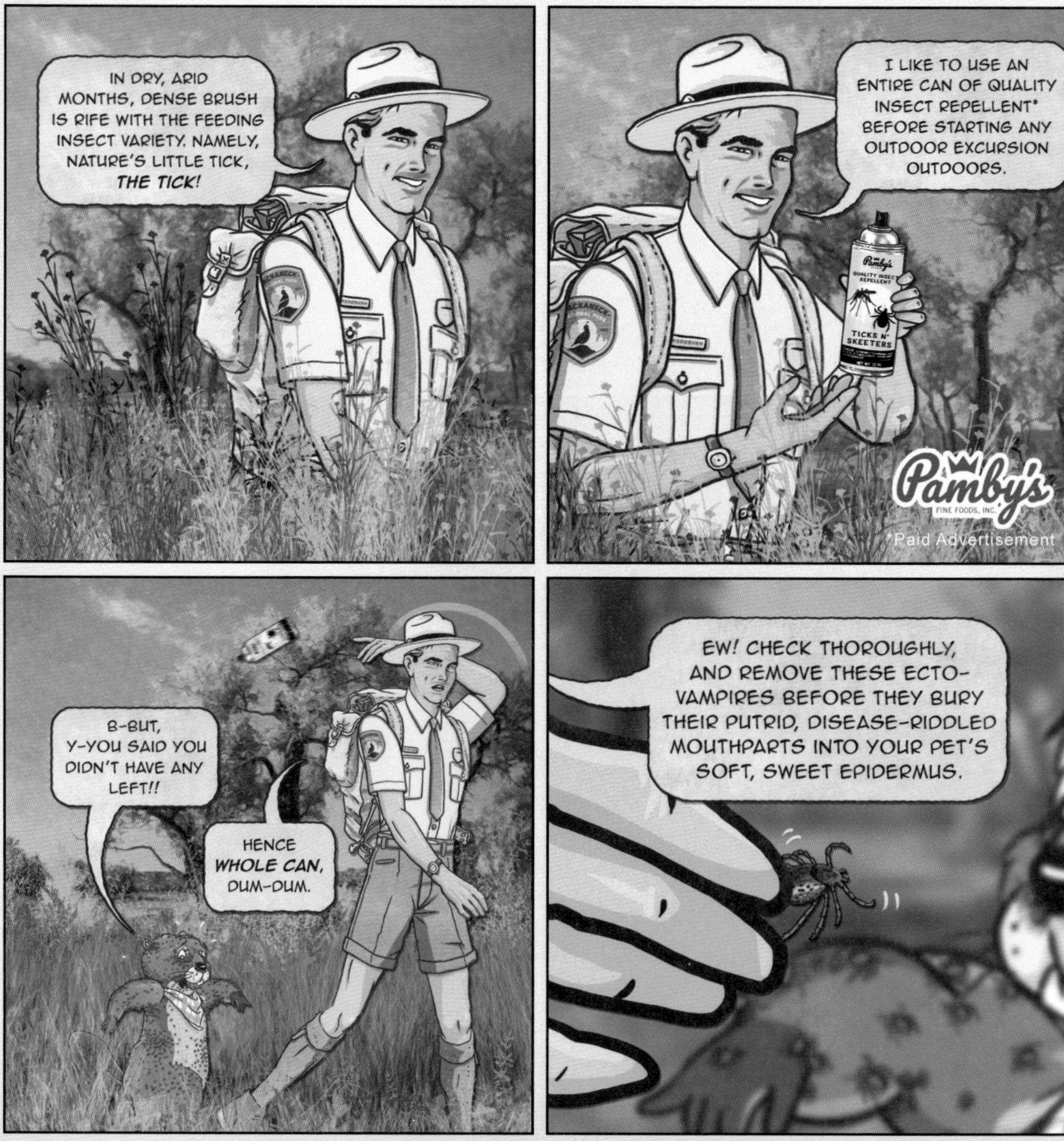

IN DRY, ARID MONTHS, DENSE BRUSH IS RIFE WITH THE FEEDING INSECT VARIETY. NAMELY, NATURE'S LITTLE TICK, *THE TICK!*
I LIKE TO USE AN ENTIRE CAN OF QUALITY INSECT REPELLENT* BEFORE STARTING ANY OUTDOOR EXCURSION OUTDOORS.
TICKS N' SKEETERS
Pamby's
FINE FOODS, INC.
*Paid Advertisement
B-BUT, Y-YOU SAID YOU DIDN'T HAVE ANY LEFT!!
HENCE *WHOLE CAN,* DUM-DUM.
EW! CHECK THOROUGHLY, AND REMOVE THESE ECTO-VAMPIRES BEFORE THEY BURY THEIR PUTRID, DISEASE-RIDDLED MOUTHPARTS INTO YOUR PET'S SOFT, SWEET EPIDERMUS.

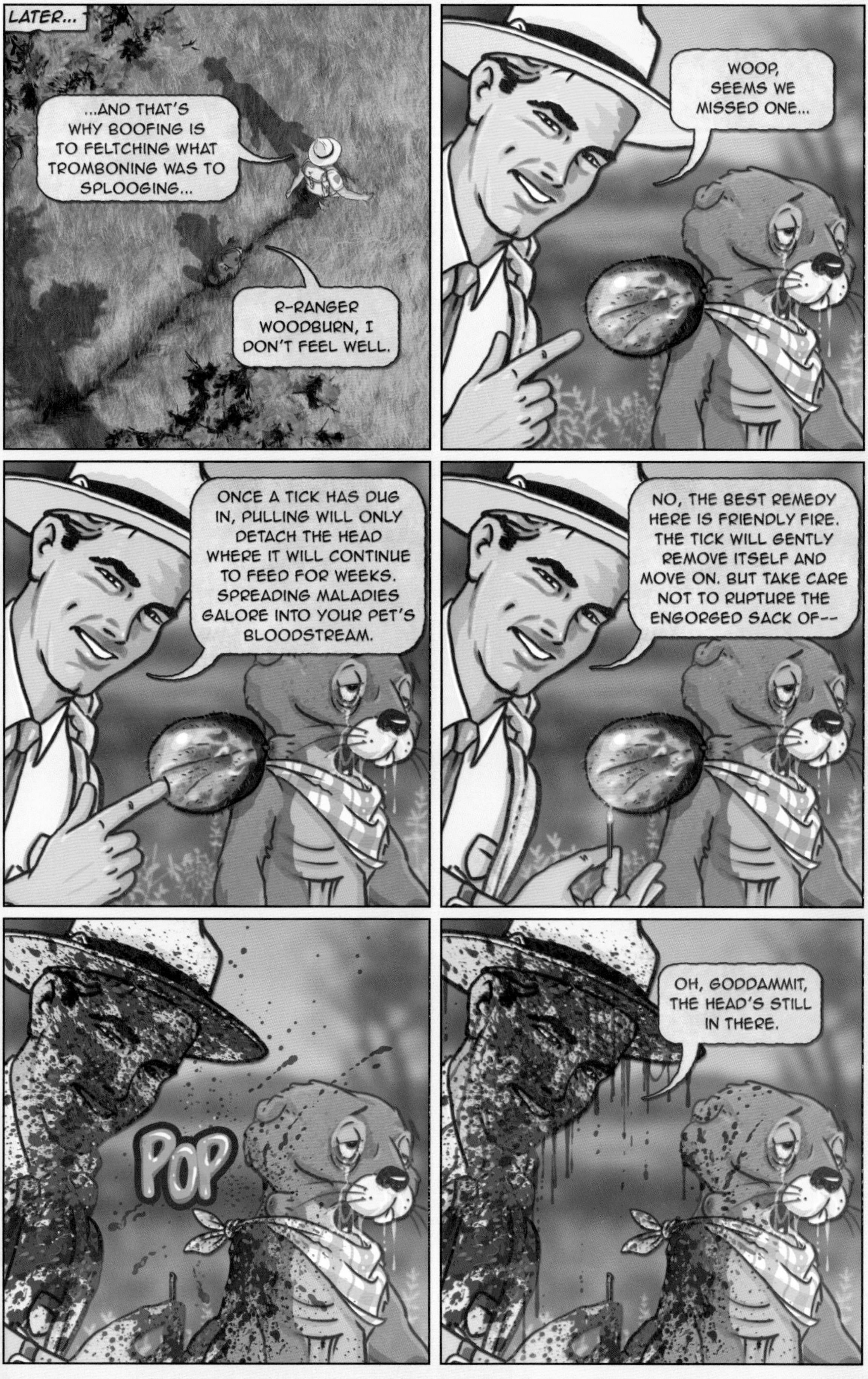
LATER...
...AND THAT'S WHY BOOFING IS TO FELTCHING WHAT TROMBONING WAS TO SPLOOGING...
R-RANGER WOODBURN, I DON'T FEEL WELL.
WOOP, SEEMS WE MISSED ONE...
ONCE A TICK HAS DUG IN, PULLING WILL ONLY DETACH THE HEAD WHERE IT WILL CONTINUE TO FEED FOR WEEKS. SPREADING MALADIES GALORE INTO YOUR PET'S BLOODSTREAM.
NO, THE BEST REMEDY HERE IS FRIENDLY FIRE. THE TICK WILL GENTLY REMOVE ITSELF AND MOVE ON. BUT TAKE CARE NOT TO RUPTURE THE ENGORGED SACK OF--
POP
OH, GODDAMMIT, THE HEAD'S STILL IN THERE.

FIRESIDE STORIES: BLOWING BIGFOOT

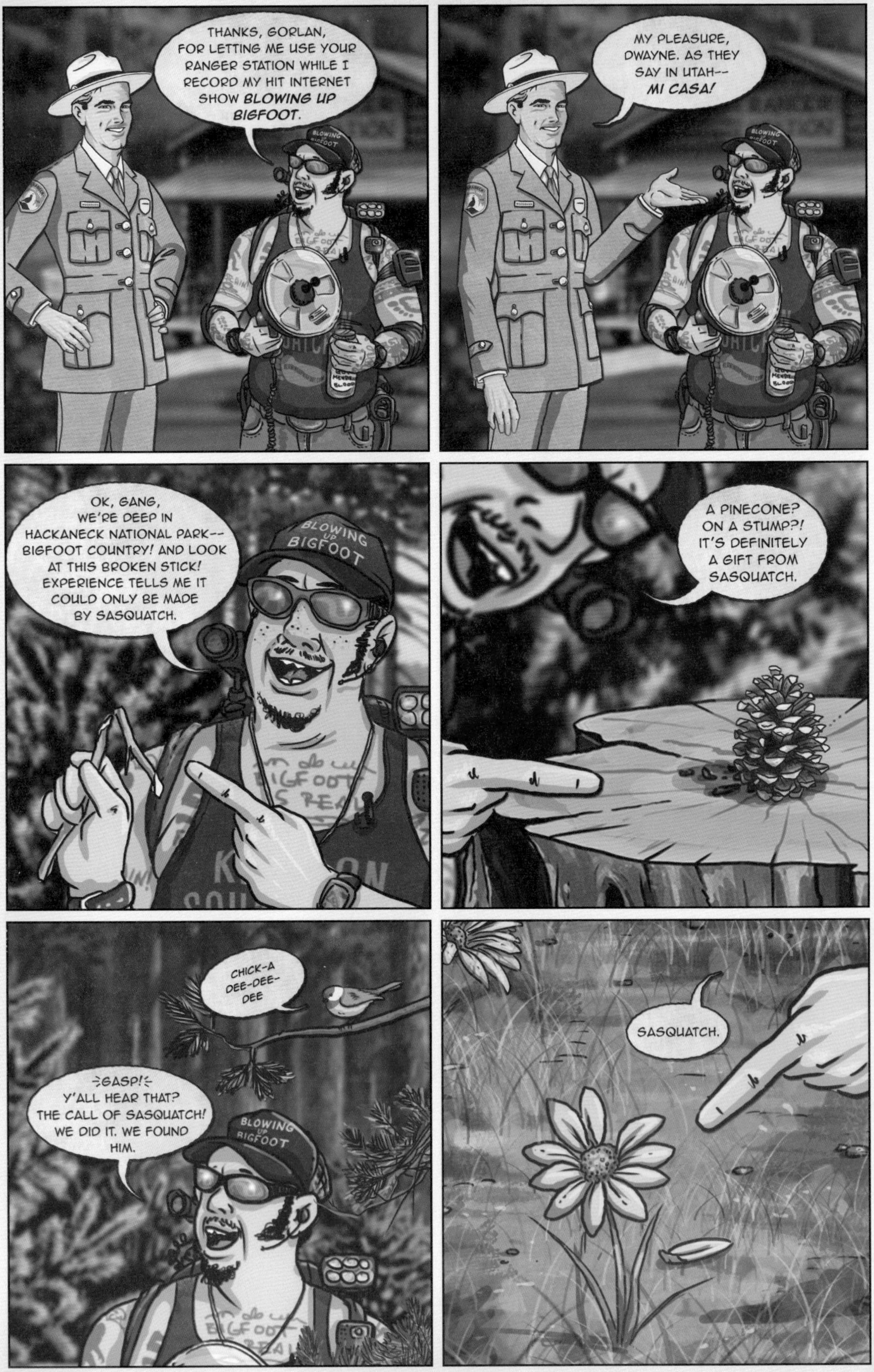
THANKS, GORLAN, FOR LETTING ME USE YOUR RANGER STATION WHILE I RECORD MY HIT INTERNET SHOW *BLOWING UP BIGFOOT*.
BLOWING UP BIGFOOT
MY PLEASURE, DWAYNE. AS THEY SAY IN UTAH-- *MI CASA!*
OK, GANG, WE'RE DEEP IN HACKANECK NATIONAL PARK-- BIGFOOT COUNTRY! AND LOOK AT THIS BROKEN STICK! EXPERIENCE TELLS ME IT COULD ONLY BE MADE BY SASQUATCH.
BIGFOOT IS REAL
A PINECONE? ON A STUMP?! IT'S DEFINITELY A GIFT FROM SASQUATCH.
CHICK-A DEE-DEE-DEE
GASP! Y'ALL HEAR THAT? THE CALL OF SASQUATCH! WE DID IT. WE FOUND HIM.
SASQUATCH.

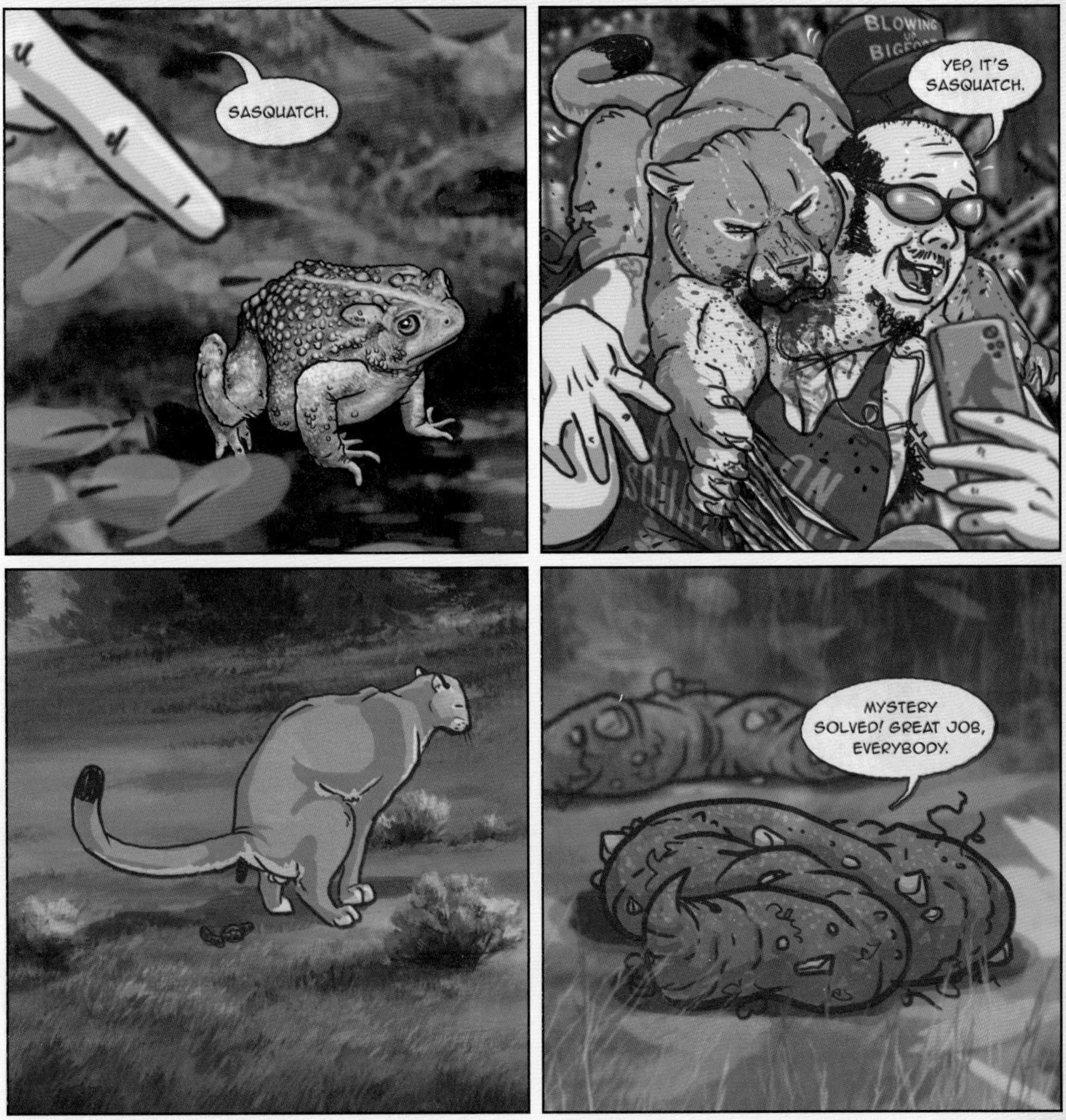
SASQUATCH.
YEP, IT'S SASQUATCH.
MYSTERY SOLVED! GREAT JOB, EVERYBODY.

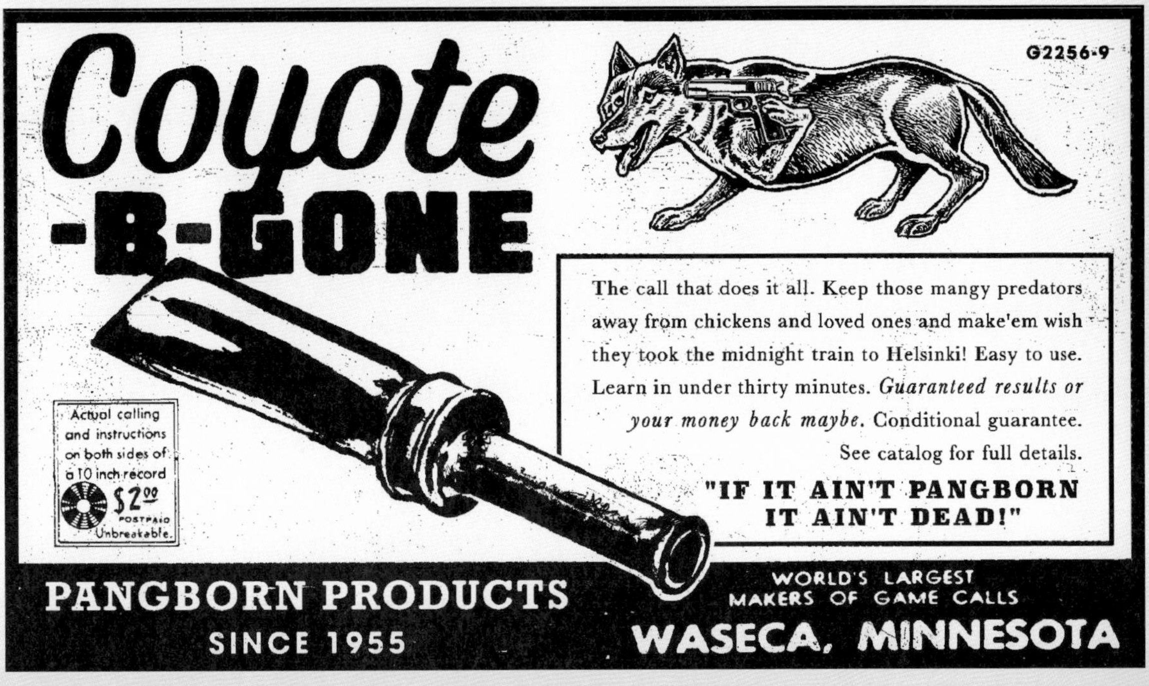
Coyote
-B-GONE
G2256-9
The call that does it all. Keep those mangy predators away from chickens and loved ones and make'em wish they took the midnight train to Helsinki! Easy to use. Learn in under thirty minutes. Guaranteed results or your money back maybe. Conditional guarantee. See catalog for full details.
"IF IT AIN'T PANGBORN IT AIN'T DEAD!"
Actual calling and instructions on both sides of a 10 inch record
$2.00 POSTPAID
Unbreakable.
PANGBORN PRODUCTS
SINCE 1955
WORLD'S LARGEST MAKERS OF GAME CALLS
WASECA, MINNESOTA

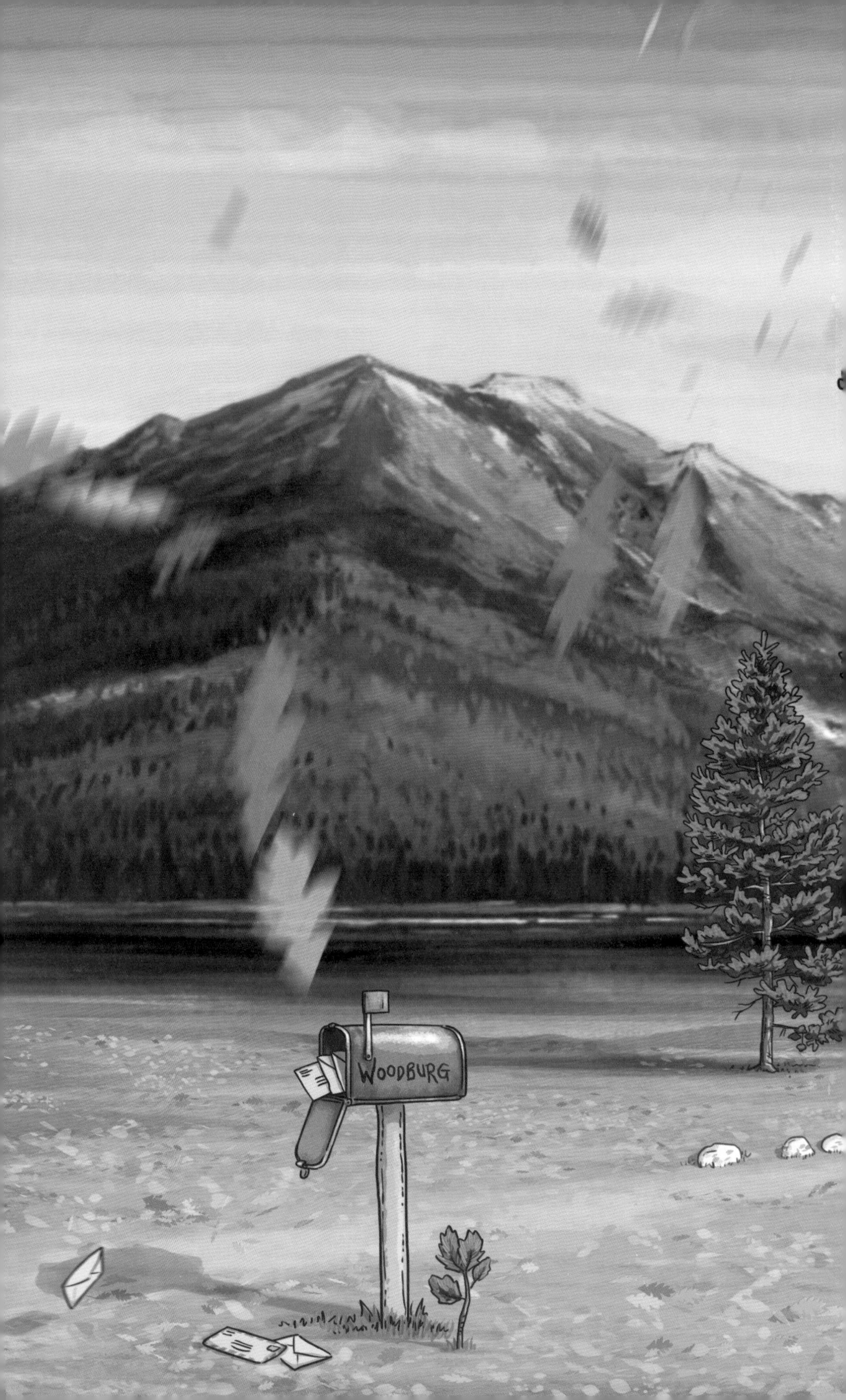
WOODBURG

FALL

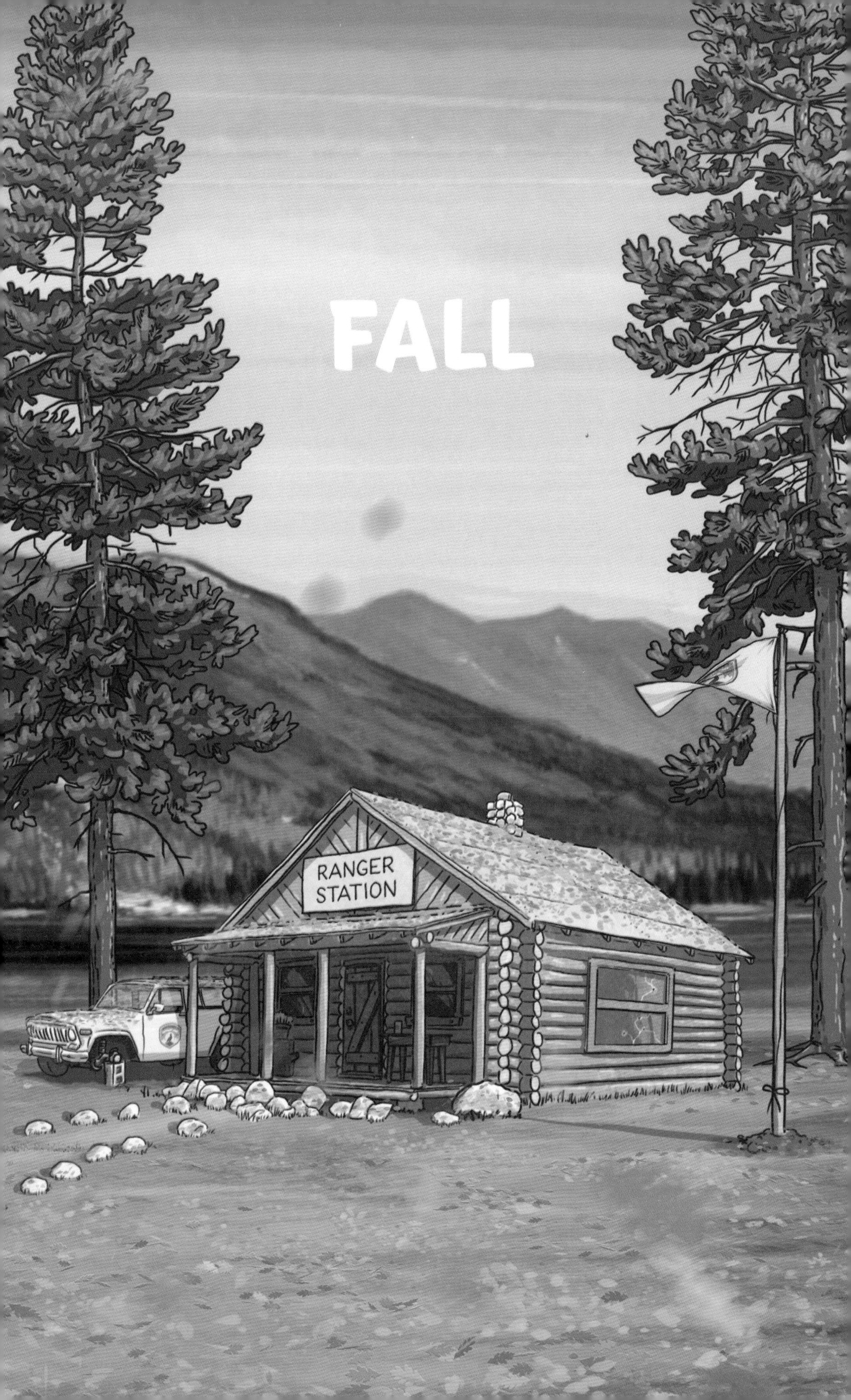
RANGER
STATION

A PORTENT TO BETTERMENT

WHAT A SUMMER, HUH? DID YOU GET AS BAKED AS WE DID? IT WAS BUSTER POINDEXTER HOT, HOT, HOT...ANYBODY? NOBODY? WONDER WHAT'S GOING ON? WHATEVER THE NEXT CATASTROPHE, IT WON'T BE NEAR AS FUN AS OUR FAVORITE SEASON--FALL. BECAUSE FALL MEANS GOURDS! WARTY GOURDS, SMOOTH GOURDS, GOURDS WITH FACES ON THEM, GOURDS SHAPED LIKE GENITALS, GOURDS SHAPED LIKE YOUR GENITALS--WHAT WE'RE SAYING IS ALL SORTS OF GOURDS, REALLY.

SO DON AGAIN THE MOTH-EATEN CARDIGAN FROM THE ATTIC, GRAB A BUTTERNUT, A SEAT ON THE DAVENPORT, AND SPREAD 'EM. THIS IS YOUR TIME. LIGHT A CANDLE, WHY DONTCHA? PLAY SOME JOHNNY MATHIS IF YOU LIKE. BUT PLAY IT LOW, YOU CAN'T BLAST THE MATHIS, YOU PSYCHO.

NOW MOVE THAT CANDLE RIGHT UP AGAINST THOSE OILY RAGS. THERE. CREATES AN ATMOSPHERE, DON'T YOU THINK? YOU'RE ALL SET. DIG IN, AND GET WEIRD WITH OUR LATEST AUTUMNAL GIFT TO YOU, DEAR READER.

RANGER GARLAND WOODBURN

HACKANECK NATIONAL PARK

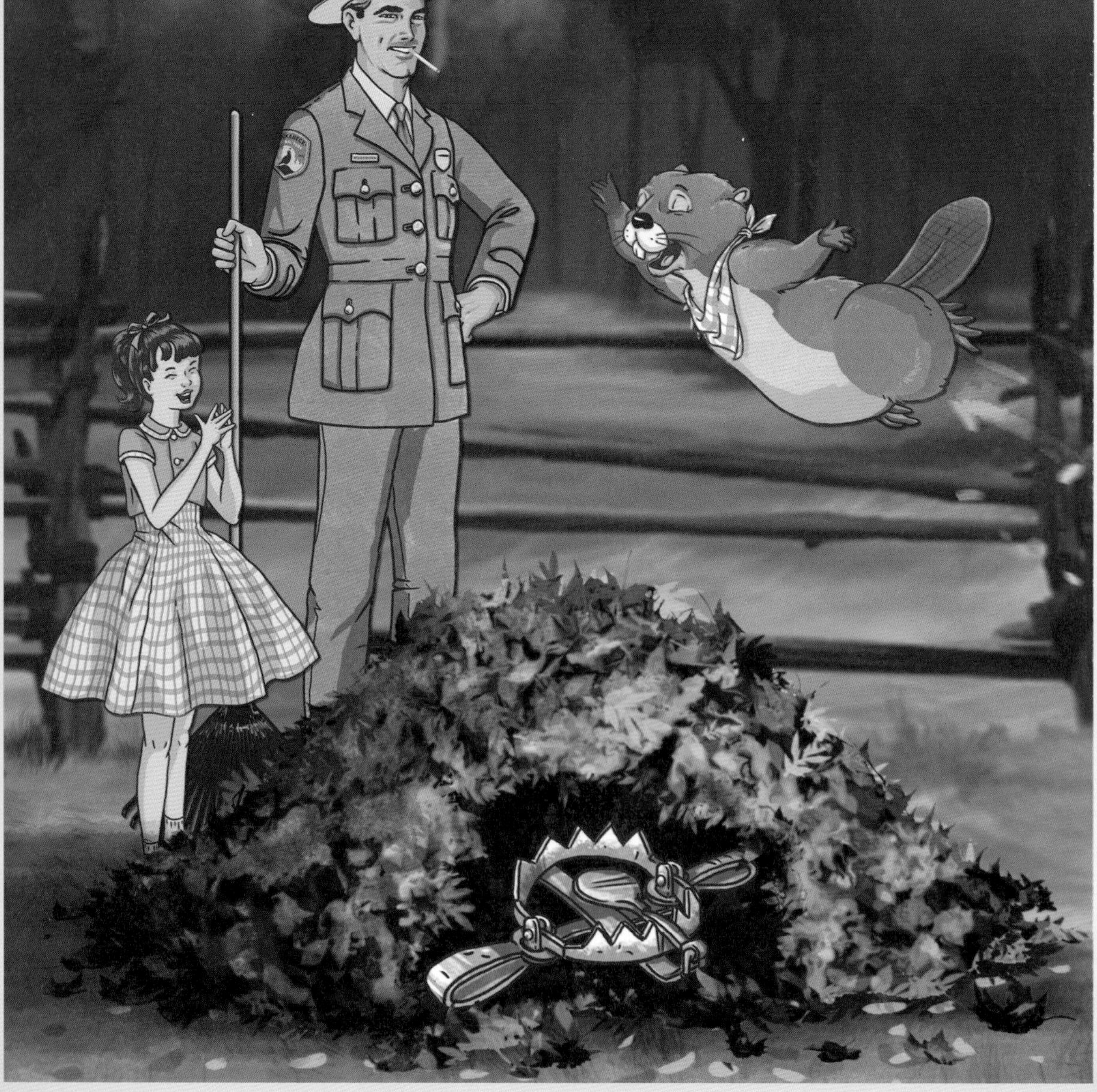

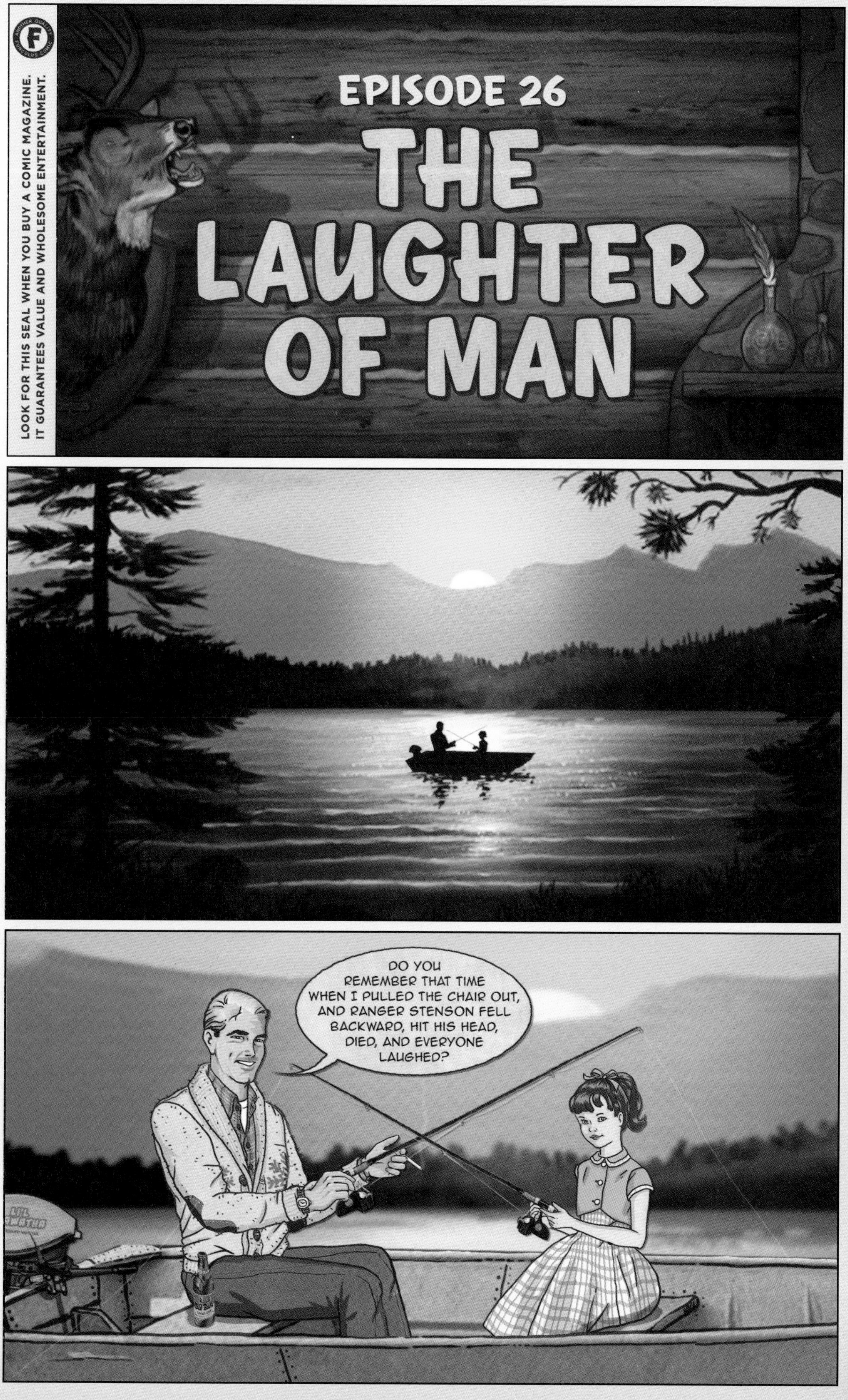
LOOK FOR THIS SEAL WHEN YOU BUY A COMIC MAGAZINE.
IT GUARANTEES VALUE AND WHOLESOME ENTERTAINMENT.
EPISODE 26
THE LAUGHTER OF MAN
DO YOU REMEMBER THAT TIME WHEN I PULLED THE CHAIR OUT, AND RANGER STENSON FELL BACKWARD, HIT HIS HEAD, DIED, AND EVERYONE LAUGHED?

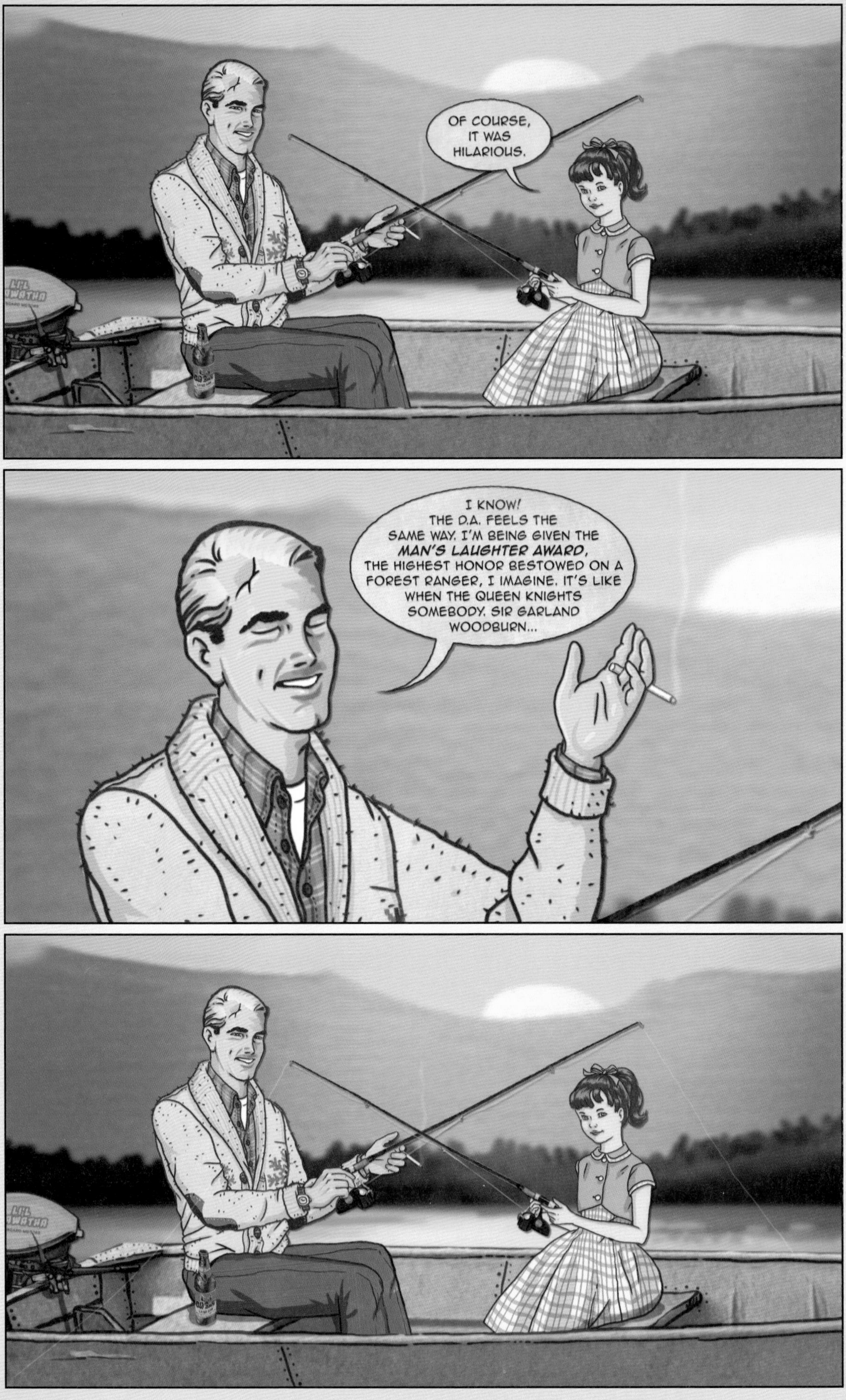
OF COURSE, IT WAS HILARIOUS.
I KNOW! THE D.A. FEELS THE SAME WAY. I'M BEING GIVEN THE MAN'S LAUGHTER AWARD, THE HIGHEST HONOR BESTOWED ON A FOREST RANGER, I IMAGINE. IT'S LIKE WHEN THE QUEEN KNIGHTS SOMEBODY. SIR GARLAND WOODBURN...

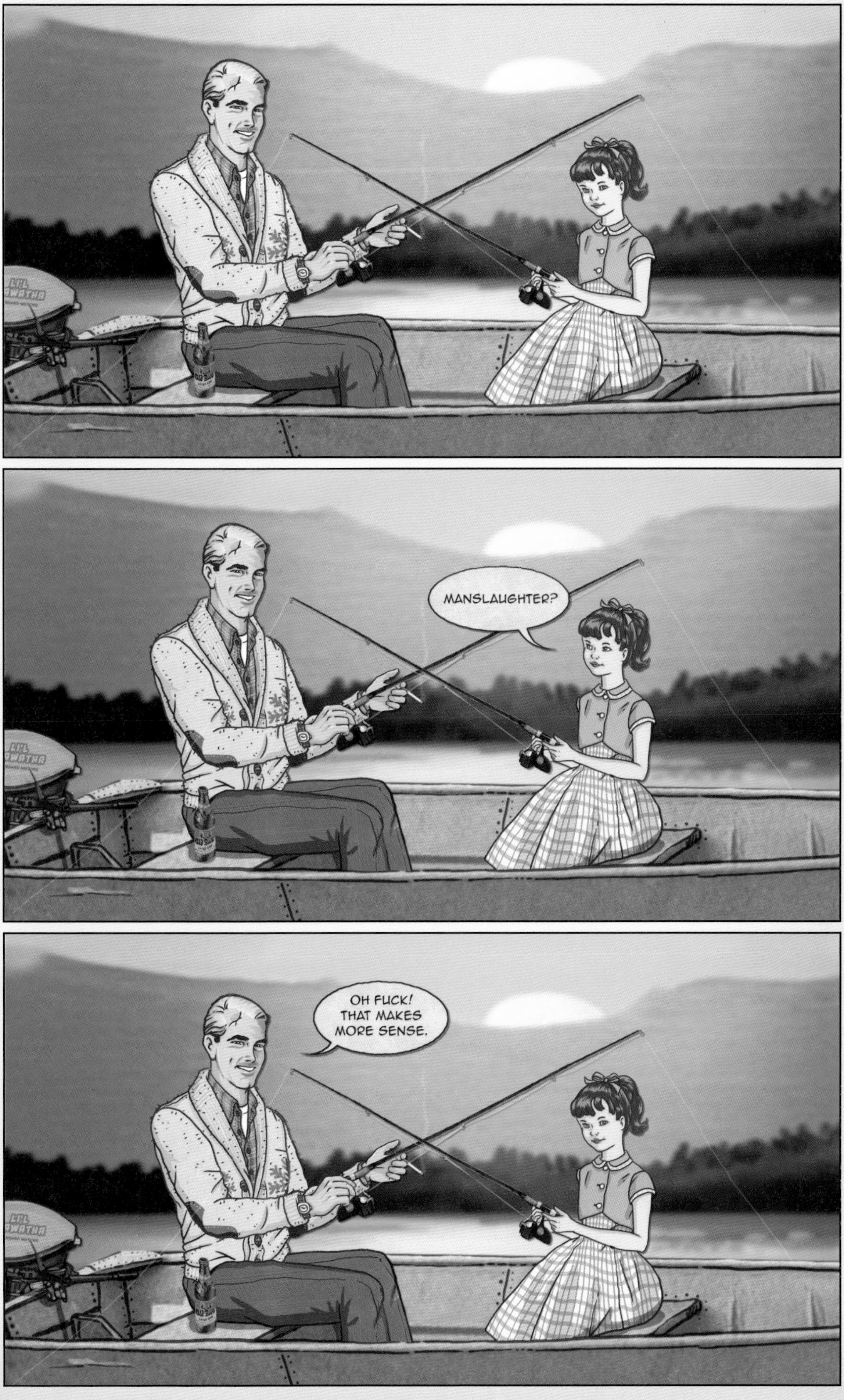
MANSLAUGHTER?
OH FUCK! THAT MAKES MORE SENSE.

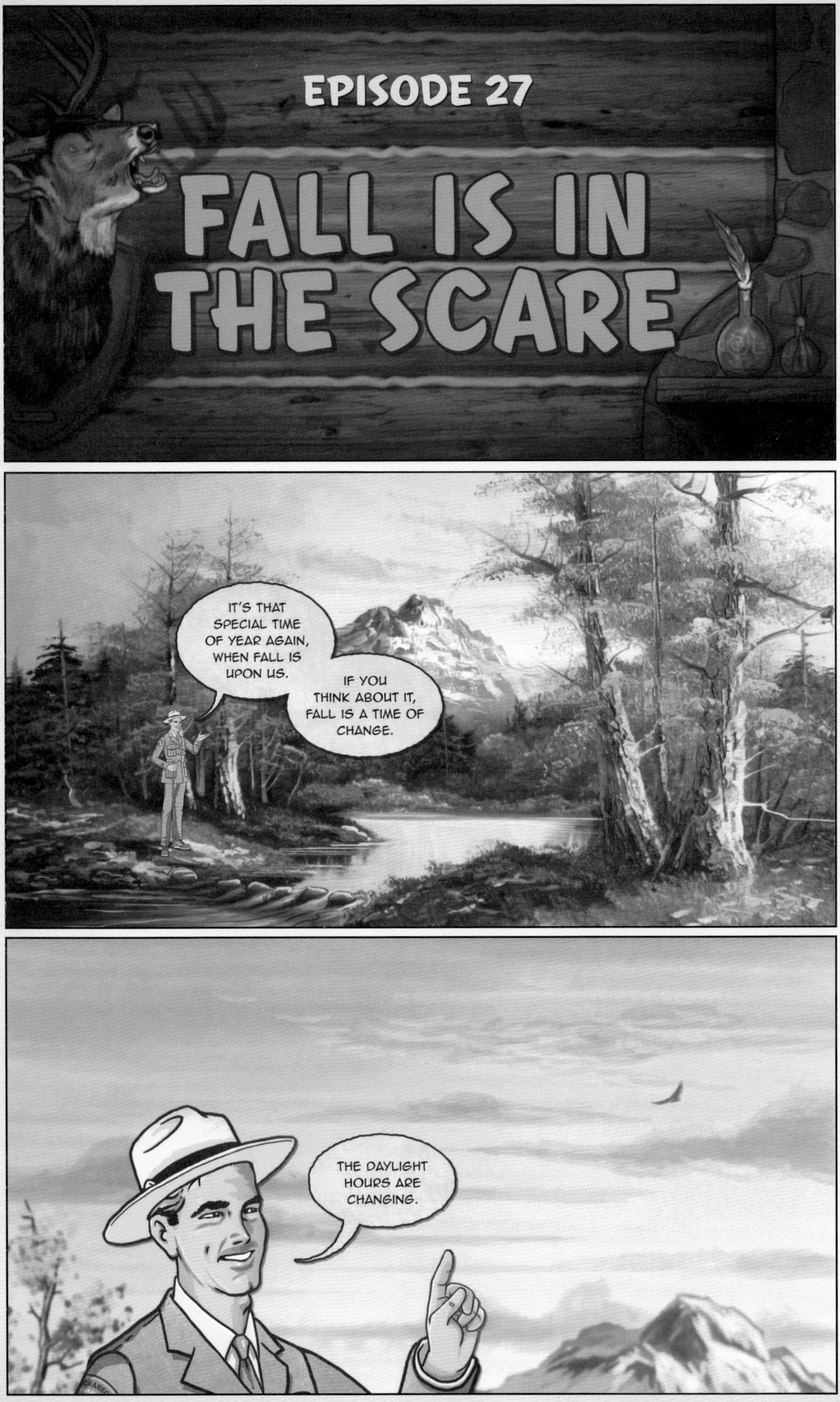
EPISODE 27
FALL IS IN THE SCARE
IT'S THAT SPECIAL TIME OF YEAR AGAIN, WHEN FALL IS UPON US.
IF YOU THINK ABOUT IT, FALL IS A TIME OF CHANGE.
THE DAYLIGHT HOURS ARE CHANGING.

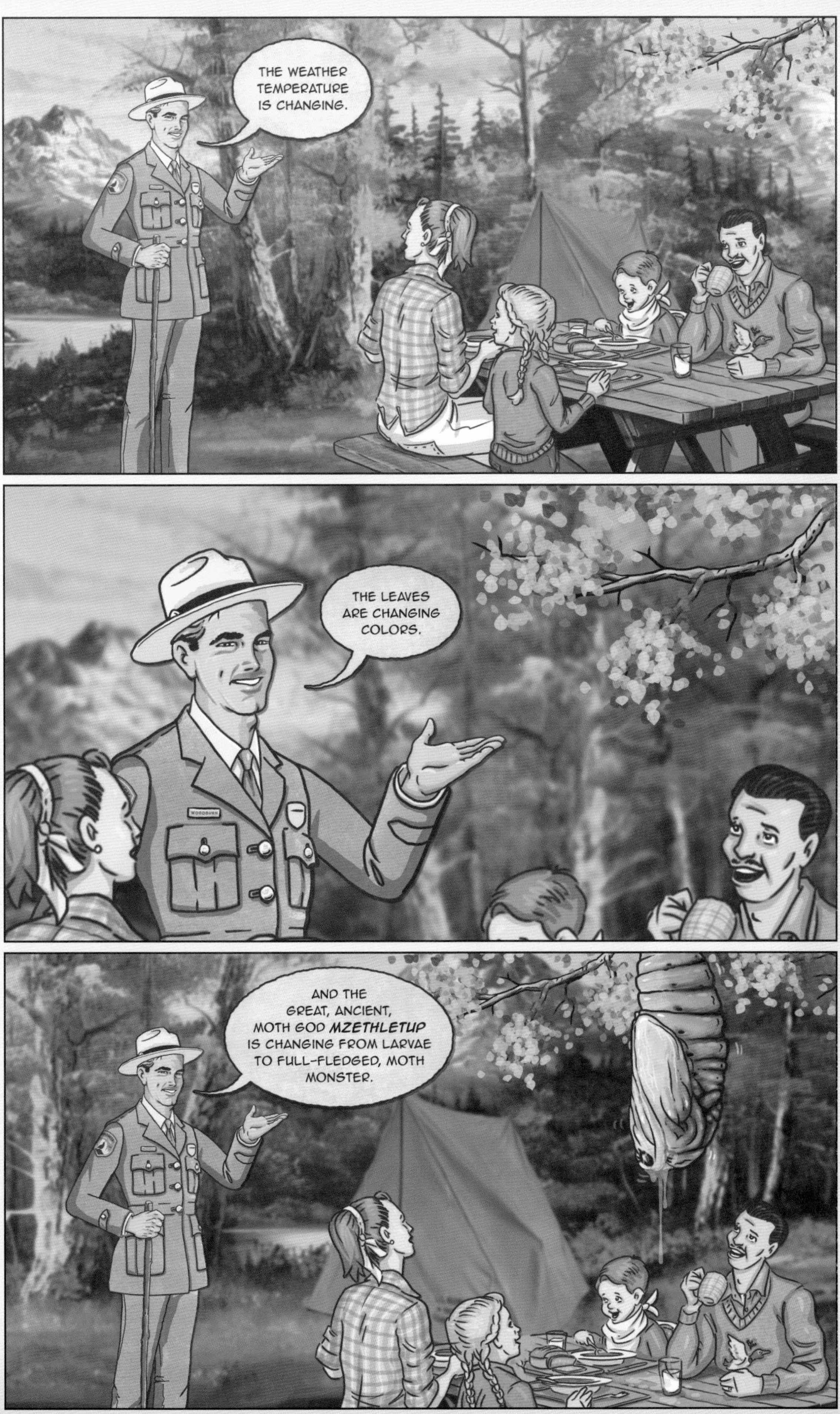
THE WEATHER TEMPERATURE IS CHANGING.
THE LEAVES ARE CHANGING COLORS.
WOODBURN
AND THE GREAT, ANCIENT, MOTH GOD *MZETHLETUP* IS CHANGING FROM LARVAE TO FULL-FLEDGED, MOTH MONSTER.

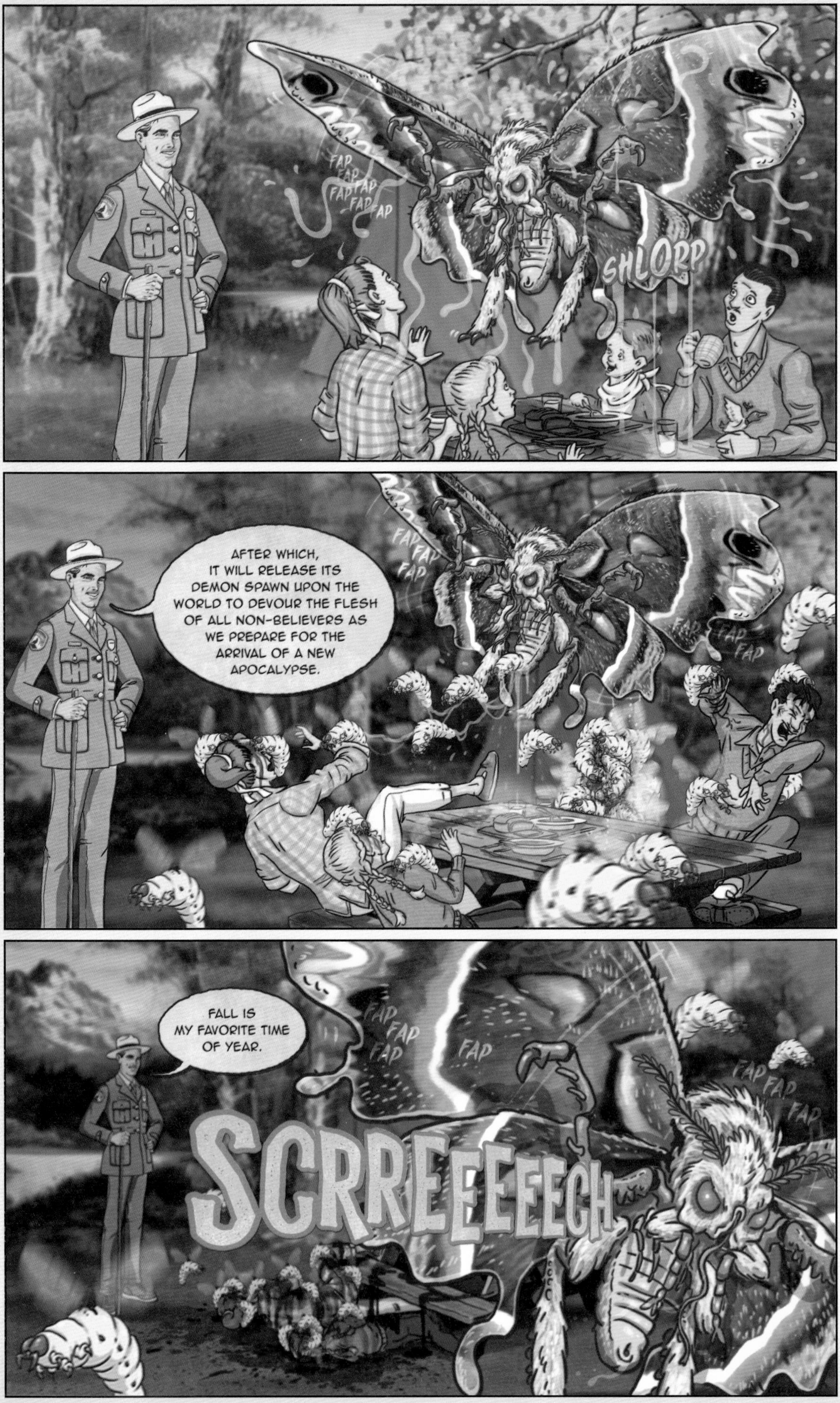
FAP FAP FAP FAP FAP FAP
SHLORP
AFTER WHICH, IT WILL RELEASE ITS DEMON SPAWN UPON THE WORLD TO DEVOUR THE FLESH OF ALL NON-BELIEVERS AS WE PREPARE FOR THE ARRIVAL OF A NEW APOCALYPSE.
FAP FAP FAP
FAP FAP FAP
FALL IS MY FAVORITE TIME OF YEAR.
FAP FAP FAP
FAP
FAP FAP FAP
SCRREEEEECH

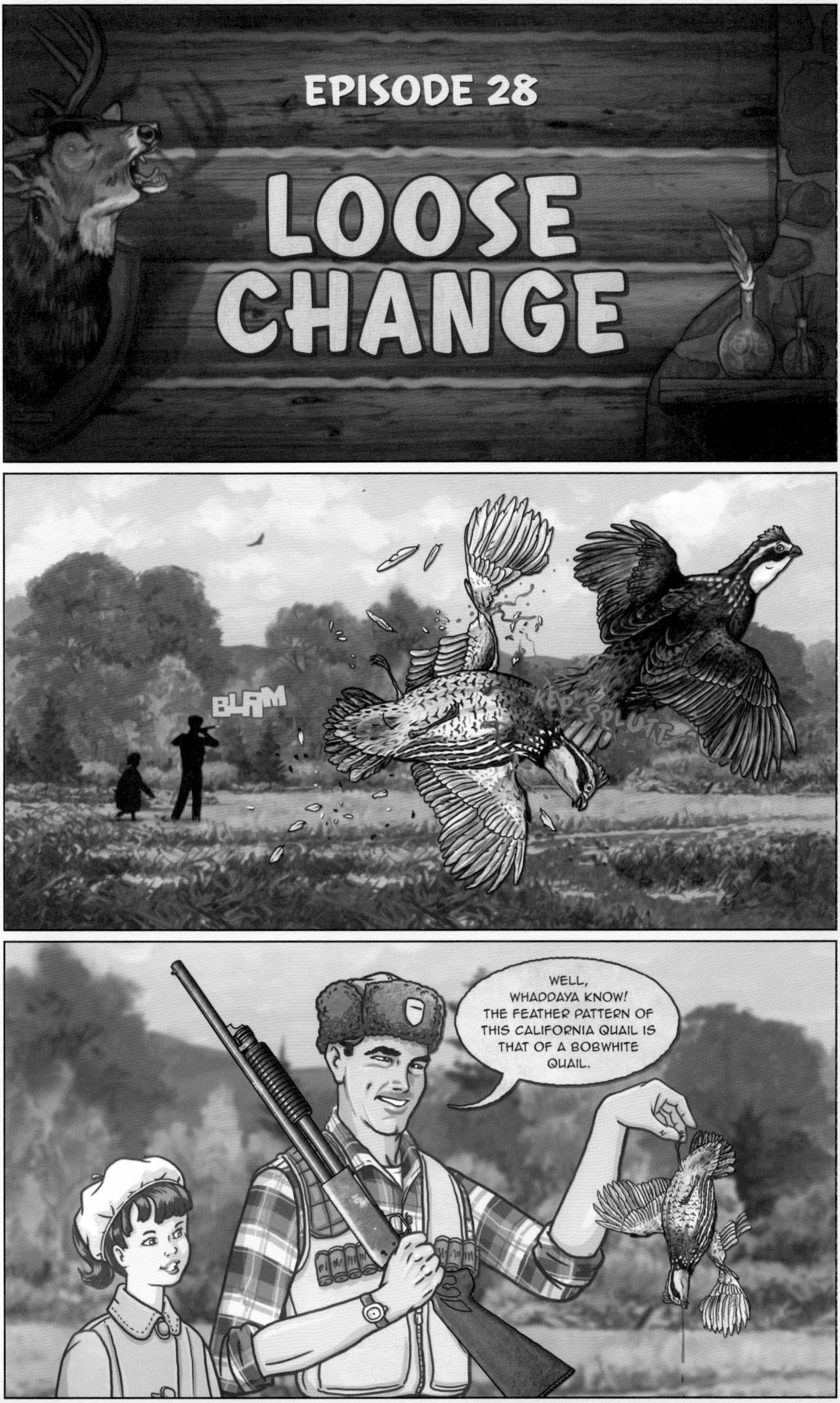
EPISODE 28
LOOSE CHANGE
BLAM
WELL, WHADDAYA KNOW! THE FEATHER PATTERN OF THIS CALIFORNIA QUAIL IS THAT OF A BOBWHITE QUAIL.

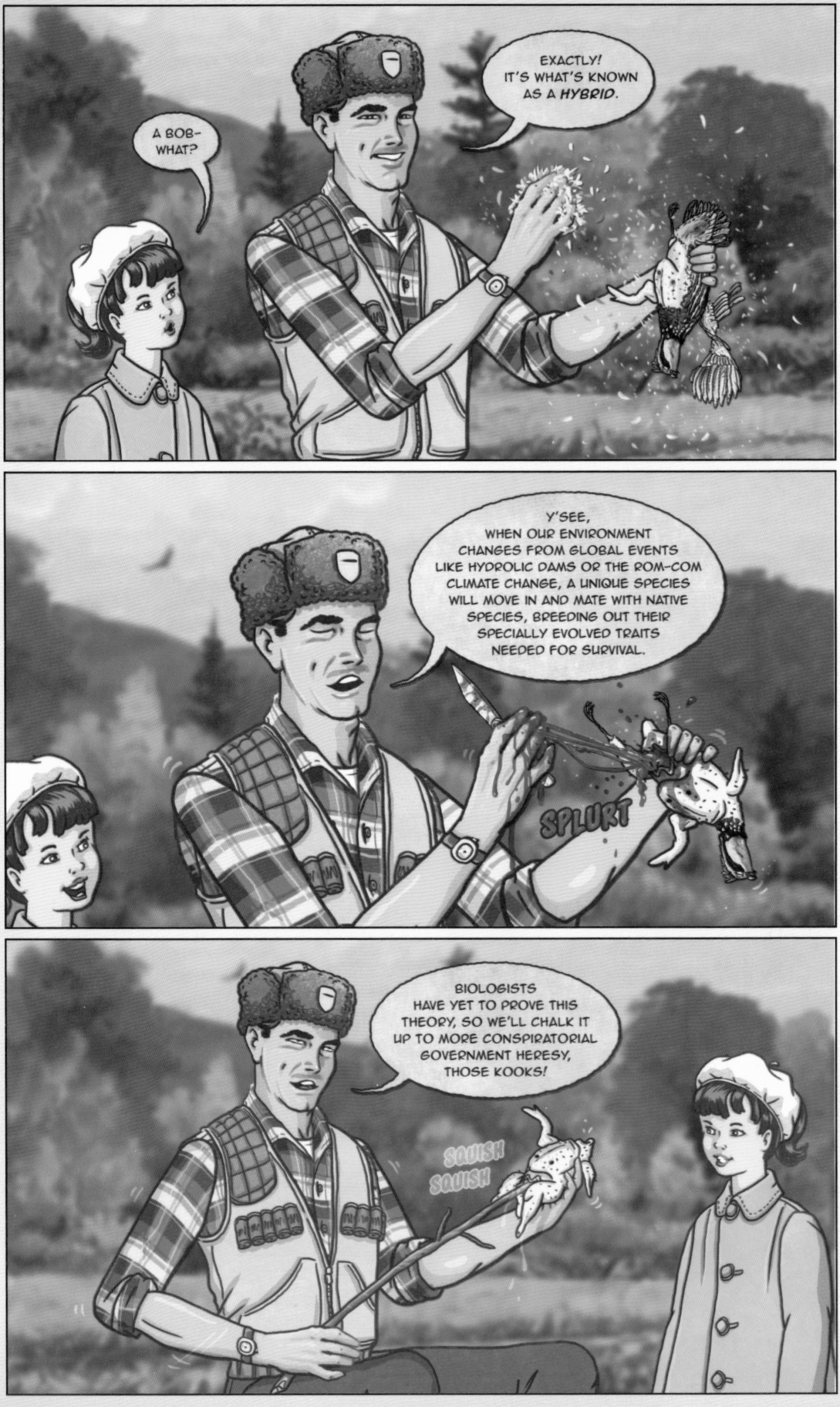
A BOB-WHAT?
EXACTLY! IT'S WHAT'S KNOWN AS A *HYBRID*.
Y'SEE, WHEN OUR ENVIRONMENT CHANGES FROM GLOBAL EVENTS LIKE HYDROLIC DAMS OR THE ROM-COM CLIMATE CHANGE, A UNIQUE SPECIES WILL MOVE IN AND MATE WITH NATIVE SPECIES, BREEDING OUT THEIR SPECIALLY EVOLVED TRAITS NEEDED FOR SURVIVAL.
SPLURT
BIOLOGISTS HAVE YET TO PROVE THIS THEORY, SO WE'LL CHALK IT UP TO MORE CONSPIRATORIAL GOVERNMENT HERESY, THOSE KOOKS!
SQUISH
SQUISH

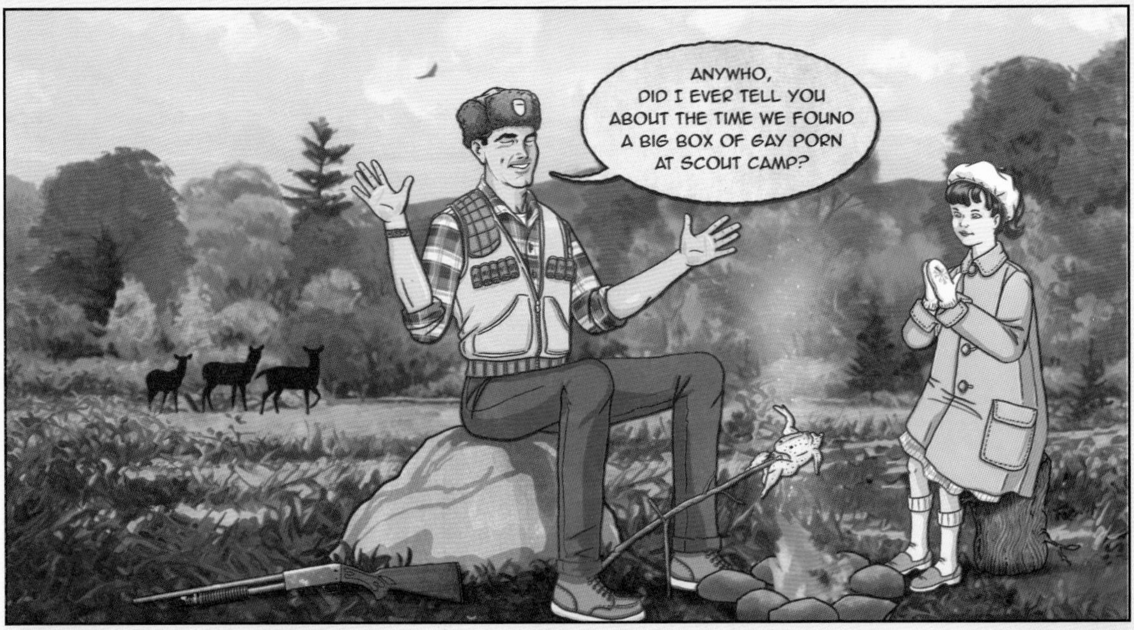
ANYWHO, DID I EVER TELL YOU ABOUT THE TIME WE FOUND A BIG BOX OF GAY PORN AT SCOUT CAMP?

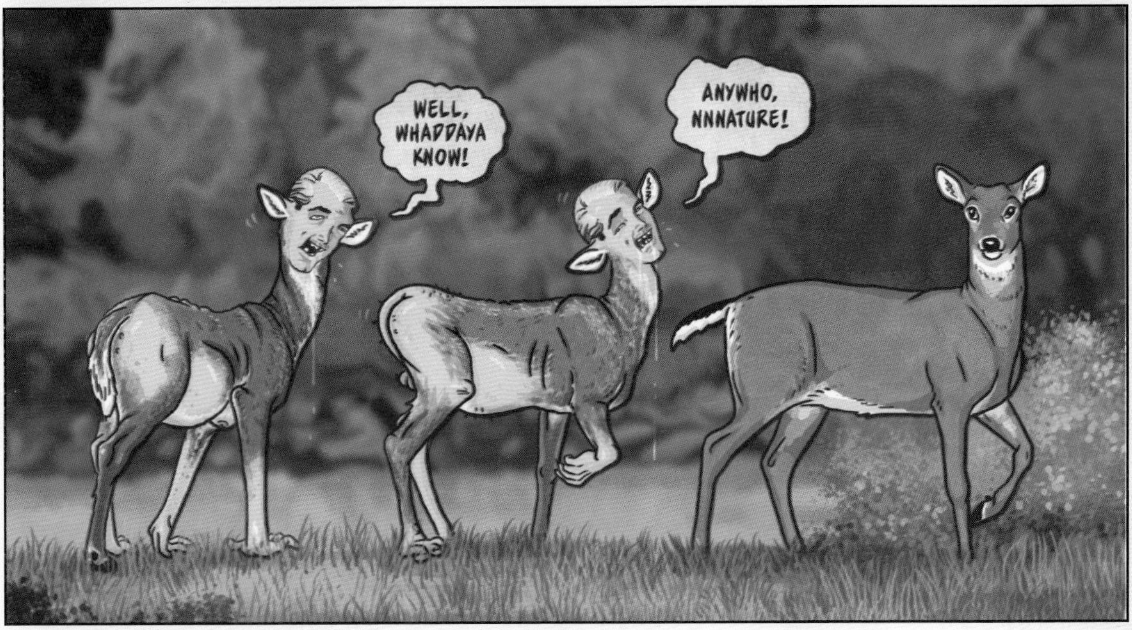
WELL, WHADDAYA KNOW!
ANYWHO, NNNATURE!

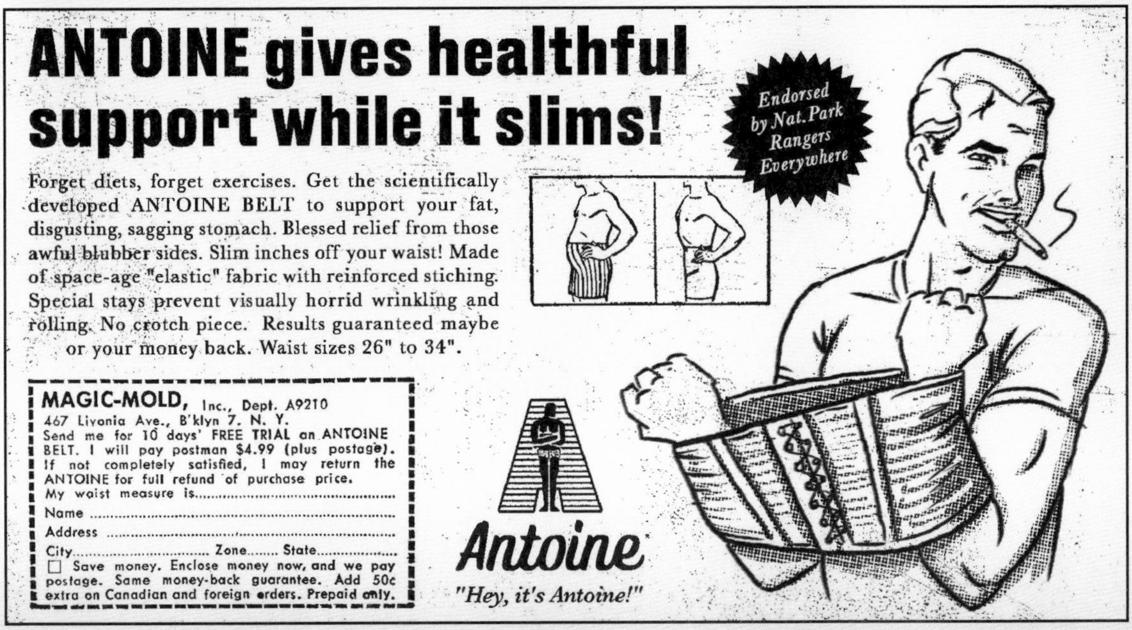
ANTOINE gives healthful support while it slims!
Forget diets, forget exercises. Get the scientifically developed ANTOINE BELT to support your fat, disgusting, sagging stomach. Blessed relief from those awful blubber sides. Slim inches off your waist! Made of space-age "elastic" fabric with reinforced stiching. Special stays prevent visually horrid wrinkling and rolling. No crotch piece. Results guaranteed maybe or your money back. Waist sizes 26" to 34".
Endorsed by Nat. Park Rangers Everywhere
MAGIC-MOLD, Inc., Dept. A9210
467 Livonia Ave., B'klyn 7. N. Y.
Send me for 10 days' FREE TRIAL on ANTOINE BELT. I will pay postman $4.99 (plus postage). If not completely satisfied, I may return the ANTOINE for full refund of purchase price.
My waist measure is....................
Name ....
Address ....
City.................... Zone....... State....................
☐ Save money. Enclose money now, and we pay postage. Same money-back guarantee. Add 50c extra on Canadian and foreign orders. Prepaid only.
Antoine
"Hey, it's Antoine!"

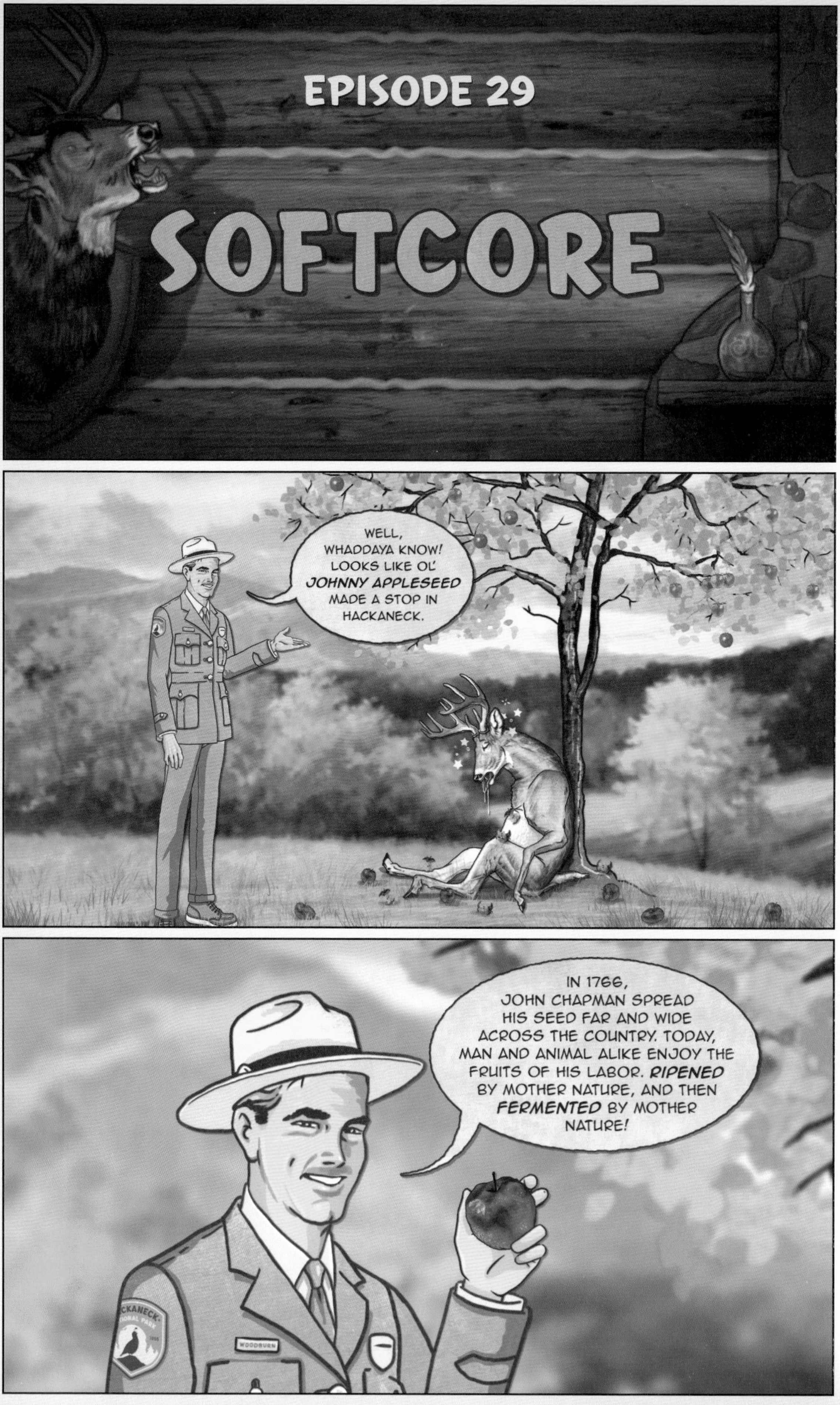
EPISODE 29
SOFTCORE
WELL, WHADDAYA KNOW! LOOKS LIKE OL' *JOHNNY APPLESEED* MADE A STOP IN HACKANECK.
IN 1766, JOHN CHAPMAN SPREAD HIS SEED FAR AND WIDE ACROSS THE COUNTRY. TODAY, MAN AND ANIMAL ALIKE ENJOY THE FRUITS OF HIS LABOR. *RIPENED* BY MOTHER NATURE, AND THEN *FERMENTED* BY MOTHER NATURE!

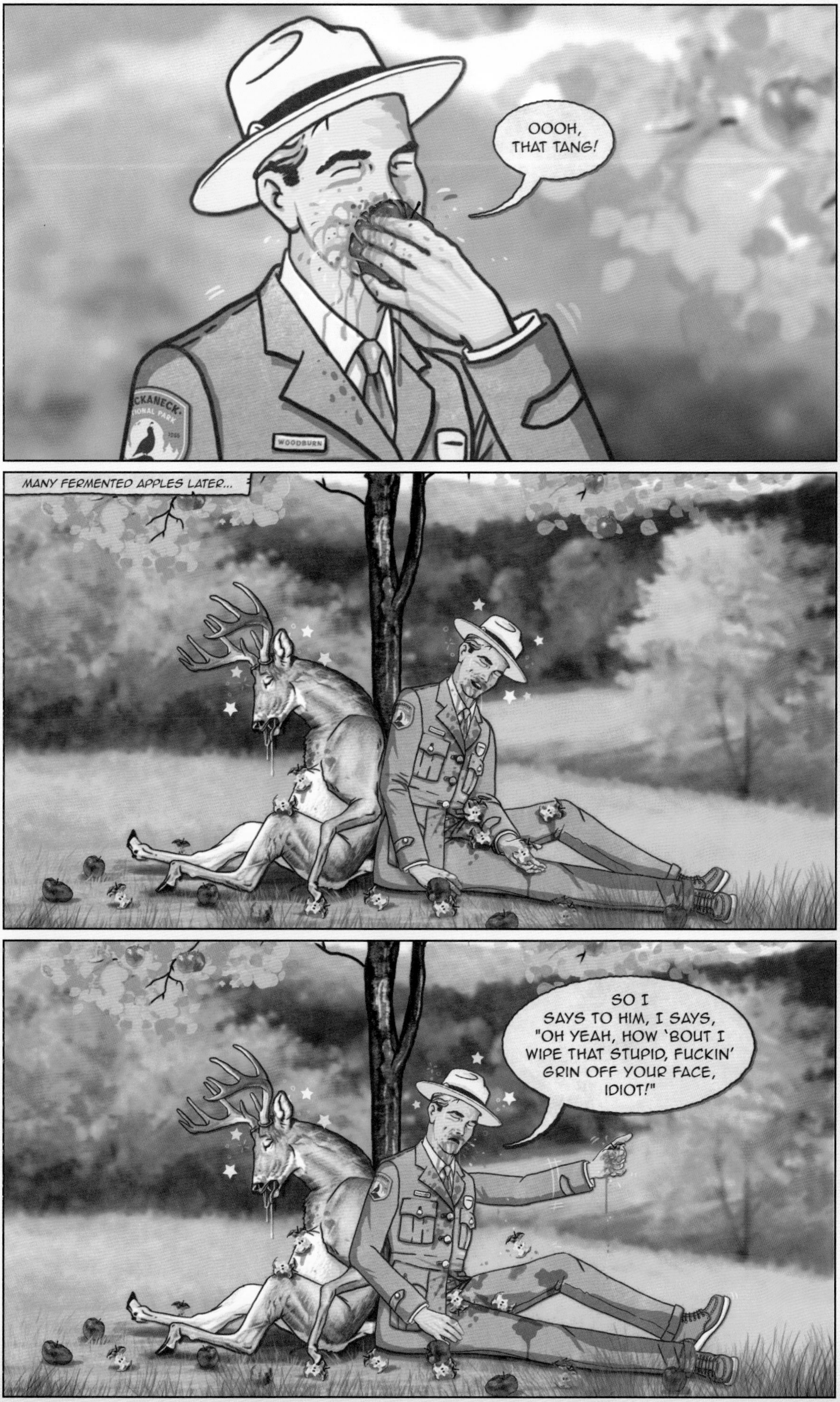
OOOH, THAT TANG!
WOODBURN
MANY FERMENTED APPLES LATER...
SO I SAYS TO HIM, I SAYS, "OH YEAH, HOW 'BOUT I WIPE THAT STUPID, FUCKIN' GRIN OFF YOUR FACE, IDIOT!"

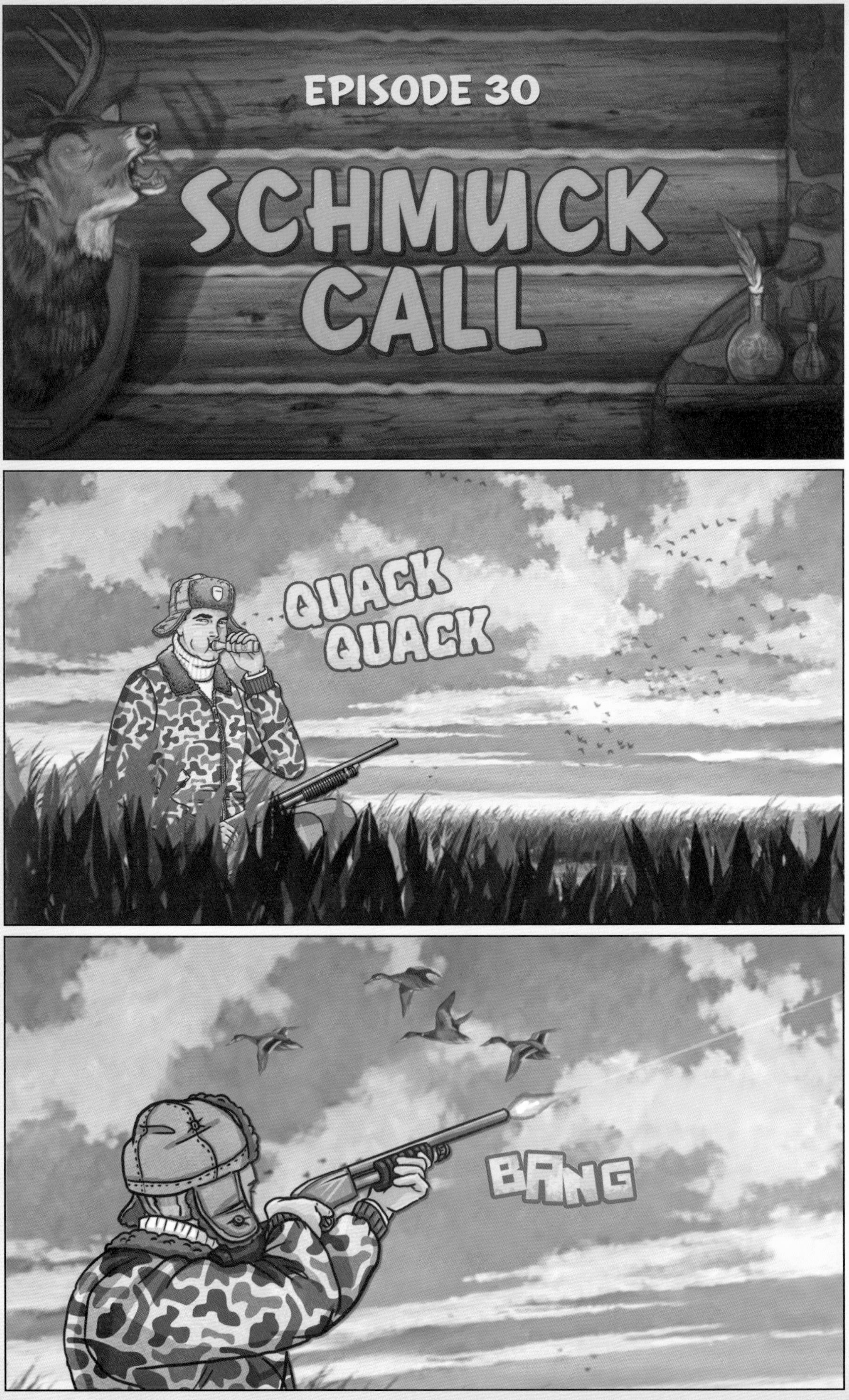
EPISODE 30
SCHMUCK CALL
QUACK QUACK
BANG

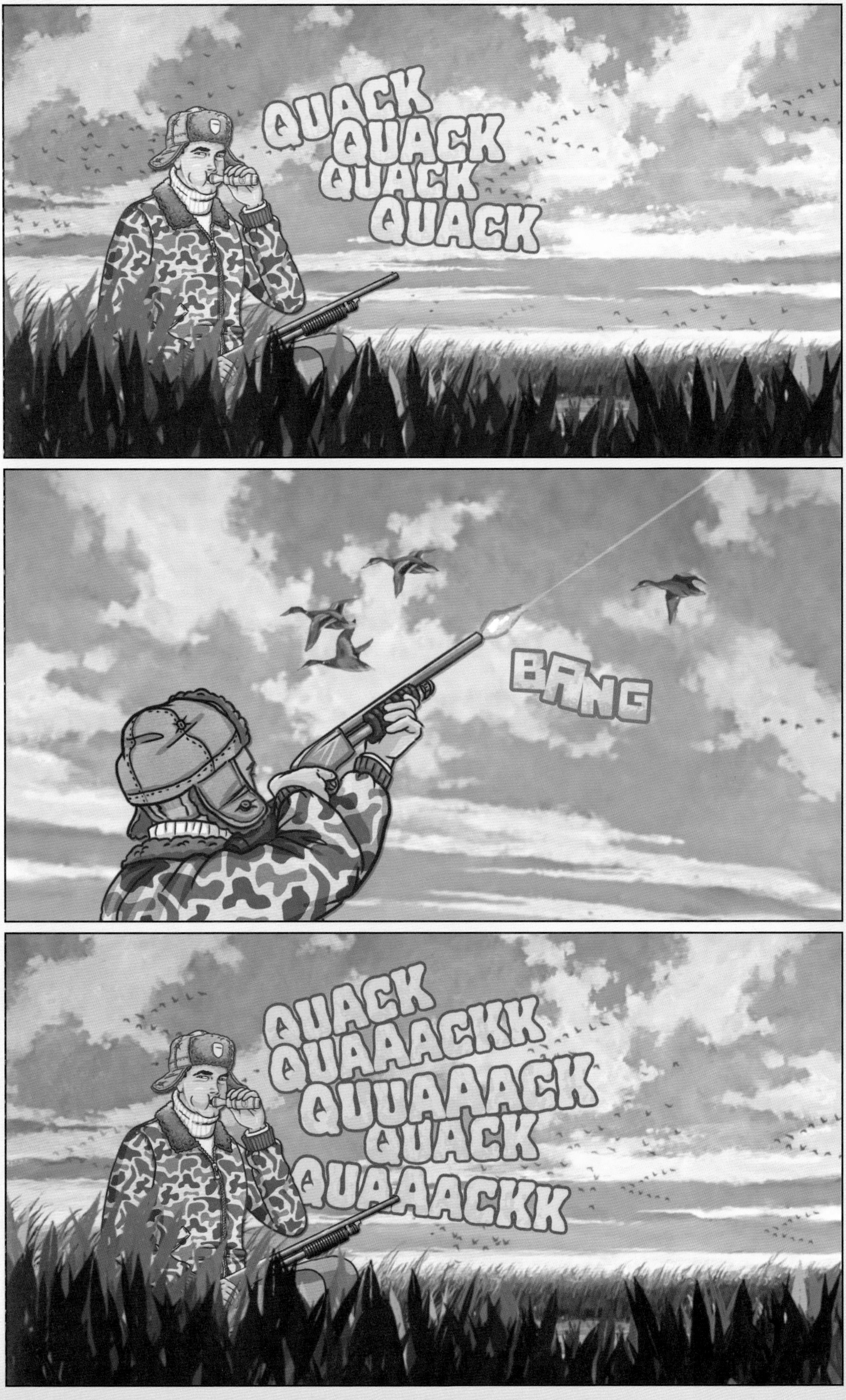
QUACK
QUACK
QUACK
QUACK
BANG
QUACK
QUAAACKK
QUUAAACK
QUACK
QUAAACKK

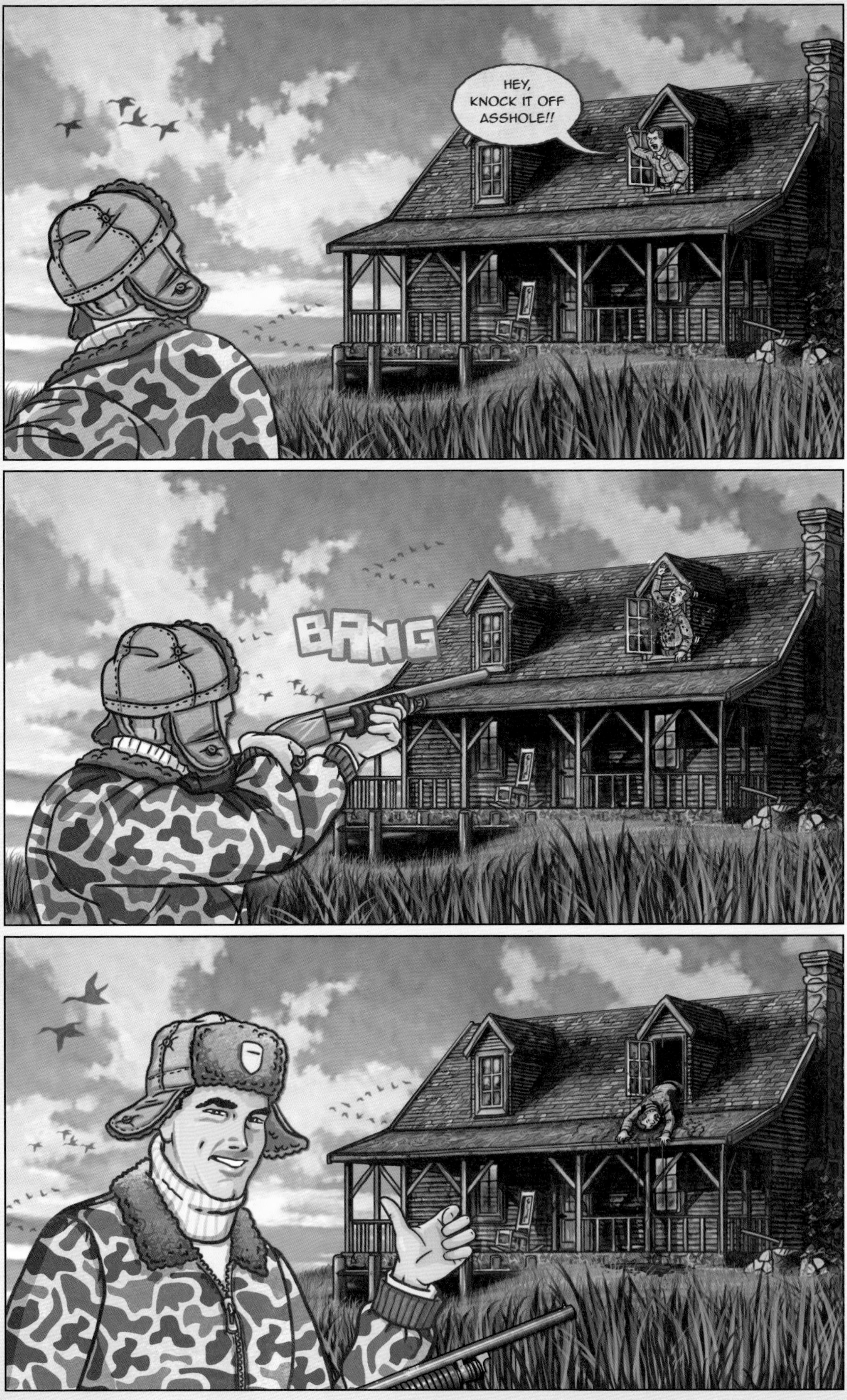
HEY, KNOCK IT OFF ASSHOLE!!
BANG

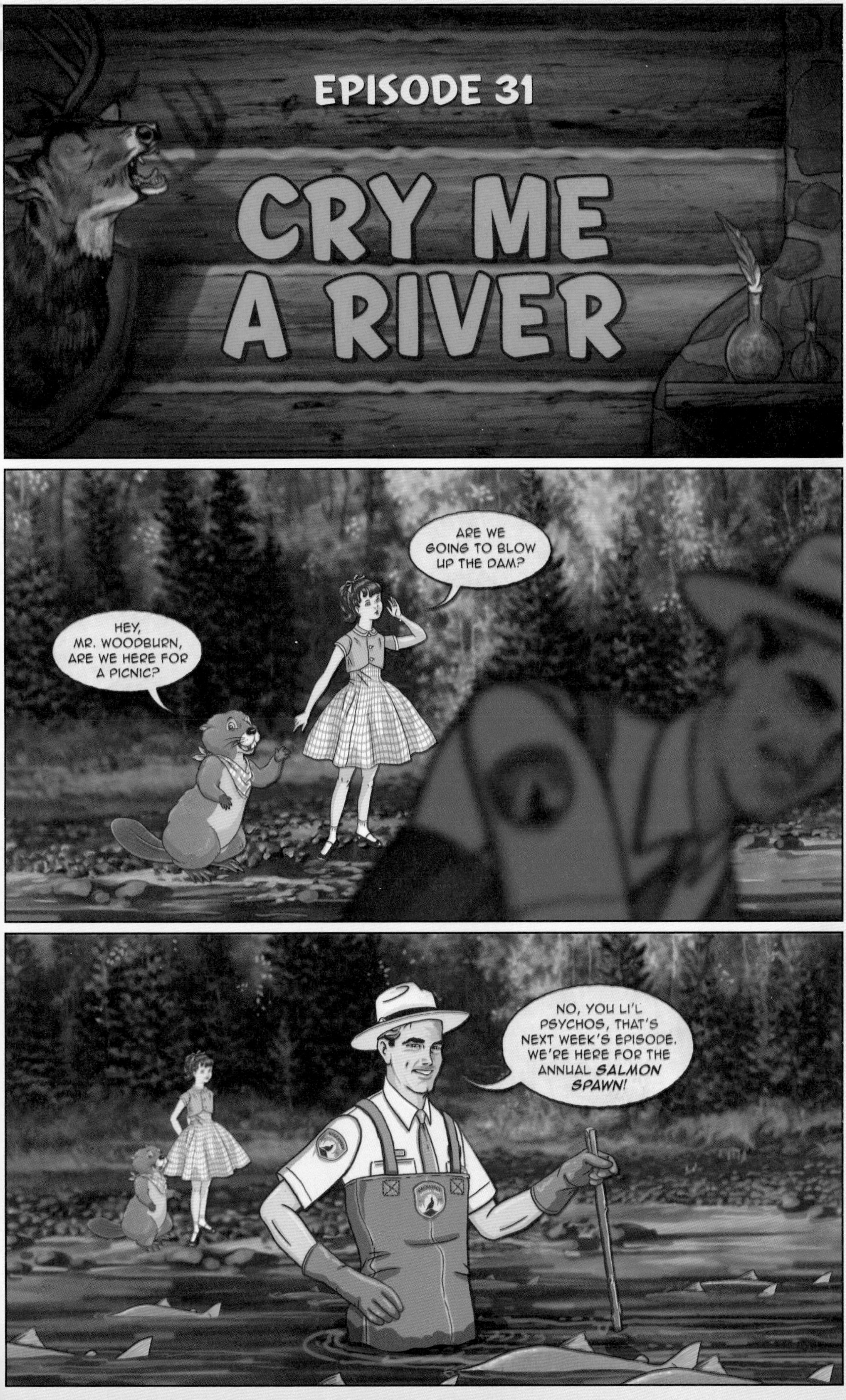
EPISODE 31
CRY ME A RIVER
HEY, MR. WOODBURN, ARE WE HERE FOR A PICNIC?
ARE WE GOING TO BLOW UP THE DAM?
NO, YOU LI'L PSYCHOS, THAT'S NEXT WEEK'S EPISODE. WE'RE HERE FOR THE ANNUAL *SALMON SPAWN!*

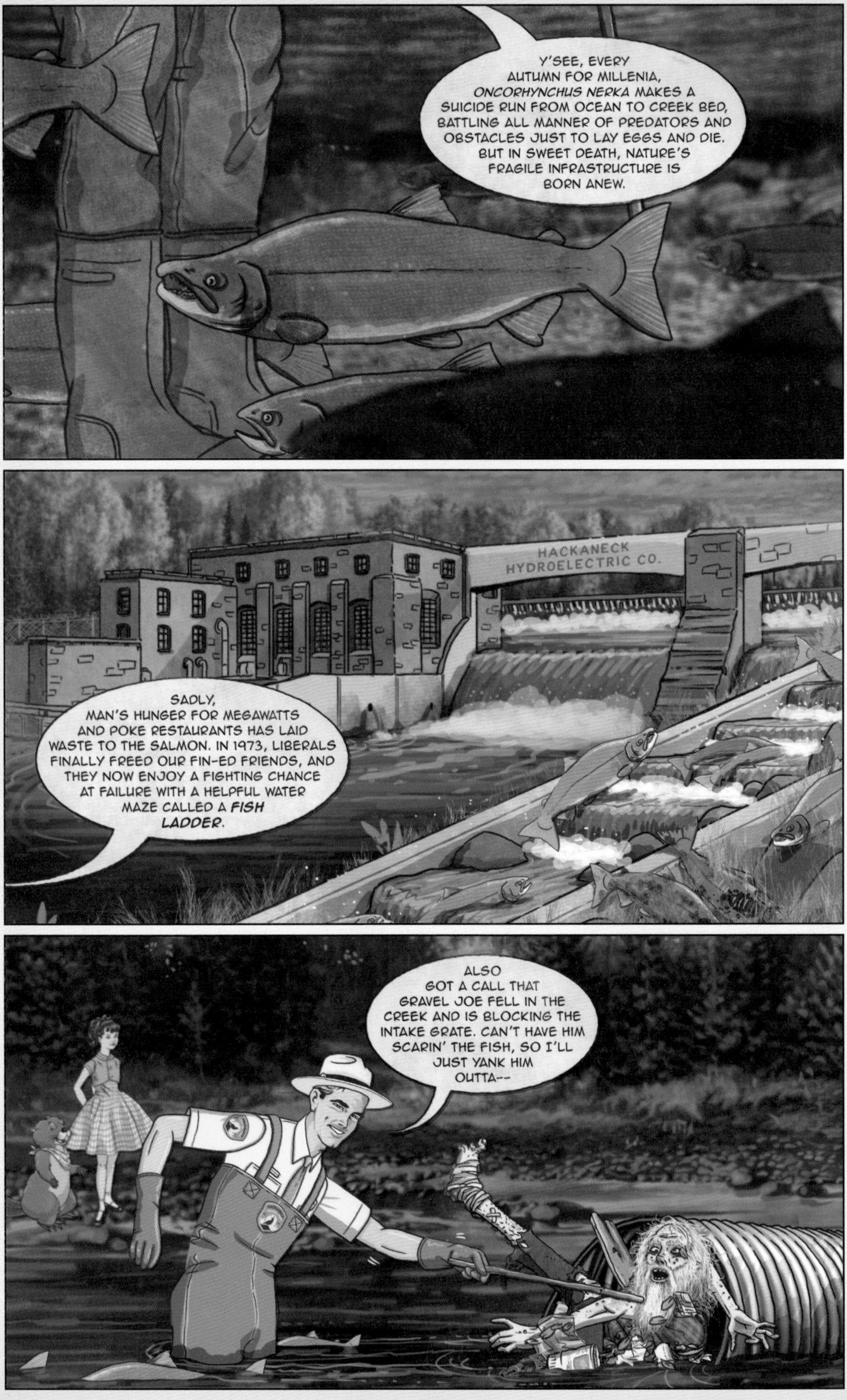
Y'SEE, EVERY AUTUMN FOR MILLENIA, *ONCORHYNCHUS NERKA* MAKES A SUICIDE RUN FROM OCEAN TO CREEK BED, BATTLING ALL MANNER OF PREDATORS AND OBSTACLES JUST TO LAY EGGS AND DIE. BUT IN SWEET DEATH, NATURE'S FRAGILE INFRASTRUCTURE IS BORN ANEW.
HACKANECK HYDROELECTRIC CO.
SADLY, MAN'S HUNGER FOR MEGAWATTS AND POKE RESTAURANTS HAS LAID WASTE TO THE SALMON. IN 1973, LIBERALS FINALLY FREED OUR FIN-ED FRIENDS, AND THEY NOW ENJOY A FIGHTING CHANCE AT FAILURE WITH A HELPFUL WATER MAZE CALLED A ***FISH LADDER***.
ALSO GOT A CALL THAT GRAVEL JOE FELL IN THE CREEK AND IS BLOCKING THE INTAKE GRATE. CAN'T HAVE HIM SCARIN' THE FISH, SO I'LL JUST YANK HIM OUTTA--

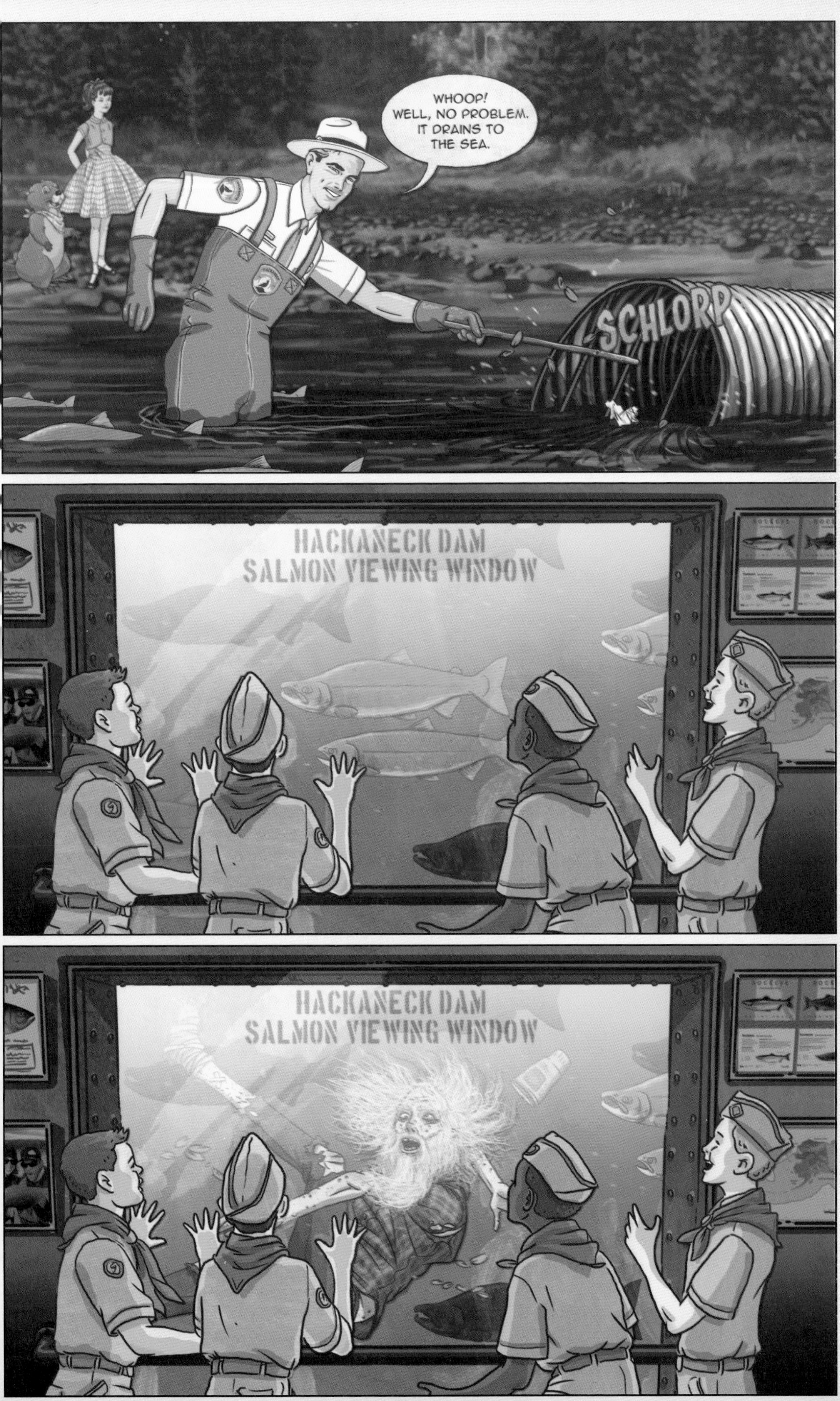
WHOOP!
WELL, NO PROBLEM. IT DRAINS TO THE SEA.
SCHLORP
HACKANECK DAM
SALMON VIEWING WINDOW
HACKANECK DAM
SALMON VIEWING WINDOW

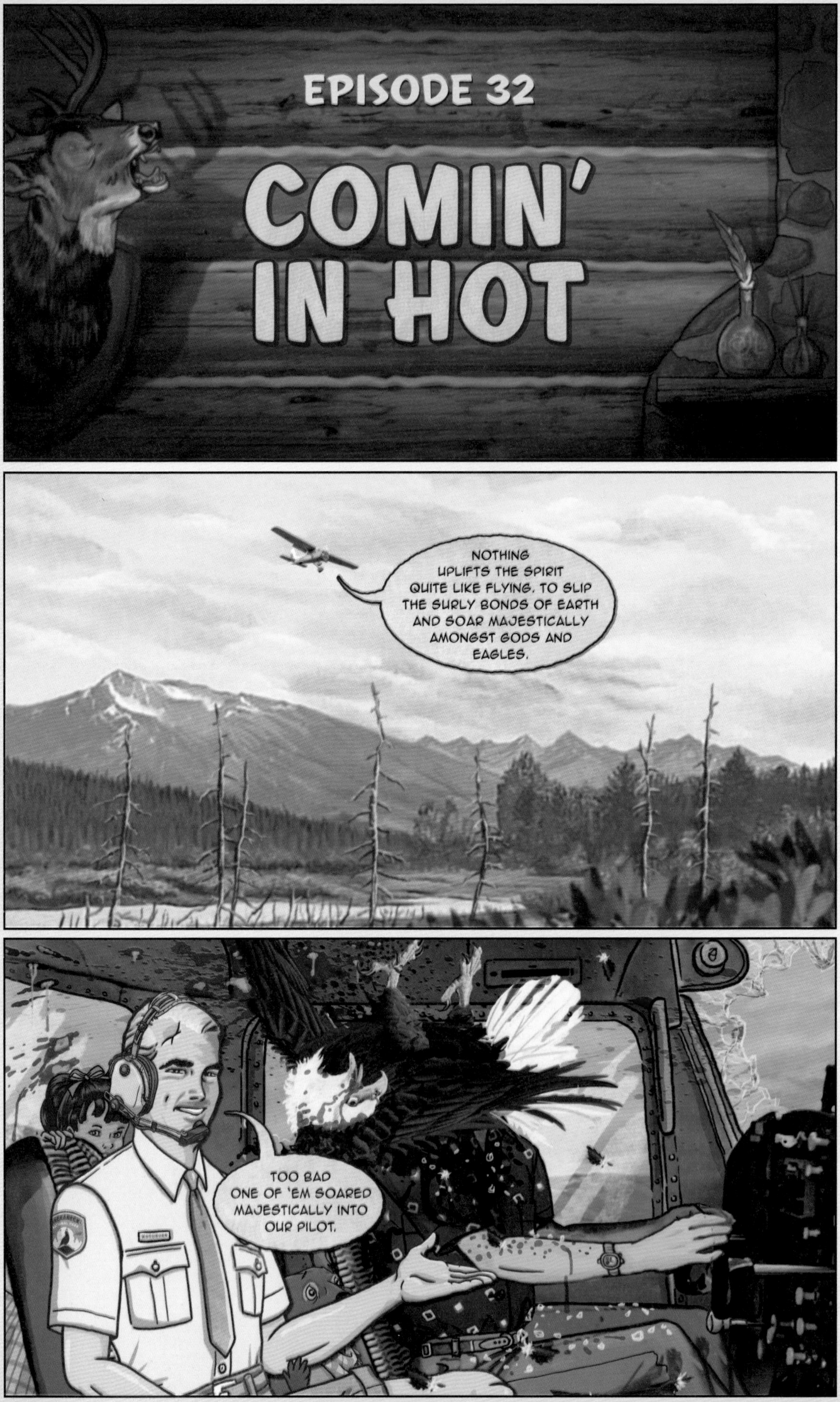
EPISODE 32
COMIN' IN HOT
NOTHING UPLIFTS THE SPIRIT QUITE LIKE FLYING. TO SLIP THE SURLY BONDS OF EARTH AND SOAR MAJESTICALLY AMONGST GODS AND EAGLES.
TOO BAD ONE OF 'EM SOARED MAJESTICALLY INTO OUR PILOT.

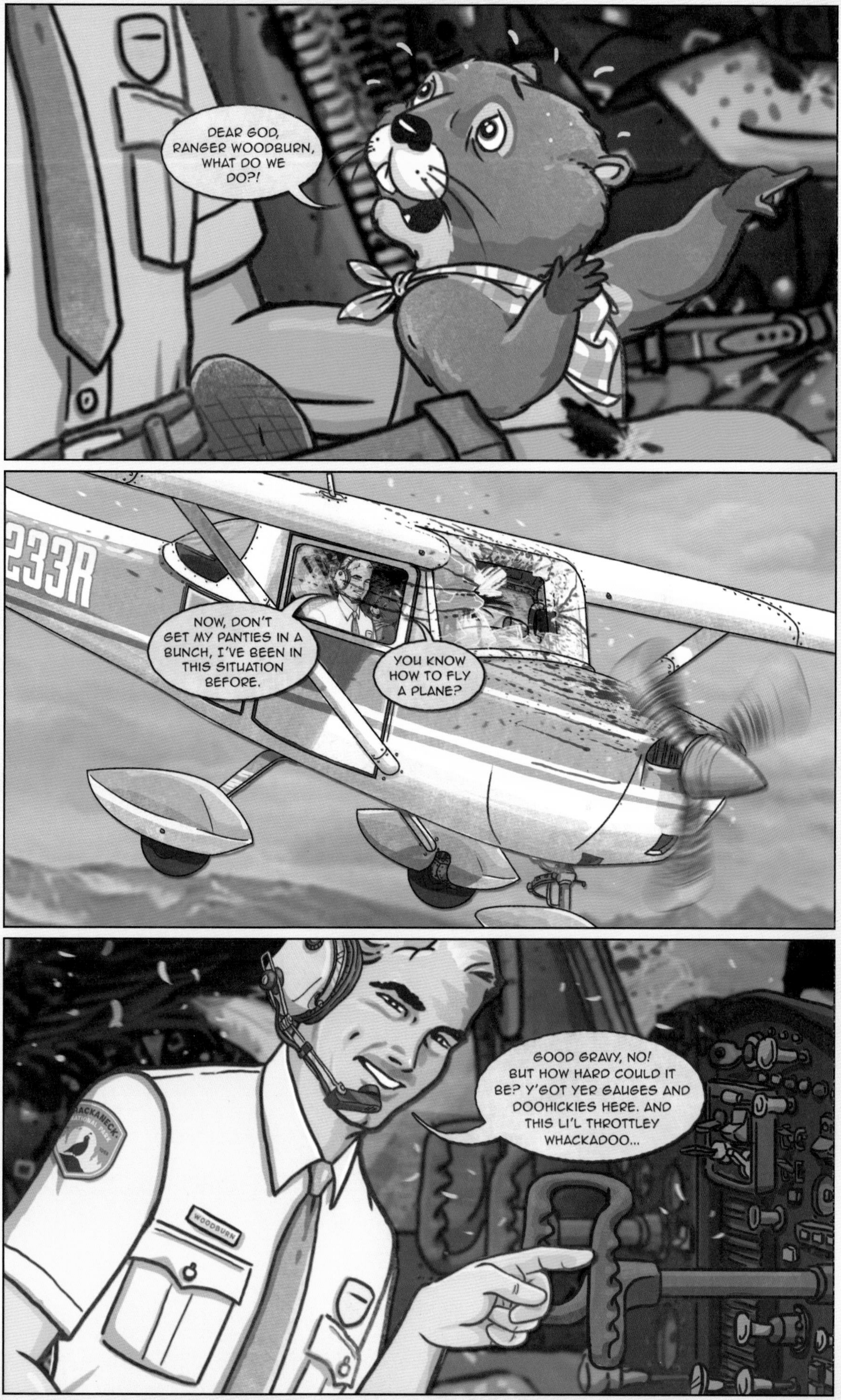
DEAR GOD, RANGER WOODBURN, WHAT DO WE DO?!
233R
NOW, DON'T GET MY PANTIES IN A BUNCH, I'VE BEEN IN THIS SITUATION BEFORE.
YOU KNOW HOW TO FLY A PLANE?
GOOD GRAVY, NO! BUT HOW HARD COULD IT BE? Y'GOT YER GAUGES AND DOOHICKIES HERE. AND THIS LI'L THROTTLEY WHACKADOO...
WOODBURN

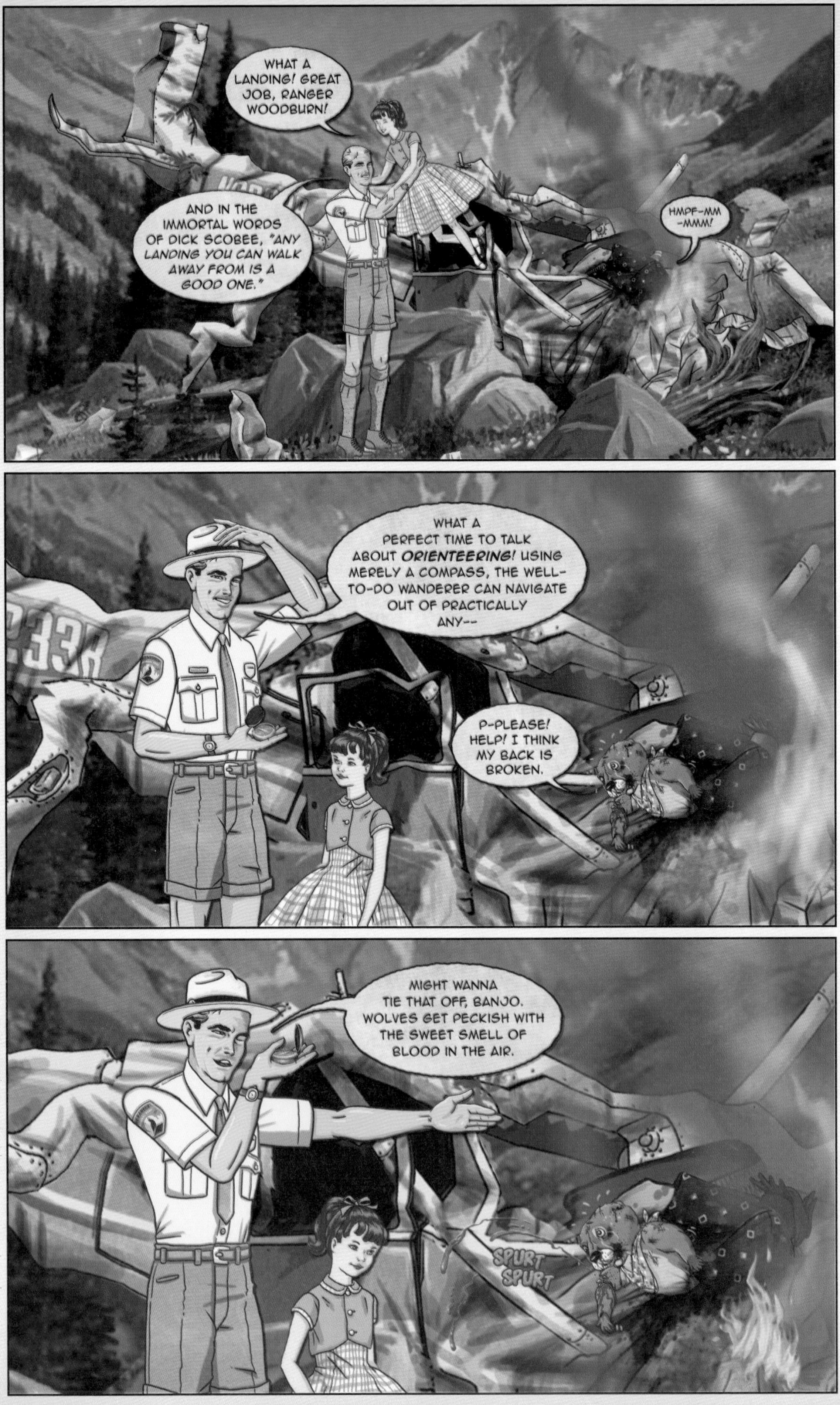
WHAT A LANDING! GREAT JOB, RANGER WOODBURN!
AND IN THE IMMORTAL WORDS OF DICK SCOBEE, "ANY LANDING YOU CAN WALK AWAY FROM IS A GOOD ONE."
HMPF-MM -MMM!
WHAT A PERFECT TIME TO TALK ABOUT ORIENTEERING! USING MERELY A COMPASS, THE WELL-TO-DO WANDERER CAN NAVIGATE OUT OF PRACTICALLY ANY--
P-PLEASE! HELP! I THINK MY BACK IS BROKEN.
MIGHT WANNA TIE THAT OFF, BANJO. WOLVES GET PECKISH WITH THE SWEET SMELL OF BLOOD IN THE AIR.
SPURT SPURT

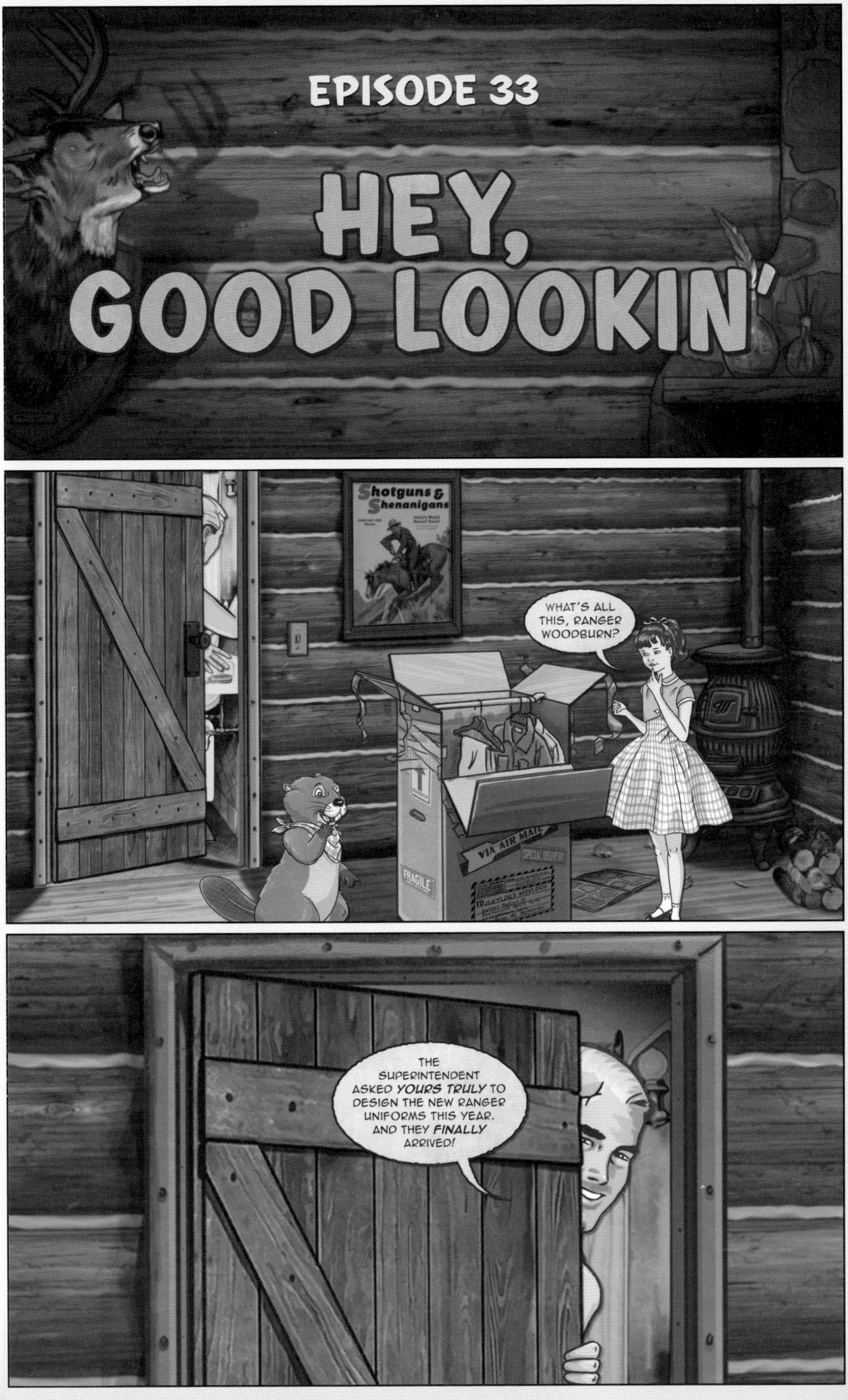
EPISODE 33
HEY, GOOD LOOKIN'
Shotguns & Shenanigans
VIA AIR MAIL
SPECIAL DELIVERY
FRAGILE
WHAT'S ALL THIS, RANGER WOODBURN?
THE SUPERINTENDENT ASKED *YOURS TRULY* TO DESIGN THE NEW RANGER UNIFORMS THIS YEAR, AND THEY *FINALLY* ARRIVED!

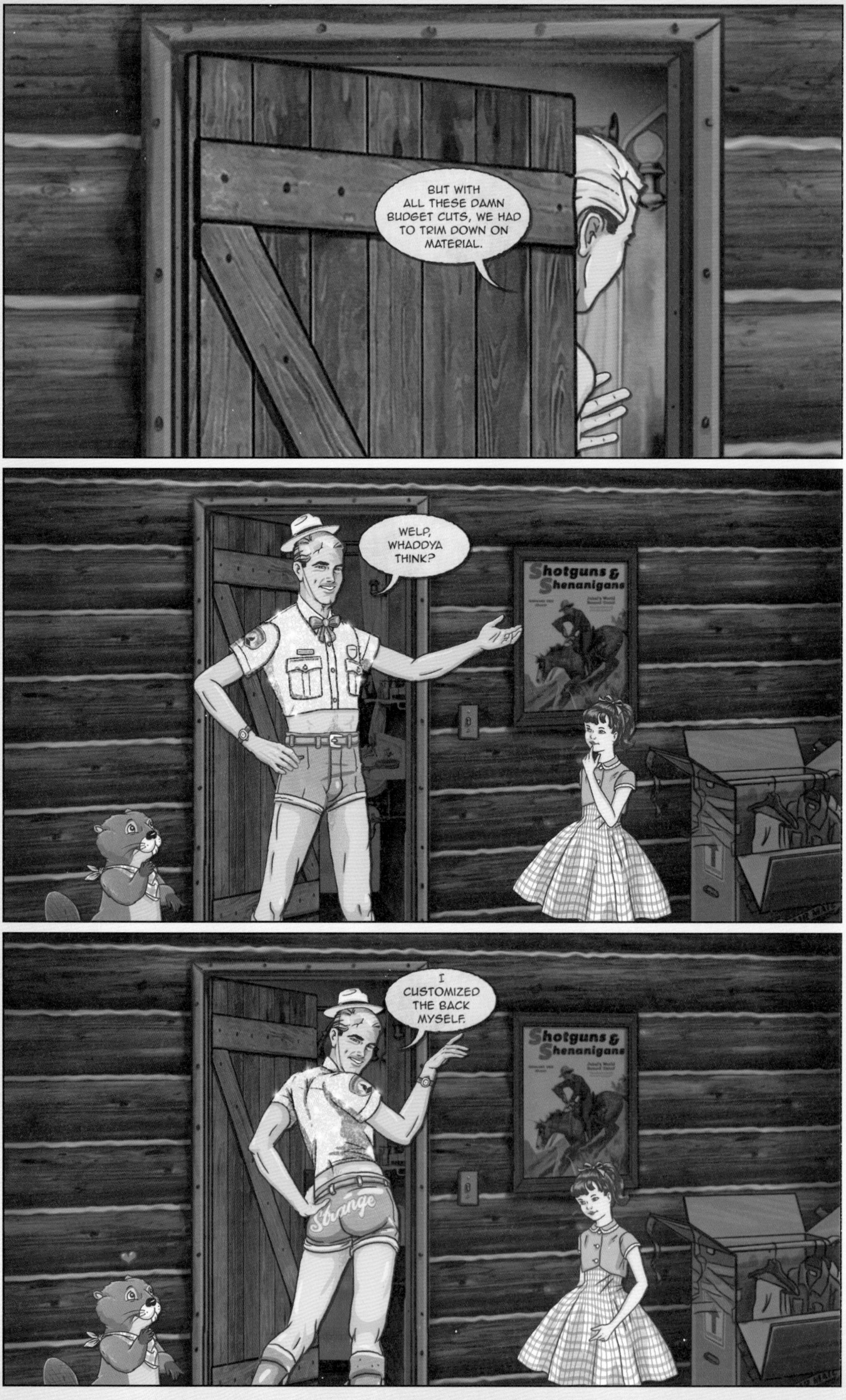
BUT WITH ALL THESE DAMN BUDGET CUTS, WE HAD TO TRIM DOWN ON MATERIAL.
WELP, WHADDYA THINK?
Shotguns & Shenanigans
I CUSTOMIZED THE BACK MYSELF.
Shotguns & Shenanigans
Strange

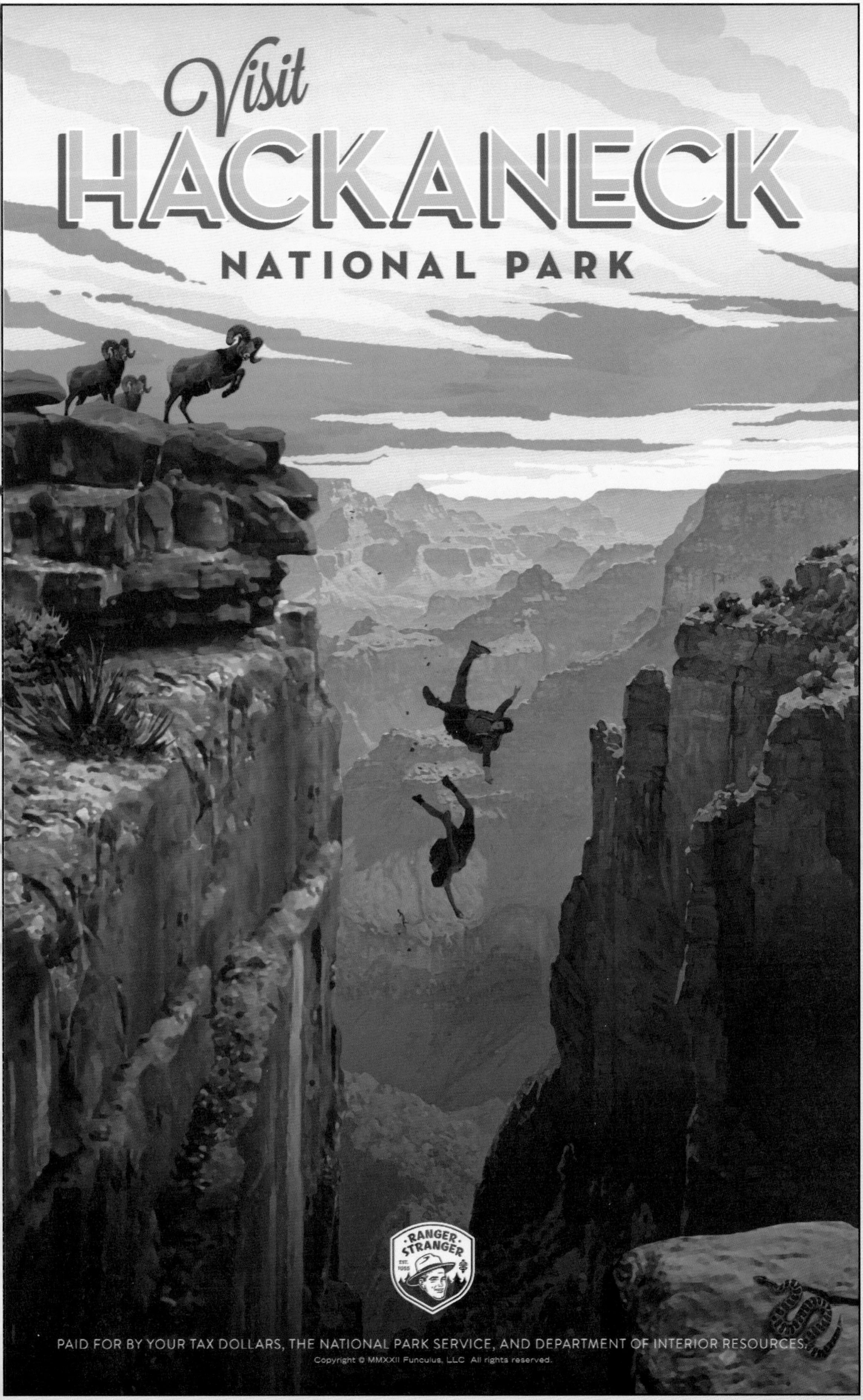
Visit
HACKANECK
NATIONAL PARK
RANGER
STRANGER
EST.
PAID FOR BY YOUR TAX DOLLARS, THE NATIONAL PARK SERVICE, AND DEPARTMENT OF INTERIOR RESOURCES.
Copyright © MMXXII Funculus, LLC All rights reserved.

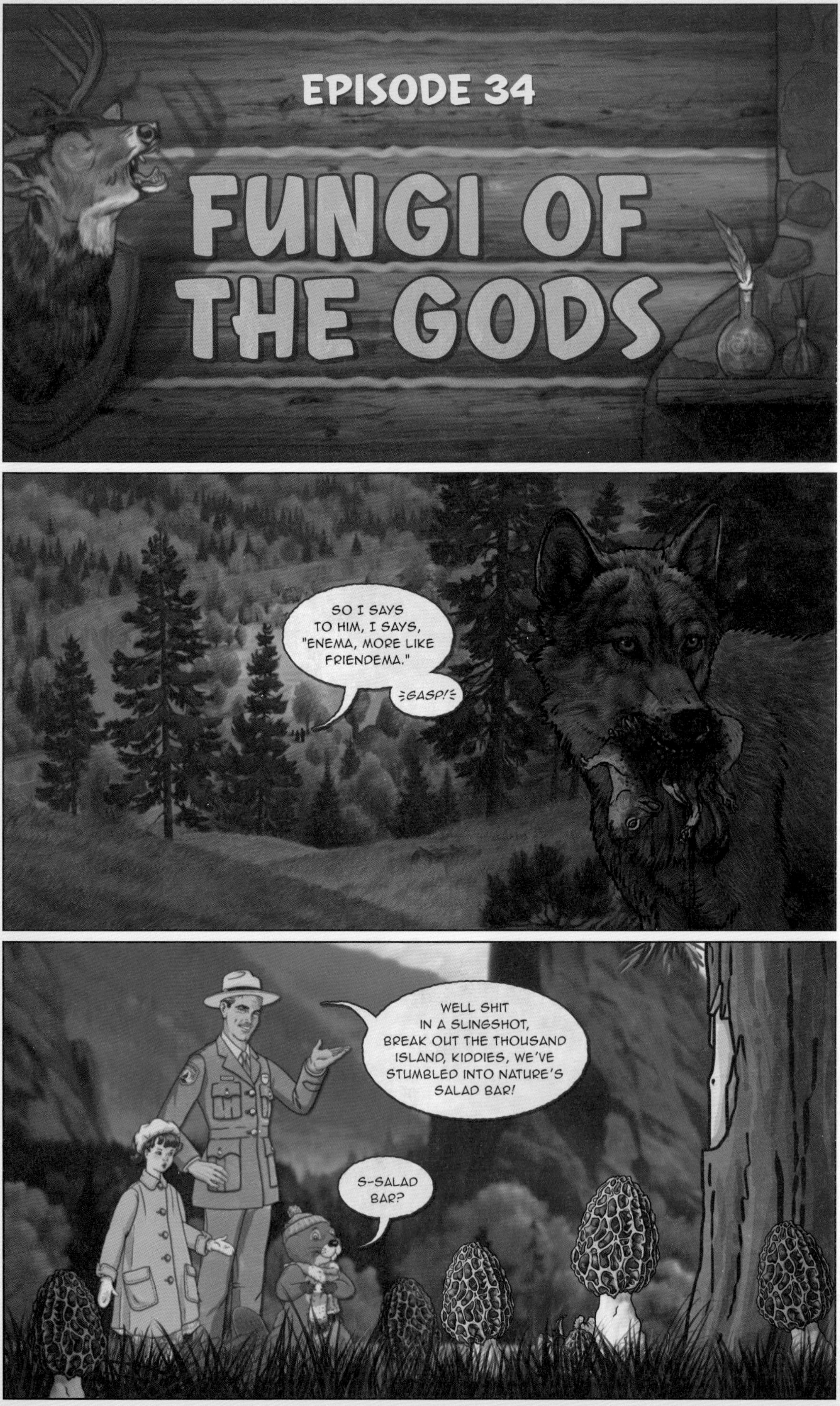
EPISODE 34
FUNGI OF THE GODS
SO I SAYS TO HIM, I SAYS, "ENEMA, MORE LIKE FRIENDEMA."
GASP!
WELL SHIT IN A SLINGSHOT, BREAK OUT THE THOUSAND ISLAND, KIDDIES, WE'VE STUMBLED INTO NATURE'S SALAD BAR!
S-SALAD BAR?

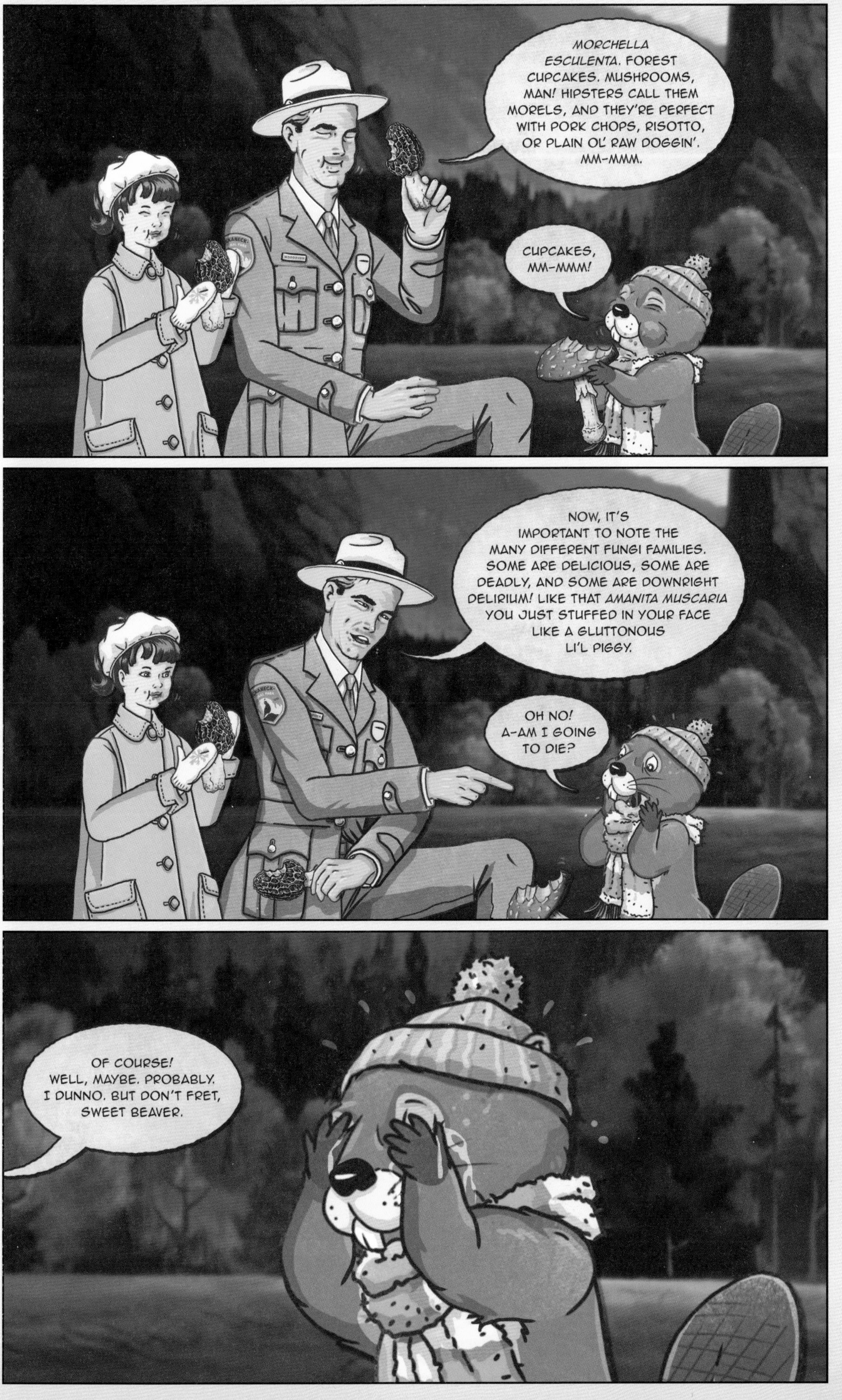
MORCHELLA ESCULENTA. FOREST CUPCAKES. MUSHROOMS, MAN! HIPSTERS CALL THEM MORELS, AND THEY'RE PERFECT WITH PORK CHOPS, RISOTTO, OR PLAIN OL' RAW DOGGIN'. MM-MMM.
CUPCAKES, MM-MMM!
NOW, IT'S IMPORTANT TO NOTE THE MANY DIFFERENT FUNGI FAMILIES. SOME ARE DELICIOUS, SOME ARE DEADLY, AND SOME ARE DOWNRIGHT DELIRIUM! LIKE THAT AMANITA MUSCARIA YOU JUST STUFFED IN YOUR FACE LIKE A GLUTTONOUS LI'L PIGGY.
OH NO! A-AM I GOING TO DIE?
OF COURSE! WELL, MAYBE. PROBABLY. I DUNNO. BUT DON'T FRET, SWEET BEAVER.

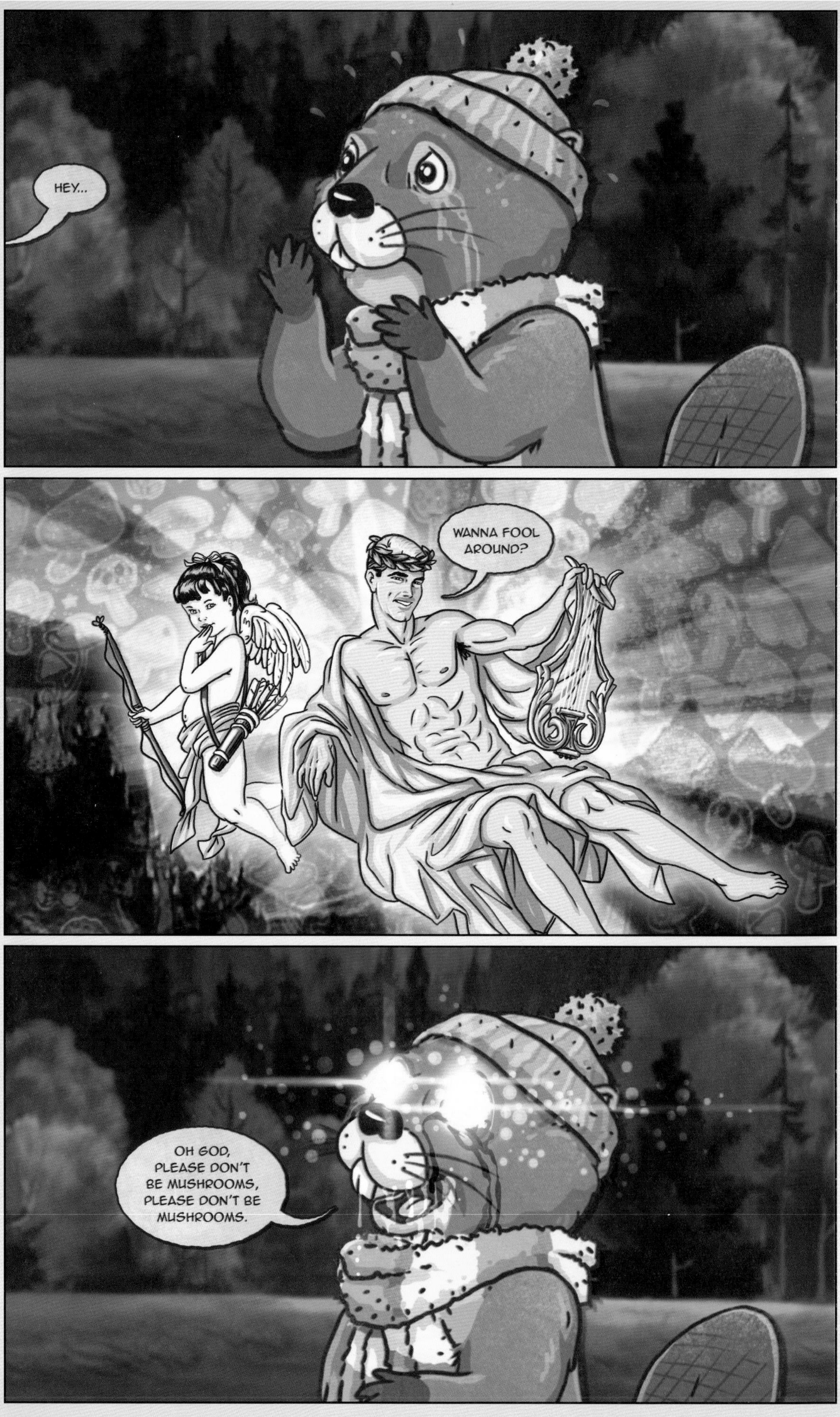
HEY...
WANNA FOOL AROUND?
OH GOD, PLEASE DON'T BE MUSHROOMS, PLEASE DON'T BE MUSHROOMS.

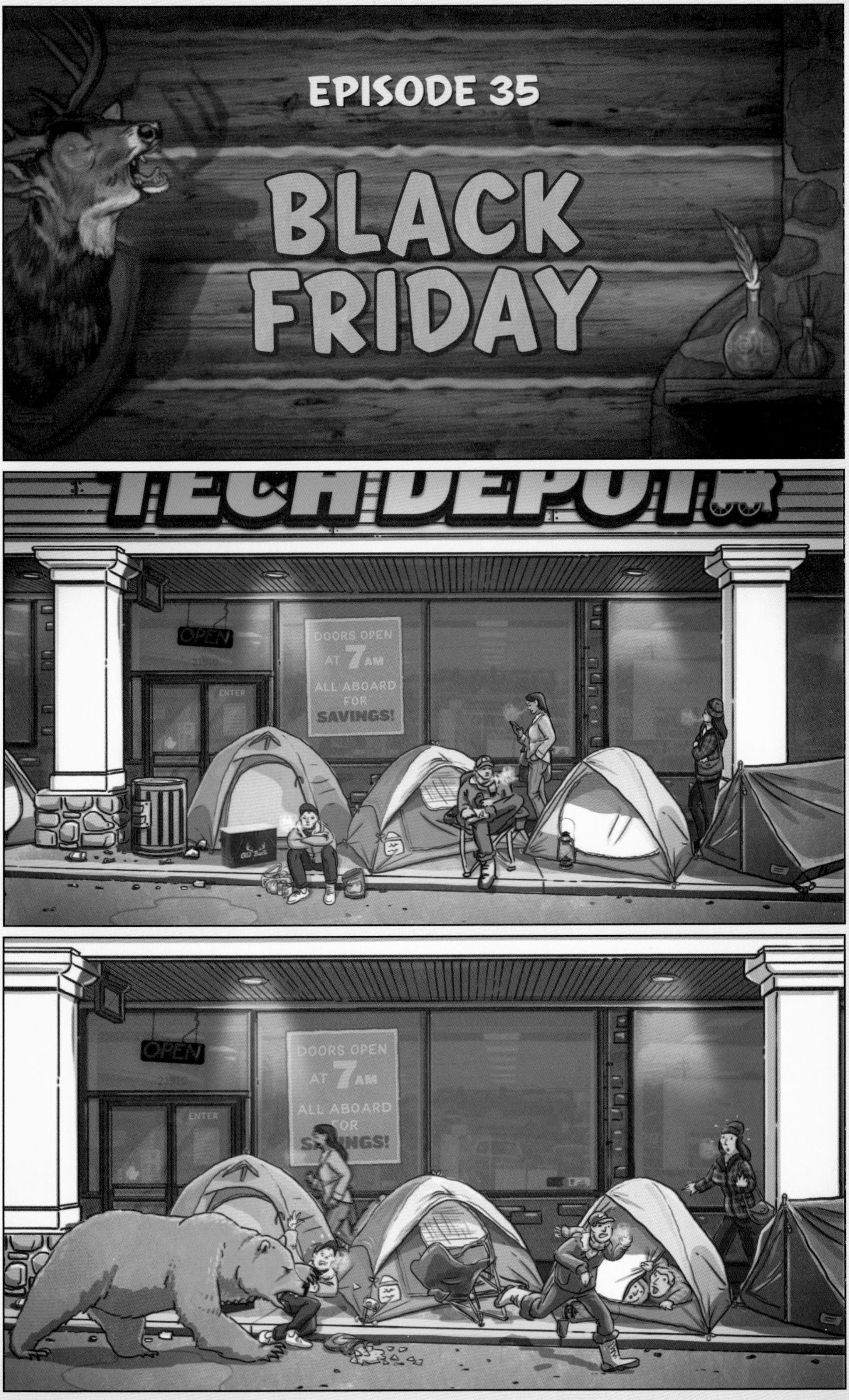
EPISODE 35
BLACK FRIDAY
TECH DEPOT
OPEN
ENTER
DOORS OPEN AT 7AM ALL ABOARD FOR SAVINGS!
OPEN
ENTER
DOORS OPEN AT 7AM ALL ABOARD FOR SAVINGS!

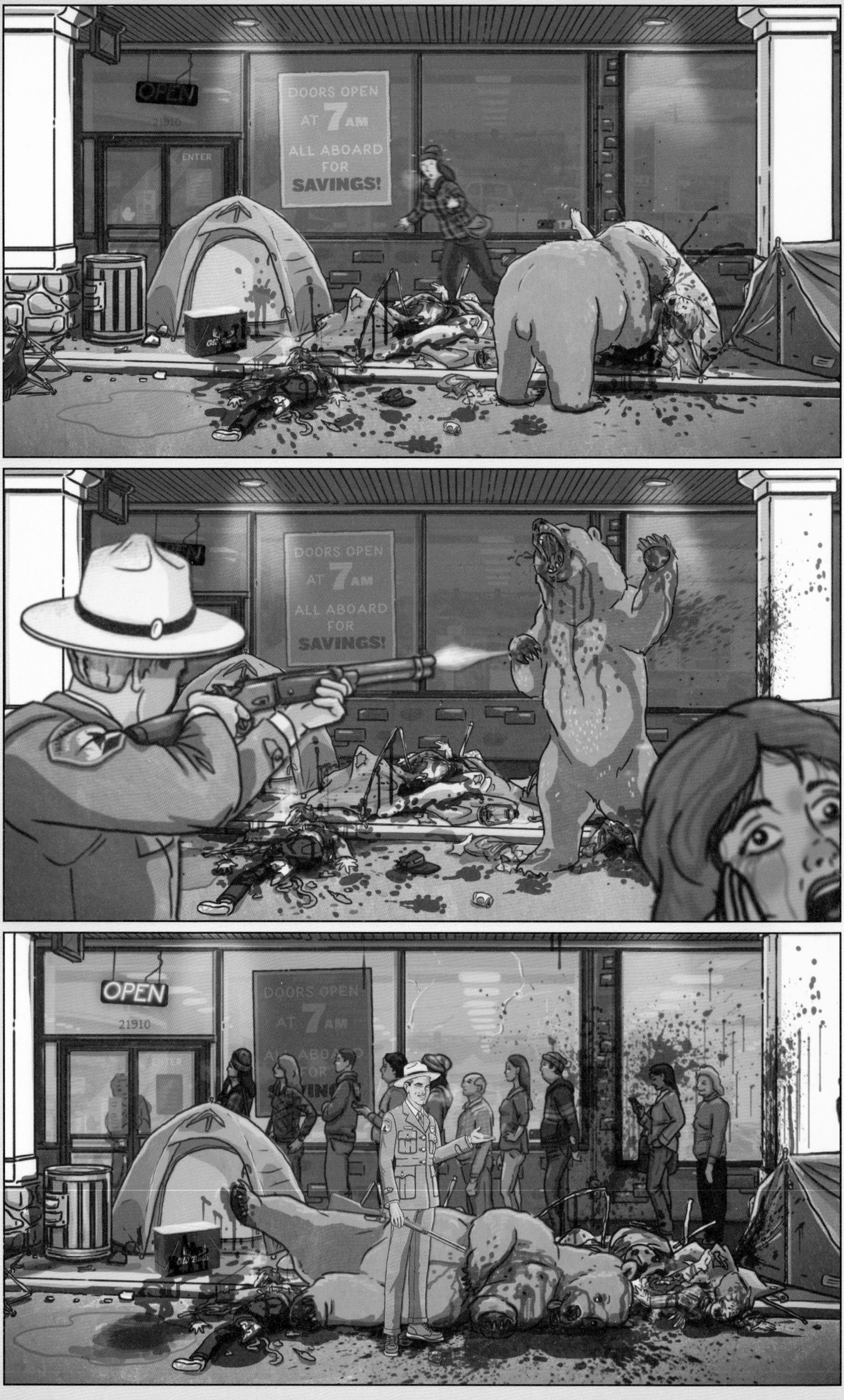
OPEN
21910
ENTER
DOORS OPEN
AT 7AM
ALL ABOARD
FOR
SAVINGS!
DOORS OPEN
AT 7AM
ALL ABOARD
FOR
SAVINGS!
OPEN
21910
ENTER
DOORS OPEN
AT 7AM

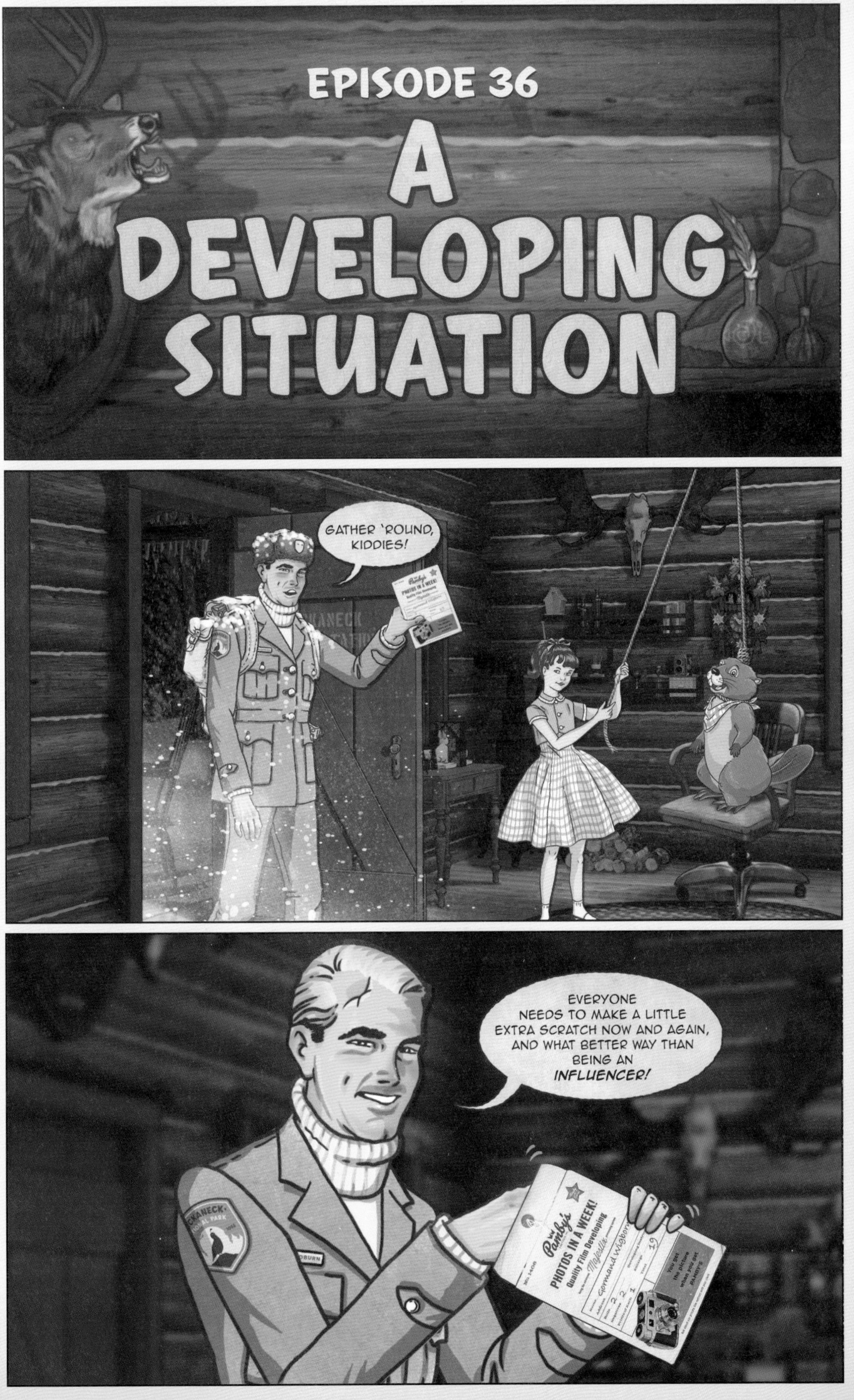
EPISODE 36
A DEVELOPING SITUATION
GATHER 'ROUND, KIDDIES!
EVERYONE NEEDS TO MAKE A LITTLE EXTRA SCRATCH NOW AND AGAIN, AND WHAT BETTER WAY THAN BEING AN *INFLUENCER!*
PHOTOS IN A WEEK!
Quality Film Developing

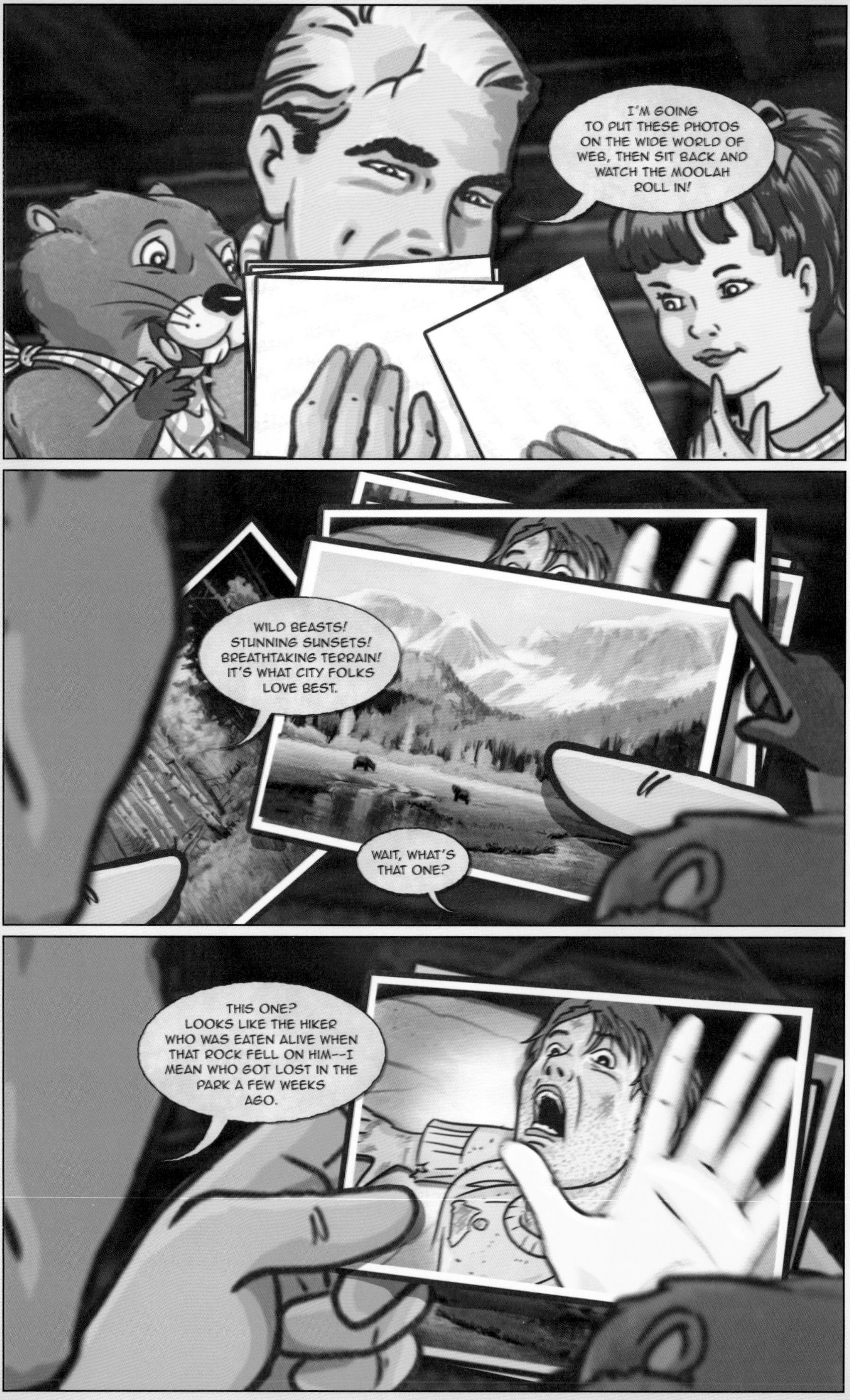
I'M GOING TO PUT THESE PHOTOS ON THE WIDE WORLD OF WEB, THEN SIT BACK AND WATCH THE MOOLAH ROLL IN!
WILD BEASTS! STUNNING SUNSETS! BREATHTAKING TERRAIN! IT'S WHAT CITY FOLKS LOVE BEST.
WAIT, WHAT'S THAT ONE?
THIS ONE? LOOKS LIKE THE HIKER WHO WAS EATEN ALIVE WHEN THAT ROCK FELL ON HIM--I MEAN WHO GOT LOST IN THE PARK A FEW WEEKS AGO.

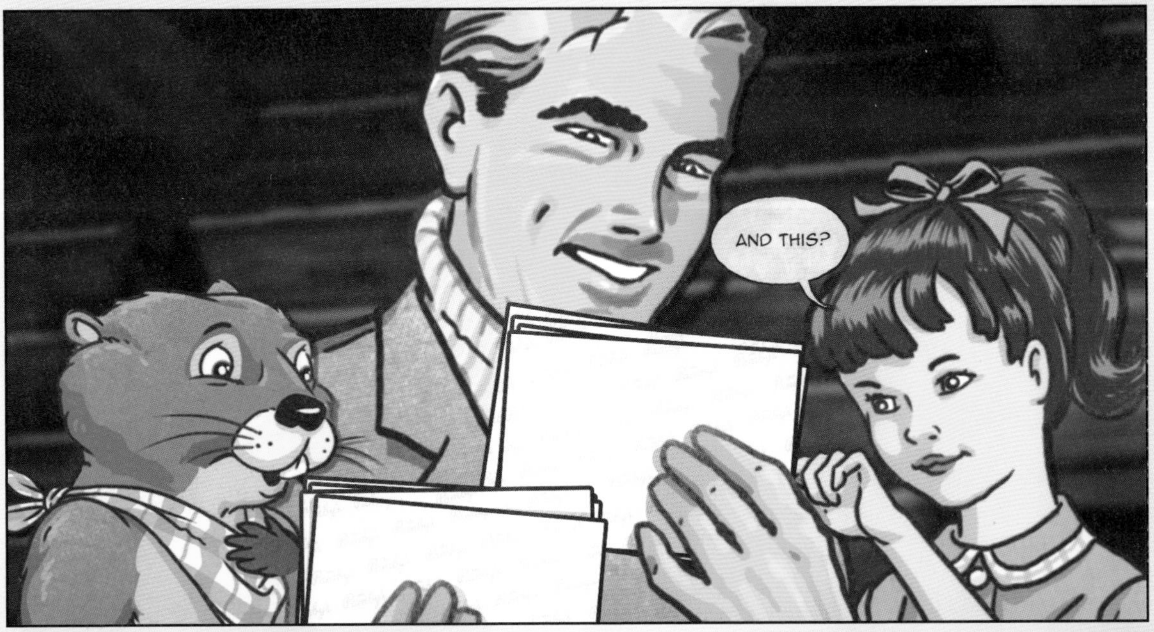
AND THIS?

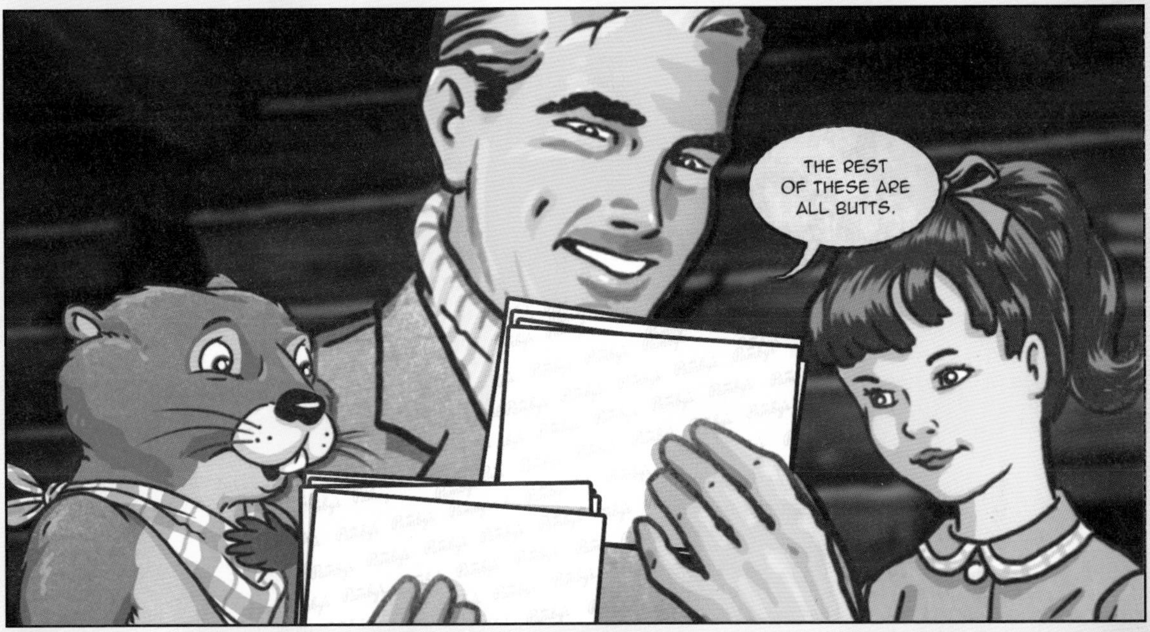
THE REST OF THESE ARE ALL BUTTS.

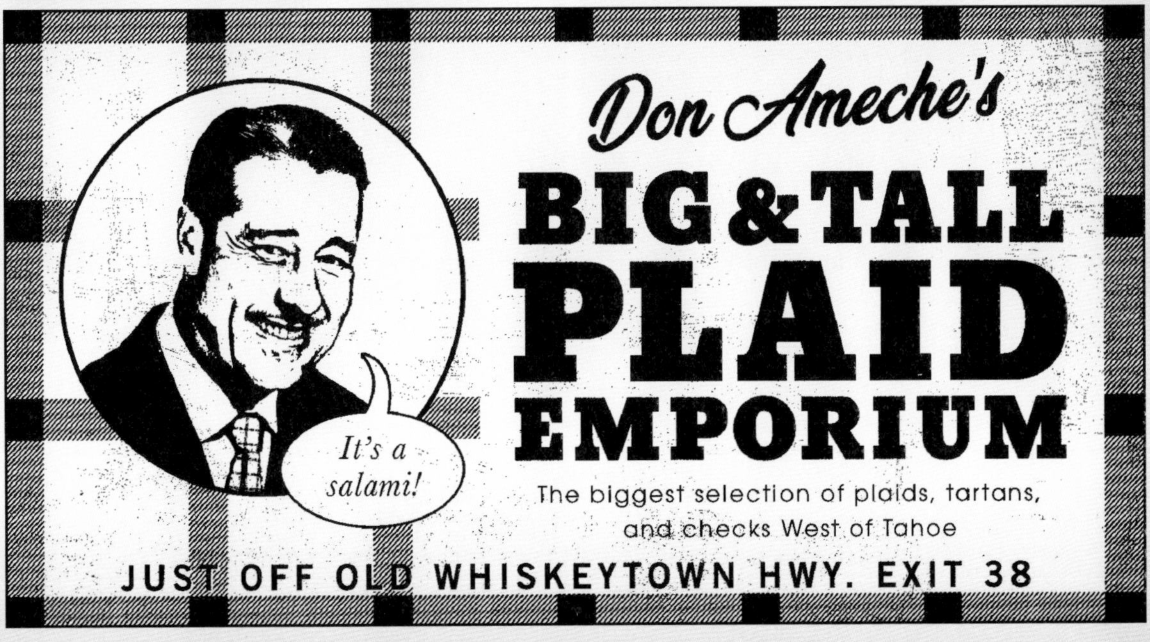
It's a salami!
Don Ameche's
BIG & TALL
PLAID
EMPORIUM
The biggest selection of plaids, tartans, and checks West of Tahoe
JUST OFF OLD WHISKEYTOWN HWY. EXIT 38

FIRESIDE STORIES: THE THIRD EYE

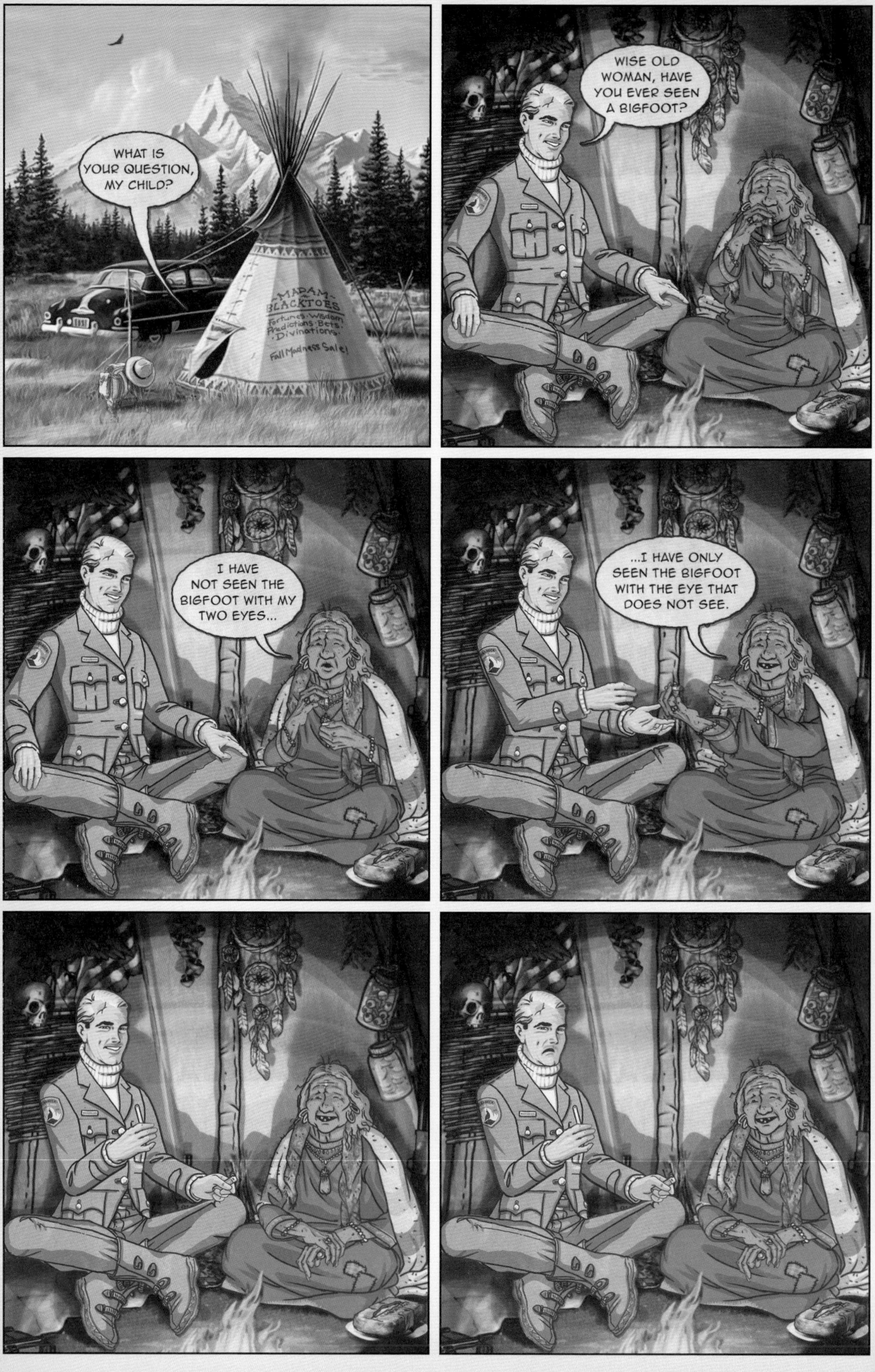
WHAT IS YOUR QUESTION, MY CHILD?
MADAM BLACKTOES
Fortunes·Wisdom Predictions·Bets·Divinations
Fall Madness Sale!
WISE OLD WOMAN, HAVE YOU EVER SEEN A BIGFOOT?
I HAVE NOT SEEN THE BIGFOOT WITH MY TWO EYES...
...I HAVE ONLY SEEN THE BIGFOOT WITH THE EYE THAT DOES NOT SEE.

A LUNKER OF A DISH!

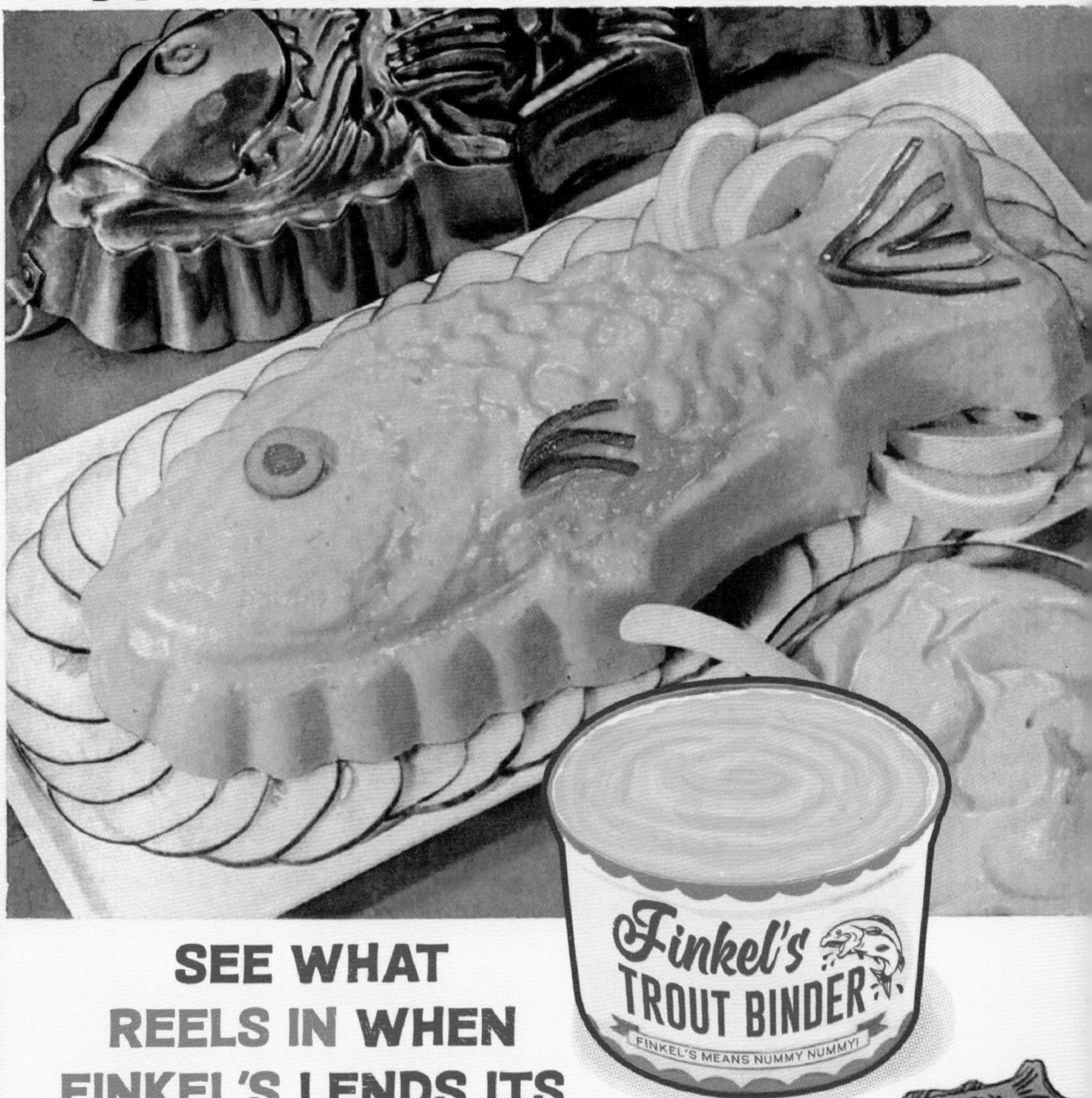

Finkel's
TROUT BINDER
FINKEL'S MEANS NUMMY NUMMY!

SEE WHAT REELS IN WHEN FINKEL'S LENDS ITS FLAVOR TO YOUR NEXT COLD MEAL!

You'll look spiffy with this attractive trout mold and Finkel's trout binder. The delicious way to add flavor and hold to any gelatinous meat serving. Easy to make and sure to compliment the family picnic, social gathering or stressful dinner when your boss comes to visit.

RAINBOW DELIGHT RECIPE (6-8 servings)

2 large scoops Finkel's trout binder gelatin
1/2 cup cold water
1 can tomato soup
2 3oz. pkgs. cream cheese
1 cup mayonnaise
2 whole fish (any species, blended to a thick paste)
1 cup chopped celery
2 tbsps. chopped onion
1/4 cup salt...dash of pepper

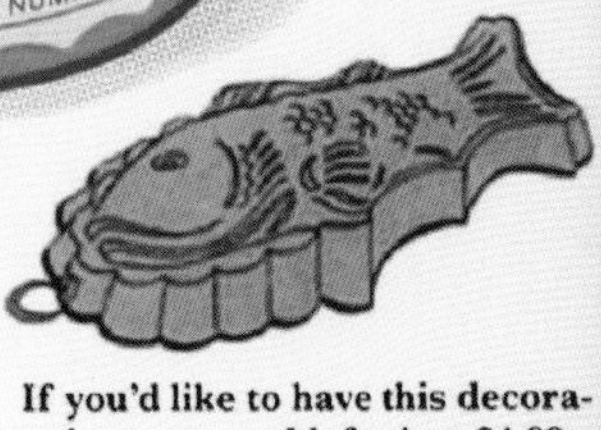

If you'd like to have this decorative trout mold, for just $4.99

MAIL THIS COUPON!

Finkel Co., Box 193, Shelton, Conn.

Please send me that copper-colored 12-inch aluminium fish mold thingy shown in the ad. I enclose $4.99 and label from the tub container of Finkel's.

Name..

Address.......................................

....

City..........................State..........

Zip...

THE FINKEL BYPRODUCT COMPANY IS A DIVISION OF PAMBY'S FOOD MANUF., BATTLE CREEK, MICH.

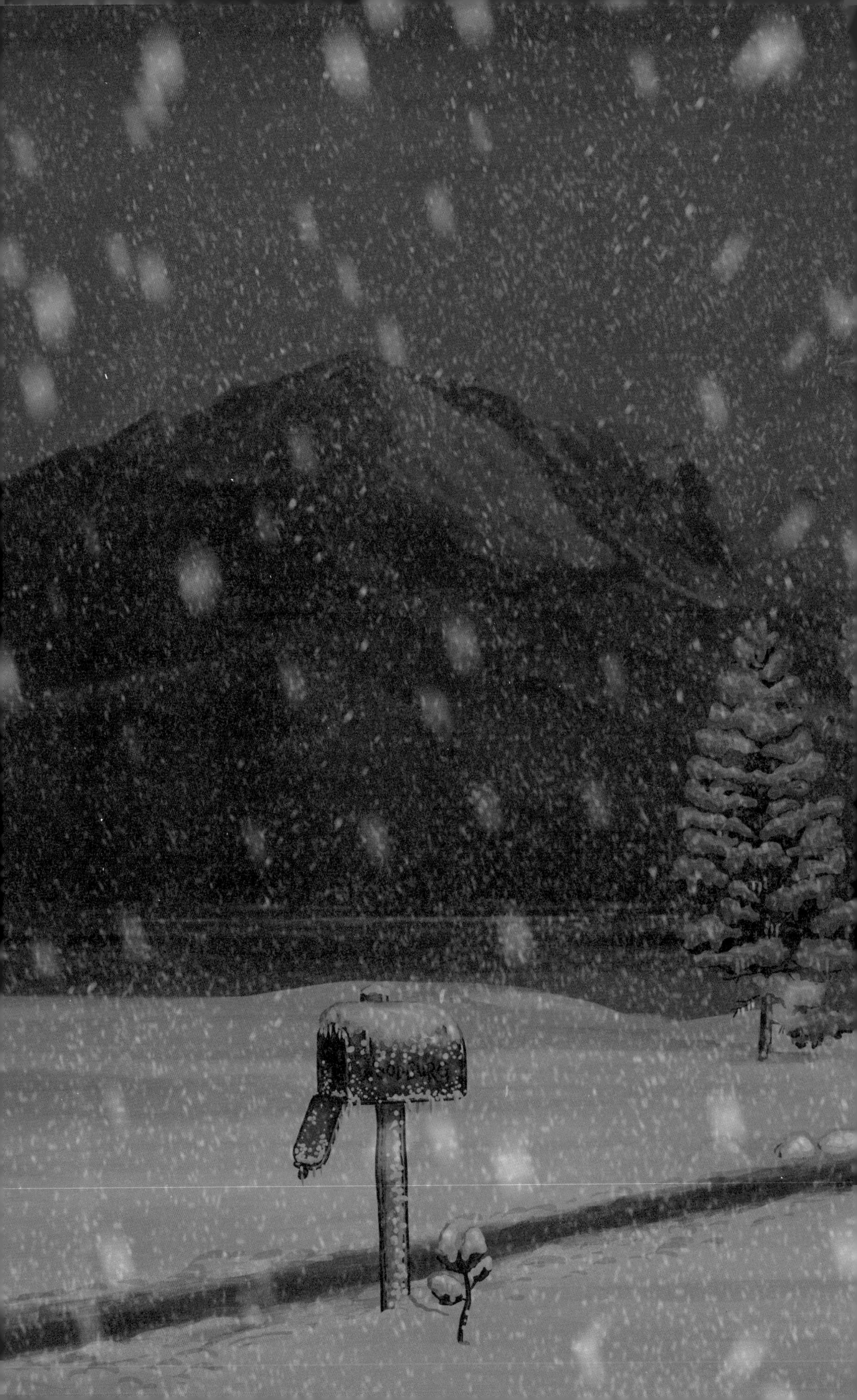

WINTER

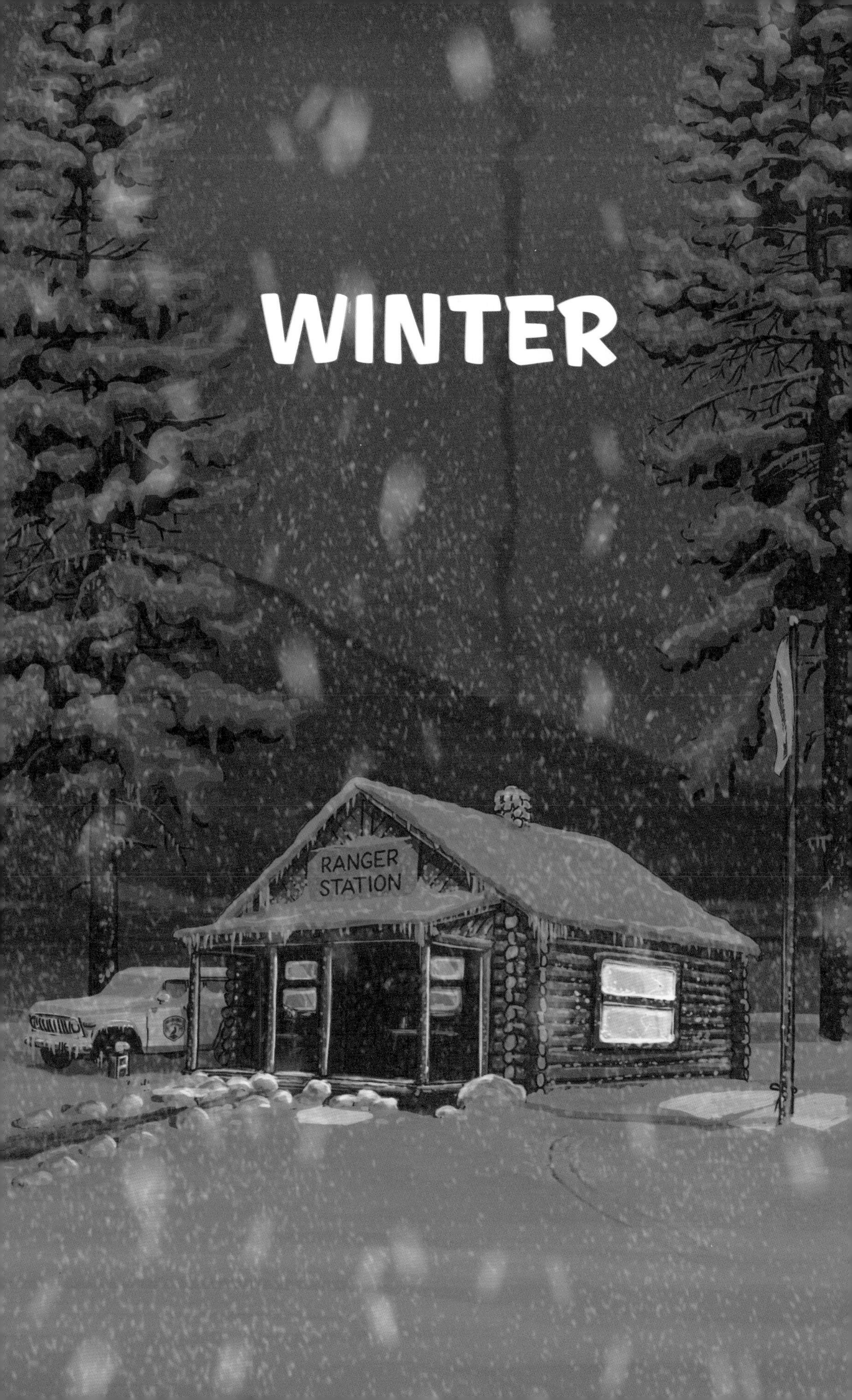
RANGER
STATION

LIGHT READING FOR THE DARKEST DAYS OF THE YEAR

GREETINGS, CAMPERS! AS THE NIGHTS GET LONG AND THE DEPRESSION LONGER, IT'S IMPORTANT TO KEEP THE MIND HAPPY AND HEALTHY. THIS IS WHY WE'RE PLEASED TO BRING YOU A VERY SPECIAL SEASONAL ISSUE OF *RANGER STRANGER*. BRIMMING WITH QUESTIONABLE CAMPING TIPS, AWFUL NATURE JOKES, OUTDOOR CHEER, AND HOLIDAY JEER, IT'S GUARANTEED TO LIFT THE SPIRITS THROUGH THE COLD, LONELY, GLOOMY, WOEFUL, MELANCHOLY MONTHS LYING IN WAIT JUST AROUND THE BEND. SO, CUT A SMILE ON YOUR FACE, TOP OFF THAT TODDY, JUMP INTO THOSE JAMMIES, AND CUDDLE UP... WITH ME. AND SOME OTHER FOLKS.

RANGER GARLAND WOODBURN
HACKANECK NATIONAL PARK

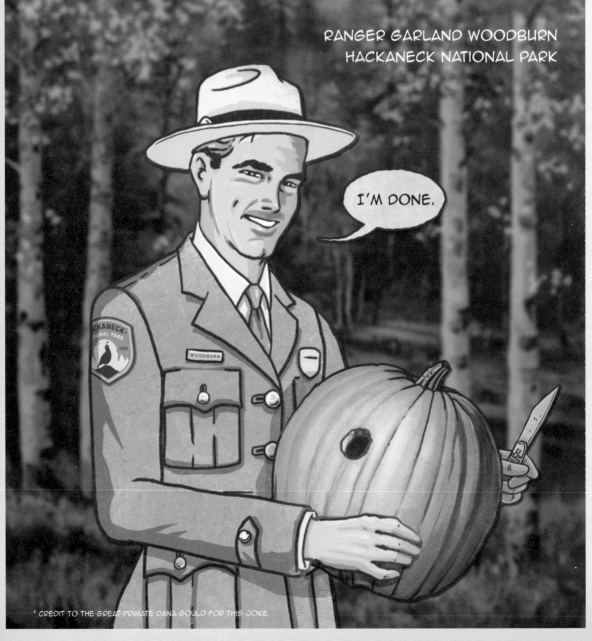

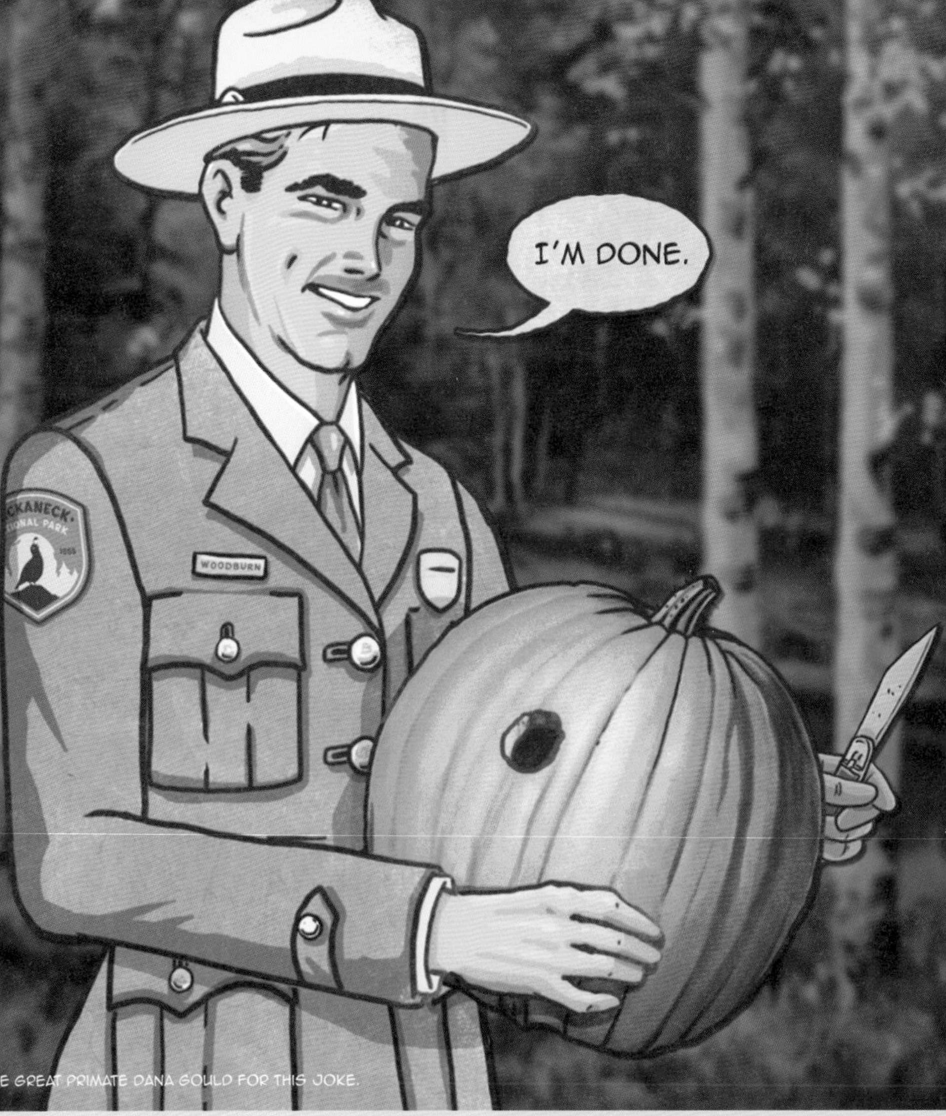
I'M DONE.
WOODBURN

* CREDIT TO THE GREAT PRIMATE DANA GOULD FOR THIS JOKE.

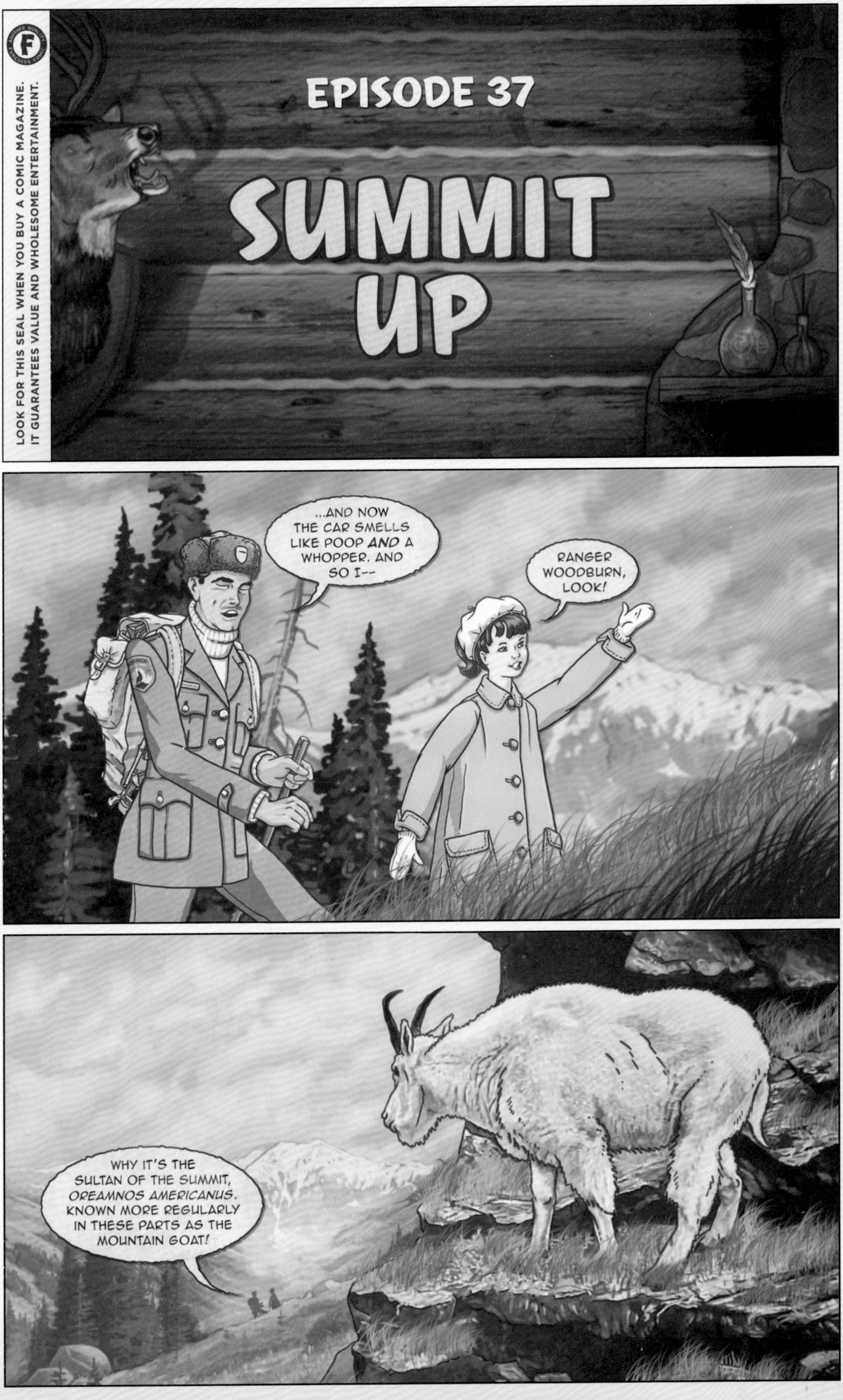
LOOK FOR THIS SEAL WHEN YOU BUY A COMIC MAGAZINE. IT GUARANTEES VALUE AND WHOLESOME ENTERTAINMENT.
EPISODE 37
SUMMIT UP
...AND NOW THE CAR SMELLS LIKE POOP *AND* A WHOPPER. AND SO I--
RANGER WOODBURN, LOOK!
WHY IT'S THE SULTAN OF THE SUMMIT, *OREAMNOS AMERICANUS*. KNOWN MORE REGULARLY IN THESE PARTS AS THE MOUNTAIN GOAT!

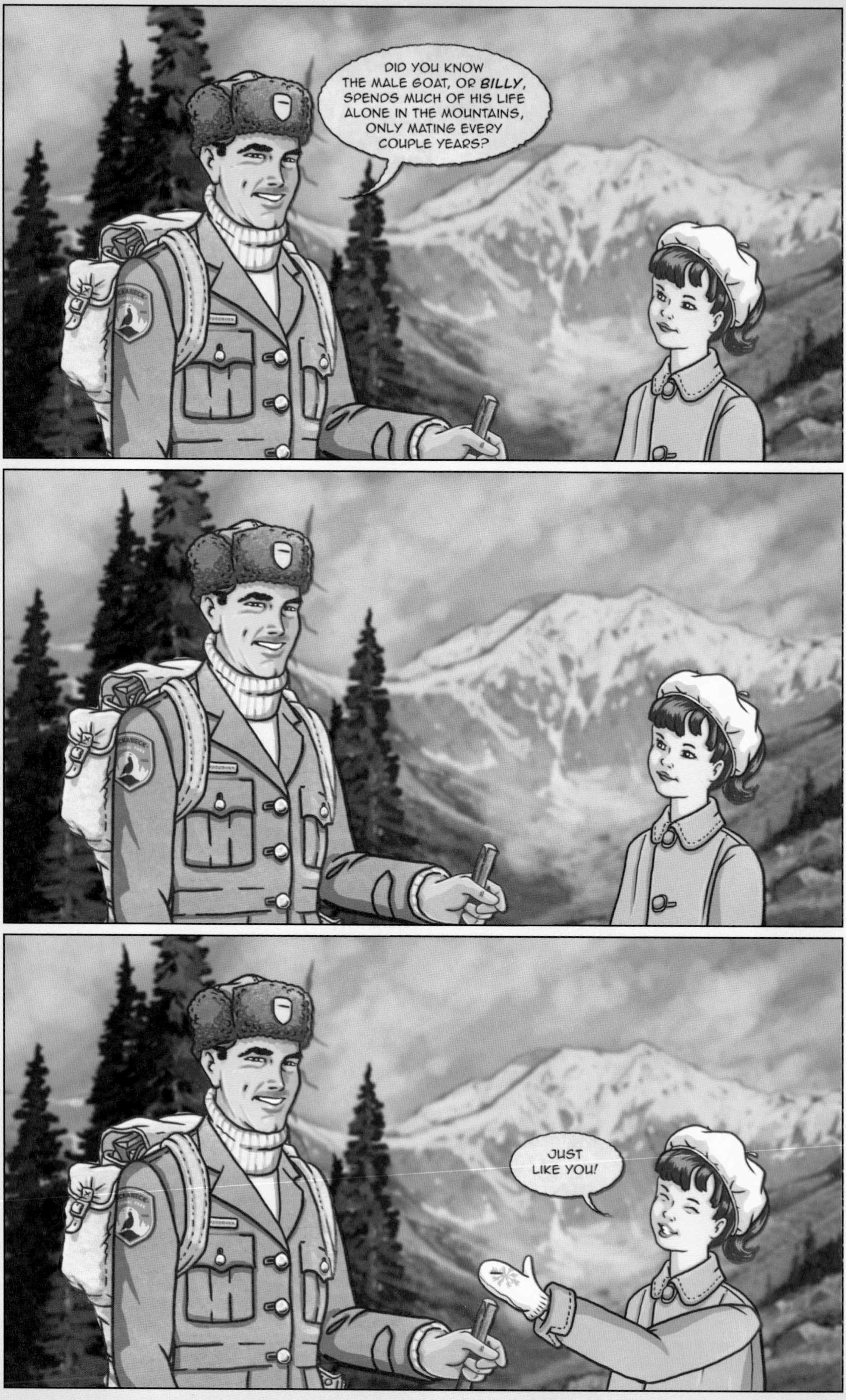
DID YOU KNOW THE MALE GOAT, OR *BILLY*, SPENDS MUCH OF HIS LIFE ALONE IN THE MOUNTAINS, ONLY MATING EVERY COUPLE YEARS?
JUST LIKE YOU!

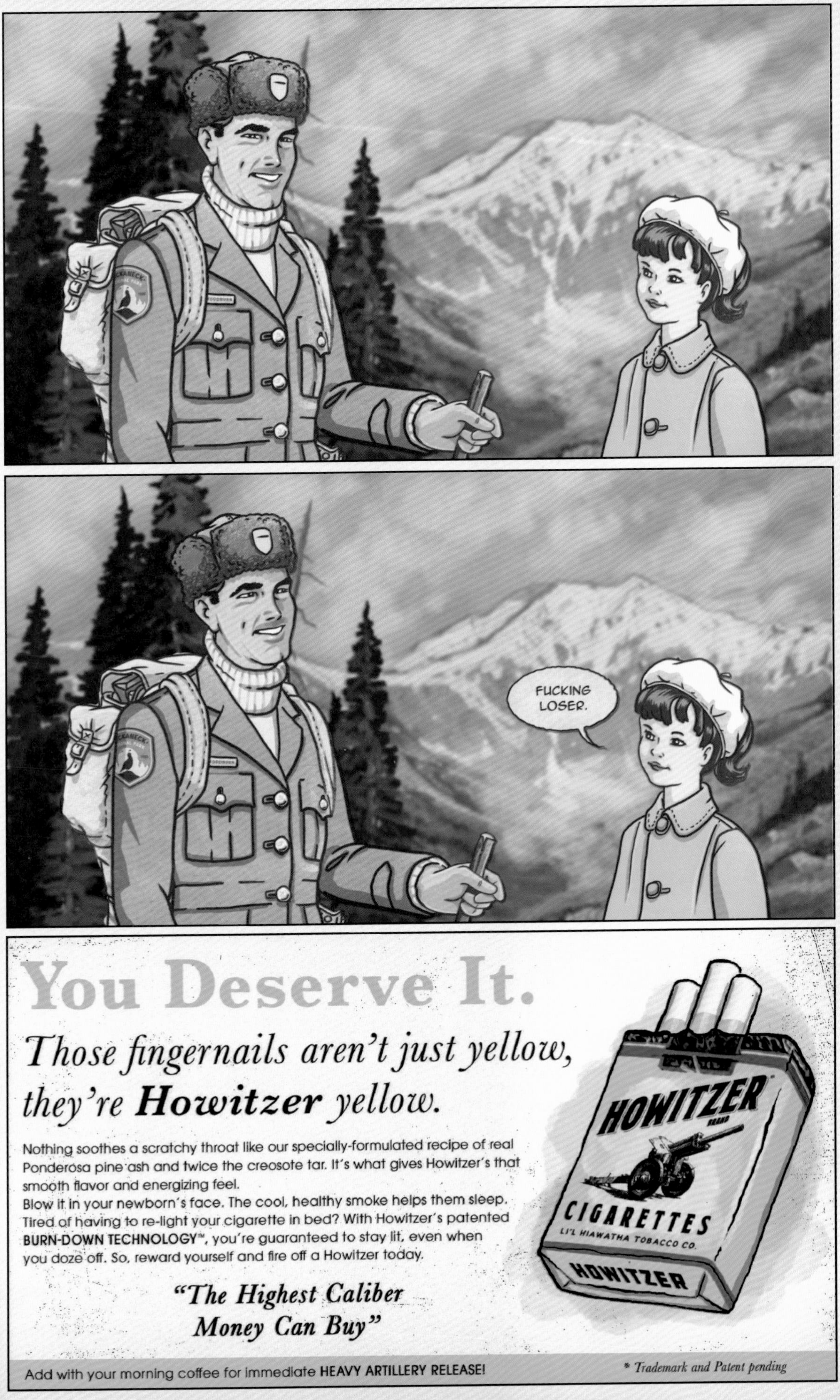
FUCKING LOSER.
You Deserve It.
Those fingernails aren't just yellow, they're Howitzer yellow.
Nothing soothes a scratchy throat like our specially-formulated recipe of real Ponderosa pine ash and twice the creosote tar. It's what gives Howitzer's that smooth flavor and energizing feel.
Blow it in your newborn's face. The cool, healthy smoke helps them sleep.
Tired of having to re-light your cigarette in bed? With Howitzer's patented BURN-DOWN TECHNOLOGY™, you're guaranteed to stay lit, even when you doze off. So, reward yourself and fire off a Howitzer today.
"The Highest Caliber Money Can Buy"
HOWITZER
BRAND
CIGARETTES
LI'L HIAWATHA TOBACCO CO.
HOWITZER
Add with your morning coffee for immediate HEAVY ARTILLERY RELEASE!
* Trademark and Patent pending

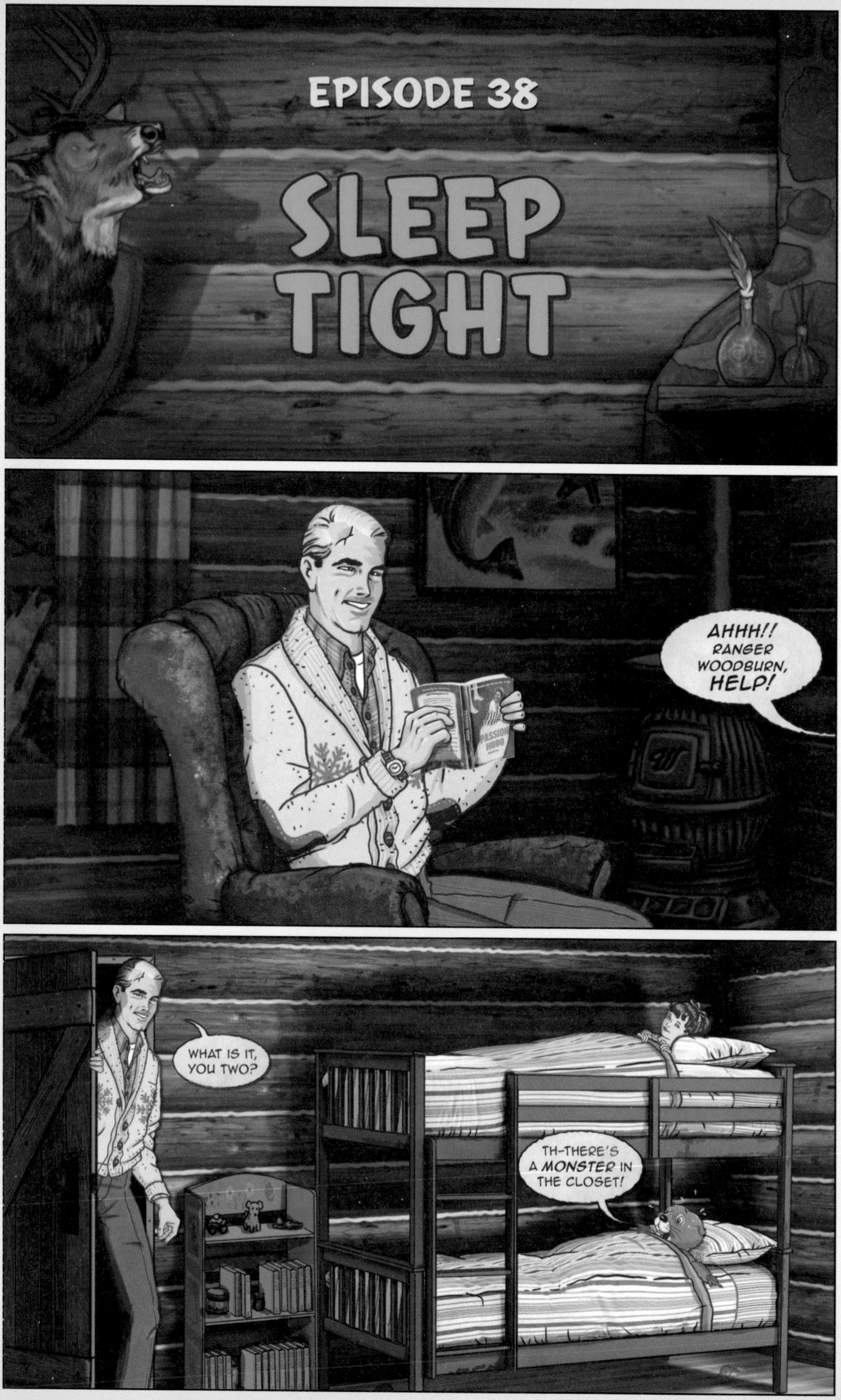
EPISODE 38
SLEEP TIGHT
PASSION HOBO
AHHH!! RANGER WOODBURN, HELP!
WHAT IS IT, YOU TWO?
TH-THERE'S A MONSTER IN THE CLOSET!

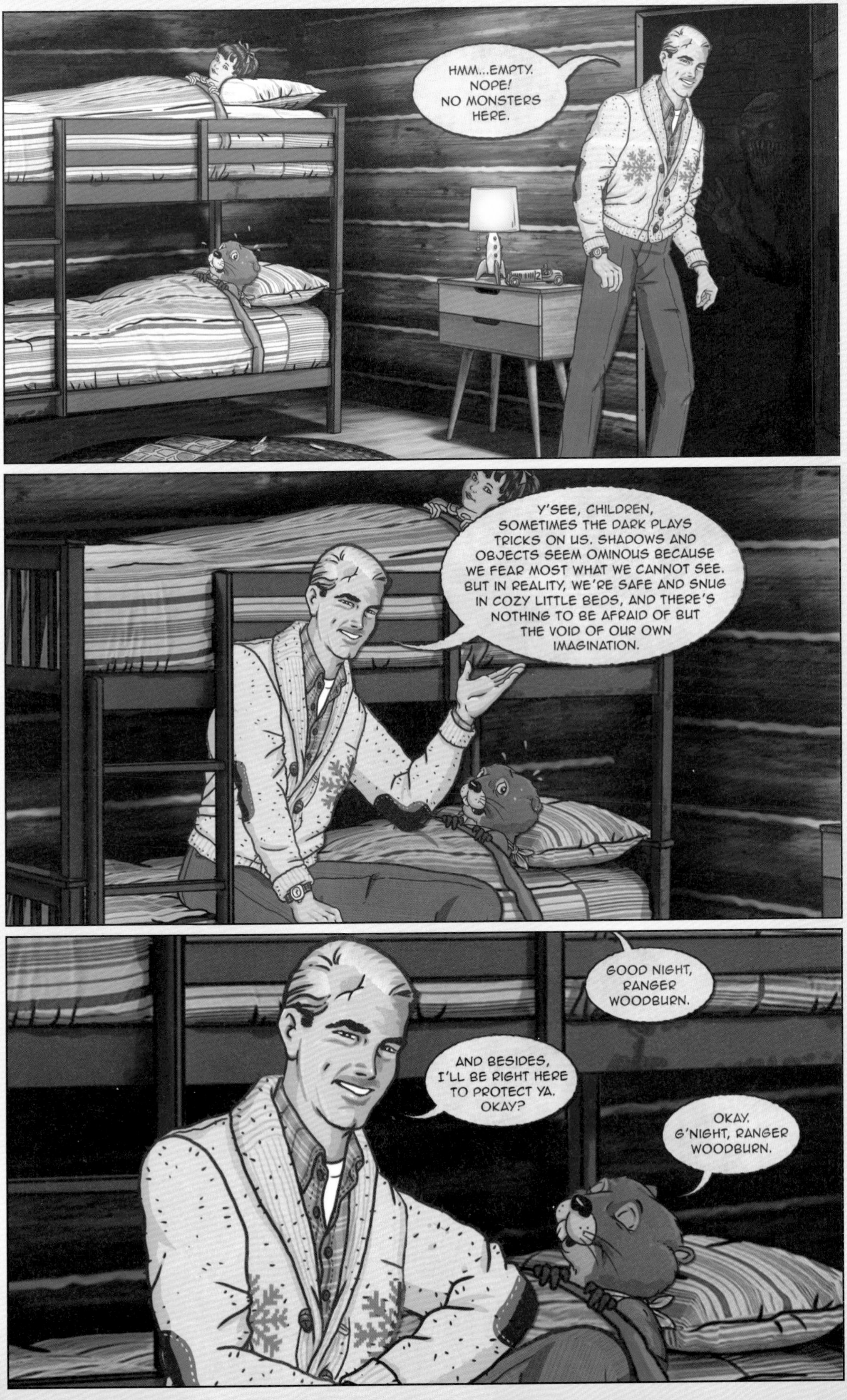
HMM...EMPTY. NOPE! NO MONSTERS HERE.
Y'SEE, CHILDREN, SOMETIMES THE DARK PLAYS TRICKS ON US. SHADOWS AND OBJECTS SEEM OMINOUS BECAUSE WE FEAR MOST WHAT WE CANNOT SEE. BUT IN REALITY, WE'RE SAFE AND SNUG IN COZY LITTLE BEDS, AND THERE'S NOTHING TO BE AFRAID OF BUT THE VOID OF OUR OWN IMAGINATION.
AND BESIDES, I'LL BE RIGHT HERE TO PROTECT YA. OKAY?
GOOD NIGHT, RANGER WOODBURN.
OKAY. G'NIGHT, RANGER WOODBURN.

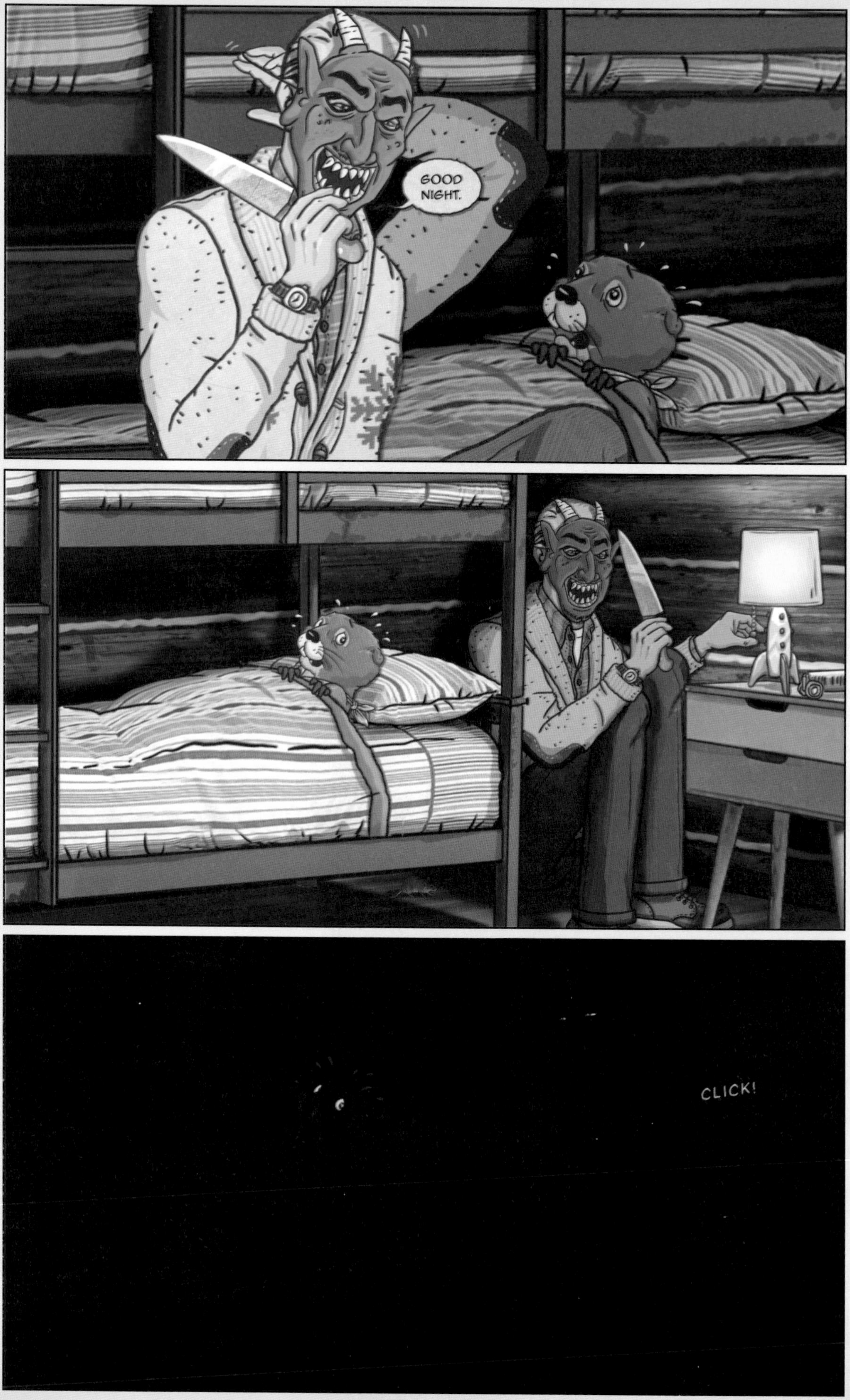
GOOD NIGHT.
CLICK!

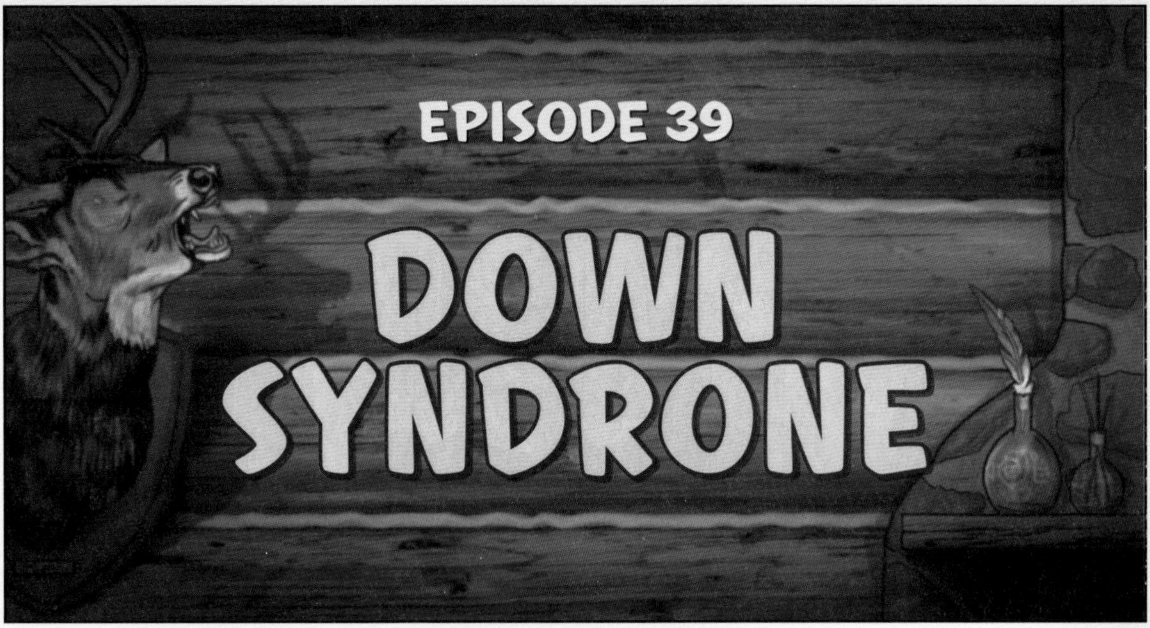
EPISODE 39
DOWN SYNDRONE

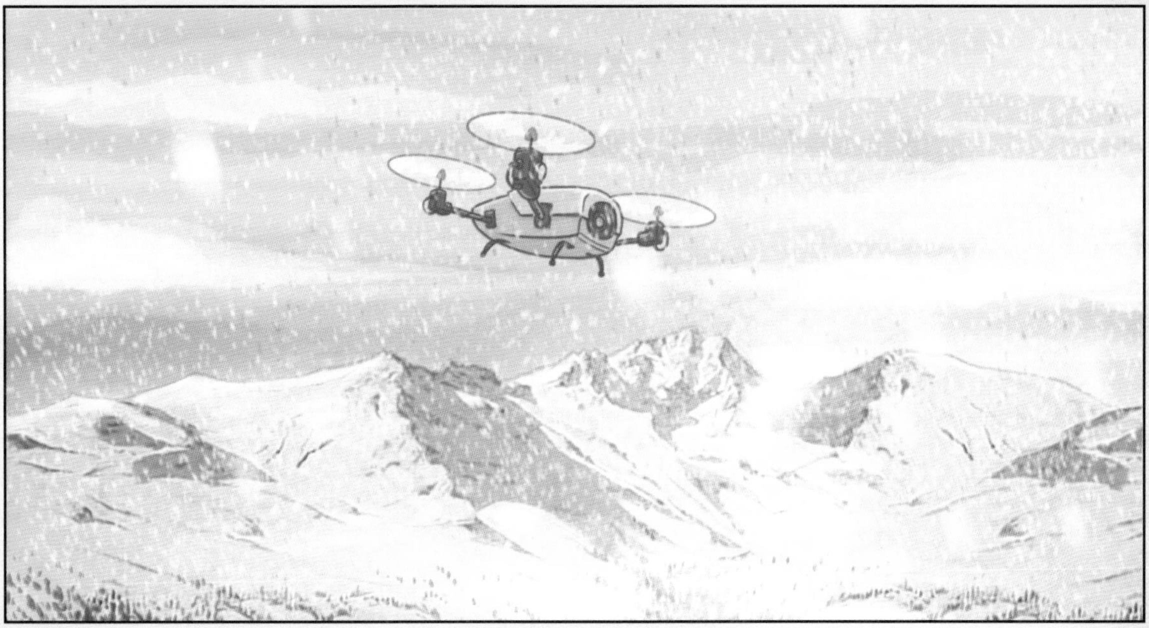

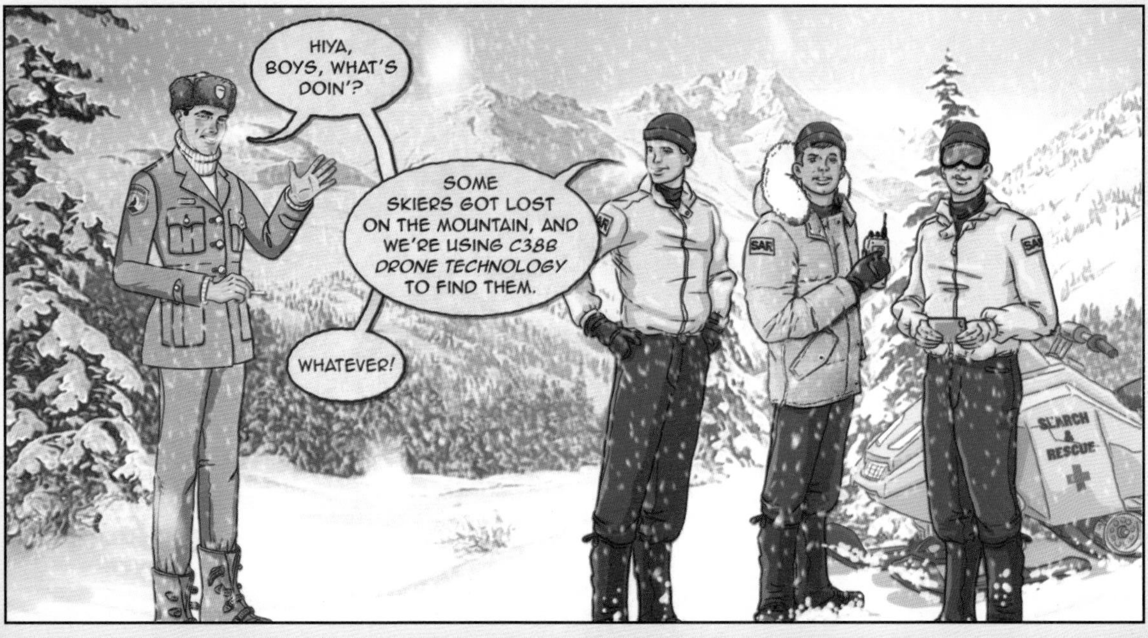
HIYA, BOYS, WHAT'S DOIN'?
SOME SKIERS GOT LOST ON THE MOUNTAIN, AND WE'RE USING C38B DRONE TECHNOLOGY TO FIND THEM.
WHATEVER!
SAR
SAR
SAR
SEARCH & RESCUE

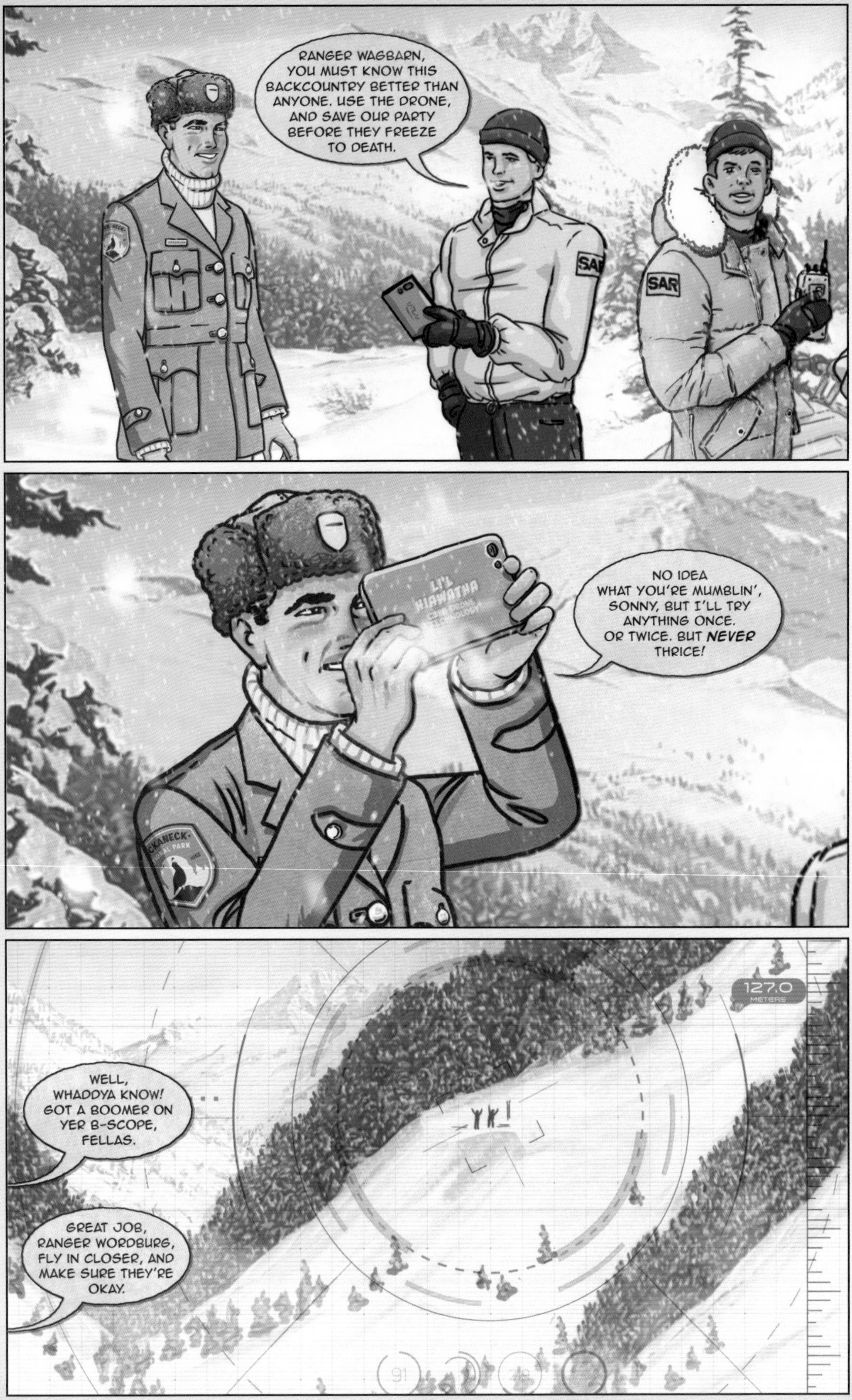

RANGER WAGBARN, YOU MUST KNOW THIS BACKCOUNTRY BETTER THAN ANYONE. USE THE DRONE, AND SAVE OUR PARTY BEFORE THEY FREEZE TO DEATH.
SAR
SAR
LI'L HIAWATHA
NO IDEA WHAT YOU'RE MUMBLIN', SONNY, BUT I'LL TRY ANYTHING ONCE. OR TWICE. BUT *NEVER* THRICE!
127.0
METERS
WELL, WHADDYA KNOW! GOT A BOOMER ON YER B-SCOPE, FELLAS.
GREAT JOB, RANGER WORDBURG, FLY IN CLOSER, AND MAKE SURE THEY'RE OKAY.

8.98
METERS
91
219
0.55
METERS
WE'RE TOO LATE, LADS. MOTHER NATURE HAS, ONCE AGAIN, CLAIMED HER VICTIMS.
0.01
METERS

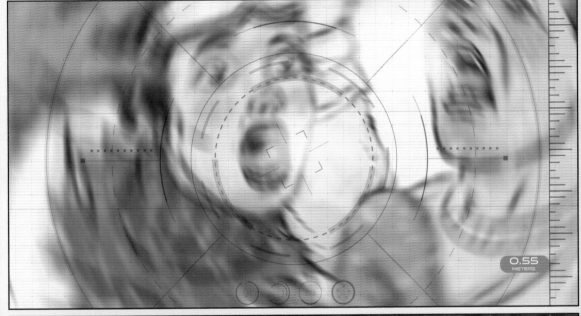

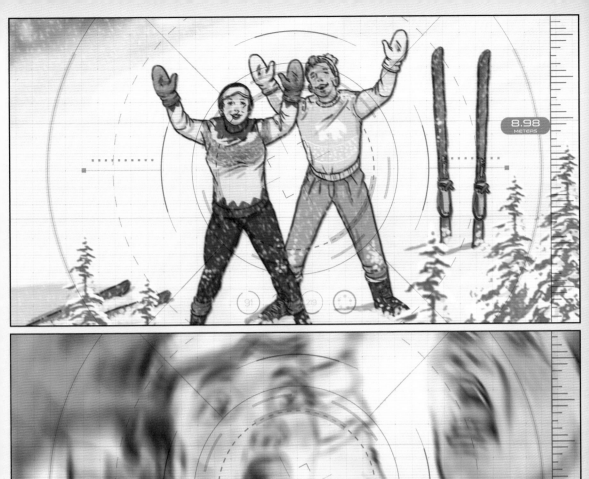

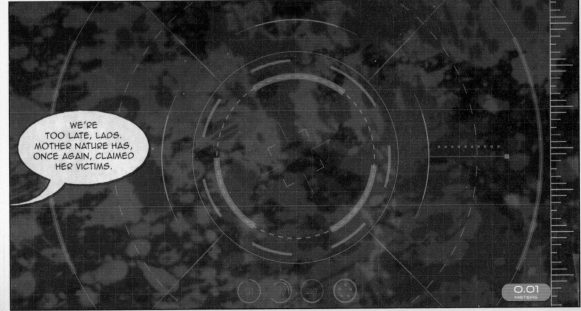

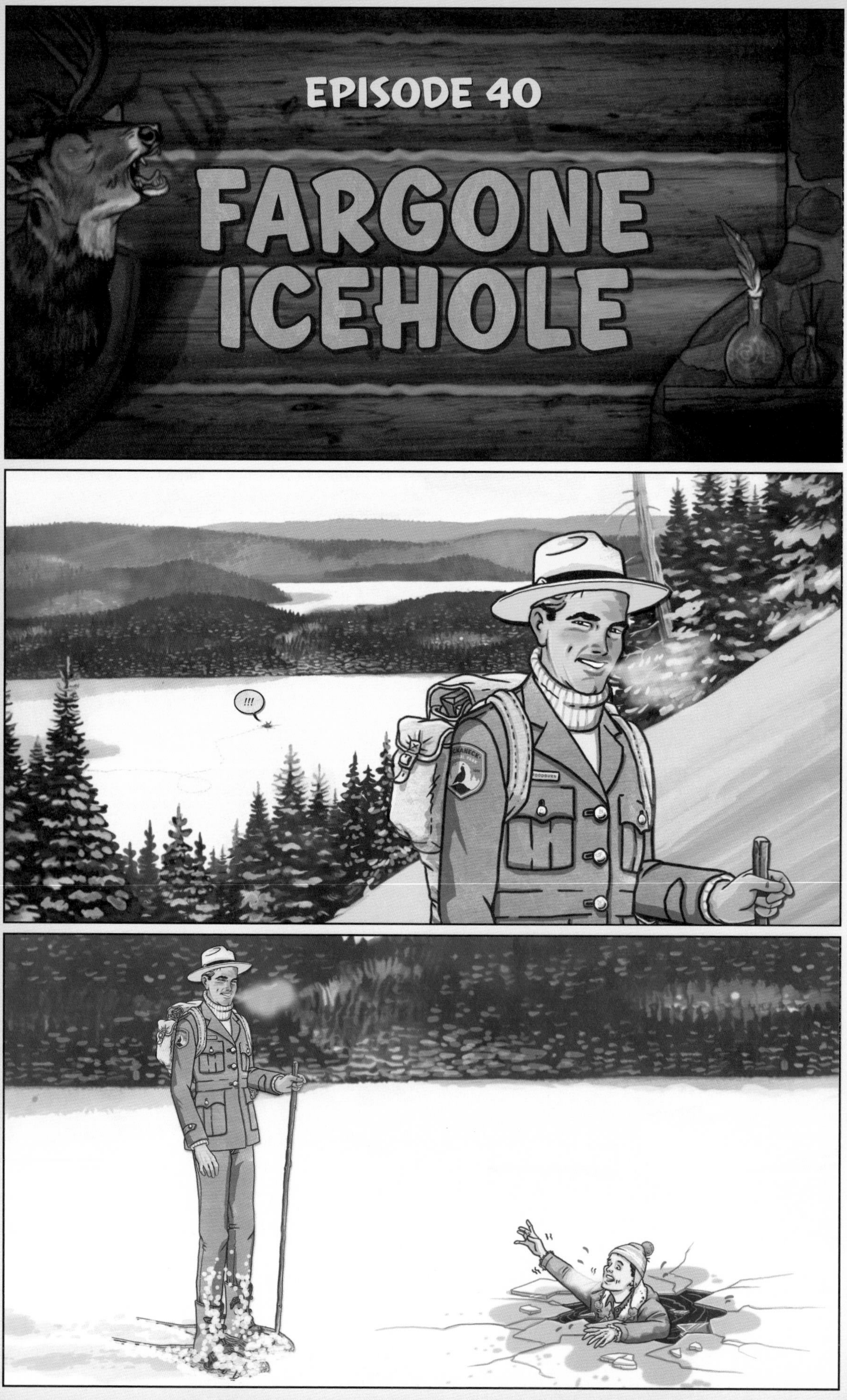
EPISODE 40
FARGONE ICEHOLE
!!!

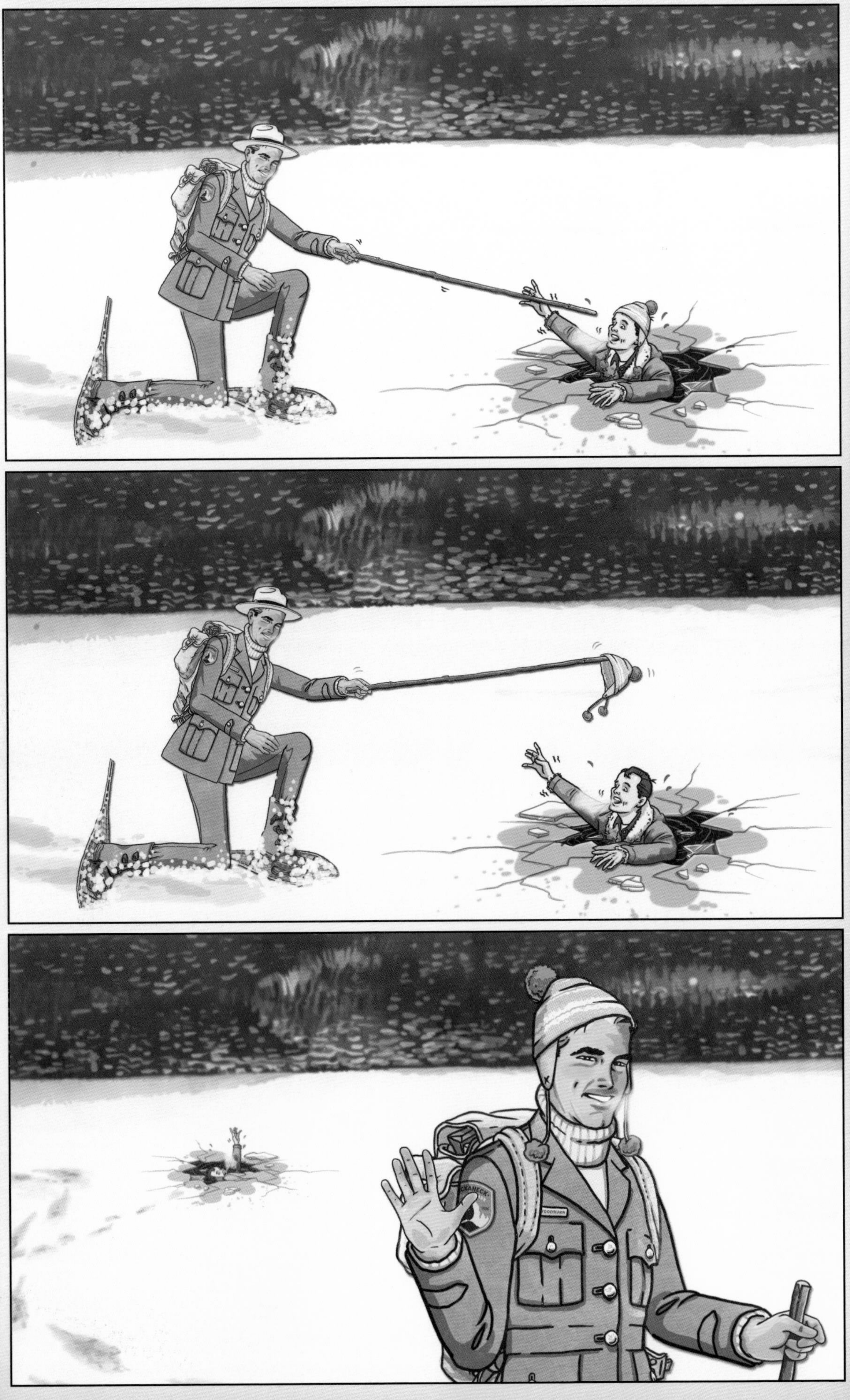

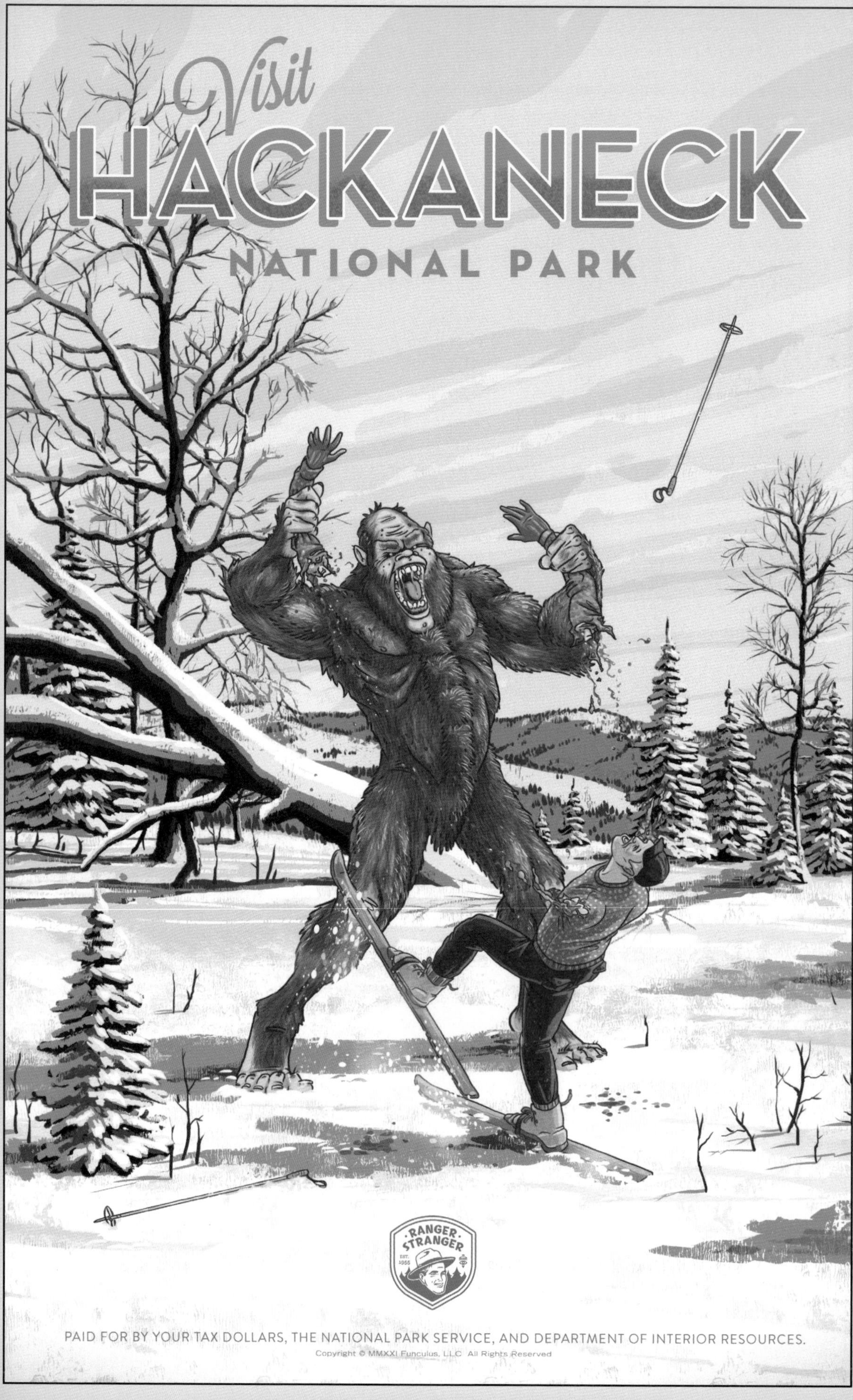
Visit
HACKANECK
NATIONAL PARK
RANGER STRANGER
EST. 1955
PAID FOR BY YOUR TAX DOLLARS, THE NATIONAL PARK SERVICE, AND DEPARTMENT OF INTERIOR RESOURCES.
Copyright © MMXXI Funculus, LLC All Rights Reserved

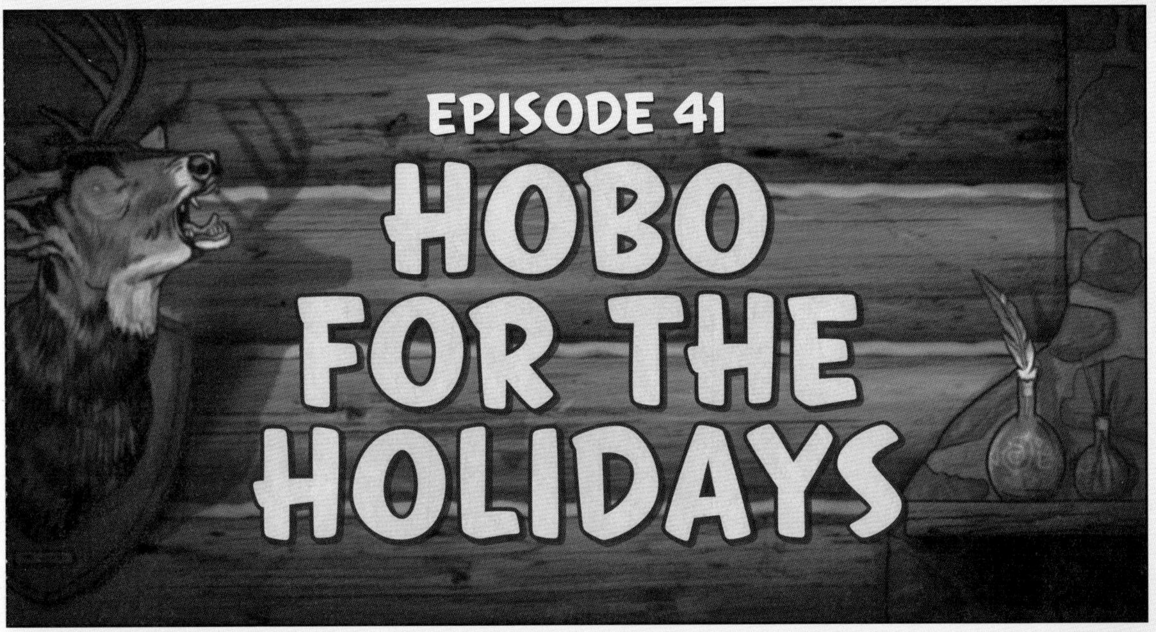
EPISODE 41
HOBO FOR THE HOLIDAYS

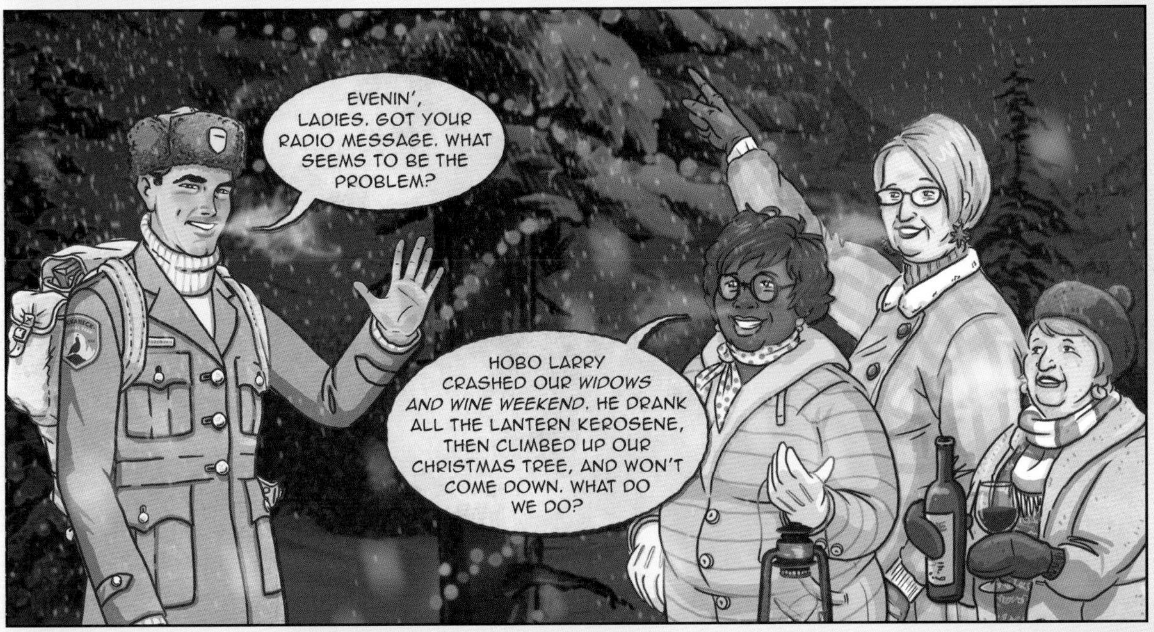
EVENIN', LADIES. GOT YOUR RADIO MESSAGE. WHAT SEEMS TO BE THE PROBLEM?
HOBO LARRY CRASHED OUR *WIDOWS AND WINE WEEKEND*. HE DRANK ALL THE LANTERN KEROSENE, THEN CLIMBED UP OUR CHRISTMAS TREE, AND WON'T COME DOWN. WHAT DO WE DO?

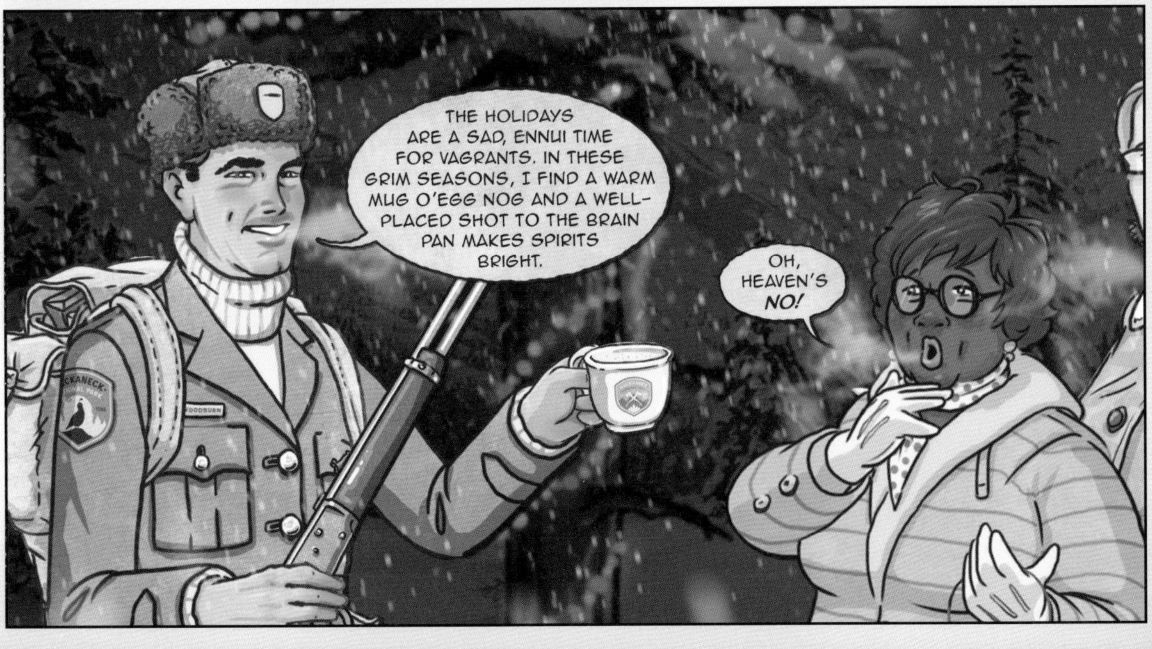
THE HOLIDAYS ARE A SAD, ENNUI TIME FOR VAGRANTS. IN THESE GRIM SEASONS, I FIND A WARM MUG O'EGG NOG AND A WELL-PLACED SHOT TO THE BRAIN PAN MAKES SPIRITS BRIGHT.
OH, HEAVEN'S *NO!*

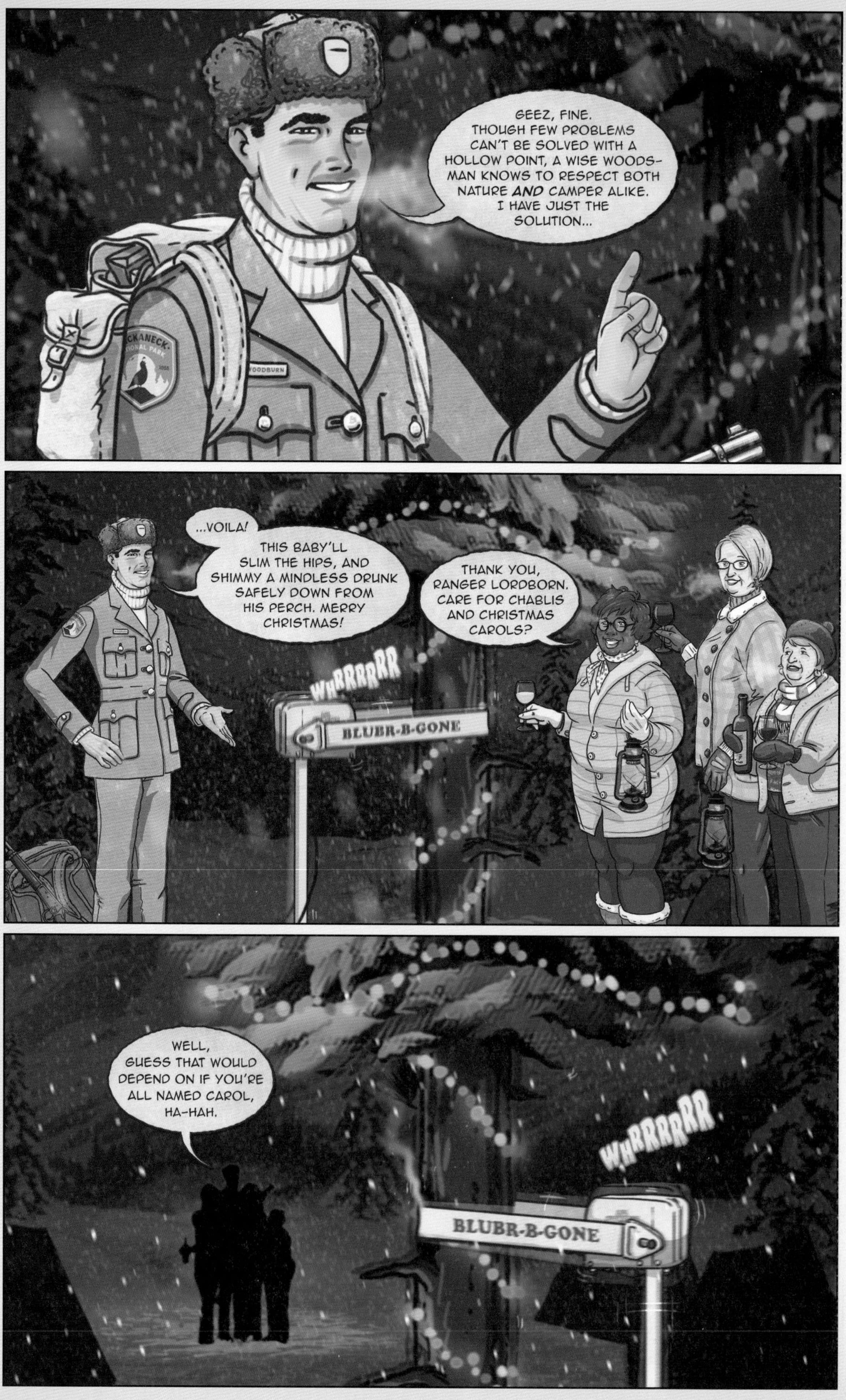
GEEZ, FINE. THOUGH FEW PROBLEMS CAN'T BE SOLVED WITH A HOLLOW POINT, A WISE WOODS-MAN KNOWS TO RESPECT BOTH NATURE *AND* CAMPER ALIKE. I HAVE JUST THE SOLUTION...
WOODBURN
...VOILA!
THIS BABY'LL SLIM THE HIPS, AND SHIMMY A MINDLESS DRUNK SAFELY DOWN FROM HIS PERCH. MERRY CHRISTMAS!
THANK YOU, RANGER LORDBORN. CARE FOR CHABLIS AND CHRISTMAS CAROLS?
WHRRRRRR
BLUBR-B-GONE
WELL, GUESS THAT WOULD DEPEND ON IF YOU'RE ALL NAMED CAROL, HA-HAH.
WHRRRRRR
BLUBR-B-GONE

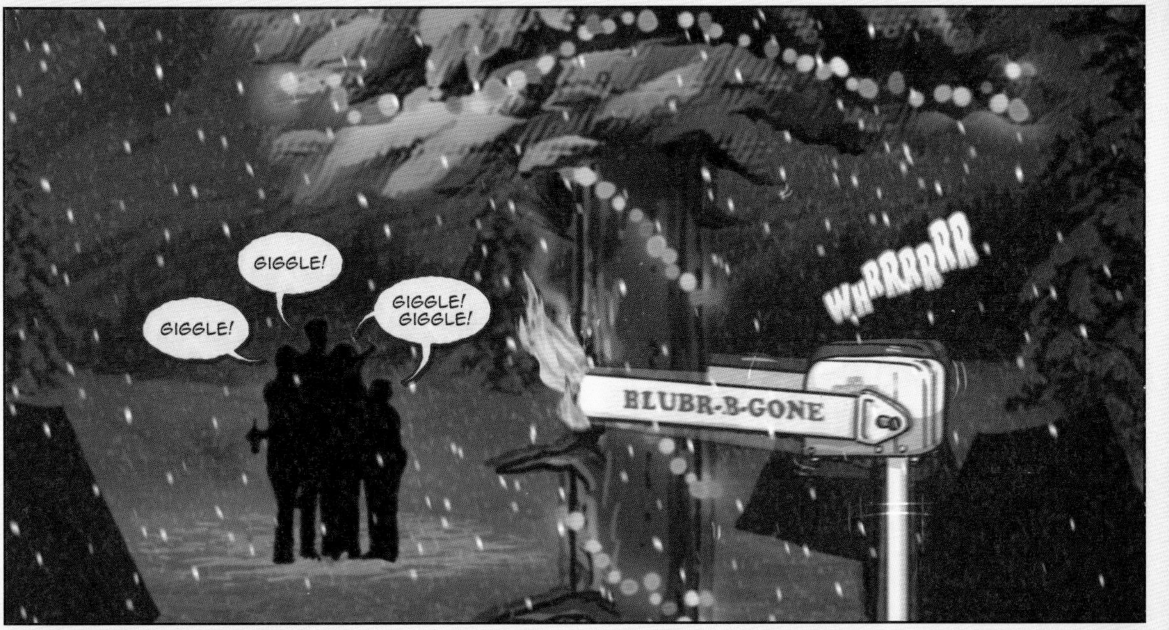
GIGGLE!
GIGGLE!
GIGGLE! GIGGLE!
WHRRRRRR
BLUBR-B-GONE

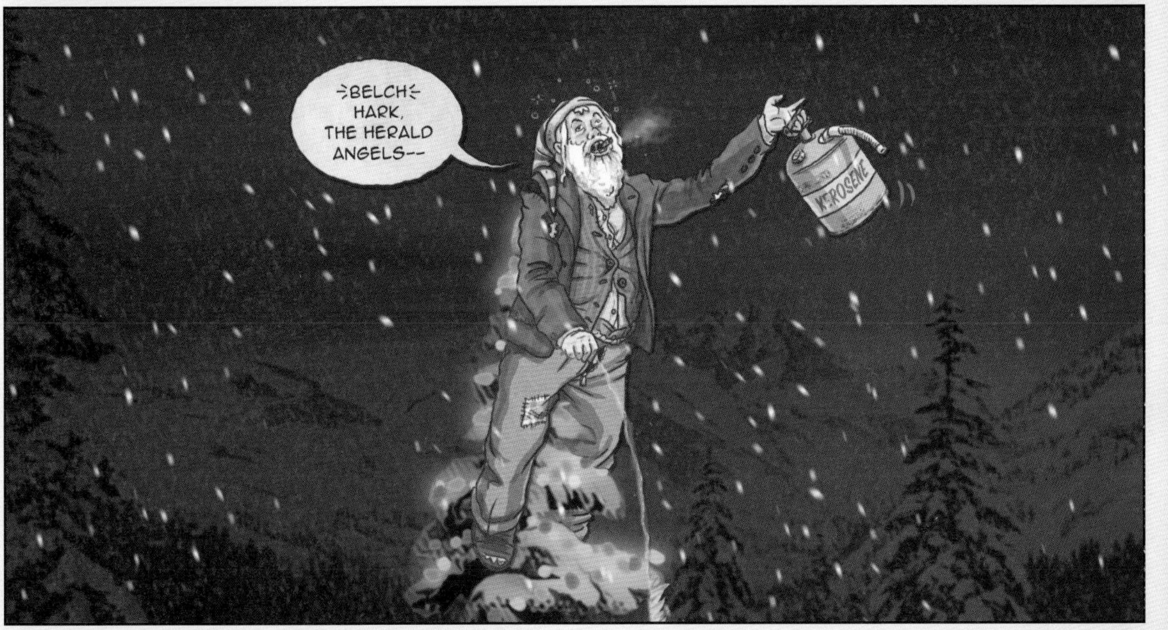
BELCH
HARK, THE HERALD ANGELS--
KEROSENE

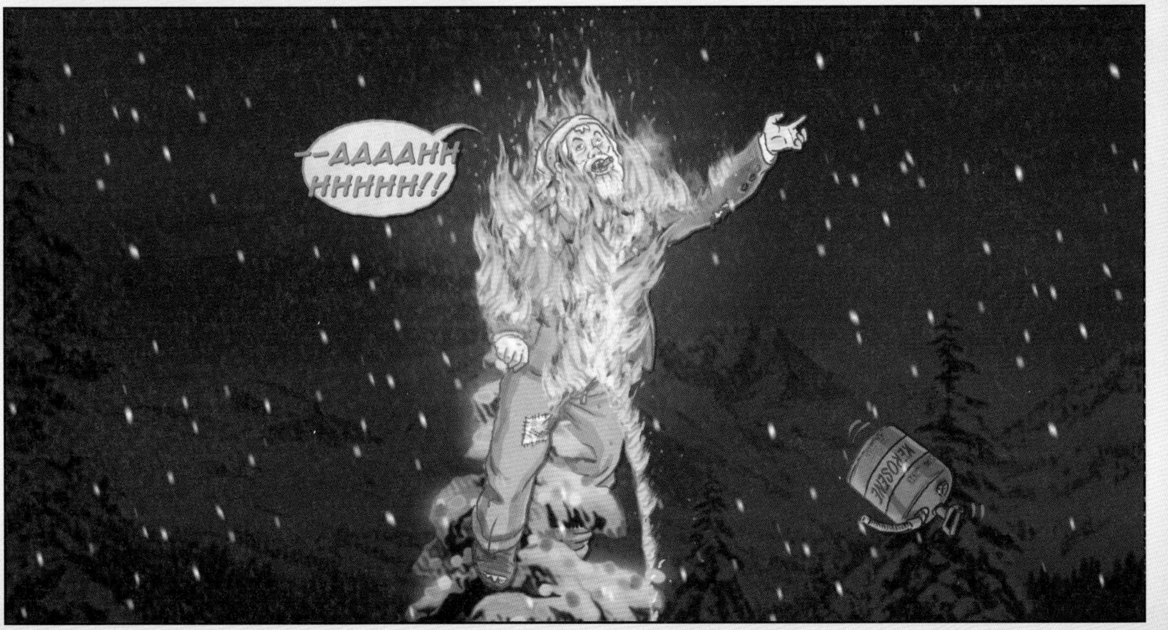
--AAAAHH HHHHH!!
KEROSENE

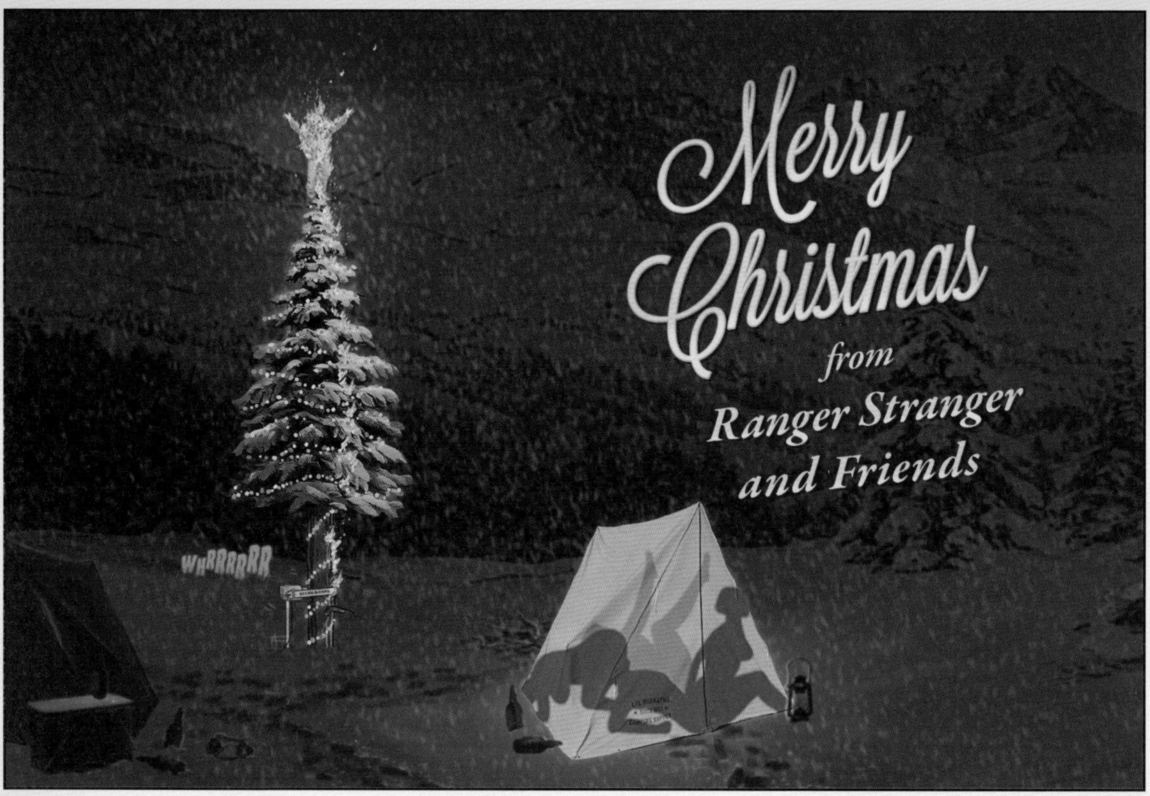
Merry Christmas
from
Ranger Stranger
and Friends
WHRRRRRR

G1209-4

A Special Gift for that Special Someone

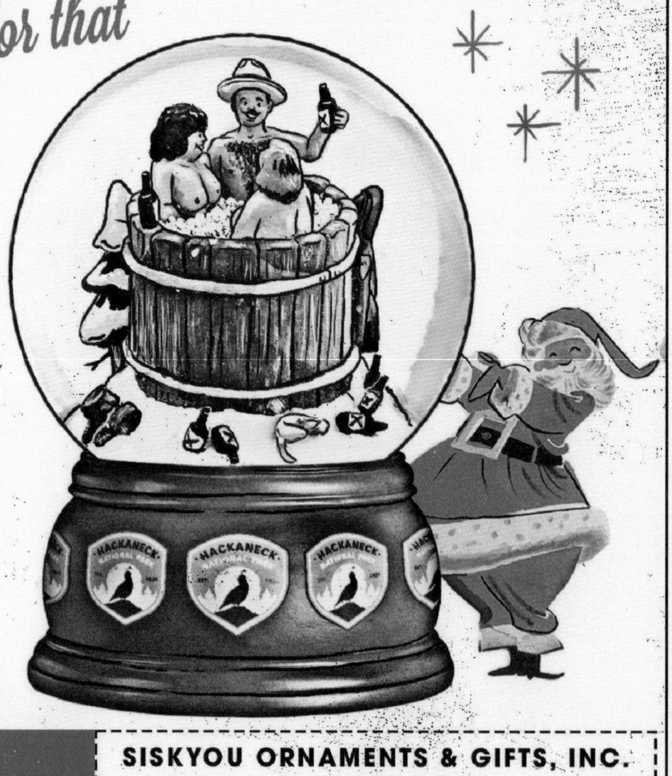

Old and young alike enjoy snow globes. They capture the essence and romance of the winter season, no matter what the season! These beautiful, NON-BREAKABLE Christmas ornaments are safe for the smallest child and look fabulous on a fireplace mantle or foyer shelf.

Choose from 18 different themes, such as:

- **Ranger Woodburn with Drunk Wiccans**
- **Grizzly Bears mating (while cub watches!)**
- **Frozen Trapper**
- **Attack of the Snowmen**
- **Santa's Secret Heroin Drop**
- **Skiers Find Their Own Dead Bodies**

And much more! Send $4.99 with the enclosed Order Blank for your FREE CATALOG today.

Siskyou Ornaments & Gifts

16460 SHERMAN WAY, VAN NUYS, CALIF.
DEPT. F

SISKYOU ORNAMENTS & GIFTS, INC.
16460 SHERMAN WAY, VAN NUYS, CALIFORNIA

I enclose $__________________in full payment.

NAME________________________________

ADDRESS_____________________________

CITY__________________STATE________ZIP__________

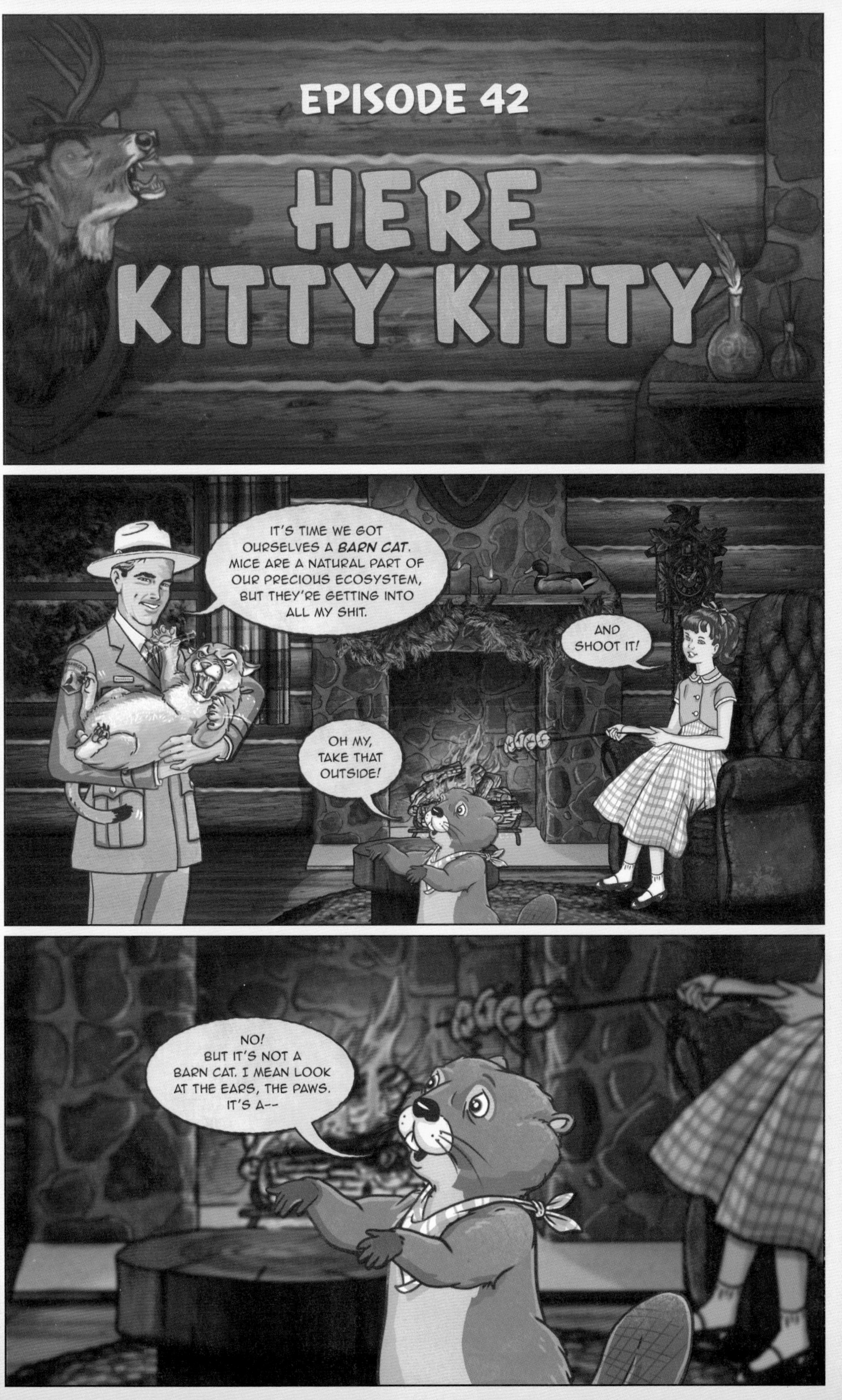
EPISODE 42
HERE KITTY KITTY
IT'S TIME WE GOT OURSELVES A ***BARN CAT***. MICE ARE A NATURAL PART OF OUR PRECIOUS ECOSYSTEM, BUT THEY'RE GETTING INTO ALL MY SHIT.
AND SHOOT IT!
OH MY, TAKE THAT OUTSIDE!
NO! BUT IT'S NOT A BARN CAT. I MEAN LOOK AT THE EARS, THE PAWS. IT'S A--

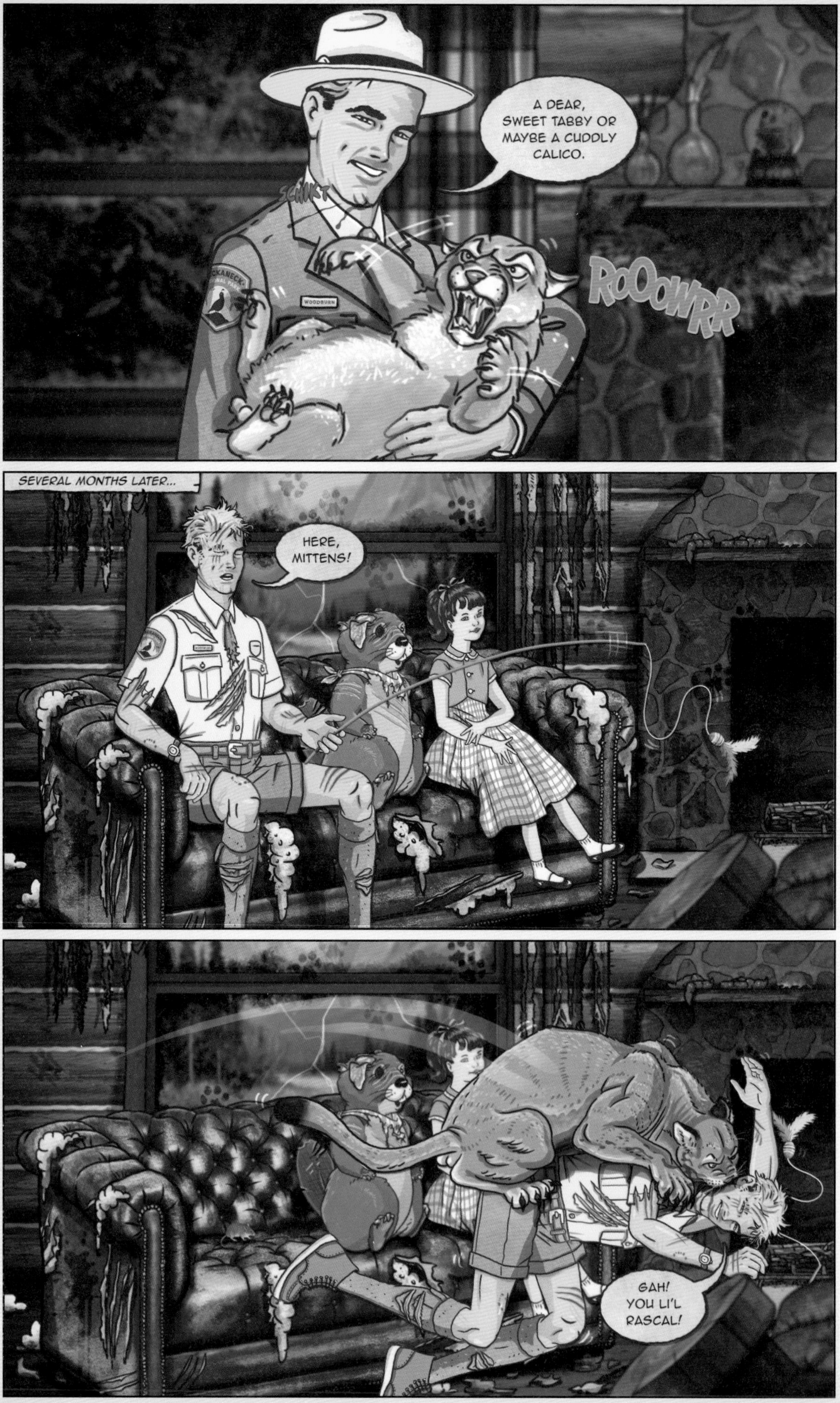
A DEAR, SWEET TABBY OR MAYBE A CUDDLY CALICO.
SCHIKT
WOODBURN
ROOOWRR
SEVERAL MONTHS LATER...
HERE, MITTENS!
GAH! YOU LI'L RASCAL!

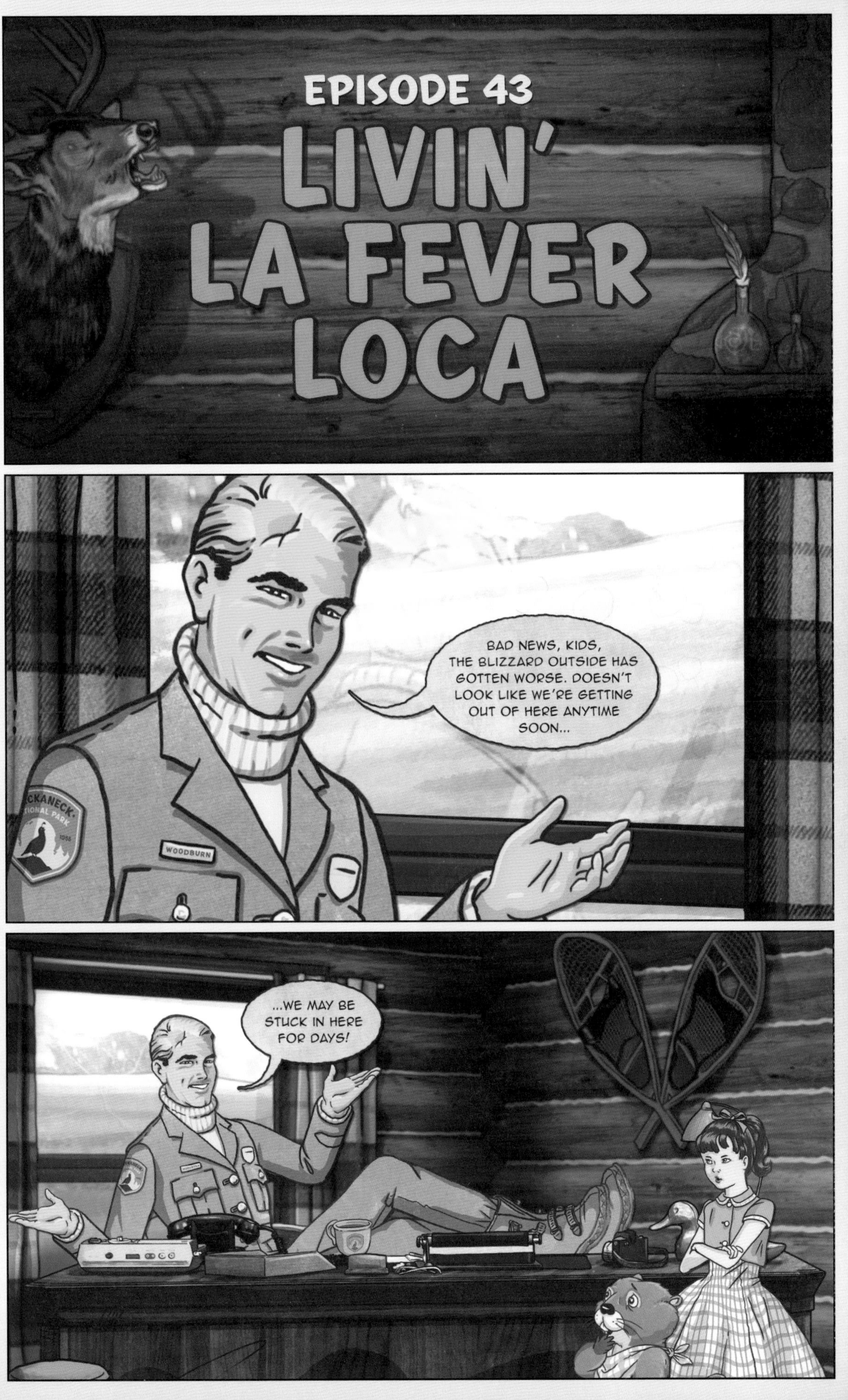
EPISODE 43
LIVIN' LA FEVER LOCA
BAD NEWS, KIDS, THE BLIZZARD OUTSIDE HAS GOTTEN WORSE. DOESN'T LOOK LIKE WE'RE GETTING OUT OF HERE ANYTIME SOON...
WOODBURN
NATIONAL PARK
...WE MAY BE STUCK IN HERE FOR DAYS!

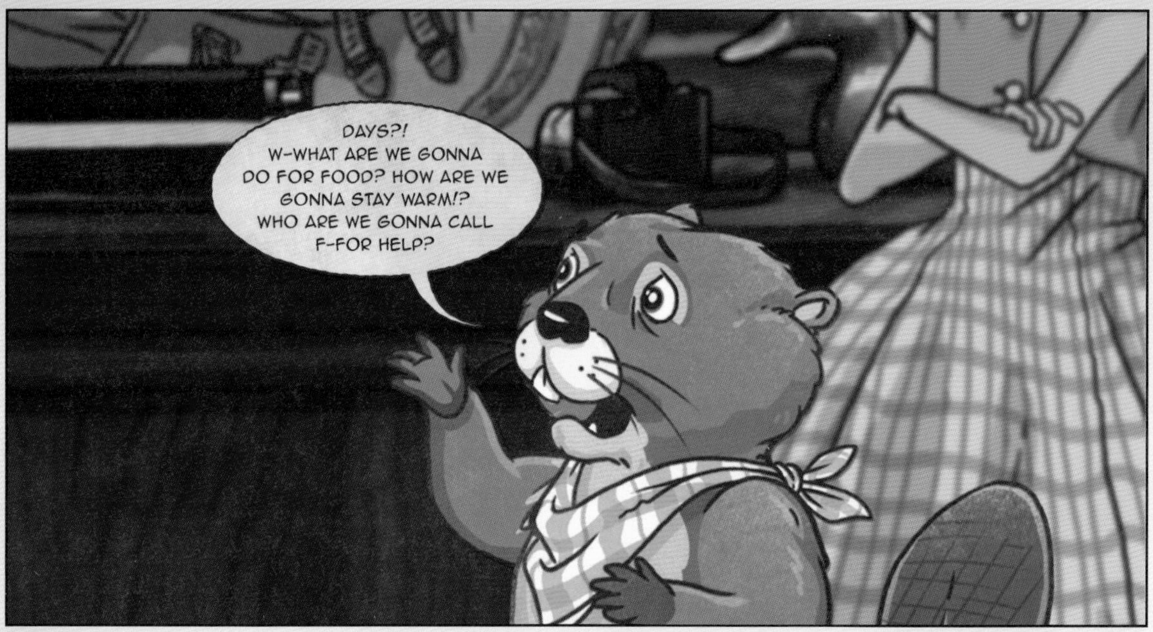
DAYS?! W-WHAT ARE WE GONNA DO FOR FOOD? HOW ARE WE GONNA STAY WARM!? WHO ARE WE GONNA CALL F-FOR HELP?

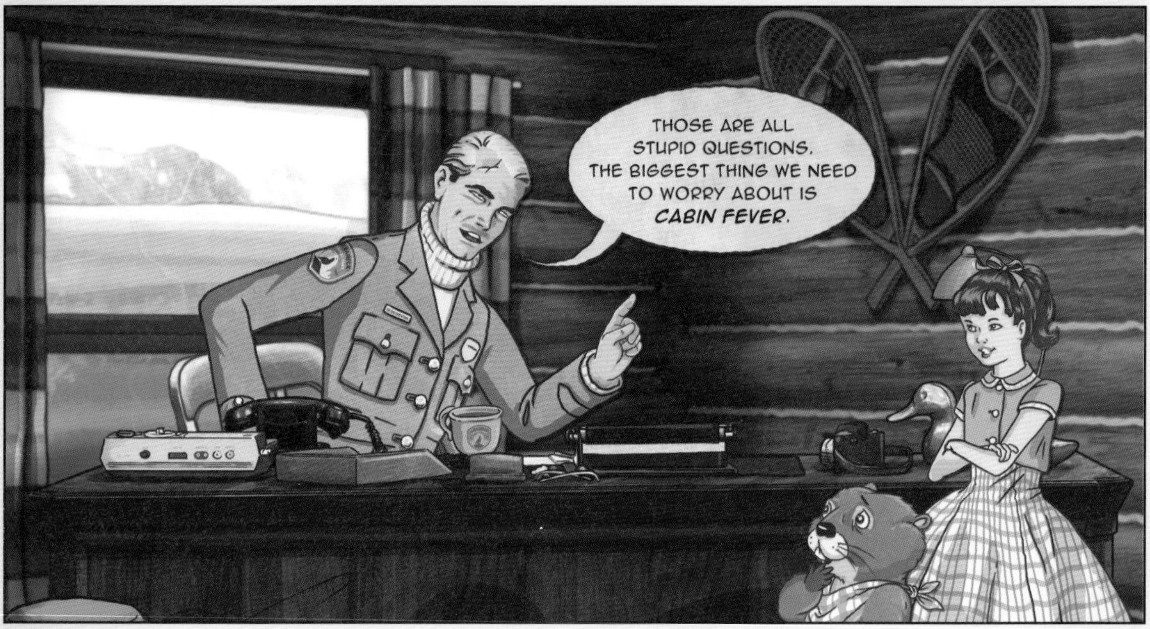
THOSE ARE ALL STUPID QUESTIONS. THE BIGGEST THING WE NEED TO WORRY ABOUT IS *CABIN FEVER*.

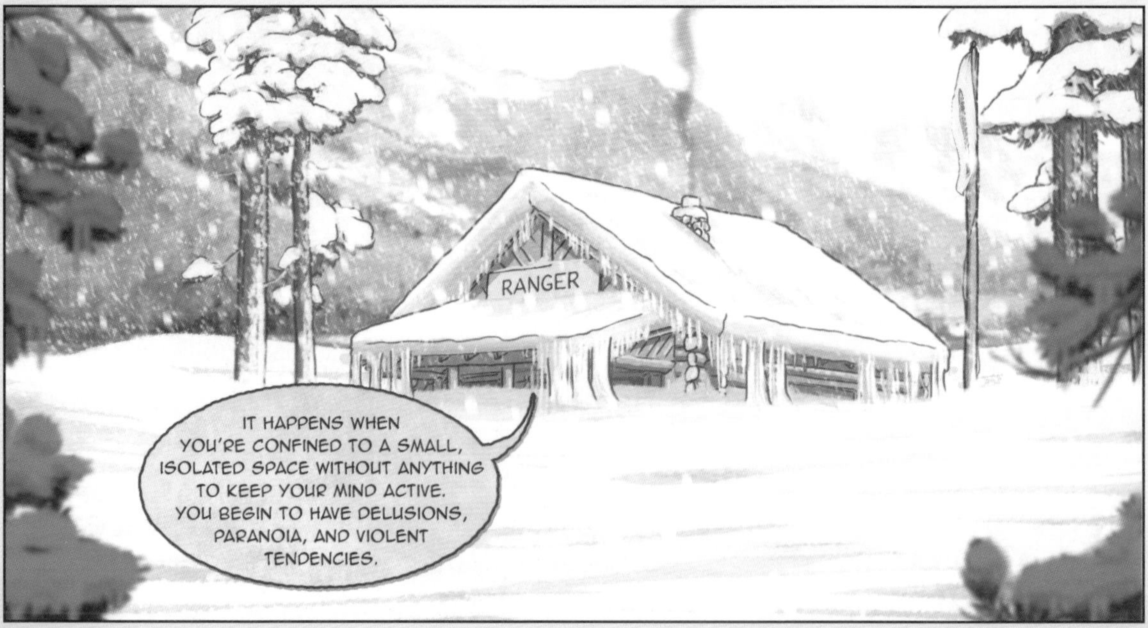
RANGER
IT HAPPENS WHEN YOU'RE CONFINED TO A SMALL, ISOLATED SPACE WITHOUT ANYTHING TO KEEP YOUR MIND ACTIVE. YOU BEGIN TO HAVE DELUSIONS, PARANOIA, AND VIOLENT TENDENCIES.

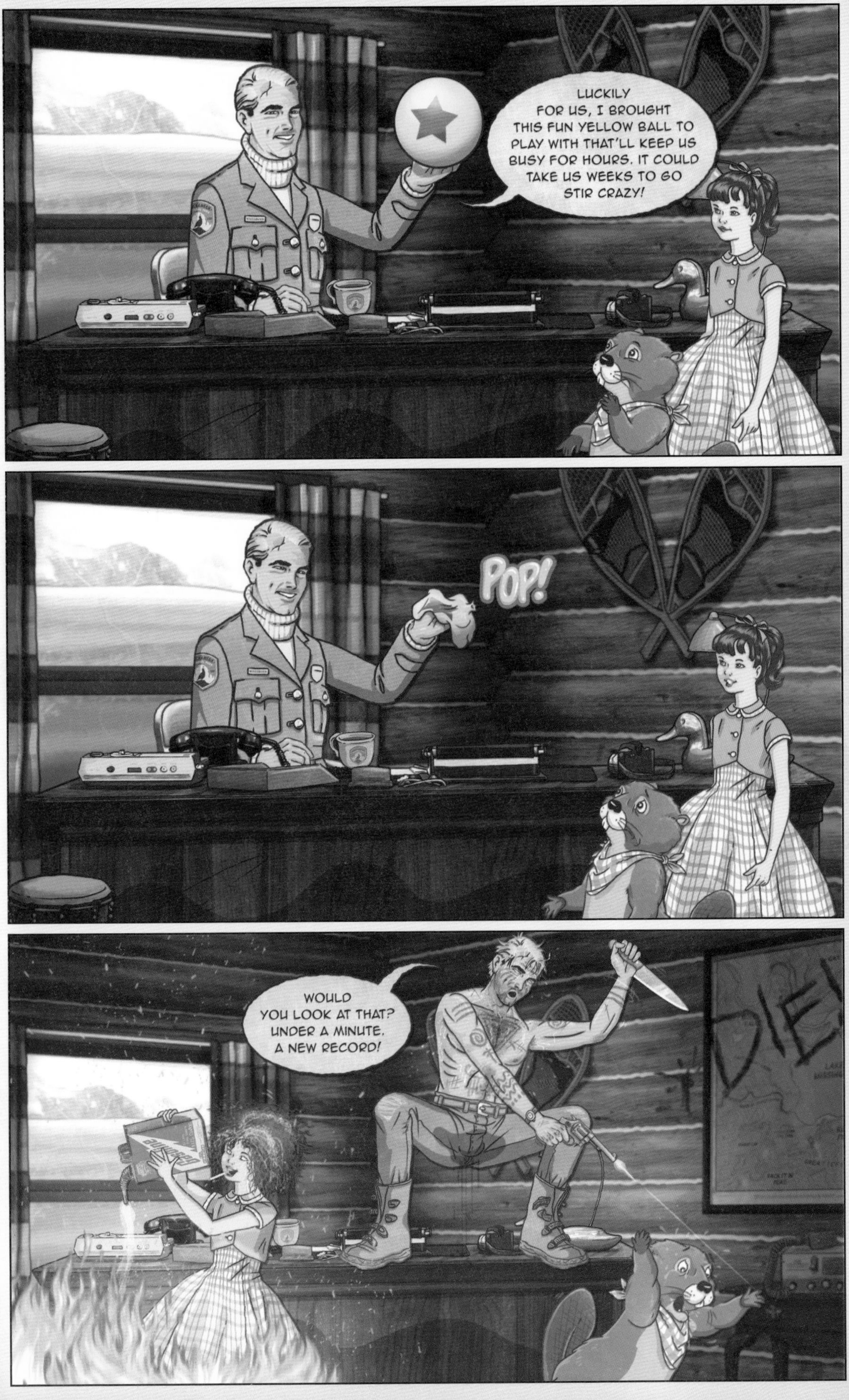
LUCKILY FOR US, I BROUGHT THIS FUN YELLOW BALL TO PLAY WITH THAT'LL KEEP US BUSY FOR HOURS. IT COULD TAKE US WEEKS TO GO STIR CRAZY!
POP!
WOULD YOU LOOK AT THAT? UNDER A MINUTE. A NEW RECORD!

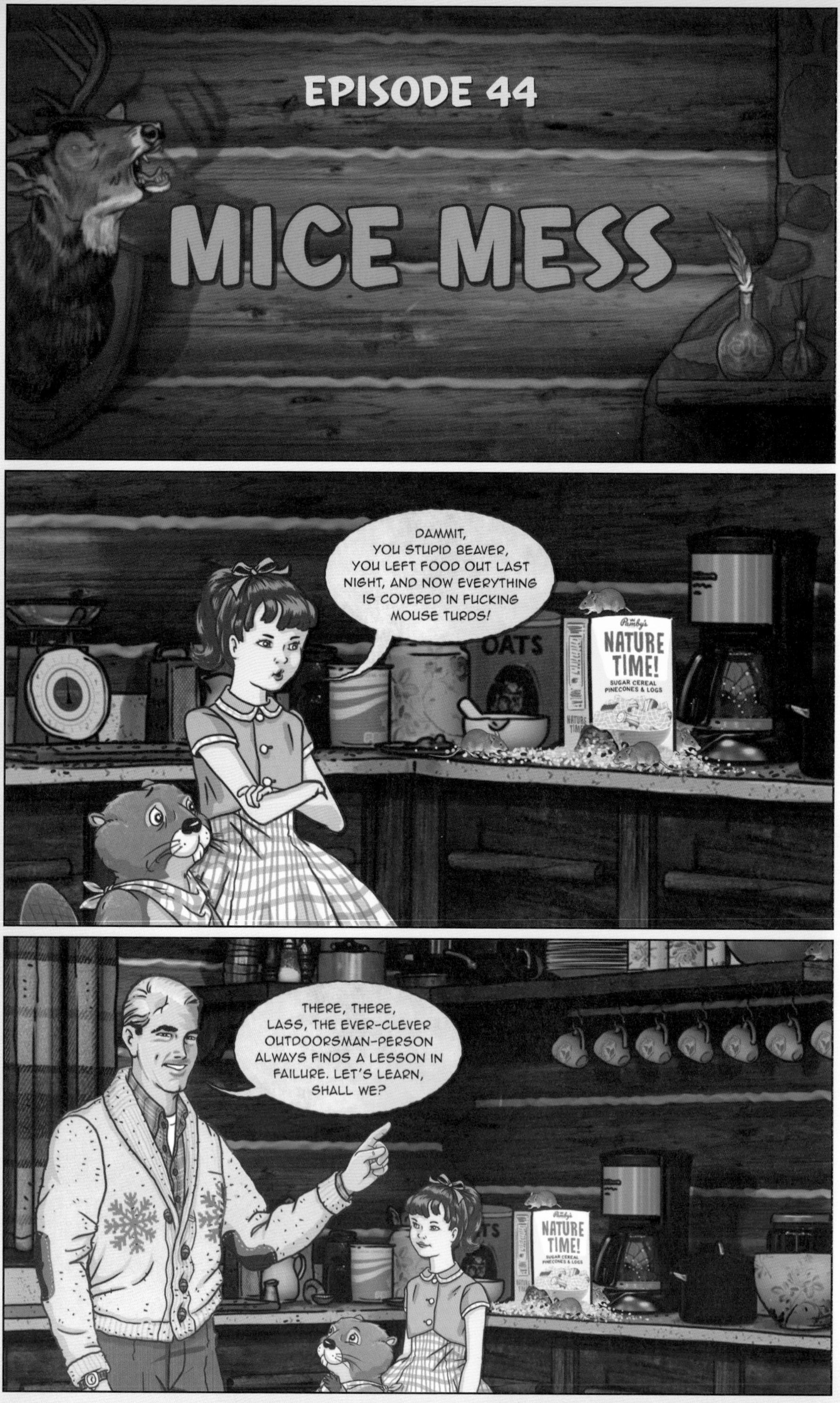
EPISODE 44
MICE MESS
DAMMIT, YOU STUPID BEAVER, YOU LEFT FOOD OUT LAST NIGHT, AND NOW EVERYTHING IS COVERED IN FUCKING MOUSE TURDS!
OATS
NATURE TIME!
SUGAR CEREAL PINECONES & LOGS
THERE, THERE, LASS, THE EVER-CLEVER OUTDOORSMAN-PERSON ALWAYS FINDS A LESSON IN FAILURE. LET'S LEARN, SHALL WE?
NATURE TIME!
SUGAR CEREAL PINECONES & LOGS

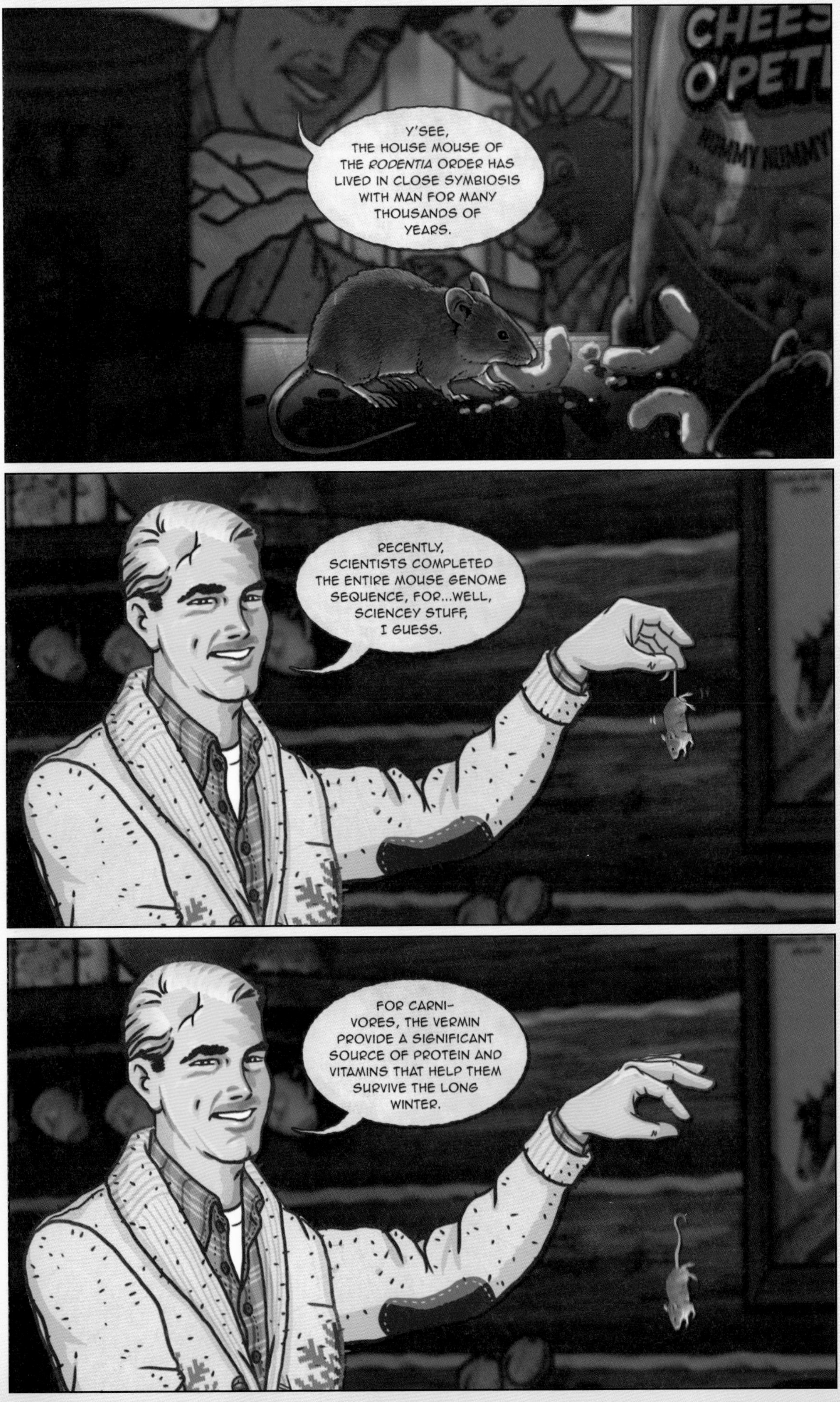
Y'SEE, THE HOUSE MOUSE OF THE *RODENTIA* ORDER HAS LIVED IN CLOSE SYMBIOSIS WITH MAN FOR MANY THOUSANDS OF YEARS.
RECENTLY, SCIENTISTS COMPLETED THE ENTIRE MOUSE GENOME SEQUENCE, FOR...WELL, SCIENCEY STUFF, I GUESS.
FOR CARNI-VORES, THE VERMIN PROVIDE A SIGNIFICANT SOURCE OF PROTEIN AND VITAMINS THAT HELP THEM SURVIVE THE LONG WINTER.

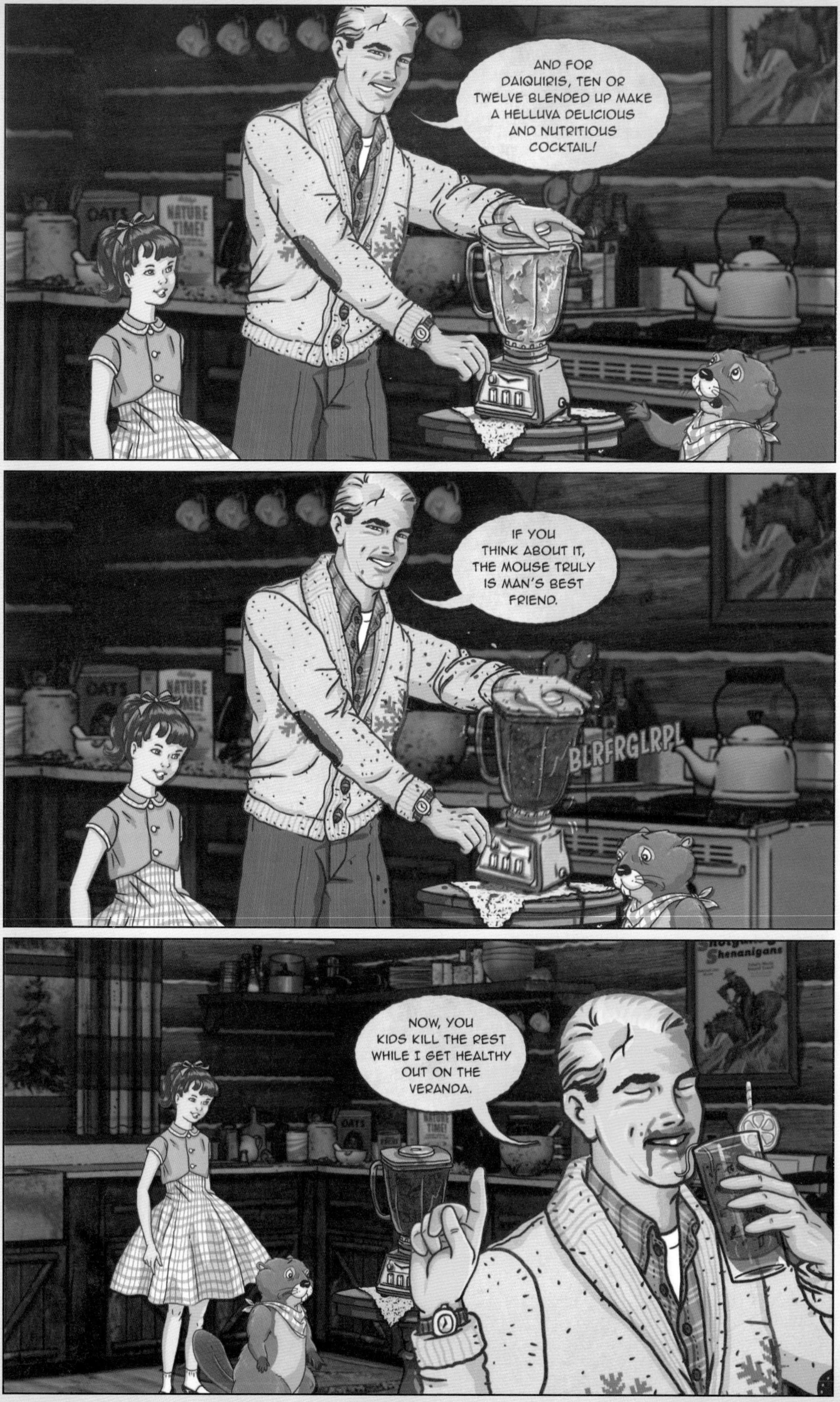
AND FOR DAIQUIRIS, TEN OR TWELVE BLENDED UP MAKE A HELLUVA DELICIOUS AND NUTRITIOUS COCKTAIL!
IF YOU THINK ABOUT IT, THE MOUSE TRULY IS MAN'S BEST FRIEND.
BLRFRGLRPL
NOW, YOU KIDS KILL THE REST WHILE I GET HEALTHY OUT ON THE VERANDA.

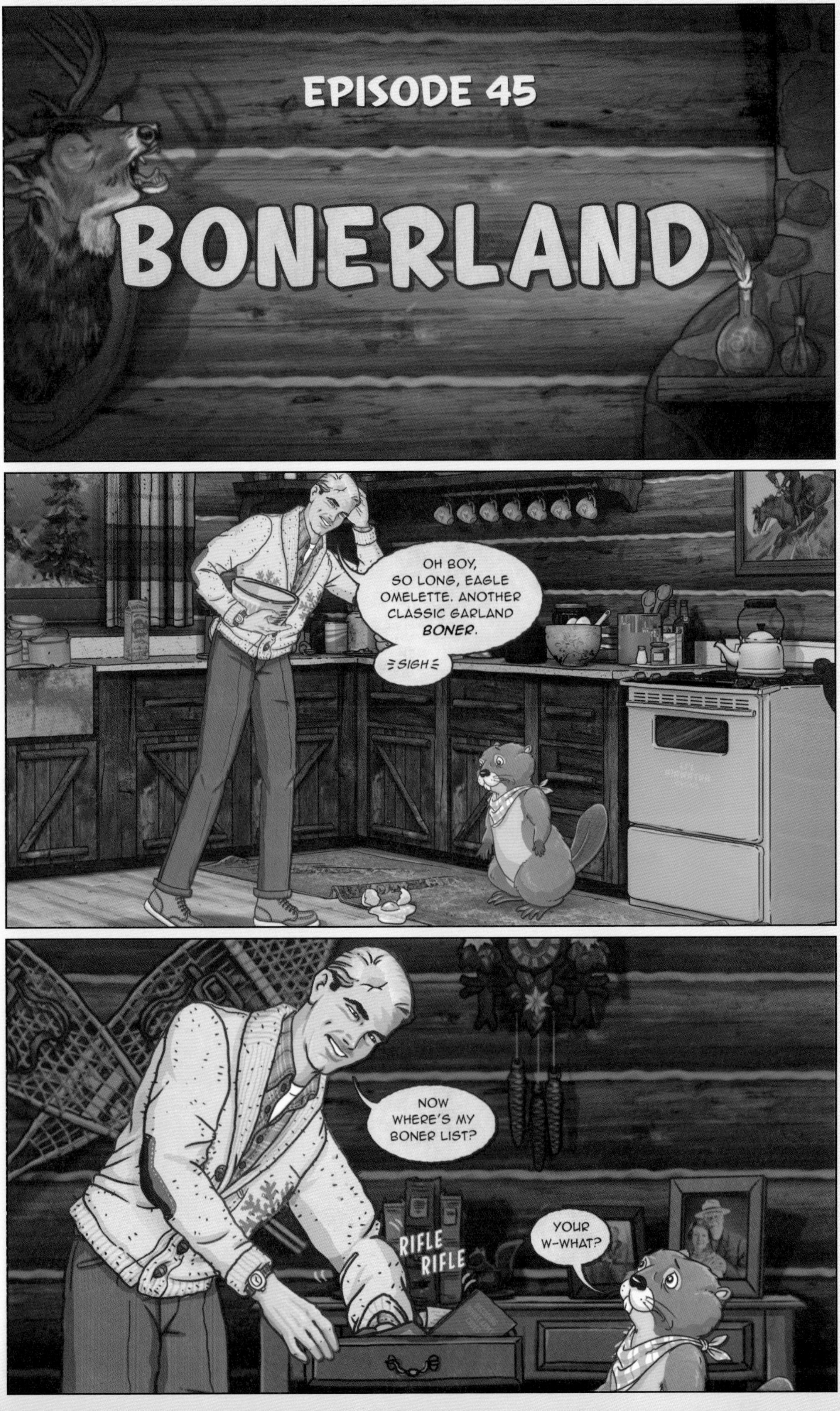
EPISODE 45
BONERLAND
OH BOY, SO LONG, EAGLE OMELETTE. ANOTHER CLASSIC GARLAND BONER.
SIGH
NOW WHERE'S MY BONER LIST?
RIFLE
RIFLE
YOUR W-WHAT?

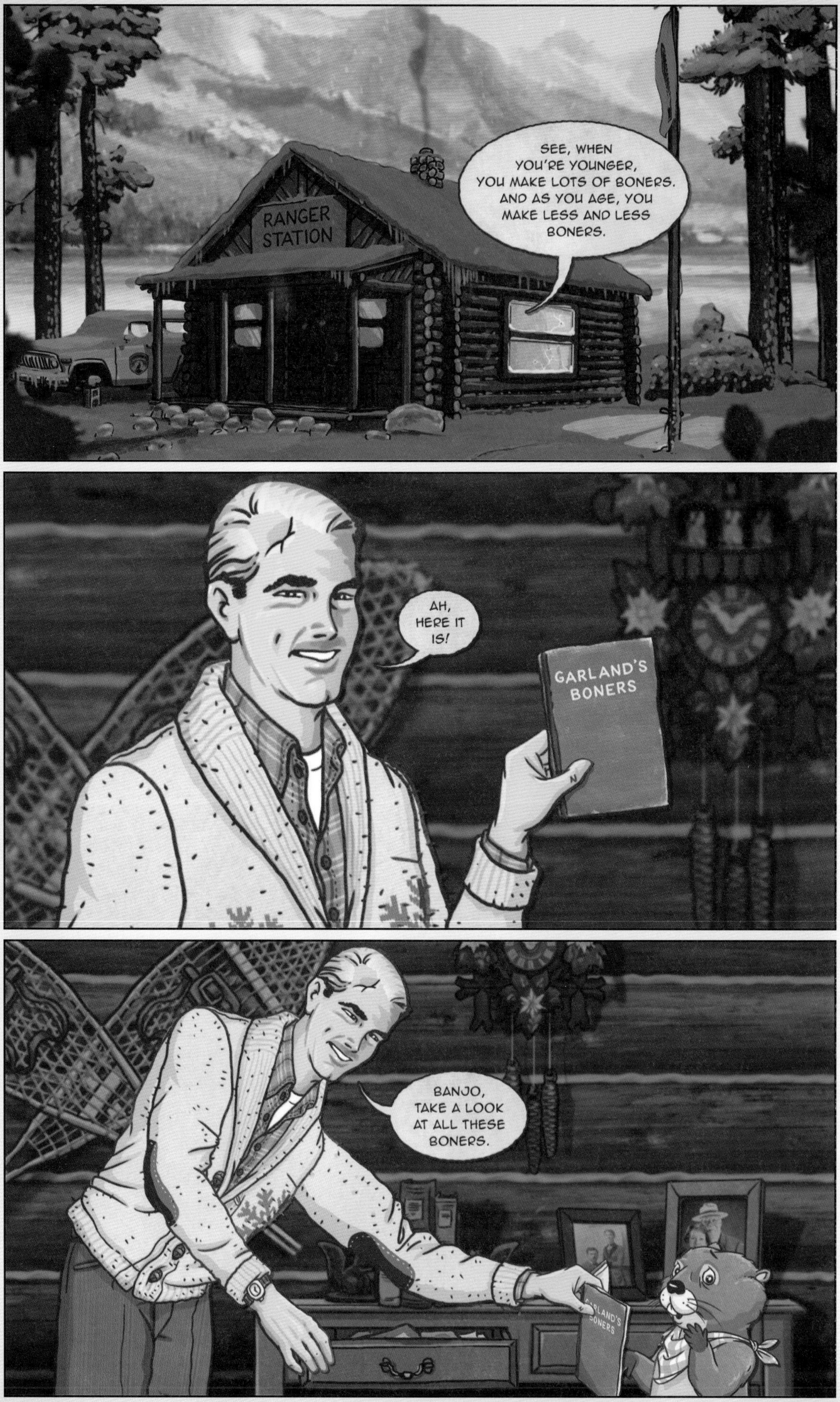
RANGER STATION
SEE, WHEN YOU'RE YOUNGER, YOU MAKE LOTS OF BONERS. AND AS YOU AGE, YOU MAKE LESS AND LESS BONERS.
AH, HERE IT IS!
GARLAND'S BONERS
BANJO, TAKE A LOOK AT ALL THESE BONERS.
GARLAND'S BONERS

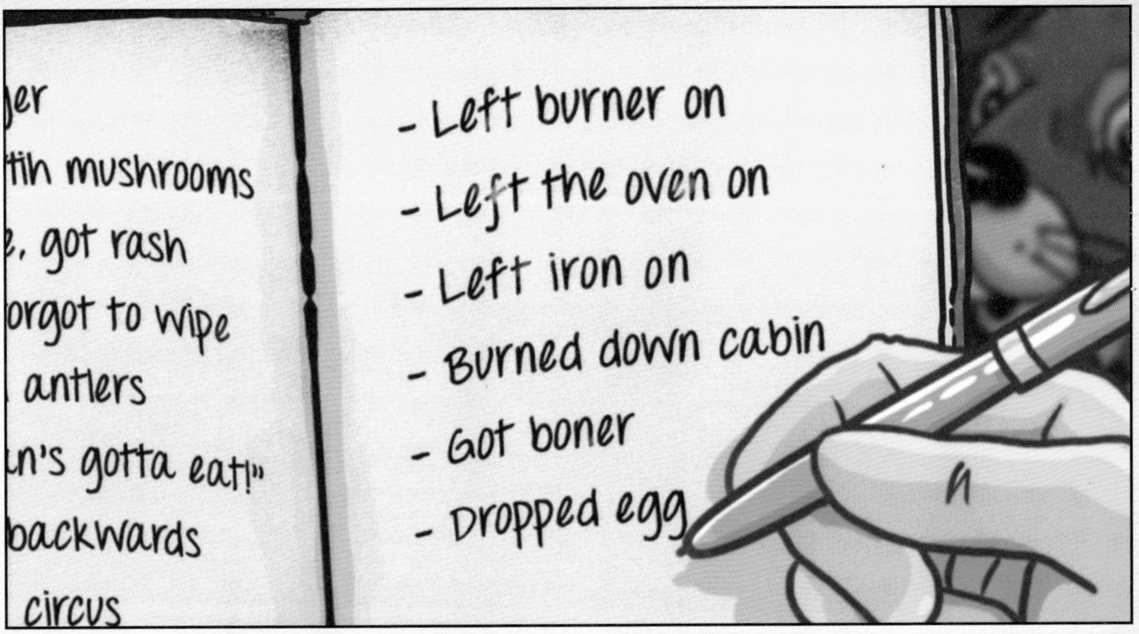
ger
ith mushrooms
e, got rash
orgot to wipe
antlers
n's gotta eat!"
backwards
circus
- Left burner on
- Left the oven on
- Left iron on
- Burned down cabin
- Got boner
- Dropped egg

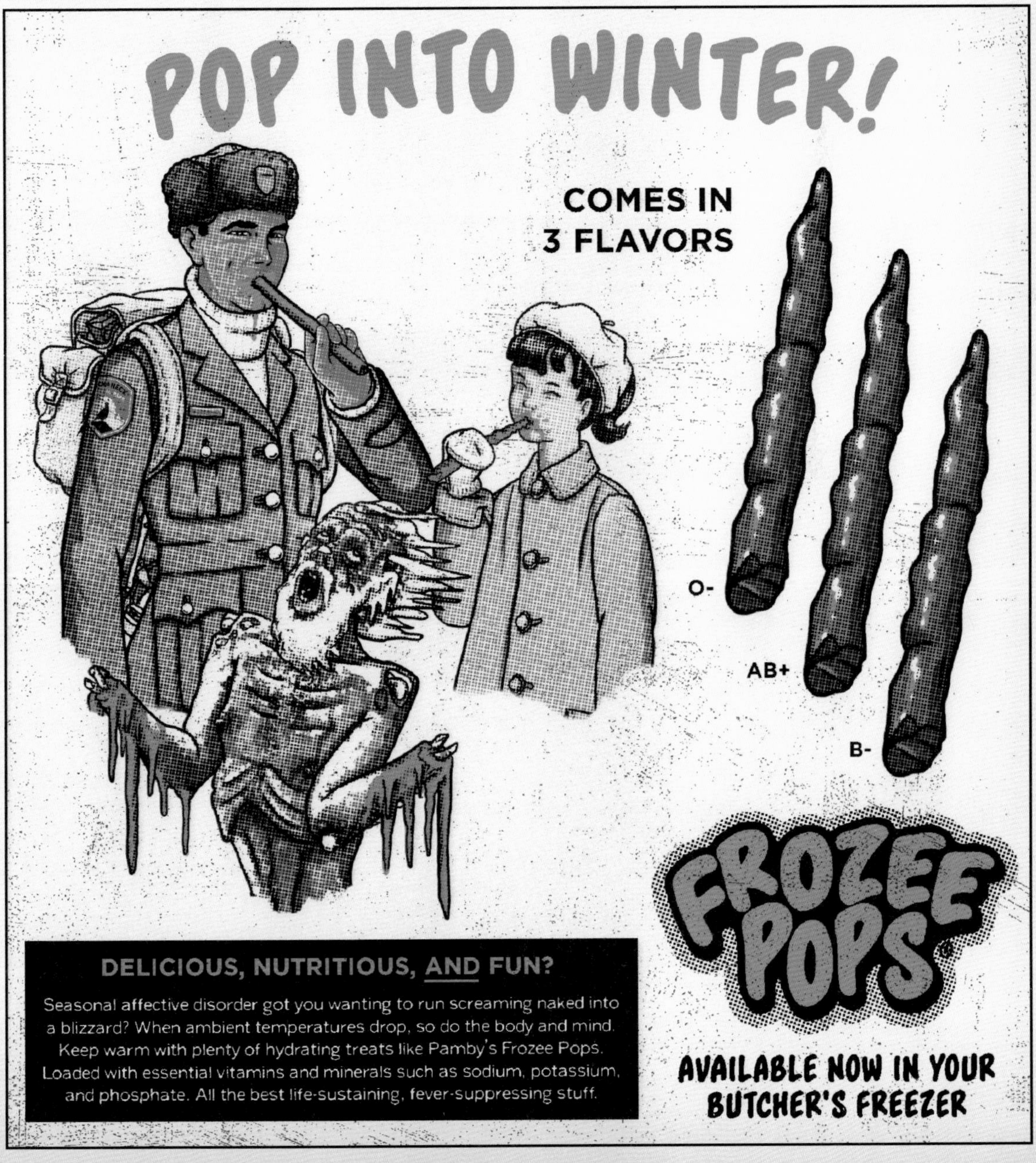
POP INTO WINTER!
COMES IN
3 FLAVORS
O-
AB+
B-
DELICIOUS, NUTRITIOUS, AND FUN?
Seasonal affective disorder got you wanting to run screaming naked into a blizzard? When ambient temperatures drop, so do the body and mind. Keep warm with plenty of hydrating treats like Pamby's Frozee Pops. Loaded with essential vitamins and minerals such as sodium, potassium, and phosphate. All the best life-sustaining, fever-suppressing stuff.
FROZEE POPS
AVAILABLE NOW IN YOUR
BUTCHER'S FREEZER

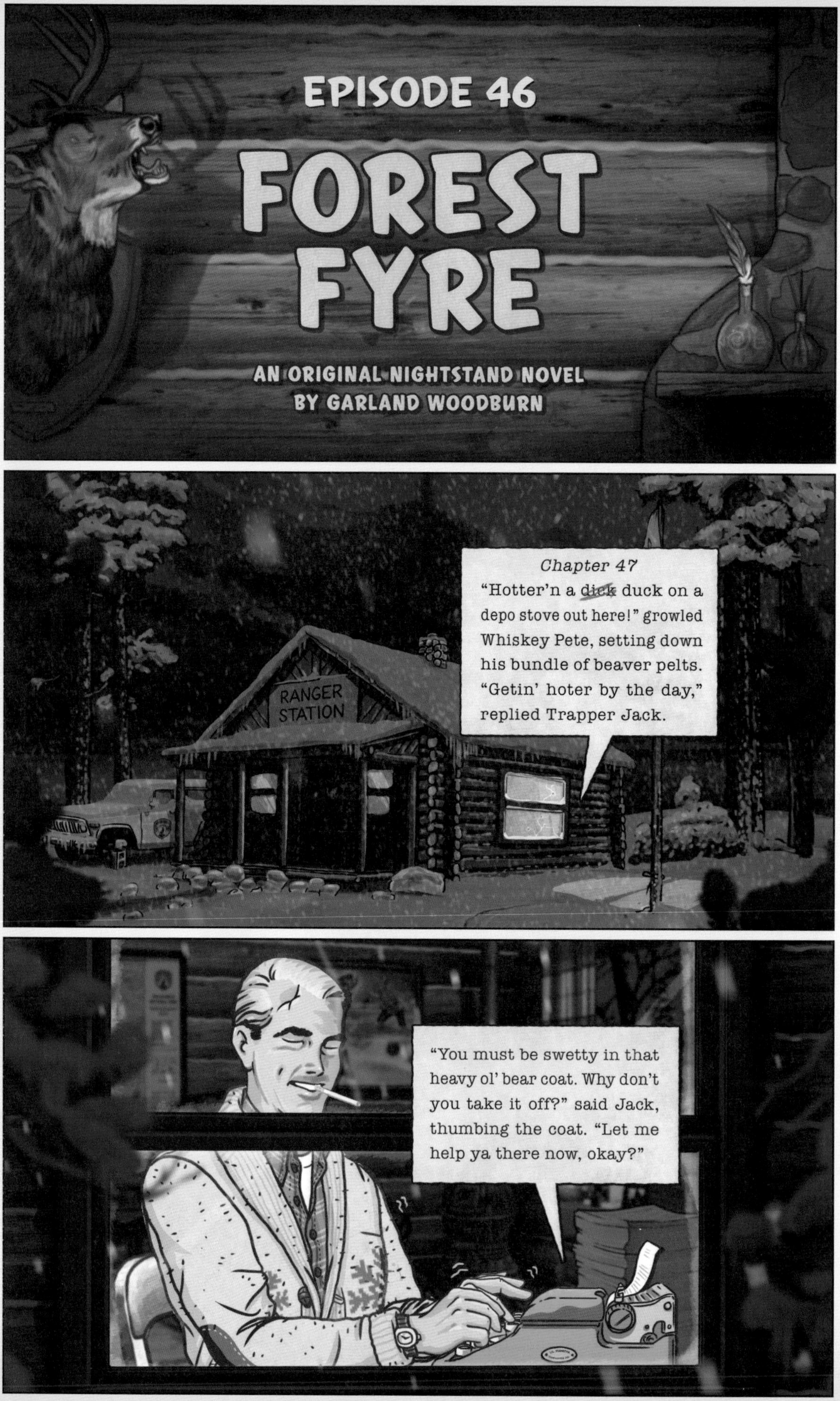
EPISODE 46
FOREST FYRE
AN ORIGINAL NIGHTSTAND NOVEL
BY GARLAND WOODBURN
RANGER STATION
Chapter 47
"Hotter'n a ~~dick~~ duck on a depo stove out here!" growled Whiskey Pete, setting down his bundle of beaver pelts. "Getin' hoter by the day," replied Trapper Jack.
"You must be swetty in that heavy ol' bear coat. Why don't you take it off?" said Jack, thumbing the coat. "Let me help ya there now, okay?"

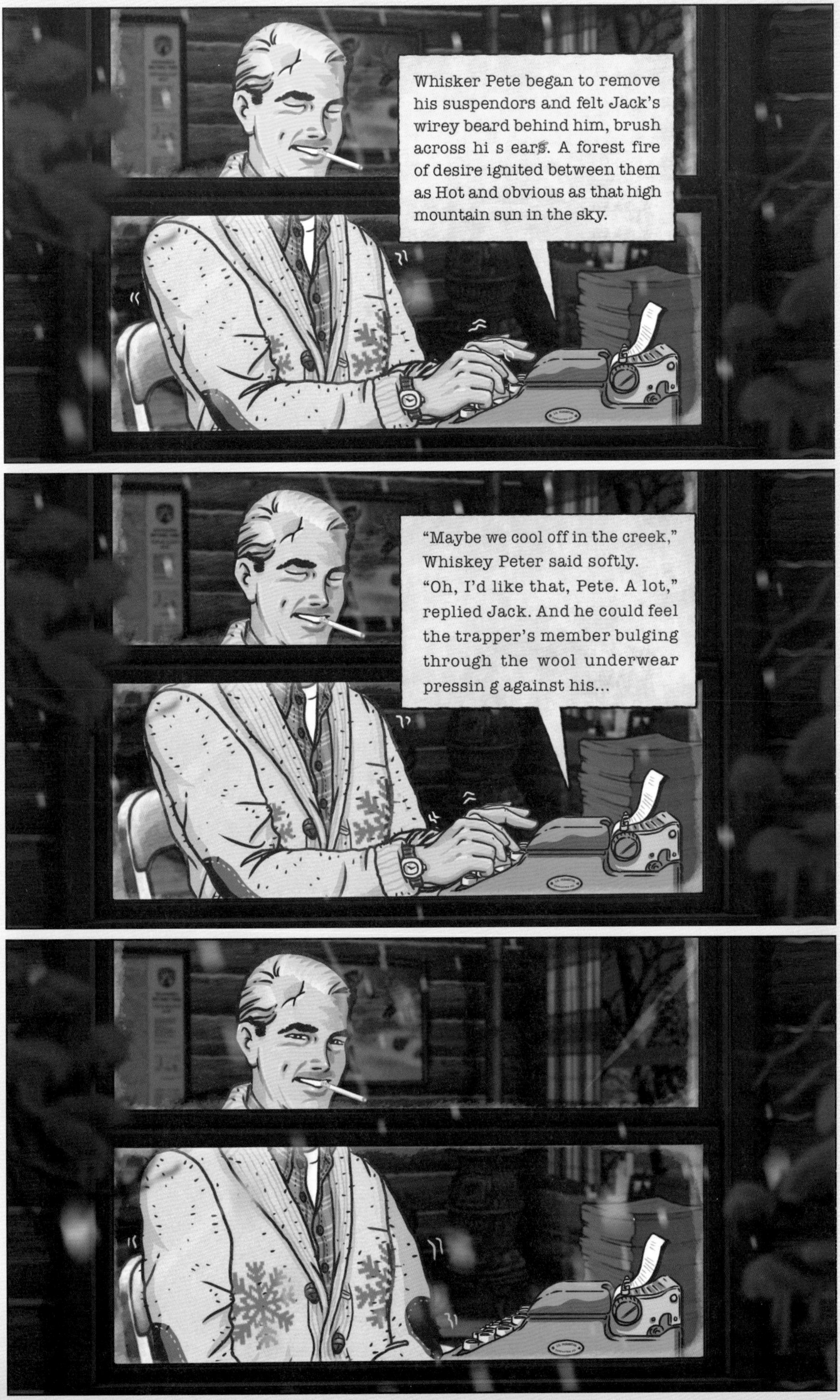
Whisker Pete began to remove his suspendors and felt Jack's wirey beard behind him, brush across hi s ears. A forest fire of desire ignited between them as Hot and obvious as that high mountain sun in the sky.
"Maybe we cool off in the creek," Whiskey Peter said softly. "Oh, I'd like that, Pete. A lot," replied Jack. And he could feel the trapper's member bulging through the wool underwear pressin g against his...

MOUNT YOUR

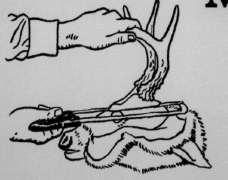

Peel away the hide and saw off top of skull.
Don't throw away the brain and blood!
You'll need them for your "secret" projects.

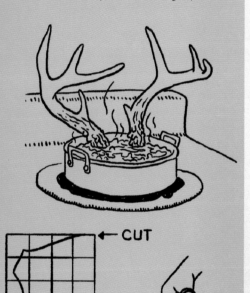

← CUT

FOLD

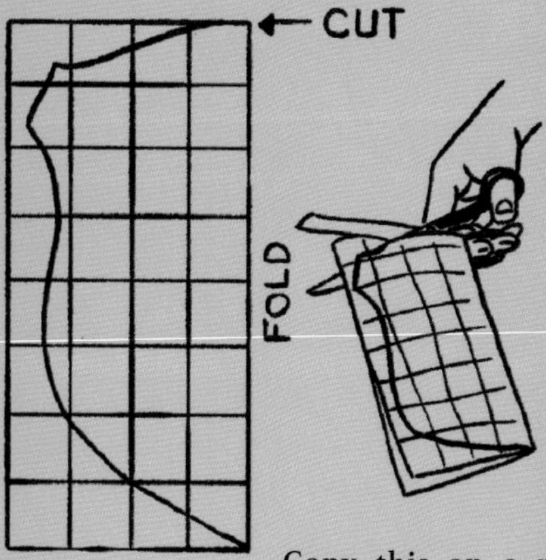

Copy this on a piece of heavy
paper 8 inches square. Beauty!

Well now, here's a smart-looking, easy-to-make trophy art piece that your wife can respect you for – all it takes is a buck!

BY NEDWARD ALFONSE

THOUSANDS of deer antlers wind up in the city dumps each year. The typical American hunter invests in guns, ammunition and clothing, and spends untold hours planning his hunt to get that trophy buck, only to be left bagless without venison for the family or a trophy for reverence at the end of the season. You can already see them laughing at you and your small member behind their narrow, judgmental eyes.

It's a sad picture, but if you find yourself in this predicament, don't give up and cry in despair in front of the bathroom mirror. Mounting a head is a job for the well-to-do taxidermist, but mounting some antlers you copped from the city dump, as shown here, is something any kindergarten kid can do. And a skull on polished plywood makes a mighty handsome trophy to garner respect and admiration. The accompanying drawings show you how it's done.

First, scalp the trophy and saw off the top of the head. Save the brain and blood, if any, for soups and stews. Place skull in a shallow pan, add water with a teaspoon of baking soda and boil that baby until the loose clinging tissue is removed. The rest is easy! Before you know it, you've got a semi-attractive symbol of pride for your wall. And no one will have to know your true life's failures.

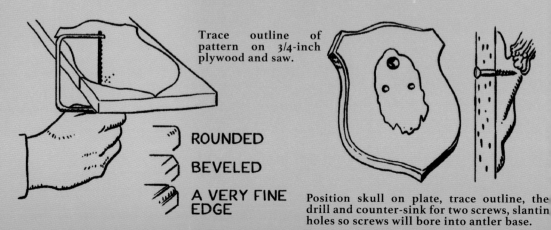

Trace outline of pattern on 3/4-inch plywood and saw.

ROUNDED

BEVELED

A VERY FINE EDGE

Position skull on plate, trace outline, the drill and counter-sink for two screws, slantin holes so screws will bore into antler base.

OWN DEER ANTLERS

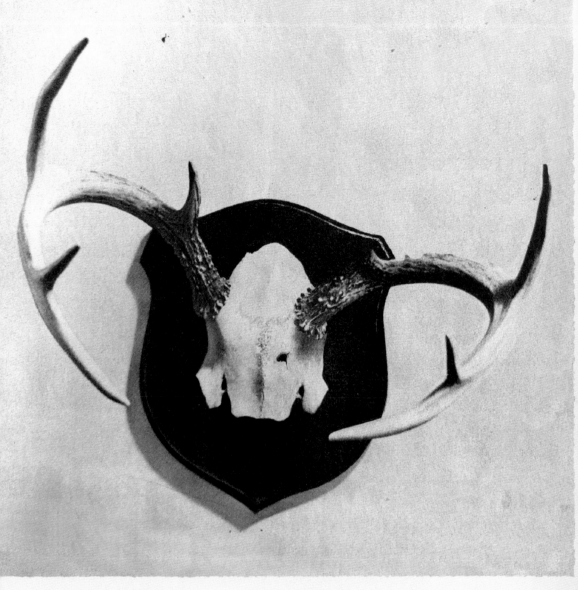

Make a hanger from a piece of sheet metal and center the notch over 1/2-inch hole in your panel. File the notch to a semicircle and chisel a 1/8-inch indentation in the wood as shown below. Just like summer school metal shop with Mr. Himler!

If you don't like a naked skull, paint it or apply flock texture to give it a nice velvety, suede-like appearance. Say--now, who's the big man of the house?

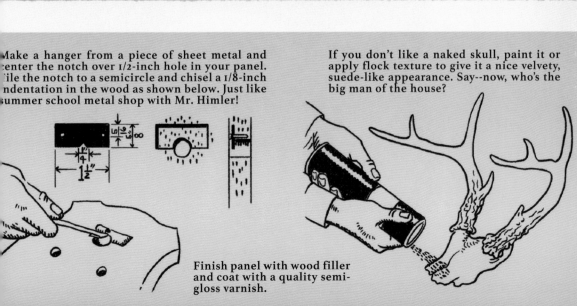

Finish panel with wood filler and coat with a quality semi-gloss varnish.

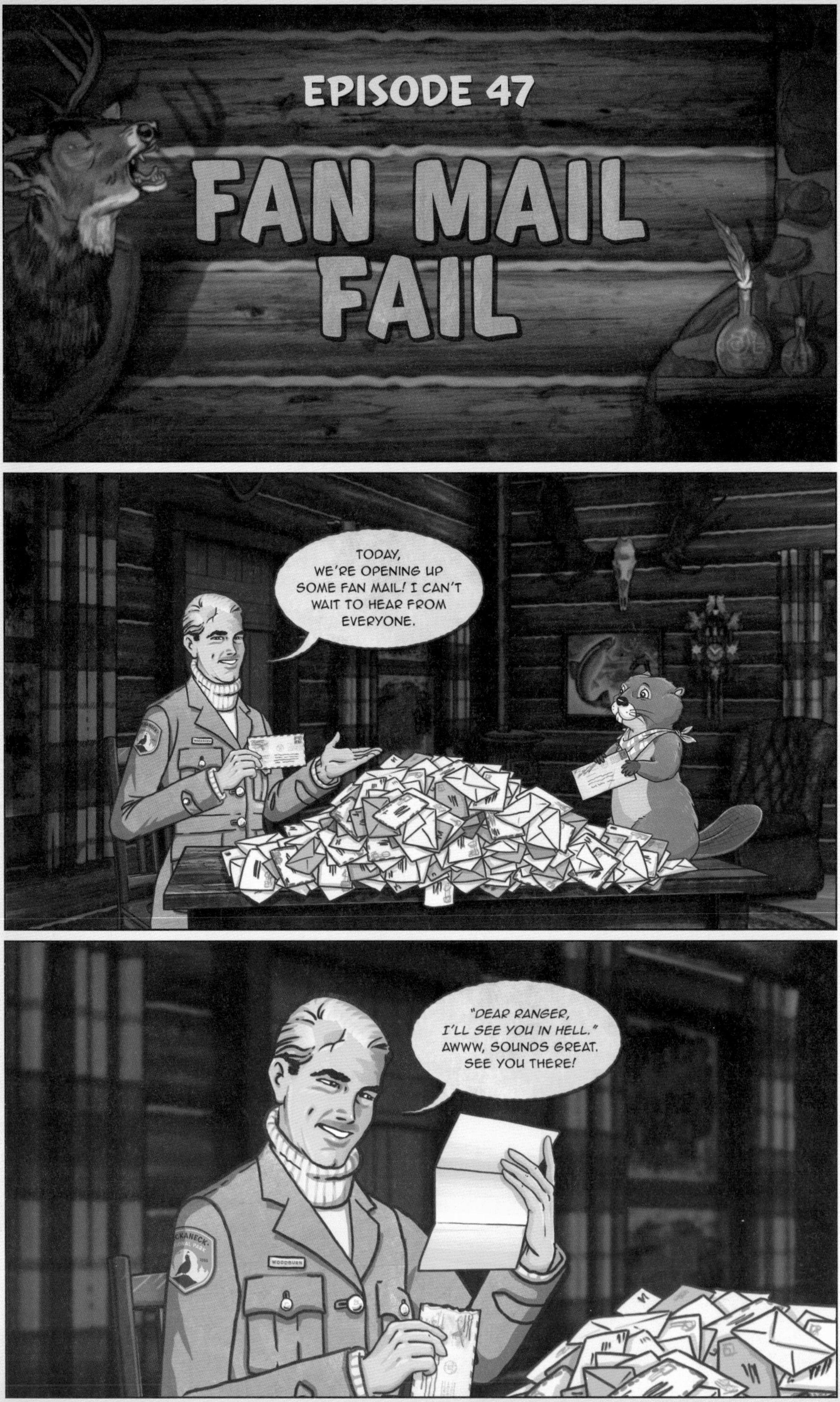
EPISODE 47
FAN MAIL FAIL
TODAY, WE'RE OPENING UP SOME FAN MAIL! I CAN'T WAIT TO HEAR FROM EVERYONE.
"DEAR RANGER, I'LL SEE YOU IN HELL." AWWW, SOUNDS GREAT. SEE YOU THERE!
WOODBURN

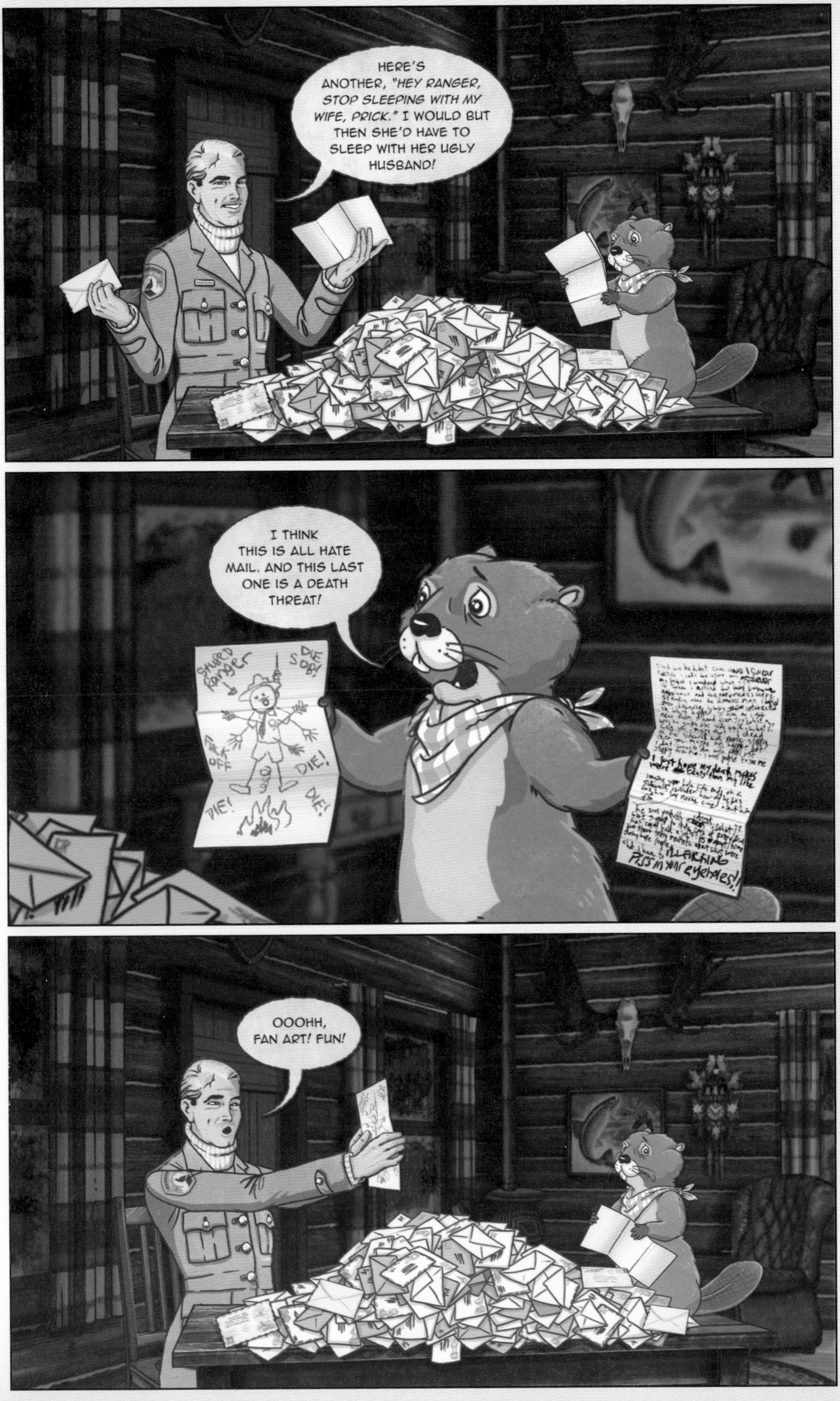
HERE'S ANOTHER, "HEY RANGER, STOP SLEEPING WITH MY WIFE, PRICK." I WOULD BUT THEN SHE'D HAVE TO SLEEP WITH HER UGLY HUSBAND!
I THINK THIS IS ALL HATE MAIL. AND THIS LAST ONE IS A DEATH THREAT!
STUPID Ranger
DIE SOB!
DIE!
DIE!
DIE!
OOOHH, FAN ART! FUN!

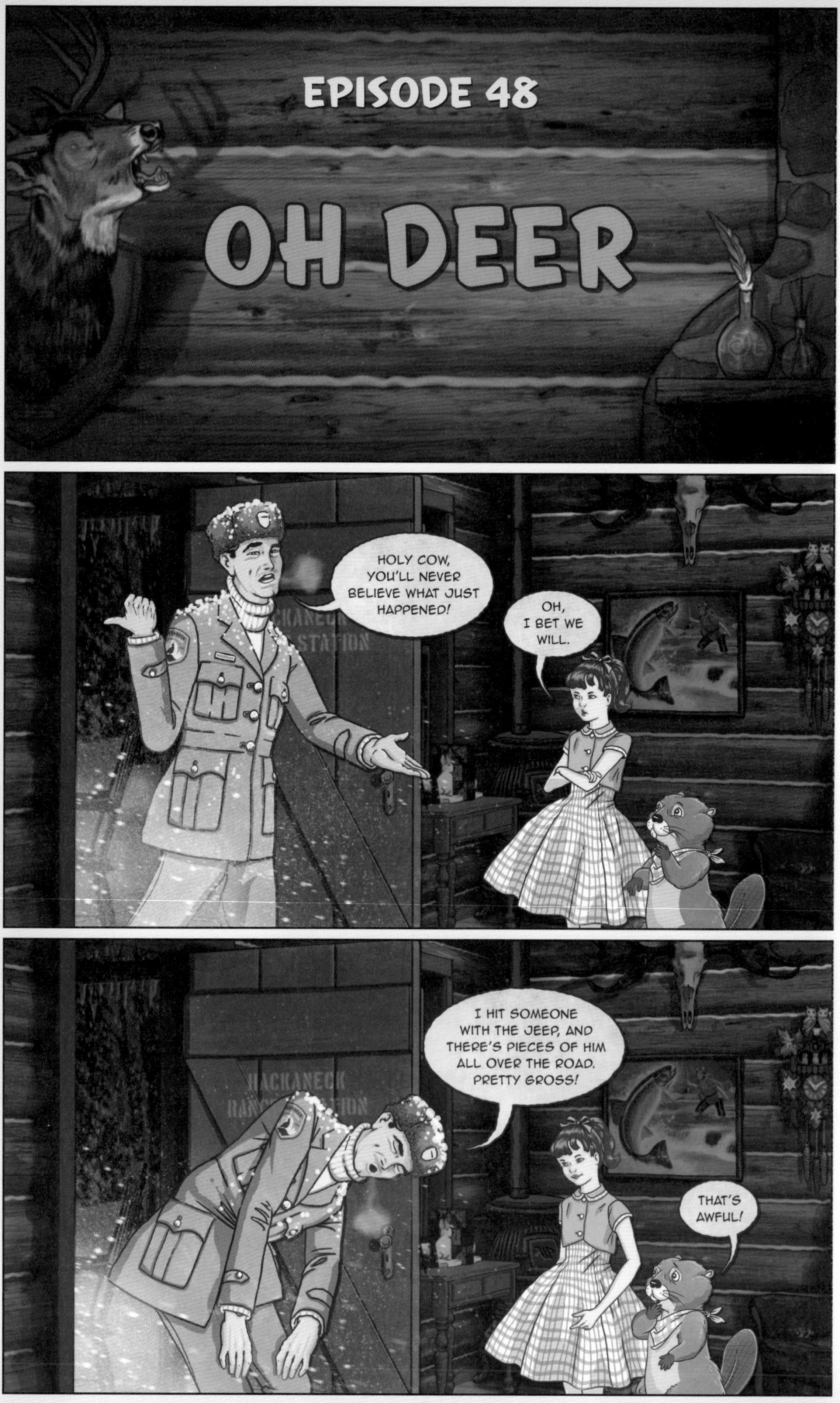
EPISODE 48
OH DEER
HOLY COW, YOU'LL NEVER BELIEVE WHAT JUST HAPPENED!
OH, I BET WE WILL.
I HIT SOMEONE WITH THE JEEP, AND THERE'S PIECES OF HIM ALL OVER THE ROAD. PRETTY GROSS!
THAT'S AWFUL!

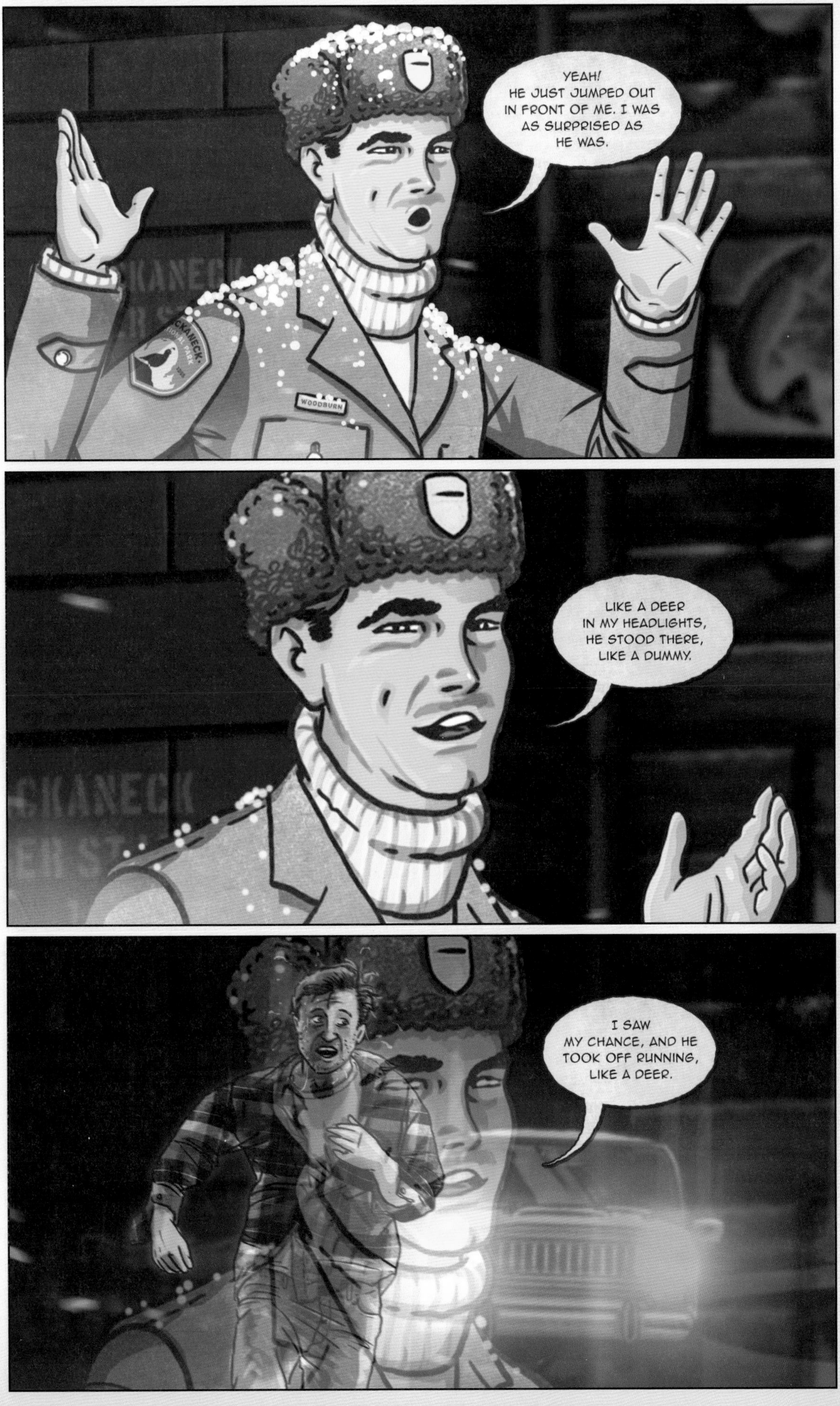
YEAH! HE JUST JUMPED OUT IN FRONT OF ME. I WAS AS SURPRISED AS HE WAS.
WOODBURN
LIKE A DEER IN MY HEADLIGHTS, HE STOOD THERE, LIKE A DUMMY.
I SAW MY CHANCE, AND HE TOOK OFF RUNNING, LIKE A DEER.

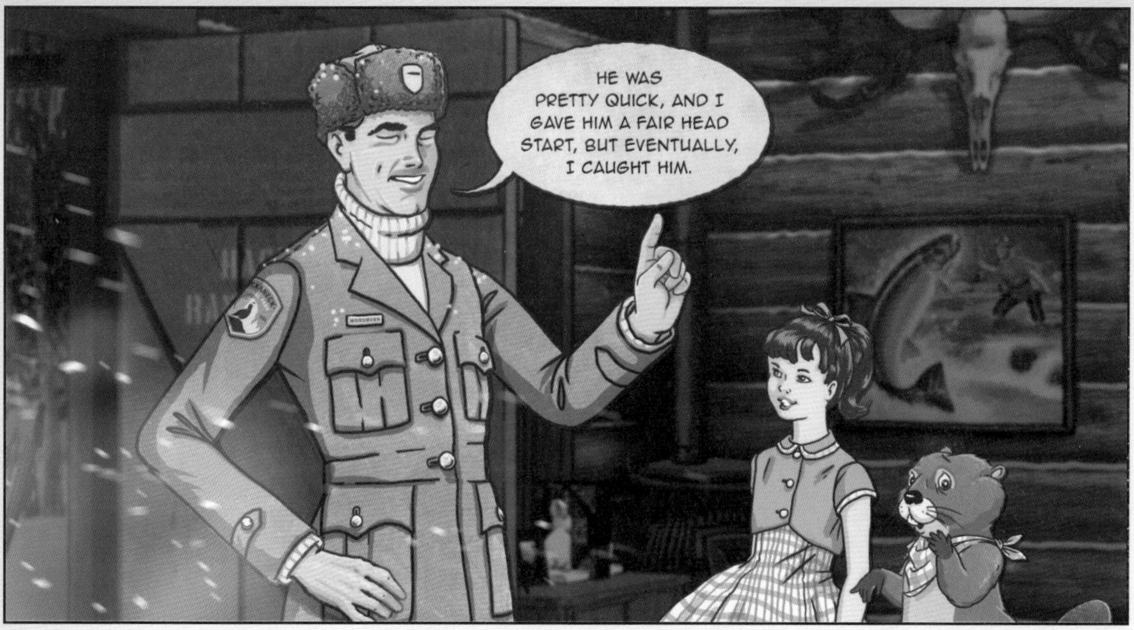
HE WAS PRETTY QUICK, AND I GAVE HIM A FAIR HEAD START, BUT EVENTUALLY, I CAUGHT HIM.

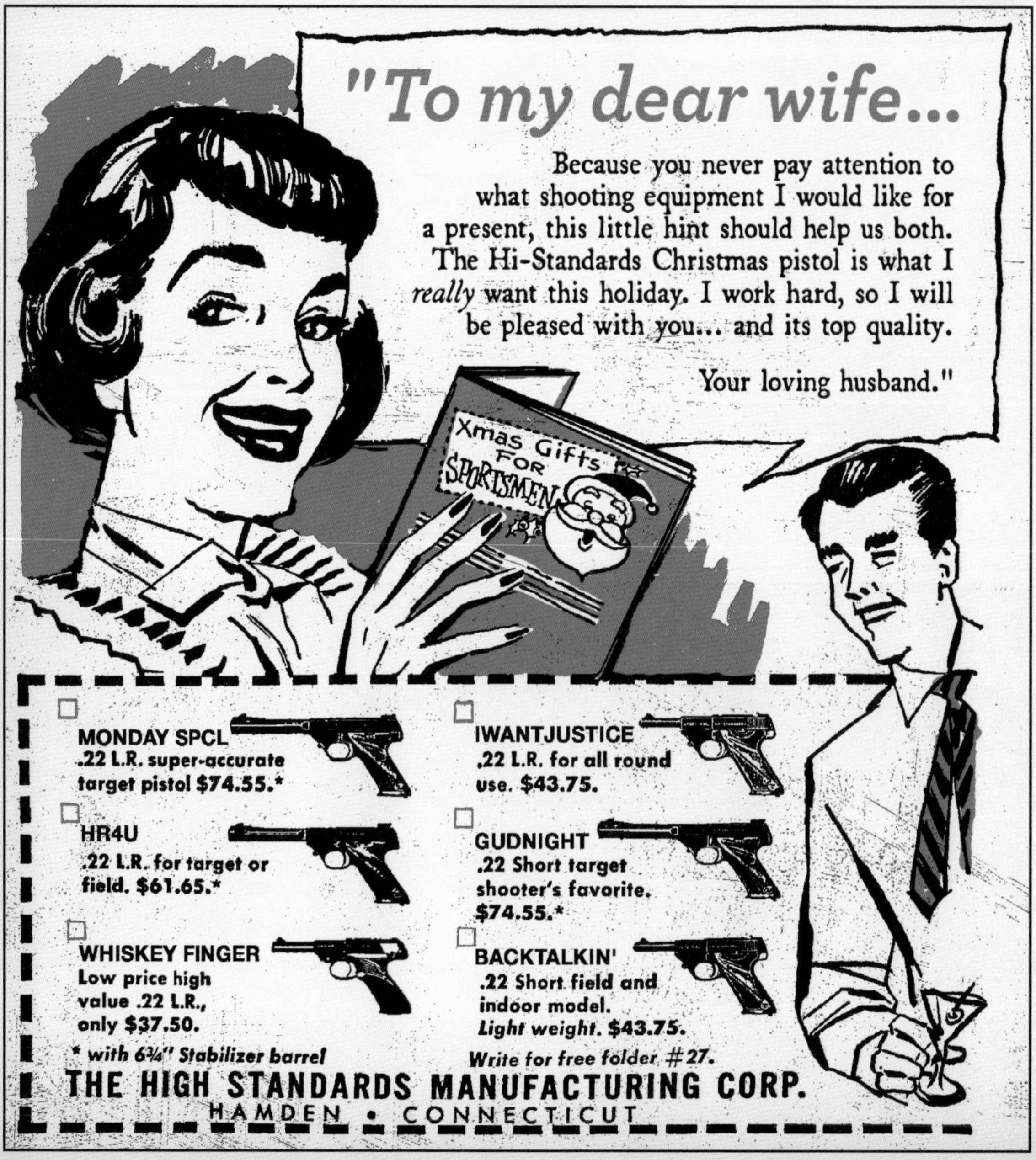
"To my dear wife...
Because you never pay attention to what shooting equipment I would like for a present, this little hint should help us both. The Hi-Standards Christmas pistol is what I *really* want this holiday. I work hard, so I will be pleased with you... and its top quality.
Your loving husband."
Xmas Gifts For SPORTSMEN
MONDAY SPCL .22 L.R. super-accurate target pistol $74.55.*
IWANTJUSTICE .22 L.R. for all round use. $43.75.
HR4U .22 L.R. for target or field. $61.65.*
GUDNIGHT .22 Short target shooter's favorite. $74.55.*
WHISKEY FINGER Low price high value .22 L.R., only $37.50.
BACKTALKIN' .22 Short field and indoor model. Light weight. $43.75.
* with 6¾" Stabilizer barrel
Write for free folder #27.
THE HIGH STANDARDS MANUFACTURING CORP.
HAMDEN • CONNECTICUT

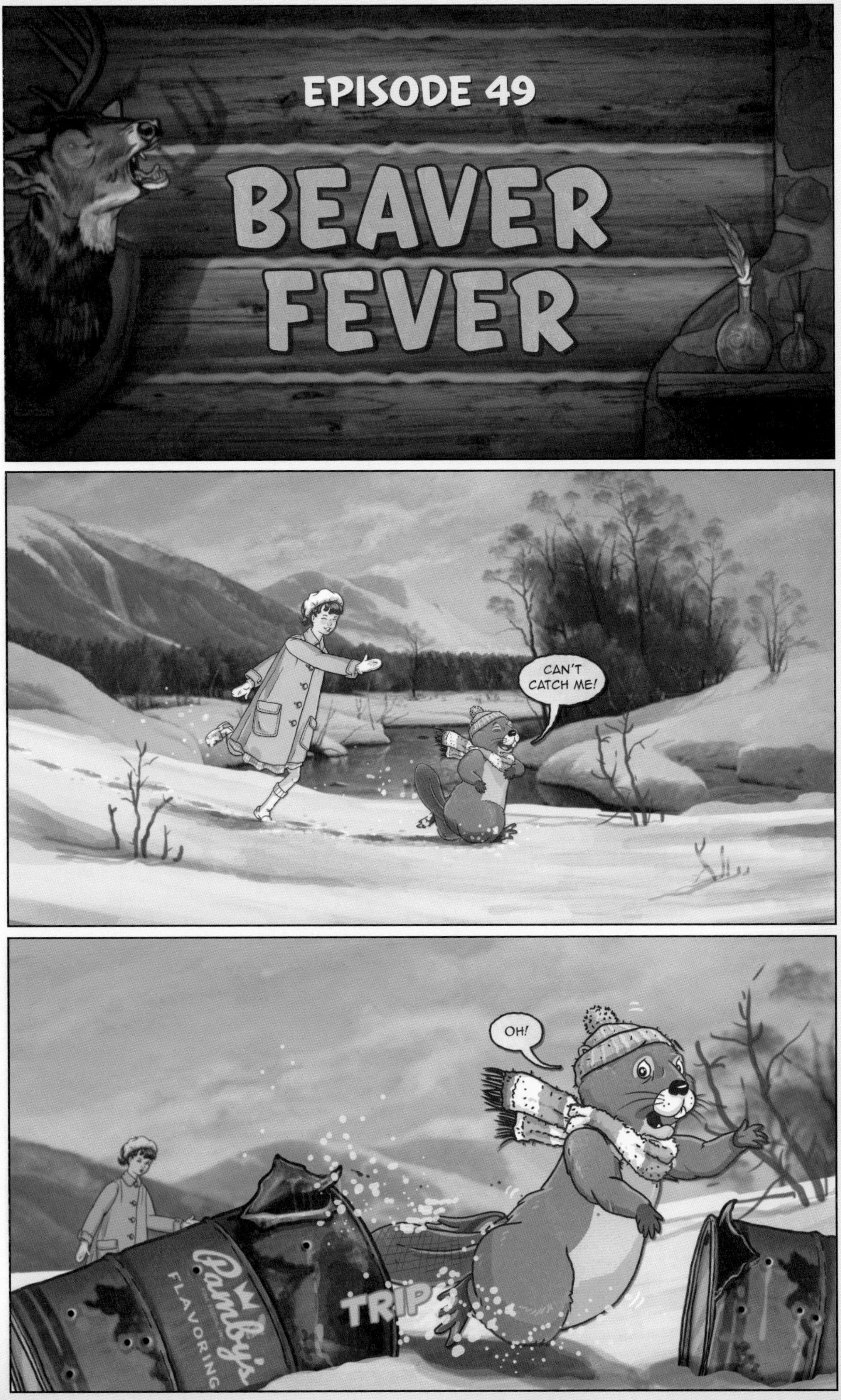
EPISODE 49
BEAVER FEVER
CAN'T CATCH ME!
OH!
Ramby's
FLAVORING
TRIP

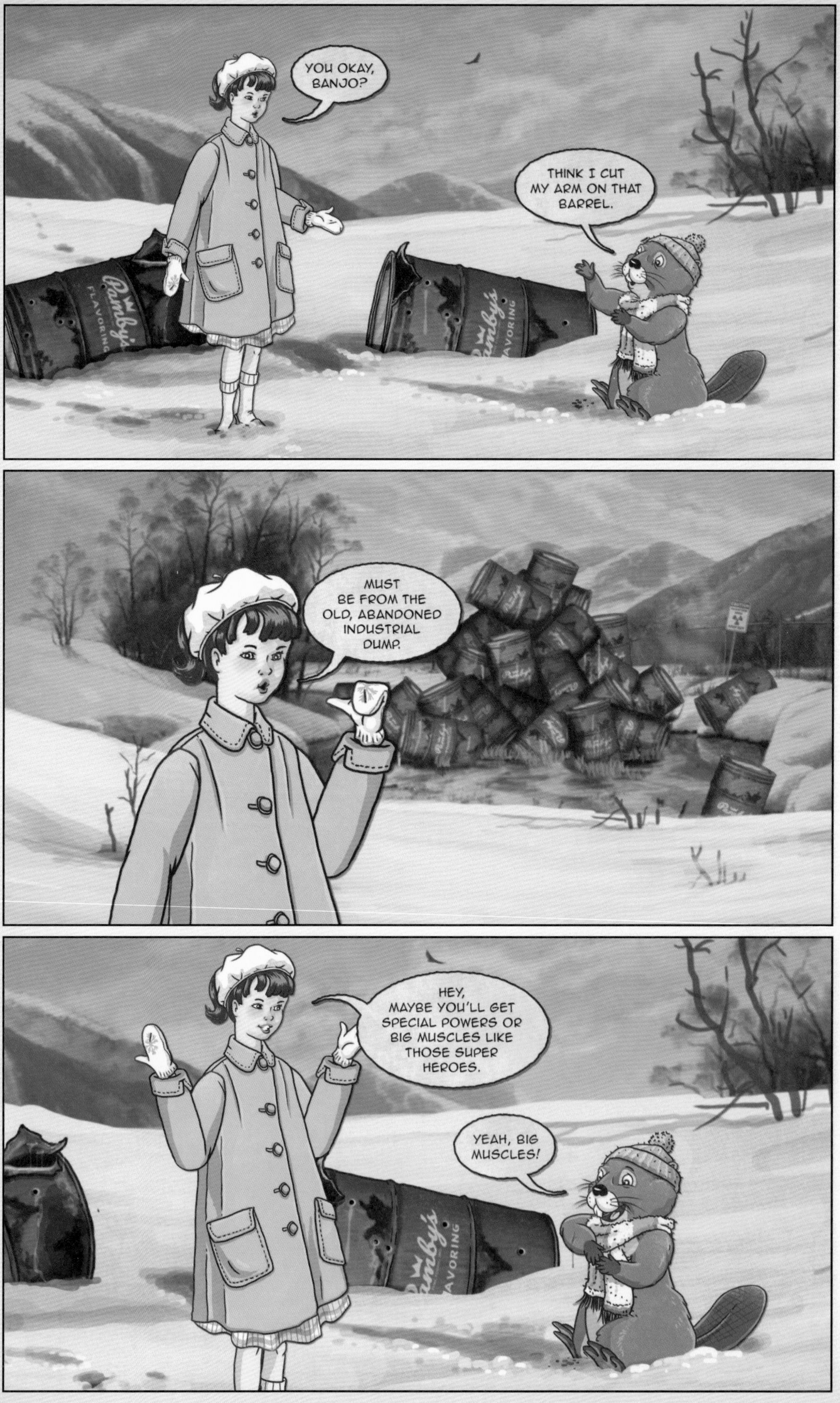
YOU OKAY, BANJO?
THINK I CUT MY ARM ON THAT BARREL.
MUST BE FROM THE OLD, ABANDONED INDUSTRIAL DUMP.
HEY, MAYBE YOU'LL GET SPECIAL POWERS OR BIG MUSCLES LIKE THOSE SUPER HEROES.
YEAH, BIG MUSCLES!

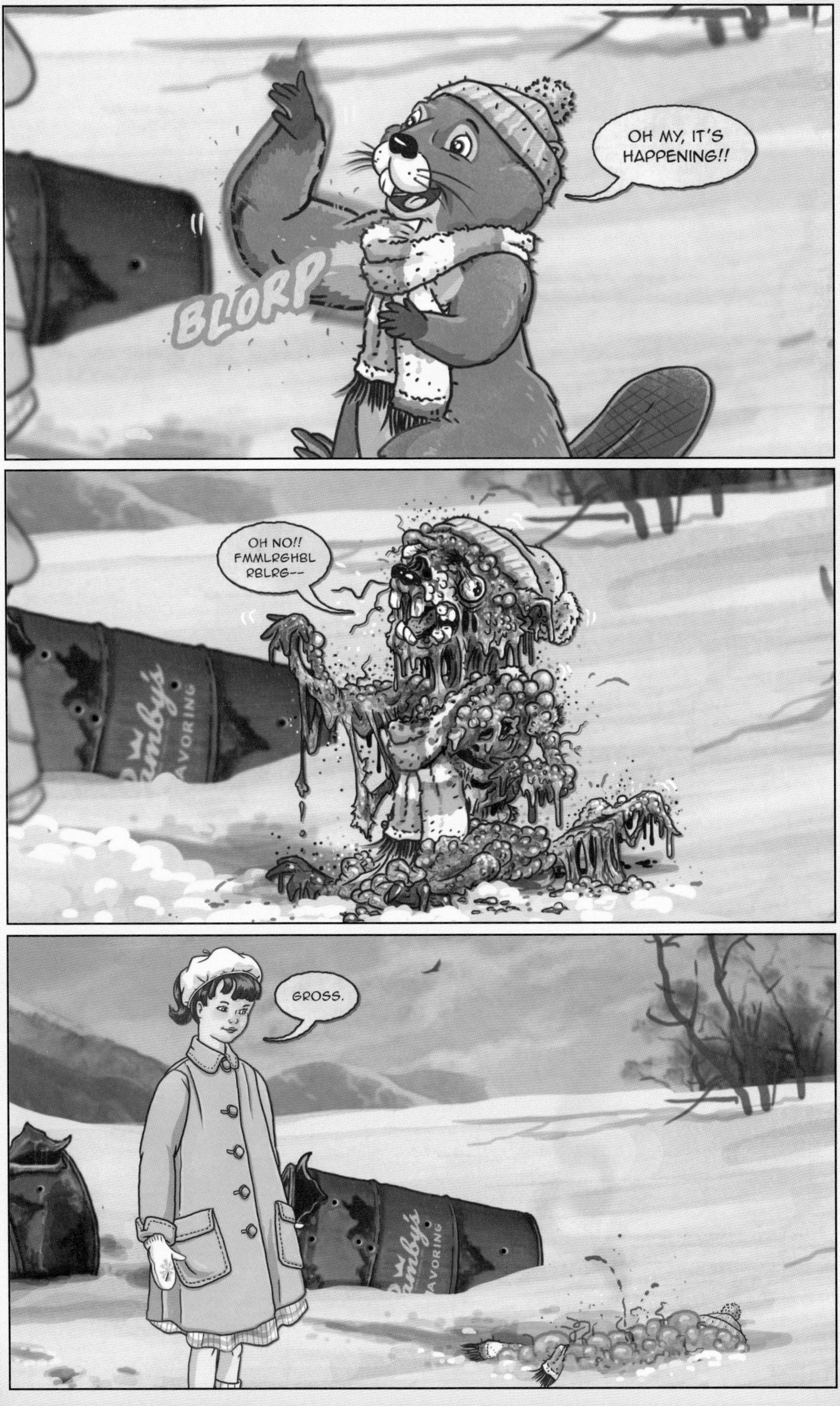
OH MY, IT'S HAPPENING!!
BLORP
OH NO!! FMMLRGHBL RBLRG--
GROSS.

FIRESIDE STORIES: REC TREK

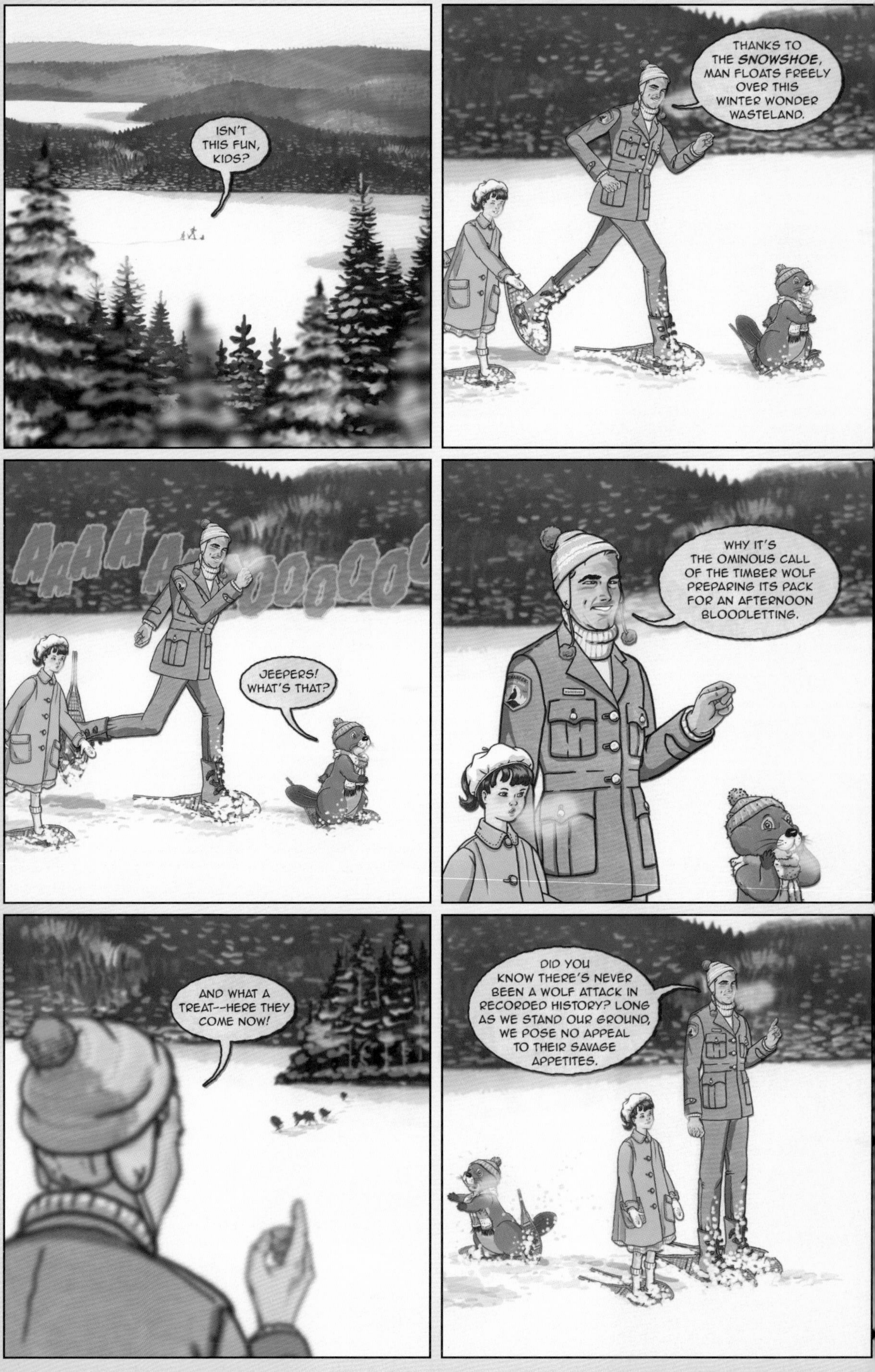
ISN'T THIS FUN, KIDS?
THANKS TO THE SNOWSHOE, MAN FLOATS FREELY OVER THIS WINTER WONDER WASTELAND.
JEEPERS! WHAT'S THAT?
WHY IT'S THE OMINOUS CALL OF THE TIMBER WOLF PREPARING ITS PACK FOR AN AFTERNOON BLOODLETTING.
AND WHAT A TREAT--HERE THEY COME NOW!
DID YOU KNOW THERE'S NEVER BEEN A WOLF ATTACK IN RECORDED HISTORY? LONG AS WE STAND OUR GROUND, WE POSE NO APPEAL TO THEIR SAVAGE APPETITES.

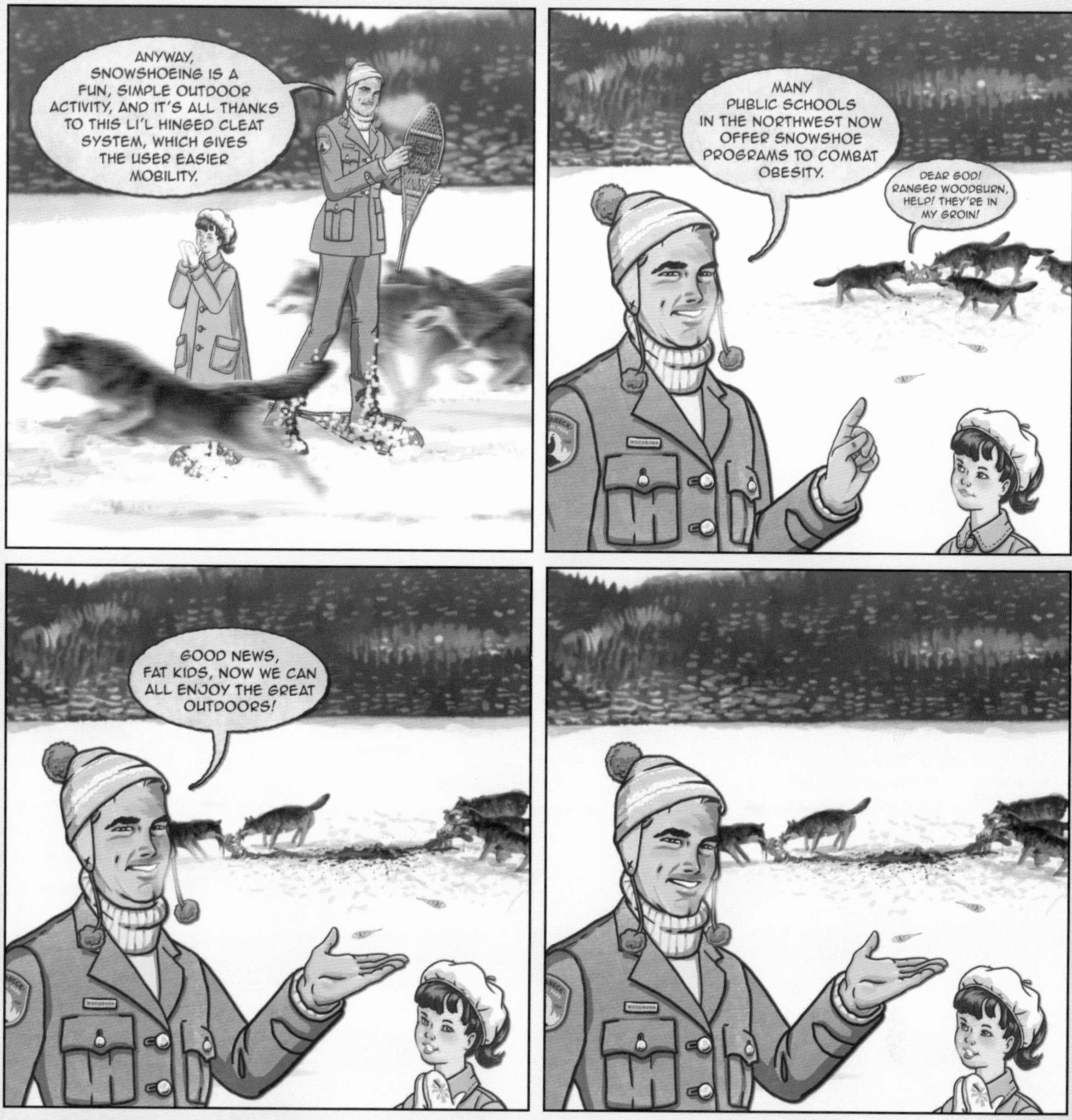
ANYWAY, SNOWSHOEING IS A FUN, SIMPLE OUTDOOR ACTIVITY, AND IT'S ALL THANKS TO THIS LI'L HINGED CLEAT SYSTEM, WHICH GIVES THE USER EASIER MOBILITY.
MANY PUBLIC SCHOOLS IN THE NORTHWEST NOW OFFER SNOWSHOE PROGRAMS TO COMBAT OBESITY.
DEAR GOD! RANGER WOODBURN, HELP! THEY'RE IN MY GROIN!
GOOD NEWS, FAT KIDS, NOW WE CAN ALL ENJOY THE GREAT OUTDOORS!

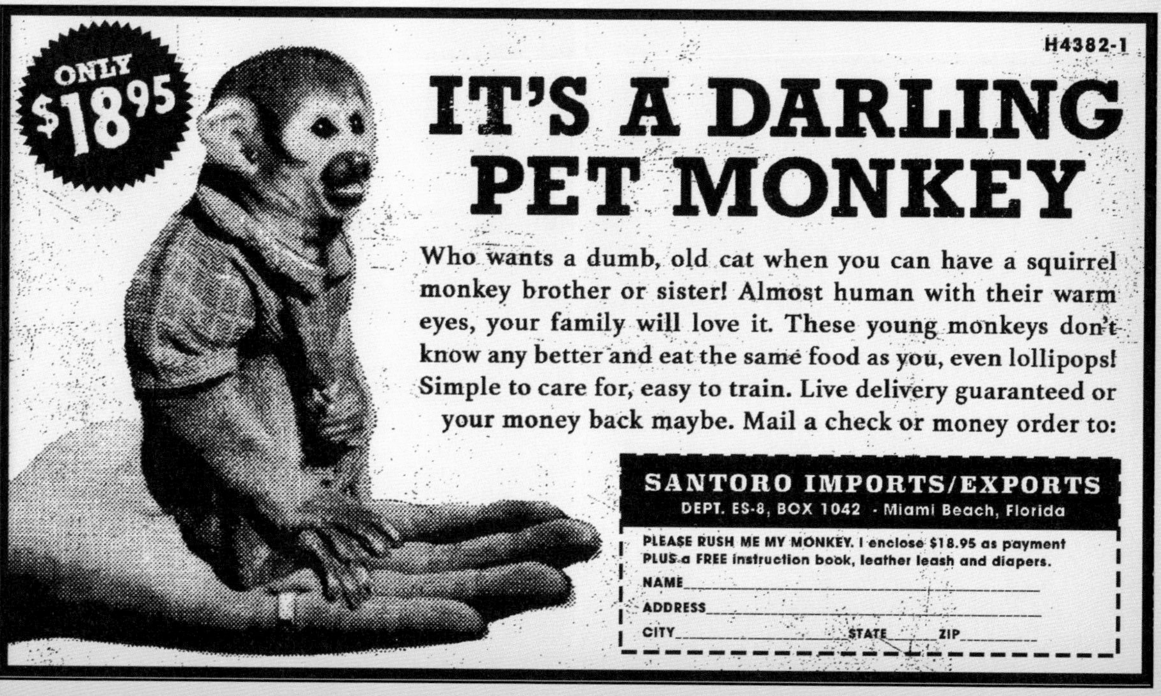
H4382-1
ONLY $18.95
IT'S A DARLING PET MONKEY
Who wants a dumb, old cat when you can have a squirrel monkey brother or sister! Almost human with their warm eyes, your family will love it. These young monkeys don't know any better and eat the same food as you, even lollipops! Simple to care for, easy to train. Live delivery guaranteed or your money back maybe. Mail a check or money order to:
SANTORO IMPORTS/EXPORTS
DEPT. ES-8, BOX 1042 · Miami Beach, Florida
PLEASE RUSH ME MY MONKEY. I enclose $18.95 as payment PLUS a FREE instruction book, leather leash and diapers.
NAME
ADDRESS
CITY
STATE
ZIP

FIRESIDE STORIES: HEYO YAYO

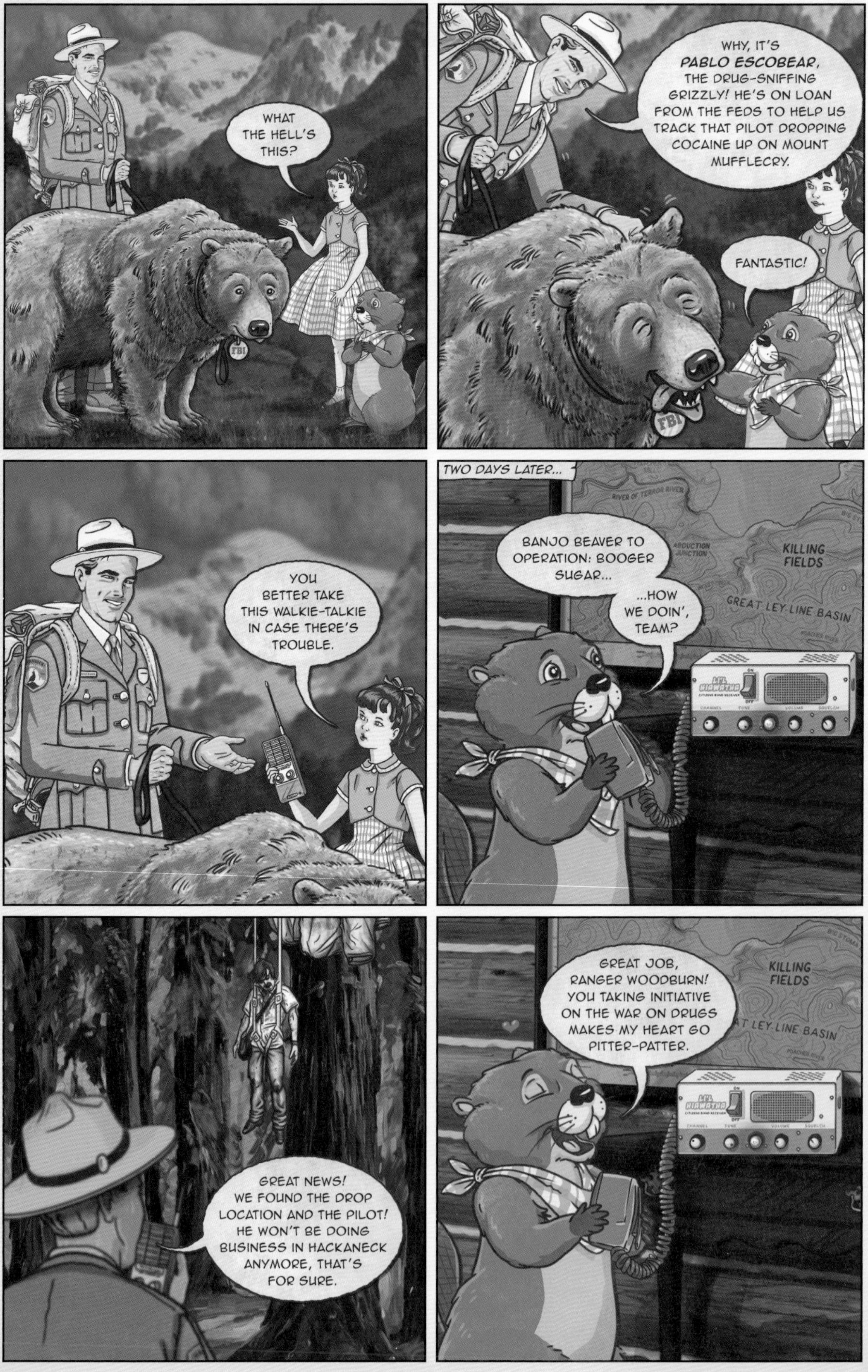
WHAT THE HELL'S THIS?
FBI
WHY, IT'S *PABLO ESCOBEAR*, THE DRUG-SNIFFING GRIZZLY! HE'S ON LOAN FROM THE FEDS TO HELP US TRACK THAT PILOT DROPPING COCAINE UP ON MOUNT MUFFLECRY.
FANTASTIC!
FBI
YOU BETTER TAKE THIS WALKIE-TALKIE IN CASE THERE'S TROUBLE.
TWO DAYS LATER...
BANJO BEAVER TO OPERATION: BOOGER SUGAR...
...HOW WE DOIN', TEAM?
ABDUCTION JUNCTION
KILLING FIELDS
GREAT LEY LINE BASIN
GREAT NEWS! WE FOUND THE DROP LOCATION AND THE PILOT! HE WON'T BE DOING BUSINESS IN HACKANECK ANYMORE, THAT'S FOR SURE.
GREAT JOB, RANGER WOODBURN! YOU TAKING INITIATIVE ON THE WAR ON DRUGS MAKES MY HEART GO PITTER-PATTER.
KILLING FIELDS

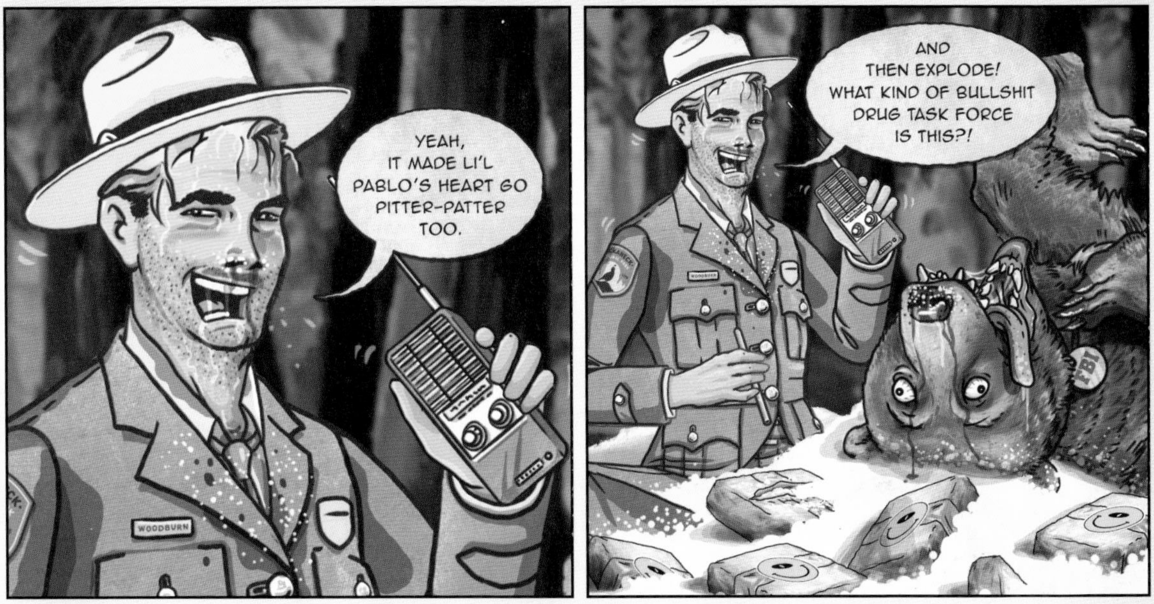
YEAH, IT MADE LI'L PABLO'S HEART GO PITTER-PATTER TOO.
AND THEN EXPLODE! WHAT KIND OF BULLSHIT DRUG TASK FORCE IS THIS?!
FBI

FIRESIDE STORIES: TRAPPINGS OF MADNESS

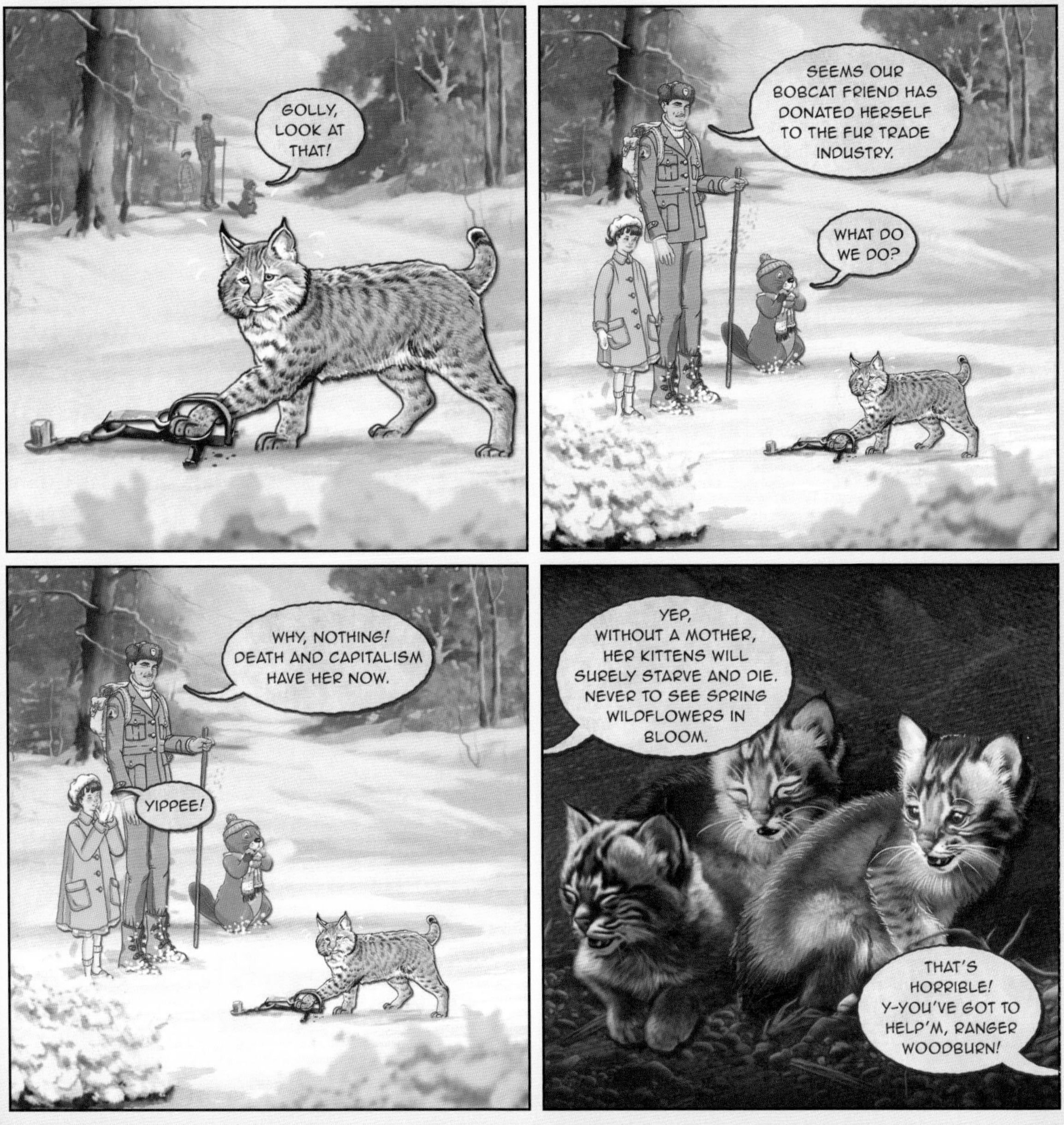
GOLLY, LOOK AT THAT!
SEEMS OUR BOBCAT FRIEND HAS DONATED HERSELF TO THE FUR TRADE INDUSTRY.
WHAT DO WE DO?
WHY, NOTHING! DEATH AND CAPITALISM HAVE HER NOW.
YIPPEE!
YEP, WITHOUT A MOTHER, HER KITTENS WILL SURELY STARVE AND DIE. NEVER TO SEE SPRING WILDFLOWERS IN BLOOM.
THAT'S HORRIBLE! Y-YOU'VE GOT TO HELP'M, RANGER WOODBURN!

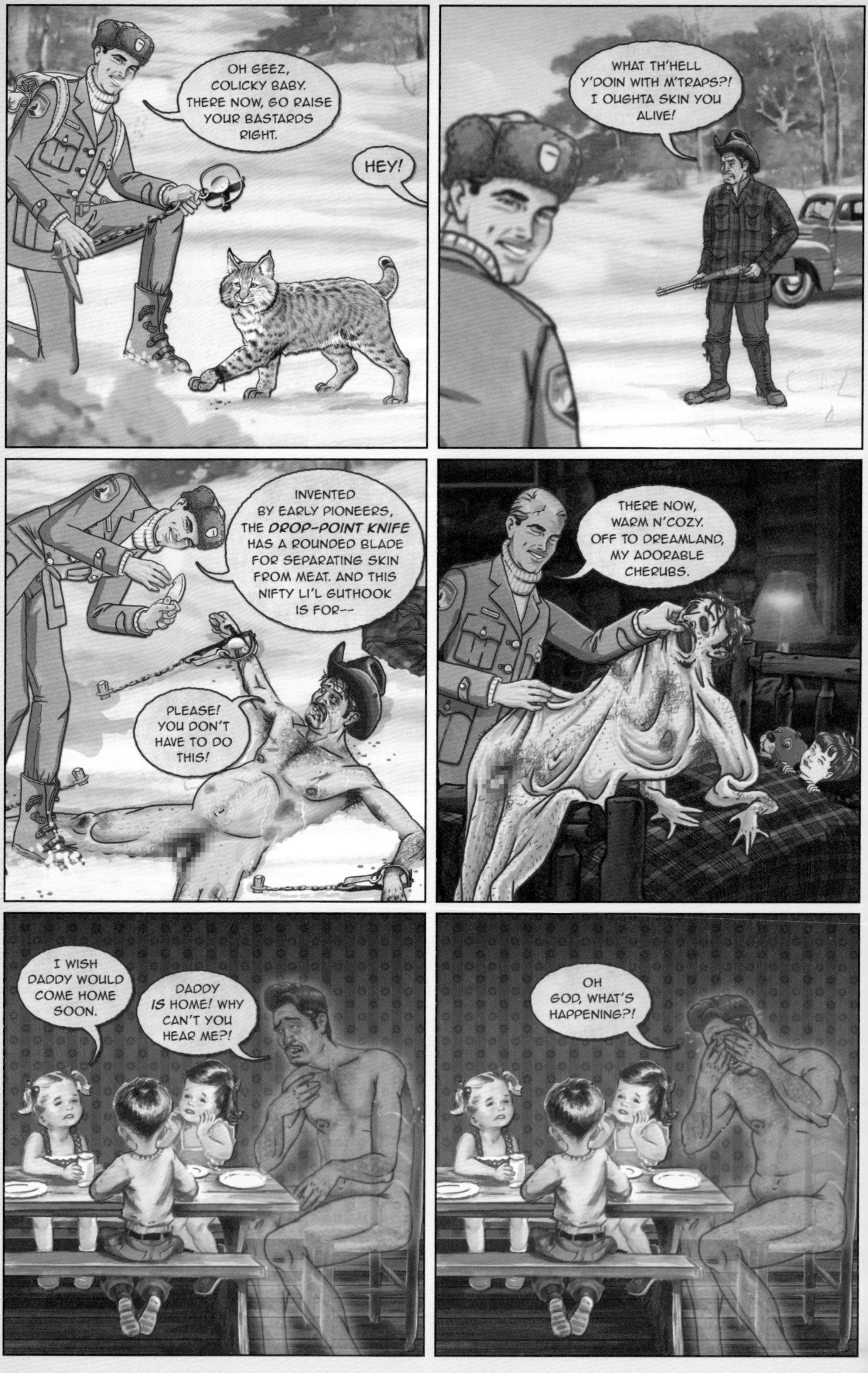
OH GEEZ, COLICKY BABY. THERE NOW, GO RAISE YOUR BASTARDS RIGHT.
HEY!
WHAT TH'HELL Y'DOIN WITH M'TRAPS?! I OUGHTA SKIN YOU ALIVE!
INVENTED BY EARLY PIONEERS, THE ***DROP-POINT KNIFE*** HAS A ROUNDED BLADE FOR SEPARATING SKIN FROM MEAT. AND THIS NIFTY LI'L GUTHOOK IS FOR--
PLEASE! YOU DON'T HAVE TO DO THIS!
THERE NOW, WARM N'COZY. OFF TO DREAMLAND, MY ADORABLE CHERUBS.
I WISH DADDY WOULD COME HOME SOON.
DADDY *IS* HOME! WHY CAN'T YOU HEAR ME?!
OH GOD, WHAT'S HAPPENING?!

FIRESIDE STORIES: WILD COFFEE BEANS

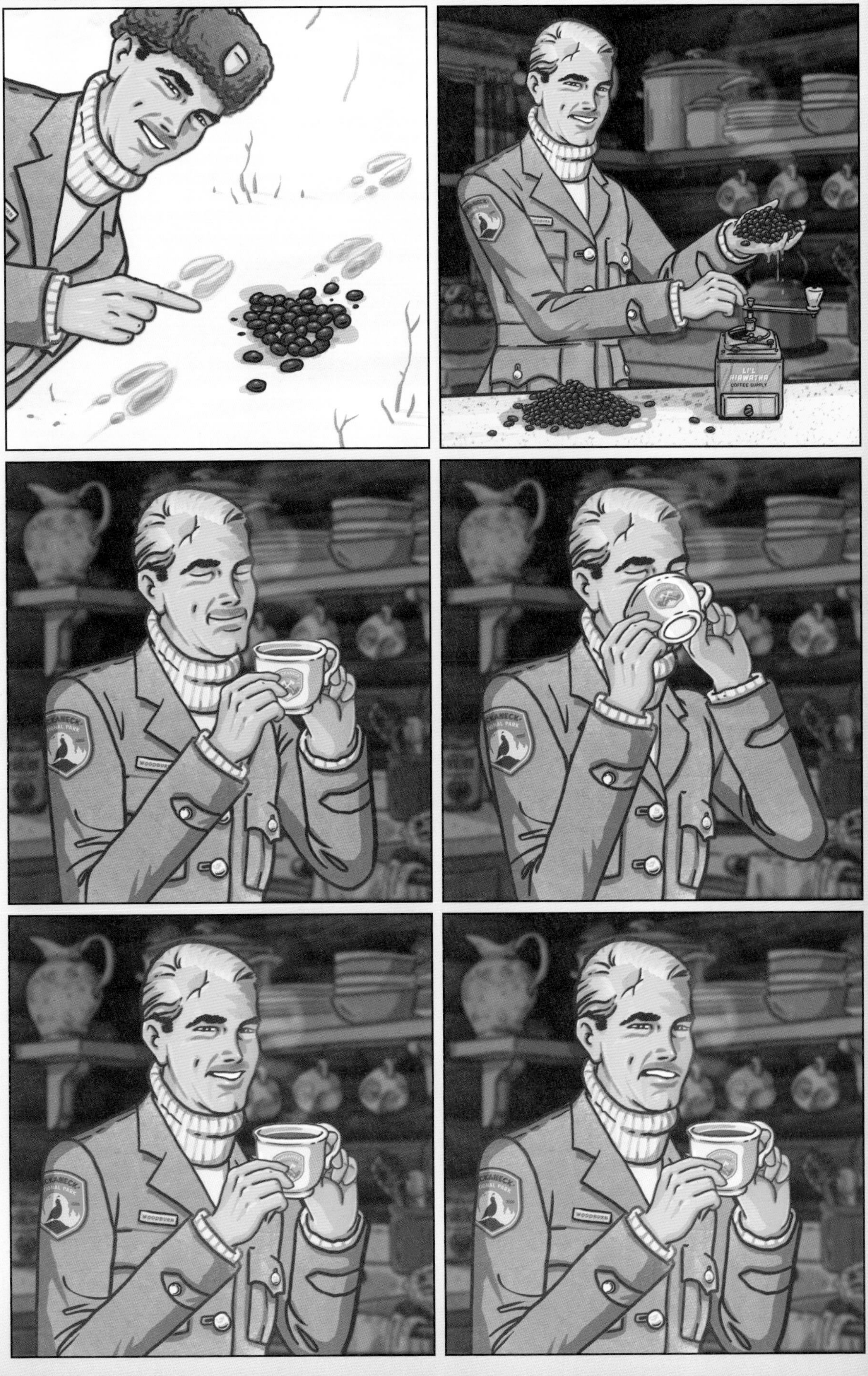
LI'L HIAWATHA
COFFEE SUPPLY
WOODBURN
WOODBURN

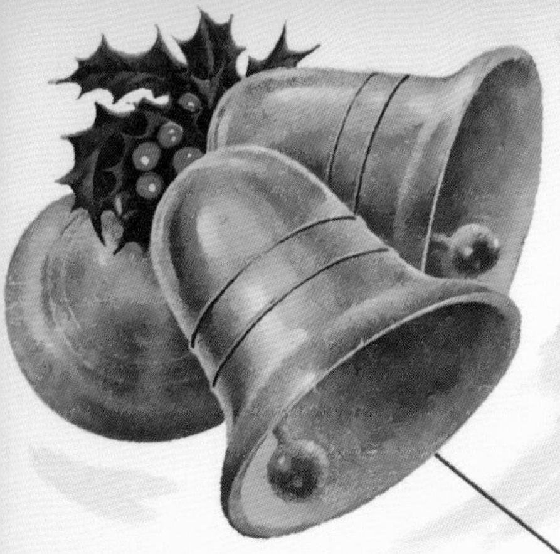

Give Bags of Joy for Christmas

The smell of fresh-brewed coffee after 9lbs of turkey and casserole. It's no wonder all the neighbors come a-runnin'! Who can resist coffee's cheery aroma– so tempting, so full of promise and friendship.

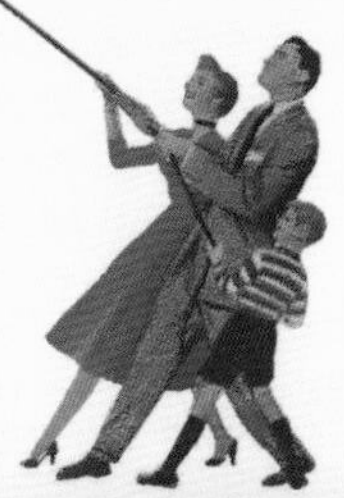

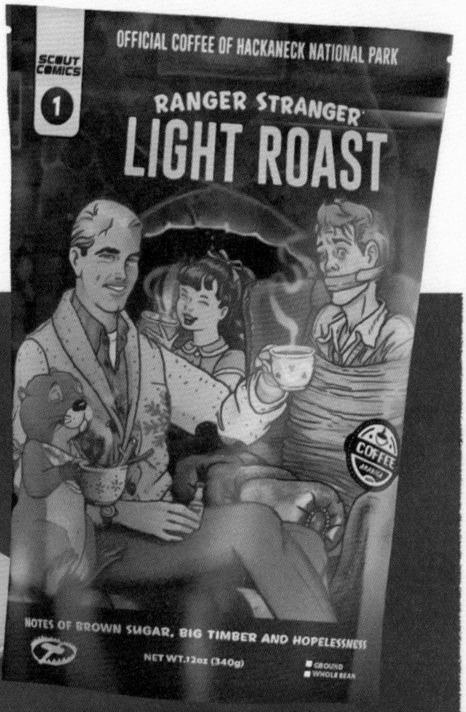

SCOUT COMICS
1
OFFICIAL COFFEE OF HACKANECK NATIONAL PARK
RANGER STRANGER
LIGHT ROAST
COFFEE
NOTES OF BROWN SUGAR, BIG TIMBER AND HOPELESSNESS
GROUND
WHOLE BEAN

M-m-m-m... nothing satisfies like coffee!

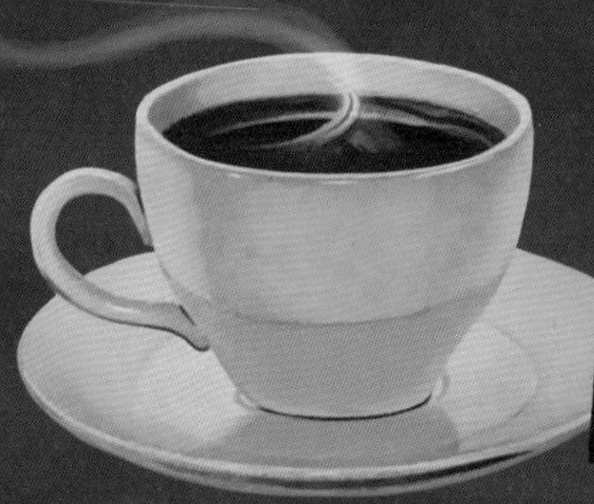

Gaily packaged

Makes a great gift

Distributed by Scout Comics Coffee Co. (scoutcomics.com) - Brazil - Colombia - Costa Rica - Cuba - El Salvador - Mexico - Honduras

FIRESIDE STORIES: COLD BLOODED

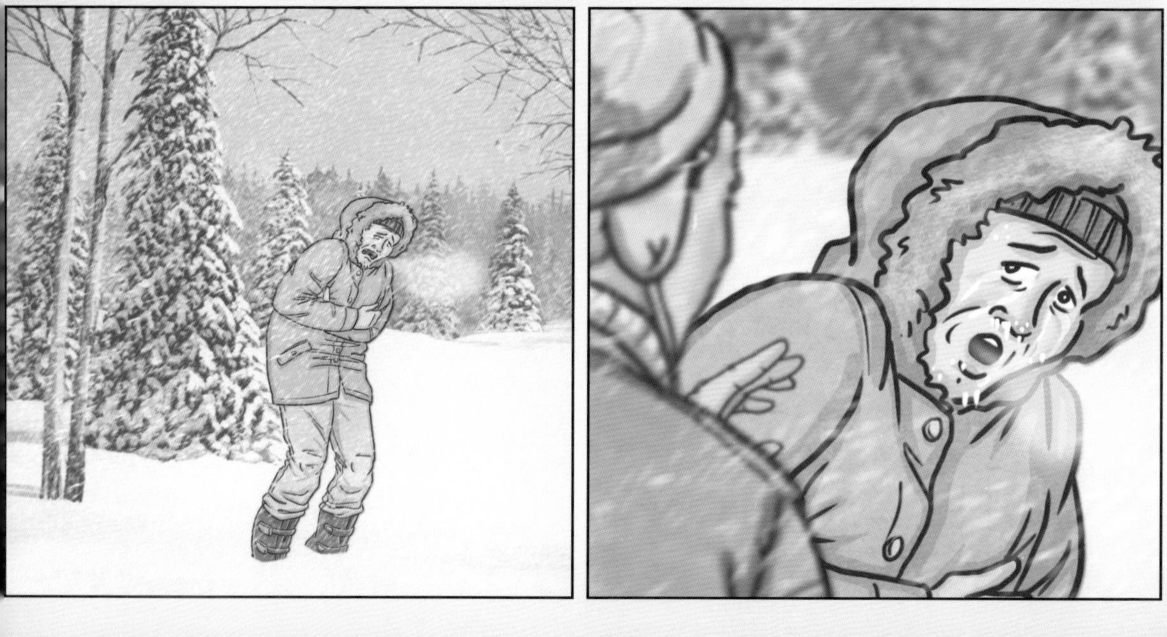

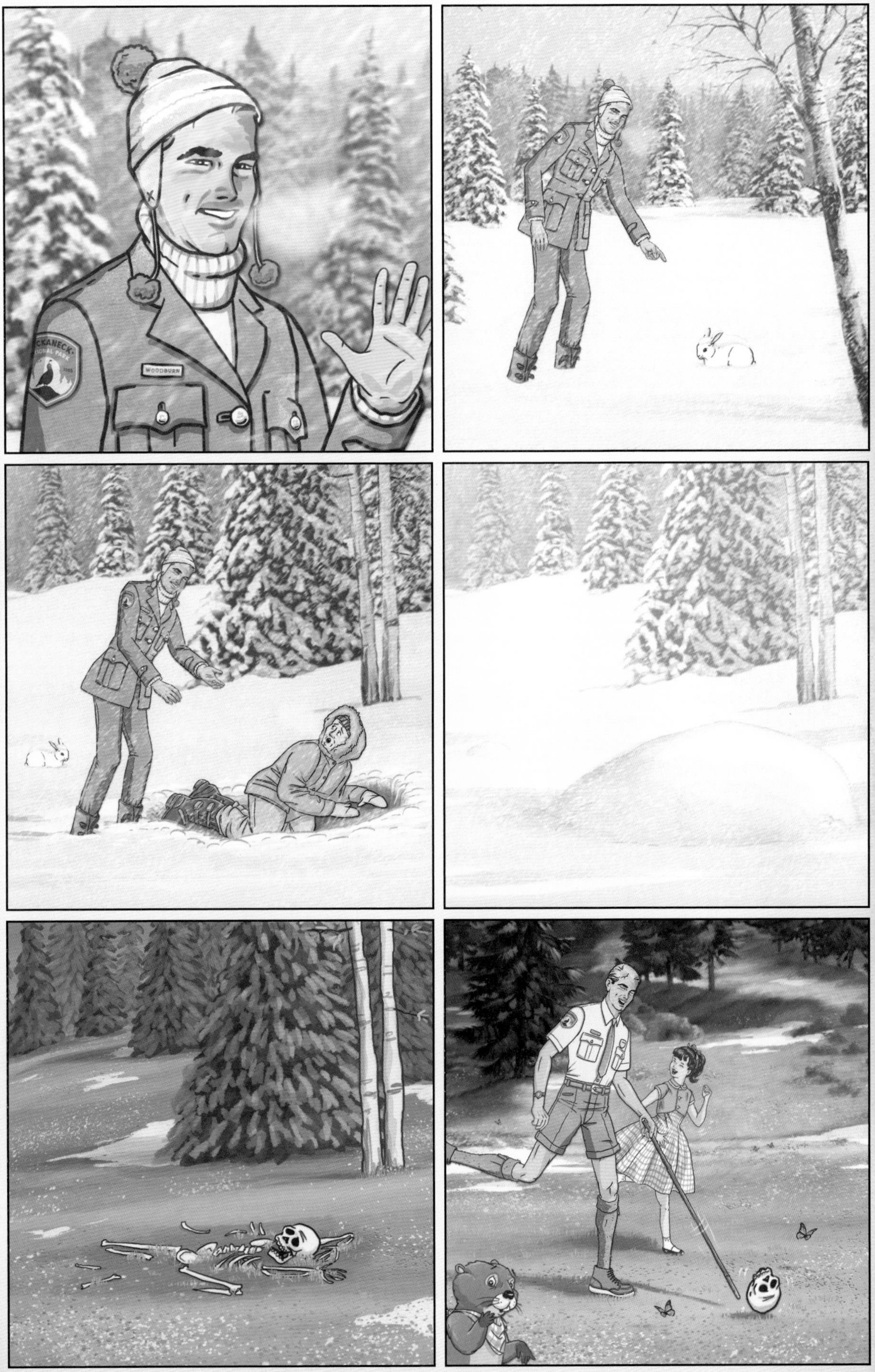
WOODBURN

CLASSIFIEDS

MEN! THIS IS IT!

Nothing like these Adult Cartoon Booklets, ever!

REAL COLLECTORS ITEMS.
1. Maggie and Diggs
2. Toots and Jasper
3. Tillie the Soiler
4. Lord Pushbottom & Emma
5. Villain & Little Nell and others.

ACT NOW!

FREE CATALOG OF TITILLATING NOVELTIES WITH ORDER

FITS VEST POCKET — 10 for $1 22 for $2!

Q. T. SALES Box 8516, Dept. 1007 Hollywood 46, Calif.

SWEATERS, SOCKS, MITTENS N'MUFFS

Handmade with love for warmth and comfort. Men's and women's sizes. Send $4.99 for free catalog.

KNANCY'S KNITS
1225 McKINLEY AVE. AKRON, OHIO

PROSPECTING

URIED Treasure - Assistant needed immediately for lost mazon gold expedition. Must be good at cyphers, digging. 're-disposed tolerance to poison darts a plus, but not reuired. H.L. Dechant, 155 Glenoaks Ave. Glendale, Calif.

FROG RAISING

ABY Frogs. Louisiana Jumbos. Grow fast and large. Multiply y the thousands. Easy to keep in your garage or backyard. 15 per hundred, $125 per thousand. Send $4.99 for full-color atalog. Ferd's Frog Farm, 88 Bohemian Rd., Jethrow, Louis.

EMPLOYMENT SERVICES

'IRED? LAID OFF? ANGRY? We'll show you HOW to conuct yourself at a job interview. Write NICE application and ositive follow up letters. Stop storming out of appointments. Ve can help! Send $4.99 Elgers, Inc. Metuchen, New Jersey.

BUSINESS OPPORTUNITY

Become a Park Ranger, Game Warden, or Lookout. Enjoy outdoor work, fresh air, miles away from bosses, nosey people asking questions. Send $4.99 for our "Self-Evaluation" test. U.S.N.P.S., Superintendant, 470 Sierra Dr. Three Forks, Calif.

Malayan THROWING DAGGER

BALANCED TO STICK! $4.99 postpaid

The MALAYAN FIGHTING KNIFE is used for self-defense, killing game, target skill. Powerful, silent, accurate weapon. Splits 1" board at 30 ft.

EASY TO THROW!

MONEY BACK GUARANTEE MAYBE

Fun, Thrills, Excitement! Indoors—outdoors Learn this Sport! Easy to throw accurately with our clear instructions. Beautiful, heavy-duty 10" knife. Tempered steel. Tough, rawhide-bound handle. Rare souvenir. If your sporting goods dealer can't supply you, send $4.99

WHOLESALE IMPORT CO. Dept. 4K, 604 Marengo, Alhambra, Calif.

ITALIAN ACCORDIONS AT LOWEST WHOLESALE PRICES

5-DAY FREE TRIAL

"PAY AS YOU PLAY" Small Down Payment As Little As $10 per month

DIRECT from Importer to You!

SATISFACTION GUARANTEED, or your money back! NOW you can save up to 50% by direct purchase from America's leading distributor of famous genuine ITALIAN ACCORDIONS. TRADE-INS ACCEPTED. *Send for FREE Illustrated Catalog!*

VORHAUER ACCORDIAN WHOLESALERS OUTLET
2003 West Chicago Ave. Dept. F5-104, Chicago 22, Ill.

PERSONAL SERVICES

Divorced? Lonely? Try again with a delightful suitor from the nation of Hungary. Naturally stout, hearty brides and grooms. All with teeth. Send $4.99 for full-color photo catalog Lagbort's Gems of Hungary, Box 42, Alhambra, Calif.

MISCELLANEOUS

VACATION in exciting CANADA! Pie eating, fly tieing, and funny-looking money. The outdoors just the way you like it. Write or wire for bulletins and a free brochure: Canada Pacific Travel Agency, Windsor Station, Montréal, Québec.

REAL Buckskin Shirts. Styled after the pioneer days. Handmade from genuine deer skin by my western craftsmen. Pliable, breathable, washable leather. Ideal for hiking, fishing, and leisure. Send $4.99 for free catalog to Norm Euker, 5092 S Barnes Rd, Portland, Oregon.

S, M, L, XL

NOW—YOU CAN EASILY RE-BLUE YOUR GUN

NEW IMPROVED
Minute Man
GUN BLUE
ONE APPLICATION

Instantly with one simple application of MINUTE-MAN GUN BLUE—a chemical bluer that actually blues the steel. Not a paint or lacquer. No heating—GUARANTEED—can't injure steel.
Your money back if not satisfied. Send $4.99

NEW METHOD MFG. CO.
FSM-96 Bradford, Pa.

MONKEYS are ALMOST HUMAN

Cheap and easy to keep! We have all kinds. Also, wild raccoons, wildcats, foxes, 'possums, snakes, owls, crows, baby alligators, and deodorized pygmy skunks. Hours of fun for the whole family. Send $4.99 for a free catalog.

PALEKIS FAMILY
WILD PET EMPORIUM
36 Caiman Rd., Destitute, FLA.
Tel: 2-1236

BUILD-YOUR-OWN ELECTRIC ENGINE!

YES! 9000 rpm MAGNETIC MOTOR. Operate small cars, boats, and so much more! Parents and teachers will love it.

Free catalog, $4.99 to: Schaatz Sciences, Inc. Dept. 129, Box 397, Rockville Centre, N.Y.

EMPLOYMENT

ASSISTANT NEEDED for KODIAK BEAR documentary. Immediate opening in exciting, dramatic Alaska. Carry equipment, make camp, scout ahead for shooting locations. No experience necessary! Must be faster than a bear. Send resume to Max Elwood Outdoor Films, Box F848, Palo Alto, Calif.

GIANT STRAIN RACCOONS 40 lbs. Maturity FOR PETS

Natural and Mutation

We produce superior quality exclusively—Famous strains you'll be proud to own. Order bred females now. Instructive, interesting art-color catalog, $4.99.

HAPPY GLENN FUR FARM
Massacre River Rd., Springfield, Minn.

PERSONAL SERVICES

LOSING hair? Send $4.99 Zeznitchia Method of Hair Prevention Clinic, 13 Hipodrom Street 06560 Yenimahalle Ankara

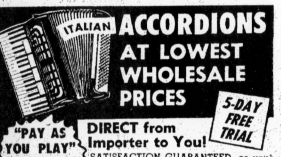

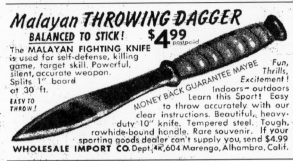

CLASSIFIEDS

Own A BABY PET MONKEY For Companionship-Fun

Illustrated brochure of species and prices. $4.99. Easy to care for.

LEVINE'S TROPICAL BIRDS & PETS
127 Main Street, Fort Lee, NJ

RAISE MINK
THE FUR BUSINESS IS ALWAYS GOOD

I ship top breeding mink in all colors on approval everywhere. Free booklet gives inside "secrets" and pen plans. There is cheap feed going to waste right in your own area. Why not turn it into valuable fur? Ask me about this feed today.

MOLGARD LAWRENCE
Brigham City 11, Utah

RAISE CHINCHILLAS! MAKE MONEY AT HOME

A Rich, Full, Profitable Future can be YOURS raising dumb Chinchillas. Top-quality, guaranteed to litter! *New, 24-page booklet, $4.99. Please send name and address to:*

CAMPOCHINO CHINCHILLA FARM N.C.B.A. 328 Pismo Beach, Calif.

DETECTIVES

DETECTIVES—NO Experience Necessary. Detective Particulars free. Write, George Frank Wagoner, 122 West 84th St., New York.

TAXIDERMISTS

START YOUR OWN TAXIDERMY BUSINESS! Fully Illustrated Instruction Manuals on Birds; Animals; Fish Mounting $4.99 each. Faartz Taxidermy School, 322 N. 15th Street, Allentown, Penn.

STOCK YOUR LAKES!

BASS·BREAM·CRAPPIE
Healthy, hardy fingerling from select brood stock. Bred to live, grow and *FIGHT!* Live delivery guaranteed, any express station in USA. *Write* for PRICE and INFORMATION NOW!

LIVE DELIVERY *GUARANTEED*

JIM REEVE CALHOUN, GEORGIA

HELP WANTED

MAKE MONEY Selling Matchbooks. Everyone needs 'em! Free Sample Kit Furnished. Matchco, Dept. MJ12, Chicago 32, Illinois.

Raise TURKEYS THE NEW WAY!

Write for free information explaining how to make up to $3,000 in your own backyard. *Address:*

NATIONAL TURKEY INSTITUTE
Dept. 272 Columbus, Kansas

FLYING SQUIRRELS

Beautiful Little Pets

Developed through expert breeding. Send $4.99 for free literature and pricing.

LINDA'S FLYING SQUIRREL FARM
905 Deschutes Rd., Richmond, VA.

LIVE BAIT

Red worms, night-crawlers, crickets, and maggots. We raise 'em by the millions! No order too big, too small. LIVE DELIVERY GUARANTEED. $4.99 for our full-color free catalog: Riggle's Bait Ranch, 12 Arliss Rd., White Bluff, Tenn.

VETERINARY SERVICES

Bitten by a wild animal or new pet? Rabies, tetanus, lockjaw, night vision treatments on-hand. House and field calls accepted. KL5-8181 or write to me: Mort's Veterinary Services, 5602 E. Del Mar Blvd., Pasadena, Calif.

MISCELLANEOUS

"X-RAY Mind," Harness the dangerous power of the brain over others. Ruin friendships, tell politicians and grocery clerks where to go. Now YOU'RE in control. Inquire. Send $4.99 to: The Kirshner Academy, Lincoln Park W., Chicago, Ill.

BE YOUR OWN ATTORNEY--Don't be left to the mercy of some scumbag lawyer. Learn it yourself! Save hundreds in fees! Simple, easy-to-understand texts and instructions. Satisfaction guaranteed. Start today! Harvey Brilstein College of Law, 3413 W. Magnolia Blvd., Burbank, Calif.

FREE Novelty Catalog--"Treasure Trove" of mirth-making novelties (for men.) Saucy, sophisticated party items. Enclose $4.99 for hilarious FREE samples to: Gold Coast Novelties & Gifts, 4557 Haskell St., Encinitas, Calif.

Serving at Sea Since 1953
SEAHAG
QUALITY MARINE PAINT

IT'S A BEAUTY!

SEAHAG PAINT & COLOR CO.
DEPT. F-3, 42nd St., New York, N.Y.

SEAHAG

TESTERS

Test new-age insect repellents, make money on the side, buy a boat! Red-heads only, ages 18-40. Send us your information to: Zorkan Chemicals, P.O. Box 3247, Tonopauh, Nevada.

TOBACK'S DUCK PICKER

PLUCK DUCKS WITH POWER!

Attaches to your 1/4" electric drill. Feather free in minutes. Won't bruise or blow feathers everywhere. *New, 24-page booklet, Send $4.99 NOW to:*

TOBACK'S OUTDOOR PRODUCTS CO.
1893 Del Moro St. Klamath Falls, Ore.

AUTHORS WANTED

No luck finding anyone to publish your autobiography, memoirs, poetry or prose? We believe in your talent! Let us publish with our successful pay-up-front plan. $4.99 free booklet. A.Q. Henckel Publishing Services. 120 W. 31st, New York.

CHIPMUNK SKIN

SKIN! WE TAN THEM YOU WEAR THEM

There's nothing quite like the soft, supple feel of chipmunk skin. Gloves, handbags, mocassins, jackets. Send $4.99 for a free catalog to:

BORGMAN'S SKINNING & TANNERY
571 Market Street Des Moines, Iowa.

HEALTH SERVICES

Piles, Fistulas, Hemorrhoids, Pustules, Colon-Stomach disorders we treat all your rectal problems using the LATEST "cutting-edge" methods. Haha, doctor joke. Send $4.99 for a free book. The McCleary Clinic, East Anchower Street, Excelsior Springs, Missouri.

TIME MACHINE

Make your own with discarded juice cans, pliers and rotary phone. See feudal Japan! Warren Klos, 5th St., Glenallen, Pa.

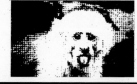

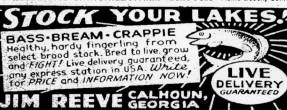

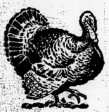

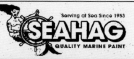

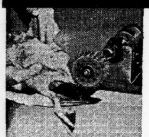

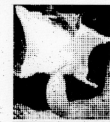

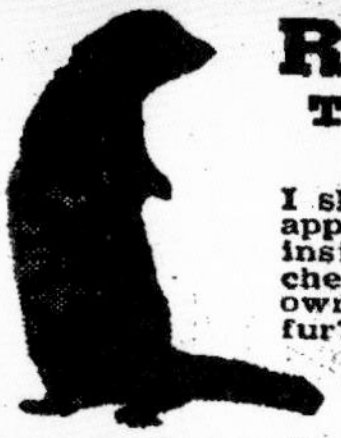

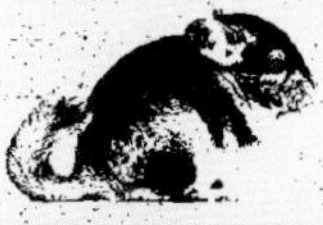

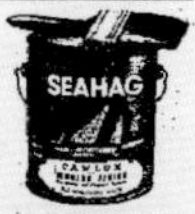

Toadlicker

QUES: *Is "Toading" good for you or bad? Ranger Wongbarn's detailed article on this topic was both confusing and compelling.*

ANSW: There's a common adage park rangers'll tell you- "Please do not lick the toads, this isn't Hollywood" as well as "Always pack your saddle bags with tuna melts." I'm not sure one has anything to do with the other, but they're both adages. Having said that, the Sonoran desert toad secrets a deadly toxin known as five-methoxy, which causes a powerful hallucination that can take you on a killer, magic carpet ride. I soak my cigarettes in it, but you didn't hear that from me.

Burnt or turnt?

QUES: *In 'Hot Potato', we clearly see that Garland has roasted his whole butt, but not one month later, we see him laying in a field of daisies with everything on display? Come on, we're all adults here, and we'd be ok if you could stick to a real timeline of events! This is ridiculous.*

ANSW: Yes, I've heard Mr. Woodburn has a penchant for nude, outdoor antics. And while I can appreciate your interest in the good ranger, I only know, and report on, nature questions. Please be sure to keep on topic.

Hot Springs

QUES: *We've seen Ranger Cockburn open a day spa where the visitors were boiled alive and made into some kind of stew. Is this a sustainable source of outdoor cooking?*

ANSW: If you've ever boiled quail or rabbit, I'm sure you'll agree the taste is much cleaner and mild. Same thing here but with high-temp hot springs you get a lot more bang for your boil without sending the power bill through the roof. This all-natural way of cooking is a forest-friendly method we've been touting for years. Throw carrots, celery and a can of Old Bay in the mix and boy howdy it's a party of four for one!!

We wear short shorts

QUES: *You want us to believe Garland can get away with those tiny shorts? Not standard issue! But he can really pull them off. Not pull them off. I mean, he could if he wants. Who the hell am I to tell him what do? Pull them off, leave them on, go even shorter, whatever.*

ANSW: We get a lot of fan mail about Garland's shorts, and I for one fail to understand what any of it has to do with nature. Do you have a question on anything specifically unrelated to Garland's groinal area? Geez.

Banjo Lovers

QUES: *What's Banjo's type? I'm asking for a friend, and that friend is me.*

ANSW: Banjo is a North American beaver also known as Castor canadensis, a fat, stupid, insecure, semiaquatic rodent that stinks. Not so much because he's unkept, but beavers have these awful scent glands (rangers call them castor sacs) near their buttholes that stink to high-heaven. I would've stretched that blubbering pantywaste into a top hat by now, but Garland seems to enjoy the smell. And incessant whining. If you're looking for love prepare for a knife fight. Or $20.

References Requested

QUES: *I'm interested in applying for a position at Hackaneck National Park, but I can't seem to find where to apply? I also can't find it on a map? A bit of help? To whet your appetite, here's a little about me: I'm real fast, I can run all the way around my whole house in 12.3 seconds, and that's not all. I'll tell you more in my resume.*

ANSW: *(sigh)* Again, this is a column about nature-related questions, folks. Do you want to know the gestation period of the hispid pocket mouse? Perhaps the spawning range of a Chinook salmon? The one thing no one wants to know, especially me, is your DJ gig at the Knaughty Pine strip club.

Midnight Run

QUES: *Some friends and I rented one of your cabins a few months back. Riann, Briann, and Dave went on your "Midnight Bilberry Picking Tour" and never came back. Is this normal? Still waiting. Let me know if you hear from them, please.*

ANSW: For Christ's sake, how should I know?! I'm just the editor of a section at the back no one gives a shit about. Maybe call "reservations," did you think of that?! Stupid. Idiot. Ridiculous. Here I am wasting an afternoon on a question that has nothing to do with nature! This is my job, you know, and you've completely turned it into a joke. Bilberry Picking is not a joke, sir. In fact, my wife and I quite enjoy spending a Sunday Bilberry picking. And now we can't. Thanks to you. Dick.

Lost in the season's worst blizzard, Cliff Yablonski stumbled onto the den of a bear. He crawled in and went to sleep. When the search party found him snuggled up with the grizzly, he begged, "Don't shoot, we're getting married in the spring!"

MORE FUN STUFF

SINGLE PANELS, FAN FAVORITES, AND CHEAPO JOKES THAT MADE US LAUGH. THEY'RE SOME OF OUR HIGHEST LOWS. ENJOY.

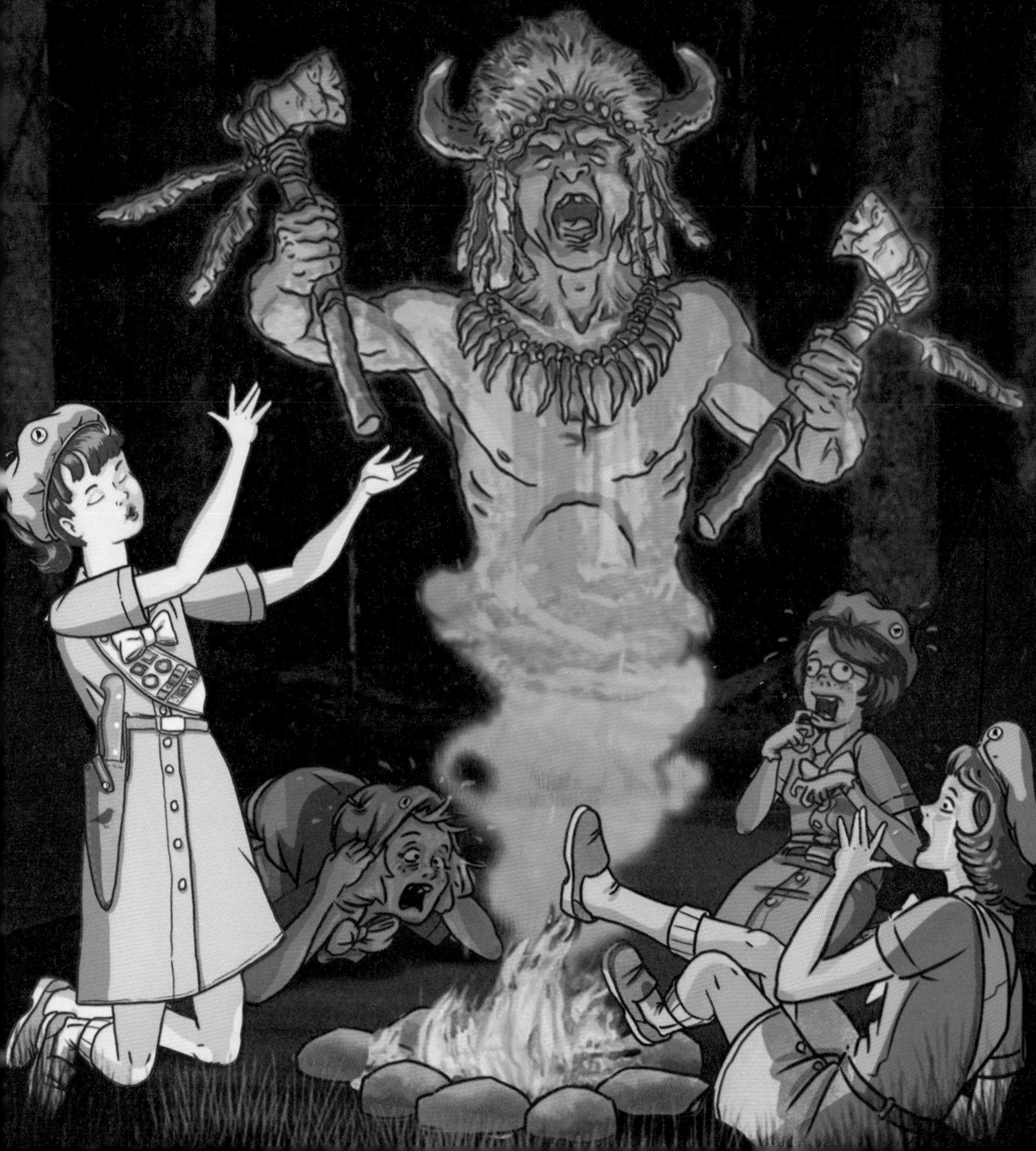

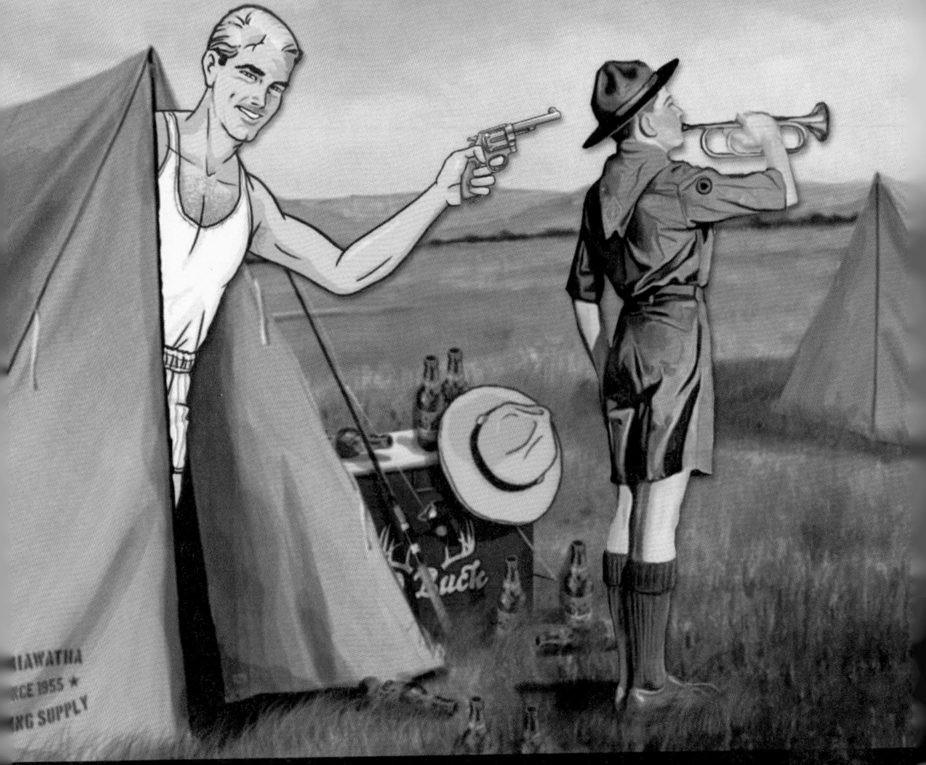

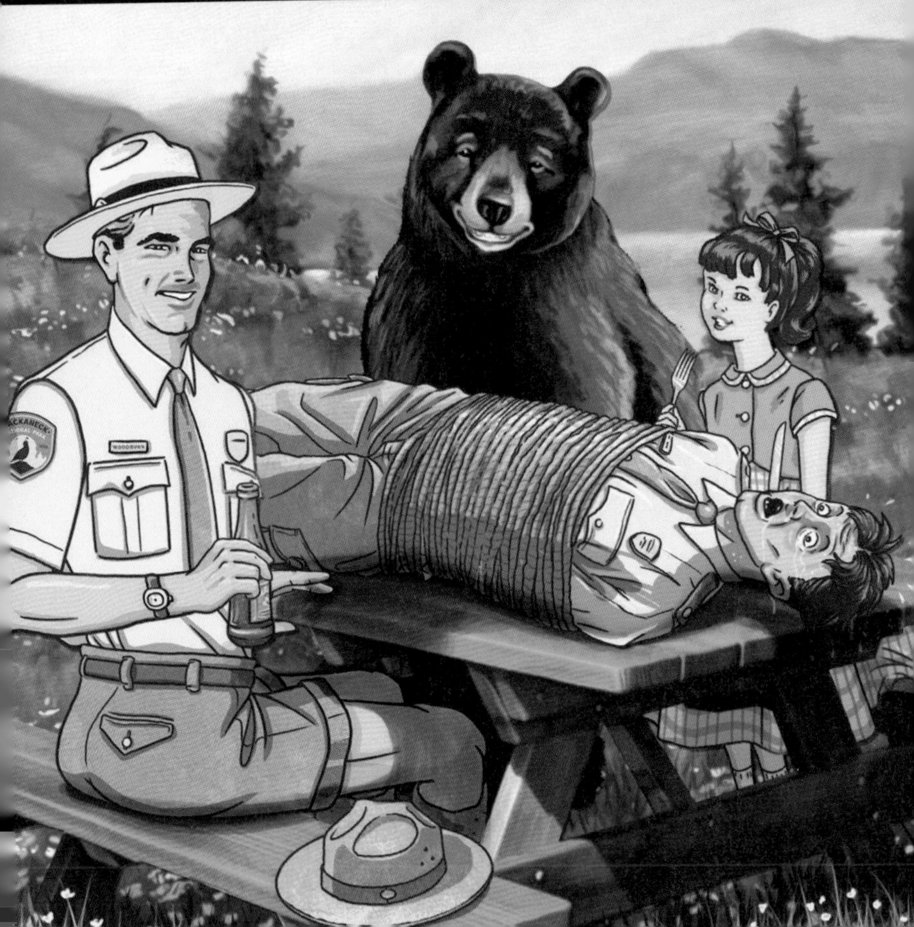

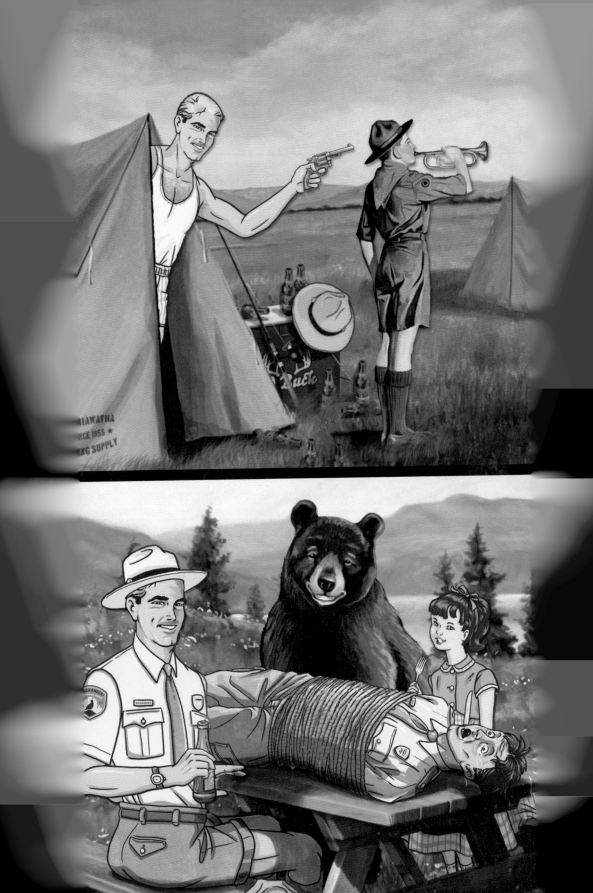

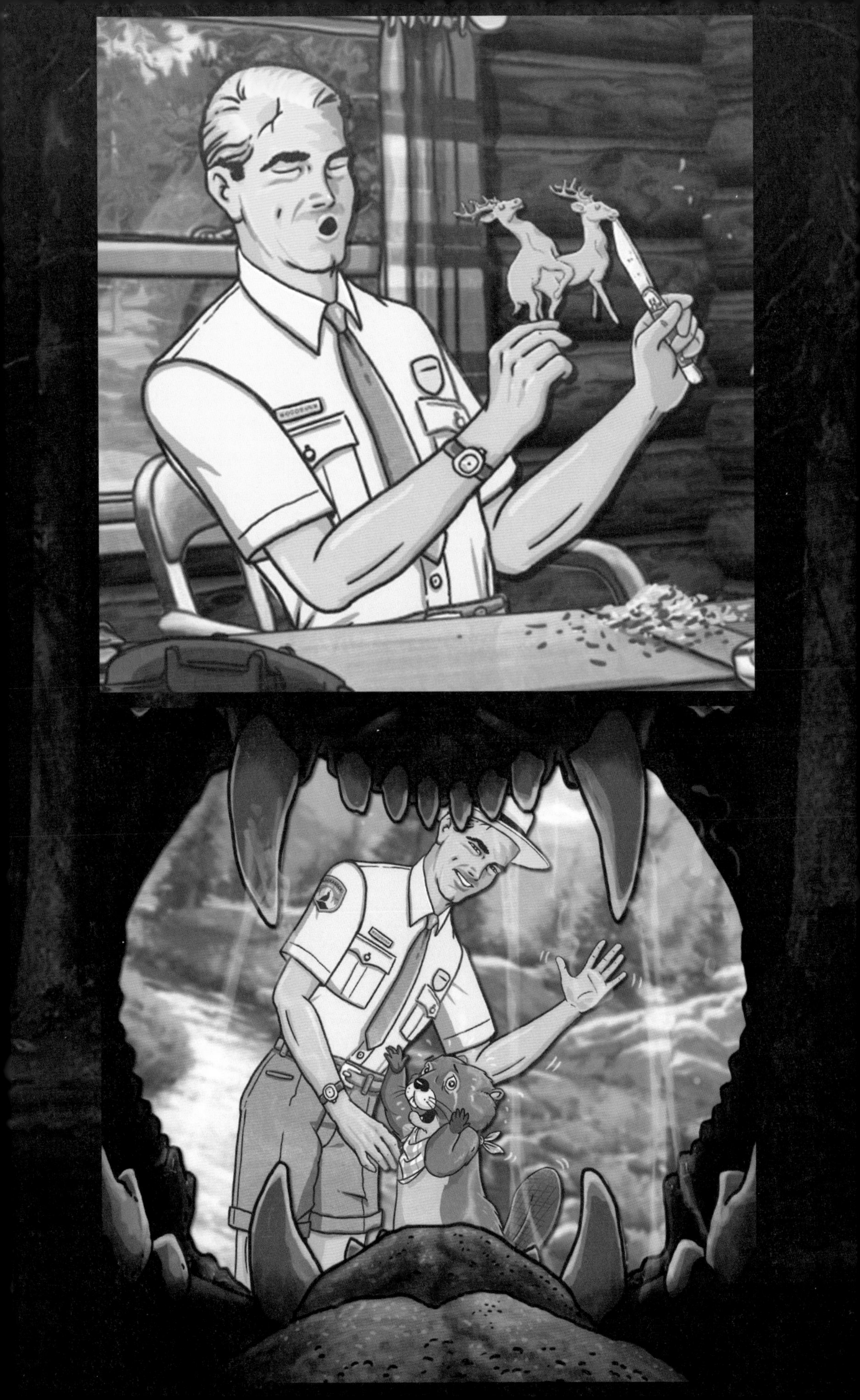

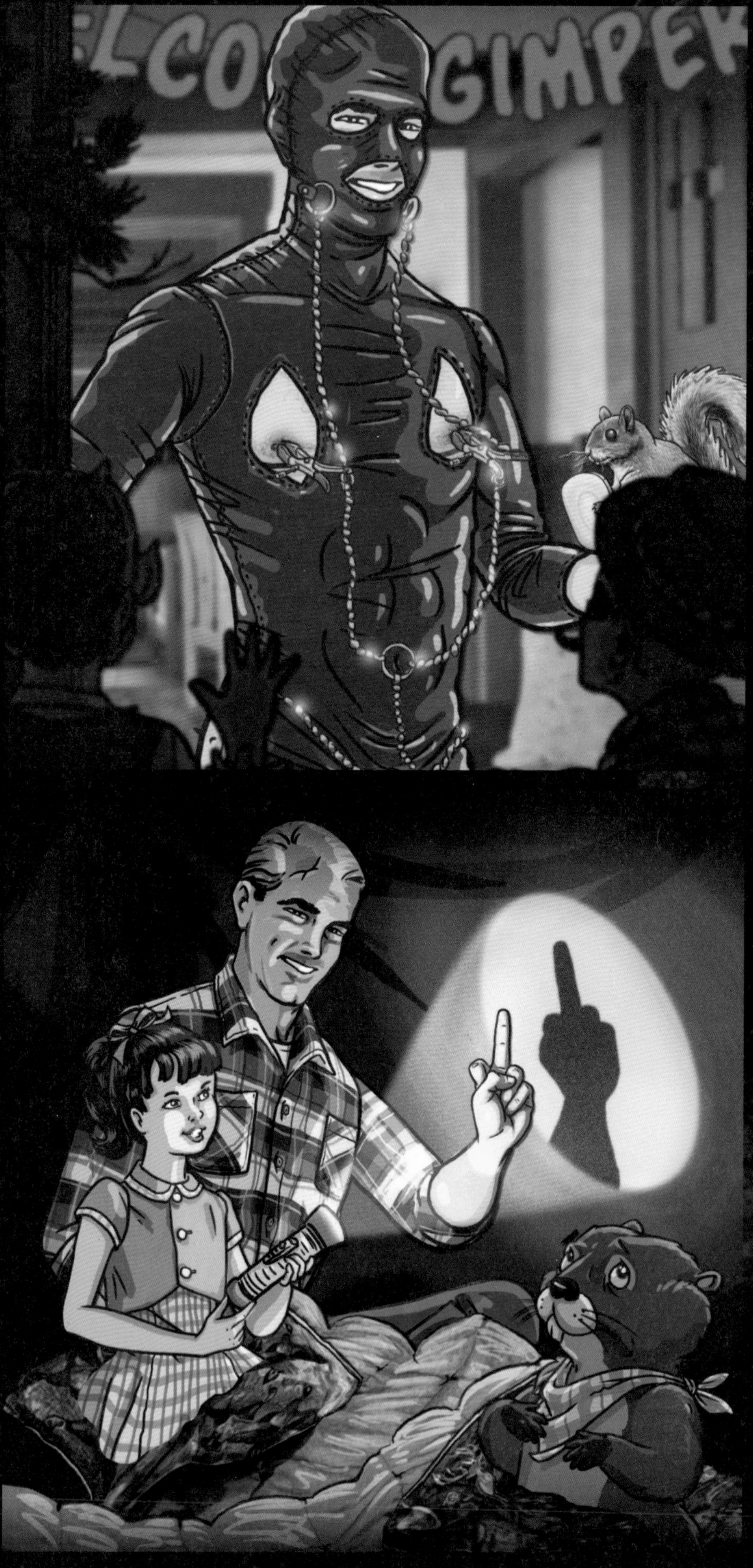

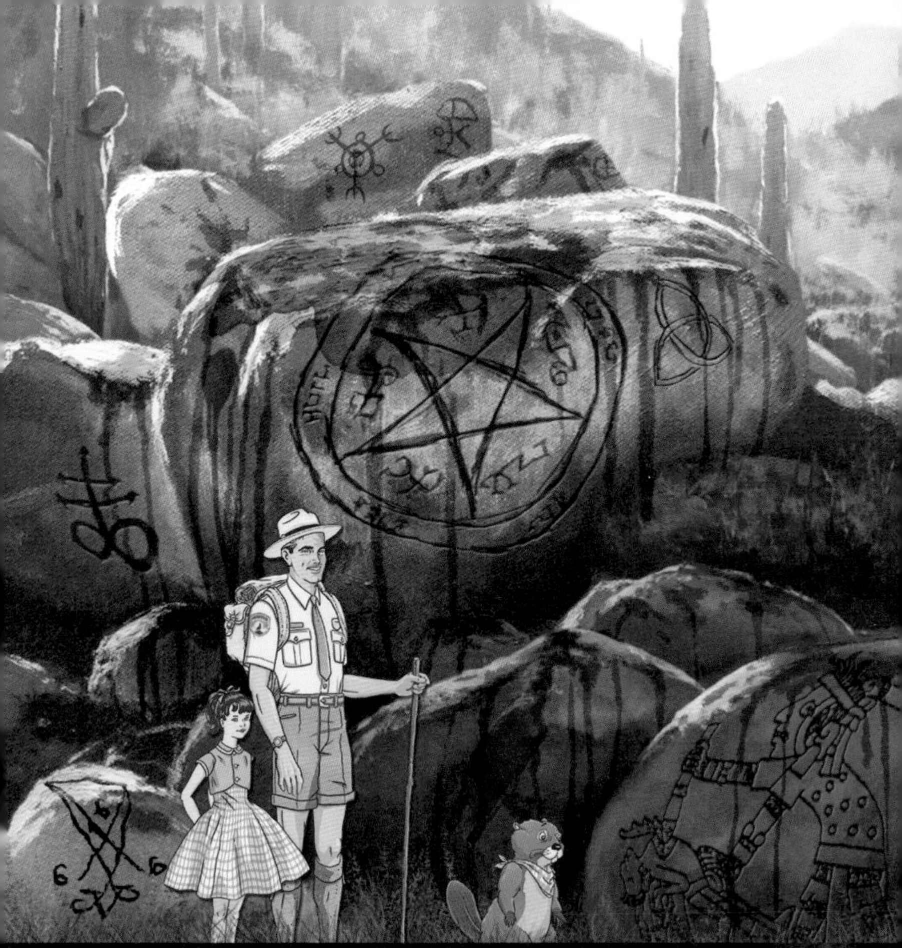

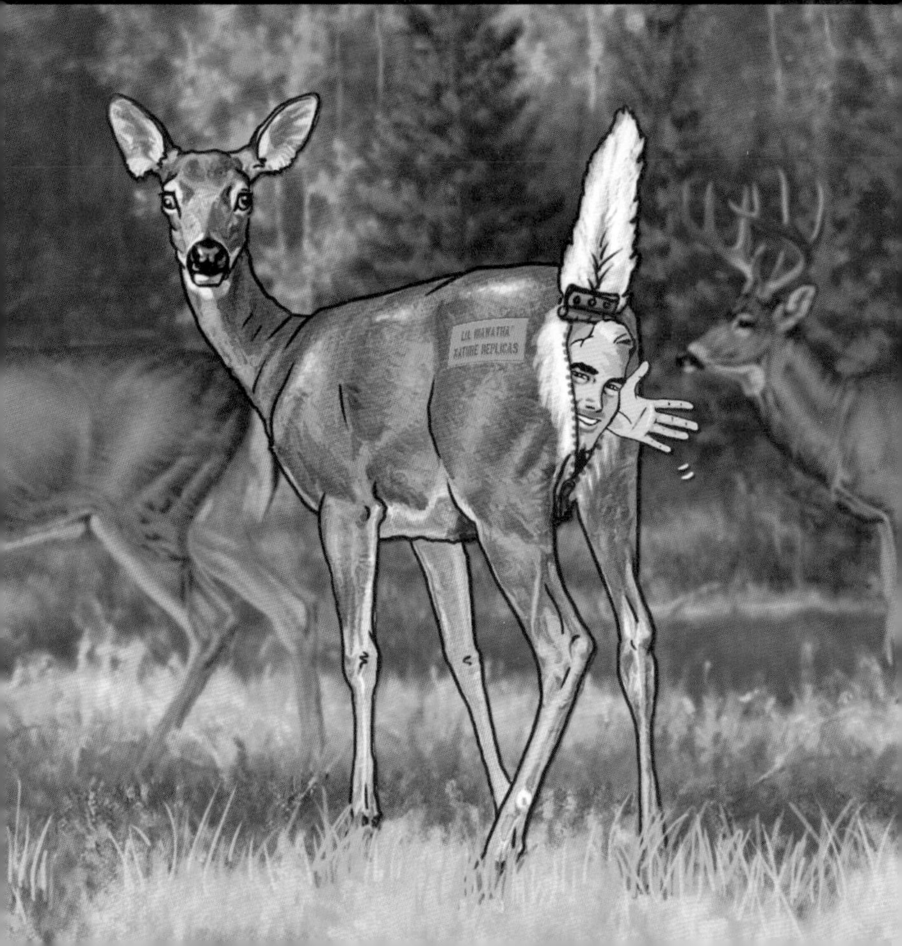
NATURE REPLICAS

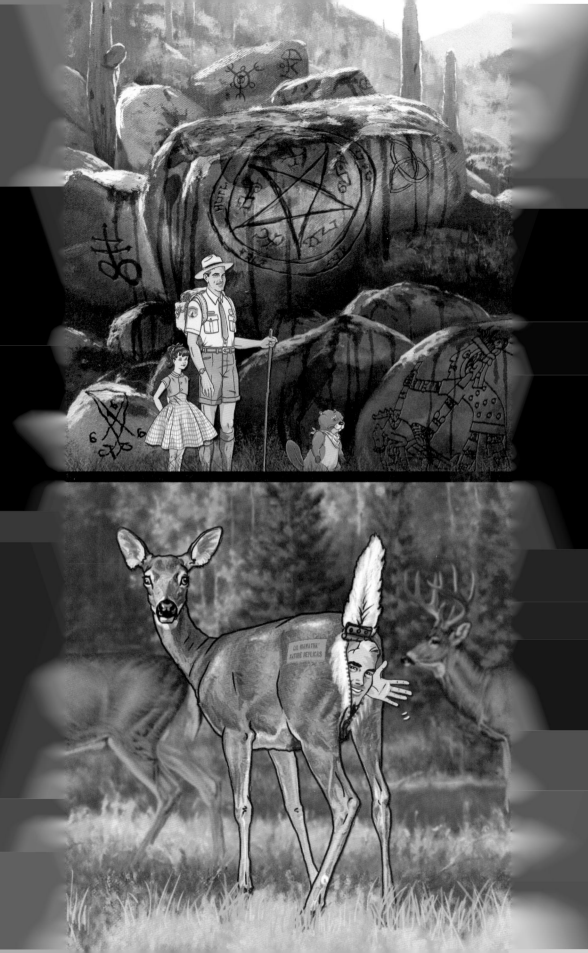

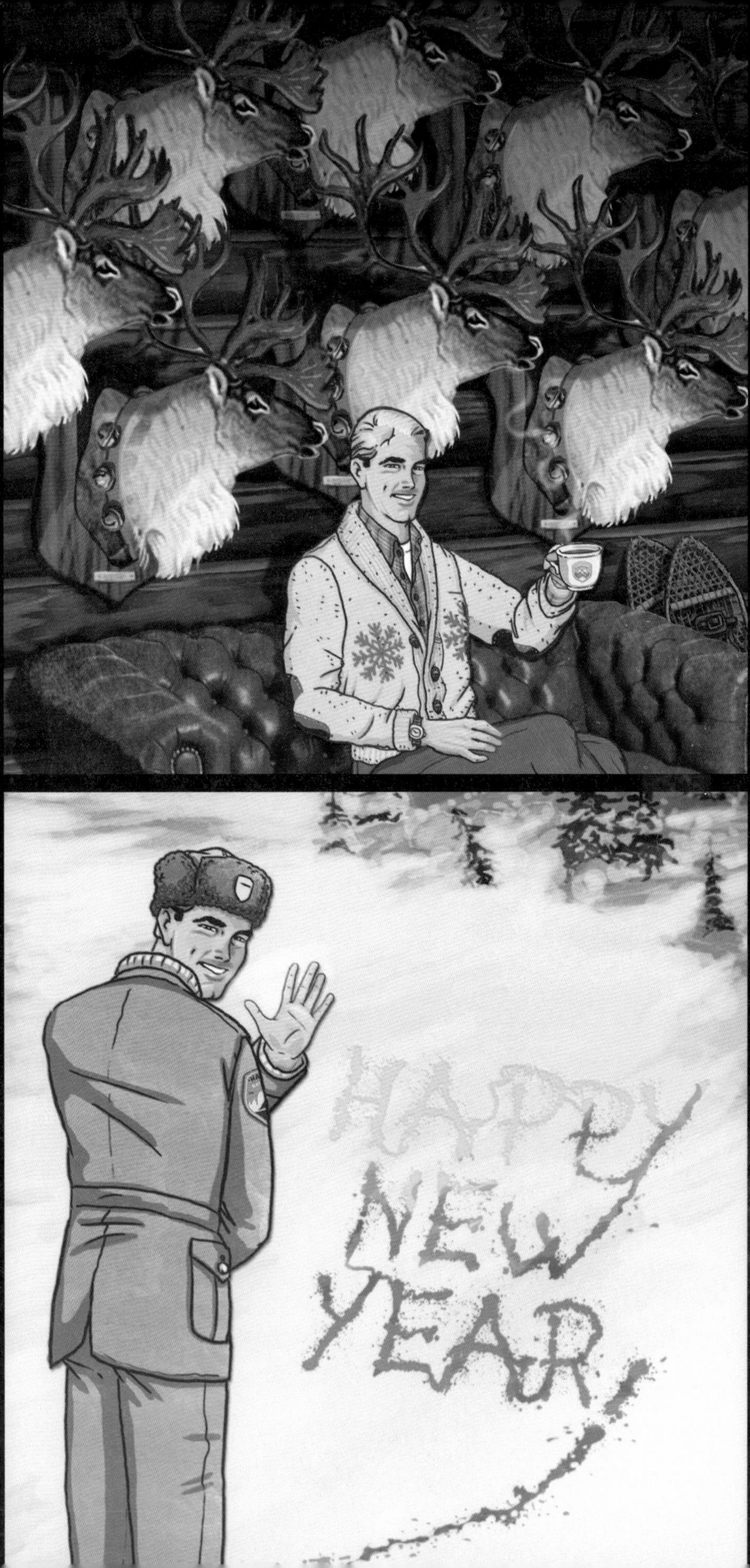
HAPPY NEW YEAR!

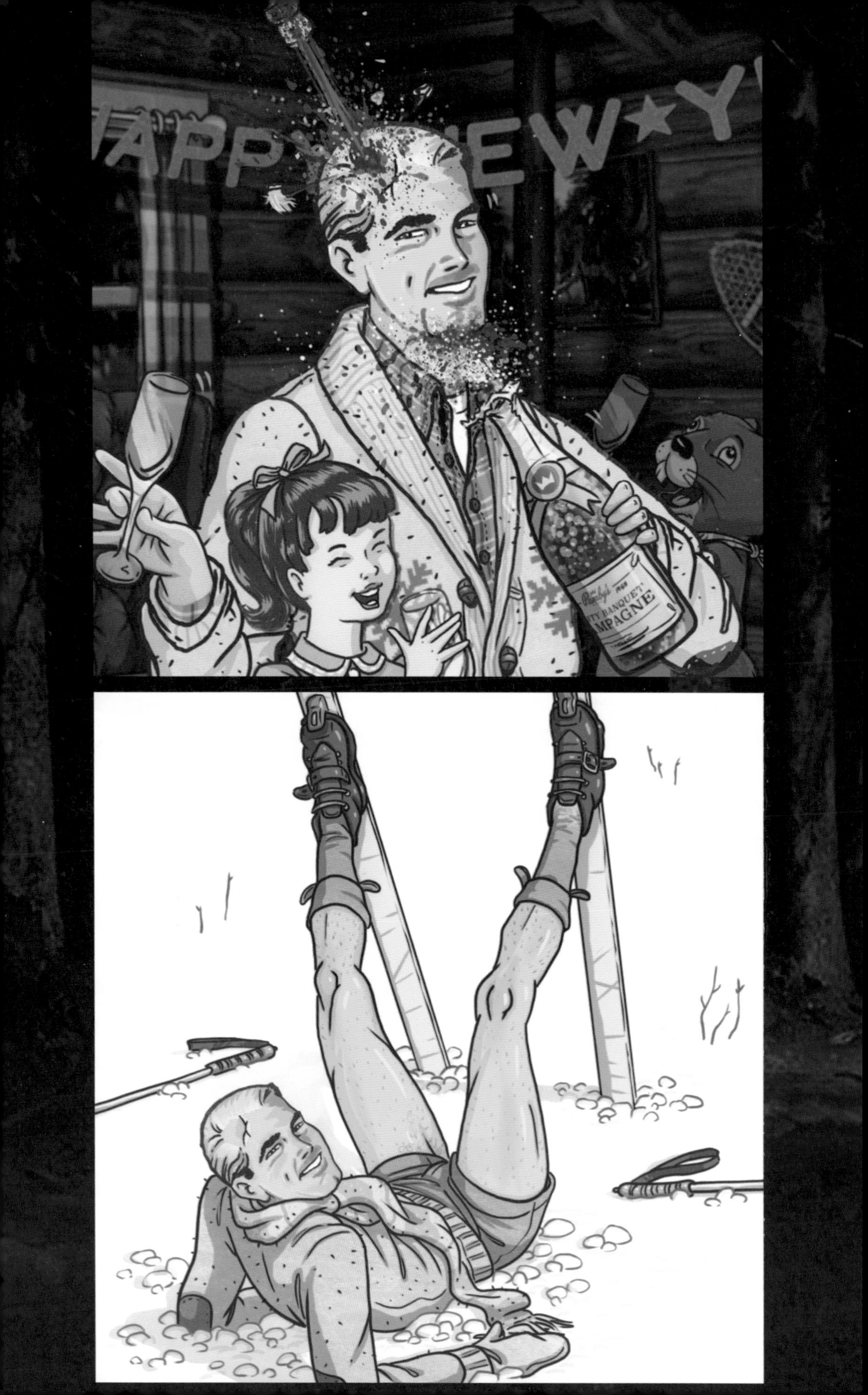

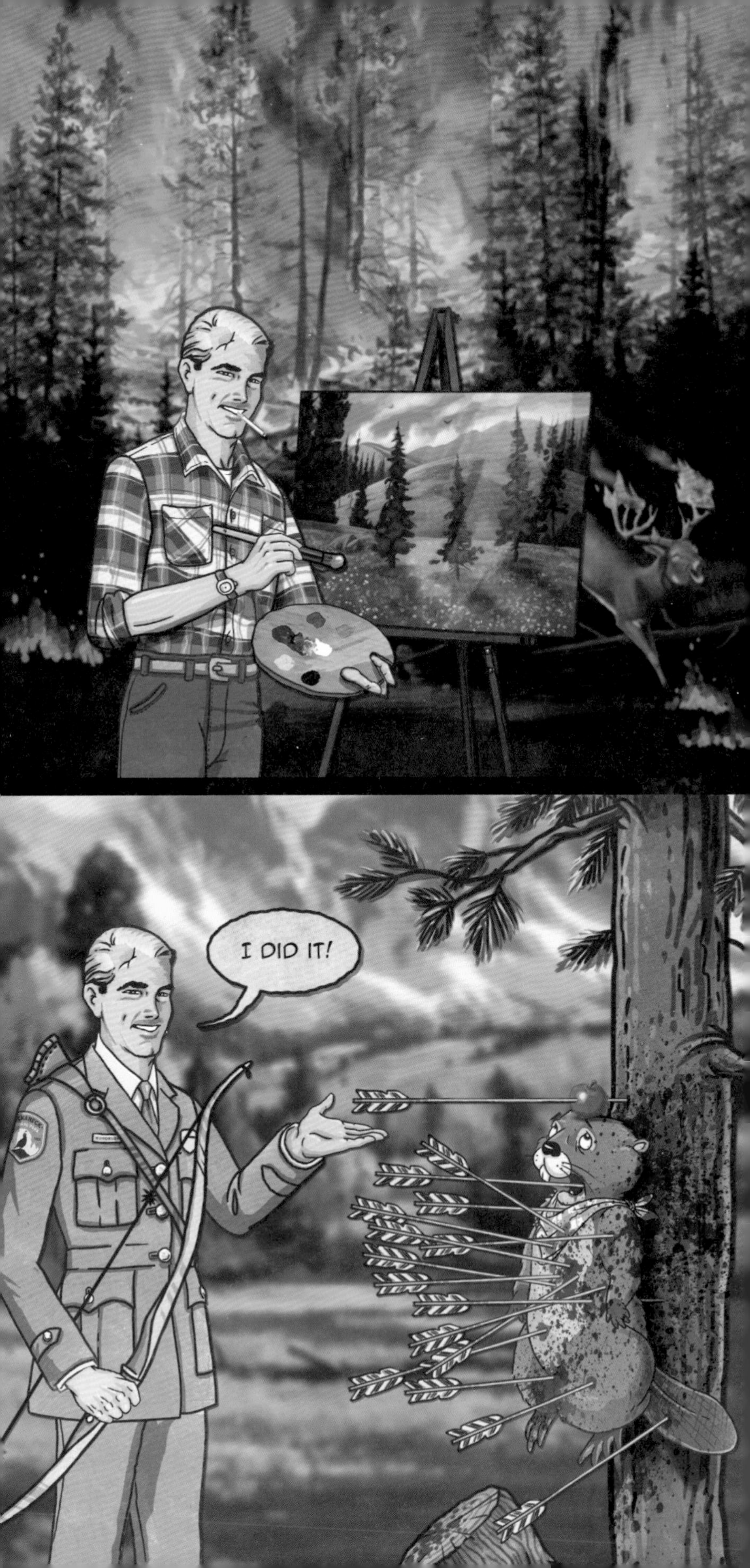
I DID IT!

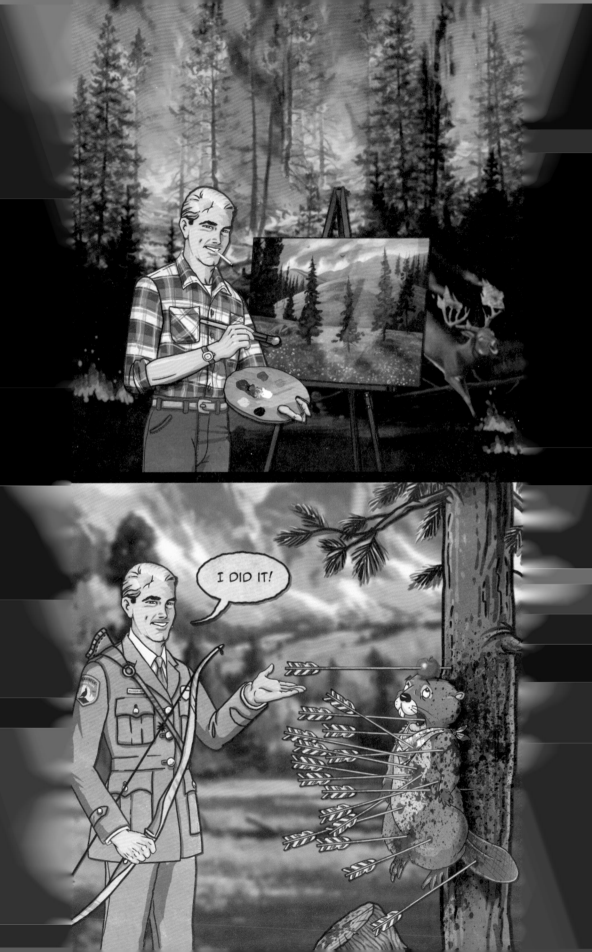

TRULY TASTELESS COMICS

If you've made it this far, congratulations! It's not going to get better. The following is more jokes and sketches we either didn't like or found simply too shameful to let anyone see... so here ya go!

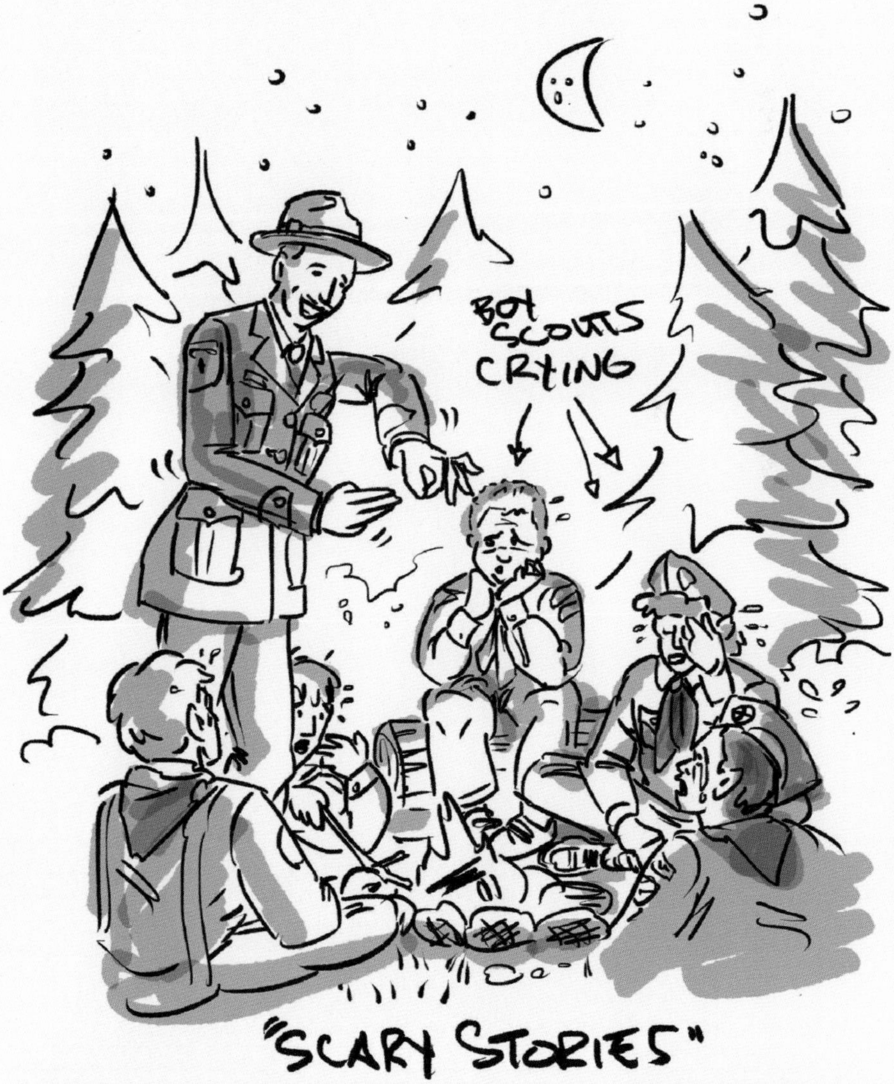
BOY SCOUTS CRYING

"SCARY STORIES"

THERE'S A NUMBER OF MANLY TOPICS OUR GOOD GARLAND COULD BE TEACHING THE BOYS HERE. HOW TO PROPERLY AFFIX CHEESECLOTH AS A MAKESHIFT COFFEE FILTER, PERHAPS. NO, PROBABLY NOT.

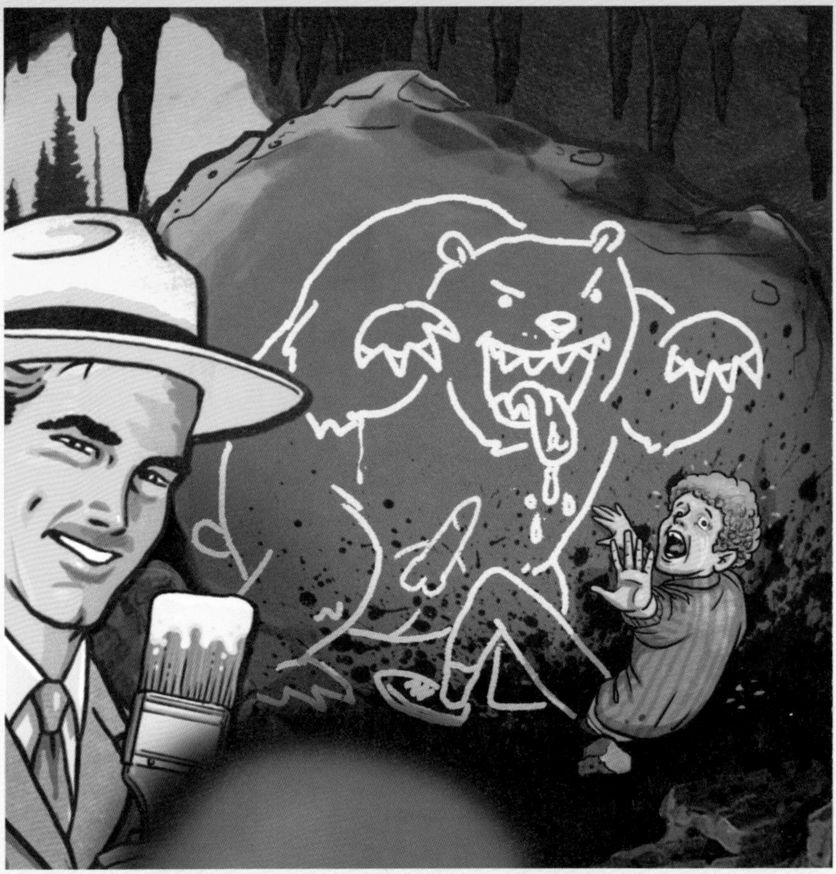

YOU CAN FIND A WATERED-DOWN VERSION OF THIS ON THE INTERNET, BUT THE ORIGINAL IDEA WAS JUST WAY...WAY TOO MUCH.

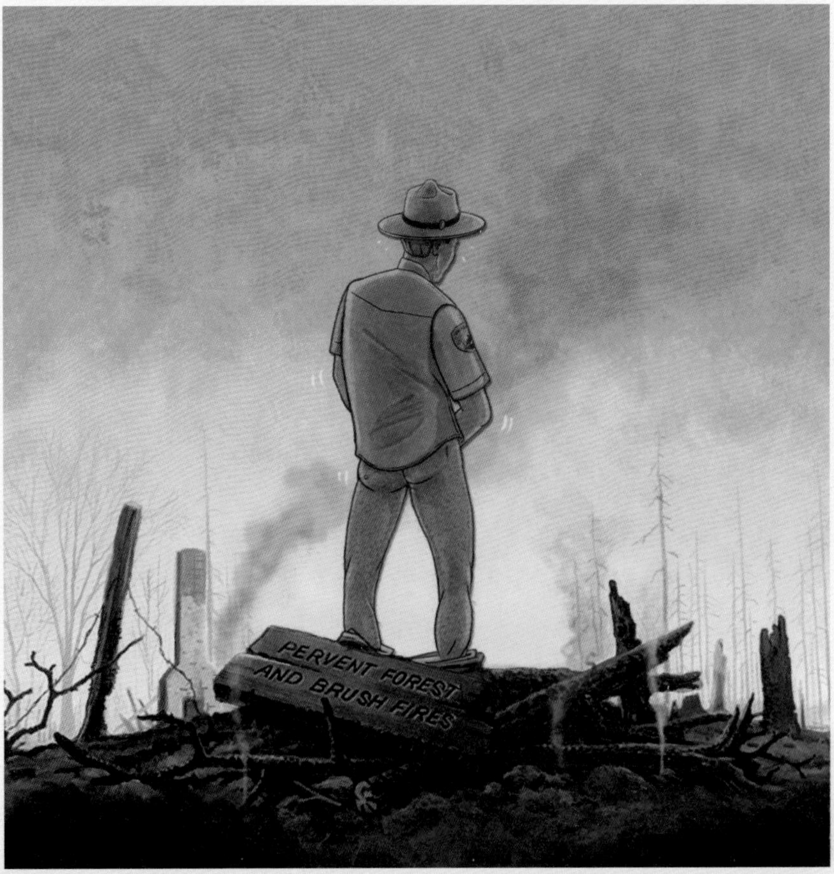
PERVENT FOREST
AND BRUSH FIRES

THIS WAS A COLD OPEN WE WROTE FOR A *RANGER STRANGER* ANIMATED PILOT. BELEAGUERED SMOKE JUMPERS CONVERSE IT'S THE WORST FOREST FIRE ON RECORD. AS THEY CREST THE HILL WE SEE THIS. HE GIVES A JOVIAL WAVE. ALAS, NO.

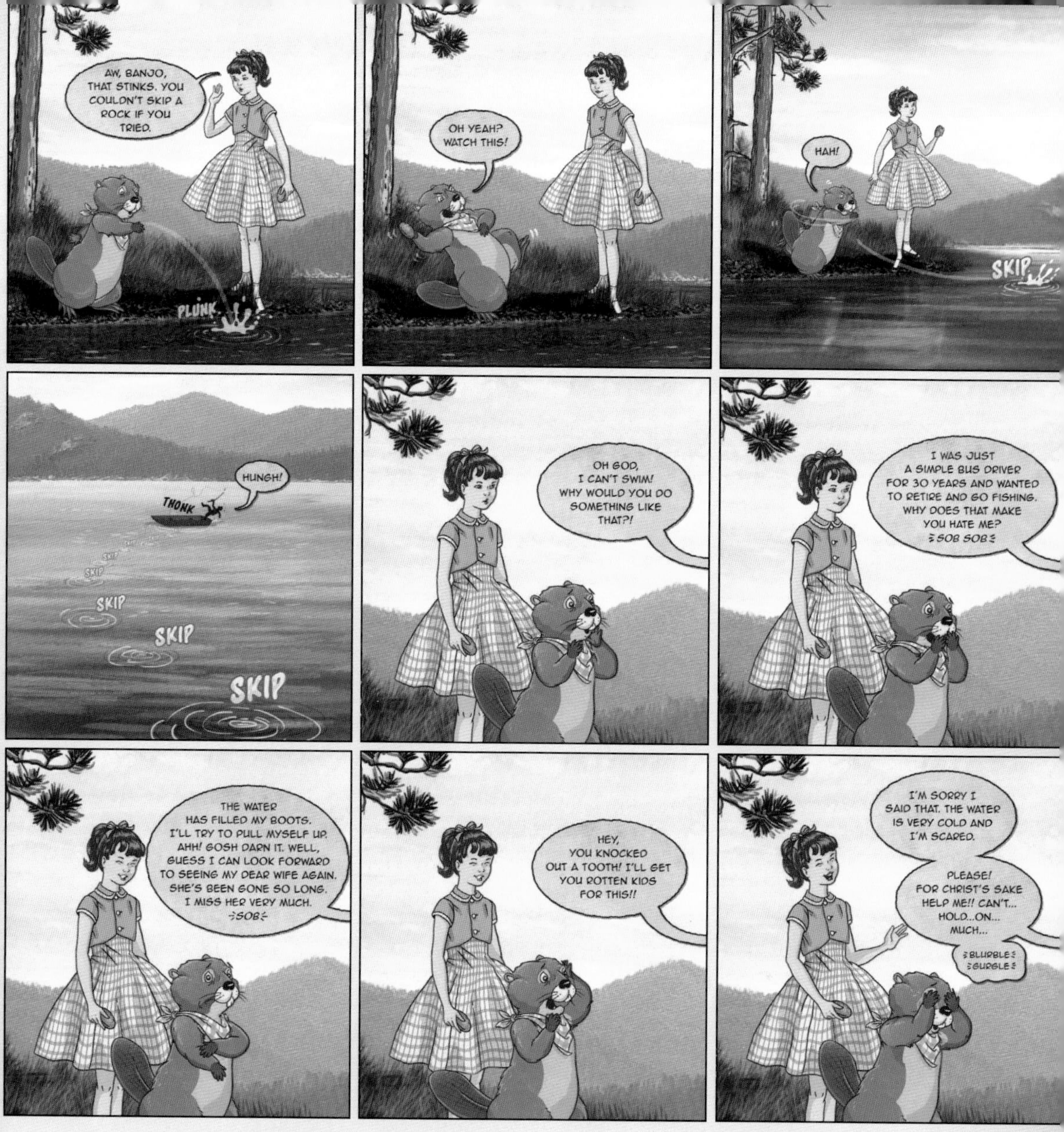
AW, BANJO, THAT STINKS. YOU COULDN'T SKIP A ROCK IF YOU TRIED.
PLUNK
OH YEAH? WATCH THIS!
HAH!
SKIP
HUNGH!
THONK
SKIP
SKIP
SKIP
SKIP
SKIP
OH GOD, I CAN'T SWIM! WHY WOULD YOU DO SOMETHING LIKE THAT?!
I WAS JUST A SIMPLE BUS DRIVER FOR 30 YEARS AND WANTED TO RETIRE AND GO FISHING. WHY DOES THAT MAKE YOU HATE ME? SOB SOB
THE WATER HAS FILLED MY BOOTS. I'LL TRY TO PULL MYSELF UP. AHH! GOSH DARN IT. WELL, GUESS I CAN LOOK FORWARD TO SEEING MY DEAR WIFE AGAIN. SHE'S BEEN GONE SO LONG. I MISS HER VERY MUCH. SOB
HEY, YOU KNOCKED OUT A TOOTH! I'LL GET YOU ROTTEN KIDS FOR THIS!!
I'M SORRY I SAID THAT. THE WATER IS VERY COLD AND I'M SCARED.
PLEASE! FOR CHRIST'S SAKE HELP ME!! CAN'T... HOLD...ON... MUCH...
BLURBLE GURGLE

AS A CRAPPY SKETCH THIS WAS FUNNY, BUT IN FINAL FORM, WATCHING A POOR, OLD MAN CRY AND SLOWLY DROWN IN A LAKE IS LESS AMUSING ALL POLISHED UP AND STUFF. PLUS, IT WASN'T VERY BELIEVABLE--GETTING HIT IN THE FACE WITH A SKIPPING ROCK.

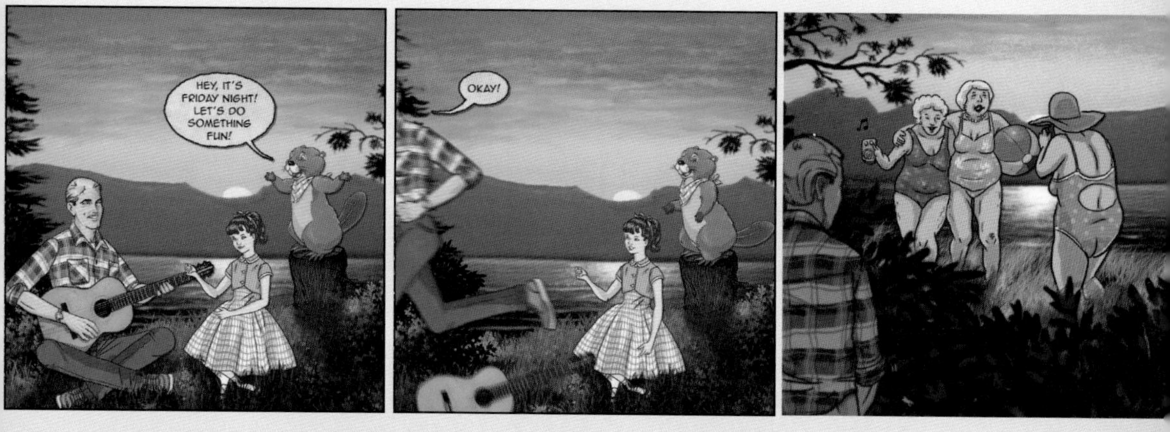
HEY, IT'S FRIDAY NIGHT! LET'S DO SOMETHING FUN!
OKAY!

AAAND, MORE MASTURBATING. I DON'T KNOW EITHER.

NAKED AMERICAN DAY

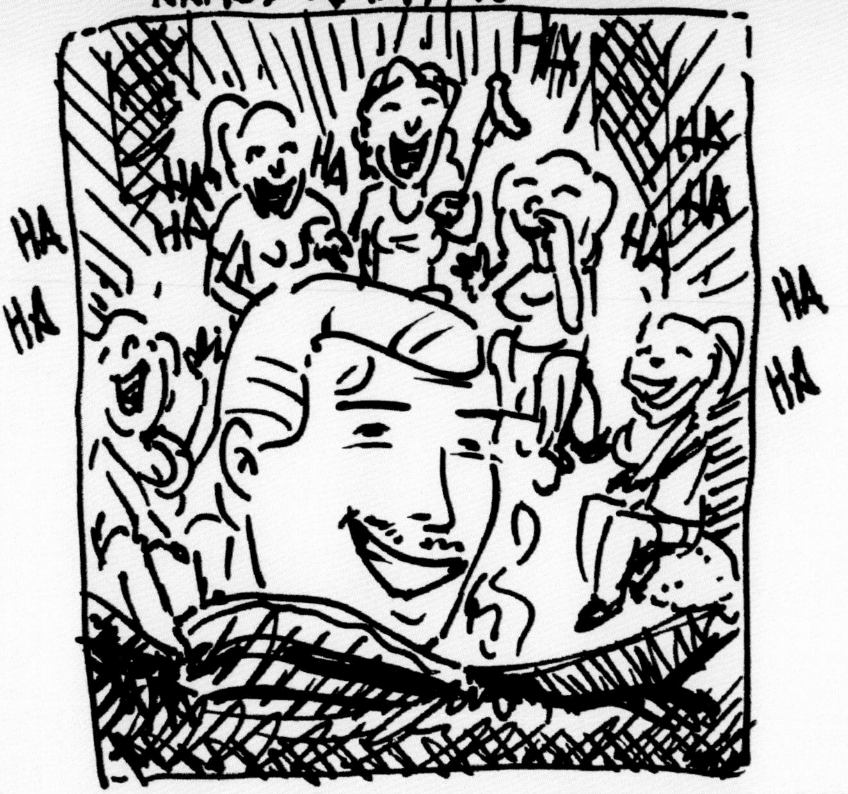
HA
HA
HA
HA
HA
HA
HA
HA
HA
HA
HA
HA

THIS IDEA HAD GARLAND FLASHING A SORORITY CAMPOUT WHO ARE LESS THAN IMPRESSED. AFTER A HEATED DEBATE ABOUT GARLAND'S GIRTH, WE CAME TO OUR SENSES AND SCRAPPED IT. SOMETIMES THE LINE BETWEEN "IS THIS FUNNY?" AND "WE SHOULD GO HOME AND GET A LIFE?" BLURS SUBSTANTIALLY.

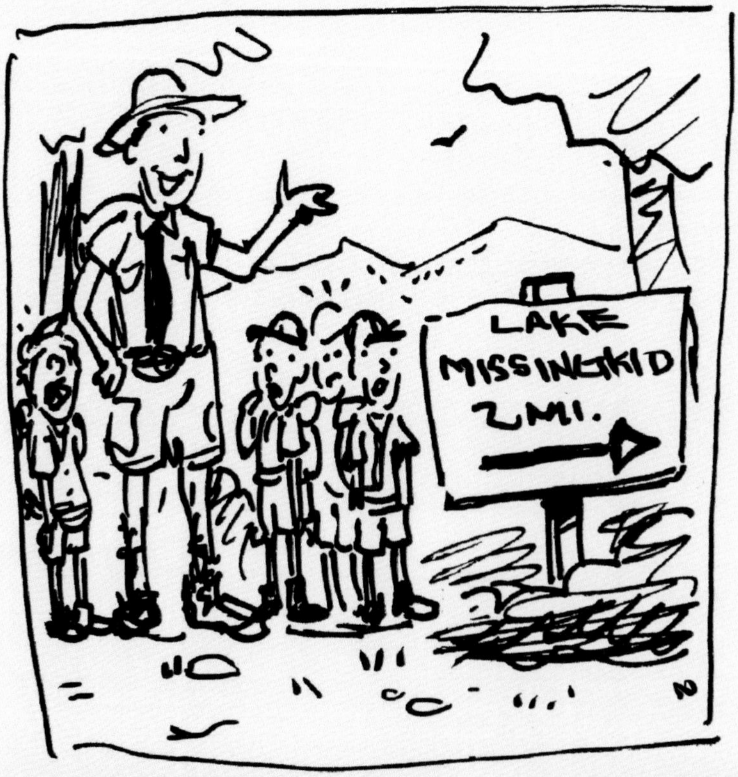
LAKE
MISSINGKID
2 MI.

YOU CAN SEE THIS LAKE MARKED CLEARLY ON THE HACKANECK PARK MAP. BUT LEADING THE INNOCENT TO A LAKE THAT ULTIMATELY SPELLS THEIR DEATH LEFT US FEELING (UNDERSTANDABLY) ICKY.

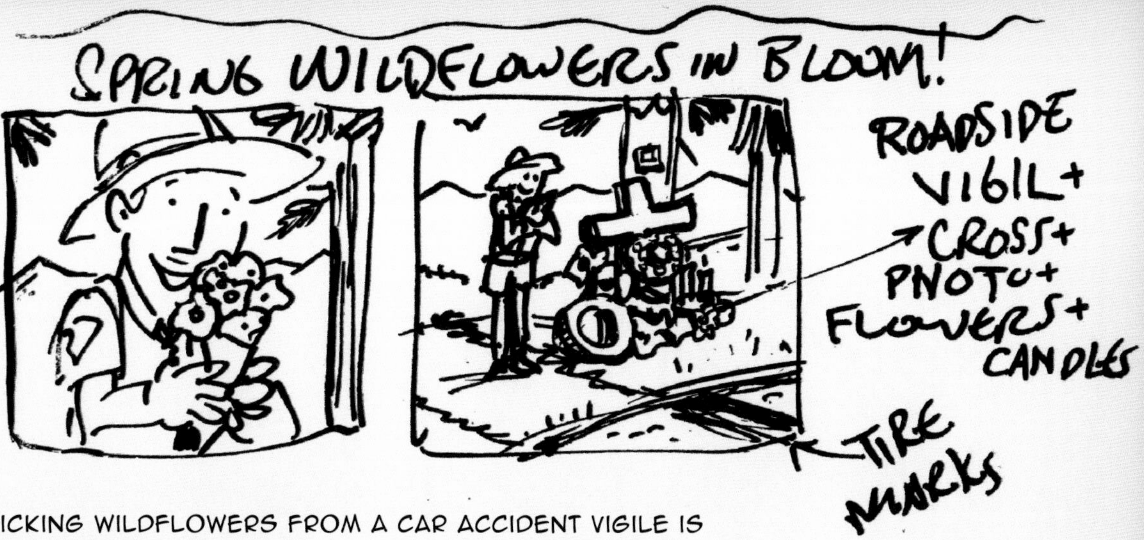
SPRING WILDFLOWERS IN BLOOM!
ROADSIDE VIGIL + CROSS + PHOTO + FLOWERS + CANDLES
TIRE MARKS

PICKING WILDFLOWERS FROM A CAR ACCIDENT VIGILE IS JUST BEGGING FOR HELL.

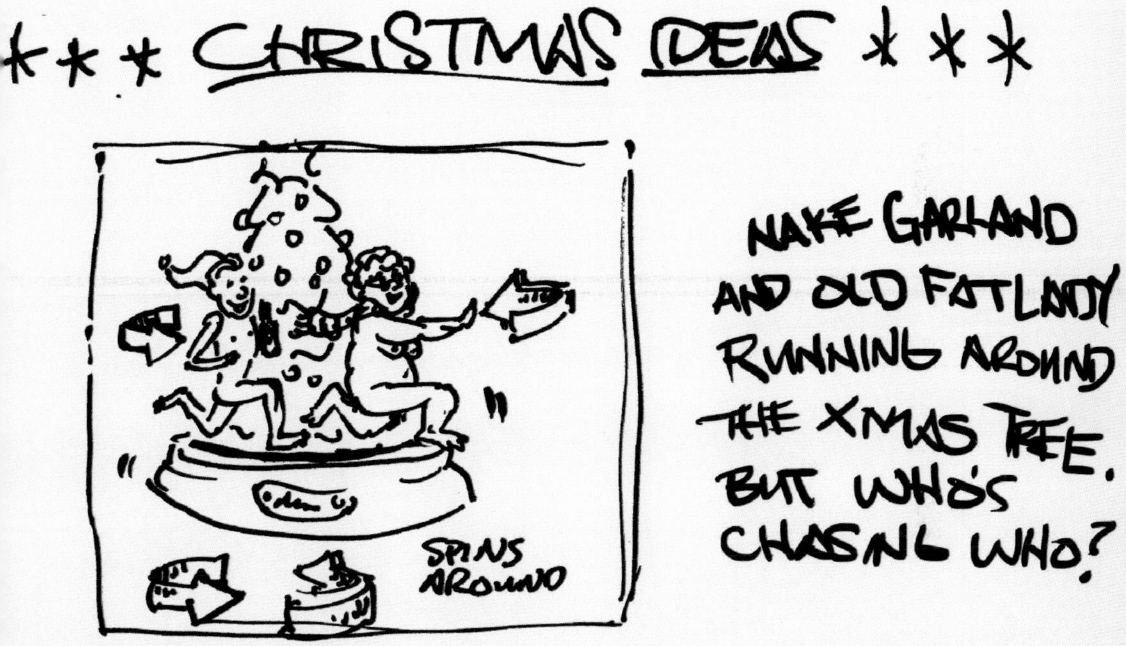
*** CHRISTMAS IDEAS ***
SPINS AROUND
NAKE GARLAND AND OLD FAT LADY RUNNING AROUND THE XMAS TREE. BUT WHO'S CHASING WHO?

HERE'S SOME CHRISTMAS COLLECTIBLES WE PITCHED TO THE BEISTLE ORNAMENT COMPANY ONE TIME. THEY PASSED, BUT I'M SURE THEY REGRET IT.

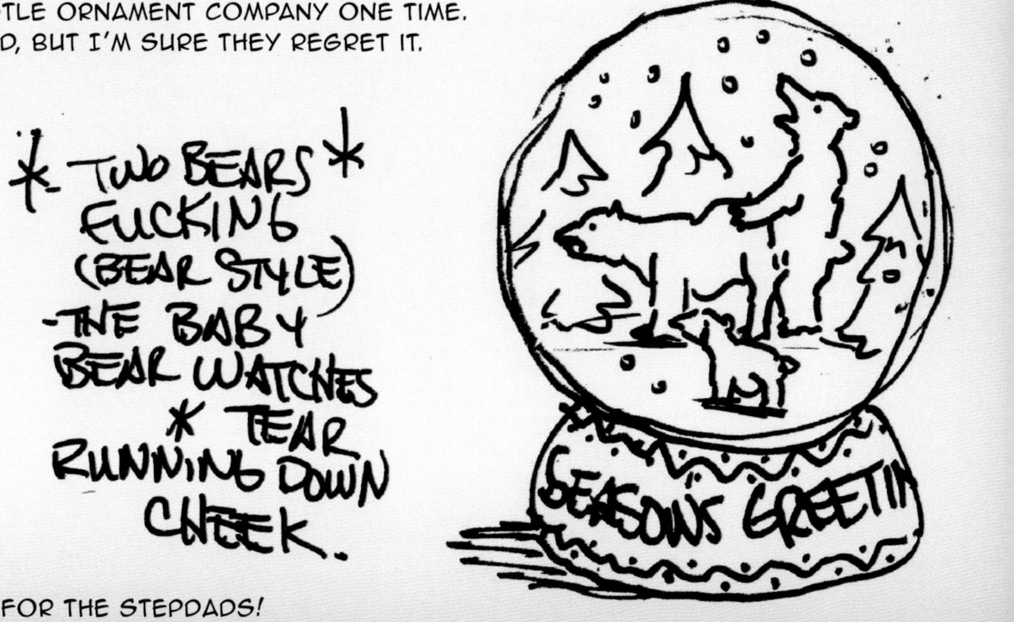
* TWO BEARS * FUCKING (BEAR STYLE)
- THE BABY BEAR WATCHES
* TEAR RUNNING DOWN CHEEK.
SEASONS GREETIN

THIS ONE'S FOR THE STEPDADS!

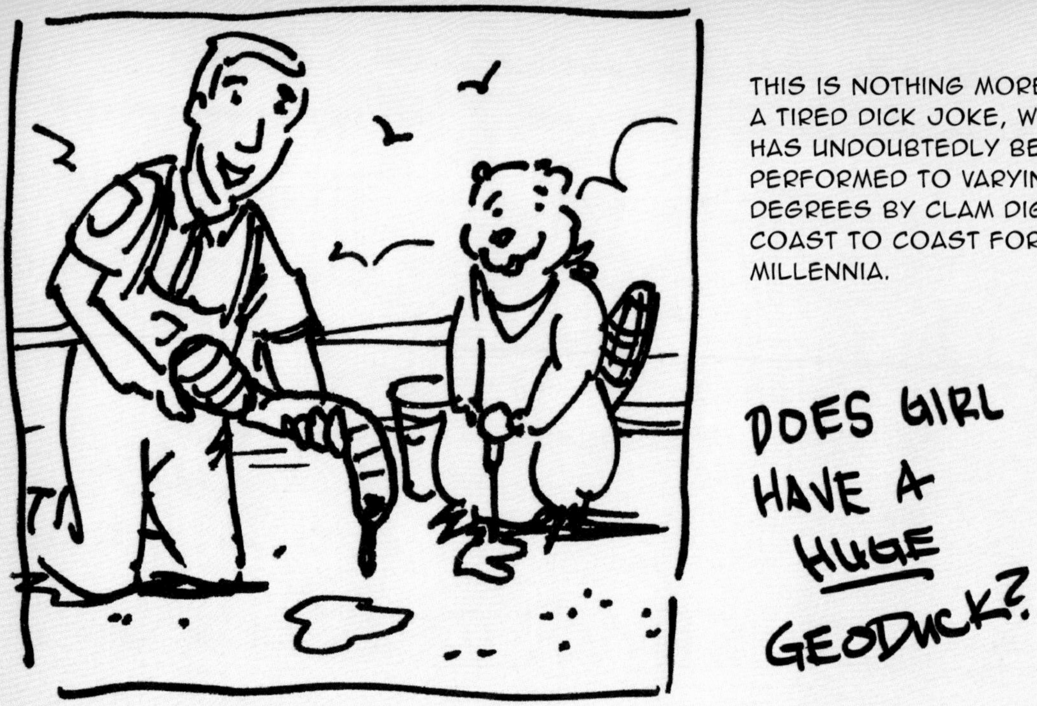
DOES GIRL HAVE A HUGE GEODUCK?

THIS IS NOTHING MORE THAN A TIRED DICK JOKE, WHICH HAS UNDOUBTEDLY BEEN PERFORMED TO VARYING DEGREES BY CLAM DIGGERS COAST TO COAST FOR MILLENNIA.

LIKE BIRD-WATCHING, LEAF PEEPING IS ABSURD AND FUNNY. THE JAPANESE SUICIDE FOREST IS THE PUNCHLINE HERE, BUT IF YOU DON'T GET THE REFERENCE, IT'S JUST PEOPLE HANGING IN TREES, WHICH, DEPENDING ON YOUR STATE, FEELS WRONG.

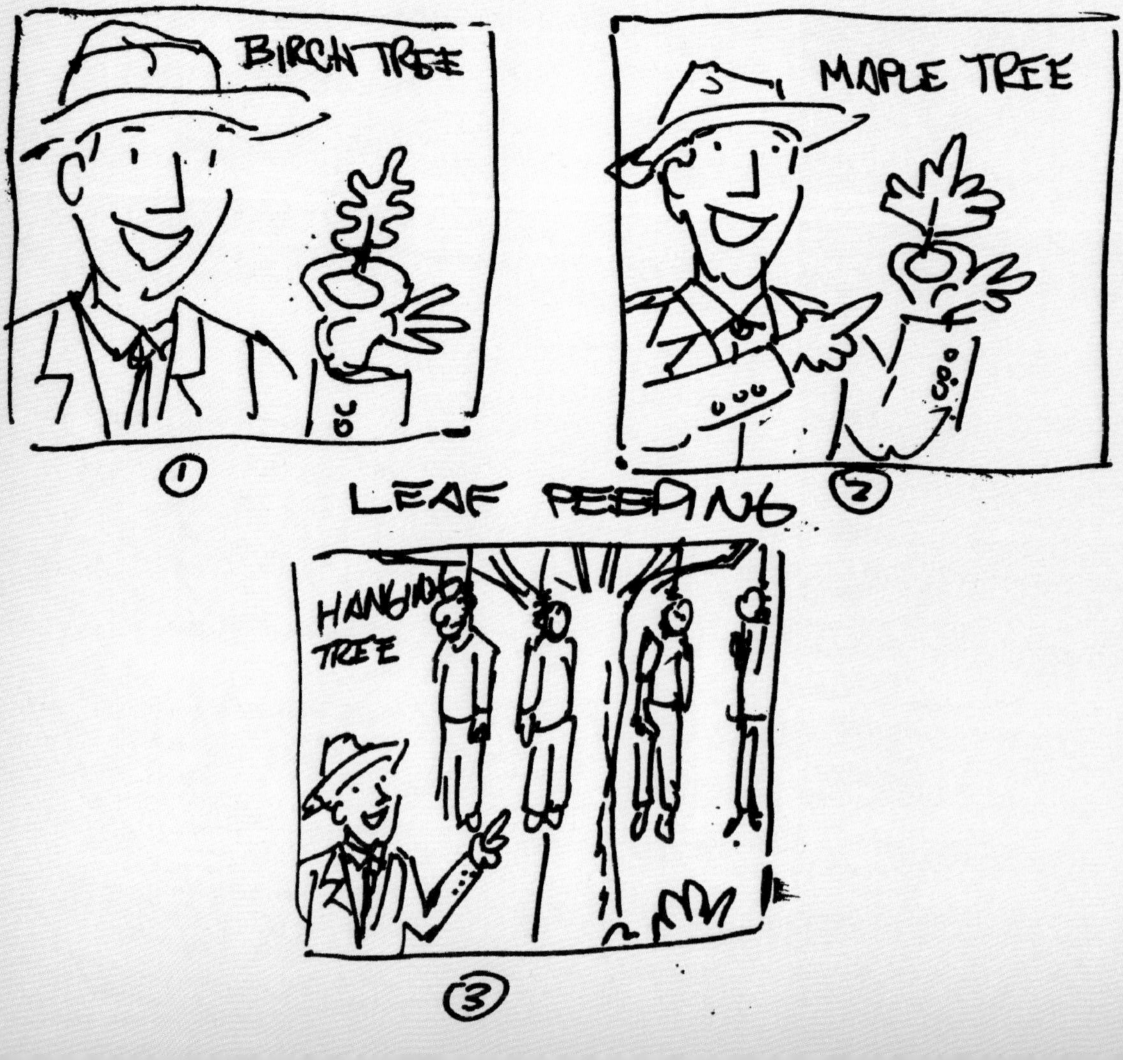
BIRCH TREE
①
MAPLE TREE
②
LEAF PEEPING
HANGING TREE
③

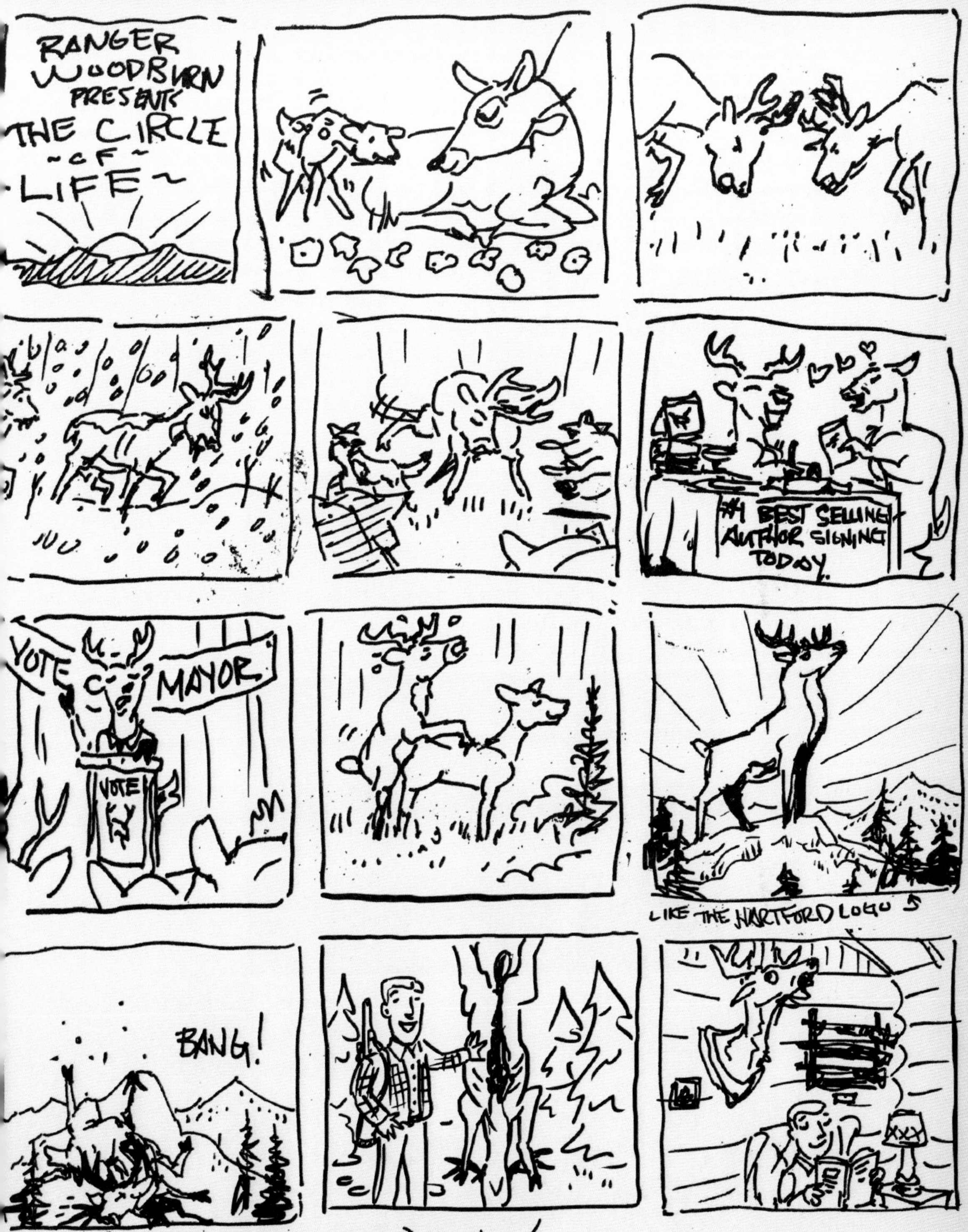
RANGER WOODBURN PRESENTS
THE CIRCLE ~OF~ LIFE~
#1 BEST SELLING AUTHOR SIGNING TODAY.
VOTE
MAYOR
VOTE
LIKE THE HARTFORD LOGO
BANG!

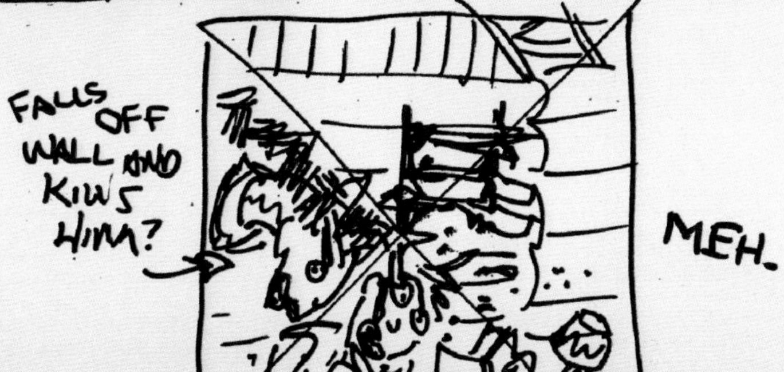
FALLS OFF WALL AND KILLS HIM?
MEH.

THIS WAS SUPPOSED TO BE AN EXISTENTIAL LOOK AT HUNTING AND THE FOOD WE HARVEST, BUT AT SOME POINT, IT WENT COMPLETELY OFF THE RAILS. PERHAPS WHEN THE DEER DECIDED TO RUN FOR MAYOR OF DEERTOWN? ANYWAY, IT MADE ZERO SENSE.

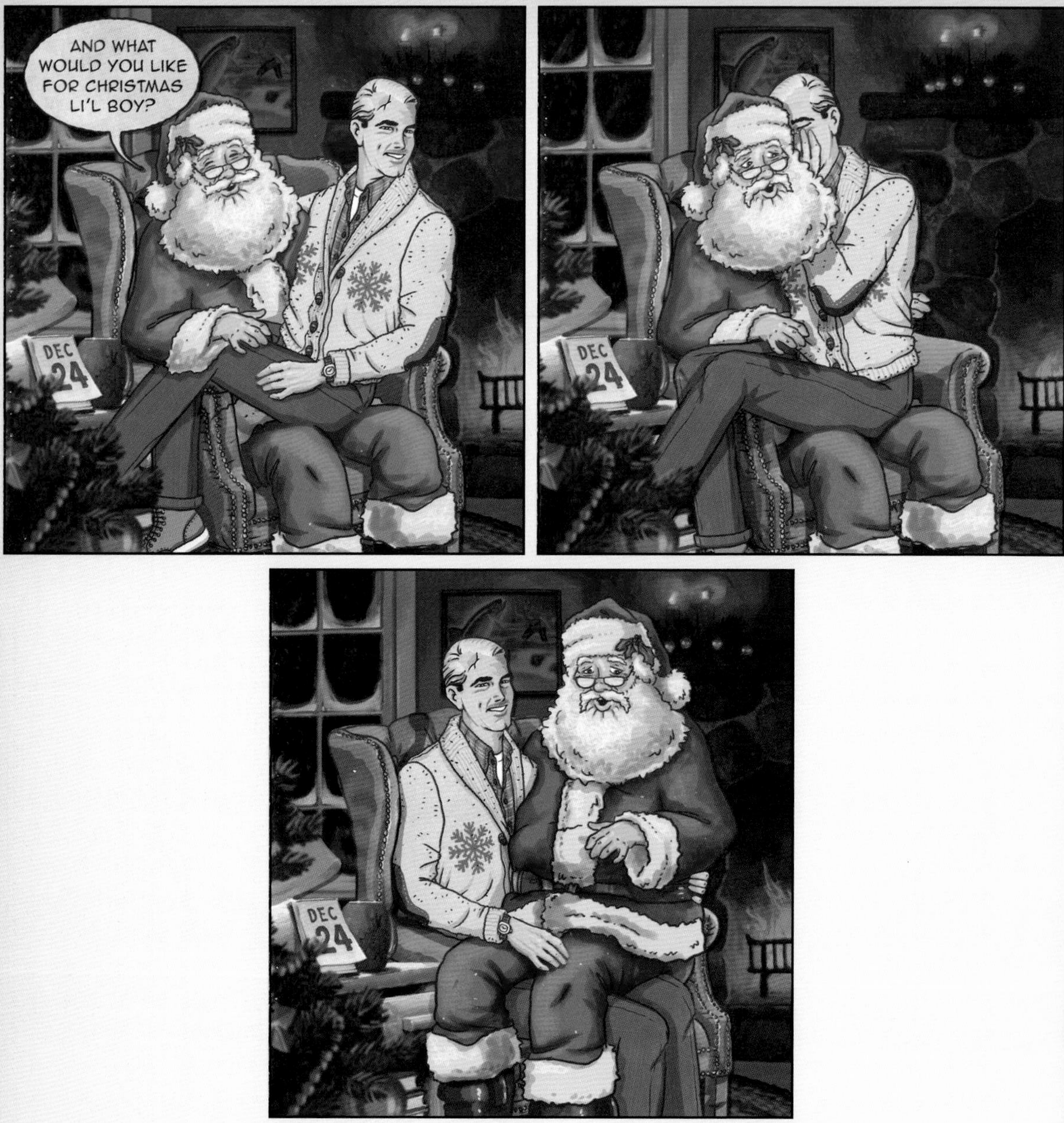
AND WHAT WOULD YOU LIKE FOR CHRISTMAS LI'L BOY?
DEC 24

ON THE RANGER STRANGER JOKE SPECTRUM, THIS IS RATHER TAME. BUT IT MADE US RATHER UNCOMFORTABLE. WHICH IS RATHER NICE.

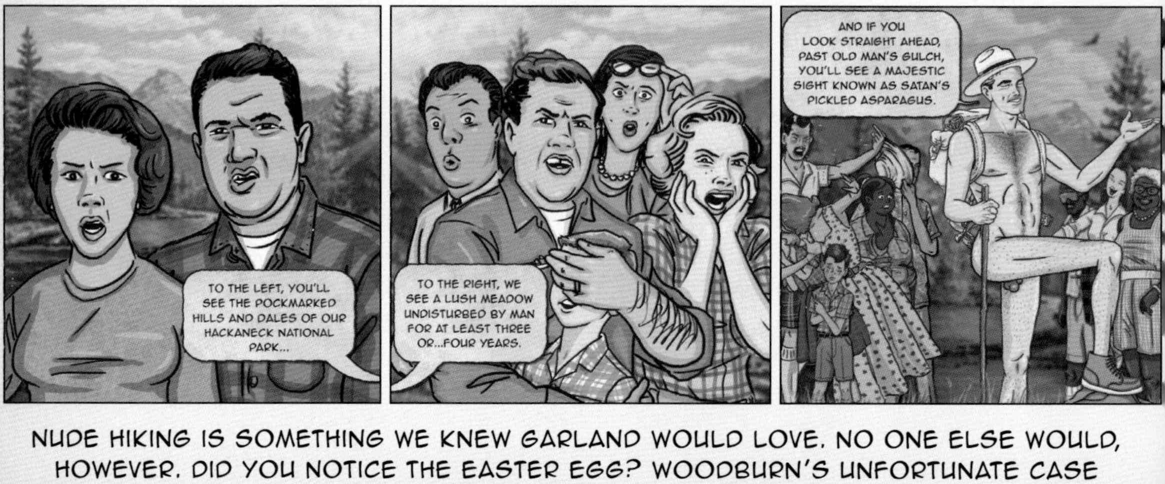
TO THE LEFT, YOU'LL SEE THE POCKMARKED HILLS AND DALES OF OUR HACKANECK NATIONAL PARK...
TO THE RIGHT, WE SEE A LUSH MEADOW UNDISTURBED BY MAN FOR AT LEAST THREE OR...FOUR YEARS.
AND IF YOU LOOK STRAIGHT AHEAD, PAST OLD MAN'S GULCH, YOU'LL SEE A MAJESTIC SIGHT KNOWN AS SATAN'S PICKLED ASPARAGUS.

NUDE HIKING IS SOMETHING WE KNEW GARLAND WOULD LOVE. NO ONE ELSE WOULD, HOWEVER. DID YOU NOTICE THE EASTER EGG? WOODBURN'S UNFORTUNATE CASE OF EPIDIDYMITIS! GOOG IT FOR MORE FUN.

GUA NO BUENO

THIS COMIC WAS ONE BIG SET UP FOR A COKE JOKE, VIA A VERY REAL AND UNFORTUNATE DISEASE OBLITERATING BAT POPULATIONS ACROSS NORTH AMERICA. THE PUNCHLINE WASN'T VERY CLEVER WITH TOO MANY DIRECTIONS THAT DIDN'T CONNECT TO EACH OTHER. WE DECIDED ON A MORE SIMPLE VERSION WHERE EVERYONE GETS RABIES. YOU CAN FIND IT ONLINE.

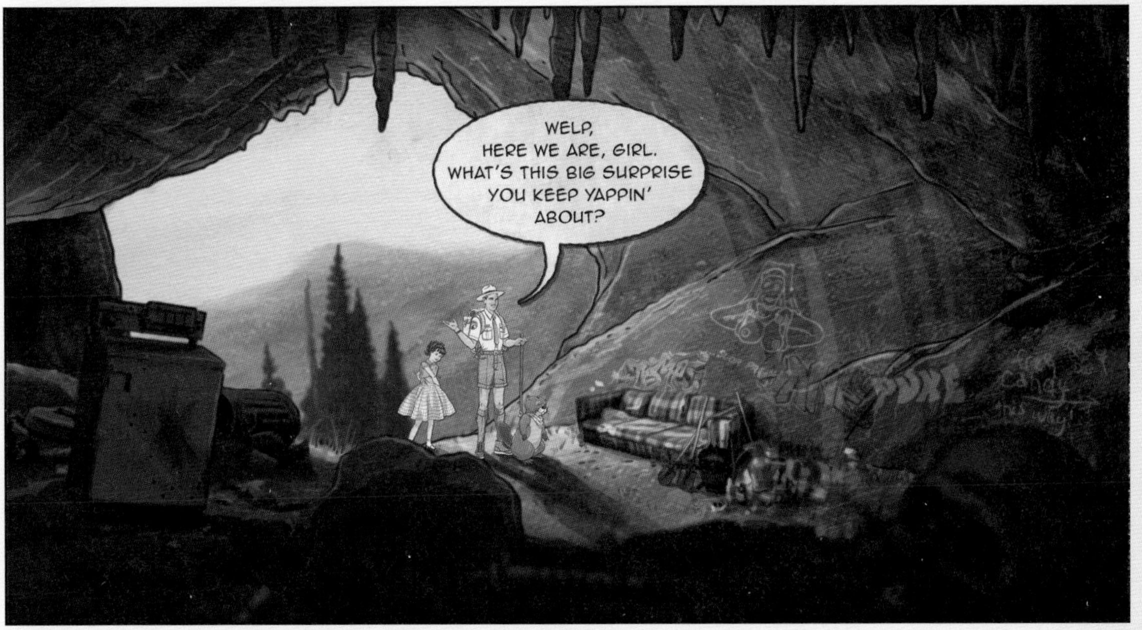
WELP, HERE WE ARE, GIRL. WHAT'S THIS BIG SURPRISE YOU KEEP YAPPIN' ABOUT?

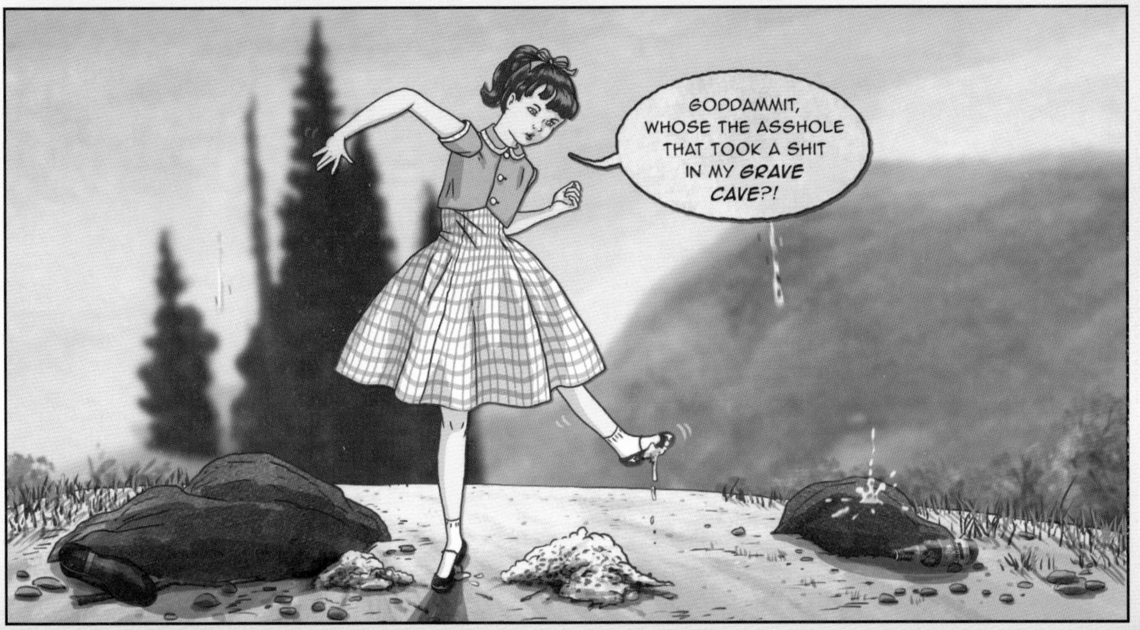
GODDAMMIT, WHOSE THE ASSHOLE THAT TOOK A SHIT IN MY *GRAVE CAVE*?!

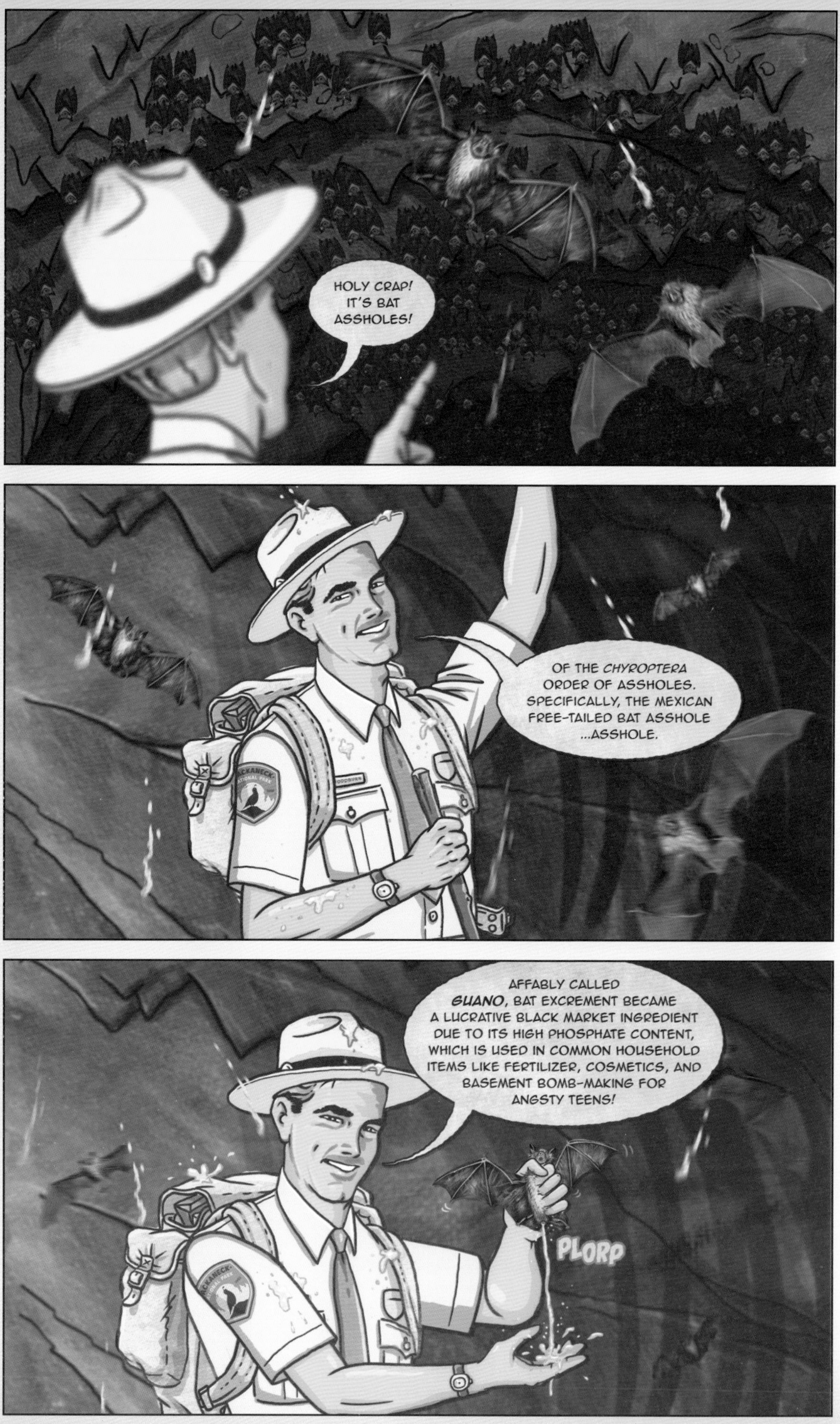
HOLY CRAP! IT'S BAT ASSHOLES!
OF THE *CHYROPTERA* ORDER OF ASSHOLES. SPECIFICALLY, THE MEXICAN FREE-TAILED BAT ASSHOLE ...ASSHOLE.
AFFABLY CALLED **GUANO**, BAT EXCREMENT BECAME A LUCRATIVE BLACK MARKET INGREDIENT DUE TO ITS HIGH PHOSPHATE CONTENT, WHICH IS USED IN COMMON HOUSEHOLD ITEMS LIKE FERTILIZER, COSMETICS, AND BASEMENT BOMB-MAKING FOR ANGSTY TEENS!
PLORP

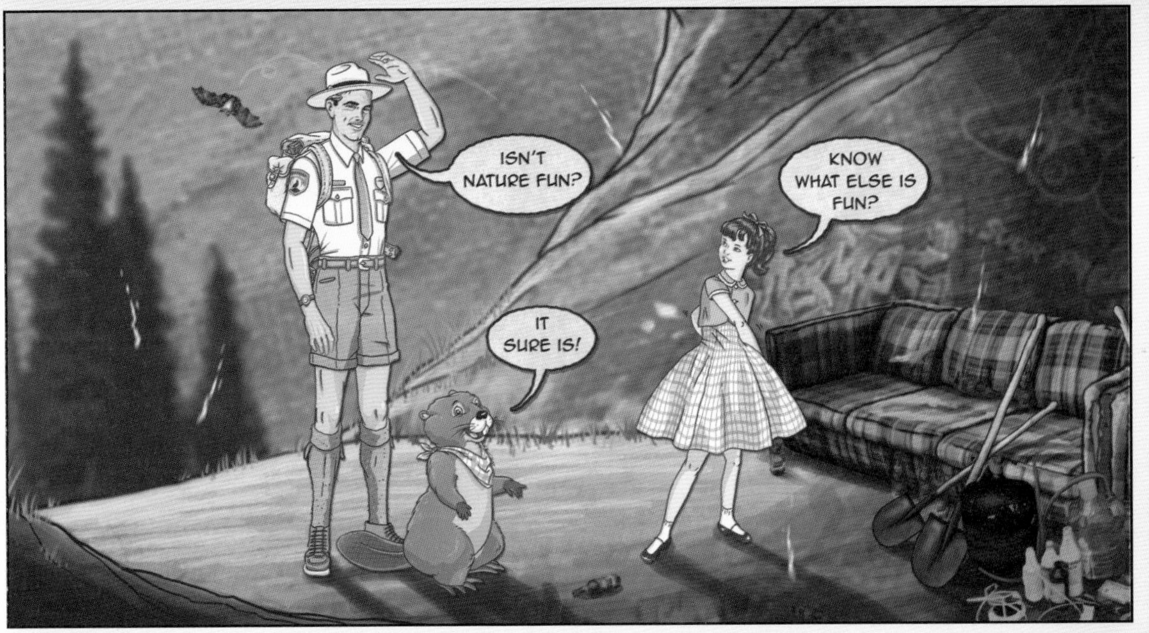
ISN'T NATURE FUN?
KNOW WHAT ELSE IS FUN?
IT SURE IS!

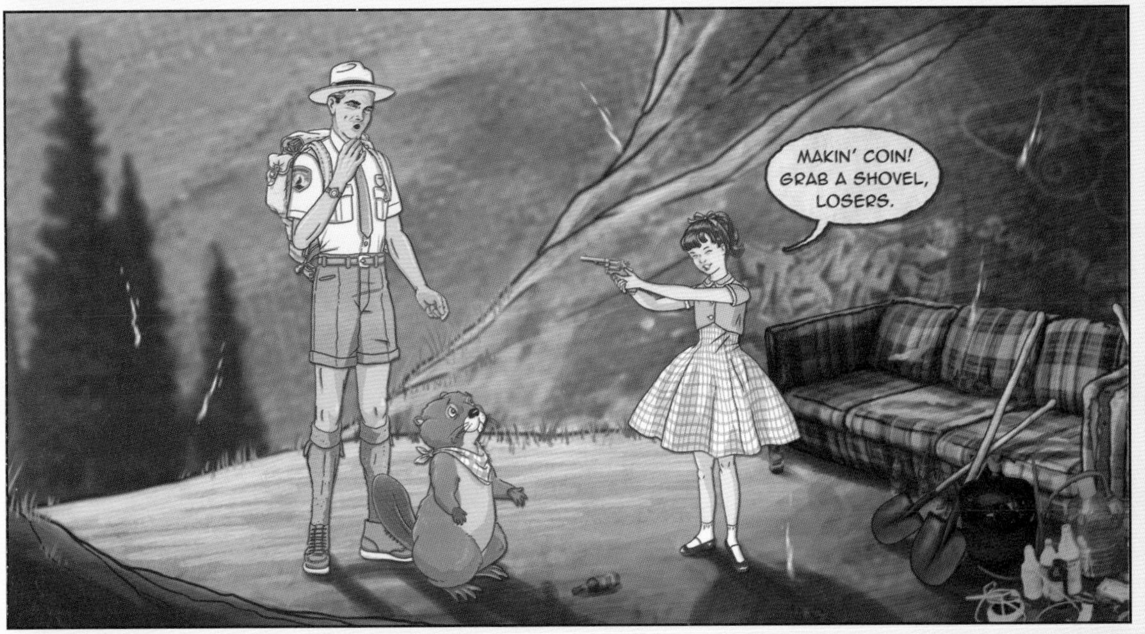
MAKIN' COIN! GRAB A SHOVEL, LOSERS.

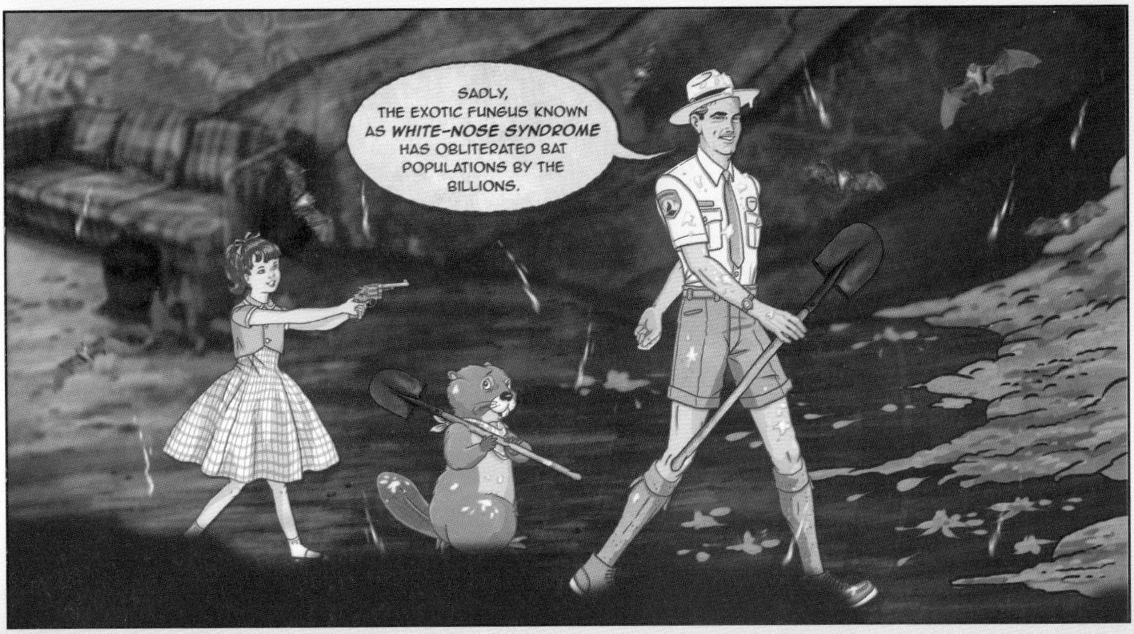
SADLY, THE EXOTIC FUNGUS KNOWN AS *WHITE-NOSE SYNDROME* HAS OBLITERATED BAT POPULATIONS BY THE BILLIONS.

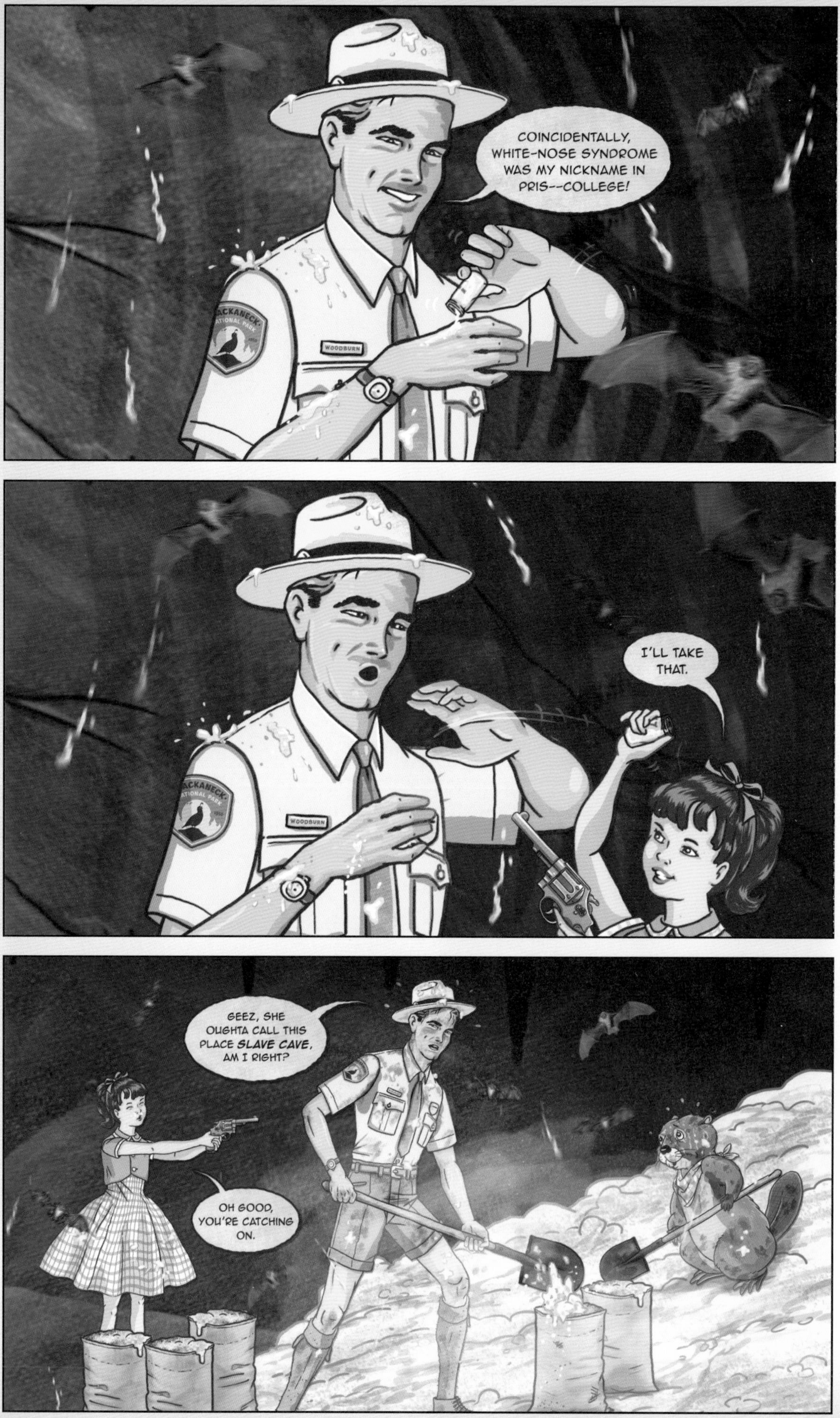
COINCIDENTALLY, WHITE-NOSE SYNDROME WAS MY NICKNAME IN PRIS--COLLEGE!
I'LL TAKE THAT.
GEEZ, SHE OUGHTA CALL THIS PLACE *SLAVE CAVE*, AM I RIGHT?
OH GOOD, YOU'RE CATCHING ON.

WE WANTED TO FIND THE SWEETEST SETTING POSSIBLE.
THEN TAKE IT TO THE DARKEST PLACE POSSIBLE...

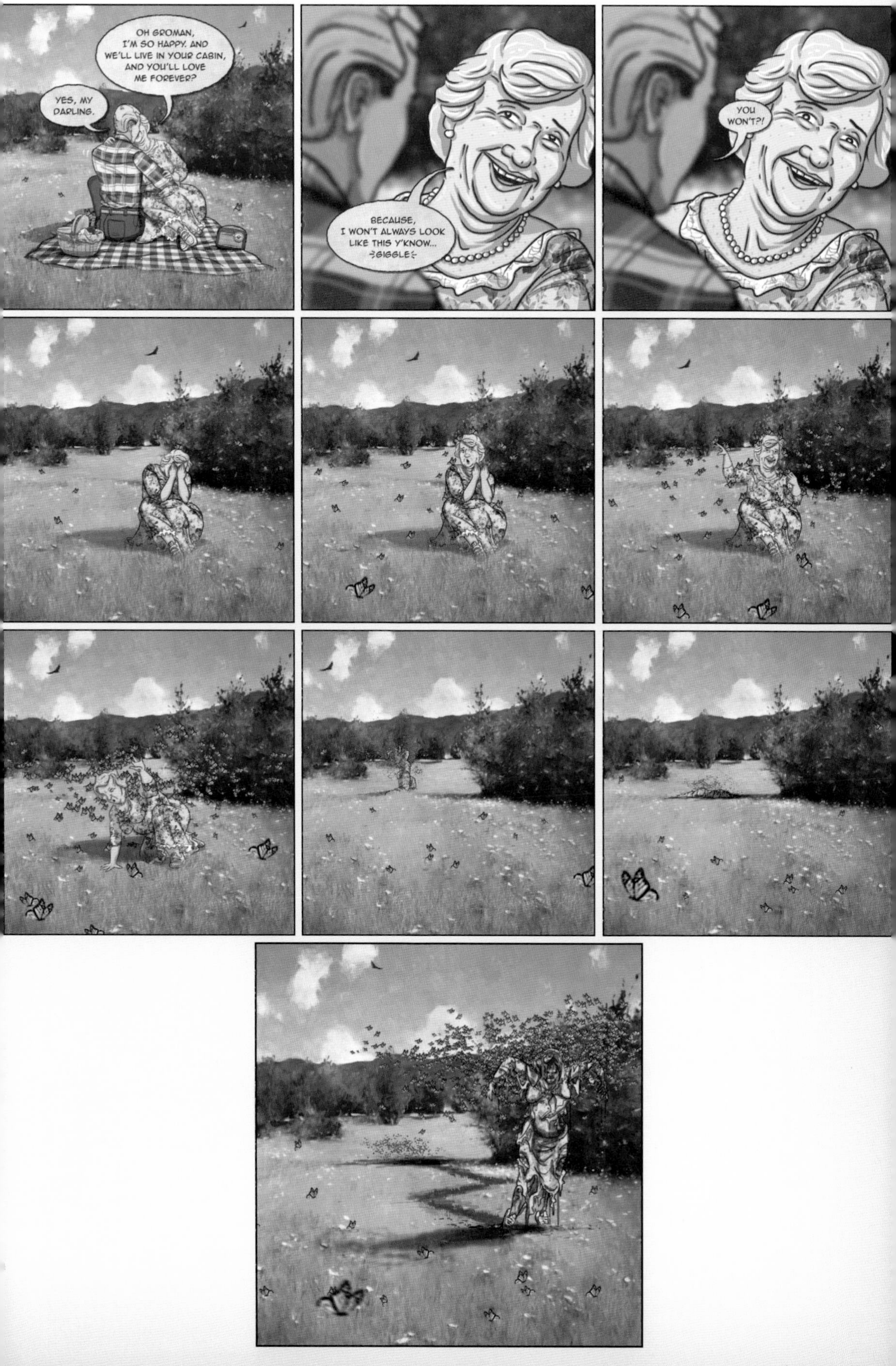
OH GROMAN, I'M SO HAPPY. AND WE'LL LIVE IN YOUR CABIN, AND YOU'LL LOVE ME FOREVER?
YES, MY DARLING.
BECAUSE, I WON'T ALWAYS LOOK LIKE THIS Y'KNOW... ⫶GIGGLE⫶
YOU WON'T?!

...AND THEN BRING'R AROUND FULL CIRCLE. NO REASON, COMPLETELY UNNECESSARY.

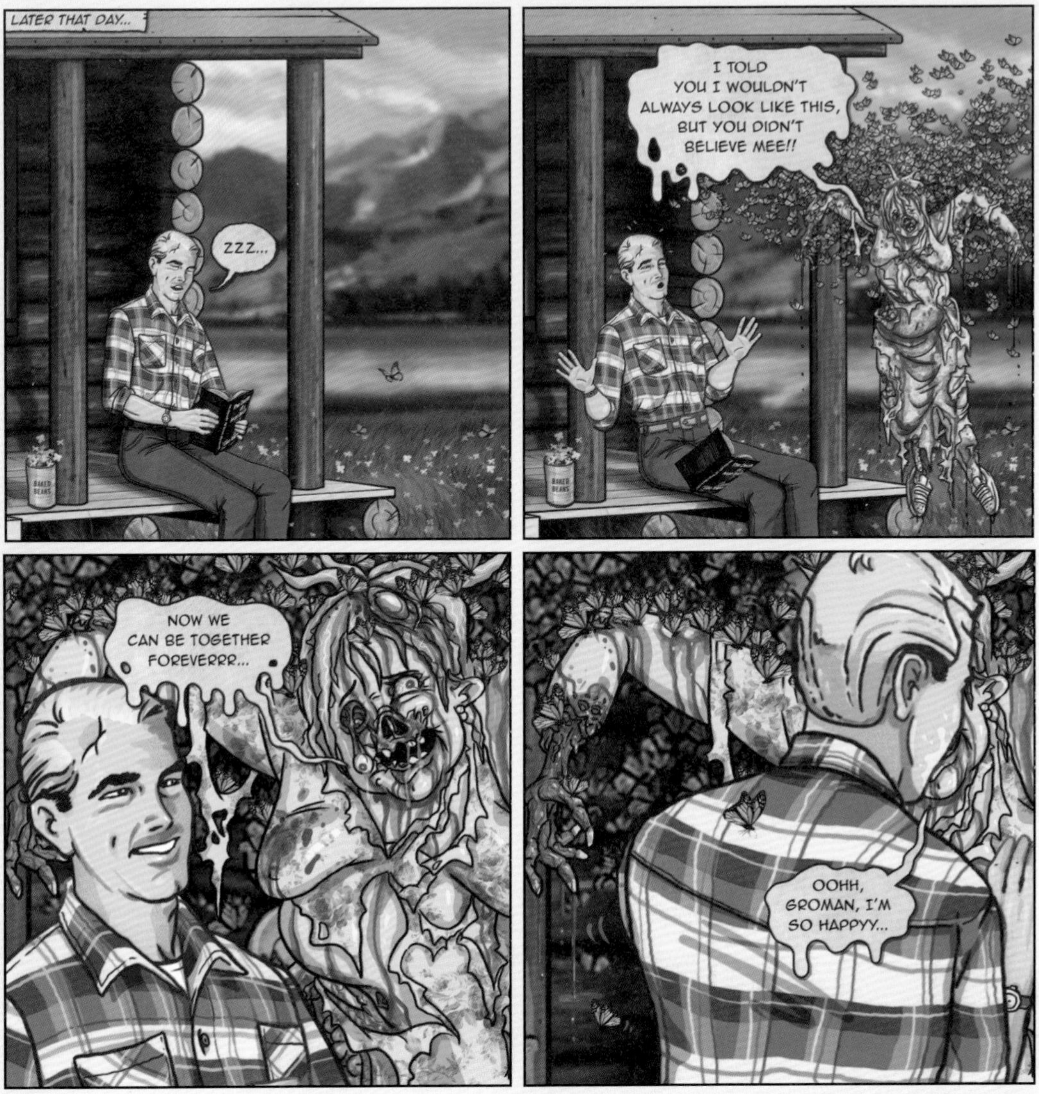
LATER THAT DAY...
ZZZ...
I TOLD YOU I WOULDN'T ALWAYS LOOK LIKE THIS, BUT YOU DIDN'T BELIEVE MEE!!
NOW WE CAN BE TOGETHER FOREVERRR...
OOHH, GROMAN, I'M SO HAPPYY...

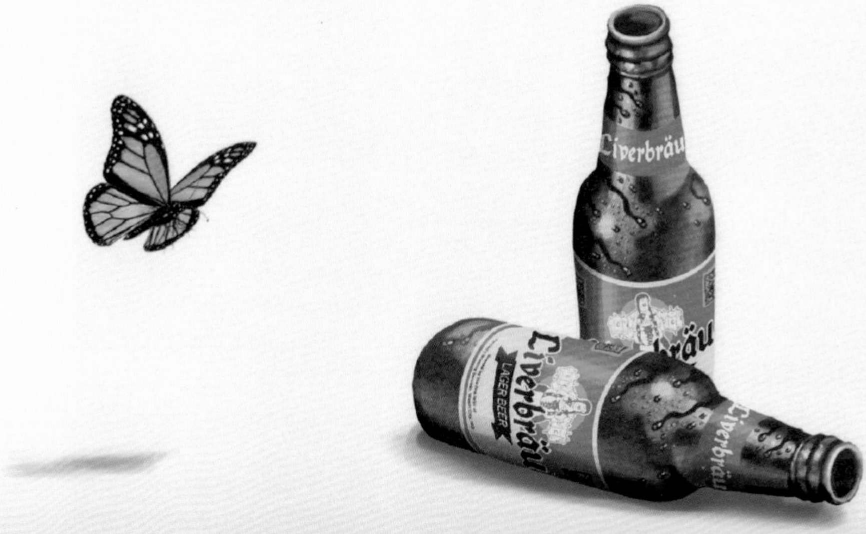
Liverbräu
Liverbräu
LAGER BEER

The LIFECYCLE of a GARLAND

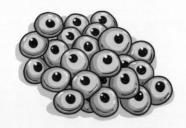

Fig. 1 – Phaseal Spawn

Fig. 2 – Early Schmeosis Tadpole

Fig. 3 – Mid Schmeosis Tadpole

Fig. 4 – Late Schmeosis Tadpole

Fig. 5 – Juvenille Zygodorphis Phase

Fig. 6 – Zygodorphis Garlet

Fig. 7 – Metadorphis Garlet

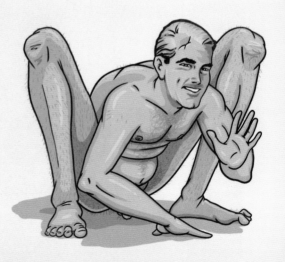

Fig. 8 – Natural Adult Garland
(Delerium Asswhipus)

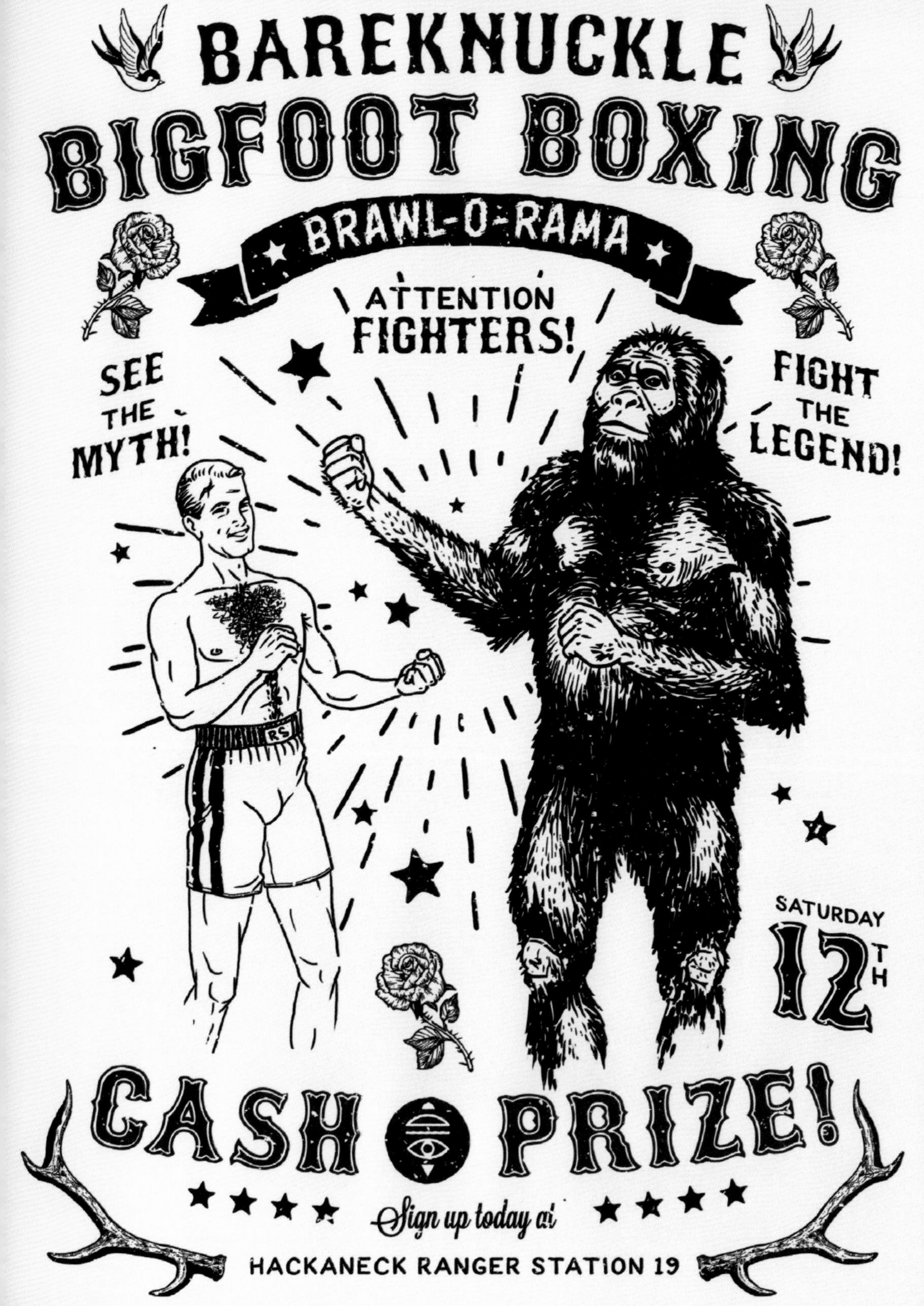
BAREKNUCKLE
BIGFOOT BOXING
BRAWL-O-RAMA
ATTENTION FIGHTERS!
SEE THE MYTH!
FIGHT THE LEGEND!
RS
SATURDAY
12TH
CASH PRIZE!
Sign up today at
HACKANECK RANGER STATION 19

MANY OF YOU ASKED WHAT THE BACKSTORY IS ON *RANGER STRANGER*. ONE WAS WRITTEN, BUT CAME OUT SO VILE AND MIND-BENDING IT WAS IMMEDIATELY BURNED IN ORDER TO SAVE OUR CONSCIOUSNESS FROM FRACKING INTO ANOTHER REALM. HERE'S A CARROT. DECIDE FOR YOURSELF.

SPECIAL ATTENTION

PHONE WALNUT 7893

GROUSE MOUNTAIN PSYCHIATRIC HOSPITAL

SCHIZOPHRENIC AND NEUROTHERAPY WARD

ASA G. LARSON, M.D.
MEDICAL DIRECTOR

CASE NUMBER: 48-271002-R
PATIENT: THOMAS J. SMUTS
DATE: September 04, 1955
TIME: 9:57 AM

Begin transcipt:

Dr. Larson: (microphone tapping) Pop pop popsicle one two. Okay, slide the mic a little closer. That looks good. All right, let's begin shall we? Please state your name and age.

Smuts: Ranger Garland Woodburn. I am 35-years-old.

Dr. Larson: For the record, the patient is Thomas Smuts, 41-years-old.

Smuts: Maybe you should be sitting here, "Doctor."

Dr. Larson: Do you know why you're here, Mr. Sm-- Mr. Woodburn?

Smuts: Of course! This is a psych evaluation. You want to determine if I'm mentally fit to continue being head forest ranger of Hackaneck National Park. I am, you know.

Dr. Larson: Why don't you let us decide that.

Smuts: I no longer believe the ancient God Samedi Mapuche instructed me to cleanse the world of sinners and usher in a golden age of love and enlightenment that heals the hearts and minds of children everywhere.

Dr. Larson: Yes, and why do you no longer believe that?

Smuts: Because those were my instructions before I was a **real** forest ranger. Now, I maintain public amenities, protect our forest lands, and keep track of campers and hikers so they don't stray from the group and get murdered, dismembered, and thrown into a thermal vent. Their blood used in seances. Or something.

Dr. Larson: I see. Mr. Woodburn, do you understand that delusions of sadism and instructions from God could be symptomatic of a serious mental illness?

Smuts: I said A God not THE God. We're just pen pals. Welp, this has been very pleasant, but I better be moseyin' on back to the ol' ranger station.

Dr. Larson: Sir, please sit down.

Page 1 of 19

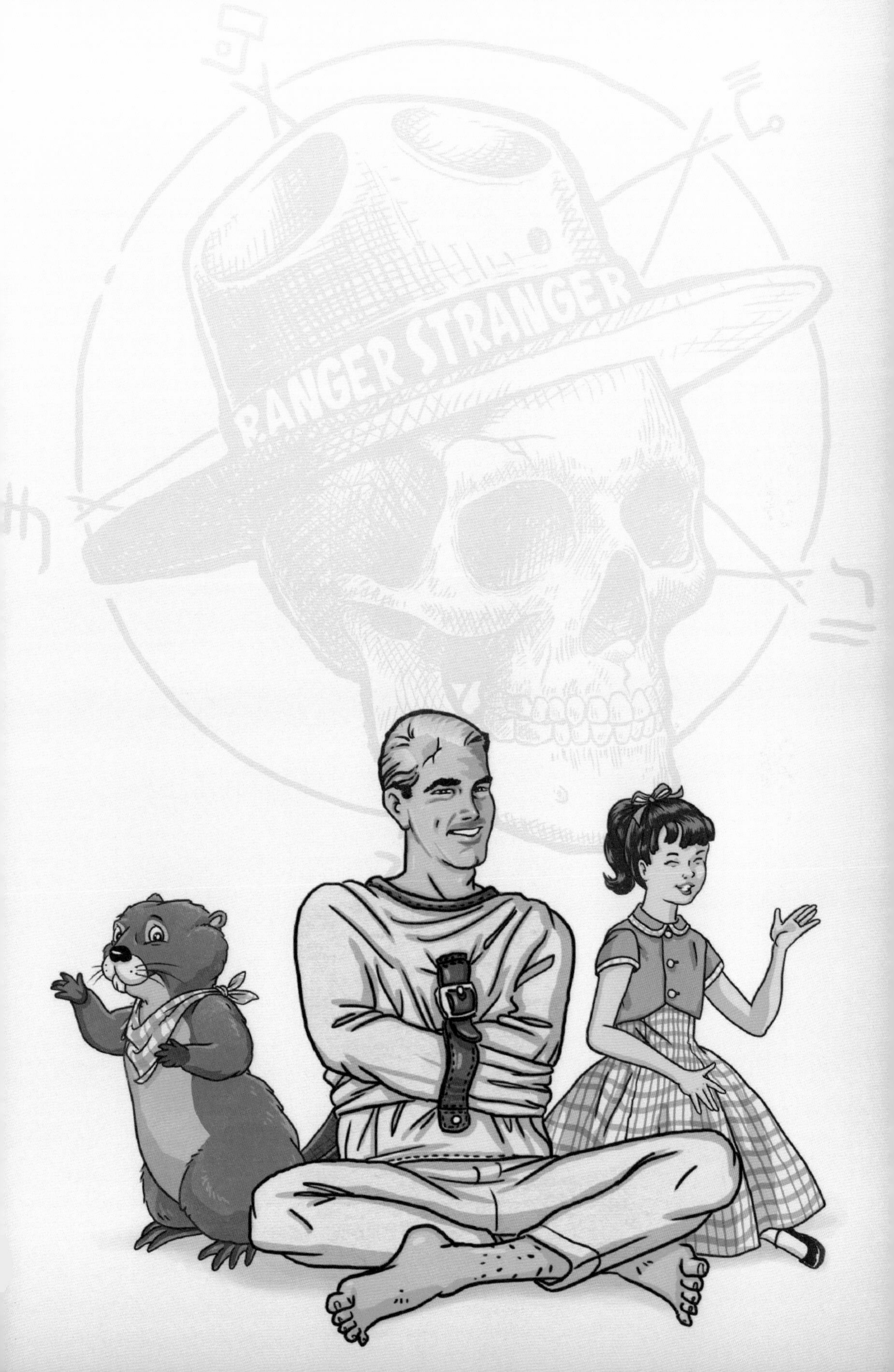
RANGER STRANGER

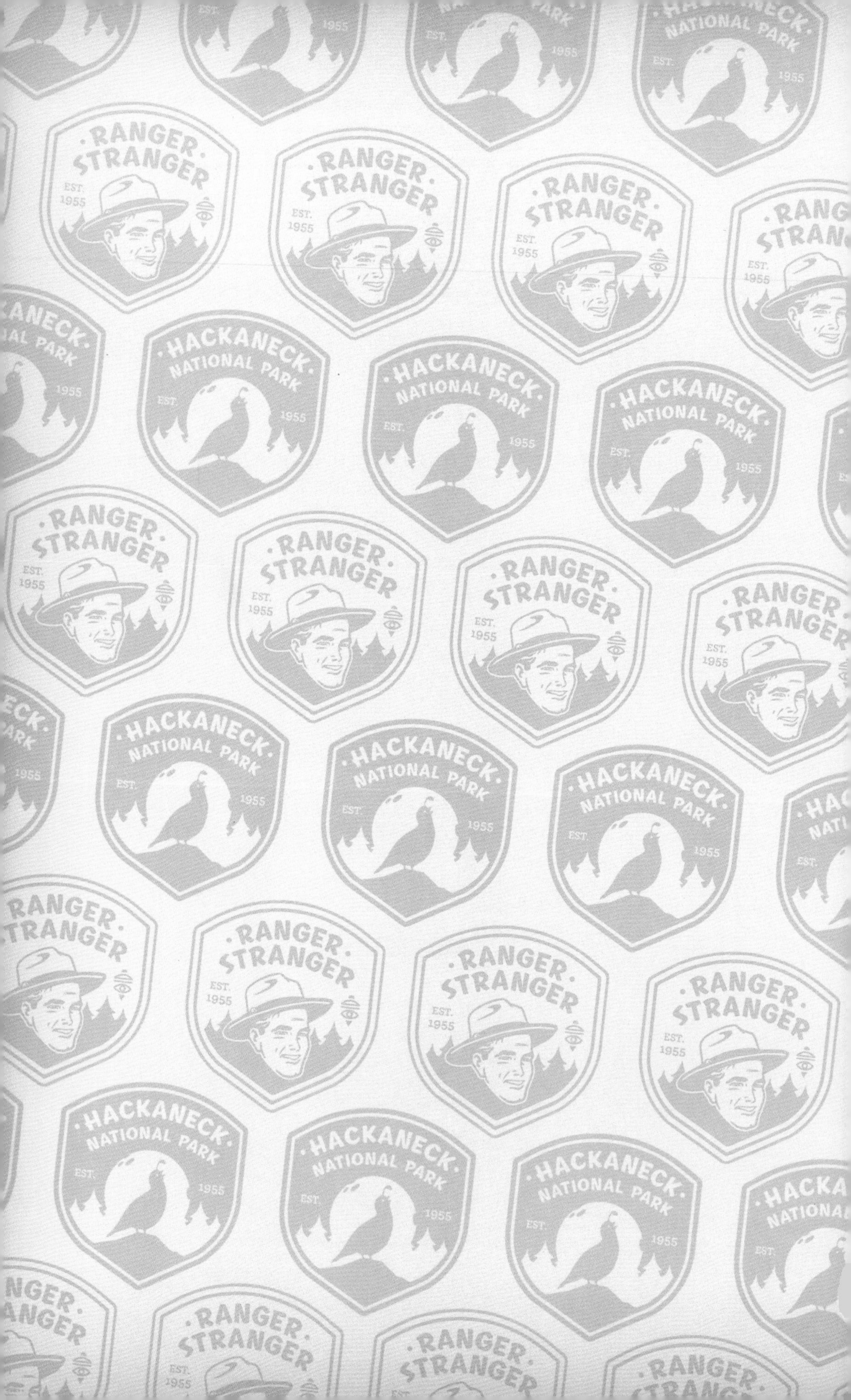
RANGER STRANGER
EST. 1955
HACKANECK NATIONAL PARK
EST. 1955